The Cattle Baron's Wife

The Cattle Baron's Wife

THE CATTLE BARON'S WIFE
BY COLLEEN COBLE

MYLES FROM ANYWHERE
BY JILL STENGL

LOGAN'S LADY
BY TRACIE J. PETERSON

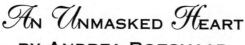

AN UNMASKED HEART
BY ANDREA BOESHAAR

HeavenSent
FROM
Crossings

All Scripture quotations, unless otherwise noted, are taken from the King James Version of the Bible.

The Cattle Baron's Wife
Copyright © 2001 by Colleen Coble

Myles from Anywhere
Copyright © 2001 by Barbour Publishing, Inc.

Logan's Lady
Copyright © 1997 by Barbour Publishing, Inc.

An Unmasked Heart
Copyright © 2001 by Barbour Publishing, Inc.

This edition was especially created in 2004 for Crossings by arrangement with Barbour Publishing, Inc.

Published by Crossings Book Club, 401 Franklin Avenue, Garden City, New York 11530.

ISBN: 1-58288-103-0

Printed in the United States of America

The Cattle Baron's Wife

THE CATTLE BARON'S WIFE

BY COLLEEN COBLE

For Steve and Paula Parks, my wonderful pastor and his precious wife, who have been there all these years to encourage and exhort.

Also for Lucile Campese in Wichita Falls, Texas, who supplied me with boxes of information about her beloved city. Any errors about the area are mine, not hers.

$$\textbf{1}$$

*L*ucy Marsh trudged up the splintered steps to the apartment of the boardinghouse. Every bone in her body ached, and she longed to throw herself across the bed and have a good cry. The paltry ten dollars in her reticule was all the money she would have coming in until she found another job. Mrs. Hanson had been apologetic about letting her go, and Lucy understood it was hard times and not her work that necessitated firing her, but that didn't keep food on the table.

She sighed. Eighteen seventy-seven had been a bad year so far, but it was bound to get better. She tried to trust in God to provide, but days like this made it hard. Sometimes it seemed no matter how hard she tried to be everything she should be, everything that God should love, she ended up failing.

She paused outside the door. She didn't want the children to see her worry. With a deep breath, she pinned a smile on her face and turned the doorknob. Before she could push the door open, Amos Cramer's gruff voice stopped her.

"One moment, Miss Marsh," he panted, hurrying toward her. He was a large, red-faced man with sparse gray hair and a handlebar mustache. He parked himself in front of her door and wheezed, struggling to catch his breath.

Her back against the door, Lucy pressed back as far as she could to escape the strong odor of stale perspiration that drifted toward her. She had tried to be kind to Mr. Cramer until he mistook her kindness for a romantic interest. Now she just tried to stay out of his way.

He crowded closer. "I'm afraid I have some bad news for you," he said. His muddy gaze slid avidly over her face and hair.

Lucy pressed tighter against the wall, though it gained her no space between the odious man and herself. What now? She didn't think she could take anymore bad news.

"I've decided to sell out and go back to New York," he said. "I've had an offer I can't refuse for this place. The new owner plans to tear it down and build a new restaurant here." He hesitated and rubbed his lips with a dirty handkerchief. "I'm afraid I must ask you to leave within the next seven days."

Lucy gasped. "A week? How can I find something else in a week?" Dismay flooded her limbs.

Amos shrugged. "I'm sorry, my dear. You might try that boarding-house over on Lincoln Avenue. They might have an opening." He pursed his lips and raked her figure with his gaze before turning and waddling away.

A great lump rose in Lucy's throat, but she fought the tears with determination. She couldn't cry, not now. She straightened her shoulders and pushed open the door. Her three-year-old sister Eileen launched herself against Lucy's legs.

"Lucy, you was late," she said, sticking out her lower lip. "Jed has company."

Lucy looked toward the single chair in the one-room apartment. A man with gray hair and penetrating charcoal eyes sat regarding her calmly before standing to his feet. There was something forbidding in his face, and Lucy gave a tiny gasp. Her gaze sought and found her brother, Jed. Twelve years old, he'd been a handful all year. His hang-dog expression did nothing to calm her fears.

"Jed?"

"Uh, Lucy, this is—"

"I'll introduce myself," the gentleman interrupted. He strode toward her and stared into her eyes. "Luther Stanton of Wichita Falls, Texas," he said. He shifted his gray Stetson in his hands, then pointed it at Jed. "Your young brother is in a heap of trouble, Miss. He lifted my wallet. I thought he'd gotten away with it, but I happened to find him in the mercantile down the street. That red hair is hard to miss."

Stealing! "Jed, no!" she wailed. "How could you?" It was too much. She couldn't take another problem. She burst into tears and sat on the edge of the bed abruptly. She buried her face in her hands and sobbed. Her shoulders heaved as she tried to get her emotions under control. Finally raising her head, she was surprised to find Luther leaning on the gold head of his walking cane with a speculative look on his face. She gulped and swiped at her wet cheeks.

"I was of a mind to call the sheriff, or whatever you call the law around here, but the youngster persuaded me to talk to you first. I hesitated to bring more trouble on you when your brother explained that you were caring for him and young Eileen. Commendable! But I can see it is of no use. Only the law will stop young Jed; you obviously have no control over him." He clapped his hat on his head and started toward the door.

"Wait," Lucy cried. "Surely we can talk about this for a few moments." Her mind raced. What could she do? How could she convince him not to prosecute? She'd promised her parents to take care of Jed; she had to keep her word. "I could work to pay back the money," she began. "I'm an excellent housekeeper. Are you in need of a maid or perhaps a cook?" What else could she do?

Mr. Stanton turned and looked at her. That odd speculation was back on his face. The silence seemed to stretch interminably before he finally spoke. "I have both a cook and a housekeeper who've been with me for years," he said. "Tell me, Miss Marsh, are you a Christian woman?"

Lucy stared at him in bewilderment. "Why, yes Sir, I am."

He smiled. "I thought as much. God has led me here for a purpose." He squared his shoulders. "There's only one thing I'm in need of."

Her heart leapt with hope. "What would that be, Mr. Stanton? I'll do anything to keep Jed out of jail." She glanced at her brother and was gratified to see him standing with his head hanging in shame. Perhaps this whole episode would wake him up.

"My son needs a wife, Miss Marsh. Have you read in the Bible how Abraham sent a servant out to find a wife for Isaac?"

"Of course," Lucy said, her heart sinking before beginning a rapid beat against her chest. Surely, he didn't think . . .

"That was my main purpose for this trip, though my son has no idea of my mission. But I've found no one suitable. I think you will do nicely."

The words fell into the silence of the room like an explosion of dynamite. Lucy's limbs went weak, and she could hardly stand. The room spun, and she sat slowly on the edge of the bed.

"I can see you don't fancy the idea," Mr. Stanton said. "That's fine. I understand completely, but you must realize that young Jed will now have to come with me. Get your gear together, Jed."

"No, wait!" Lucy put out a shaking hand to stop him. "Is—is your son a Christian? Can you give me until tomorrow to at least pray about it?"

Mr. Stanton smiled slowly. "That just confirms the Lord's leading me here. As soon as I soon as I clapped eyes on you, something reared up inside me. I knew you were the right one for my Caleb. Yes, my boy is a Christian, and I can see you would need time to confirm this is God's will. Very well, I will return at precisely nine o'clock tomorrow morning for your decision." He put a hand on her shoulder. "I have my son's signature to act as his agent in all business matters for this trip, so if you agree, I will arrange a proxy marriage. Right after the ceremony, we'll leave for Texas. A train leaves at one o'clock tomorrow afternoon, and I aim to be on it with or without you." He clapped his hat on his head and turned toward the door.

When the door closed behind him, Lucy clenched her hands in her lap and turned to her brother. Too angry to speak, she just looked at him.

Jed swallowed hard and took a step back. "It was just a dare, Lucy. I didn't mean to do anything wrong. I would have given it back to him."

"A dare? You have ruined our lives over a dare, Jed? One of us will pay, either you with an eternity in jail or me in bondage to some man I've never met. A jail of a different sort." She buried her head in her hands. "Lord, help me," she whispered. There was no way out. She couldn't fail her parents and her brother.

She tossed and turned all night as she pleaded with God for a way out. At three in the morning, she finally slid out of bed and lit a lantern. She opened her Bible to Genesis 12.

> Now the LORD has said unto Abram, Get thee out of thy country, and from thy kindred, and from thy father's house, unto a land that I will shew thee: And I will make of thee a great nation, and I will bless thee, and make thy name great; and thou shalt be a blessing.

A blessing? She could be a blessing? Peace washed over her in a warm blanket. God was behind this; it had to be so. Marriage was an honorable thing. And this had come at a time when she saw no way to support the children and herself. Marriage was something God had ordained, and Mr. Stanton said his son was a Christian. She closed her Bible and crawled back into bed with Eileen. She would marry this Caleb and make him a good wife. Caleb meant faithful. That thought comforted her.

❧

After a frantic morning, they all found themselves aboard the train heading west. Mr. Stanton had arranged for comfortable accommodations, but the luxury car couldn't still the trepidation in Lucy's heart. What had she done? She stared down at the simple gold band on her left hand. She was a married woman, and she'd never even met the man. What if he was cruel or physically repulsive to her? What if he expected her to come right to the marriage bed? She suppressed a shudder.

But she had had no choice. When she looked into Mr. Stanton's level gray eyes, she had known he meant what he said. He would summon the authorities if she didn't agree to the marriage. Why was he so set on finding a wife for his son anyway? Was Caleb so repugnant he couldn't find a wife for himself? Lucy shuddered, then relaxed as a sense of peace calmed her frantic heart. God had given her direction. She would trust Him.

Eileen nestled against her arm, her breathing deep and easy. Jed was next to the window, staring morosely out at the bleak winter landscape. He hadn't had much to say all day. Lucy knew he felt terrible about what his actions had caused. She had been too angry to talk to him since he explained why he'd stolen Mr. Stanton's wallet. She knew she had to forgive him, but it was hard to do, especially before she met this Caleb and her own fate. Jed had been thoughtless and irresponsible. She sighed and said a silent prayer for the strength to forgive her brother. God had forgiven her many times; could she do less?

Jed's red hair fell across his forehead, and his freckles stood out on his pale skin. Lucy felt a wave of love well up for him. He'd had a rough year. He and Papa had been so close. The trauma of seeing their parents swept away by a flood had devastated him. Jed had clung to a tree and watched the flood sweep Papa right past him. He'd tried to grab Papa's arm, but the raging river had carried him out of Jed's reach. In one crushing blow, they'd been orphaned. The bodies of their parents hadn't been recovered for three days. Jed hadn't been the same since.

Jed looked up gratefully when she began to talk to him, and by the time they reached Pittsburgh, he had relaxed and was sleeping. Lucy wished she could sleep, but the thought of what awaited her in Texas kept her staring into the swirling snow outside the window. Mr. Stanton tried to talk to her several times, but he gave up when she answered in monosyllables.

❧

Caleb pushed his broad-rimmed Stetson back on his forehead and leaned back in his saddle. Whew, what a day he'd had. He'd lost ten head of cattle from the frigid cold in the past twenty-four hours. He couldn't remember ever enduring cold like this. And snow! The most they usually got was an inch or two that quickly melted away, not six inches like that covering the ground now. Then his favorite bay mare, Skyler, had broken a leg and had to be put down. He still winced from that. Skyler had been with him since he was fifteen. She was aging but still a good cattle horse. It would be hard to replace her. His mount,

Maxi, was a good workhorse, but Caleb didn't have the rapport with him that he'd enjoyed with Skyler.

Pa should have been home two days ago. A dart of worry kept Caleb on edge. He hoped this sudden and unusual snowstorm hadn't trapped Pa somewhere. Turning Maxi's head, he plodded toward the house. Smoke curled from the chimney, and his mouth watered at the aroma of stew that blew in with the smoke. It had been a long time since breakfast. He rode into the barn and curried Maxi before heading to the house.

Not for the first time, he wondered if he should take a wife. Someone strong and knowledgeable about cattle. The only one he knew of in the area who fitted that description was Margaret Hannigan, Luke's daughter. She was almost as tall as Caleb was himself and could rope a calf nearly as well, too. She was no beauty, but he tried to tell himself that had nothing to do with his reluctance. Still, the thought of staring at that horsy face of Margaret's over breakfast every morning for the next forty years was enough to quell any man's appetite.

He sighed and put his speculation away. Bounding up the steps, he had his hand on the door when he heard the rattle and clank of a wagon coming across the snow-covered meadow. He turned and shaded his eyes with one hand while he studied the approaching convoy. Three wagons. It had to be Pa with provisions. His spirits lifted. Supper wouldn't be such a lonely affair with Pa home. Percy, their cook, didn't talk much, and there had been no one to share his thoughts with.

As the wagons neared, he recognized his father's gray head. Caleb lifted a hand in greeting and went to meet him. The welcoming grin faded when he saw the young woman clinging desperately to the wagon seat beside his father. Her youth and beauty seemed to bring sudden color to a dreary landscape.

He stared harder. What had Pa done? With a sinking heart, he remembered his father's ramblings about the place needing a woman's touch. Pa had gone and gotten himself hitched to a young filly! This woman was young enough to be Pa's daughter and Caleb's sister. How could he do this? Caleb gritted his teeth. The little hussy probably took one look at Pa and saw him for a rich sucker. Well, if she thought she was getting any money out of this ranch, she was sadly mistaken.

Silently, he waited for his father to step down from the wagon and explain. Maybe he hadn't married her yet. Maybe there would be a chance to talk him out of such a fool notion. Caleb's thoughts were interrupted when his father enveloped him in a bear hug. Caleb tried to return the embrace, but his rising anger kept his shoulders stiff.

"Caleb, Boy, you did good while I was gone. We passed the south pasture and saw the herd there. They look fat and sassy." He gripped his son's arms and stared into his face. "Help Lucy down while I get her luggage." He didn't wait for an answer, but then he never did. Caleb was used to his father's peremptory tone.

Caleb suppressed a sigh and offered his hand to the young woman. Lucy, his father called her. She was a cute little thing. Tiny, barely five feet if he had to hazard a guess, with huge blue eyes and fine blond hair. He could see how she might get to someone inexperienced in dealing with a little gold digger like her. But he would make sure his father saw through her wiles.

She took his arm and nearly fell when she tried to step down. He caught her in his arms and the contact sent a shock of awareness through him. He hastily set her on her feet and backed away. "Miss Lucy," he said, tipping his hat.

She stared at him with those enormous blue eyes. He'd never seen eyes so big and blue. A man could get lost in those eyes. She caught her full, pink lips between perfect white teeth. Was that fear in her eyes? She had cause to fear him, he thought grimly. He'd see her packed up and heading east if it was the last thing he did.

He heard an excited shout and turned to look at the last wagon. A boy of about twelve came bounding through the snow, his cheeks red from the cold. His amazingly red hair stood up on end, and he carried a little girl who looked like a tiny version of Lucy.

"Did you see how big everything looks out here, Lucy?" He turned his brown eyes on Caleb. "How far's the nearest neighbors, Mister?"

Caleb softened a bit at the lad's exuberance. "Nearest would be Mitchells', about two miles away. They have some young 'uns close to your age." He frowned. Why had he bothered to tell the boy about neighbors? It wasn't like he was going to be here long enough to make any friends. Who was this kid anyway?

As if she had read his mind, Lucy introduced him. "Uh, Mr. Stanton, this is my brother Jed and my sister Eileen."

Caleb shook the boy's hand brusquely and turned to lead the way to the house. That boy might be her brother, but he'd bet the little girl was her own daughter. Percy and Luke, the foreman, had come to help with the provisions and the luggage, and he followed them into the house. Lucy had a bit of difficulty walking through the heavy drifts of snow. Caleb's lip curled in contempt. What had Pa been thinking? If he wanted a wife, why hadn't he picked one that would be a real helpmeet like the Bible said? This pale lily wouldn't last long out here.

He took her elbow and helped her along near the house where the drift went clear up on the porch. She shot him a grateful look from those blue eyes again, and his heart sped up. *Stupid, stupid*, he told himself. He was much too cautious to be caught in her little web of deceit. Frowning, he glared at his pa's back. Was Pa getting senile? It wasn't like him to be taken in like that. Caleb would get him alone and point out a few facts to him.

Lucy sighed and sank into the rocker near the fire. She held out her arms for Eileen and took off the little girl's coat, then spread it out in front of the fireplace. Setting Eileen on her feet, Lucy stood to take off her own cloak, bonnet, and mittens. When she pulled her small, white hands from the mittens, his heart sank when he saw the plain gold band on her left hand. She'd gotten Pa to marry her! Pa always was a sucker for a hard luck story. And there was a hard luck story lurking here somewhere. Why did she have her brother and sister with her? She probably gave Pa some story about being an orphan. If little Eileen wasn't her own daughter, he'd eat his hat.

Caleb's eyes met hers, and he saw the fear in them again. He narrowed his eyes and stared her down with a contemptuous curl to his lips. She paled and looked away. Good. She'd better be afraid of him. He was about to be her worst nightmare. No one made a fool of a Stanton.

His father came into the room, rubbing his hands. "I'm famished. We haven't eaten anything since breakfast. Let's eat while it's hot."

"Aren't you going to introduce me properly?" Caleb asked.

"There's time for all that after supper," his father answered. He avoided Caleb's gaze. "After we eat a bowl of the stew, we'll have some coffee here in the parlor by the fire, and I'll explain everything."

Supper was a stilted affair. Caleb saw the glances Jed kept tossing his way. Lucy grew more strained and silent. Her knuckles were white from gripping her fork, and she kept her eyes trained on her plate throughout the entire meal. His father tried to draw her into the discussion several times, but she wouldn't look at him and answered in the briefest of words.

Finally, his father pushed back his chair and gave a satisfied sigh. "I missed that good grub of yours, Percy. Now how about some of your famous coffee? They just don't know how to make the stuff out east. Bring it to the parlor when it's ready." He stood and led the way down the hall to the parlor.

Lucy pleated her dress nervously. "Could I put Eileen to bed? She's exhausted."

"Of course, dear girl." Luther turned to Caleb. "Show her to the little guest room, Son. The coffee should be ready by the time you get back."

Caleb had been watching for an opportunity to talk to her alone all evening. He led her up the stairs and down the hall, swinging open the door to the smallest guest room. Silently, Lucy slipped past him into the room. A blue quilt his mother had made covered the bed, and a small cot was pushed up against the wall. Lucy sat Eileen on the bed and slipped the little girl out of her dress and into her nightgown.

Caleb watched her practiced movements. She acted like a mother. He took a step closer and lowered his voice. "I know what you're up to, so you might as well give up now."

Lucy turned an anguished white face up toward him. "I don't think you do, Mr. Stanton."

"I've seen your kind blow through here before. You're just out for all the money you can bleed out of Pa, but you'll have to go through me first," he said through gritted teeth. "So why don't you just pack your things and get out before you get hurt?"

Lucy smiled wearily. "It's a bit late for that," she said softly.

"You can't mean you actually *care* for Pa," he said derisively. "He's an old man."

"It's not what you think," she said.

"Oh, I think it is." He spun around and stormed out of the room. He hadn't handled that well. She'd stayed too calm, as if she knew something he didn't. Had Pa already given her money?

Moments later, Lucy joined them in the parlor. Caleb stood staring morosely out the window at the driving snow. He turned when she entered the room and glared at her. He thought he saw tears shimmering on the tips of her lashes, but told himself he was imagining it. She was much too calculating to cry.

Luther rubbed his hands together. "Ah, Caleb, I guess I've got some explaining to do."

Caleb gave him an ironic smile. "I reckon so, Pa."

Pa stared at him with a steady gaze and a hint of compassion in his eyes. "This is Lucy, your wife."

2

*C*aleb's face wavered through the tears that rimmed Lucy's eyes. She had felt a thrill of joy at her first sight of her handsome husband, so strong, so manly, his feet planted apart like the king of his realm here in Texas. But with his rejection of her, all those hopeful wonderings had vanished like yesterday's sunshine.

"You mean, *your* wife," Caleb corrected. But his lips went white, and Lucy saw the shocked comprehension settle over his face.

Mr. Stanton shook his head. "No, Son, I mean *your* wife. It's time you settled down and saw to raising a family. I won't be around to help you forever. You need a passel of strong sons to begin to build our cattle empire."

Caleb sat heavily on the sofa, and the lines deepened in his tanned face. "Pa, what have you done?" he whispered.

Mr. Stanton hunched his shoulders and raised his voice defensively. "If I waited for you to find a wife, I'd be too old to enjoy my grandchildren. Lucy here, she's a good Christian girl. She'll make you a fine wife."

Lucy saw the shudder that passed through Caleb's frame. A lump grew in her throat. Did he find her so unattractive? She knew she had no claim to great beauty, but he had barely glanced her way to even know what she looked like.

Caleb waved a hand in her direction. "Look at her, Pa! What were you thinking? Any sons she bears will likely be as small and spindly as she is. The work here is hard. The vision we've talked about will take a woman who can carry her own weight."

Small? Spindly? Lucy's tears dried up with the bolt of rage that shot through her. She drew herself up to her full height of just under five feet and glared at her new husband. "I'm stronger than I look, Mr. Stanton. I've worked long hours at the millinery shop, and I'm not afraid of hard work. I can tackle any chores you care to throw my way!"

She was wasting her breath; he was determined not to give her a chance. She could see it in the hard line of his jaw and the fierce glare in his eyes. But something inside her screamed to be allowed to prove her worth.

His eyes widened, and his jaw dropped. "You aren't staying long enough to find out, Miss Marsh. I aim to put you on the first stage back east."

"We *are* married," she reminded him. "I don't believe in divorce." She glared at him. He would not send her away; she had a brother and sister to care for. Her appearance might disgust him, but marriage was more than physical appearance. She would prove herself to him.

Another shudder passed through his frame. He took a deep breath. "Neither do I," he said. "But this is no real marriage. I never agreed to any such arrangement. You should have known better, Pa."

"For once in your life, listen to me, Caleb! This ranch needs a woman's touch. *You* need a woman to soften you before you turn to granite. If we're going to build a cattle empire in this place, we need sons. Strong sons. Lucy has the grit to raise sons you'll be proud of. You don't really know her yet."

"If you want a woman around the house so bad, *you* marry her," Caleb shot back.

Mr. Stanton opened his mouth to reply, then his face turned red and darkened to nearly purple. He gasped, then clutched his left shoulder. The color drained from his face, and a gargle escaped from his open mouth.

"Pa?" Caleb's voice rose, and he jumped to his feet and rushed toward his father. Luther Stanton gasped, then reeled away, crashing to the floor like a great tree felled by a logger's axe.

Lucy bit back a shriek and ran toward her new father-in-law. Caleb arrived at his father's side first. He rolled Luther over onto his back and peered into his face. The older man was still breathing, but his pallor was pronounced, and he was unconscious.

"Let me," Lucy said, pushing her way closer to Luther. "I know something of nursing."

Caleb clenched his jaw. "If he dies, his blood will be on your head. He was just fine until you came along."

Lucy ignored him. "Is there a doctor in the area?"

Caleb nodded. "Doc Cooper in Wichita Falls."

"Send Percy to fetch him, and you help me get him into bed." She checked his breathing and was relieved to see a bit of color coming back to his face. Snatching a quilted throw from the chair, she tucked it around Luther.

Bellowing for Percy, Caleb's voice echoed down the hall as he ran to do what she said. Lucy pressed her fingertips against her father-in-law's chest and frowned when she felt Luther's irregular heartbeat. He'd had some kind of a heart spasm. Her heart sank, and she was ashamed to admit that her first thoughts were of her own situation. If this man died, she would be at the mercy of her new husband. "Please God, please keep him alive," she whispered.

Caleb returned and lifted his father's shoulders. "Grab his feet," he ordered.

Lucy grabbed Luther's feet, and Jed jumped in to assist as well. They carried him up the stairs.

"His room is the first on the left," Caleb gasped. Lucy pushed open the door with her foot, and they laid Luther on the bed. Caleb jerked his father's boots off. Lucy pulled the quilts up around him.

"We need to keep him warm," she told Caleb. "His color looks bad."

Caleb nodded, then ran his hand through his sandy blond hair. His gray eyes held a deep fear that brought a hint of sympathy to Lucy's heart. She laid a hand on his arm. "We should pray for him," she said.

He nodded and moved so her hand fell away. She couldn't help the stab of disappointment at his rejection of her comfort. Suddenly aware that Jed and Eileen hovered at the doorway, she straightened her shoulders and moved away from Caleb. She had to be strong for the children's sakes. "I'll fix us all some tea," she said.

"No thanks," Caleb said. "I can't abide that sissy drink, and I'm not about to start drinking it now."

Hot words bubbled to her lips, but she choked them back. No wonder Luther had to find a wife for his son. No woman in her right mind would choose to put up with him.

Luther stirred, and his eyes fluttered open. "Quit your wrangling," he said in a weak voice. "I can't endure petty quarreling." He struggled to sit up. "Besides, the sight of Caleb sipping tea like a woman would finish me off for sure. Fetch me some coffee. That's all I need." A hint of color was returning to his face.

"I'll just be a moment," Lucy said. Away from her new husband's stern presence, she felt reprieved. She hurried down the stairs to the kitchen, with Jed and Eileen on her heels.

"I don't like it here, Lucy," Jed whispered once they were out of earshot. "I want to go back to Boston."

Eileen began to cry, and Lucy scooped her up into her arms. "Hush, Darling, it will be all right. There's flour for biscuits and beefsteak for dinner. That's more than we had in Boston. I know it's going to be an adjustment, but let's wait and see how things are tomorrow. We're all at sixes and sevens with Mr. Stanton's illness and the long trip. God hasn't brought us this far to let us down."

Jed crossed his arms and glowered at her. "Caleb acts like this was all your fault. I'd like to slug him."

"Jed, that's not respectful to your elders." She wanted to remind him that if it weren't for his foolishness, they would not be here, but she bit the words back. Recriminations would serve no purpose now.

"Caleb is just shocked at what his father has done," Lucy said. She hoped that was true. She was willing to give Caleb the benefit of the doubt, but her charity was growing thin. The thought of their single room in the boardinghouse, rude though it might be, filled her with a sense of nostalgia and longing. Not that it was there anyway. It had probably already been razed into a pile of rubble.

Lucy put Eileen down and went to the stove. Wrinkling her nose at the strong smell, she poured the black coffee into a cup. Taking a sip, she shuddered at the bitterness. A sugar container was on the table, so she took it, then dumped some sugar in it and stirred it.

Sugar. What a luxury. There seemed to be plenty, too. She dipped her finger into the coffee and tasted it. Shivering at the still-bitter taste, she added more sugar, then poured another cup for Caleb and added sugar to that cup, too. At least it might be drinkable now. From the strong, acrid taste, it must have been made this morning. There was no time to make more now, though.

She carried the coffee back to Luther's bedroom. Luther was sitting up against the pillows. Though he looked wan and weak, his eyes were not so dull. He took the coffee eagerly, and she handed the other cup to Caleb. Both men took a big gulp. Caleb's eyes widened, and he choked but managed to keep it down. His father was not so charitable. Sputtering, Luther spewed the coffee from his mouth. The dark liquid pooled on the quilt in front of him.

The eyes he turned to Lucy were full of reproach and betrayal. Luther shuddered. "Sugar! You put sugar in my coffee?"

"I'm sorry." Lucy took a step back toward the door. "It was bitter."

Caleb wiped his mouth. "It's supposed to be bitter!" He took the cup from his father and brushed by Lucy on his way to the door. "Pa, I told you no good would come of having a woman around," he growled. "She's too little to be of any use on the ranch, she doesn't know coffee from syrup, and she's bound to nag us both to death. We've gotten along just fine, the two of us."

Luther scowled. "That's enough, Caleb. Lucy is your wife, and the sooner you adjust to that fact, the better. You were too young to remember what a different place this house was with your mama here, God rest her soul. We need her, try to remember that."

"She's not my wife, Pa! I never gave you permission to bring me back a bride."

"You signed a proxy statement, Caleb. It's all legal, and you'd best make the most of it."

The two men glared at one another, and Lucy thought they looked like two roosters squaring off for a fight. She should douse them both with cold water. If she had the nerve, she would. They deserved it. Luther for bringing her here without telling her his son hated women, and Caleb for not giving her a chance to prove herself. Well, she would show them! She wasn't afraid of hard work, and when Caleb realized it, his apology would be sweet.

Still lost in a pleasant daydream of Caleb groveling at her feet, she didn't notice Luther's gray color until he choked. Sinking weakly back against the pillows, he clutched his left arm again. Lucy started to his side, but Caleb beat her to it.

"Pa!" Caleb hurtled forward and crouched at his father's bedside.

Drops of perspiration beaded Luther's face. "Quit fussing," he muttered. He rallied a bit and clutched his son's hand. "Promise me you'll try to care for your new wife, Son," he whispered. "I would turn over in my grave if I thought I'd done anything to harm her and those children."

"You're not going to die, Pa!"

Luther tried to raise in the bed. "Promise me!"

Caleb stilled, and his shoulders slumped. "I promise." He shot a dark glance toward Lucy as if it were her fault his father was so truculent.

"I want her and the children to move in with you," Luther said. "I'm not sure the noise would be good for the old ticker." His voice was weak, but the odd gleam in his eye made Lucy wonder if he was using the situation to his own advantage. "Once I'm well, we'll see about getting you a decent house for a family."

Caleb's brows drew together, but he bowed his head and nodded. "Whatever you want, Pa." But the look from his gray eyes as he turned toward Lucy was anything but meek.

The time ticked by slowly. When Lucy had finally begun to wonder what had become of the doctor, he came bustling in. A stringy man with grizzled hair, Doc Cooper reminded Lucy of a miner rather than a doctor.

"What's this nonsense, Luther? You're too ornery to die on us. Let's take a look at you." Dr. Cooper jerked his head at Caleb, Lucy, and the children, and they obeyed the silent admonition to leave him alone with Luther.

In the hall, Caleb crossed his arms and leaned against the wall. "I have to hand it to you, Miss Marsh—"

"Mrs. Stanton," she corrected, unable to stop the smile that tugged at her lips. She wanted to laugh aloud at the consternation that raced across his face. Caleb had likely never had anyone buck his will. He was a spoiled child, used to getting his own way.

Caleb straightened, his face going white as he stared at her. "You laugh now, but you won't be laughing long. Life on a ranch is not the fancy parties and teas you're used to in Boston. It's hard, smelly, and dirty. Those lily-white hands won't look so pretty in a few weeks."

Lucy found it difficult to breathe. Before she could respond, Jed stepped between her and Caleb. His fists clenched, he thrust his face into Caleb's.

"My sister is worth two of you! Eileen and me would be in the or-phanage if she hadn't found a job at the millinery and kept us all to-gether. She's come home with her fingers bleeding from the pins. And she's small 'cause when there's not enough food, she makes sure me and Eileen eat first. Lucy may not be big, but she's all heart, Mr. Stan-ton. You don't deserve her!"

Lucy put a hand on her brother's arm. "Hush, Jed," she mur-mured. "God told me to do this, that it was His will."

Caleb gave a short bark of laughter. "I find it hard to believe the Almighty told you to agree to such a plan. I don't need a wife."

A slight smile tilted Lucy's lips. "No, you don't *want* a wife, and that's a completely different situation. God sees things we don't, Mr. Stanton. I don't believe in divorce, so we must make the best of this situation. You should respect your father enough to do that much. I haven't known Luther long, but he seems a wise man. Maybe he knows more about what you need than you do."

Caleb ran a hand through his hair, and Lucy's heart softened at the vulnerability she saw on his face. This had taken him by complete surprise. She'd had time to get used to it, but Luther's actions had left Caleb reeling. "We'd better get that coffee for your pa, or he'll take a switch to you."

Surprise flickered across Caleb's face, and he lifted one eyebrow. "Figured him out already, huh?" He stared into her eyes, then his shoulders slumped. "I guess we'd best declare a truce for now. But don't think this situation will stand, Miss Lucy. You're not up to the task of building the Stanton cattle empire."

Lucy bit her lip and held out her hand. "Truce, Mr. Stanton. I see I shall have to prove myself to you."

Her small hand was enveloped by his large, calloused one. The contact sent a thrill of awareness through her, and she nearly jerked it away. Searching the gray depths of his eyes, she wondered if he felt the awareness she did. If he did, he hid it well.

Caleb released her hand and turned toward the kitchen. "I reckon your first lesson better be coffee. A cattleman can't live without it. It warms him up on those cold nights on the cattle drive and wakes him up after a night spent tossing on the hard ground."

Lucy followed him into the kitchen. Caleb grabbed the handle of the battered coffeepot and poured the dark liquid into a tin cup. "Sugar ruins the taste." He handed her a cup. "Take a swig."

Repressing a shudder, Lucy took the cup of coffee and raised it to her lips. She mustn't let him think she was too weak to even stand up to the taste of coffee. If learning to like the vile liquid was a necessity, then she would do it. She took a gulp of coffee, and the bitter taste nearly made her gag. Managing a smile, she lowered the cup.

"That wasn't so bad, was it?"

"Do you want the truth?" A smile tugged the corners of her lips.

"Yeah."

"It's not as bad as cutting my finger off with a dull knife, but that's about all I can say for it."

Caleb stared at her for a moment, then a laugh rumbled in his throat. Lucy's heart jumped at the sound. With his face lit with amusement, he was entirely too appealing. A dimple in one cheek and the white flash of his teeth softened the tanned planes of his face, and even his towering height and broad shoulders seemed less intimidating.

Caleb poured a cup for Jed. "Here, Boy. If you aim to be a cattleman, you'd best learn, too."

Jed took it cautiously, then sniffed it. His nose wrinkled, but he took a big swallow. His eyes widened, and he coughed. "Good," he choked.

Lucy and Caleb both burst into laughter. The moment of camaraderie warmed Lucy's aching heart. Maybe things would turn out right yet. She would trust God.

3

*L*ucy and her siblings on his heels, Caleb pushed open the door to his father's room. What would he do if something happened to Pa? It had been just the two of them so long, ever since he could remember. Cholera had carried off his mother when he was two, and he had only vague memories of a gentle voice singing to him and a soft lap that smelled of something sweet. Maybe Pa was right, maybe it was time for him to take a wife. But he wasn't some greenhorn who needed his father to pick out a wife for him!

His pa was sitting up in the bed, some color in his face. He smiled when he saw the cup in Caleb's hand. "Coffee, just what the doctor ordered. And Lucy's pretty face will help as well." He winked at Lucy, and Caleb heard her soft laugh.

"I don't remember ordering any such thing, Luther." Doc Cooper put his stethoscope into his black bag and closed it with a snap. "I reckon one cup won't hurt, but don't go drinking too much of it. You need to rest. I'll be back in the morning." He jerked his head, and Caleb followed him into the hallway.

"How is he, Doc?"

"I won't lie to you, Caleb. He's getting old, and his ticker is just wearing out. See that he starts to take it easy, even if it means hiring more help. And try not to get him excited or upset. I know that's not easy to do with a man as active and vital as Luther has been."

Caleb's heart squeezed with pain. "I can't lose him, Doc!"

"Death comes to all of us eventually, Caleb. Lord willing, your pa will be around a few more years, but he's got to step back and learn to enjoy life. That new wife of yours will help. Luther thinks a lot of her, and she'll make him slow down, you mark my words." Doc Cooper pulled on his coat and went toward the door. "I think he'll be fine if you follow my instructions."

Caleb walked the doctor out and stood staring at the closed door, his mind numb. He couldn't make himself believe that his pa was getting old.

A soft hand touched his, and he jumped. Turning, he stared into Lucy's anxious face. "What did the doctor say?"

"Pa's heart is weak. Doc says he needs to cut back and take it easy." He blurted out the words, but it didn't ease the pain.

Lucy's eyes filled with tears. They looked luminous, like sapphire gems. "I'll take care of him," she said.

"He's my pa. I don't need any help." He regretted his words when he saw her bite her lip. He didn't know how to act around women, which was probably the reason he was still unmarried at thirty. He'd had no lack of partners at the county dances, but he invariably said the wrong thing and ended up riding home with Pa. He swallowed hard at the realization that he was no longer unmarried. This young woman with the dazzling blond hair and luminous blue eyes was his wife. His wife. He couldn't get his mind around it.

Lucy straightened her shoulders and stared into his face. "Well, you're going to get my help, whether you want it or not, Caleb Stanton! I'm your wife, and your father is now my father. The kids and I have already learned to love him. This isn't about you. It's about your pa. Our problems can wait."

She was right. He wanted to apologize, but the words stuck in his throat. He knew so little about women. Lucy was entrancing with her golden curls and pink cheeks. Her full lips looked soft and inviting. Caleb jerked his thoughts away from that direction. His priority was to see Pa better; then he could worry about getting rid of Miss Lucy and her siblings.

The next morning Caleb went to his pa's room and found it empty. Panic made his mouth go dry. He rushed down the hall and found him in the kitchen with Jed and Lucy.

"There you are, my boy." Luther pointed to a seat across from him. "Breakfast is ready. Lucy fixed the best flapjacks I've ever feasted upon."

Caleb eased into the seat and looked at the platter of flapjacks. They did look good. His stomach rumbled, and he scowled. "How'd you get Percy to give up his kitchen?"

"He didn't give it up. He shared it." Lucy's smile seemed to brighten the sunshine flooding through the window. "He fixed the coffee and eggs and let me do the flapjacks."

Truly, Lucy was a miracle worker. Percy guarded his kitchen like a dragon guarded gold. Caleb transferred a heap of flapjacks to his plate and spread jam on them. The flapjacks were light as thistledown, and Caleb dug in with gusto. "I'll say one thing," he muttered. "You sure can cook." He aimed a glance at his pa. "You're looking better, Pa."

"I feel fine. Dr. Cooper is an old woman. I aim to rest up another day, then get out to the barn and shoe the horses."

Caleb saw Lucy open her mouth, but he shot her a look of warning, and she quickly closed it. Arguing with Pa would do no good. "Good idea," he said with a shrug. "But don't you reckon it would be bad manners to leave Lucy alone all day?"

"You're probably right. You get your chores done, then get back in here to entertain her," Luther said.

He gave a sly grin, and Caleb had to grit his teeth to keep from spewing his thoughts out. He still hadn't changed his mind over Pa's fool-headed scheme to marry him off to this pale lily of a girl. When she saw the cabin, she'd soon be hightailing it back to Massachusetts.

"I'll take her to the cabin when I get done with chores."

"I was going to suggest that," Luther said. "Lucy here is eager to see her new home."

"She may change her mind when she sees it."

"Now don't you go scaring her, Caleb. That place just needs a woman's touch. It's what your ma and I had when we were first married. You'll build her something better soon."

"It's fine like it is, but if she's expecting something like Boston, she's in for a shock."

"You needn't discuss me as though I'm not here," Lucy said.

Caleb felt a shaft of grudging respect. She knew how to hold her own.

"Can we ride a horse there?" Jed shot to his feet and practically pranced around his chair.

Caleb aimed a glance at Lucy. "Can you ride?"

"A little."

A little. A tenderfoot, just as he suspected. He shrugged and got to his feet. "Wanda is real gentle; you'll be okay on her. And Jed can ride Buck. I'll put Eileen in front of me."

Lucy stood and began to clear the dishes. "By the time you get the chores done, I'll have these dishes cleared away and Eileen fed and dressed."

"Let Percy see to those dishes. You young 'uns run along." Luther waved a hand. "You need to start settling into your new life."

His new life. Caleb slanted a glance toward Lucy. Maybe once he got used to it, the idea might not be so bad. If he just hadn't been dragged to it like a roped calf.

～❧～

An hour later Lucy watched the play of emotions across her new husband's face. One minute she thought he might be warming up to her, and the next, he pulled away again. If he ever loved a woman with the fierce loyalty he showed his pa, she would be a lucky woman.

"I really should help Percy," she told Caleb as she followed him from the kitchen.

"Pa won't rest until he knows we're on our way. So we'd best get it over with, then check back and see how he's doing."

Lucy nodded and fetched her bag. Jed carried his belongings, and Caleb hoisted Eileen's case to his shoulder. The snow nearly blinded her when she stepped outside.

"I hadn't been expecting snow," she told him.

"Don't get much," Caleb said. "I don't remember ever having this much. A skiff of snow is about all we ever see." He strapped the luggage to the back of a mule, then led Lucy toward a black and white horse whose markings reminded Lucy of a cow. Its forlorn stance with its shaggy back to the wind softened her heart.

"This is Wanda. Riding her is like sitting in your mama's rocking chair. She won't let you fall." The horse nuzzled Caleb's hand, and he laughed, then dug his hand into his pocket and pulled out a lump of sugar for the mare. The mare nuzzled it with soft lips from his hand.

Lucy's trepidation eased. Wanda glanced at her with gentle brown eyes, then dropped her head again. Lucy let Caleb help her into the saddle. He'd had the foresight to saddle her with a lady's sidesaddle. It was old but well oiled and in good condition. This high up, she could see out across the land. Stanton land. And she was as much a possession of Caleb's as these boundless acres. In that moment the thought terrified her.

Jed bounded onto his horse, a small buckskin that shied nervously at Jed's exuberance. Caleb lifted Eileen in his arms and showed her how to pet his horse. "This is Maxi, Eileen. Would you like to give him a lump of sugar?"

Eileen's face was white with fright, but she nodded, and Caleb gave her a lump of sugar. The gelding's lips closed gently around the sugar, and Eileen gave a squeal of delight. "I feeded the horse, Lucy!"

Lucy gave her an encouraging smile, full of pride. "You're a brave girl, Eileen," she said. So he was good with kids. That was a mark in his favor, but he had a lot of black marks to overcome.

Caleb set Eileen at the front of his saddle, then swung up behind her. "Follow me," he told Lucy and Jed.

Clutching the reins, Lucy managed to get her horse to follow Caleb's lead, but she had a sneaking suspicion it had more to do with her mare's determination not to be left behind. As the horses labored through the snowdrifts, Lucy kept stealing glances at Caleb's firm jaw. She had so many questions she wanted to ask him, but her tongue seemed stuck to the roof of her mouth.

They traveled over a hill, and she saw a frozen creek in the valley below. A building crouched beside it, the siding gray and worn. A small, leafless tree, shaking in the wind, seemed to cower under the small house for cover.

Lucy smiled. The way he'd talked, she was imagining a soddy or something even worse. He didn't know how rude their former lodgings were. This little place was simply waiting for her. Its forlorn appearance warmed her with the desire to make a difference. This would be home, and she would make Caleb glad his father had found her. She would earn his admiration and respect yet.

Caleb pulled his horse to a halt and jumped down, then pulled Eileen down against his chest. His gaze scanned Lucy's face, and puzzlement clouded his face when she gave him a serene smile.

"It's not much," he said. There seemed to be regret in his voice, and Lucy wondered if he was ashamed of the little cabin.

Her smile warmed. "It's charming."

His eyes widened, and he gave her a sharp look, then turned to go inside.

Jed dismounted and thrust his hands into his pockets. Surveying the small shanty, he turned to Caleb with a grin. "This doesn't look so bad, Mr. Stanton. Lucy's real good at fixing stuff up. You should see the apartment we used to live in."

Lucy felt the heat of a blush on her cheeks. Such faith was humbling. Her gaze was drawn to the cabin again. It seemed to call her like a long-lost child. In her mind's eye, she could see a small garden patch out front and wild roses climbing on a trellis under the kitchen window where she could enjoy the fragrance.

Eileen sidled closer to Lucy and thrust her small hand into Lucy's larger one. "I have to go potty, Lucy," she whispered.

Caleb's expression softened. "Outhouse is out back," he said. "I'll show you, Eileen."

The little girl shrank back and put her thumb in her mouth. Her blue eyes sought her sister's face. "I want Lucy," she whispered.

Caleb nodded. "Let's get inside, and then you can go out the back door instead of traipsing through the snow."

His voice was gentle when he spoke to Eileen. Studying him, Lucy thought he might make a good father once he lost that gruff exterior. He wasn't nearly as hard as he tried to convince everyone he was. She followed him into the cabin and looked around.

Her first impression was of dark, dingy wood and dust. The floor was unpainted plank. It needed a good cleaning more than anything else. A hastily constructed table and a single chair were shoved against the wall by the wood stove. A wood box beside the stove was heaped with kindling that had spilled over onto the floor.

She walked to the kitchen. The stove needed scrubbing and several dirty plates and cups sat in a dishpan on the dry sink. She shivered, not so much from the temperature as from the coldness of the room's atmosphere. But she would fix that.

"I know there aren't enough chairs, but I wasn't expecting company." Caleb pulled the single chair out from the table and nodded toward it. "Have a seat."

"I need to take Eileen out back," she said. Without waiting for a reply, she took Eileen's hand and quickly stepped to the back door. The privy was sturdy and well made. While she waited for Eileen, Lucy glanced at the back of the cabin. It was well constructed, too. She thought he seemed competent in whatever he decided to put his hand to.

Eileen came from the privy, and Lucy took her hand and led her back inside. She found Caleb poking at the fire in the stove while Jed handed him kindling. Heat was already beginning to ease the chill of the room.

"Good, I'll need hot water for my work," Lucy said.

"Work? There won't be anything to do today. The cattle have been fed, and I'll take Jed out with me to break the ice for them to water. You and Eileen can stay inside and keep warm."

Lucy waved a hand. "Look at this place. We can't sleep in this filth."

Caleb's brows drew together. "Filth?" His voice went up at the end of the word. "There's nothing wrong with my cabin. It's not the fanciest home in the Red River Valley, but it would suit any other woman who was used to homesteading. But I knew a city girl like you would turn your nose up at it."

Lucy refused to let him rile her. "The accommodations are fine, Caleb. It's the lack of cleanliness I object to. Now you and Jed just run along. We're going to need some beds, too. See what you can do. When you get back, you'll see how much better it looks with a woman's touch."

Caleb's mouth hung open, and he just stared at her.

"I wouldn't argue with her, Mr. Stanton," Jed said.

Lucy didn't wait to see if Caleb would take Jed's advice. Taking

Eileen by the hand, she grabbed a bucket and headed for the door. "I'll need some water for scrubbing."

"I'll get it." Caleb roused from his stupor and snatched the pail from her. "The pump is out back, but it might be hard to start. I haven't used it for a few days. Just stay put and don't touch anything."

Lucy nearly smiled at the alarm in his voice. Caleb now had a family to look out for, and he seemed to be taking the responsibility seriously. Jed followed him out the door. Putting her hands on her hips, Lucy turned and surveyed the room. They could put some beds against the west wall and there was space for some extra chairs by the fire. The loft overhead was empty. It would serve as the main bedroom.

Heat scorched her cheeks at the thought of sharing a room with Caleb. Not yet, she prayed. She wasn't ready yet. It was a blessing from God that Caleb was so uncertain about the marriage. Time would help them both to adjust to the thought that they were tied for life.

She found an apron in her bag and tied it on. "Eileen, would you like to help me?"

The little girl nodded. "I can do the dishes."

"All right. As soon as Mr. Stanton gets back with the water, I'll heat some, and you can wash up." Lucy looked around again. There wasn't even a broom! No wonder the place needed a woman's touch.

The front door blew open, and Caleb and Jed stumbled inside with the scent of moisture and a blast of cold air. Stomping the snow from his feet, Caleb carried a bucket of water to her. "Where do you want it?"

"There by the stove. Do you have a pan to heat it in? And I need a broom."

"A broom?" Caleb said the words as if he'd never heard of a broom before. He looked around the room as if a broom might materialize from the mere thought.

"I need to sweep."

"It's just a rough plank floor. Sweeping won't do any good."

"Even a plank floor can be kept clean, Mr. Stanton."

His bewildered expression deepened. "But why? You just walk on it. It's not like it's fine hardwood or carpet."

The corner of Lucy's mouth turned up, and she bit her tongue to keep from laughing. The poor man had no clue. "Just find me a broom, and you'll see what I mean."

Caleb scowled. "Let's go, Jed. There's no pleasing a woman."

"I'll be very pleased with a broom," she called after them. Chuckling, she went to heat the water. By the time the water was hot, Caleb was back with a makeshift broom of straw.

When he gave it to her, she handed him the bucket again. "I need more water."

He rolled his eyes but didn't protest. Jed giggled. "I think you're getting domesticated, Mr. Stanton."

Caleb widened his eyes. "I'm just doing what needs done for my own protection, Jed. Your sister may be small, but she's determined." He dropped the bucket and swung Eileen into his arms. "Hey, Sweetheart, there's a new calf in the barn, you want to see?"

Eileen squealed with delight. "Can I pet it?"

"He might suck your fingers."

Eileen looked doubtfully at her hand, then turned her sunny smile back to Caleb. "I don't mind."

"Okay, get your coat."

"Can I come, too?" Lucy asked. The thought of a new calf was suddenly much more appealing than cleaning.

"Sure you can spare the time from your sweeping?" Caleb's grin clutched at her heart.

"I'll take the time."

"Just don't blame me if you have to sleep with the spiders."

Spiders? Lucy eyed the room. There *were* a great many cobwebs. "Maybe tomorrow," she said.

"The cleaning or the calf?"

"The calf," she said reluctantly.

His grin widened, and he went to the door with Eileen in his arms. "You don't know what you're missing."

Lucy was sure that was true. This was a side to Caleb she hadn't seen before. But sometimes duty was more important than fun. She had to earn her keep and show Caleb she could be the wife he needed. He would never love her unless she could prove herself.

Holding the broom like a sword, she swept through the cabin like an avenging angel. Spiders scuttled from her attack. Stomping and shouting, she killed all she could find and swept the room clean of dirt and cobwebs. When the water was hot, she washed the dishes, then used the still-warm water to scrub the floors, swirling the water around with her broom before mopping it up on her hands and knees.

She was almost afraid to check the loft; there were probably even more spiders there. With shaking knees, she climbed the ladder. Poking her head over the top, she looked around. It was as she feared. The entire loft was crisscrossed with spider webs laden with fat bodies, alive and dead. Shuddering, she backed down the ladder. There was no way she could do that herself. She would get Jed to make the first pass. Or maybe even Caleb.

Caleb. The thought of his derision was almost enough to make her go back up, but she couldn't quite make herself mount that ladder again. She should have cleaned upstairs first. Now some of those spiders would probably come down here.

Her earlier euphoria vanished. Maybe she really wasn't cut out to be a cattleman's bride. If she couldn't face up to something as small as a spider, what would she do with a bull? But the thought of a bull wasn't nearly as daunting as those plump bodies upstairs.

She looked around her new kitchen. She could at least start a meal. She went to the small pantry and opened it. Something black moved in the corner, and Lucy stared at it for a moment before it moved again. She backed away, a scream lodged in her throat. It couldn't be what it appeared. Spiders didn't grow that big or that hairy. Then it scuttled toward her, and the paralysis in her vocal chords broke. She shrieked with all the breath in her lungs and bolted for the door.

4

*H*e likes his nose scratched." Caleb guided Eileen's small hand to the calf's nose.

"What's his name?" Eileen scratched the calf's nose, then giggled when its mouth opened and it began to suck on her finger.

"He doesn't have one. This is a working ranch. We can't get attached to our livestock."

"Why? She's pretty." Eileen patted the calf with her small hand. "Can I call her Elsie?"

Before Caleb could explain why it wasn't a good idea to get attached to the calf, a shriek echoed from the house. Caleb jerked and knocked over a pitchfork. The scream was full of panic and terror.

"Stay here and hide!" he ordered the children. Jed instinctively grabbed his little sister and pulled her behind a feed barrel. Grabbing a shotgun by the door, Caleb pelted toward the house. The blood thundered in his ears. Just last month the Landers family had been wiped out by Indians.

Lucy screamed again, and the sound made his blood curdle. He reached the front of the house and stood for a moment collecting his wits. Maybe he should try getting in the back door. The Indians likely were watching this one. But before he could move toward the back, the front door flew open, and Lucy came stumbling out.

Her face was white, and her blue eyes mindless with terror. Those eyes widened when she saw him; then the next thing he knew, she was burrowing into his arms. She barely came to his chest, and still holding his rifle, he held her close. Her shoulders shook, and she made frantic little mews of panic. Holding her close, he tried to peer into the cabin as he steered her to the safety of the side yard.

"Indians?" he whispered, patting her back awkwardly.

She shook her head so hard pins flew from her hair, and golden strands fell to her shoulders. "Spider," she gasped. She shuddered again, and his arms tightened around her.

"A spider?" he asked, pushing her away.

Lucy shuddered again, returning to his grasp. "It was as big as my hand. And—and *hairy*." She burrowed deeper into his jacket.

"Probably a tarantula," he said. The corner of his mouth lifted, and he felt almost giddy with relief. His chest rumbled with the effort to hide his mirth.

Lucy lifted her head. "Are you *laughing*?"

A chuckle escaped. "It's probably Pete. He was in the pantry, right?"

Her eyes wide with horror, Lucy took a step back. "This spider *lives* there? And you *named* him?"

Caleb was surprised to find he regretted letting go of her. "Sure, he eats the bugs."

Lucy shuddered. "You have to kill it."

He shook his head. "Nope. Pete stays."

She crossed her arms. "Then I go. I'm not sharing my home with a hairy spider."

Caleb narrowed his eyes. "Fine. I didn't want you here anyway."

"I'll stay with your father until you get that, that *thing* out of there."

His father. Caleb gritted his teeth. If she went back to the big house, it might upset Pa. He would think Caleb wasn't being a proper husband. And maybe he wasn't, Caleb admitted. He would be the first to admit he had no idea of what women found important. But what gave this little woman the right to waltz into his home and start giving orders?

"I'll take Pete to the barn," he said.

"Then I won't go in the barn!"

Caleb let out an exasperated sigh and shook his head. Women. There was no pleasing them. "I thought you wanted to learn to be a proper rancher's wife. That includes helping out in the barn. And making peace with beneficial bugs like tarantulas."

"Spiders aren't insects; they're arachnid. And they're hideous." Lucy shuddered.

Tears shimmered on her lashes, and Caleb realized for the first time that she was truly terrified. This was not some power ploy. She was petrified. Backing away from him, a sob rose from her chest, and she hiccupped. Remorse smote Caleb. She would think he was a fiend.

He put a hand on her shoulder. "I'm sorry, Lucy. Pete won't hurt you."

Lucy burst into tears and covered her face with her hands. "I've been trying so hard," she sobbed. "I want to be a blessing to you, Mr. Stanton. You must think you've been saddled with some weak woman who needs pampering. Truly, I can carry my side of the bargain, but I can't abide spiders. Especially ones who need a close shave. Preferably with a very sharp blade."

Caleb suppressed his grin when she shuddered. He pulled her back into his arms. She seemed to fit there. He rested his chin on her head and breathed in the fragrance of her hair. It smelled clean with a hint of something sweet, maybe lavender. Something stirred in his heart. Whether he'd planned it or not, this woman was his wife. He might not love her, but he had to make accommodations for her in his life, even if it meant ridding the house of creepy crawlies.

He hugged her gently. "I'll get rid of Pete," he said.

She turned her wet face up to him. "You will? It won't even be in the barn?"

"I'll take him out somewhere and let him loose."

She smiled, and it was like the sun burst through the storm clouds. "Thank you, Mr. Stanton," she whispered. A shadow darkened her eyes.

"What's wrong?"

"Um, there're other spiders in the loft. Could you get rid of them, too?"

He grinned. "Those I can kill." He released her and went inside.

"I'll just stay out here until the spiders are gone," she called.

Caleb stepped inside the room and stopped short. His eyes widened. Was this the same place? It was spotless. He whistled softly through his teeth. Maybe this marriage thing wouldn't be so bad. He hadn't even noticed all the dust and cobwebs until they were gone.

He strode through the house until he found Pete crouched in a corner of the pantry. "Sorry, old friend, you have to go out into the cold." He held out his hand, and the tarantula crawled onto his sleeve. He carried the spider out the back door and walked out into the field until he couldn't see the cabin anymore, then shook Pete off into the melting snow. The spider seemed to look at him reproachfully, then scurried off toward a stand of cottonwood trees by the river.

Now for the rest of the spiders. Caleb hurried back to the cabin. Grabbing the broom, he climbed the ladder to the loft. He swatted and squashed spiders until all that was left were dead remains, then swept them all up onto a piece of tin he found. He carried them out the back door so Lucy wouldn't see them and tossed them into the field.

He was still smiling when he went looking for Lucy. She was in the barn with the children, and she jumped when he stepped through the door. Her face was still pale, but she met his gaze bravely.

"It's gone," he said. "So are the ones in the loft."

Relief flooded her face, and she gave him a tremulous smile. "Thank you, Mr. Stanton. Are you hungry?"

"Starved. Let me show you where the root cellar is. I have smoked meat down there as well as some vegetables." Taking the shovel, Caleb led the way to the back of the cabin and shoveled away the snow to reveal a cellar door. He tugged it up. "Get me the broom, and I'll make sure you don't have to deal with any unwanted guests down there, either."

She gave him a grateful smile, and he felt as tall as Paul Bunyan. They would learn to rub along together. All they needed was time.

While Lucy fixed the meal, he took the children back to the barn, where he had them help him muck out the horse stalls. Before long the aroma of beef and potatoes wafted across the yard. His mouth watered. Usually all he managed was a slice of cold smoked meat. He rarely bothered with more than that.

He tossed the pitchfork into the pile of straw. "That's it, kids. Let's go get some grub." He lifted Eileen in his arms, and they trooped toward the house. As they neared the house, he heard Lucy scream his name. "Must be another spider," he told Jed. Grinning, he set Eileen down at the front door and grabbed the broom. It sounded like it came from the backyard. Maybe Pete had found his way back.

As he rounded the corner of the house, he heard snarling. The hair on the back of his neck rose. That was no spider. It sounded like a wolf or a dog, and he'd left his rifle in the barn. He heard a whimper from Lucy and broke into a run.

A large mongrel, half wolf, half dog, blocked Lucy's way to the house. A twig clutched in her hand, she stood with her back pressed to the outhouse. Caleb raised the broom like a club, but before he could swing it, the animal launched itself at Lucy's throat. Caleb let out an involuntary cry, then a golden shape came hurtling across the yard and crashed into the mongrel in midair. Mongrel and dog rolled over together, both snarling and growling. Fur flew like blowing snow. The ruckus brought the two children to the back door.

"Get back inside!" Lucy shouted. She eased away from the outhouse and ran to Caleb. "Do something," she panted. "It will kill the dog."

The children stood paralyzed in the doorway. "Jed, get my rifle!"

The boy nodded and shut the door. Caleb propelled Lucy toward the door. "I'll handle this. You get inside." He opened the door and pushed her inside.

Her eyes pleading and frantic, she stood in the doorway. "That dog saved my life. You can't let that—that wolf or whatever it is—kill him."

She was right. He nodded and turned with the broom. When he whacked the mongrel wolf across the head, it turned toward him, its jaws open in a snarl. It lunged at him, but the dog renewed the attack and seized the wolf by the back leg. They rolled together again, snarling and spitting.

Caleb brought the broom down on the mongrel wolf's head with all his might, and the broom handle broke. The wolf yelped and shook the dog off, then launched itself at Caleb.

A gun boomed, and the mongrel fell at Caleb's feet. Stunned both by the suddenness of the attack and the loud crack of the rifle, he stood there a moment with the snow turning to crimson at his feet. The air was acrid with the scent of gunpowder. Turning his head, he found Lucy holding the smoking rifle.

Lucy dropped the rifle and ran into the yard to the dog. It was a golden retriever. The dog's ribs showed through its mangy, bloodied coat, and it licked her hand when she knelt beside it.

Lucy turned a pleading gaze to Caleb. "Can you help the poor thing?"

Caleb knelt beside her and ran gentle hands over the dog. It whimpered when he touched its wounds but made no move to bite him. "Good girl," he soothed. He scooped the dog up in his arms and stood. "Let's get her inside."

Lucy held the door open, and he carried the dog inside and laid her down by the fire. "I need some hot water and old rags. There should be some in the pantry."

Lucy hurried to find what he needed while he opened his toolbox and found some scissors. He cut away as much of the fur as he could and winced at the deep bites and lacerations on the dog. He washed the wounds with the water and rags Lucy provided, then bandaged the worst of the bites on the dog's leg.

"How'd you learn to shoot like that?" He felt a curious mixture of pride and curiosity.

"Lucy can shoot a walnut out of a tree," Jed said with obvious pride. "Pa said she took to hunting and shooting like most women take to meddling."

Caleb's mouth lifted in a smile. "Sounds like your pa had some bad experience with women."

Lucy flushed. "He liked to tease Mama. She was always helping out the neighbors. Pa called it meddling, but he was really very proud of her. She showed Christ's love wherever and whenever she could."

"I never knew my ma," Caleb said. "I was only two when she died, and all I remember is the scent of her hair and her soft lap." He regretted the words as soon as he saw Lucy's face soften. He didn't want pity. She'd already saved him from the mongrel wolf; he didn't want her to unman him anymore.

He stood. "She should be all right. We'll keep her inside until she's well enough to turn outside again."

"Can I keep her?" Eileen asked. Her small hands patted the dog's head, and the dog licked the little girl's fingers feebly.

Caleb hesitated. "I reckon so. I don't have a dog right now, since Rolf died last fall. This lady doesn't look like she belongs to anyone; she's much too thin. But we should put out in Wichita Falls we've got her. She looks to be a valuable animal."

Eileen's face clouded. "She's mine. No one else can have her."

Lucy patted Eileen's head. "I doubt anyone will claim her. What are you going to name her?"

Eileen kept patting her head. "What would be a good name for such a brave doggy?"

"How about Bridget? It's Irish for strong." Lucy put a bowl of water near the dog.

"Good girl, Bridget," Eileen crooned, patting the dog again. Bridget thumped her tail on the floor, and Eileen flung her arms around Bridget's neck.

"Looks like she approves," Caleb said. "Now if we're all finished with the dog, can we eat? My stomach is gnawing on my backbone."

Lucy's lips curved in a smile, and he found himself fascinated with the way her teeth gleamed and the smooth pink of her cheeks. He shook himself out of his reverie. A lucky shot with the rifle wasn't enough to get past his guard. He would bide his time and see where her true character lay.

After the meal, Lucy put Eileen down for a nap on a mat beside Bridget. Caleb took Jed and went outside to bury the mongrel wolf and to knock together some beds in the barn. He had Jed take some feed sacks in to Lucy to stitch together for mattress covers. They built two beds, one for Lucy and Eileen and one for Jed. Lucy was beautiful, but he knew it was much too soon for her to share a bed with him, even if he wished it. And he didn't. Not yet. She had shown some courage today, but she still wasn't the wife he'd envisioned for himself.

It would take more than a pretty face and a good meal to win him over.

As if the thought had brought her, Lucy stepped into the barn with the feedbags over her arm. "Eileen is still sleeping. Could I get some straw to stuff the mattresses?"

Caleb pointed to the stack of clean straw at the back of the barn. "Help yourself."

He watched her kneel and begin to stuff the bags full of straw. A shaft of sunlight shone through a crack in the barn siding and lit her hair with gold. He dragged his glance away. Pa would be smirking at the easy way he was letting his defenses down.

"We've got the beds done," he said, standing to his feet.

"Are we staying here tonight?"

"I want to check on Pa, but we'll come back here afterwards. That's what he wants, and Doc says we need to humor him."

Her cheeks pink from exertion, she turned to face him. "There are many things we need to set up a home. Would your pa have extra he could share?"

Caleb stiffened. "I'm no pauper, Lucy. Give me a list of what you need, and I'll get it in Wichita Falls."

She inclined her neck. "I would like to go with you, if I might."

Great. Now the whole town would gawk at her like she was his prize filly. He shrugged. "Suit yourself. When Eileen wakes up, we'll go see Pa, then take a quick run to town." He hefted an end of the bed and nodded for Jed to pick up the other end. Carrying the bed to the house, he reflected on how the day had turned out nothing like he expected.

5

ucy wanted to sit in the corner and wail like a baby. Discouragement slowed her steps as she trudged after Caleb to the barn. Not only had she gone into hysterics over a spider, but she had let a mongrel corner her. Why hadn't she faced the animal down and forced it to back off? Instead, she had acted like a damsel in distress. What would Caleb think?

Mounting her horse, she glanced at Caleb from the corner of her eye. He didn't seem to be upset by her failure. But he had to be wondering if she was entirely too frightened and sissified to be of much use on the ranch. The Triple S would never take its place with the big cattle empires with her slowing him down.

Caleb was a fine man, and he deserved a strong wife, one who faced up to the challenges of this wild land instead of screaming for help over a spider a fraction of her size. She wished she could get over her fear of spiders, but it had dogged her ever since she could remember. A warm feeling enveloped her when she remembered the way he'd taken care of the spiders and faced up to the mongrel.

"Will Bridget be all right?" Eileen asked. Her blue eyes were enormous in her pale face as she peered around Caleb from her perch in front of him. It had been a hard day for such a little girl. She'd never gotten a full nap, and the terror of the mongrel wolf had taken its toll on them all.

All except Caleb. His face tanned and strong, he rode easy in his saddle, his knees hugging the horse as though it was an extension of himself. His sandy hair blew in the wind, and his gray eyes looked luminous in the sun. He was a man a woman could depend on. Lucy had learned that much already. Not many men would have displayed his sense of humor over her fear of spiders. And he hadn't hesitated to rush to defend her from the mongrel.

No other man, and a stranger at that, had ever offered to protect her before. The warmth she felt toward Caleb for that unconscious gesture baffled Lucy. She'd always prided herself on taking care of everyone else, yet her deepest being longed for someone like Caleb to nurture and protect her. How could she earn his love if she wasn't all he wanted in a wife? She would have to work harder.

She realized she hadn't answered Eileen. "The dog will be fine, Sweetheart. I left her water and some food. We'll be back in a few hours."

In a few hours it would be bedtime. Lucy's mouth went dry at the thought of the coming night. She'd fixed Caleb's bed in the loft, but what would she do if he expected her to join him there? She would just have to tell him the children needed her close for awhile. And it was the truth. But he seemed too aloof to expect her company in bed.

They rounded the bend in the road, and the ranch house came into view. It felt like home to Lucy already. The two-story house sprawled in several directions, and the front porch beckoned her like an old friend. Over the crest of the hill, she could see several riders rounding up cattle, and Lucy straightened in her saddle. Craning her neck, she wished she could go watch them, but there was no time today. But someday, she promised herself, she would learn just what cowboys did.

Caleb stopped at the barn and dismounted, then pulled Eileen down. He tossed his reins to a ranch hand, then stepped over to help Lucy. She lost her balance when she slid out of the saddle, but he caught her before she could tumble to the ground. Pressed against his hard chest, she caught the aroma of the bay rum he'd used to wash his hair. The pleasant, masculine scent, combined with his proximity, brought the heat to her cheeks.

His gray eyes lingered on her lips while his hands spanned her waist. Lucy had never been this close to a man before, with the exception of her father. Looking deep into his eyes, she felt a connection she'd never felt. In spite of his casual manner, her nearness affected him more than she'd realized. She stepped away and put a trembling hand to her hair to make sure it was still in place.

Caleb's hand dropped, and Eileen took it as though he had put it down for her. Caleb exchanged an amused grin with Lucy.

"Watch it or she'll have you wrapped around her little finger," Lucy whispered.

"Too late," Caleb whispered back. "I was lost when she let the calf suck her fingers. She has a lot of spirit like her sister." He looked away. "I never did say thank you for your sharp-shooting."

Heat scorched Lucy's cheeks again. "It was the least I could do for making you give up your pet." A slight shudder passed through her frame.

"You replaced Pete with Bridget."

"At least Bridget looks good with hair."

Caleb grinned. "Pete would be offended that you didn't care for his haircut."

"He's lucky I didn't have my way. If I had, he would have been bald and flattened."

Caleb chuckled. He opened his mouth, but the door swung open, and Doc Cooper let himself out. His lean face held a trace of worry, and Lucy tensed with concern.

The mirth left Caleb's face as well, and he reached out to touch the doctor's arm. "How's Pa?"

Doc pressed his lips together. "Weaker than I'd like to see him. He had another spell a few hours ago."

Caleb's face went white. "I should have been here."

"No, no, Percy fetched me, and your pa is resting comfortably."

"We'd better stay here instead of at my place."

Doc nodded. "Couldn't hurt. That's providing the old coot will let you coddle him a bit. I'm not telling you anything you don't know when I say your pa is the most stubborn man I know."

A ghost of a smile lifted one corner of Caleb's mouth. "He's ornerier than a newly branded calf when he's sick. I'm not sure my—my wife is up to this."

The doctor's eyebrows went up to his hairline. "I wondered who this pretty lady was, Caleb. Where you been hiding her?" He turned to Lucy and nodded. "These two cowpokes have needed a woman's hand for a long time. It's a big job, though, Missus. I'll be praying for you to withstand the strain."

Lucy laughed and took hold of his hand. "Until you've faced matrons determined to fit into clothes two sizes to small for them, you don't know what strain is, Dr. Cooper. I think I can handle two cantankerous men. But the prayers would be most welcome."

The doctor guffawed and slapped his hat on his leg. "You've got your work cut out for you handling this little woman, Caleb. I wish I could be a fly on the wall and watch." Still grinning, he went toward his buckboard. "Call me if you need me," he said before climbing into the seat.

Lucy's face burned. Sneaking a peek at Caleb, she caught his stare fixed on her with an expression on his face she couldn't read. "I'm sorry, Mr. Stanton, I didn't mean to cause you embarrassment," she whispered. "When will I ever learn to watch my tongue?"

"I thought you handled yourself right well. Doc's sense of humor can be pretty intimidating. I was proud of you."

A lump grew in Lucy's throat. He was proud of her! No one had ever told her that. Her parents were stern disciplinarians and were stingy with their praise. And for three years now, her life had been consumed with the thankless task of putting enough food on the table for her brother and sister. Caleb's pride, for she recognized that emotion on his face now, was heady stuff.

She struggled to answer him, but the lump grew larger not smaller, and for a moment she was afraid she would cry. Then Caleb pushed open the door and motioned for her to go in. The aroma of beef and potatoes and the warmth of the fire welcomed them. Caleb strode straight toward the hall to the bedrooms. Lucy and the children trailed behind him.

Before they reached Luther's bedroom, they could hear his voice raised in disgust. "Look at this food, Percy, it's not fit for man nor beast. Bring me some of that stew I smell cooking. A man needs more than this thin broth! I'll waste away to nothing."

"Doc Cooper thinks you need to shed a few pounds, Boss. This is good for you. He told me not to let you have none of that stew just yet," Percy said.

Lucy crowded behind Caleb to peer into the bedroom. Luther turned his head and saw them at the door. "Give me that spoon." He snatched it from Percy's hand. "I'm not so far gone I can't feed myself. Get in here, all of you; don't stand there gawking.

Lucy followed Caleb into the room and went to the bed. "Can I help you, Mr. Stanton?"

He waved a hand. "I've had all I can take of Doc and Percy treating me like an old woman. Tell me about your day. How do you like your new home?"

What could she say? That it was better than she'd ever imagined herself mistress of? That much was true. But she'd always imagined sharing a home with a man who loved her, not some stranger, kind though he had been today.

"I didn't get much of a chance to see it until I cleaned it," she said. "Your son is not the best housekeeper."

Caleb pulled up a chair and propped a booted leg on it. "She didn't cotton to Pete. I had to take him to the back forty and let him go." Though his tone sounded injured, the glance he sent Lucy's way was full of mirth.

"Good for her. I never did understand why you had a spider as big as a dinner plate wandering around your place."

Caleb shrugged. "Oh, and she saved my hide when she shot a mongrel wolf aimed straight at my throat."

A bit of color came back to Luther's pale face, and he sat up a bit straighter. "I told you our Lucy would make you a fine wife, Caleb. Sometimes your old dad knows what he's doing."

Lucy saw Caleb press his lips together, and her earlier euphoria vanished. He was trying to be a good sport, but he still wished she'd never shown up with his father. Suppressing a sigh, she spent some time talking with Luther, urging him to eat his broth with a promise that he could have some more at suppertime.

When she saw Caleb stirring restlessly, she stood. "We must be going, Mr. Stanton. There are some things we need in town."

"We'll be back for the night in a few hours," Caleb said.

"I thought you were going to stay at your place," his father grumbled.

"We will when you're better."

Luther pointed a bony finger at his son. "You'll do no such thing. I won't be coddled, Caleb. When the good Lord calls me home, I'll go, but until then I intend to get on with my life and have you get on with yours. If you want to do something for me, produce me a grandchild before I die."

Caleb's nostrils flared, and Lucy dropped her gaze to the floor. Her face was hot, and she didn't dare look at Caleb again. She wanted to run from the room in mortification. Gritting her teeth, she lifted her head and mustered her strength enough to smile sweetly at her father-in-law. "We'll be going now, Mr. Stanton. We'll check in on you tomorrow."

"Do you think you could bring yourself to call me Pa or at least Luther?" the old man asked.

Lucy's heart softened. She already cared for him; how could she deny such a heartfelt request. "All right, P-Pa."

Luther's cheeks gained a bit of pink, and he relaxed against the pillows. "You're a good girl, Lucy. If I was thirty years younger, I would have married you myself. Lucky for Caleb I was too old to compete with a young buck like him." His voice trailed away, and he fell asleep, his mouth open in a soft snore.

Still churning inside from Luther's mention of children, Lucy almost flinched when Caleb touched her elbow and guided her out of the room. She found the children in the parlor and had them get their coats, all the while conscious of Caleb's overwhelming presence beside her. She longed to be back in Boston, away from these confusing emotions that ravaged her as that mongrel wolf had ravaged Bridget. The coming night terrified her. What if Caleb took his father's request seriously and demanded his husbandly rights? Swallowing hard, she threw her cloak about her shoulders and went outside.

"How about we take the buckboard to town? The snow is almost melted, and we'll need the space to bring our supplies home," Caleb asked.

"Whatever you say," Lucy said.

Caleb went to hitch the horses to the buckboard, and Lucy turned to stare out at the land. Though the day had warmed enough for the snow to melt, the air still held a crisp edge. Lucy wondered if she would still be here when spring finally came. She didn't know whether to pray for that or not. Taking her place as this man's wife, in all ways, brought the blood hammering to her face and left her trembling.

But her mama hadn't raised her to be a coward. She drew herself up to her full height and marched toward the buckboard. Following behind her, Jed and Eileen were strangely quiet, as if they sensed her mood. Caleb tossed Eileen up onto the second seat, and Jed joined her there. Caleb's big hands spanned Lucy's waist as he lifted her to the seat. His grip held on a moment longer than necessary, and Lucy saw the same trepidation in his eyes that she felt.

Her face softened, and she yearned to touch his cheek with her fingertips, but she resisted the impulse. They had much to learn about one another, and she didn't want to rush anything.

The trip to town was silent, broken only by Eileen's chatter. Lucy tensed as the buckboard rattled nearer the cluster of buildings that was Wichita Falls. She dreaded the pleasantries she would have to face as Caleb's new wife. Just from looking at their holdings, she guessed the Stantons were a prominent cattle family.

Caleb stopped the buckboard in front of the general store. "Ready?" he asked.

"About as ready as a chicken is to get its neck wrung off," Lucy muttered.

Caleb grinned. "It won't be as bad as what you've already faced today. Come on, let me introduce you, and you can pick out everything you need." He jumped out of the wagon and held up his arms for Lucy.

He helped her down. "Jed, collect your little sister and meet us inside. You all need some new clothes, so we might as well get them while we're here."

Lucy stopped in her tracks. "I'll not have you buying us all these things, Mr. Stanton. People will say I married you for your money."

"That's pretty accurate, though, isn't it?" he asked quietly. "If you'd had enough money, you wouldn't have agreed to my father's plan. You would have found some other way around it."

Lucy's eyes stung with outraged tears, though she knew what he said was true. She *would* have spurned Luther's offer if she'd had any recourse. She would have paid whatever was necessary to get Jed out of trouble and gone on with her life in Boston.

Caleb held up a hand. "I didn't mean to insult you, Lucy. What's done is done. Now we have to see if we can work this marriage out so we're not at each other's throats like Bridget and the mongrel."

Choking back the tears, Lucy pinned a smile in place and took hold of his arm. Caleb led her into the general store, milling with people, mostly women. The familiar scents of cinnamon and mint mingled with leather and perspiration. It smelled just like the general store she frequented back in Boston, and a wave of homesickness gripped her.

The chatter in the store ceased as they stepped to the middle of the large room that was crammed with everything from food stuffs to notions to tools. Every gaze in the room pinned Lucy in her tracks. Gathering her courage, she managed to smile as Caleb introduced her.

"While you're all here, I'd like to introduce you to my wife, Lucy," he announced.

A collective gasp went around the room, and Lucy couldn't help noticing the way several women turned to look at a tall, rawboned woman standing near the glass jars of candy. Her thick red hair was caught carelessly in a tail at her neck, and she wore leather boots similar to Caleb's under her heavy skirt. Though not at all pretty, she exuded an animal magnetism that held Lucy's attention.

At Caleb's words, the woman's head snapped back as though she were slapped. Her deep green eyes, her one claim to beauty, looked almost feverish, but she was the first to offer her congratulations. Hectic spots of red in her cheeks, she held her head high as she stepped forward with an outstretched hand. "Congratulations, Lucy. You've succeeded where so many of us have lost. We thought Caleb here would die a bachelor. I'm Margaret O'Brien, your neighbor to the south."

Margaret's handshake was firm, almost like a man's. Lucy's heart sank like an anvil in water. This was the woman Caleb should have married. Lucy felt like an incompetent child next to her. No wonder Caleb was upset. This woman could have been his partner in every meaning of the word. Lucy would never manage to fill those large boots.

"Pleased to meet you," she choked.

Margaret raised her gaze to meet Caleb's. "I wish you well, Caleb," she said. Then her composure failed, and tears filled her eyes. With a muttered apology, Margaret fled the store with an almost palpable wave of sympathy behind her. Lucy felt small and mean that she had hurt this woman, even unknowingly.

Once the store door slammed, the glares from the other women should have cowed Lucy, but she couldn't let them. Too much depended on her fitting in here. She managed a smile. "I do hope you'll feel free to call on us whenever you can. I look forward to learning much about ranching from you."

Several of the women looked at one another, then one by one the women grudgingly welcomed her to the community. After a pause bordering on rudeness, they then scuttled out the door, no doubt to find Margaret and commiserate with her. And who could blame them? Lucy was an interloper here. She glanced at Caleb. He wore a bewildered smile, and she wondered how much he'd kept company with Margaret. But Lucy was Caleb's wife, and she offered a silent prayer of thanks for that as she took her list to the counter.

6

The wagon, laden with food stuffs, fabric, and planks of wood, lumbered along the road. Bits of mud, left from the melted snow, flew up from the wagon wheels. Caleb risked a glance at Lucy. She hadn't said much, and Caleb had to wonder if she was angry. She didn't look angry, though; she looked tired and sad. Guilt smote him, but he pushed it away. He hadn't asked her to come here. Maybe she had gotten it into her head that he needed her because he couldn't find a wife for himself. Pa had probably led her to believe that.

He hated that Margaret had acted so hurt. There had never been any promises between them, but he had danced with her more than any other woman at the last county dance. And to be honest, his manner had probably indicated his interest. He glanced at the woman beside him. His wife. It still didn't seem real.

She was such a tiny thing, but she was stronger inside than any woman he'd ever met. A tiny Titan. The way she'd shot that mongrel wolf had shocked him to the core. But she still wasn't the wife he wanted. And why was that? Was it because he hadn't picked her for himself? A man wanted to choose his own wife. Not that she wasn't attractive. Maybe that was half the trouble. Being around her made his palms sweaty.

Caleb cleared his throat. "I thought me and Jed would build some more chairs with this lumber. Anything else you can think of, Lucy?"

"Trying to make amends?" she asked softly. "I'm not the one you should apologize to."

So much for extending the olive branch. He scowled. "What do I have to feel guilty about?" Women. Why had Pa gotten him into this predicament?

"What promises did you make that poor woman?"

"I never promised Margaret anything," he said. "I never even asked to call on her."

Lucy tipped her head to the side and looked at him with those clear, honest eyes. After a long moment in which he held her gaze, she nodded. "I see that's true. Poor Margaret."

There was true compassion in her voice, and Caleb had to wonder about this woman who was his wife. He would have felt rivalry toward another man, but Lucy seemed to see right to a person's heart and feel something that mattered. She truly was sorry about Margaret's pain.

Eileen nestled her head under his arm, and Caleb looked down in surprise. The little girl's long lashes lay soft against her pink cheeks, and his heart softened. His life was changing already, and parts of it felt mighty good. He wrapped his arm around Eileen and pulled her close so she didn't jerk so badly when the wagon hit the ruts in the road.

Lucy brushed the blond hair back from Eileen's face. "She's tuckered out. I think we all are."

"I shouldn't have made you come to town so quick."

"It's all right. I had to face them all sooner or later."

"Later would've been better. I should've given you time."

"It wasn't your fault. I'm the interloper, the one who snatched a handsome, eligible man out from under their noses."

Lucy's voice was matter-of-fact, but Caleb caught his breath. Was that really the way she saw him? A warm glow of pleasure spread through his chest. Women had flirted with him before, but he'd always thought it was simply because he was a Stanton. He didn't want to be loved because of who his pa was, but for who he was.

He hunched his shoulders and stared ahead at the road. Her words were likely a ploy to make sure he didn't send her packing. His lips tightened. How could he do that? If what Pa said was true, he was tied to this woman for life. Divorce wasn't an option, in spite of his blustering when he'd first learned of his pa's actions. He ducked his head deeper into his coat. If there was a way out of this tangle, he didn't see it.

The cabin looked cold and forlorn when they stopped at the barn. This probably wasn't what she expected when Pa told her of all their holdings. And he had never intended to bring a bride to this hovel; it was only a temporary cabin until he built a real house. It might have been good enough for his parents once, but that was in the frontier days. Lucy probably wouldn't have agreed to Pa's ridiculous offer if she'd realized she would be living in a small cabin.

Clouds gathered overhead, and cold drops of rain splashed onto Caleb's face. The wind freshened, and he squinted at the sky. "Storm's coming."

He jumped to the ground and held out his arms for Eileen. Lucy passed her down to him, and he held the little girl close to protect her from as much wetness as he could.

"Jed, help your sister down, then see to the animals," he said. "When you're done, start bringing in the supplies. I'll be right out to help you."

"Yes, Sir." Jed jumped from the wagon. He helped Lucy down, then led the horses inside the barn.

The rain began to come down in earnest, hard droplets that chilled him instantly. Caleb took Lucy's arm, then they ran toward the house, splashing through the rivulets of mud that were already beginning to fill the yard.

He threw open the door and followed Lucy inside. It wasn't as cold as he had expected; heat still radiated from the last of the fire. The rain drummed on the tin roof as he handed Eileen to Lucy, then went to stir up the embers of the fire.

As he poked at the fire, he heard Lucy humming in a low voice as she rattled pans at the cookstove. It was a homey sound that he found he rather liked. He spent little time here, usually only sleeping on his pallet after a hard day with the cattle. The cabin was changed already after just a few hours.

He pushed the thought away and went out to join Jed in the barn.

The lad had already curried the horses and unloaded the wagon. The house supplies were stacked in one corner, and he'd put the feed in the grain bins.

"Good job, Jed," Caleb said.

The boy flushed, and his eyes brightened. "Thank you, Sir."

"You don't have to call me Sir, Boy. Call me Caleb."

"Does that mean you're going to keep us?" Jed's voice was anxious, but he held Caleb's gaze without looking away.

Caleb hesitated. What did he say to that? He really didn't have a choice. He was coming to realize that after only two days. Pa's health wouldn't take any more upheaval, and the marriage was legal. The best thing was to make do with the situation as best he could. And he had to admit having a pretty wife to come home to might not be such a bad thing.

Jed's face fell as the silence went on. "Don't blame Lucy for us being here, Mr. Stanton. It was my fault." He hung his head. "I stole from your pa as a dare. That's how he met Lucy."

Caleb caught his breath. He would never have guessed Jed would do something like that. He studied the boy's downcast face, then gently touched his shoulder.

"Pa is a pretty good judge of character," he said. "If he thought you weren't a budding Jesse James, I reckon I should give you a second chance as well."

When Jed raised his head, his eyes were glistening with tears. "You won't be sorry, Mr. Stanton. I know Lucy is little, but you don't know her very well yet. Mrs. Thomas at the millinery shop was always going on about how quick she was to learn something new. She'll learn to help you here at the ranch. And I'm a hard worker." He flexed the muscles on his arm. "See here? I can heft a bale of hay by myself. And me and Eileen will try to stay out of your way as much as possible so you can have time with Lucy."

A lump grew in Caleb's throat. Lucy inspired a lot of love in her brother. He squeezed Jed's shoulder. "I'll be glad to have the help, Son. You don't need to stay out of the way. I don't have much experience with young 'uns since I never had a brother, but I'll try to be a dad to you as well. Tomorrow I'll start teaching you how to rope and brand. We'll be taking the cattle to market come summer, and I'll need all the hands I can get."

Jed's lip trembled, and the tears spilled over onto his cheeks. He scrubbed at his face with the back of his hand. "I ain't usually a bawl baby, Mr. Stanton. I'll work hard and make you glad you married us. Lucy's worked so hard to try to keep us together. Now it's my turn."

Us. He reckoned a package deal was what it was, too. He had a ready-made family. It was a little overwhelming.

Caleb cleared his throat. "How about helping me carry this stuff to your sister? She may be a miracle worker, but she has to have something to work with."

"Yes, *Sir!*" Jed hefted a sack of flour to his shoulder and marched toward the house. He looked back at Caleb. "Uh, Mr. Stanton, I'd sure be glad if you didn't say nothing to Lucy about our talk. She hates for people to say nice stuff about her."

"She does?"

Jed nodded vigorously. "There was a guy hanging around all last summer who went on and on about how pretty she was. She finally got fed up and told him the only beauty she was interested in was that on the inside, and since all he could see was the outside, he'd best mosey on down the road."

Caleb squelched a grin. "I'll keep mum."

"Thanks, Mr. Stanton." Jed started for the door.

"Jed."

The boy stopped. "Yes, Sir?"

"Call me Caleb. Mr. Stanton is my pa."

Jed's eyes grew bright. "Yes, Sir, I mean Caleb." He was still grinning as he dashed out into the driving rain.

Caleb grabbed a gunnysack full of food and slung it over his shoulder. Lucy was quite a remarkable young woman. How many women would have worked so hard and sacrificed so much for their siblings? His respect for his new wife went up a notch.

When he got to the house, Jed was jabbering excitedly while Lucy listened. "I'm going to learn to rope a steer and brand, Lucy. Maybe I'll even get to go on the cattle drive up north. You know how good I can ride."

"We'll see, Jed. That's a big job, and you're not hardly old enough."

"Old enough to do a man's job," Caleb observed, setting his burden on the floor. "Jed's going to be a fine ranch hand."

"He's only twelve, Mr. Stanton."

"I was ten when I went on my first cattle drive."

Lucy's eyes narrowed. "He's my brother, and I'll decide what's best for him!"

Caleb's warm, fuzzy feelings toward Lucy evaporated like the morning dew. She would make a sissy of the boy. "You want Jed to turn into a man or young hoodlum?"

Lucy's face whitened, and she held up her hand as if to ward off a blow. Jed made a small sound of protest, and Caleb realized he'd said too much. "I'm sorry, I didn't mean that. Jed is a fine boy, but he's almost a man, Lucy. You have to let loose those apron strings a tad."

Her sober blue eyes regarded him for a moment, then she nodded. "You may be right. But Jed and Eileen are my whole life. I couldn't bear for anything to happen to Jed."

"You have to trust someone, Lucy. I'm your husband now. I'll take care of Jed."

Her eyes examined him again. "I'm sure you will, Mr. Stanton," she said softly. "I'm sorry if I made you think I didn't trust you." She turned back to her task of stashing the supplies.

What had Pa been thinking? Did he have any idea how hard it was to be married to a stranger? It would take years to know all about Lucy. Yet Caleb found the thought was not at all unappealing.

❧

Emotions she didn't know she had churned in Lucy's stomach. Anger and jealousy—over her brother, of all things! For so long, she was the one Jed looked up to, the one whose approval he sought. The adoring look Jed gave Caleb had hit her hard. For a moment she felt adrift, a waif in a foster home. Without a needy brother and sister giving her life purpose, what would happen to her? The thought filled her with panic.

Eileen stirred from her pallet on the floor beside Bridget. The little girl sat up and rubbed her eyes. "I'm hungry, Lucy," she said plaintively.

At least Eileen still needed her. "Supper will be ready in about a half an hour," Lucy told her. "Why don't you take Bridget outside until it's ready? The best thing for that hurt leg is some exercise. Otherwise it will stiffen up."

The dog wagged her tail at the mention of her name. She was smart, Lucy observed. She'd figured out they were talking about her.

"Do you need me for anything right now?" Jed asked. His gaze followed Eileen and the dog longingly.

"No, just keep an eye on your sister," Caleb answered before Lucy could.

Outrage churned again. It was *her* job to give or deny permission. She bit her lip and looked down at the biscuits she was making. *Help me, Lord. My attitude is not worthy of You. I should be glad Caleb is taking an interest in the children. Help me to let go.*

Her heart a bit calmer, she patted the dough, then used her knife to cut the dough into square biscuits. Transferring them to a baking sheet, she slid them into the oven and closed the door. Jed followed Eileen and Bridget outside.

Lucy didn't dare meet Caleb's gaze. She was acting like a shrew, hardly the type of helpmeet she'd wanted to be. She had longed for someone to help her carry the load, so why was she now resenting it when Caleb offered to share some of her burden? Tears blurred her vision.

She heard movement behind her, then Caleb put his hands on her shoulders and turned her to face him. His fingers tilted her chin up, but she stubbornly kept her eyes fastened on his shirt.

"Don't fight me, Lucy. If this marriage is going to make it, we have to work together."

Her heart jumped. He almost sounded as though he *wanted* them to work things out, as if he wasn't planning on shipping her back to

Boston the minute his father was well enough to handle the news. She dared a glance into his face. His gray eyes were gentle.

"What are you saying?" she whispered.

He took off his cowboy hat with a swipe of his big hand. "I'm saying that I'm willing to try if you are." He gave a heavy sigh. "We haven't gotten off on a very good start, Lucy, but it seems this marriage is square and legal. We may not love each other, but we can at least be friends and see what happens. I like you, Lucy. You've got guts, even if you are small and spindly."

He grinned, and she smiled back feebly. She wet her lips. "What do you expect of me?" Against her will, she glanced at the ladder leading to the loft.

His cheeks reddened. "Not that," he said hastily. "Not yet, at any rate. You stay with Jed and Eileen. Jed can help in the field while you and Eileen take care of the house."

"I thought you wanted a wife who could rope and shoot as well as a man." She didn't want him to settle for her if she wasn't what he needed in his life.

He grinned. "You sure shoot as well as any man I ever saw." Her cheeks burned, and she ducked her head. He laughed out loud. "I don't think either one of us knows what we want in a mate. We're going to have to discover that as we go along. You willing to try?"

Her throat felt tight, and she struggled not to cry. "I'll try, Mr. Stanton," she managed.

"Like I just told Jed, Mr. Stanton is my pa. Think you can see your way clear to calling me Caleb? Seeing as we're married and all."

Her gaze searched his, and she nodded. "I'll try, Caleb."

"I will, too." His gaze was soft and roamed down to her lips. His grin widened, then his eyes grew sober. "Can I kiss you, Lucy?"

Her heart fluttered like a frightened bird. She'd never been kissed, and she wanted to wait until she felt more than mere liking for a man. But this was her husband; how did she refuse him such a natural request? Before she could answer, his fingers tightened on her shoulders, and he bent his head. His lips grazed her cheek.

Her stomach felt funny, all nervous and fluttery. Then he pulled away.

"That's all for now," he said. "When you're ready for a real kiss, you let me know." He sauntered to the door with a smug grin as if he knew her knees were almost too weak to hold her.

When the door closed behind him, Lucy sank into a chair. If a kiss on the cheek affected her like this, what would a real kiss do? She was almost afraid to find out. She'd had no experience with men to gauge her reaction; maybe this was how a woman always felt. But she didn't think she'd feel like this if her old landlord, Amos Cramer, kissed her on the cheek.

7

*C*aleb heard every sound in the room below him all night long. Jed groaned several times in his sleep; Lucy was up taking Eileen to the outhouse several times, and he thought he heard soft weeping at one point near dawn. He thought about climbing down from the loft to see who it was, but he knew he didn't have the right words to fix the problem if it was Lucy.

He rolled over and punched his straw pillow into shape. It was prickly and uncomfortable; he was used to the feather pillow, now propping Lucy's head. How did he get into this situation? Pa must be going senile to have come up with this plan. He and Lucy were worlds apart in their temperaments and goals. He tended to think things through, to plod along with careful plans. Lucy seemed to rush in with no thought for consequences. Look at the way she'd demanded he get rid of his pet tarantula, just an instant decision with no forethought.

Marriage should be a partnership like a business. He would have been better off with someone who knew ranching and intended to help him reach his goals, someone who wasn't so flighty and emotional. Emotion made him antsy. He grimaced, remembering the fear he'd seen in her face. When he'd asked to kiss her last night, she'd obviously thought he intended to claim his husbandly rights. Her blue eyes had been huge, and she looked as though she wanted to bolt for the door.

She was a pretty little thing. He'd have to be a eunuch not to think about what it would be like to be truly married to her in every sense of the word, but he wasn't an ogre. Caleb didn't like being thought of that way, either. Still, he had to admit he'd liked the reaction his impersonal kiss had brought. Those soft cheeks had bloomed color like the first rosy blush of dawn. Maybe they had physical attraction going for them, but that was all. In every other way, they were just too different. And he didn't know what to do about it.

He'd either have to change or she would. And he had the feeling they were both a little too set in their ways to do much changing. Cheeper, the rooster, crowed from the chicken coop out back, and Caleb sighed. Those cattle weren't getting herded into the south pasture by themselves. In spite of having little or no sleep, he had to get up.

As he swung his feet to the floor, he heard the rattle of pans in the room below. He raised an eyebrow. Who was up so early and why? He pulled on his boots and climbed down the ladder. Jed yawned at the kitchen table while Lucy, her glorious blond hair still hanging down her back, poked life into the cookstove fire. She was already dressed in a blue gingham dress.

Jed saw him first. "Morning, Mr. Stanton."

"Call me Caleb, remember?" he said, his eyes on the way the lamplight lit Lucy's hair with shimmering lights.

"Yes, Sir."

Lucy turned and caught his stare. A becoming bloom of color raced up her cheeks, but she bravely met his gaze. He saw the muscles in her neck move as she swallowed, then she turned around quickly and took some eggs out of a bowl.

"Jed got me some eggs this morning. I hope that's all right," she said without looking at him.

"Of course. I wasn't expecting you to get out of bed so early. You had a busy day yesterday."

"So did you. I heard you tossing and turning all night."

"You didn't seem to get much sleep, either," he pointed out.

Bridget nosed his leg, and Caleb looked down. "You want out, Girl?"

The dog whined, and he went to the door and pushed it open. Bridget gave a deep bark and sprang out the door. Barking furiously, she raced to the road and planted her feet wide as she growled and barked at a dim figure by the gate.

Caleb squinted through the dim light of predawn. A rider on a horse. Not willing to take any chances, he shut the door and stepped to the back door, where his rifle leaned against the wall. He checked to make sure it was loaded, then swung open the front door.

Drew Larson pushed past him. "Put the peashooter away. We need to talk."

Scowling, Caleb tightened his grip on his rifle. "I've got nothing to say to you, Larson. You've stolen the last of my cattle. The next time I'll shoot first and ask questions later." Drew wasn't listening. His mouth hung open as he stared at Lucy. Then a slow smile lit his swarthy face. "Hello, Honey, where did you come from?" He started toward Lucy.

Caleb stepped in front of him. "You're not welcome here, Larson. And that's my wife you're ogling." It took all his effort not to plant his fist in the man's face.

Drew's chin dropped further. "Your wife? I didn't hear nothing about no wedding. When I worked here just five days ago you didn't say nothing about getting hitched. What are you trying to pull, Stanton? Her kind is fair game."

Caleb clenched his teeth, his throat tight. He grabbed Drew by the collar and propelled him back toward the door. "She's a lady, Larson, and my wife. Now get your slimy presence out of our house and don't come back."

"I'm working for the Burnett ranch now, and I got a proposition for you."

"I'm not interested in anything you have to say. Does Burk know you're a cattle thief? I'd venture he would be interested in that piece of information."

Drew's mouth curled in a snarl. "You keep your trap shut if you know what's good for you, Stanton! You spill any of your lies, and I'll tell him about that bull of his you let stay with the herd last summer."

Caleb's brows drew together. "I'd ask what you were talking about, but I'm in no mood to hear more of your lies. You know as well as I do that I've never taken so much as a blade of grass that didn't belong to me. Now get your lazy carcass out of my sight. If I see you on Stanton land again, I'll shoot."

Drew gave a derisive laugh. "You don't have the guts, Stanton.

Now your pa, that would be a different story, but I got nothing to fear from you. Your religion has made you too soft." He touched his hat, his gaze again on Lucy. "Morning, Miss. I'm sure we'll run into each other again."

Lucy was backed up against the stove, her eyes wide and her lips white. She didn't answer Drew, and he gave a short laugh and spun on his heel. He slammed the door behind him.

Caleb let out the breath he didn't even realize he was holding. His jaw hurt from clenching it, and his heart was stuttering like a faulty steam engine. "I'm sorry, Lucy," he said. "He won't bother you again."

Lucy gulped. "Can he get you in trouble, Caleb?"

Caleb laughed, a mirthless sound. "He can spread his lies, but Burk isn't one to go off half-cocked. He'd come to me for an answer. And by the time he hears any of Drew Larson's lies, he will have found out what kind of man he has working for him and fired him, most likely. Larson is—well, I won't say what I really think. You just see you avoid him if he happens to be in town the same time as you." His scowl deepened as he thought of the way the man had talked about Lucy. No one talked about his wife like that!

His wife. When he was least expecting it, that fact reared up and hit him in the face again. He stared at Lucy. No wonder Larson was bowled over. She looked delectable. No one who looked that good could be a wife. Small, but exquisitely proportioned, she looked like a china doll come to life with her golden ringlets and perfect skin. He stared into her eyes and wondered what she would do if he took a step nearer.

He mentally shook himself. He had work to do; there was no time to be inside mooning over a woman. This was going to have to be a working relationship, and he was glad to see Lucy was determined to hold up her end of the bargain.

"I could use some of those flapjacks I smell cooking," he said.

Lucy blinked as though she had forgotten what she was doing, then blushed and turned back to the stove. "The gravy is done, and the eggs will be in a minute. Jed fetched some clean water for you to wash up in."

He stared at his hands. "I don't need the water."

Lucy whirled and pointed a spatula at him. "Caleb Stanton, this may be Texas, but where I come from, we wash up for meals. I won't have dirty hands at my table."

"My hands are clean. See." He held them out for her inspection.

She didn't look at his hands but stared him in the eye and pointed to the bowl and pitcher. "The soap is there as well."

"If you think we're running a cattle ranch like a millinery shop, you'll soon find out different. I don't have time to fuss with soap and water every time I want to eat. You can get that through your head right now!"

Her eyes welled with tears, but she put her hands on her hips and faced him down. "And your father wants some genteel manners brought to this spread. You'll wash your hands, or you'll go without breakfast."

He weakened at the sight of her tears. Caleb gritted his teeth, then stalked to the bowl of water. Snatching up the cake of soap, he lathered his hands, then poured water over them. "Satisfied?" He held them up. "Next time you want to 'genteel' someone, try Pa. He's the one who signed on for this nonsense, not me."

"Thank you, Caleb. Please sit down and eat your breakfast while it's hot." Lucy's voice was composed, but he could still see a suspicious wetness in her eyes.

"That's what I wanted to do an hour ago," he muttered.

He caught a glimmer of a grin on Jed's face. "What are you grinning about?" he demanded.

"Nothing," the boy said hastily, stuffing a flapjack into his mouth.

"Jed, what have I told you about talking with your mouth full?" his sister said. "And I didn't hear either of you pray."

Caleb exchanged a commiserating smile with Jed. At least he wasn't the only one in hot water, he reflected as he bowed his head.

❧

Lucy kept a small plate of flapjacks hot on top of the cookstove. Eileen would be hungry when she awakened. Tomorrow, she would make sure they all ate together. Eileen had been awake most of the night, though, and she would be cranky without her rest. Lucy felt a little cranky herself. Maybe she had come off too domineering over the washing up, but she wasn't about to start off this marriage by letting a man eat at her table without washing his hands. She'd worked for years to get Jed in the habit, and Caleb could destroy all her hard work in the blink of an eye.

She had her work cut out for her. Caleb was used to being around only men; he had no concept of the niceties of life. But she would set such a good spread for him; he would be willing to do whatever he had to do to eat her cooking. She'd learned to cook at Mama's knee, and she was good at it.

Lucy heated water on the stove to wash the dishes, then got out the ingredients to make bread. Kneading it with practiced hands, she put it on to raise, then went through the cabin and collected all the dirty clothes. She'd noticed a pile of Caleb's clothes in the pantry, of all places.

By the time Eileen had gotten up, Lucy had hauled in wood and water to do laundry. She fed her sister, then set her to helping hang the clothes up to dry on some string Lucy strung up by the fire.

Humming as she worked, she baked a raisin pie, then rolled out noodles and left them on the table to dry. What a blessing it was to have chickens and eggs in the backyard. God had truly blessed her. As she'd tossed in the night, she had come to that conclusion. Caleb was a fine man, a bit rough around the edges, but he just wasn't used to women. She would be patient and be the helpmeet she was created to be. Caleb would be glad for his father's meddling in the end.

Dinner was ready by one. In fact, if the men didn't come in soon, the noodles would be overcooked, and the chicken would be dry as chalk. Lucy kept glancing worriedly through the window, but saw no sign of her menfolk. By one-thirty she was becoming angry, and by two, she was downright livid. It was the height of inconsideration to let this fine food go to waste. She couldn't help but wonder if Caleb had done it deliberately to get her back for making him wash his hands.

"We might as well eat without them, Eileen," she said. Lifting her sister onto the chair, she ladled up rubbery noodles and stringy chicken. It tasted as bad as it looked. Eileen picked at her plate, and Lucy finally gave her a piece of warm bread spread with butter and jam. By the time she put Eileen down for her nap, Lucy's anger was white-hot. She rehearsed all the things she would say to Caleb when he got in. And Jed. He knew better.

She started to dump the remains of the meal into a dish to give to Bridget when she got back with the men, then stopped and stared at the food. They would just have to eat it. Where she came from, food was a precious commodity; it didn't deserve to be dumped out. If it was not the best now, maybe that would teach Mr. Caleb Stanton to be on time for a meal next time.

Lucy put the pan back on the stove to stay warm, then felt the clothes hanging around the cabin. They were dry, so she took them down and folded them. She carried Caleb's up the ladder to his room. His bed had not been made, and she clicked her tongue at her forgetfulness. She would have to remember tomorrow.

She threw the covers up over the bed, and her foot hit something under the bed. Curious, she knelt and peered in the darkness. A battered metal box, about six inches by eight inches was the only thing under the bed. She laid a hand on the cool surface and pulled it to her. For a moment she hesitated. Maybe it was something private. But she was his wife, and they should have no secrets from one another, she told herself.

Slowly, she opened the lid. Inside was a journal and a daguerreotype. Lucy picked up the photo. It was of a young woman holding a baby. She had a look about her that reminded her of Caleb, and Lucy realized she was looking at Caleb's mother. She was lovely, with a cloud of thick, dark hair and Caleb's stubborn mouth and expressive eyes.

A lump in her throat, Lucy dropped the picture back into the box and picked up the journal. It looked old, too old to be Caleb's personal journal. The battered leather cover felt loved and worn in her hand, and the pages smelled old and stale.

She opened the first page. Mary Elizabeth Stanton. His mother's journal. Tears stung Lucy's eyes. Poor motherless boy. This was all he had of his mother, all the experience he had of women as well, just some brief memories of a long-dead mother. No wonder his father was determined to find him a wife.

Lucy put the journal back into the box. She couldn't read it, not without Caleb's permission and knowledge. It was too private, almost sacred. Her anger mostly evaporated, she finished making the bed, then dropped the freshly folded clothes into a box that served as Caleb's chest.

She had just finished putting the clothes away when she heard a horse neigh in the yard. Compressing her lips, she glanced out the window. Jed was still mounted, but Caleb had jumped to the ground and was opening the barn door. Lucy lifted the watch that hung around her neck. The watch had belonged to her mama and offered her some comfort as she checked the time. Four o'clock, almost time for supper, and the uneaten dinner sat congealing on the stove. Her anger raged again, and she went down to meet them.

8

*C*aleb was bone-weary, and his stomach was gnawing on his backbone. Jed had made several pointed comments about dinner around about one o'clock, but he'd ignored him. The lad needed to grow up and realize that a man didn't go running home when his belly got a little empty. He didn't go home until the work was done.

"Help me curry the horses, and we'll see if Lucy can rustle us up some grub," he told Jed.

The boy's shoulders drooped wearily, and Caleb almost relented, then remembered he was supposed to be teaching Jed how to be a man. He was responsible for Jed now. He shoved open the sliding door to the barn and led his horse inside. He grabbed a curry brush, then handed one to Jed. They quickly curried the horses and turned them out into the stable. Caleb tossed a pitchfork full of hay over the fence, then clapped Jed on the back.

"You did a man's work today, Jed. I was mighty proud of you."

Jed's chest visibly swelled, and if his grin were any bigger, it would have split his face. "Thank you, Sir."

"You as hungry as I am?"

Jed nodded. "Lucy is probably wondering where we are."

"We're early, why should she wonder?"

"We usually eat at one at home."

"She knew we were working." Caleb started toward the house.

A strange aroma wafted toward him when he pushed open the door. It smelled a bit like something charred and a bit like glue. Whatever it was, it didn't smell good. Jed had been bragging on his sister's cooking, but it must have been the youngster's love talking. Still,

Caleb would put a good face on it and force it down. He was hungry enough to eat whatever she threw at him.

He forced a smile. "Smells like something's cooking."

Lucy stood and put her fists on her hips. "Something *was* cooking. Now something is burned. But help yourself." She made a sweeping gesture toward the cookstove. "If you dare." Her eyebrows lifted in challenge.

Caleb looked at Jed, and Jed looked at Caleb. Caleb knew he wore the same expression the boy did. A look of panic and dismay. He sidled over to the stove and looked in the pan. It might have been chicken and noodles once, but now it more resembled a sticky gob of glue.

"Uh, looks good," he said lamely. Lucy almost visibly swelled, and he was reminded of an outraged mother hen.

"It *was* good around one o'clock. Even at two it was still edible. Now it looks—it looks like porridge!" Lucy stalked toward the fireplace and sat beside Eileen. Even her back and neck looked outraged.

Caleb scratched his head and looked at Jed. The boy's eyes were round and pleading, and he stared from the mess on the stove to Caleb.

"Do we have to eat it?" he whispered.

"I heard that, and the answer is yes!" Lucy jumped to her feet again. "Maybe it will help you remember to come home in time to eat tomorrow."

Caleb frowned. This was not going the way he had pictured the evening. He'd planned to eat a hot, home-cooked meal, then take the buggy over to the main house and check on Pa.

"I see I need to explain the way a ranch works," he began.

"No, I need to explain the way a cook works," Lucy said, springing to her feet. "When food is ready to be eaten, the men come and eat it. Jed is a growing boy. He needs to eat three square meals a day. Look at him, Caleb. He's skinny as a pitchfork and needs fattening. That's one reason I agreed to marry you. And you need to eat three square meals a day. If you can't be bothered to come home for dinner, then you need to tell me, and I'll pack you a lunch or bring it to you."

He looked at Jed. She was right. His heart clenched at the boy's thinness. He bit his lip and looked back at Lucy. Her cheeks were rosy with anger, and her blue eyes sparkled. Her beauty tugged at him. If the children weren't there, he would have pulled her into his arms and kissed her.

His anger subsided and he grinned. "A bit riled, aren't you? You sure look pretty that way. Maybe we'll have to try this again tomorrow, Jed."

Her brother grinned, though his eyes were still anxious. He'd obviously been made to toe the line by his sister before.

For a moment, the color in Lucy's cheeks deepened. Then the corner of her mouth lifted, and she bit her lip. Her dimple appeared, and she clapped a hand over her mouth. A chuckle squeaked past her lips.

"Don't think fake compliments will make me forgive you," she said. Though her tone was severe, her eyes held a hint of mirth.

He held up his hands. "Uncle!" He turned to Jed. "She has me, Boy. I should have realized you would need to be fed. But we'll take our punishment like men, what do you say?"

Jed gave a doubtful glare at the mess in the pan. "Do we have to?"

"Are you a man or a rabbit? Come on, this will taste better than it looks." He grabbed the ladle and tried to scoop some out of the pan. It stuck to the spoon and refused to drop to the plate.

"I think I'll be a rabbit today," Jed said.

Lucy sighed and got to her feet. "Since you're truly contrite, I'll see if I can find something edible for you."

Caleb shook the spoon again. The glob clung steadfastly to the spoon. He dropped it back into the pan with a sigh of relief. "Jed and I will rise up and call you blessed, won't we, Boy?"

"I'll even tell everyone she's the prettiest woman in Boston, if I don't have to eat that slop," Jed said.

"Boston, my foot! She's the prettiest woman in the Red River Valley—in Texas even," Caleb said. He caught Lucy by the waist as she sashayed past him. She smelled good, kind of like fresh-baked bread. "Do you forgive us?"

"I forgive Jed. I haven't decided about you yet," she said. Her lashes lowered to her cheeks, then she raised them, and he was dazzled by the light in her eyes.

For the second time, he wished the kids weren't here. How was he supposed to woo his wife with a constant audience? It would be a challenge, but for the first time Caleb realized he intended to do just that. Almost against his will, his hands tightened around her waist, and he pulled her against his chest and rested his chin on her head.

"You're staying right here until you tell me I'm forgiven," he said softly.

She struggled to get free for a moment, but then her arms circled his waist, and she stood content in his arms. "I'm not complaining," she said too softly for the kids to hear.

His heart soared. She must find him attractive. Maybe even as attractive as he found her. The Bible admonished him to love his wife. He was beginning to realize that might not be too difficult.

❧

The days sped by in a blur of busyness. Lucy had so much to learn she felt her head must surely explode with the knowledge she stuffed in. She and Caleb were still wary around one another, but they were slowly learning to know one another.

Spring had finally come to Texas. Wildflowers brought welcome bits of color to the landscape, and the air was filled with the fragrance of spring. Lucy carted her washtub outside and scrubbed the clothes while Eileen occupied herself planting her own small garden.

Lucy rubbed at a spot on Caleb's dungarees. Her hands were red and chapped, but who would have thought she would find such satisfaction in caring for a man and his belongings? Caleb's prediction about the softness of her hands had proven true, but Lucy didn't mind. Her red hands were proof of the effort she was putting into this marriage.

She hung the clothes on the line Caleb had put up for her and went to the house to start dinner. Caleb had told her he would be in the south pasture all day and had asked her to bring the meal to him. Since that one missed meal, he had been conscientious about keeping her informed of his mealtime activities. She suppressed a grin.

"Eileen, it's time to come in," she called.

She went inside and took the bread from the breadbox. Cutting thick slices, she made egg sandwiches, then wrapped them in cloth and put them in a box. To that she added cheese and pie she'd made earlier in the day.

She cocked her head and listened. Eileen still hadn't answered her. She went to the back door. "Eileen, come in now!" There was still no answer, so she stepped outside. She sighed when she saw no sign of her sister. Eileen was probably in the barn petting the calf.

Lucy hurried across the yard to the barn. They would have to hurry, or Caleb would accuse her of ignoring his mealtime. She shoved open the barn door and stepped into the dimly lit barn. A shaft of sunlight illuminated the dust motes, and the straw made her sneeze.

"Eileen?"

The only answer she got was the snort of the horse in the far stall and the rustle as the calf shuffled in the hay. Beginning to be alarmed, Lucy turned and ran back to the front yard. "Eileen! Where are you?" She raced around the house several times before she could admit the obvious to herself. Eileen was nowhere to be found.

Her heart was racing like a runaway train, and her mouth was dry with panic. Shading her eyes, she stared out at the horizon. Where could Eileen be? Lucy was torn between wandering out to find Eileen herself or going for help. Her heart screamed for her to find her sister now, but wisdom dictated finding Caleb. He knew the area; she didn't.

She threw the sidesaddle on Wanda and clambered atop the mare's broad back. Digging her heels into Wanda's sides, she clung desperately to the pommel as the horse broke into a canter. Within minutes, she was in sight of the herd of longhorn and could make out Caleb's familiar broad shoulders.

At the sight of her husband, tears sprang from her eyes, and she began to sob. "Caleb!" she screamed. The sound that came out of her mouth was closer to a croak.

Caleb's head came up, and he kicked his horse into a run, with Jed right behind him. "What is it? What's wrong?" His gaze darted past her. "Where's Eileen?"

"She's gone! I was doing laundry, and she was playing with Brid-

get. When I called her for lunch, she was missing." Aware she was beginning to babble, Lucy took a deep breath. "I didn't know where to
look."

Caleb turned and whistled. "Bridget, come here, Girl!" The dog
came bounding to him.

Hope lifted its head for a brief instant. "Do you think Bridget can
find her?"

"She loves Eileen. She'll find her."

They turned and rode back to the cabin.

"I'll look around just to make sure," Caleb said. "Did you check
the privy?"

"No, I didn't think of that." Lucy rushed to the privy and threw
open the door. Empty. Her shoulders drooping, she followed Caleb as
he quickly walked around the yard and then checked the barn.

He knelt and took Bridget's head in his hands. "Find Eileen, Bridget." He released her. "Go, find Eileen!"

Bridget barked and began sniffing the ground. She circled the
privy, then went around to the front. She paused at Eileen's small garden plot and then tore off toward the north.

"Quick, get the horses, we'll follow her!"

Lucy wanted to just run after her, but she realized she'd never
keep up with the dog. She grabbed Wanda's reins and managed to
mount by herself. Caleb and Jed were already ahead of her. She
bounced hard in the saddle as Wanda strove to catch them.

She could hear Bridget barking as she made her way toward a
meadow by the river. The river! Eileen loved water. Her heart in her
mouth, Lucy bent low over Wanda's neck and smacked her hand on
the horse's rump.

"Eileen!" she shouted.

Caleb and Jed reached the grove of trees, and Lucy got there a
moment later. Panting nearly as hard as Wanda, she looked around for
her sister. Nothing.

"We'll check the river. You look around," Caleb said. His voice
was grim, and Lucy's eyes filled with tears as she watched him and Jed
stalk purposefully toward the river. She could hear the rushing water
from here. The Red River could be deadly this time of year.

Then she heard Bridget give a joyful bark. The dog was leaping happily into the air. Lucy looked closer and saw the still form of her sister on the ground. She rushed to Eileen and reached her just as the little girl sat up and rubbed her eyes sleepily. Bridget licked her face, and Eileen began to cry.

Lucy scooped her into her arms and hugged her fiercely. "Here she is," she shouted.

"Lucy, you're hurting me," Eileen complained.

Lucy wanted to loosen her grip, but she couldn't let go. "I thought I'd lost you," she whispered. "Don't ever do that again, Eileen. You know better than to go off without telling me."

Jed and Caleb came running. Jed's face was streaked from tears, and Caleb's eyes were bright with relief. Jed took his sister from Lucy, and she wrapped her arms and legs around him.

"I looked for you, Jed, but you was hiding," she said reproachfully. "I walked and walked, but you weren't there."

Caleb held out his arms for Eileen, and she went to him. He set her on the ground and knelt beside her. "Eileen, what did I tell you about watching out for Lucy?"

She hung her head. "You said to stay close to her all the time, so's I could see her."

"That's right. What did you do today?"

Eileen started to cry. "I just wanted to find you and Jed. I wanted Jed to see my flowers."

"I know, Sweetheart, but you disobeyed me. You know what that means, don't you?" Caleb's voice was gentle but firm.

"I have to be punished?" Eileen said hesitantly. Her tears flowed in earnest now.

Caleb nodded. "I'm afraid so."

"Caleb, no!" Lucy said. "I'm just glad to have her back safe and sound."

He took Lucy's hand and led her away from the children. "Eileen knew the rules, Lucy. If we let her get away with it this time, she might not remember how important this rule is the next time. The next time she could drown or Indians could find her first. I'm responsible for her now, and this is the way it has to be."

Lucy's eyes burned from all the tears she'd shed. "I can't stand to hurt her, Caleb. You'll have to do it."

"If that's what you want." He turned and went back to Eileen. He picked her up and went to his horse. "We'll discuss what the punishment is to be when we get home."

Lucy's mouth was dry with dread as she mounted her horse and followed Jed and Caleb home. She knew Caleb was right, but that didn't make it easier. It had always been hard for her to discipline Eileen, who was so small and engaging. But this had been willful disobedience. She knew she wasn't to leave the yard.

They reached the cabin, and Jed took the horses to the barn. Caleb carried Eileen inside while Lucy followed, her footsteps dragging. He sat on a chair and pulled Eileen onto his lap, then motioned for Lucy to be seated next to him.

"What do you have to say, Eileen?"

"I'm sorry," she wept. "I shouldn't have gone out of the yard. I knew I wasn't s'posed to. I'se sorry, Lucy."

"Lucy was very sad when she found you gone. And we didn't make the rule to be mean. You remember when the mongrel wolf came?"

Eileen nodded. "Lucy shooted it with the gun."

Caleb nodded. "Another wolf could come when Lucy wasn't there with the gun. There are Indians and snakes, too. All kinds of things that could hurt you. We make a rule because we love you. And Jesus is sad when we disobey. Do you want to tell Him you're sorry, too?"

Eileen nodded and clasped her little hands together. "Jesus, I'm sorry," she sobbed. "I didn't want to make You sad, and I didn't want to worry Lucy. Help me be a good girl next time. Amen." She sniveled and wiped her nose with the back of her hand.

Tears burned Lucy's eyes. Wasn't that good enough?

"Am I going to be punished now?" Eileen's voice was pitiful.

"Do you think you should be?" Caleb stroked her hair.

Eileen hesitated before she nodded. "You have to 'cause you said. I wouldn't want God to think you was a liar."

Lucy thought she saw a hint of moisture in Caleb's eyes. He put

Eileen down and rose. Stepping across the floor, he took a wooden spoon from the utensil crock.

"I don't want to discipline you, Eileen. Just like God doesn't like to discipline us. Bend over the chair."

Tears streaming down her face, Eileen rose slowly and bent over the chair. Caleb bit his lip and looked at Lucy helplessly. She could see the toll this was taking on him.

He knelt beside Eileen and whacked her three times across the bottom. The licks weren't hard, but Lucy winced each time.

After it was over, Caleb pulled Eileen into his arms. "I love you, Sweetheart. Let's pray and promise God we'll try to obey next time."

Eileen wound her arms around his neck and kissed him. "I love you, Caleb. I'se glad you married us."

"So am I," Caleb said, his gaze meeting Lucy's.

9

ucy touched the cow with one hand gingerly and wrinkled her nose at the unlovely aroma of cow and manure. Positioning the bucket under the cow, she grabbed the cow's udder and squeezed. Nothing. She huffed and got a firmer grip. This couldn't be that hard. She'd already watched Caleb do it for two months. If he could do it, she could. Maybe if she sang to the animal. . . .

She cleared her voice and thought of the words to that song Caleb sang. She raised her voice in melody.

"From this valley they say you are going. We will miss your bright eyes and sweet smile. For they say you are taking the sunshine, that brightens our pathway awhile."

She felt stupid singing a love song to a cow. But Bessie seemed to like it. The cow snorted, then swished her tail, and a drop of milk squirted the next time Lucy squeezed. Heartened, she leaned her head against the cow and tried to get a rhythm going. *Squirt, squirt. Ping, ping.* She smiled. She was getting it!

Then Caleb's deep baritone chimed in with her soprano.

"Come and sit by my side if you love me. Do not hasten to bid me adieu. But remember the Red River Valley and the one who has loved you so true."

His gray eyes were smiling as he pulled up a stool beside hers. Did he love her? She was beginning to think he felt something, even as this feeling grew in her own heart. Was it love? She hoped so. She wanted to love her husband. But she'd had so little experience with men. Maybe it was merely physical attraction. Whatever it was, she wanted to nurture it.

"I reckon you're getting the hang of this," Caleb said. "Almost half a bucket."

"You usually get over a bucket."

"I didn't at the beginning. Once those fingers get stronger, you'll be great at it."

Her fingers *did* ache. She flexed them. "You want to finish? Bessie might appreciate being totally emptied." She scooted over to make room for him. His broad shoulder grazed hers, and she could smell the clean scent of the soap he'd used to wash. She wanted to lean against him and have him gather her in his arms the way he'd done that night he'd been too late for dinner. So far there'd been no repeat of that.

Though it was only late April, the weather had turned hot. She could hear Jed shouting to Eileen as he tossed a ball with her in the yard. Bridget ran barking from one to the other. She and Caleb were alone, a state that came so seldom she felt tongue-tied.

"I thought we'd go check on Pa after supper," Caleb said. "We haven't been over for two days. That okay with you?"

"Of course. I made some pies today. I'll take one to him."

"He'll enjoy that. All he's done lately is eat, Percy says. I think Percy is getting tired of cooking for him."

"I wonder if we should take dinner to him for a few days to give Percy a break? I could go over in the morning to cook." She almost hated the thought of leaving her little cabin. It had quickly become home.

"We can ask him." Caleb rose and took the bucket of frothy milk. Lucy followed him, and they crossed the yard to the house. She'd opened the windows to take advantage of what wind there was, and the new yellow gingham curtains blew in the breeze.

"You've done wonders with the house," Caleb said. "I never realized before how much this place needed something. Pa hasn't even seen it yet."

"He'll just say, 'I told you so.'" Lucy smiled and took Caleb's hand.

He gave her a surprised glance, then laced his fingers through hers. A warm glow spread through Lucy's stomach. She prayed every day for the relationship between them to blossom and flourish. It looked as though God was answering that prayer.

The next day Caleb showed Lucy how to hitch the horse to the buggy. "Are you sure you know how to get to the main house?"

"I've been there many times, Caleb," she said with a toss of her head. "I may be small, but I'm not a child." She was an adult and his wife. Sometimes he could be so sweet, and then the next day he would treat her like she was Eileen's age. Lucy tightened the strings on her bonnet and squared her shoulders.

"Sorry." Caleb grinned and put an arm around her.

The hug he gave her felt like one he'd give Eileen, and it irritated her. After the closeness of last night, she wanted him to cradle her in his arms and kiss her, really kiss her. Not that light peck on the cheek he'd taken to giving her every night. How did a woman go about letting a man know she was ready for more than he was offering? Would he think she was wanton? Lucy gave a tiny sigh.

"What's wrong?"

"Nothing." She pulled away and climbed into the buggy without his assistance. She stared into his perplexed gaze and stretched out her arms. "Could you hand Eileen up to me?"

He ran a hand through his hair and sighed. Scooping up Eileen, he handed her to Lucy. "You girls be careful. Don't forget there's a rifle under the seat if you need it."

"I remember." She stared straight ahead and slapped the reins against the mare's back. "Dinner will be at one. Try not to be late."

Caleb reached up and grabbed the reins. "Lucy, what's wrong? Did I do something?"

Shame twisted in her gut. It wasn't his fault she was feeling so blue and rejected. He was doing everything he could to make this work. How was he to know she was ready for a deeper relationship? She bit her lip and raised her gaze to his. "We'll talk tonight, after the kids are in bed."

Relief lit his eyes, and he nodded, though a perplexed frown still marred his forehead. He slapped the mare's hindquarters, and she set off at a trot. As she guided the horse, Lucy stewed about what to say to him. Their relationship seemed to be stagnating. She didn't want a big brother; she wanted a husband. Caleb was trying so hard, too. Half the time she didn't know what she wanted, so how was he supposed to know?

The recent rains had left the ground muddy. Lucy tried to keep the buggy in the driest areas, but she still got bogged down several times. Eileen fell asleep, and Lucy breathed a sigh of relief. Now she could concentrate on where she was going and on her own thoughts. She rounded a curve and hit a deep patch of mud. The mare whinnied and thrashed in the mud, flinging up bits of muck onto Lucy's dress with her hooves.

"Whoa, Girl!" Lucy pulled on the reins and clambered down. The mud sucked at her boots, and she almost fell as she made her way to the horse's head. She patted her and tried to back the horse out of the mud. The horse reared in terror, and Lucy scrambled back. She lost her balance and sat awkwardly in the mud. Struggling to get up, she fell forward. Near tears, she tried to get on all fours, but the mud sucked at her.

She might have to send Eileen for help. She could see the smoke from the main house from here. Then she heard a horse whinny behind her. She turned and looked up into the smiling, swarthy face of Drew Larson.

He tipped his hat. "Morning, Miss."

"That's Missus," she corrected.

His grin widened. "Whatever you say, Ma'am. You need some help? Looks like you're in a bit of a predicament."

His smirk raised Lucy's ire, but she was in no position to refuse help. "I would appreciate it," she said coldly.

"Say that like you mean it, and I might see my way clear to helping you." He put his hands on his hips, and his white teeth flashed.

"Mr. Larson, give me your hand!" She wasn't about to play games with him.

His eyes widened, and he stepped forward and offered his hand. She gripped it with her mud-covered one, and he hauled her inelegantly to her feet. Before she could thank him and release his hand, he gave a tug and jerked her into his arms.

"Now I'll take my appreciation," he said. He bent his head.

Lucy didn't take time to think, she just walloped him upside the head with a glob of mud she'd inadvertently clutched in her other hand. It hit him in the eye, and he let out a yelp. He was so startled, he let loose of her, and she sprang to the buggy and wrested the rifle from under the seat.

"I won't hesitate to use this on a coyote like you, Mr. Larson. I appreciate your help, but not enough to offer more than a handshake and a thank you. Now mosey on down the road. My father-in-law is expecting me, and his men would be rather put out to find you'd manhandled me."

Drew's face suffused with red, and he narrowed his eyes. "We'll meet again, Miss."

"That's *Missus*!" she shouted after him as he vaulted to his horse and wheeled angrily away.

Lucy snapped the whip over the mare's head. "Giddup!" She flipped her filthy skirt around her legs and hunched forward. She couldn't wait to get out of this mud-encased dress. The horse and buggy cantered into the yard. Lucy pulled hard on the reins to halt the horses, then she flung herself from the buggy and scooped up Eileen. Several ranch hands gaped as she hurried to the house. She was wet and scared, but she was determined not to let that bully cow her.

Luther, his spectacles perched on his nose, looked up from where he sat by the window with a book in his hand. His bushy eyebrows rose when he saw her condition, and he stood. "Lucy, what's happened to you?"

"My buggy got bogged down in the mud," she said. He didn't need to worry about Drew; she would take care of her own battles.

"My dear girl, you must get out of those wet clothes." He stood and went to the hall. "Percy, fetch the trunk with Mrs. Stanton's things in it." He turned back to Lucy. "I kept some of my wife's nicer things, since they were all I had of her. You're about the same size. I think they'll fit."

"Oh, I couldn't wear them," Lucy said. "An old pair of dungarees and a shirt will do until I get home."

"Absolutely not!" He gestured for her to sit. "Percy will bring the trunk, and you can take whatever you like."

"Your cushion will be soiled if I sit down. I'll just stand here," she said. She hated to feel like she was asking for anything.

"Here, then." He pulled a ladder-back chair out from the desk.

Gingerly, she eased onto the chair. Flecks of mud fell to the carpet, and she grimaced and sprang to her feet. "I'll get it." She crouched and began to pick up the bits of debris.

"Lucy, please." At the pained look on his face, she stood. "You're not a servant here; you're my daughter. I don't want you acting like you're here on suffrage."

Tears welled in Lucy's eyes. She'd always been so used to carrying her own weight, of trying not to be a bother, that it came hard to accept what he was offering. "Thank you, Mr. Stanton."

Luther smiled. "Do you think you could ever see your way to calling me Pa, like Caleb does? Or even Father would do. I've asked before, but you seem to forget each time that I'm not an ogre."

Lucy's throat closed. "I'd like that—Pa."

Luther colored with pleasure. He knelt beside Eileen's chair. "I'd like you to call me Grandpa, if you'd like, Eileen."

The little girl stared into the older man's face. She put a small hand on each side of his face. "I like you," she announced. "You can be my grandpa."

Luther kissed her, then rose to his feet and fished for his handkerchief. "You've made me very happy, Lucy. I know it hasn't been easy for you. My Caleb can be like a penned bull when he feels he's being forced into something. But I've seen the way he looks at you. You two are a good match." His voice was full of satisfaction.

"I hope you're right," Lucy said quietly.

Percy came in dragging a chest behind him. He dropped it with a thump in front of Lucy. "Took me forever to find this, Boss. It was in the attic."

Luther reached over and opened the chest. Inside, shimmering silk dresses caught the sunlight.

Lucy gasped at the glorious array of color and texture. "These are far too grand to wear to cook in," she said, fingering a pale pink fabric.

"Nonsense, they've been tucked away far too long. You heard Percy. They were in the attic not doing a body any good." He pulled out the dress she had touched. "This will look lovely on you. You might as well surprise Caleb when he comes."

Lucy gasped at the reminder. She didn't have time to argue. "I must get busy. Thank you, Pa, I'll try to be careful of it." She gathered it in her arms and hurried to the spare bedroom. Water stood in the pitcher, so she quickly slipped out of her soiled dress, washed, and stepped into the clean dress. It was only as she began to button up the tiny seed pearls on the bodice that she realized it was the same dress Caleb's mother had worn in the picture in the box in his room.

She slid her hands over the smooth fabric. Would it bother him to see her in this dress? Maybe she should choose another. She bit her lip. There wasn't time to change. She would barely be ready for the men as it was. No, she would just have to wear this one.

Her boots were too muddy to put back on; she would just stick them on the porch to dry so she could knock off the hardened mud before she went home. In her stockings, she padded to the kitchen, depositing her boots on the porch along the way. Percy stood amid the pots and pans waiting for her.

Together they whipped together a beef stew with dumplings and apple pie using canned apples from the larder.

Percy tasted the stew. "You sure know how to cook, Miss Lucy. It does a body good to eat someone else's cooking for a change."

She smiled. At least this was one wifely duty she knew how to do. Before she could answer Percy, the door banged, and she heard the sound of men's voices. She could make out Caleb's voice amidst the babble, and her heart leapt.

"I'll set the table." Percy grabbed a handful of plates and dinnerware and rushed off to the dining room.

Lucy picked up the pot of stew and followed him. The men's voices stilled when she entered the room. Her gaze picked out Caleb from the crowd of men. His laughter died when he saw her, and he frowned.

"Why are you wearing my mother's dress?" he demanded.

"My—my dress was soiled. I fell in the mud when the buggy got stuck."

"The bad man yelled at her," Eileen said. She slipped her hand in Caleb's.

His glower deepened, and he knelt beside the little girl. "What bad man, Sweetheart?"

Lucy bit her lip. She hadn't wanted Caleb to know.

"Lucy hit him with some mud. He was mad." Eileen spoke in a confiding tone of voice as Caleb lifted her into his arms.

"Lucy, what's this all about?" Still carrying Eileen, Caleb stepped next to Lucy. "Did someone threaten you?"

"Drew Larson stopped to help me get out of the mud," Lucy admitted. She would not tell him anymore than she had to. A range war had been started over less.

Caleb's expression darkened like a lowering storm cloud. "Did he touch you?"

Before Lucy could answer, Eileen piped up again. "Uh, huh. But Lucy got the gun."

"Lucy? What did he do?"

The entire roomful of men seemed to be holding their breaths. Lucy sighed. "He thought I ought to show a bit of appreciation for his help."

"I see. What kind of appreciation?" Caleb's voice was dangerous, and Lucy shivered.

"A—a kiss was what he had in mind."

Caleb ground his teeth together. "He's gone too far this time. Stealing my cattle is one thing, but messing with my wife is another thing altogether. Monk, get the men together. We're riding to Burnett's ranch."

Lucy laid a hand on Caleb's arm. "Please, Caleb, I handled it. I warned him off with the gun. He knows I'm not easy prey."

"A man like that will be back." He shook off her hand. "Come on, men."

"Not Jed!" Lucy cried out in alarm when her brother moved as if to go with the rest of the men.

Caleb paused, then nodded. "You're right. It might be dangerous."

Dangerous! Lucy's heart clenched. She couldn't bear it if something happened to Caleb. It was all her fault. She should have told Eileen not to say anything, but she hadn't realized the little girl had seen so much. She had been sleeping when Drew rode up.

"What about dinner?" she called.

"Keep it warm."

Lucy sighed. She knew better than to berate him this time. But she could pray.

∼❧

Caleb's muscles were strung as tight as a tanning rawhide. His hands clenched the reins, and he urged his horse faster along the muddy road to the Burnett ranch. He prayed Burk Burnett was home. He didn't want to wallop the tar out of one of his men when he wasn't around.

Part of his anger was rage at himself. He should never have allowed Lucy to go out by herself; this was still very unsettled territory. Even Burk himself had only moved into this area last year. In addition to rough men like Drew Larson, Indians still roamed, burning out the occasional settler. He needed to remember he was a family man now. His wife and her family depended on him to make proper decisions. This morning's had obviously been a bad one.

Several ranch hands milled around the corral as he stopped at the hitching post. He dismounted and tied his horse, then motioned for the men to stay where they were while he went to the door. He pounded on it with his fist. Only silence answered his knock. Pounding again, he took a deep breath. He had to stay calm and present his case to Burk in a reasonable fashion.

There was still no answer at the door, so he strode to the corral and watched two men working to saddle break a young mare. Peering through the dust and commotion, he finally spied Burk leaning against the fence by the barn as he watched the action in the corral. Clenching his fists, Caleb made his way to Burk's side.

Burk jerked his head up in surprise when he saw Caleb. In his early thirties, he had the keen eyes of a cattleman and a genial grin. Caleb had always liked him from the moment they met.

Caleb held out his hand. "Burk, I got some business with one of your hands."

Burk regarded him with a sober gaze. "Serious business, looks like."

"Drew Larson manhandled my wife today."

Burk's mouth pressed into a straight line, and his nostrils flared. "That so? Care to tell me about it?"

Caleb ignored the questions. "Where can I find him?"

Burk cocked an eyebrow. "I fired him yesterday. Caught him rustling cattle. That why you fired him?"

"Yep."

"I sure would have appreciated it if you would have let me know that. It would've saved me a heap of trouble."

"I reckon I should have, but I never like to meddle in another man's business." Caleb gritted his teeth. His quarry had flown the coop. "Got any idea where he is?"

"Town, most likely. He's probably trying to find some other sucker to hitch up with. I'm putting the word out not to hire him, though. We don't need his kind around here."

"I reckon I'll mosey into town and see if he's still around. I can't have my wife tormented."

"Congratulations on your marriage, by the way. I heard you got hitched, and she's a pretty little thing." Burk grinned and held out his hand.

Caleb shook it. "Thanks. I'm a lucky man." And as he walked back to his horse and mounted, he realized how true that was. How many other wives would have drawn a gun on a man like Drew Larson? And it wasn't just her fire and spirit that drew him or her exquisite beauty. It was something else, something that was all Lucy. Her fierce caring for her brother and sister, her determination to learn everything she needed to know to be a good rancher's wife, her moral backbone.

It had thrown him to see her in his mother's dress. He'd fingered that picture until it was about worn out. Until he'd seen her in Ma's dress, he hadn't realized how tiny his mother must have been, too. No wonder Pa wasn't afraid Lucy wouldn't make a good rancher's wife. He was always talking about how Ma had loved the ranch and how the men had adored and protected her. Lucy had that way about her, too. She drew people to her as naturally as bees to flowers. He glowered at the thought of how Drew Larson had dared to touch her. Digging his knees into his horse's side, he headed to town.

When he reached Wichita Falls, he stopped at the saloon and pushed inside. Larson was there, as he'd expected. He was talking to Curly Milton, a ranch owner from the other side of the county.

Larson flushed when he saw Caleb and the men behind him. His hand went to his holster, but he paused when Caleb pulled his gun first.

"No need for gunplay," he said, holding his splayed fingers out to show he held no weapon.

"Not this time, maybe," Caleb said. "But I'll not say the same if you dare come near my wife again." It was all he could do to not grab the man by the throat and throttle him.

Larson laughed, but it was forced and without humor. "I got no reason to seek out the pretty lady, Stanton. I merely stopped to help her out of the mud. If she says I did more than that, she's lying."

Rage tightened Caleb's throat. He seized Larson by the collar and hauled him to his feet. "My wife doesn't lie," he snarled. "I'm giving you just one warning, Larson. Stay away from Lucy. Better yet, you'd best seek employment somewhere else. You've just been blackballed in this county."

He turned to Curly. "This man stole cattle from me, Curly. I'd suggest you talk to Burk Burnett as well. He fired him yesterday for the same thing."

The man's bald head went pink, and his brows drew together. "In that case, I'll take my leave of you two." He stood and tossed some coins onto the table where they rolled against the plate and stopped.

"Hey, what about my job?" Larson called.

"I'm not interested in hiring a rustler." Curly clapped his hat on his head and strode out of the saloon.

Larson's lips drew back in a snarl like that of a rabid dog. "You'll pay for this, Stanton. You and that so-called wife of yours." He jerked out of Caleb's grip and ran from the building.

Caleb shouted and took off after him, but he had vanished. Frowning, Caleb ran for his horse. He would have to be more vigilant with Lucy. Larson was a dangerous man.

10

he Wichita River, swollen from spring rains, rushed along beside their picnic spot in a tumble of water and flotsam. Lucy watched as Caleb tossed a ball with Jed and Eileen. Since he'd come back from confronting Drew Larson two weeks ago, things had been pleasant between them. Too pleasant. His gaze was admiring and gentle, but it was as though he was waiting on a sign from her. Several times she'd opened her mouth to talk to him about their relationship, then closed it just as quickly. She was a coward, and she couldn't bear for him to think her wanton.

They had family devotions each night, and Lucy was impressed at the amount of Scripture Caleb knew and at the depth of his wisdom. She'd wanted Jed to have a godly role model, and he adored Caleb. They attended worship every Sunday, making the drive to town like a normal family. But as she looked around at the other families who filled the pews, she knew they were like none of them. But she longed to be like the other wives, secure in a husband's love. She looked at Caleb playing with the children and smiled. God had been good to them so far. He would bring them the rest of the way to the fulfillment of all He planned for them. She could hold onto that certainty.

Caleb's hair fell across his forehead as he laughed and feinted away from Jed. Eileen squealed and threw herself against his leg. A smile tugged at Lucy's lips. She caught her breath at the wonder of her feelings. For the first time, she loved him as a wife should love a husband. Looking at his masculine arms, she desired them around her. He looked at her, and she felt the heat of a blush on her cheeks. Did he know?

Caleb reeled over with Eileen still clinging to him and collapsed on the quilt beside her. He closed his eyes. "I'm beat. We're supposed to be resting up before starting the roundup tomorrow, but I don't think this is the way to do it." He scooted over and put his head in Lucy's lap.

Lucy's cheeks heated, but she ran tentative fingers across his forehead, then lightly touched his thick hair. Caleb's eyes were still closed, and for that she was thankful. She stroked his hair, enjoying the feel of it between her fingers. She didn't want to think about the roundup tomorrow. Especially the branding. Her stomach congealed with dread at the thought. But Caleb needed all the help he could get.

"What time do we start tomorrow?" she asked.

"I told the boys to meet at the south pasture at six. Lord willing, we'll be done by suppertime on Wednesday. Since we're starting so early, Pa suggested we bring Eileen to him tonight."

"She'll keep him running."

"It was either that or he'd insist on helping with the roundup. At least this way, he feels useful, and Percy will help him. Eileen will be fine." Caleb sat up and sighed. "I reckon we should be going. Pa is expecting us for supper, and Bessie will be caterwauling to be milked."

Their idyllic day was at an end. She gathered up the remains of their dinner, then folded the quilt. Jed carried the things to the wagon.

That night she could hardly sleep for worrying about the coming three days. What if there were spiders when they slept out on the ground? And what if the ranch hands realized she was a tenderfoot and despised her for it? She wanted Caleb to be proud of her. Lucy sighed and rolled over. She could hear Caleb's soft snore above her head in the loft. He obviously wasn't worried about the roundup. And why should he be? He wasn't the one on display, the one everyone would be judging. An image of Margaret, tall and competent, floated before her like a gray cloud in the sky. Margaret would know how to handle herself on a roundup. All Lucy could do was disappoint.

Cheeper, the rooster, crowed at five, but Lucy was already awake. She hurriedly dressed in a pair of Jed's dungarees and one of his flannel shirts. They were both too big, but they would have to do. She couldn't do a man's work in a dress.

Caleb's brows lifted when he saw her attire, but he grunted in approval. "Glad to see you showing some sense about it," was all he said.

She fixed breakfast while he loaded the bedrolls into the wagon. The three of them ate breakfast in silence. Lucy kept stealing glances at Caleb's distracted face. He already had the cattle in his mind, she saw. After breakfast she followed him and Jed outside. The wagon was laden with the supplies for meals. At least part of her day would be spent with something she knew and loved. Bridget jumped into the wagon to join the fun.

The scene at the roundup was already chaotic. Cattle bellowed, and thick clouds of dust hung in the air. The air was fetid with the scent of cattle and manure. Lucy felt faint and nauseated, and the real work was yet to begin.

The men began to herd the longhorns together. Lucy mounted her mare and found her horse knew what to do better than she did. The mare cut and wheeled among the melee of horses and cattle while Bridget followed, nipping at the heels of the calves who tried to get away. They cut out the unbranded calves and herded them toward a corral the men had built.

Lucy took a deep breath as Rusty, the Stanton foreman, knelt to drop the branding irons in the fire. A movement to her right caught her eye, and she turned. Margaret Hannigan, her generous curves evident in her dungarees and shirt, laid her hand on Caleb's arm. His head was bent attentively to her.

Jealousy, hot and unexpected, swamped Lucy. What was Margaret doing here? She looked completely at home in those clothes. She laughed and tilted her head coquettishly to listen to something Caleb said, then walked toward the branding fire. Picking up a branding iron, she nodded for Rusty to ready the first calf.

The calf bucked and tried to run, but the two men holding bore it to the ground. Margaret walked to the calf and applied the Triple S brand. The calf bawled, and the sound smote Lucy's heart. She bit her lip so hard she could taste blood. The calf bawled again, and bile rose in her throat. Lucy turned to run, but her feet wouldn't obey her. A mist blocked her vision, and the ground rose up to meet her.

"Lucy!"

Hands shook her, but she kept her eyes shut. She didn't want to wake up; it was too early. She would just sleep a few more minutes, then get up to fix breakfast.

"Lucy, wake up."

Gradually she became aware of the hard chest she rested against and the feel of gentle hands holding her. The sounds around her penetrated her consciousness. Cattle lowing, men yelling above the din. Lucy opened her eyes and blinked. Caleb's anxious face swam into focus. Over his shoulder she could see Jed, and just past him, Margaret's concerned face.

Memory flooded back. That calf, the awful bawling, and the stench of burning hair. She felt faint again, and she closed her eyes. Tears stung her eyes and slipped from her closed lids.

Caleb's strong arm lifted her to a more upright position. "Would you like a drink of water?"

She nodded. Anything to avoid looking at the pity in Margaret's face. Pity for Caleb, for the burden he carried having such a sissified wife. He would be sorry he married her now. She sneaked a peek at his face through her lashes.

"Here, take a sip of water." He held a canteen to her lips, and she gulped it, then coughed as it went down the wrong way.

"Careful." He held it to her lips again, and she took another drink before she swiped the back of her hand across her mouth.

"Thanks." She finally dared to meet his gaze. "I'm sorry, Caleb," she whispered.

"Sorry for what? It's a bit overwhelming the first time. You're doing fine."

"The calf." Lucy gulped and broke off.

"I know. But the calf is fine. Look." He pointed to the little blaze-faced calf on the other side of the fence. It nuzzled its mother, then scampered off to play with a friend.

Relief flooded her, but the entire procedure still left a bad taste in her mouth. She let Caleb help her to her feet. Wooziness rushed over her again, and Caleb caught her as she would have fallen.

"Hey, Boss, 'spect you'll be having a little one scampering about, huh?" One of the men laughed, and heat flooded Lucy's face. If they only knew.

Caleb ignored the impolite comment and escorted Lucy to the wagon. She sank weakly onto the ground and leaned against a wagon wheel.

"You should have married Margaret," she muttered. She sensed Caleb go still.

"What's she got to do with this? Are you upset she's here? She always helps with our branding, and I help with theirs. She's just a friend, Lucy." His voice was stiff. "If you don't know I'm an honorable man by now, you don't know me at all."

She winced, and shame flooded her face. "It's not you; it's me," she said almost inaudibly. "I'm useless as a ranch wife. Margaret wasn't just watching, she participated. I will never be able to do that, Caleb." Her shoulders slumped, and she buried her face in her hands.

Caleb knelt beside her, and his breath whispered on her neck. His big hands took hers and pulled them from her face. "Lucy, I never asked you to do that. You're the one who's so determined to prove yourself. You don't have to prove anything to me."

She stared into his gray eyes doubtfully. "You said I was little and puny, that I couldn't be a good rancher's wife," she whispered.

"I was angry then, and wrong. Size doesn't matter, heart does. And you've got the biggest heart I've ever seen." His eyes were tender, and his hands cupped her face.

Her heart surged with hope. Did he mean it? His face came nearer, and her eyes fluttered shut. She held her breath and lifted her face. His breath touched her face. She waited in almost unbearable anticipation.

"Is she all right, Caleb?"

Lucy's eyes flew open at the sound of Margaret's voice. Caleb rocked back on his heels, then stood.

He held out his hand to Lucy. "She's fine, Margaret. Thanks for your concern. I'd best get back to the men."

His warm palm left Lucy's with obvious reluctance. Lucy forced herself to smile at Margaret. The other woman's gaze followed Caleb as he strode back to the dusty, noisy scene. She tore her gaze from Caleb's back with obvious reluctance and smiled distractedly at Lucy.

"I'd better get back, too." She dashed off without waiting for Lucy to reply.

Lucy turned her back on the commotion and began to sort through her supplies. She would not watch the woman ogle her husband. God would not be pleased at her jealousy. Caleb said he was happy with her the way she was. She would cling to that.

Dinner was nearly ready when she saw a buggy come rolling across the field. Shading her eyes, she waved at Luther and Eileen. Luther stopped the buggy at the chuck wagon and hoisted his bulk to the ground. Lucy went to get Eileen.

"Couldn't stay away, could you?" Lucy asked Luther with a teasing smile.

"In the ten years we've been ranching here, I've never missed a roundup. I'm not going to start now." Luther's color was good, and his eyes were bright with excitement. "I think I'll go see if my boy is doing it right." He strode eagerly toward the men and animals.

"It smells," Eileen said. She wound her arms around Lucy's neck.

"I know, Sweetheart. But we'll stay here and get dinner ready." She put Eileen on the end of the wagon and stirred the stew one last time. She heard Eileen gasp and whirled to see what was the matter.

An Indian brave, dressed in buckskin and moccasins, stood by her sister. His brown hand was touching Eileen's shining golden locks. Eileen's blue eyes were wide, and tears trembled on the ends of her lashes.

Lucy sprang to her side and thrust her body between Eileen and the Indian. "Would you like something to eat?" she asked in a shrill voice.

The Indian's dark eyes narrowed, and he touched Lucy's blond hair with a curious hand. Lucy flinched away, and he frowned.

"How much?" He gestured at Eileen. "I give two fine horses for girl child."

"No! She is not for sale."

"I give you five horses." He reached for Eileen.

"No!" Lucy knocked his hand away. Trembling inside, she was determined not to show her fear. Where were the men? Didn't they see the danger?

The Indian scowled and stepped back. He crossed his arms over his chest. "Ten horses."

"No, not for a hundred horses." She scooped Eileen into her arms and dashed toward the safety of the men and cattle. Was he following? Risking a glance back, she didn't see a rock in her path. Her foot struck it, and she went tumbling through the air. Lucy desperately tried to hang onto Eileen and to protect her with her own body.

Twisting as she fell, her arm hit the ground first, and she felt a sickening jerk inside. Crushing pain and nausea dimmed her sight to a pinpoint. She held Eileen against her with her good arm. A moan escaped her mouth.

Eileen began to sob and wail. Moments later Caleb knelt beside her. "What happened? Are you all right?"

"My arm. The Indian," she babbled.

Caleb ran his hand over her arm, and she cried out when he touched her elbow. He bit his lip. "You've dislocated your elbow. I'll have to put it back in place." He stood and waved. "Margaret, could you help me?"

Lucy gritted her teeth. They wouldn't hear her cry out! She would show them what stuff she was made of.

Margaret held her hand while Caleb took hold of Lucy's arm, one hand on either side of her elbow. "Ready?" His face was white, and beads of perspiration stood out on his forehead.

"Yes," Lucy whispered. She closed her eyes and pressed her lips together.

Caleb jerked, and Lucy thought she would be sick. A scream hovered on her lips, but she refused to let it out. The pain was excruciating, and her vision wavered for several long moments. Then the pain began to ebb until it was a manageable dull throb.

Caleb helped her to sit. "You're a brave woman," he said. "What happened?"

Peering past his shoulder, she realized the Indian was gone. Her shoulders eased, and she sighed. Eileen was safe. She told Caleb about the Indian's offer for Eileen.

He sucked in his breath, and his face went white. "You're both beautiful and rather exotic looking to him. I'll have the men keep an eye out, and I want you to stay close to me."

He smiled, but his expression seemed forced to Lucy. She shuddered. He wouldn't have to tell her twice to stay close.

He stood. "You rest that shoulder. Margaret can see to finishing dinner."

"I'll do it." Lucy managed to get to her feet. Margaret wasn't taking over her job. She knew this competitive spirit she had toward the other woman was a sin, but she couldn't seem to help herself. Her elbow throbbed, but she pressed it against her side and hurried to finish dinner. She would prove to Caleb she was a better wife than Margaret if it was the last thing she did.

11

*C*aleb limped a bit as he walked toward the campsite. A blister had formed at his heel, his back felt like someone had stuck a pitchfork through it, and his left hand throbbed from a burn left by the branding iron. His bedroll was going to feel mighty good tonight.

The sight of the firelight on Lucy's golden hair made the glow of the campfire even more welcome. My, she was a beautiful sight. Her radiant hair fell to her waist, and he wondered what she would do if he walked up and plunged his hands into that glorious mass. Scream, probably. He was filthy, and he stank of cattle.

But he was blessed to call her his wife. His bemused grin faded. Unfortunately, that's all she was. A woman he called his wife. He'd watched for a sign from her that she was ready to move forward into a deeper relationship with him, but just when he thought there might be hope, she stepped back again.

She looked up as he approached. Her blue eyes were shadowed, but he didn't think it was from the pain of her dislocated elbow. She seemed to be using that arm a bit.

"I heated some water for you," she said. "Jed already washed up and went to bed."

"He worked as hard as a man today. You've done a good job with him." Caleb thrust his hands into the kettle of hot water, splashing it over his face and neck. "Whew, that feels mighty good."

"I brought a piece of pie from the chuck wagon. I thought you might be hungry."

"I'm almost too tired to be hungry. But pie sounds good." He took the pie from her outstretched hand and gulped it down in four bites.

All he really wanted to do was crawl into his bedroll and rest his weary body.

The April air was muggy, even as late as it was. Staring into his wife's lovely face, Caleb felt all thought of sleep leave him. He pushed a log over to the fire and sat on it, then patted the spot next to him. "Let's jaw awhile. I'm not as tired as I thought I was."

She came toward him and perched on the log next to him. Her arm brushed his, and the contact sent a tingle up his back. "How's your arm?"

"Better. It still aches some, but the more I use it, the better it gets." She leaned forward and poked at the fire with a stick. Tiny sparks escaped the flames and shot upward into the dark night.

Caleb reached over and captured her hand. She jumped but didn't pull away. Instead, her slim fingers curled around his and returned his pressure. "I was proud of you today," he said softly.

Lucy jerked her head up, and her eyes went wide. "How could you be proud? I fainted at the sight of a simple branding, I ran shrieking in fear at the sight of an Indian, and then stumbled over my own feet and dislocated my elbow." Her voice was low and anguished. "I'm sure the men were laughing at the boss's poor choice in a wife. I came here to be a helpmeet, but it seems all I've managed to do is to be a hindrance."

"That's not true, Lucy. I'm glad you're here."

"Truly?" She turned to face him, and the movement brought her face only inches from his own. Her breath touched his face, and he caught a glimpse of perfect white teeth in the moonlight. Her breath was sweet and enticing. Something stirred in his heart; some new emotion had sprung to life.

He couldn't help himself. His fingers traveled up her arm to her mane of hair, and he pulled her into his arms. Caleb heard her soft gasp, and it only served to inflame the passion he felt for her. She fit into his arms as though she were made for him.

Her face turned up to his, and he pressed his lips against hers. At first Lucy was stiff, then she wound her arms around his neck and returned his kiss. His heart hammered against his ribs as he tasted the sweetness of her kiss for the first time. Caleb had never kissed a woman before, and the wonder of holding his wife in his arms this way drove all thought from his head.

He wanted to go on kissing her, but he felt her pull away a bit. "Did I hurt you?" he muttered in a hoarse whisper.

Keeping her face turned away, she shook her head. Was she crying? Caleb touched Lucy's chin with his fingers and turned her to face him. Her face was wet with tears, and his throat tightened. "What is it, Lucy?"

"Now you kiss me," she said softly. "Now when I've failed so miserably. I don't want your pity, Caleb. I want your love and your respect. You expected certain things from a wife, and I don't think I can ever meet those expectations."

"I don't have any expectations. I was wrong to lash out at you that way. Wrong and pigheaded."

Lucy shook her head and knuckled away her tears. "You and Pa are building an empire here. An empire takes an empress, someone who can stand at your side and fight whatever comes without fear. Today has shown me I can never be that woman. I was wrong to think I could."

"This doesn't sound like the Lucy I know. Where's that spunky little woman who faced down the mongrel? Where's that gal who made me toe the line at mealtimes? I need you, Lucy. I just didn't realize it before." He twined a long curl around his finger.

"I wish that were true," she muttered. "You're so self-sufficient, Caleb, a self-made man. I have nothing I can bring you that you don't already have. I just didn't realize that until today."

He tried to pull her close again, but she stood and evaded his grasp. "Is this because Margaret is here? She's not the woman I want. You are."

"I don't want pity, Caleb. Margaret would have made a much better wife for you."

Caleb jumped to his feet. "I don't want Margaret," he shouted.

Several ranch hands glanced their way, and he lowered his voice. "The day I ever let you go, Lucy, is the day the Red River runs backwards." He turned and stalked away. Women! He didn't understand them. She was just getting tired of the isolation and hard work. Well, that was too bad. She was stuck with him.

He wandered through the maze of bedrolls and campfires until he reached the outskirts of the camp. Caleb wished Pa was here; maybe he knew more about how to handle women. Lucy likely needed wooing, but he just didn't know how to do it, especially encumbered by her brother and sister. Not that he didn't love them, but sometimes a man needed space to say those things that only a wife should hear.

All he knew were cattle and horses, and they were easily handled by a cattle dog. He was out of his element here. If one of the newfangled universities offered a course on women, he would be the first to sign up. Lucy made his head spin with all her jawing and emotional turmoil. Next time she started talking like that, he'd just pull her into his arms and kiss her until she shut up. He grinned at the thought. She would likely toss a clump of mud at his head like she did Drew Larson.

He flopped down under a cottonwood tree. "I could use some help here, Lord," he said softly. "What do I do about this?" Caleb buried his face in his hands. In the stillness of the night, thoughts of Scripture crept into his mind, Scripture he thought he'd never need to apply to his own life.

> *Husbands, love your wives, even as Christ also loved the church, and gave himself for it.*

The words wrapped around his heart. He'd admitted he cared for her, but did he love her? Caleb examined his heart. With dawning wonder, he realized he loved Lucy. She was the best thing that had ever happened to him. He didn't care if she never came on another roundup or ever learned to rope a calf. He loved her fire and determination, her desire to do right, just the essence of who she was. What she did was unimportant.

But with a sinking heart, he realized he hadn't done a very good job of letting Lucy know that. All she'd heard was how important the ranch was to him, not how important she was, not how vital her happiness was to him. No wonder she was all wrapped up in performance and ability. He had to tell her how he felt and make it right.

But as quickly as the notion struck, he knew that was wrong. Words wouldn't convince Lucy. Actions were the only thing she would understand now. His actions had told her she was unimportant next to the ranch. Only actions would convince her she was the most important thing in his life. She would have to see the difference in him; then he would tell her he loved her. Not before.

❧

Lucy's heart ached in a most peculiar way. It was a good kind of hurt, the kind she felt when she probed a wound and brought out a splinter, the way she felt when her stomach burned with hunger but Jed and Eileen got up from the table with a full belly. At least she'd been honest with him. And he would come to agree. Maybe she could just be his housekeeper and give up any expectations of more. They could learn to get along that way somehow.

From here she could see Margaret's strong body, could hear her robust laughter. Margaret would have bred strong sons for Caleb. She could have stood at his side, shoulder to shoulder, and carved an empire out of this desolate place. Tears pricked Lucy's eyes, but she pushed them away. She was such a failure in all that she'd set her mind to do.

All her dreams of being a blessing to her husband were gone. She had brought him nothing but aggravation. How had it come to this? Her high hopes and dreams of just last week lay in ashes from one day as a cowhand.

She kicked open her bedroll and sat down to take off her boots. Crawling under the blanket, she groaned at the hardness of the ground. She'd gotten spoiled in that soft bed Caleb had made for her.

As if the thought had brought him out of the fog, Caleb came through the smoke of the fire with an intent smile on his face. He said nothing, simply picked up his bedroll from the other side of Jed and laid it down beside her. He shifted it closer to her, then took off his boots and crawled under the blanket.

His arm snaked out from the covers and his fingers grasped hers. She waited for him to speak, to explain his intentions, but moments later she heard the even sound of his breathing. But even in his sleep, his hand still gripped hers. Lucy rolled over on her side and watched his face in the moonlight. She'd longed to watch him sleep for months. Now that she had the chance, there were dozens of people around. Lucy was so bewildered, she found it hard to fall asleep, in spite of her fatigue. But Caleb's presence beside her eased the fear she'd had of sleeping on the ground. No tarantula would dare bother her with his strong arms next to her.

Jed and Caleb were already gone by the time she awakened. Lucy sat up and rubbed the sleep from her eyes. The morning air was heavy with the promise of heat and humidity. A single spray of some kind of yellow wildflower lay on top of her bedroll.

"Caleb," she murmured. She picked up the flower. What had gotten into him? He was acting almost romantic, which was totally out of character for him. She lifted the flower to her nose and breathed deeply of its fragrance. Sighing, she laid it aside and scrambled to her feet. There was a lot to do today.

She rolled up her bedroll and pulled on her boots, shaking them first to make sure no creepy crawlies had found their way inside. Taking her comb, she tugged it through her hair, then wadded her long tresses up on top of her head. Good thing she didn't have a mirror; the sight of her bedraggled state would surely be depressing.

When she made her way to the chuck wagon, most of the men were already out with the herd. She took a tin plate and scooped up a bit of the congealed gravy and hard biscuits. Lucy shook her head. If she'd awakened in time, she would have made some flapjacks. If the illustrious Margaret had made this breakfast, she wasn't as perfect as Caleb thought. She winced at her own unattractive thoughts. No wonder Caleb couldn't love her.

The mess had been left dirty, so she scraped the scraps onto a plate for Bridget and heated water to wash up. The bawling of the calves made her wince, and she thought about going back to the cabin. She was never going to be a proper rancher's wife anyway, so why prolong the agony? But Lucy couldn't force herself to go. Quitting was against her nature. Maybe today would be better. Caleb's gift of the flower had given her fresh hope somehow.

Lucy had just finished the dishes when Margaret came toward her. Striding like a man, her hair carelessly braided and tossed over one shoulder, she was the picture of health and vitality. Her white teeth flashed in her tanned face, and Lucy had to smile back.

"I need a break," Margaret said. "My throat is as dry as gypsum. Any water handy?"

"Of course." Lucy grabbed a tin cup and scooped some water into it.

Margaret drank thirstily and wiped her mouth with the back of her hand. Lucy watched in fascination; she'd never met a woman who was so vital and alive. Margaret made no pretense of femininity, but she was attractive in spite of it.

Margaret plopped onto the ground at Lucy's feet. "You don't like me, do you, Lucy?"

Lucy blinked. "I—I don't really know you, Margaret. I'm sure you're a very nice person."

Margaret snorted. "Nice? That's the first time anyone ever accused me of that. Overbearing, manly, outspoken, those are terms I'm more familiar with."

Lucy opened her mouth, then closed it again. What could she say to that? It was all true, after all.

Margaret grinned at her obvious discomfiture. "Don't worry; you won't hurt my feelings none. Your problem with me is that you think I'm after your husband. You wouldn't be far wrong. But I know when I'm licked. He's in love with his pretty, genteel wife, and someone like me will never tempt him away."

In love with her? For a moment Lucy's heart soared, then thumped back to ground. Not likely. He felt something for her; she would allow that. But love? He loved his ranch, not her.

Margaret leaned forward. "I'm sorry to be so blunt, but we're going to be neighbors, and we need to clear the air between us. Yes, I was hurt when you came waltzing in the store on the arm of the man I had claimed as my own. Not that Caleb realized he was claimed, mind you, but I'd staked him out just the same. But I'm now sure it's for the best. Caleb and me are too hardheaded to rub along very well together. We would have always been clashing heads." She grinned. "Not that you haven't had your share of clashes from the sound of that argument last night."

Heat scorched Lucy's cheeks. "I—I do have a temper myself," she admitted. "You would make him a much better wife. Unfortunately, it's too late."

Margaret's eyes narrowed. "He loves you, Lucy. If you think there's anything between us, I'm telling you there's not."

"I believe you. I just can't be the helpmeet I should be. I wish I could be like you."

"So you're just going to give up like a yellow-bellied coward? Since when is marriage supposed to be perfect? Everyone goes into it with unreal expectations." Margaret shook her finger in Lucy's face. "Sounds to me like you're expecting more of yourself than Caleb expects from you. You need a dose of reality. Loving one another through arguments and sickness, through lean times and child rearing, that's reality. Perfection is like trying to catch a moonbeam."

Lucy stood. "You're not even married, Margaret. How can you presume to counsel me on marriage?"

"You're acting like a spoiled child who runs away when the other kids don't play her game. Grow up."

Lucy gasped. The woman had a nerve! Before she could think of a suitable retort, Margaret rose to her feet and swept her up in a bear hug.

"We'll be friends one of these days, Lucy. Give us both some time to lick our wounds. I like you; you got spunk. It's about time you showed it."

*L*ucy stirred the beans and then began to make cornbread for supper. The roundup was almost over, and she would be glad to get out of the dust and noise. And the smell! She wrinkled her nose. Margaret's words echoed in her mind. Did she expect too much of herself? Her parents had always expected her to be the best at everything she did. And she had to admit she took pride in doing more and giving more than other people.

Tears welled in her eyes, but she pressed her lips together and beat the cornbread batter as if it was the cause of all her turmoil. Tears never solved anything, but lately it seemed she was on the verge of them all the time.

While the cornbread was baking, she walked over to watch the last of the roundup. A thrill of joy shot through her as she watched Caleb astride his black gelding. He'd only bought the horse last week. A magnificent animal, man and horse were well matched. Caleb's powerful arms controlled the huge creature as an ordinary man would a pony, while his muscular thighs dared the horse to try to throw him.

Caleb's sandy hair was already beginning to lighten from the spring sunshine. He was a man who would turn heads no matter where he lived or what he did. No wonder Lucy couldn't measure up. She was a pale shadow of the kind of woman he should have.

Margaret rode next to him. She had that same vitality and vigor that Caleb possessed. But Margaret said she didn't want Caleb. How could any woman say that and mean it? Caleb had but to crook his finger, and any woman would want him. Lucy's heart clenched. She would never measure up; she would never be able to earn his love.

He wheeled on his horse and saw her. A tender smile accompanied the hand he lifted in greeting. Cantering over to her, he sat looking down at her from his saddle. "You've been in hiding all day. You getting used to the noise and commotion?"

She smiled. "I just thought I'd look to see how Jed was doing." And she had a need to see her husband, but she couldn't tell him that. She couldn't get enough of looking at him lately. What would he think of that, if he knew?

Caleb pointed out a group of riders across the field from them. "Rusty is teaching him to rope. He's picking it up pretty well, though on his first few attempts he managed to rope the fence post instead of the calf."

"You've done so much for him," Lucy said. "He actually likes work, and he's got a confidence I've never seen him show before. Thank you, Caleb."

The tenderness in Caleb's gaze sucked the breath from her lungs. The expressions on his face and the solicitousness of his manner for the past two days had Lucy pondering what was going on in his head. Was he really not disappointed in the bargain anymore? She was afraid to hope for that.

"Jed's a good boy. He'll be an asset on the cattle drive next week." He looked over her head. "Here comes Pa with Eileen."

Lucy turned and waved.

"I've missed her; she keeps things lively."

Lucy laughed. "I think things have been plenty lively around here."

"At least Pete didn't show up."

Lucy gasped. "Um, just where did you turn him loose?"

Caleb pointed to the far clump of trees. "Right there. Want to take a walk in the moonlight tonight and look for him? He might come if I call."

In spite of herself, Lucy felt the corners of her mouth turn up. "No thanks. I might have to ask you to stomp on him."

"I'd do it for you."

His gray eyes seemed to reach into her soul with an emotion she hadn't seen there before. What was going on in his head? A lump formed in Lucy's throat. "You—you would?"

His gaze caressed her face. "I reckon I'd do most anything for you, Lucy."

How did she answer that? A pulse beat high in her throat. Before she could make a fool of herself, Eileen and Luther reached them.

"This little girl is pert near pining herself to death for you," Luther said in a booming voice. "I tried reading her a story, and even Percy offered to let her help bake cookies, which was a big sacrifice since he never lets anyone in his kitchen." He caught Lucy's gaze. "Except for you, Lucy."

Eileen threw herself at Lucy's legs and began to clamber up them like she would a tree. "Lucy, we baked-ed cookies with raisins. Percy let me put the raisins in."

Lucy hugged her, relishing the feel of her small body. "You're getting to be a big girl, Eileen. Did you thank Percy?"

Eileen nodded her head, and her blond ponytail whipped in the breeze. She gazed up at Caleb's horse. "Can I pet him?"

"How about a ride on Morgan?" Caleb said. "Want to come, too, Lucy?"

Lucy glanced back at the chuck wagon. "I really should check on the cornbread." But the thought of being next to her husband for just a few minutes was almost too enticing to resist.

"I'll watch it," Luther said. "You go ahead with Caleb."

The pleased expression he wore brought a smile to Lucy's lips. Then the lightness in her heart faded. If he only knew the truth.

Caleb held out a hand. "Pa, you hold Eileen until I get Lucy up here, then she can put Eileen in front of her."

Eileen held out her arms to Luther. "Grandpa, you want to come, too?"

Luther lifted her into his arms. "No thanks, Pumpkin. That horse of Caleb's won't let just anyone ride him. You and your sister are special."

Eileen preened. "We're special, Lucy."

Caleb slid into the saddle, then gripped Lucy's hand and lifted her up in front of him on Morgan. Luther handed Eileen up to her, while Caleb reached around Lucy's waist and took the reins. He smelled of horse and leather with a hint of spice from his hair tonic. His breath ruffled her hair, and without thinking Lucy leaned back against his chest.

The shock of contact slicked her palms with perspiration, and she swallowed. She needed to stay away from close contact with Caleb. Touching him just made her realize all she was missing. Taking a deep breath, she started to ease forward, but his left arm came around her waist and pulled her closer. She could feel the hard muscles of his chest against her back, and he rested his chin on her head.

"Faster, Caleb!" Eileen kicked her little legs and giggled.

Caleb obliged by digging his heels into Morgan's ribs. The horse broke into a canter. Eileen loosened her grip on Lucy's arm and clapped her hands. They rode with the wind blowing the scent of sage and creosote in their faces.

Finally Eileen tugged on Lucy's arm. "I have to go potty, Lucy," she said in a loud whisper.

Lucy nodded and told Caleb. He pulled on the reins and stopped beside a rocky outcropping on the far side of the men. He slid to the ground and reached up to lift Eileen down.

"Wait for your sister," he told her.

His big hands spanned Lucy's waist as he lifted her from the saddle. Setting her on the ground mere inches from him, she had to fight an urge to wrap her arms around his waist and rest her head on his chest. What would he do if she did that? His gray eyes were somber, and his hands still held her. She swallowed and stepped away. Tearing her gaze from his, she turned to take Eileen's hand.

She was gone.

A rattle sounded to their right. Lucy turned and saw Eileen only two feet from a coiled rattler. "Eileen, no!" Lucy hurtled toward her sister. A split second later, the rattler struck at Eileen, but Lucy got there first. The snake's fangs sank into Lucy's right forearm, then pulled back for another strike. Eileen was shrieking, but Lucy felt nothing at first. Then a boom sounded, and a bullet slammed into the snake, driving its still writhing body away.

Caleb was there instantly, kneeling beside her. Two tiny puncture wounds oozing blood was all the damage Lucy could see, so she didn't understand why his face was so white. She felt fine; the snake must not have had much venom.

"Let me see." His voice was terse.

She cradled Eileen with her good arm and held the right one up like a child offering a gift. Dizziness suddenly swamped her. Then the pain struck, deep, burning pain. Lucy bit her lip in an effort not to cry out. She gritted her teeth against the pain.

Caleb took her arm in one hand, reaching into his pocket with the other. "Pa!" he bellowed across the field.

The rowdy, boisterous calls of the roundup faded until there was just Caleb's white face and Eileen's keening cry. Lucy held onto both to keep herself conscious. She mustn't frighten Eileen. Her sister clung to her, and she patted her hand weakly.

Caleb scooped Lucy up in his arms. Luther took Eileen, and they both ran with their burdens toward the fire. Caleb pulled his pocketknife out of his dungarees and heated it in the fire. He held it poised over Lucy's arm, an apology in his eyes.

His fingers bit into her flesh, but Lucy didn't cry out; the deeper pain of the poison was too great. She fought nausea and breathed deeply.

"This will hurt," he said softly. "I'm sorry, Love." Then the knife plunged down into Lucy's arm, and he made two slits over the puncture wounds.

The pain bit into her, and she cried out. Circles of blackness came and went in her vision. Caleb brought the cuts to his mouth. He sucked, then spat bright blood. Again he sucked the poison from her wounds and spat it out.

Time lost all meaning for Lucy as she watched her husband battle to save her life. She felt far away, as if this was all happening to someone else. Her vision blurred, and chills ravaged her. She tried to speak, to tell him not to do this. Caleb was risking his own life to save hers. If he had a cut in his mouth, the poison would kill him. She had brought him no blessing; she'd been a curse instead. But the words wouldn't come; her numb tongue was thick in her mouth. She closed her eyes and welcomed the blackness.

～❧

"Yeehaw!" Caleb lashed the whip over the head of the horses as he drove the rig toward home. Her head on Jed's lap, Lucy lolled bonelessly in the back. Caleb didn't know another time he'd been this afraid. Not when the fire burned down the barn, not when the Wichita River flood came almost to the house. His knuckles white, he urged the horses to go faster.

Dust kicked up behind him as he jerked the team to a halt in front of the main house. Scooping up Lucy in his arms, he carried her into the house and up the steps to his old bedroom. His boot heels echoed emptily on the polished wood floors. Lucy's welfare landed squarely on his own shoulders.

He laid her in the bed. "Bring me that bowl and pitcher of water," he told Jed. Jed sprang to obey and brought the washcloth as well. Caleb loosened the buttons on her dress and began to sponge her with the damp cloth.

Lucy thrashed and cried out. Caleb felt helpless as he watched her agony. He wished he could take it for her. Rattler venom could kill even a hardy man, let alone a tiny thing like Lucy. She was hardly bigger than a child.

The front door banged, and a minute later he heard his father's voice.

"Caleb, how is she?" His father's voice was loud in the quiet room.

"Still unconscious."

"Doc will be here shortly; I sent Rusty after him." His pa stood at the foot of the bed, his big hands gripping the bedpost.

"Where's Eileen?"

"Percy has her. He'll be along with her in a few hours, once we're sure Lucy is out of danger."

"*Will* she be out of danger, Pa? What if she doesn't make it?" The question was an anguished cry from his heart. He felt like a child again, needing assurance from the one stable thing in his life.

"She's in God's hands, Boy. It's up to the Lord. But we can pray right now and ask Him to spare her."

"What if He doesn't? How did you bear it when Ma died?"

Luther was silent for a moment, his gray eyes moist and faraway. "One day at a time, Caleb. I held onto God's hand and made it one day at a time." He leaned over and gripped Caleb's hand. "Let's pray, Son."

Caleb felt Jed's fingers creep into his hand, and he squeezed it with more reassurance than he felt. He bowed his head. "Oh, Lord, we can only ask for Your mercy right now. Don't take Lucy from us." His throat closed, and he couldn't speak. Jed gave a slight sob.

His thoughts were too jumbled to even voice out loud, but he knew the Holy Spirit was there to speak them to the Lord. His father sniffled, and Caleb raised his head. They all stared at Lucy until the door banged again, and the doctor came bustling down the hall.

"How's my patient?" Doc asked, setting his black bag on the foot of the bed.

Lucy was so tiny; her feet came just past the halfway point of the bed. Her face was ashen against the white of the pillow. Doc examined her pupils, then pressed his stethoscope to her chest. Caleb held his breath and continued to pray.

Doc straightened up. "Her heart is pretty irregular, Caleb. I won't lie to you. It's going to be pretty touch and go through the night. Keep sponging her off with water and try to get some water down her as well." He gripped Caleb's hand and peered into his face. "How about you? Suffering any ill effects from sucking out that poison? Any sores in your mouth?"

Caleb shook the doctor's arm off impatiently. "I'm fine. Do you think she'll make it, Doc?"

The doctor shrugged, his brown eyes kind. "Do I look like God, Son? Sometimes I feel all I do is travel around to watch Him work. It's like offering a thimble of water to help the ocean. You are already appealing to the only One who can decide that." He snapped his bag closed. "There's nothing I can do for her, Caleb. She'll likely wake up soon, but she'll be hurting some. I'll leave some laudanum here to give her. If she gets worse, send Percy for me."

Caleb nodded, and Luther walked the doctor to the front door. Jed sighed and sat in the chair beside his sister. Putting his face in his hands, he gave a huge sigh. Caleb put a hand on his shoulder. "We'll get through this together, Jed."

Jed raised wet eyes to meet his gaze. "What will happen to us if— if Lucy dies?" he whispered.

Caleb knelt beside him. "Jed, we're a family now, no matter what. But Lucy will be fine. We have to believe that. But I'll take care of you and Eileen. Don't you worry about that. I love you, Jed. You and Eileen both."

Jed flung his arms around Caleb's neck and burst into noisy sobs. Caleb pulled him tight against his chest and patted his back.

"What's all that caterwauling?" Lucy's voice was weak. She struggled to sit up, then whimpered. Gasping, she gripped her stomach, and her face went a shade whiter. "Water," she whispered.

"I'll get it!" Jed rushed from the room.

Caleb knelt beside the bed and touched Lucy's cheek. "Feeling pretty bad?"

"Like the barn fell on me." She tried to smile but moaned instead.

Caleb smoothed the hair back from her forehead. "You're going to be fine," he said. "The doctor was just here. We'll have some rough next few hours, but you hang on."

Her fingers crept across the top of the quilt and gripped his hand. "If I don't make it, Caleb—"

"Hush, don't even think that way." Now that she was awake, he felt a surge of hope, and not even Lucy could be allowed to dampen it.

"Jed and Eileen—"

"Don't worry about them. They'll be fine."

"But if something should happen, if I don't pull through this—"

Caleb caressed her cheek. "Rest, Love. I'll take care of Jed and Eileen."

Relief lit her face, then cramps struck her, and she doubled up in agony. Caleb felt helpless watching her suffer. Remembering the laudanum, he snatched it up and uncapped the bottle. He slid an arm under her and managed to get a swallow down her. Gasping, she fell back against the pillow.

Jed brought back the water, and Caleb gave Lucy a drink. Once she was sleeping again, he talked Jed into getting some rest, promising to call him if there was any change.

❧

For three days Caleb sat for long hours in the chair beside Lucy, offering her sips of water between bouts of sickness and sleeping. Her chills finally eased, and a bit of color began to come back to her cheeks. Caleb was bleary-eyed with fatigue, and when she closed her eyes, he dropped to the floor and rested his head against the mattress.

Lucy's fingers entwined in his hair. "There's room in the bed for you," she whispered.

He raised his head and stared down into her blue eyes. She'd made it over the hump; he could see it in her tender smile and pink cheeks. Without another word, she pulled back the quilt and scooted back against the wall. Caleb pulled off his boots and crawled into the bed.

He stretched out his arm, and Lucy curled up against his side. The sensation of someone else in the bed was a strange one, but something he thought he could get used to pretty quickly. Her breathing evened out, and he relaxed himself. She was asleep. Now if he could do the same. His mind whirled. When she was fully recovered, they would have to have a long talk. It was time to take up their lives together in earnest.

13

*A*n unfamiliar weight pressed against Lucy's waist, and she opened her eyes to find herself facing the wall in an unfamiliar room. She tried to move her arm and winced. The pain brought the memories flooding back. She looked down to see what pinned her in place and found an arm. A man's arm. Caleb's arm.

Shock rippled through her, and she eased away and sat up. Last night, his face had been tight with worry and fatigue. Now sleep had eased the lines and tension. A wave of love swept over her, and she reached over and smoothed the hair back from his face. His eyes flew open, and she stared deep into their depths.

A smile curved his firm lips. "Good morning. How do you feel?"

"A little sore and weak, but better I think."

He lifted his hand, and his fingers grazed her cheek. "You look lovely."

Heat flooded her cheeks, and she tore her gaze away. He couldn't mean that tender look he was giving her. She had to remember Margaret was his true love. It would be easy to mistake his concern for love.

"When do you leave for the cattle drive?"

"You eager to get rid of me?"

Her gaze flew to meet his again. "No, I want to go along."

His eyebrows arched, then he frowned. "The Chisolm Trail isn't for tenderfoots. I'll have my hands full looking out for Jed without worrying about you and Eileen."

"Someone will need to cook, why not me?"

"You just got bit by a rattlesnake. You hated the cattle and the dust of the past few days. The trail to Wichita will take three months." He crossed his arms. "You'll stay here and work on gardening and making curtains like a normal wife."

She laid a hand on his arm. "Please, Caleb. Am I that hateful to you that you can't stand to be with me?"

He groaned. "That's not fair, Lucy, and you know it. I've been trying to show you that I want this marriage to work. But the stress of the trail is not the way to do it." He swung his legs out of bed and stood. "It's out of the question. Now you rest while I fetch you some breakfast."

Lucy didn't answer, but a hard rock of determination grew within her. She'd failed at the roundup, but she would prove to him she could stand toe-to-toe with Margaret. Earning his love might not be easy, but it would be worth it. With God's help, she would conquer this weakness and go with him.

❧

By the end of the day she was longing for home. Home. Funny how she had begun to think of the cabin as her home so quickly. She hadn't had a home since her parents died, not a real home. Now she did. But it would never be the home she really needed until she could show herself worthy of Caleb's love.

Caleb brought the buggy to the front of the house, then escorted her out. His steadying arm around her waist would be easy to get used to. Jed helped Eileen clamber into the backseat while Caleb swung Lucy up onto the front seat. She felt naked without her bonnet, but it had been lost somehow in the excitement. The sun on her bare head was a welcome sensation. She still felt chilled and weak.

Was going on the cattle drive such a good idea in the condition she was in? She pushed away the doubts. This was her chance to prove herself; she had to go. She would enlist Jed's help and hide herself among the cowboys until it was too late to send her back. She shivered at the thought of Caleb's anger.

"Cold?"

She forced a smile. "Not really. The sun feels good."

"You won't say that come July and August. At least you won't be on the trail with the dust mixing with the perspiration until you look like you're covered in mud."

Doubt assailed her again. That didn't sound like much fun. But it surely wasn't as bad as he made out. He was just trying to make certain she didn't ask to go again.

They crested a hill, and the cabin came into sight. A curl of smoke rose in a welcoming spiral from the chimney. "Someone's started a fire," she said.

Caleb frowned. "Maybe one of the hands came over." He stopped the buggy in front of the house instead of the barn. Jumping out, he lifted Lucy down. His manner was brusque and businesslike as if he had something else on his mind. He helped her to the door.

The door swung open as they reached it, and Margaret's strong form filled the doorway. "Welcome home," she said with a smile. "Now, I'm not staying, mind you. But I thought after your ordeal you wouldn't feel up to cooking. There's a roast and potatoes in the oven, and your bed is all ready for you." She stepped aside to allow them to enter.

"How thoughtful," Lucy stammered. And it was. So why did she feel so resentful? Margaret's overwhelming presence and many abilities just made Lucy feel even more inadequate.

"We sure do appreciate it, Margaret," Caleb said. There was affection in the nod he gave her.

Lucy saw the gesture, and tears pricked her eyes. How could Caleb ever grow to love her when she failed to attain Margaret's perfection? She was small and weak; she hated the noise and smells of the cattle; she needed rescuing every time she turned around. No wonder Caleb looked at Margaret with such admiration.

Weakness slowed her walk, and Caleb's grip around her waist tightened. He led her to the bed and made her sit down. Kneeling beside her, he slipped her boots off.

"Lie down. I'll get a quilt." He pulled a quilt from the rack and pulled it over her.

Margaret's face was filled with concern. "Can I do anything for you, Lucy?"

"No, you've done quite enough. Thank you so much, Margaret." Lucy lay back against the pillow with a sigh.

"If there's anything you need, just send Jed after me." Margaret picked up her basket and went to the door. "I'll check in on you tomorrow. Like I said, if there's anything I can do, send Jed to fetch me. Hopefully, you'll be almost yourself again by the time we leave for the cattle drive next week. Doc says your recovery has been nearly miraculous. And that's saying something for that old reprobate to let God take the credit for anything."

"You—you're going on the cattle drive?" Caleb hadn't mentioned that little detail.

"Of course. We're taking our cattle to Wichita, too. We always drive them together."

Hopeless. It was hopeless. How could she compete with Margaret's supreme competency? Lucy gritted her teeth. She *would* compete. She would compete and win!

Jed fixed her a cup of tea, and Eileen curled up beside her on the bed while Lucy read her a story from one of the books they'd brought in the trunk. If Lucy forgot the fact that Caleb wished he'd married Margaret, she could almost imagine they were the happy family they seemed. When they returned from the cattle drive, maybe they would be. She had to cling to that hope.

The scent of the roast and potatoes began to fill the air. Eileen had fallen asleep beside her, and Jed had gone outside to practice his rope throwing. He'd taken Bridget with him. The long-suffering dog would be his "calf."

She heard Caleb overhead in the loft. Scraping and banging, he seemed to be moving furniture. Curious, Lucy eased out of bed without awakening Eileen and went to the ladder leading to the loft. Though her head was still spinning, she clung to the ladder with clammy hands and managed to make her way to the loft. Peering over the top, she found Caleb with a broom in his hand.

He saw her and gave a sheepish grin. "I thought I ought to make sure there are no spiders up here before I leave."

"Why? You're not afraid of them."

"No, but you are. I'd like you to sleep here while I'm gone." His gray eyes were intent.

Lucy carefully finished the climb into the loft and stepped onto the rough floor. What did he mean? Her gaze probed his, and neither of them looked away.

"Then when I get back, I'd like us to share this room." His gaze never left hers as he took a step nearer.

Lucy's mouth went dry, and she was afraid to breathe.

"I reckon it's time we tried to make this marriage work." He was right in front of her now. He took a ringlet and twisted it around his finger.

But without love? Lucy wanted to ask him how he really felt about her, but the words stuck in her throat. Maybe he could grow to love her through the intimacy of marriage. He'd been different lately; maybe he was already beginning to love her. But no, she couldn't let herself hope. Hope always seemed to disappoint her.

"I love Jed and Eileen, but I want our own kids, too. I reckon that can't happen the ways things are right now." His thumb traced her jawline.

"I—I want children, too." She barely managed to get the words out past the lump in her throat.

"Girls with this pretty hair and your blue eyes."

"Strong sons," Lucy whispered. "With broad shoulders and gray eyes."

Those gray eyes crinkled in a smile, and his rough fingers caressed her cheek. "I won't mind if those girls are small and dainty like their mama," he said softly.

His face came closer, and Lucy closed her eyes and leaned against his chest. She was almost too weak to stand.

The front door banged, and Jed's voice rang out. "Hey, Lucy, Caleb, where is everybody?" His shout woke Eileen, and she began to cry.

Caleb sighed and stepped back. "I can't seem to woo my wife no matter how hard I try," he muttered. "Will you think about it, Lucy?"

Lucy opened her eyes. Unable to speak, she nodded, then went to the ladder and climbed down to see to Eileen. It would likely be all she thought about.

"Crown me." Caleb pushed his black checker toward Jed with an air of triumph. From the corner of his eye he could see Lucy moving about the cookstove. She seemed a little weak and shaky, but he thought she was mostly recovered from her snakebite. She'd insisted on fixing the meal. All evening the tension between them had grown. Should he ask her to share his room tonight, before he left for such a long trip?

He mentally shook his head. It was a fool notion. It wouldn't be fair to start a new life together, then leave her. Words of love seemed trapped behind his lips. In the loft he'd wanted to tell her she was his sun and moon, the one thing he would give all his possessions for. But such romantic words would have seemed strange pouring from the lips of a cowboy like him. He was no poet. But why couldn't he manage the simple words "I love you"?

Caleb had never thought of himself as a coward. But when it came to matters of the heart, he was at a loss. He dragged his concentration back onto the game before Jed could notice his preoccupation.

"Supper's ready," Lucy said. Eileen put her doll into the little bed Caleb had made for her.

Caleb stood. "Come with me, Eileen, I'll pump the water for us to wash up." He took the little girl's hand, and they went to the back door. As Caleb pumped the handle and water gushed over Eileen's then Jed's hands, he was struck with how dear this little family had all become to him. It wasn't just Lucy. God had surely blessed him; he'd just been too stupid to see it.

If he hadn't been so pigheaded at first, would things be different now? Maybe Lucy would not feel this fierce desire to prove she was as good as Margaret. He could see that was what drove her.

He sluiced water over his own hands and dried them on the towel that hung over the pump. As he went back inside with the children, he decided to just table all thought of his marriage until he got back. God would help him find his way through this morass of doubt.

After supper, they had their evening devotions together as usual, and then he climbed the ladder to bed. Tomorrow he would leave for Wichita, Kansas. Normally, he was full of excitement the night before a cattle drive. Now he hated to leave Lucy and Eileen behind. Maybe he should have allowed her to go, but she was so small and slight. He wanted to protect her; surely that was a normal response for a husband. He punched the pillow into shape and closed his eyes. He couldn't worry about it now; it was too late to change anything.

The next morning he was awake before Cheeper crowed. Noiselessly, he dressed and slipped down the ladder. He touched Jed's shoulder, but the lad was already awake. He sprang out of bed, a smile on his eager face.

Caleb looked at Lucy, still sleeping peacefully, one arm flung under her head. He knelt at the side of the bed and touched her forehead with his lips. Her eyes flew open, and he stared into the depths of her blue eyes. Every time he looked at the sky this summer, he would think of her. It would be hard to be away so long.

"I'm leaving now."

Pushing her heavy hair from her face, she sat up. "I'll fix you some breakfast."

"Don't bother. Jed and I will grab some biscuits. I'm not really hungry, and I don't think Jed could eat a mouthful. He's too excited." He leaned over and pressed his lips against hers, savoring their softness. Her arms went around his neck, and she clung to him.

"Pray for me. I'll be praying for you and Eileen."

A shadow darkened her eyes, and she nodded and averted her gaze.

He frowned. "Is something wrong?"

"No, no, of course not." She scrambled out of bed in a flurry of voluminous nightgown. "I'll walk you to the door."

At the door, he took her in his arms properly and buried his face in her sweet-smelling hair. "I reckon this will be the longest cattle drive in my life with a pretty wife waiting for me at home. I'll be back as quick as I can."

She nodded, and he gave her a lingering kiss before he stepped through the door. "Come on, Jed, we'll be late." With a final wave, he and Jed went to the barn and saddled their horses.

As soon as Jed and Caleb were gone, Lucy flew into a flurry of activity. She dragged on a pair of Jed's dungarees. They were too big for her, but she cinched them in with a belt. The blue flannel shirt she had found in the bottom of the chest. It had been Jed's last year and fit her fairly well now. She stuffed her hair up in a kerchief to hide her hair, then covered it all with an old hat of Caleb's she had found in the barn. It was stiff and smelly, but it hid her identity fairly well. She stuffed extra clothing for her and Eileen in a bag, and then she woke Eileen.

"Where are we going, Lucy?" the little girl complained.

"A great adventure! We're going with Jed and Caleb."

Eileen thrust out her bottom lip. "I'm sleepy. We'll go tomorrow. And I don't like the cattle. They smell."

"If we don't go now, we won't see Jed and Caleb for a long, long time. Would you rather stay with Grandpa Luther?" Lucy had been toying with the idea of leaving her anyway. It would be a hard trip for a little girl. But Eileen had never been away from Lucy more than overnight.

Eileen considered, then nodded. "I love Grandpa."

Maybe she would be all right. Lucy had to make an instant decision. "All right. I'll run you over there."

She took Eileen's hand in one hand and snatched the bag with the other. She would have to hurry. Luckily, she could join the end of the herd and avoid Caleb for a few days that way. Saddling up Wanda, she hefted Eileen to the saddle, strapped on her bedroll and bag, then clambered up behind her. She'd never get used to riding this way. No matter how much she did it, she felt awkward and strange.

Cantering across the track, she headed for the main house. Minutes later, she pulled Wanda to a halt and slid down. Practically running, she hurried into the house. Luther was reading in the parlor.

His face brightened when he saw her, then his gaze took in her strange apparel. A smile tugged at his lips. "You're going with Caleb, aren't you? I knew you had spunk, Girl. You got any more clothes than that?"

"Only a couple of dresses."

"I got a trunk of Caleb's old clothes in the attic. Some of them will fit you." He rose and took Eileen from her. "I reckon I'm babysitting for young Eileen here. You and me will have fun, Chickadee." He tossed her in the air, and Eileen squealed.

"I really don't have time to look for more clothes," Lucy began.

"You got hours yet, Girl. The end of the herd won't pull out of here until close to ten by the time they all get rounded up and moving." He carried Eileen to the back stairway and opened the door. "It's that trunk at the top of the stairs. There's clothes there going back to when Caleb was a baby."

Rather than argue anymore, Lucy raced up the stairs. She threw back the lid of the trunk and rummaged through it. She would have to come back when there was time; the trunk was full of mementoes of Caleb's childhood. Rifling through small dungarees that would fit Eileen and tiny boots that she could imagine on her own child someday, she found three pair of dungarees she thought would fit her and four shirts. Hurrying back down the stairs, she went out to her horse and pulled down the bag. Pulling out Eileen's belongings, she stuffed the things she'd found for herself into it and carried Eileen's clothing inside.

"I have to go," Lucy told Luther. She knelt beside Eileen and hugged her. "You be good for Grandpa."

"Grandpa says I'se always good," Eileen said. She wrapped her arms around Lucy's neck. "Bye, Lucy. Don't cry. I'll take care of Grandpa."

"And I'll take care of our little girl. Now run along before all this blubbering is useless and Caleb is gone without you." Luther took Eileen from her and gave Lucy a slight shove.

After one final look, Lucy ran for her horse. Her heart pounded against her ribs, and she prayed to escape discovery. She had to make this work.

14

he lowing of the longhorn cattle and the stench they left in their wake made Lucy begin to question her decision almost as soon as she arrived. The air was thick with red dust, and it was hard to breathe. Lucy coughed and pulled a red bandana up to cover her mouth.

"Hey, Cowboy, over here!" A weathered man Lucy didn't recognize waved to her, and she turned her mare's head to join him.

"You're late, Tenderfoot. You'll have to ride in the rear. You'll soon go runnin' home to mama." His face cracked in a grin, and the smile made him resemble someone, but Lucy couldn't decide who it was. "Round up them strays over there and watch to make sure they don't get away. My name's Bo, and you'll be answering to me this trip." Digging his knees into his horse's ribs, he wheeled and rode away.

Well, there was no time like the present to learn this cowboy business. Lucy set her chin and rode toward the stray cattle. They resisted her efforts to make them go the right way, and by the time she got them turned the right direction, she was wilting with dust and heat. The sun beat down in a merciless glare, and she longed for some shade and a drink of cold water. She'd remembered a canteen, but the water was warm and brackish.

Wiping her mouth, she pulled her bandana up again and got back to work. At times she felt as though she was barely clinging to the pommel as she grimly fought to do what was expected of a cowboy. Once she thought she saw Jed in the distance, but she pulled her hat down lower over her face and went the other direction. She couldn't risk even Jed's discovery.

When night fell, she was so stiff she almost fell from the saddle.

Now she knew why cowboys walked bowlegged, she told herself with a grim smile. Hunkering down around the fire, she got her plate of beans and bread and retreated to the shadows again.

She wolfed down her food, then unrolled her bedroll and crawled under the blanket. She should wash up, but she couldn't find the energy. Lucy fell asleep to the sound of the men laughing and singing camp songs.

Morning came way too early. "Breakfast, Tenderfoot."

A hard boot in the ribs roused Lucy from sleep. She groaned and tried to sit up, but every muscle in her body cried out in pain.

Bo prodded her with his boot again. "Get up, or you can just head on back where you came from. We don't need no lazy boys on this trip. You're awful puny, Tenderfoot. I'm surprised your mama let you out to come with us. You're no bigger than a grasshopper. What's your name, Boy?"

Her name. She tried to pitch her voice low. "Uh, Luke, Sir."

"Sir. I like that. You are learning, Boy. Now get your lazy hide out of bed and get your breakfast. We pull out in half an hour." He walked away without waiting for an answer.

If she could just escape detection for one more day, she should be safe. Caleb wouldn't waste that much time to send her back. She forced herself to her feet and went to find breakfast.

The second day was a repeat of the first, with Lucy growing more confident on the back of the mare. She watched the others and learned to cut a steer out of the herd and how to drive strays back to the main group. Feeling rather smug, she stopped to take a swig of water and noticed a man driving two steers behind a rock. Thinking they would exit the other side of the rock, she watched, but they didn't emerge.

Alarmed, she rode over to see if something was wrong. A man was tethering the cattle together behind the rock. In a flash Lucy understood what was happening. A rustler! Anger gripped her, and she started to pull her rifle from its sling on her saddle, but then her hand stilled. What rustler would be afraid of a boy by himself, rifle or not? She wheeled her horse around.

But her movement had caught the rustler's attention. "Hey! Stop or I'll shoot!"

A bullet whizzed over her head, and she bent low over Wanda's neck. Another bullet whined by close to her cheek, and then she was out of range. Shaking with reaction, she saw Bo on the other side of the herd and made her way to him.

"A rustler!" she gasped.

Bo jerked his head up. His eyes narrowed as he stared at her. "Where?"

"Behind that rock." She pointed. "He has two cattle tied up. He shot at me," she added.

His lips thin with rage, Bo rode off to where she pointed. Before he got there, a man on a horse tore out from behind the rock. He lashed his horse ferociously as he tried to get away. Bo shot over his head, and the man hunched down. Another cowboy rode to intercept the rustler, then another. Within minutes, he threw down his gun and surrendered.

Bo was berating him as he herded him back to camp. "I should have drowned you when you were born. How am I going to explain to Ma that you're a no-good cattle thief?"

The rustler turned his head and spat. "Shut up, Bo. I left home when I got tired of your lectures, and I'm in no mood for one now."

Drew Larson! That's who Bo reminded her of. They were brothers. Lucy hunched in her saddle. He might recognize her.

When his horse drew level to hers, he sneered at her. "A boy! Why couldn't you mind your own business, Kid? Stanton owes me; he would never miss a few head of cattle."

Lucy didn't speak; she was afraid her voice would give her away. Bo drove his brother on, pausing long enough to give her an approving nod. Lucy swelled with pride. She'd done well today. Wait until Caleb heard about it. Margaret herself couldn't have done better.

It was nearly dark when Bo rode back. Bo made his way to her side. "The boss wants to see you," he told her.

Lucy barely contained her gasp. "What for? It's bedtime."

"When the boss calls, there ain't no bedtime, Kid. You head on over there now." Bo's voice brooked no argument.

"I'll go in the morning."

Bo grabbed Lucy by the collar and raised her to her feet. "You'll go now. You got a lot to learn, Tenderfoot, and this is the main lesson. When the boss says jump, you ask how high." He released her, and she fell to the ground.

She rose, dusting herself off. "Yes, Sir." There was no help for it. She lifted her chin in the air. Caleb wouldn't send her back, not now. Her heart beat loudly in her ears as she saddled her horse and rode to the front of the herd. Maybe she had proved herself today; that's all she could hope for.

She found Caleb at the chuck wagon with Margaret beside him. Pulling her hat over her brow, Lucy dismounted and walked toward them. Staying in the shadows, she listened for a moment. They seemed to be reading the Bible.

"You mean, no matter how good I am, God won't let me into heaven?" Margaret's voice was indignant. "I've proven my worth to anyone who dared question it, Caleb Stanton!"

"God loves us for who we are, Margaret. We can't work our way to His love. That doesn't work here on this earth, either. You either love someone for who they are, or you can forget it. Love that is earned is no love at all. It won't last."

Caleb's word struck at Lucy's heart like an anvil. Was that what she'd been trying to do all her life? Even with God, she tried to be good, to be worthy of His love. Though she was certain of her faith, she realized she tried to prove herself worthy of His love and care. He loved her in her sin; why wouldn't He love her always?

And now with Caleb . . . she'd tried to work her way to his love as well. He either loved her or he didn't. And with Caleb's words, she realized she desperately wanted to be loved just for being who she was, not for being like Margaret or like anyone. Just for being herself.

Her blood surged. She would find out now where she stood. If Caleb chose to love her, wonderful. If not, she would go on being the best wife she could, but with the gifts God had given *her*, not the ones He had given Margaret.

"You wanted to see me, Sir?" She kept her face turned down.

"You're Luke?"

"Yes, Sir."

"I reckon I owe you some thanks, young man. You've got sharp eyes."

"That's more than I can say for you, Caleb," Margaret observed. "That's no lad—that's a girl." She rose and knocked the hat off Lucy's head.

Lucy had wrapped a bandana round her hair to keep it from falling out while she worked and while she slept. But with the hat out of the way, she knew Caleb would recognize her anyway. Lifting her head, she whipped the bandana off and let her hair flow free.

Caleb gasped, and Margaret echoed it.

"Lucy!" Caleb rose to his feet. "What are you doing here? And where's Eileen?"

"I left Eileen with your father," she said. "I wanted to come with you, to prove I could do it, to prove I was as worthy a wife as Margaret."

"I think it's time for me to get another cup of coffee," Margaret murmured. She rose and left Lucy staring into Caleb's eyes.

"This was very foolish," Caleb said with a frown. "You're in no shape for this trip. I'll have to send you back."

"We've come too far. If you do, the drive will be delayed."

"I'll take you back myself," Caleb said. He rose and went to speak with Percy.

Lucy's spirits flagged. He wasn't even going to give her a chance; he was just sending her back without listening. Her shoulders drooped. She should have let Drew steal those stupid longhorns. At least she could have avoided detection until they were farther away.

Caleb came back. "We'll leave in the morning. You'd better get some rest."

There was a strange gleam to his eyes Lucy didn't understand, but right now she was too angry to care. She wheeled and stormed off. He could take her back, but he would have to listen to her on the way.

Before she'd gone ten steps, Caleb grabbed her arm and hauled her against his chest. "Where do you think you're going?"

"To bed!" she spat. "You don't want to hear what I have to say; you just want to pack me off home like a child."

Caleb gave an exasperated sigh. "Lucy, this just isn't the time or place. When we have this discussion, I don't want a camp full of observers."

Lucy glanced around, and heat crept up her neck. At least ten men were watching them with great interest. "Fine," she snapped. "We'll talk tomorrow."

"You're staying here. I'll send Jed for your bedroll and horse."

Lucy clenched her fists. "I've been doing just fine doing my job. I'll continue with it until I go back."

"I reckon not. While I trust my own men, there are some here who signed on just for the drive. I'll not have you vulnerable."

"Fine. But keep away from me." She stalked over to a tree and flung herself down. If he thought he was holding her hand tonight, he could think again.

When Jed brought her bedroll, she kicked it open and clambered into it. But it was a long time before she slept.

By the time Caleb came for her the next morning, she was sitting on a tree stump sipping a cup of vile coffee. She'd coaxed some sugar from the cook, which was easier this morning than it had been yesterday, now that the cook knew she was the boss's wife. She longed for milk, though. Then the coffee might be drinkable.

When she saw Caleb, she poured out the rest of the bitter brew and rose.

"I'd pour it out, too, if it had sugar in it," he said with a teasing grin.

She shrugged. He needn't think he could smile at her and she would get over her pique with him. "I should have brought some tea."

His grin widened. "That would have given you away for sure."

Lucy's stiffness eased, and she chuckled. "That's what I thought."

He walked her to Wanda. "Those britches never looked that good on me," he whispered as he helped her mount.

Heat crept up her neck. What had gotten into him today? He seemed almost happy to be leaving the cattle drive.

They rode in silence to the south, back toward the ranch. At only twenty miles from home, they should reach the cabin by early afternoon. The cattle were only able to make ten miles a day, but the horses could do forty. Lucy wouldn't mind, she had to admit. That bedroll was hard.

Caleb finally broke the silence. He began showing her wildflowers along the way and told her their names. He pointed out the hawks flying overhead and the eagles atop the bluff they passed.

The landmarks began to be familiar to Lucy. They would be home soon. Would Caleb listen to her then?

Caleb cleared his throat. "Was Pa in on this all along?"

"No, he had no idea until I showed up that morning with Eileen. I had planned to take her with me, but she was sleepy and cranky, and I realized it wouldn't work."

"At least you showed *some* sense." He turned in the saddle and stared at her. "Why do you feel this need to prove yourself, Lucy? You have many talents; they just aren't with the cattle. I'm not saying you didn't do a good job as a cowboy. Bo said you were better than most of the tenderfoots he's worked with. But you hate it."

"But it's part of your life, and I want to share your life, Caleb. I don't want to be an appendage who has no relevance to your real life. Your real life is the cattle empire you're building. You said when we first met that you needed a wife who would work alongside you with the cattle."

Caleb sighed. "I was wrong, Lucy. I've told you I was wrong. I didn't know what I needed, but God did. I needed you."

Tears stung her eyes, but she sniffed and wiped her nose on her sleeve.

They crested the hill, and Lucy saw the cabin in the distance. It looked abandoned and forlorn after only three days. The horses plodded to a stop in front of the barn, and Lucy slid to the ground.

"I'll go fix some dinner."

"I'll put the horses up." Caleb grabbed both halters and headed into the barn.

Despondent and heartsick, Lucy walked inside. Back again. She was a failure. After dinner she would have to go get Eileen. Her spirits lifted at the thought. She had missed her baby sister.

She opened a can of beef and added some potatoes and carrots from the cellar. It was hot by the time Caleb came in.

"Smells good," he said, shutting the door.

They ate in silence, then Caleb pushed back his chair and stood.

He grabbed Lucy by the hand, and they walked to the sofa. That strange glint was back in his eyes as he sat on the sofa and pulled Lucy down onto his lap.

With his arms wrapped around her waist and his face buried in her hair, Lucy didn't know what to make of his strange behavior. Her heart was pounding so loud she found it hard to think, even hard to breathe.

Caleb pulled away and stared into her face. "What would it take for you to believe I love you, Lucy? Just like you are, warts and all."

"What warts?" Lucy smiled, but her smile faded at the gravity in his eyes. "What about Margaret?" she blurted out.

"What about Margaret? She's a childhood friend and a neighbor. Nothing more. You're my wife, Lucy. I love you."

Lucy gulped the tears in her throat. "You do? Truly? I overheard you talking to Margaret about love that is earned is no love at all. I realized that's what I've been doing my whole life. With everyone, not just with you. I've always felt I had to earn love. I think it started with my parents. Mama was always so strict and cold. I was the oldest, and I was supposed to do more, to give more. I always felt like a failure. But I want so badly to be loved for myself, for who I am."

Caleb's gray eyes grew solemn. "I love everything about you, Lucy. Everything that makes you who you are. Your fire and spirit, your determination to right any wrongs, your love for people, your compassion. I love you even if you hate tending cattle."

Lucy uttered a tiny cry and buried her face in his neck. He pressed his lips against her hair. "I'm so blessed God brought you to me," she whispered. "You're what gives meaning to everything I do."

His fingers lifted her chin, and he gazed into her eyes. "I love you, Lucy Stanton. I only hope our children are just like you."

His lips found hers, and she was lost in his kiss. It promised all the things she'd longed for all her life. A home, acceptance, and approval. She rubbed her hands across the rough stubble on his face, relishing his maleness and strength.

"I love you, Caleb. I've loved you for a long time, but I was so afraid you would never accept me. I'm never going to be like Margaret."

"I reckon I had plenty of opportunity to marry Margaret. I always knew something was missing. You're more important than anything, Lucy, more important than the ranch even. What would you say if I told you I wasn't going back to the cattle drive?"

Lucy's eyes widened. "You have to go back!"

Caleb shook his head. "No, I don't. I have a good foreman and good cowboys. Percy will watch out for Jed. There's no reason to go back and a very good reason to stay." He cupped her face in his hands. "You are that reason, Lucy. It's been hard trying to woo you with Jed and Eileen in the house. We have that time now. Let's take it and get to know one another better. I love you, Lucy Stanton. I wish I was a poet, and I'd be able to tell you how much I love you."

With an inarticulate cry, Lucy burrowed into his arms. "I love you so much, Caleb," she sobbed. "I wanted to be a blessing to you, just like the Bible says."

"You already are," he murmured. "My life was empty without you. I can't imagine living without you. If you couldn't adapt to ranch life, I'd leave it all behind and find a job in the city. You're all I want, Lucy. You and Jed and Eileen. And our own kids, of course." He smiled crookedly.

"I love the ranch," Lucy said. "As long as I don't have to share it with Pete."

Caleb grinned. "Pete's gone, but you're here, and I'm here, Lucy. Can we have a honeymoon here or would you like to travel somewhere? I have money tucked away, if that's what you want."

"Keep your money, Caleb Stanton. All I want is you. This cabin with you is where I want to be. I won't have to share you with anyone here."

Caleb's eyes grew bright, and his lips came down to claim hers. Lucy reveled in his love and in who she was in his sight. She was the cattle baron's bride and proud of it.

$\mathcal{M}$YLES FROM
$\mathcal{A}$NYWHERE

BY JILL STENGL

———◆———

With love to Tom, Annie, Jimmy, and Peter Stengl. I thank God for each of you every day. Every mother should be so blessed!

Thank you again to Paula Pruden Macha and Pamela Griffin—two living proofs that long-distance friendship is possible. Love you both!

PROLOGUE

1872

*C*hild Prodigy Missing. Statewide Search Underway for Myles Van Huysen, Musical Star, read the headlines of the August 21 edition of the city paper. A passerby stepped on the newspaper where it lay crumpled beside the tent door, and a breeze lifted the top page, sending it drifting across the midway.

A boy glared at the paper from beneath the brim of his cap, hoping his prospective employer had not read it closely. Why did Gram have to make such a big deal about everything?

"You say you're willing to work hard, Kid? How old are you, anyway?"

"Eighteen. Ain't got no family." He struggled to sound illiterate yet mature enough to merit the two extra years he claimed.

"Kinda puny, ain't ya?" The owner of the traveling circus chomped on his unlit cigar. "You're in luck, Red. One of our fellas went down sick a week back, and we've been struggling since. It ain't easy work, and the pay is peanuts, but you'll get room and board, such as it is. Go see Parker in the animal tent and tell him I sent you."

"Yes, Mr. Bonacelli. Thank you, Mr. Bonacelli."

"You may not be thankin' me when you find out what you'll be doin'. What's yer name, Red?"

"Myles Trent." It was his name minus its third element. If he so much as mentioned "Van Huysen" the game would end for certain.

"Hmph. I'll call ya Red."

Visions of becoming an acrobat or animal trainer soon vanished from Myles's head. During the next few months, he worked harder than he had ever worked in his life, cleaning animal pens. It was nasty and hazardous work at times, yet he enjoyed becoming friends with other circus employees. Whenever the circus picked up to move to the next town, everyone worked together, from the clowns to the trapeze artists to the bearded lady. It wasn't long before Myles began to move up in the circus world.

Bonacelli's Circus made its way south from New York, then west toward Ohio, playing in towns along the highways and railroads. During the coldest months, the caravans headed south along the Mississippi; spring found them headed north. Months passed into a year.

Lengthening his face to minimize creases, Myles wiped grease paint from his eyelids. Behind him, the tent flap was pulled aside. Someone came in. "Antonio?" he guessed.

"Hello, Myles."

His eyes popped open. A handsome face smiled at him from his mirror.

Myles froze. His shoulders drooped. He turned on the stool. "Monte."

The brothers stared at each other. Monte pulled up a chair and straddled it backward. "I caught today's show. Never thought I'd see my musician brother doing flips onto a horse's back. You've built muscle and calluses. Look healthier than I can remember." There was grudging admiration in his voice.

"The acrobats and clowns taught me tricks."

"I've been hanging around, asking questions. People like and respect you. Say you're honest and hardworking."

Myles's eyes narrowed. "I love the circus, Monte. I like making people happy."

"You're a performer. It's in your blood."

Myles turned to his mirror and rubbed blindly at the paint. "Why so pleasant all of a sudden?"

Monte ignored the question. "Gram wants you back. She's already spent too much on detectives. I'll write and tell her I found you before she fritters away our fortune."

"I'm not going back."

"I didn't ask you to. The old lady sent me to keep an eye on you. She never said I had to go back . . . at least not right away." One of Monte's brows lifted, and he gave Myles his most charming smile.

"The Van Huysen Soap Company and fortune will wait for me. No reason to waste my youth in a stuffy office, learning business from a fat family friend. I think I'd rather be a circus star like my runny-nosed kid brother."

"You've seen me. Now get lost." Hope faded from Myles's eyes. "You'll spoil everything."

"Believe it or not, I do understand. That was no life for a kid. I've often wondered how you endured it as long as you did. Getting out of that Long Island goldfish bowl is a relief. Always someone watching, moralizing, planning your life—whew! You had the right idea. I could hardly believe my luck when Gram sent me after you."

"She trusted you," Myles observed dryly. "What are you planning to do?"

"Does this circus need more workers? I'm serious. This looks like the life for me."

Myles huffed. "Nobody needs a worker like you, Monte. Why don't you go find yourself a gaming hall and forget you ever had a brother?"

"Gram would never forgive me if I returned without you."

"You could tell her I'm dead."

Monte pondered the idea in mock gravity, dark eyes twinkling. "Tempting, but impossible. Family honor and all that. You'd show up someday, then I'd look the dolt at best, the knave at worst. Part of the family fortune is yours, you know. I wouldn't try to filch it from you. I'm not as rotten as you think, little brother. I do feel some responsibility for my nitwit prodigy sibling."

The next morning when Monte left his borrowed bunk, Myles was gone. No one had seen him leave. Running a big hand down his face, Monte swore. "Gotta find that crazy kid!"

❧

"Are you here with good news or bad, George Poole?" the old lady grumbled from her seat in a faded armchair. A few coals glowed upon the hearth near her feet. "I trust you have disturbed my afternoon rest for good reason."

"Yes, Mrs. Van Huysen. You may see for yourself." He thrust a newspaper into her hands and pointed at a paragraph near the bottom of the page. "An associate of mine in Milwaukee—that's a town in Wisconsin—heard of my quest, spotted this article, and mailed the paper to me."

"Kind of him," Mrs. Van Huysen said, fumbling to put on her glasses. Holding the folded-back paper near her face, she blinked. "For what am I looking?"

"This, Madam. The article concerns a small-town farmer who, years ago, served a prison sentence for robbery and murder. Last summer, new evidence was discovered and the man's name was cleared of the crimes. Judging by the article's tone, this Obadiah Watson appears to be a fine Christian man. It is a pleasure when justice is served, is it not?"

"Yes, yes, but what has this to do with my grandsons?" Virginia Van Huysen struggled to keep her patience.

"Let me find the line . . . ah, right here. You see? The article mentions a certain Myles Trent, hired laborer on Watson's farm." Poole's eyes scanned his client's face.

"I fail to see the significance, Mr. Poole. You raised my hopes for this?"

"Don't you see, Madam? Your grandson's name is Myles Trent Van Huysen. Oftentimes a man in hiding will use a pseudonym, and what could be easier to recall than one's own given name?"

"Have you any proof that this man is my Myles? And what of Monte? There is no word of him in this article. The last I heard from the boys, they were together in Texas. Isn't Wisconsin way up north somewhere? Why ever would Myles be there?" Pulling a lacy handkerchief from her cuff, Virginia dabbed at her eyes. "In Monte's last letter he told me that he had surrendered his life to the Lord. Why, then, did he stop writing to me? I don't understand it."

Poole tugged his muttonchop whiskers. "I cannot say, dear madam. The particular region of Texas described in your grandson's most recent letters is a veritable wasteland. Our efforts there were vain; my people discovered no information about your grandsons. It was as if they had dropped from the face of the earth."

"Except for the note your partner sent me about the game hunter in Wyoming." Virginia's tone was inquisitive.

"An unfortunate mistake on Mr. Wynter's part. He should have waited until he had obtained more solid information before consulting you. Be that as it may, Madam, unless this Myles Trent proves to be your relation, I fear I must persuade you to give up this quest. I dislike taking your money for naught."

"Naught?" Virginia lifted her pince-nez to give him a quelling look.

Poole nodded. "We at Poole, Poole, and Wynter are ever reluctant to admit defeat, yet I fear we may be brought to that unfortunate pass. It has been nine years since Myles disappeared and nearly six since Monte's last letter reached you. If your grandsons are yet living, they are twenty-five and twenty-eight now."

"I can do simple addition, Mr. Poole," Virginia said. "Have you given up entirely on that hunter?"

"The fellow disappeared. He was probably an outlaw who became nervous when Wynter started asking questions. You must keep in mind that your grandsons are no longer children to be brought home and disciplined. They are men and entitled to live the lives they choose. I fear Myles's concert career will never resume."

Virginia clenched her jaw and lifted a defiant chin. "I would spend my last cent to find my boys. Look into this, Mr. Poole, and may the Lord be with you."

1

Shall not God search this out?
For he knoweth the secrets of the heart.
Psalm 44:21

Summer 1881

"Move over, Marigold."

The Jersey cow munched on her breakfast, eyes half closed. When Myles pushed on her side, she shifted in the stall, giving him room for his milking stool and bucket. Settling on the stool, he rested his forehead on Marigold's flank, grasped her teats, and gently kneaded her udder while squeezing. His hands were already warm since she was the sixth cow he had milked that morning. Marigold let down her milk, and the warm liquid streamed into the bucket. Myles had learned that it paid to be patient with the cows; they rewarded his kindness with their cooperation.

"Meow!" A furry body twined around his ankle, rumbling a purr that reminded Myles of a passing freight train. Other cats peered at Myles from all sides—from the hayloft, around the stall walls, from the top of Marigold's stanchion. Their eyes seldom blinked.

The plump gray and white cat had perfected her technique. She bumped her face against Myles's knee, reached a velvet paw to touch his elbow, and blinked sweetly.

"Nice try, you pushy cat, but you've got to wait your turn. I'll give a saucer to all of you when I'm finished."

"Why do you reward them for begging? It only makes them worse." A deep voice spoke from the next stall where Al Moore was milking another cow.

"Guess I like cats."

"I . . . um, Myles, I've got to tell you that I'll be heading over to

Cousin Buck's farm after dinner. I've got to talk with Beulah today . . . you know, about my letter."

"I'll be there too. I'm working in Buck's barn this afternoon—mending harnesses and such."

"Things have changed since Cousin Buck married Violet Fairfield last year and took over her farm, Fairfield's Folly," Al commented sadly. "I mean, in the old days he kept up with every detail about our farm, but he's too busy being a husband and papa these days."

"He doesn't miss much. Must be hard work, running the two farms." Myles defended his friend.

"I run this place myself," Al protested. After a moment's silence he added, "You're right; I shouldn't complain. I just miss the old days; that's all. Anyway, to give Cousin Buck credit, being Beulah's stepfather must be a job in itself, and now with Buck and Violet's new baby . . ." His voice trailed away. "Buck has made major improvements at the Folly farm this past year. Guess that's no surprise to you."

"I do have firsthand knowledge of those improvements," Myles acknowledged. "Working at both farms keeps me hopping, but I don't mind. I'm glad Buck is happily married. I've never worked for better people than you and your cousin."

"Since I'm taking the afternoon off, I'll handle the milking this evening. How's that?" Al asked. "Don't want you to think I'm shirking."

Myles smiled to himself. "Don't feel obligated, Boss. You always do your share of the work. Be good for you to take a few hours to play."

"But you never do. Wish you'd relax some; then I wouldn't feel guilty."

"Maybe you and I could toss a baseball around with Samuel this afternoon." The prospect lifted Myles's spirits. He liked nothing better than to spend time with Obadiah "Buck" Watson's three stepchildren. The retired cowboy preferred to be called "Obie," but Myles had known him for years as "Buck" and found it impossible to address or even think of his boss by any other name.

"That would be great!" Al sounded like an overgrown schoolboy.

Myles stripped the last drops from Marigold's teats. Rising, he patted the cow's bony rump. "You're a good girl, Goldie." He nearly tripped over the pushy gray cat as he left the stall. With a trill of expectation, it trotted ahead of him toward the milk cans, where several other felines had already congregated.

Myles found the chipped saucer beneath a bench. Sliding it to the open floor with one foot, he tipped the bucket and poured a stream of milk—on top of a gray and white head. Myles smiled as the cat retreated under the bench, shaking her head and licking as much of her white ruff as she could reach. Another cat began to assist her, removing the milk from the back of her head. "Pushy cat, Pushy cat, where have you been?" Myles crooned.

He filled the saucer until it overflowed; yet it was polished clean within seconds. A few cats had to content themselves with licking drops from the floor or from their companions. Myles tried to count the swarming animals but lost track at twelve.

"Too many cats," Al remarked, emptying his bucket into a can.

"They keep down the rodent population," Myles said.

"I know, but the barn's getting overcrowded. There were a lot of kittens born in the spring, but most of them are gone. I don't know if they just died or if something killed them."

Myles squatted and Pushy cat hopped into his lap, kneading his thigh with her paws and blinking her yellow eyes. She seemed to enjoy rubbing her face against his beard. He stroked her smooth back and enjoyed that rumbling purr. Myles knew Al was right, but neither man had an answer for the problem.

"Say, Myles, what if . . . I mean, are you . . . do you have any plans to move on? Might you be willing to stay on here over the winter and . . . I'm not sure how to say this." Al ran long fingers through his hair, staring at the barn floor.

Myles rubbed the cat and waited for Al to find the words. He had a fair idea what was coming.

"I'm hoping to marry Beulah and take her to California with me— to meet my parents, you know. We would probably be gone for close to a year, and I can't leave Cousin Buck to run both this place and Fairfield's Folly alone. I would take it kindly if you would . . . well, run my farm as if it were yours, just while I'm away, you understand.

I would make it worth your while. You don't need to answer me now; take your time to think it over."

Myles nodded. In spite of his determination to keep his own counsel, one question escaped. "Have you asked her yet?"

"Asked Beulah? Not yet." Al's boots shifted on the floorboards. "That's the other thing that worries me. She's . . . uh . . . I don't know that she'll take to the idea of a quick wedding. We've never discussed marriage . . . but she must know I plan to marry her. Everyone knows."

Myles glanced at his young boss's face. "Will you go if she refuses?"

Al looked uncertain. "I could marry her when I get back, but I hate to leave things hanging. Another man could come along and steal her away from me. Maybe I could ask her to wait." He collapsed on the bench, propped his elbows on his spread knees, and rested his chin on one fist. "She's really not a flirt, but I can't seem to pin her down. Every time I try to be serious, she changes the subject. What should I do, Myles?"

Myles rose to his feet and began to rub his flat stomach with one hand. "You're asking an old bachelor for courtship advice?" He hoped the irony in his voice escaped Al's notice. "I've got no experience with women."

"No experience at all?" Al's face colored. "I mean . . . uh . . . Sorry."

Myles shrugged. "No offense taken. I left home at sixteen and bummed around the country for years."

"What did you do to keep alive?"

"Any work I could find. No time or opportunity to meet a decent woman and had enough sense to avoid the other kind. When I drifted farther west it was the same. You don't see a lot of women wandering the wilderness."

"So where are you from?"

"Anywhere and everywhere." His lips twitched into a smile that didn't reach his eyes. "When your cousin hired me and brought me here to Longtree, that was the first time I'd been around women since I was a kid. Guess I don't know how to behave around females."

"I didn't know you were afraid of women. Is that why you almost never go to church or socials?"

Myles lifted a brow. "I didn't say I was afraid of them. More like they're afraid of me."

"If you'd smile and use sentences of more than one syllable, they might discover you're a decent fellow."

This prompted a genuine smile. "I'll try it. Any other advice?"

Al cocked his head and grinned. "That depends on which female has caught your eye. Want to confide in old Al?"

"I'd better cast about first and see if any female will have me," Myles evaded.

Al chuckled. "Too late. I know about you and Marva Obermeier."

"About me and . . . whom?"

"Don't look so surprised. Since the barn raising at Obermeiers' when you and she talked for an hour, everyone in town knows. She's a nice lady. If you want a little extra to hold and like a woman who'll do all the talking, Marva is for you."

"But that was—" Myles began to protest.

"Things aren't progressing the way you want, eh? You ought to spend evenings getting to know her family, getting comfortable in the home. Try teasing her and see what happens. Nice teasing, I mean. Women enjoy that kind of attention from a man."

"They do?"

A collie burst through the open barn door. Panicked cats scattered. Both men chuckled. "Good work, Treat."

Treat grinned and wagged half her body along with her tail, eager to herd the cows to pasture. "Cats are beneath your notice, eh, Girl?" Al said, ruffling her ears.

Al carried the milk cans to the dairy. Myles untied the cows and directed Treat to gather them and start them ambling along the path.

Udders swaying, bells clanging, gray noses glistening, the cows did their best to ignore the furry pest at their heels. While Myles held the pasture gate open, Treat encouraged the little herd to pass through. Myles gave one bony bovine a swat before latching the gate behind her. "As usual, last in line. No wandering off today, my ornery old girl."

The sun was still low in the sky and already the temperature was rising. Myles swung his arms in circles to relieve the kinks. He glanced around. No one watching. He performed a few cartwheels, a round off, then a front flip to back flip in one quick motion. He straightened in triumph, flushed and pleased, arms lifted to greet the morning. The cows and Treat were unimpressed.

"Good thing you're used to my antics. Hey, Treat, maybe I'll see Beulah today." Myles slapped his thighs until the dog placed her front paws on them. He ruffled her fur with both hands. "What do you think, Girl? Think Beulah will smile at me?"

Then his grin faded and his heavy boots scuffed in the dirt. Little chance of that while Al was around. Of all the stupid things Myles had ever done, falling in love with his boss's girl was undoubtedly the worst.

～❧

Deep in thought, Beulah Fairfield dumped used dishwater behind her mother's gladiolus. Something jabbed into her ribs, and the last of the water flew skyward. "Oh!" She spun around, slapping away reaching hands. "Al, stop it!"

Al took the two back steps in a single bound and held the kitchen door for her. "Testy woman. Better make myself useful and return to her good graces."

She was tempted to suggest that he choose another time to visit, but her mother had chided her several times recently for rudeness. "Thanks." Beulah forced a smile as she entered the kitchen before him. His return smile seemed equally fake. "Is something wrong, Al?"

He let the door slam behind him. "Nothing much."

Beulah hung the dishpan on its hook and arranged the dishtowels on the back of the stove to dry. "Would you like a cup of coffee?"

"Uh, sure. Yes, please."

"Please take a seat at the table, and I will join you presently."

In another minute, she set down his coffee and seated herself across the table from him. His forehead was pale where his hat usually hid it from the sun; his dark hair looked freshly combed. Beulah knew her apron was spotted, but she was too self-conscious to change to a fresh one in front of Al. Her hair must be a sight—straggling about her face. "I've been canning tomatoes all morning." She indicated the glowing red jars lining the sideboard.

Before Al could comment, Beulah's sister Eunice burst into the room. The hall door hit the wall and china rattled on the oak dresser. "It *was* your voice I heard in here! Why did you sneak around to the back door, Al? I was watching for you out front."

A black and white dog slipped in behind Eunice and thrust her nose into Al's hand, brushy tail beating against the table legs. "Watchful, shame on you! Get out of the kitchen." Beulah attempted to shoo the dog away.

"She's all right." Petting the dog, Al gave Eunice a half-hearted smile. "I didn't sneak. My horse is in the barn, big as life. I rode over with Myles. He's mending the whiffletree the horse kicked apart while we were pulling stumps."

"Myles is in our barn?" Beulah asked.

"Still want to go for a ride today, do you?" Al asked Eunice as if Beulah had not spoken.

The girl flopped down in the chair beside him. "Of course we want to ride with you. My brother has to finish cleaning the chicken pen, but he's almost done. I finished my chores. Won't you teach me to jump today? Please?" She laid her head on Al's shoulder and gave him her best pleading gaze, batting long lashes.

He chuckled and roughed up her brown curls. "Subtle, aren't you, Youngster? We'll see. I'd better talk to your parents before we try jumping. To be honest, Blue Eyes, I want to talk with your sister in private for a minute, so could—"

The door popped open again, this time admitting Violet Fairfield Watson, the girls' mother, with a wide-eyed baby propped upon her shoulder. "Would one of you please take Daniel while I change his bedclothes?" She transferred the baby to Beulah's reaching arms. "Thank you, Dear. Hello, Albert. Will you stay for supper tonight?"

"I . . . um, thank you, but no, not tonight, Ma'am. I . . . I've got to do the milking. I promised the kids we'd go for a ride this afternoon, but then I've got to get home and . . . and get some work done."

Violet gave him a searching look. "Hmm. Is something wrong, Al?"

Blood colored his face right up to his hairline. "Actually, yes. I got a letter from my mother yesterday. She wants me to come home to California. I'm the oldest son, you know. It's been five years since I was last home, and my folks want to see me again."

"I see." Violet Watson sent Beulah a quick glance before asking Al: "Do you plan to leave soon?"

"I'm not sure, Ma'am. That depends . . . on a lot of things. I'll have to work out a plan with Cousin Buck—Obie—for care of the farm. I can't expect Myles to handle everything alone for so long. I mean, he's just a hired hand."

"How long is 'so long'?" Eunice asked, her expression frozen.

"I don't know. Could be up to a year. The train fare between here and California is no laughing matter. I have to make the visit worth the price."

"Yes, you do need to speak with Obie about this, Al." Violet looked concerned. "That is a long time to leave your farm."

Al held out his hands, fingers spread. "I know, but what else can I do? They're my parents."

"But, Al, a whole year? What will we do without you?" Eunice wailed.

Wrapping one long arm around the girl, Al pressed her head to his shoulder. "Miss me, I hope. I'll be back, Blue Eyes. Never fear."

Rocking her baby brother in her arms, Beulah watched Al embrace her sister. *No more pokes in the ribs, no more mawkish stares. I wonder how soon he will leave?*

Baby Daniel began to fuss. Beulah took the excuse to leave the kitchen and wandered through the house, bouncing him on her hip. He waved his arms and kicked her in the thighs, chortling. She heard the others still talking, their voices muffled by intervening doors.

My friends all think I'm the luckiest girl in the world because Al likes me. He is handsome, nice, loves God, has his own farm—he'll make a great husband for someone. But that someone isn't me!

She strolled back into the hall, studying the closed kitchen door. No one would notice if she slipped outside. Snatching a basket from a hook on the hall tree, she headed for the barn. Her heart thumped far more rapidly than this mild exertion required. Shifting Daniel higher on her hip, she reached for her hair and winced. No bonnet, and hair like an osprey's nest. Oh, well; too late now. If she didn't hurry, Myles might finish his work and leave before she had a chance to see him.

A tingle skittered down her spine. Without turning her head, she knew that Myles stood in the barn doorway. The man's gaze was like a fist squeezing her lungs until she gasped for air. Daniel squawked and thumped his hand against Beulah's chest. He managed to grasp one of her buttons and tried to pull it to his mouth, diving toward it. Beulah had just enough presence of mind to catch him before he plunged out of her arms.

One ankle turned as she approached the barn, and she staggered. Daniel transferred his attention to the basket hanging from her arm beneath him. He reached for it and once more nearly escaped Beulah's grasp. "Daniel, stop that," she snapped in exasperation, feeling bedraggled and clumsy.

"Need a hand?"

Swallowing hard, Beulah lifted her gaze. A little smile curled Myles's lips. One hand rubbed the bib of his overalls. The shadow of his hat hid his eyes, yet she felt them burning into her.

"I came for eggs," she said, brushing hair from her face, then hoisting Daniel higher on her hip. "For custard."

"Your brother Sam headed for the house with a basket of eggs not two minutes back."

"He did?" Beulah felt heat rush into her face. "I didn't see him."

Daniel grabbed at a button again, then mouthed Beulah's cheek and chin. She felt his wet lips and heard the fond little "Ahh" he always made when he gave her kisses. Unable to ignore the baby's overtures, she kissed his soft cheek. "I love you, too, Daniel. Now hold still."

When she looked up, white teeth gleamed through Myles's sunbleached beard. "Thought Al was with you."

"He's in the kitchen with my mother and Eunice. Daniel and I came out for the eggs. Are you—will you be here long?"

"Might play baseball with Samuel and Al. Glad you came out for a visit."

Myles appeared to choose his words with care, and his voice . . .
that rich voice curled her toes. Did he know she had come outside in
hope of seeing him? Why must her mind palpitate along with her
body whenever Myles was near? She was incapable either of analyzing
his comments or of giving a lucid reply.

"You haven't been to our house for awhile, and I haven't seen you
at church all summer."

His smile faded. He took a step closer, then stopped. Did Myles
feel the pull, almost like a noose tightening around the two of them
and drawing them ever closer together? She had never been this close
to him before. Only five or six feet of dusty earth separated them.

Tired of being ignored, Daniel let out a screech and smacked Beulah's mouth with a slimy hand. Pain and anger flashed; she struggled
to hide both. "Daniel, don't hit."

The baby's face crumpled, and he began to wail. Sucking in her
lip, Beulah tasted blood. "I think it's time for his nap." She spoke
above Daniel's howls. "I'll try to come back later."

Myles nodded, waved one hand, and vanished into the barn's
shadows. Beulah trotted toward the house, patting Daniel's back.
"Hush, Sweetie. Beulah isn't angry with you. I know you're tired and
hungry. We'll find Mama, and everything will be fine."

Al held the door open for her. "What are you doing out here?
What's wrong with the little guy?"

"Where's my mother?"

"Upstairs. You going riding with us?" he called.

"No, you go on. I've got work to do." She barely paused on the
bottom step.

"Play ball with us later?"

"Maybe." Beulah hid her grin in Daniel's soft hair.

Once Daniel was content in his mother's arms, Beulah returned to
the kitchen to work and ponder. Sure enough, a basket of brown eggs
waited on the floor beside the butter churn. Samuel must have entered the kitchen right after she left it.

Beulah found her mother's custard recipe on a stained card and
began to collect the ingredients. *I'm just imagining that Myles admires
me. Probably he watches everyone that way. I scarcely know the man. No*

one knows much about him. *He could be from anywhere—a bank robber or desperado for all we know. It is ridiculous to moon about him when I can have a man like Al with a snap of my fingers. Myles is beneath me socially—probably never went to school. Could never support a family—we would live in a shack . . .*

Al's words repeated in her mind: *Just a hired hand. Just a hired hand. Just a hired hand . . .*

And when ye stand praying, forgive,
if ye have ought against any:
that your Father also which is in heaven
may forgive you your trespasses.
Mark 11:25

*C*ustard cooled on the windowsill. Untying her apron, Beulah peeked through the kitchen window. Outside, a baseball smacked into a leather glove. She heard her brother Samuel's shrill voice and good-natured joking between Al and Myles. *He's still here!* She hung her apron on a hook, smoothed her skirts, and straightened her shoulders. Once again, her heart began to pound.

Eunice slammed open the kitchen door. Damp curls plastered her forehead; scarlet cheeks intensified the blue of her eyes. "We had a great ride, Beulah! You should have come."

Beulah wrinkled her nose.

Eunice splashed her face at the pump. "It hurts Al's feelings that you never want to ride with us."

"I'm sure I don't know why."

Lifting her face from the towel, Eunice protested, "But you're supposed to want to spend time with him. People in love want to be together all the time, don't they?"

"How would I know?" Beulah said. "And I can't see how being in love would make me want to ride a horse. Hmph. You need a bath. I can smell horse from here."

"You're mean, Beulah." Eunice rushed from the room.

Beulah rolled her eyes. Pinching her cheeks, she checked her reflection in the tiny mirror over the washbasin. "Guess I didn't need to pinch my cheeks. They're already hot as fire."

Beyond Beulah's kitchen garden, the two men and Samuel formed a triangle around the yard. The ball smacked into Al's glove. He tossed it to Samuel, easing his throw for the boy's sake. Samuel hurled it at Myles, who fielded it at his ankles, then fired another bullet toward Al. Around and around they went, never tiring of the game.

"Hi, Beulah!" Al greeted her with a wave. "Want to play? We've got an extra mitt."

"No, thank you." *He must be crazy.* "Don't want to spoil your fun."

"We would throw easy to you," Samuel assured her.

"I'll watch." Beulah moved to the swing her stepfather Obie had hung from a tall elm. After tucking up her skirt lest it drag in the dust, she began to swing. The men seemed unaware of her scrutiny. They bantered with Samuel and harassed each other. Her gaze shifted from Myles to Al and back again.

Al's long, lean frame had not yet filled out with muscle. A thatch of black hair, smooth brown skin, beautiful dark eyes, and a flashing smile made him an object of female fascination. How many times had Beulah been told of her incredible good luck in snaring his affection? She had lost count.

Leaning back in the swing, she pumped harder, hearing her skirts flap in the wind. Overhead, blue sky framed oak, maple, and elm leaves. A woodpecker tapped out his message on a dead birch.

Sitting straight, she wrapped her arms around the ropes and fixed her gaze upon Myles. He was grinning. Beulah felt her heart skip a beat. Myles had the cutest, funniest laugh—a rare treat to hear. What would he look like without that bushy beard? He had a trim build—not as short and slim as her stepfather Obie, but nowhere near as tall as Al.

The ongoing conversation penetrated her thoughts. "So are you planning to go, Al? Will you take me with you? I've always wanted to see a circus. I bet my folks would let me go with you," Samuel cajoled.

Al glanced toward Beulah. "I was thinking I might go. It's playing in Bolger all weekend. The parade arrives tomorrow."

Samuel let out a whoop. "Let's all go together! Eunice wants to go, and you do, don't you, Beulah? Will you come, too, Myles? Maybe they'll ask you to be a clown. Myles can do lots of tricks, you know. Show 'em how you walk on your hands. Please?"

Beulah's eyes widened.

Myles wiped a hand down his face, appearing to consider the request. "Why?"

"I want you to teach me. C'mon, Myles! Beulah's never seen you do it."

She saw his gaze flick toward her, then toward Al. He fired the baseball at Al, who snagged it with a flick of his wrist. "You can walk on your hands? Where'd you learn that trick?"

"I worked for a circus once. The acrobats taught me a thing or two."

Beulah fought to keep her jaw from dropping.

"No kidding? I'd like to see some tricks. Wouldn't you, Beulah?" Al enlisted her support.

Beulah nodded, trying not to appear overly interested.

Myles studied the green sweep of grass. "All right." He removed his hat. "Can't do splits or I'll rip my overalls," he said with a sheepish grin.

"If I tried splits, I'd rip more than that," Al admitted.

Myles upended and walked across the yard on his hands, booted feet dangling above his head. He paused to balance on first one hand, then the other. With a quick jerk, he landed back on his feet, then whirled into a series of front handsprings, ending with a deep bow. His audience cheered and clapped.

"Amazing!" Al said. "I never knew you could do that."

"Your face is red like a tomato," Samuel said.

Beulah met Myles's gaze. Did she imagine it, or did his eyes reveal a desire to please? Heart pounding again, she managed an admiring smile. "Who needs to see a circus when we have Myles?"

He seemed to grow taller; his shoulders squared. "You would enjoy a real circus."

"So let's go!" Samuel persisted. "Beulah, you've gotta help me ask Mama. With Myles and Al taking us, I'm sure she'll say we can go."

"Do you want to take us?" Beulah asked, carefully looking at neither man.

"It might be fun," Al wavered.

"I do." Myles's direct answer took everyone by surprise. "I'm going for the parade and the show."

❧

Beulah and Eunice hurried into the kitchen. Beulah tied her bonnet beneath her chin, setting the bow at the perfect angle. "Does this bonnet match this dress, Mama?"

Violet cast her a quick glance. "It's sweet, Dear."

"Now you stay close; no wandering off by yourself," she warned Samuel while combing back his persistent cowlick. "Being ten does not mean you're grown up." The boy squirmed and contorted his face.

Obie watched them from his seat at the kitchen table, his chest supporting a sleeping baby Daniel. Amusement twitched his thick mustache.

"I'll behave, Mama," Samuel said. "Do you think there will be elephants in the parade, Pa? Maybe bears and lions! Myles used to be in the circus. He says it was lots of work. I think I'd rather be a preacher when I grow up."

His stepfather lifted a brow. "Preachers don't have to work, you figure?"

"Reverend Schoengard doesn't work much. He just drives around visiting people and writes sermons."

Obie chuckled. "Our pastor more than earns his keep. You don't get muscles like his by sitting around all the time."

Eunice was still braiding one long pigtail. "I'm so glad it stopped raining! Now it's all sunny and pretty—the perfect day for a circus. Are they here yet?" She hurried to the window and peered toward the barn.

Obie tipped back his chair and balanced on his toes. "They're hitching the horses to the surrey. Should be ready soon."

"Can I go help, Pa?" Samuel begged.

"Ask your mother."

"You may. Try not to get too dirty." Violet released her restless son. "I'm trusting you to keep your brother in line, girls. Don't get so involved with your friends that you forget to watch Samuel."

"We won't, Mama," Beulah assured her mother. A crease appeared between her brows. "Our friends? I thought just the five of us were going."

Obie grinned. "I imagine half our town will head over to Bolger this afternoon. Circuses don't come around every day."

"Here come Al and Myles!" Eunice announced, bouncing on her toes.

Beulah bent to kiss Daniel's soft cheek. "Bye, Papa and Mama. Take care and enjoy your free day."

Al was less than pleased when Samuel squeezed between him and Beulah on the surrey's front seat. "Can't you sit in the back? It's crowded up here, and I need elbow room."

The boy's face fell. "Can't I drive a little? Papa lets me drive sometimes. The horses know me."

"I'll climb in back," Beulah offered quickly, rising. When she hopped down, one foot tangled in her skirt and she sat down hard in the dirt, legs splayed. Her skirt ballooned, displaying a fluffy white petticoat and pantaloon. Horrified, she clapped her arms down over the billowing fabric and glanced toward Myles. He was loading the picnic basket behind the surrey's rear seat. Had he seen?

"But, Beulah," Al protested. "I wanted to—Are you all right?"

Beulah scrambled to her feet and brushed off her dress, cheeks afire. "I'm fine."

"I'll drive, if you like," Myles said. "I don't mind sitting with Samuel."

Al looked abashed. "I don't either. It doesn't matter, really." He settled beside the boy and released the brake. "Climb in."

In the surrey's back seat, Eunice had one hand clamped over her mouth. Her shoulders were shaking. She looked up, met Beulah's eyes, and started giggling again. Beulah felt a smile tug at her mouth. Frowning to conceal it, she climbed up beside her sister and smoothed her skirts. "Stop it!" she hissed.

"You looked so funny!" Eunice nearly choked.

Myles hauled himself up to sit on the other side of Eunice. He must have visited the barber that morning. His beard and hair were neatly trimmed. He watched Eunice mop her eyes with a crumpled handkerchief, but made no comment.

Beulah leaned forward. "Are you excited to see a circus again, Myles?"

He looked at her with raised brows. "Guess I am. It's been a long time."

Conversation flagged. While Samuel chattered with Al, the three in the back seat studied passing scenery with unaccustomed interest. Beulah longed to talk with Myles, but about what? Her mind was blank.

After awhile, Myles cleared his throat. "Lots of traffic today."

"Must be for the circus," Al said. "I think I see the Schoengards up ahead."

Samuel's ears pricked. "Scott is here?"

"You're sitting with us, Sam." Beulah leaned forward to remind him.

"I know. I know," he grouched, pushing her hand from his shoulder.

The streets of Bolger were already crowded. People lined the road into town, standing in and around buggies and wagons. Al parked the surrey beside a farm wagon, easing the team into place. "We can see better from up here," he explained, "and we've got shade." He indicated the surrey's canvas top. "Did you bring water, Beulah?"

Samuel stood and waved his arms, shouting. "Here it comes! I see it!"

A roar went up from the crowds, and Beulah clutched her seat. The horses objected to the commotion. Al had his hands full quieting the rearing animals.

"May want to drop back," Myles advised. "Especially if this circus has elephants."

"You all climb out," Al growled. "Don't want Sam to miss the parade."

Beulah climbed down, but Eunice chose to remain in the surrey. "Al needs company," she said. "You three can find us after the parade."

Grabbing Samuel's hand, Beulah tried to find a place with a clear view. "This way," Myles said, waving to her. He found a front row spot for Samuel, and Beulah clutched her brother's shoulders from behind.

Two elephants wearing spangled harnesses led the parade. Pretty women rode on the beasts' thick necks, waving to the audience. A marching band followed, blaring music that nearly drowned out the crowd's cheers. Beulah watched clowns, caged beasts, a strong man, fat lady, a midget, and several bouncing acrobats. Costumed men shouted invitations. "Come and see the circus! Come to the show!"

Beulah clapped and waved, smiling until her cheeks ached. The crowd pressed about her and waves of heat rose from the dusty road, but she was too enthralled to care. Samuel hopped up and down, waving both arms. "It's a real lion, Beulah! Do you see it? And that huge bear! Was it real?"

When the music died away and the last cage disappeared into the dust, Beulah stepped back—right on someone's foot. Hands cupped her elbows; her shoulder bumped into a solid chest. "Oh! I'm so sorry," she gasped.

"We'd better find Al and Eunice," Myles said. His eyes were a dusty olive hue that matched his plaid shirt.

Beulah shivered in the heat. "Yes. Yes, of course." He turned her around and started walking, guiding her with one hand at her elbow. Beulah walked stiffly; she was afraid to wiggle her arm lest he remove his hand.

Samuel capered beside them, turning cartwheels in the trampled grass. "Have you ever seen a bear that big, Myles? And they've got two elephants, not just one. This is the greatest circus! Did you see those men wearing long underwear do back flips? Why don't they wear clothes, Myles?"

Myles chuckled. "Not underwear, Sam. They wear those snug, stretchy clothes to make it easy to move. It's a costume, you could say. There's the surrey." He waved an arm at Al.

Samuel took off running toward the surrey. "Did you see it? Weren't the elephants great, Eunice?" His sister agreed.

Al's smile looked forced. "We could see pretty well from here. Too well for the horses' peace of mind. They don't care for elephants and lions. I'm hungry. Ready to dig into that supper basket?"

❧

Myles followed the Fairfields and Al into the big tent and took a seat at one end of a bench. Ever since the parade, Al had hovered over Beulah like a dog over a bone. Now he made certain she sat at the far end of the bench. Beulah looked up at Al just before he sat beside her. Myles lifted a brow. That pout of hers was something to see.

Although Myles knew he was a far from impartial observer, he was certain something had changed between Al and Beulah. True, they had never been a particularly affectionate pair, but they appeared to enjoy an easy camaraderie.

No more. Beulah seemed almost eager to escape Al's company. Her attention wandered when he spoke, and her gaze never followed his tall form. Al's dark eyes brooded, and his laughter sounded strained.

Perhaps they had quarreled. It was too much to hope that their romance had died away completely. Everyone in town knew that Al and Beulah would marry someday. Everyone.

Myles studied the sawdust center ring, arms folded across his chest. There was a tightness in his belly. He tried to rub it away. Not even the familiar sounds and smells of the circus could alleviate his distress.

"Are you hungry again, Myles?" Eunice asked over Samuel's head. "We could buy some popcorn."

He tried to stuff the offending hand in his pocket, then crossed his arms again. "I'm not hungry, but I'll buy you a snack." Rising, he approached a vendor and returned with a sack of buttered popcorn. "Don't know how you can eat again so soon, but here you go." Eunice and Samuel piled into the treat, knocking much of it to the floor in their haste.

"Hey, look. Isn't that Marva Obermeier?" Al pointed across the tent. "If you hurry, you could find a seat with her, Myles. We'll join up with you later."

The well-meaning suggestion was more than Myles could endure. Without a glance at Al or Beulah he turned and left the tent. Stalking around the perimeter of the big top, ducking under guy wires, he made his way toward the living quarters.

Evening shadows stretched long on the trampled grass between tents and wheeled cages. From the shadows of one caravan, a large animal gave a disgruntled rumble.

"You there! Mister, the public is not going back here," an accented voice called from behind him.

Myles froze. It couldn't be! He turned slowly, studying the approaching clown. No mistaking that green wig and the wide orange smile. "Antonio? Antonio Spinelli!"

The clown halted. Myles saw dark eyes searching his face. "Who are you?"

"Myles Trent. I'm the boy you taught how to tumble years ago. You used to call me Red, remember?"

Antonio stepped closer, his giant shoes flopping. "Red? The bambino who feared the heights and the bears?" He held out a hand at waist level then lifted it as high as he could reach, and gave a hearty chuckle. "My, how you grow!"

Myles gripped the clown's hand and clapped his shoulder. "I never expected to see you again, Antonio. You're a sight for sore eyes! How's your wife?"

"Ah, my Gina, she had a baby or two or three, and now she stay in the wagon while the show it goes on. We do well, we five—two boys and a dolly." The proud father beamed. "I teach them all to clown as I did you, Red." He scanned Myles once more. "You looka different with that beard on you face. And your hair not so red anymore. You marry? Have a family?"

Myles shook his head. "No. I've got a girl in mind, but she doesn't know it yet."

Antonio laughed again. "You wait until my act, she is over; then you come and see Gina. Tell us all about your ladylove. Yes?"

Myles nodded. "For a quick visit. I'm here with friends."

"This girl in your mind?" Antonio guessed.

"Yes. Problem is, another fellow has her in mind, too."

Antonio pulled a sober face, ludicrous behind his huge painted grin. "That a problem, yes. Now you must put yourself into the lady's mind, that's what! I must run. You stay." He pointed at Myles's feet.

"I'll wait." Myles nodded.

The little clown hurried toward his entrance. Soon Myles heard laughter and applause from the big top, then screams of delighted horror. The aerialists must be performing. He imagined Beulah watching the spectacle, and his smile faded. *If only I could sit beside her, enjoying the show through her eyes.*

The Spinelli family lived in a tiny red coach parked behind the row of animal cages. Myles had to duck to keep from bashing his head on the ceiling, and his feet felt several sizes too large. The redolence of a recent spicy meal made his eyes water.

Antonio's wife Gina was thrilled to see him, kissing him on both cheeks. She shoved a pile of clothing from a chair and told him to sit, then plied him with biscotti, garlic rolls, and a cup of rather viscous coffee. Myles took one sip and knew he wouldn't sleep all night. It was a pleasure to hear the Spinellis' circus stories, yet he could not completely relax and enjoy their company.

A tiny girl with serious dark eyes claimed his lap and played with his string tie while he talked. "This is our Sophia," Gina explained. "The boys, they are helping with the horses. Such a crowd tonight! Never did I expect it in the middle of nohow."

"Nowhere," Myles mumbled.

"We had a problem with the bear today. Did you hear?"

"Gina." Antonio shook his head. "We are not to speak of this."

She touched her lips with red tinted nails. "Oh, and I was forgotting. You will not think of it." She shook her dark head and changed the subject. "So you work at a farm? You are happy at this farm, Red?" Gina had put on weight over the years, yet she was still an attractive woman.

Myles shifted little Sophia to his other knee. "I am. I hope to acquire land of my own before long and raise a family along with cattle and crops."

Gina nodded. Her mind was elsewhere. "And you were such the performer in those days! Our Mario is much like him, don't you think, Antonio? Such a fine boy you were, and how we missed you when you disappeared. It was that brother who chased you off, no? Never did I care for him, though he was your flesh and blood. What become of that one?"

A tide of bitterness rose in his soul. "Monte is dead." Antonio's intense scrutiny produced an explanation. "He was shot by bandits in Texas. Gambling debts and cattle rustling."

The little clown nodded. He had not yet removed his wig and greasepaint. "And you cannot forgive this brother."

Myles sniffed. "Why should I forgive him? He's dead."

"For your own peace of mind. You have the look of a man carrying a heavy load, Red. It will break you, make you bitter and old while you are young."

Myles made a dismissive movement with one hand and watched his own leg jiggle up and down. "I'm starting over here in Wisconsin. The past is gone, forgotten."

"You have not forgotten; oh, no. Grudges are heavy to carry. The past will haunt you until this burden you give to God. Remember how the good Lord tells us that we are forgiven as we forgive others? Why should God forgive you when you will not forgive your fellowman?"

Myles placed the dark-haired "dolly" on her feet and rose. "I'd better return to my companions. It was a pleasure to see you again, Gina." Gloom settled over his soul.

After Myles made his farewells, Antonio accompanied him back to the midway. Darkness had fallen, making support wires and ground stakes difficult to see. Myles felt the need to make casual conversation. It would not be right to leave his old friend in this dismal way.

"This seems like a successful circus," Myles said, ducking beneath a sagging cable. "Are you satisfied with it?"

Antonio shook his head. "Ever since Mr. Bonacelli, he sell out, things not go so well. Lots of us come from Bonacelli's Circus—some of the animals, even. The new owner, he cut the pay and the feed to make a profit. The animals not so happy anymore."

"Is the bear the one that came at me while I was cleaning his cage?" Myles grimaced at the memory of falling through the cage doorway with hot breath and foam on his heels.

"The very same." Antonio frowned. "He's a bad one, sure. You were right to fear the beast. He only get meaner as he get old. He ripped up our animal trainer we had who liked his corn liquor too well."

"I can believe it. Was it the same bear that made trouble today?"

Antonio glanced around. "Not to speak of this!" he whispered.

"Those cages don't look sturdy. I wouldn't want my little ones playing near them if I were you."

Antonio nodded and pushed Myles toward the main entrance.

"Gina keeps the bambinos to home. You not to worry, my friend. Ah, it looks like the show, she is over. You had best find your friends quick. Is this lady with the yellow hair the one who lives in your head?"

Myles glanced up to see Marva Obermeier approaching. "No. She's just a friend." But a moment later Marva was attached to his arm. Myles introduced her to Antonio, attempting to be polite. The clown's eyes twinkled.

"I didn't know you knew any clowns, Myles," Marva chattered in her amiable, mindless way. "Wasn't that a tremendous show? It was so exciting when . . ." Myles tuned her out, scanning the passing crowds.

He spotted Al's broad gray hat. "Al!" Waving his free arm, he gave a sharp whistle and saw his friend's head turn. "Over here!"

Marva was excusing herself. "My papa is beckoning—I must go. It was nice to meet you . . ."

Myles tuned her out again, focusing on Al until he spotted Beulah behind him. "Here she comes—the tall girl in the blue dress. Beulah Fairfield."

Antonio regarded Myles with evident amusement. "Your other lady friend is gone. Did you notice?"

Myles glanced around. Marva had disappeared. "Did I tell her good-bye?"

"You did." Still grinning, Antonio turned to study Beulah.

Myles made his introductions all around. Samuel was thrilled to meet a real clown and plied the man with questions. Antonio answered the boy patiently.

"How long ago did you two know each other?" Beulah asked.

"This fine fellow was but a lad with hair like fire," Antonio said, eyes twinkling.

"It has been about eight years," Myles said. "Antonio and his wife were newly married. Now they have three children."

"Myles tells me he has thoughts of family for himself." Antonio wagged one finger beside his ear. "Time, she is passing him by."

Myles felt his face grow hot.

Al gruffly reminded them that home was still a good drive away. Antonio bade the Fairfields and Al farewell. Beulah held the clown's hand for a moment. "It was so nice to meet an old friend of Myles. His past has been a mystery to us, but now we know you, Mr. Spinelli."

Beulah's smile had its usual effect: Antonio beamed, shaking her hand in both of his. "But mine is the pleasure, Miss Fairfield, to meet such a lovely lady. Red is a mystery to Gina and me always—so secretive and shy! But in him beats a man's heart, I am knowing. He is needing a great love to banish these burdens he carries and fill his life with laughter and music."

Myles knew a sudden urge to hurry the little clown away before his heart's secret was broadcast to the world. Al relieved his distress by hustling Beulah away. "Give them time alone, Beulah. They haven't seen each other in years. We'll meet you at the surrey, Myles."

As soon as they were out of earshot, Antonio shook his head mournfully. "And this Al, your fine friend, is the other whose heart beats for Beulah. For him it is a sad thing, Red. She must be yours."

Myles lowered one brow. "What makes you say that?"

Antonio waved at the starry sky. "I read it in the stars? But maybe the stars, they are in a young lady's eyes." He laughed and patted Myles's arm. "You will have joy, Red. Gina and I, we will remember you and your Beulah in our prayers each night. Remember what I say about forgiveness—I know this from living it, you see. Don't imagine you are alone. Everyone has choices in life. Think of Beulah—you cannot offer her an unforgiving heart. The poison in you would harm her."

The man was like a flea for persistence. Nodding, Myles pretended to ignore the stinging words. "You will write to me? I live in Longtree, the next town over."

"I not write so good, but Gina will do it. Maybe when the season ends, we come to see you and your little wife."

Myles smiled and hugged the smaller man's shoulders. "Thank you, Antonio. You have given me much-needed encouragement."

❧

Buck met the tired travelers in front of the barn and helped unhitch the horses. "Why are you up so late, Papa? Is Mama still awake?" Eunice asked sleepily.

"Mama and Daniel are asleep. Get ready for bed quietly, children. Go on with you now." Buck shooed his flock toward the house. "We've got church in the morning."

"Thank you, Al. Thank you, Myles. It was a wonderful circus," Beulah paused to say. Her eyes reflected the surrey's sidelamps.

"You're welcome," they each replied.

"See you at church," Al called after her. "May I come pick you up?"

Myles jumped. That would be a sign of serious courtship. Hidden in the shadows behind the surrey, he gritted his teeth and braced himself for her reply.

"Thank you for the offer, but no, I'll see you there," Beulah's voice floated back. "Good night."

Al smacked a harness strap over its peg and tugged his hat down over his eyes. Without a word, he led his horse from its stall and saddled up. Myles felt a pang of sympathy for his friend.

Buck finished caring for the team while Myles saddled his mare. "Got a job for you Monday," Buck said.

"What's that?" Myles asked.

"We got two pasture fence posts snapped off; musta been rotted below ground level. I found Mo among our cows. He may be only a yearling, but he's all bull. I propped up the fence well enough to hold him temporarily; but we've got to replace those posts soon."

"I'll run the materials out there," Al promised.

"And I'll fix the fence," Myles said.

3

Let all bitterness, and wrath, and anger, and clamour,
and evil speaking, be put away from you, with all malice.
Ephesians 4:31

*C*lutching a novel under one arm, Beulah peeked into her mother's room. "I'll be at the pond if you need me, Mama."

Bent over the cradle, Violet finished tucking Daniel's blanket around his feet. Straightening, she turned to smile at her daughter. "Enjoy yourself, Honey. Would you bring in green beans for supper tonight? Samuel caught a dozen bluegill this morning, and beans would be just the thing to go with fried fish."

"He's getting to be quite a fisherman," Beulah observed. "Whatever will we do when school starts up and we lose our provider? You're right, beans sound delicious—or they would if I were hungry. Is Papa around, or did he go into town today?"

Violet led the way downstairs. "He went to help Myles repair the fence the bull broke. Which reminds me . . . I know it's asking a lot of you, Dear, but would you be willing to carry water to the men? They're way out at that northwest pasture beyond the stream."

Beulah followed her mother into the parlor. "Of course I will, Mama. I'm going out anyway."

"You're a dear! You might take along some of those cookies you baked."

Beulah felt slightly guilty about her mother's gratitude, since her motive was not entirely altruistic. "That's a good idea. If I hurry, I'll still have time to read a chapter or two."

Violet settled into a chair and picked up her mending. "Darling, I want you to know that I've noticed your efforts to be cheerful and kind, and so has Papa Obie. You're my precious girl—I want other people to see and appreciate your beautiful spirit along with your pretty face."

"Do you really think I'm pretty, Mama?" Beulah tried to see her reflection in the window. "Everyone says I look like my real father, and he was homely. At least, I remember him as kind of ungainly and bony with big teeth."

"You have your father's coloring and his gorgeous brown eyes. Your teeth may be a bit crooked, yet they are white and healthy. You have matured this past year, and I think you must have noticed that boys find you attractive. Al certainly does."

Beulah looked down at her figure. "I guess so. I wonder why men are attracted by a woman's shape. When you think about it, we're kind of funny looking."

Violet laughed. "Trust you to say something like that! As for me, I'm thankful that men find women attractive and vice versa. It makes life interesting."

"So it isn't wrong for a girl to enjoy looking at a man?"

"Wrong? Of course not," Violet answered absently. "I enjoy looking at my husband."

"When a girl is interested in a man, what is the best way for her to let him know it?" Beulah perched on the edge of the sofa. "A subtle way, I mean. Without actually saying so."

Violet looked at the ceiling, touching her needle to her lips. "Hmm. Subtle. How about meeting his gaze and smiling? A touch on his arm, perhaps. Touching can be hazardous, however. A lady doesn't want to touch a man too much or he will lose respect for her."

Beulah's lower lip protruded and her brows lowered as a certain memory of a clinging blond recurred. Her mother's advice seemed faulty. A shy man like Myles might be different. He might prefer a woman who took the initiative. "How does a lady know if a man returns her interest?"

Violet's lips twitched. "She will know. Most men are straightforward."

"But how will she know for certain? If a man stares at a girl, does that mean he is interested?"

"That depends on the stare." Violet frowned. "Who has been staring at you?"

"It's a respectful gaze. Don't worry." She hopped to her feet. "Thank you, Mama. I'd better hurry before the day is gone."

Although she took a shortcut through a stretch of forest, the trek to the back pasture was more arduous than Beulah had anticipated. She crossed Samuel's log bridge over the brook, then hiked up the steep bank, nearly dropping the water jug once.

"Why did I think this was such a good idea?" she grouched, hoisting the jug on her hip. "I'll be a sweaty mess again before he sees me." Mosquitoes and deerflies hummed around her head, dodging when she slapped at them. Her arms ached until they felt limp, and her feet burned inside her boots.

Through the trees she caught sight of Papa Obie's mustang Jughead and open pastureland beyond him. The horse's patches of white reflected sunshine as he grazed. Wherever Jughead was, Beulah was certain to find Obie nearby.

Sure enough, there were Obie and Myles, ramming a new post into a hole. Both men had removed their shirts; their damp undervests gaped open to reveal sweaty chests. Suspenders held up faded denim trousers, and battered hats shaded their eyes.

"Hello," she greeted, picking her way between stumps. "I brought water and cookies."

"Beulah!" Obie straightened. "You're an angel of mercy. We've needed a drink yet hated to stop before we finished this post." He exchanged a glance with Myles. "Let's take a break." Myles nodded, and the two men sat on nearby stumps.

Wiping his face with a red kerchief, Obie drained the dipper in one long draught. "Thanks."

Beulah's hands trembled as she handed Myles the dipper. Hazel eyes glinted in his dusty face. He, too, poured the water down his throat and wiped his mustache with the back of one hand. "Thank you."

"More?"

Each man accepted two more drinks, and the jug felt much

lighter. Then they gobbled up her molasses cookies. "These are delicious, Beulah . . . but then your cookies always are," Obie said.

She peeked at Myles to see if he agreed. "My favorite." He lifted a half-eaten cookie.

Satisfied, she settled upon a low stump near Obie's feet and arranged her skirts. "How much longer must you work in this heat? Is this the last post?"

"Yes. Once we brace this post and attach the crossbeams, we'll be done. Nasty work." Obie shook his head, betraying a former cowboy's natural aversion to fences. "Myles did most of it before I got here. Planned that well, didn't I?" He grinned at the hired man, and Myles acknowledged the teasing with a smile.

"Ready?"

Myles nodded, and the two returned to their work.

Beulah stayed. Myles never spoke to her, but several times she caught his eye and smiled. He did not smile back. Her heart sank. *He is in love with Miss Obermeier! Whatever shall I do?*

"Beulah, would you bring me the hammer?"

She hurried to comply.

"If you would hand me that spike . . ." Obie requested next.

This time she hovered. "May I help?"

"Not now," Obie puffed. "Better stay back."

Myles lifted the rails into place and Obie hammered in the spikes. The hair on the hired man's forearms and chest was sun-bleached. Sweaty hair curling from beneath his hat held auburn glints. His trousers bagged around slim hips.

From this close range Beulah could locate his ribs and shoulder blades. Sinews protruded in his neck and chest as his muscles strained. When Mama was pregnant with Daniel, Beulah once sneaked a peek at a human anatomy book in the doctor's office. Myles might have posed for the model of muscles and bones, so many of them were visible beneath his skin.

He glanced up; Beulah looked away, too late. Her body already dripped sweat; now she burned on the inside. *What must he think of me, staring at him like a hussy?* She strolled away, fanning her apron up and down. Grasshoppers fled buzzing before her.

When the last rail was in place, Beulah helped the men gather their tools. Obie loaded his saddlebags. "Thanks again, Myles." He swung into Jughead's saddle. A wisp of grass dangled from the gelding's mouth. "Will you see Beulah home, then check on Cyrus Thwaite for me? He hasn't been eating well since his wife died, and I want to make sure he's all right."

"Yes, Sir, I will."

Obie's silvery eyes smiled, and one brow arched. "You two take your time. Behave yourselves."

Now what did he mean by that? Beulah wondered.

Jughead sprang into motion, hurdling brush and stumps in his way. Within moments he had disappeared from view.

Beulah looked at Myles. "Why didn't you bring a horse? I thought cowboys preferred to ride. Or are you really a clown?" she tried to tease.

Wiping one sleeve across his forehead, he clapped on his hat. Every inch of exposed skin glistened red-brown, and his undervest was sopping. Though he was pleasing to behold, Beulah tried to remain upwind.

"First a clown, then a cowboy, now a farmer." One grimy hand began to rub his belly. "No point in making a horse stand around while I work. The boss was in town this morning; he needed a horse."

"Don't forget your shirt." She scooped it up and held it out.

"Thanks." He slung it over his shoulder and picked up her water jug.

He wouldn't even meet her eyes. Beulah's temper rose. "You don't need to escort me home. You must be tired." She picked up her book.

"Let's cut through Mo's pasture."

Not twenty yards down the sloping pasture, placidly chewing his cud, lay Mo. Shading her eyes, Beulah cast a wary glance at the dormant bull. "Is it safe?"

"He knows me." Myles bent to step through the fence rails. "Come on."

She slipped through the fence easily enough, but her skirt caught on a splinter and Myles had to release it. Beulah kept glancing toward Mo. The bull watched them walk across his field. Slowly he began to rise, back end first.

"Myles, he's getting up!" Beulah caught hold of Myles's arm.

He looked down at her hand on his arm, then back at the yearling Jersey.

Clutching his arm, she let Myles direct her steps and kept both eyes on the bull. Mo began to follow them, trotting over the rough ground.

"Any cookies left?" Myles asked.

"Some broken ones. Why?"

"Mo likes sweets. Don't be frightened, Child. He's too small to harm you."

Child!

When the bull approached to within a few yards, it bawled, and Beulah let out a yelp. "Here, give him the cookies!" She shoved the sack into Myles's hands, then cowered behind him. The man's cotton undervest was damp beneath her hands, but the solid feel of him was reassuring. Beulah could hear her own heartbeat.

Myles extended a piece of cookie. "Come and get it, Li'l Mo. You've had your fun, scaring Beulah. Now show her what a good fellow you are."

Shaking his head, the young bull pawed the ground and gave a feinting charge. Myles held his ground. Mo stretched toward the cookie, nostrils twitching. When the bull accepted the treat, Myles took hold of the brass ring in its nose. "Good lad." He stroked Mo's neck and scratched around the animal's ears. "This is one fine little bull."

Beulah began to relax, peeking around Myles's shoulder. "I can't believe he was once a tiny calf. Samuel named him 'Moo-moo.' Remember that day when my mother drove us to your farm—Al's farm—by mistake? Or were you there that day?"

"I was there. I helped deliver this fellow that very morning." With a farewell pat for Mo, Myles turned to Beulah. "I remember how cross you looked that day. You've got a pretty smile, but your pout is like nothing I've ever seen." His grin showed white through his beard.

Beulah gaped, hands dangling. She took a step back and tucked her hands under her elbows. "I—I was not cross; I was worried."

"With your lip sticking out and your eyes stormy, just like now." His hat shaded his face, yet Beulah caught the glint in his eyes.

She covered her mouth with one hand, conscious of her overbite. Eyes burning, she turned and picked up the water jug. If Myles knew how she felt about him, he would laugh, and the whole town would know about Beulah's infatuation within days. Marva would regard her with pity and mild amusement.

"Are you all right, Beulah?" Myles took two steps in her direction. "I didn't mean to hurt your feelings."

"I'm not angry; I'm hot." Water sloshed in the jug. Beulah eyed the sweaty man. "You look hotter." Without pausing for reflection, she dashed the water into his face.

Water dripped from his nose and beard and trickled down his chest. "Did I deserve that?"

He didn't seem angry. A nervous giggle escaped before Beulah could stop it. "You needed a bath."

His eyes flared, and Beulah knew she had better get moving. Picking up her skirts, she dashed for the fence, intending to vanish into the forest. But an arm caught her around the waist. "Not so fast." Without further ceremony he tossed her over his shoulder and picked up the empty jar. Her book flew into the tall grass.

"What are you doing?" she gasped. "Put me down!" He surmounted the fence without apparent difficulty and headed into the woods.

Beulah found it hard to breathe while hanging head down over his shoulder, and her stomach muscles were too weak to lift her upper body for long. In order to draw a good breath she had to put both hands on his back and push herself up. "Myles, a gentleman doesn't treat a lady this way! Please put me down. This is . . . improper," she protested. The grasp of his arm around her legs was disturbing, the solid strength of his shoulder beneath her stomach even more so. There was a roaring in her ears.

"Very well." He hefted her and flung her from him. Beulah fell with splayed arms and horrified expression only to land with a great splash. She had enough presence of mind to shut her mouth before water closed over her head.

Flailing her arms, she managed to right herself, but her face barely cleared the surface when she stood on the rocky bottom. The source of the roaring sound was now clear: The stream poured into this little pool over a lip of rock suspended twelve feet above the surface. The churning water tugged at Beulah's billowing skirts, and bubbles tickled her arms.

"How dare you!" she gasped, sudden fury choking her. "I could have drowned!"

An exaggeration, but the sharpest accusation she could think of at the moment. She had to shout for him to hear her.

Myles stood above her, his boots planted wide, arms folded on his chest. Dapples of sunlight played across his hat and shoulders. "It's not deep," he protested. "I swim here often." His smile was infuriating.

"I can't swim with my boots and clothes on," she blurted, then choked on a mouthful of water. "You . . . you monster! You are no gentleman!"

"I had not observed you behaving like a lady."

"Ooooh!"

Desperate for revenge, she thrashed over to the steep bank and reached for his boots. One frenzied hop and she caught hold around his ankles. No matter how hard she tugged, he remained unmoved. She paused, gasping for air. "Where are we? I've never seen this place."

"Just over half a mile above the beaver pond. The waterfall made this hole, perfect for swimming. It's one of my favorite places on earth."

Beulah tried to look over her shoulder at the lacy waterfall, but her bedraggled sunbonnet blocked her view. Hoping to catch Myles unaware, she gave his feet another sharp jerk, lost her grip, and slid back into the pool. Sputtering with fury, she surfaced again, arms thrashing. Her teeth chattered, although the water was not terribly cold. "Help me out of here!"

He frowned, considering, then removed his hat and boots. After stacking his garments well out of Beulah's reach, he dove into the pool and disappeared.

Beulah let out another little screech, then scanned the pool for him with narrowed eyes. He should pay for this outrage.

He did not come up. Beulah began to feel concerned. Had he hit his head on a rock? "Myles?" she inquired.

"Myles, where are you?" She stepped forward, took a mouthful of water, and coughed. "Myles!" Her hands groped, searching for his body. This pool was too shallow for safe diving. Panic filled her voice. "Myles!"

" 'Ruby lips above the water blowing bubbles soft and fine, but, alas! I was no swimmer, so I lost my Clementine.' " The voice in her ear was a rich baritone.

"Oh!" Beulah's anger revived. "You are dreadful! I thought you had drowned—that's what you wanted me to think!" Even more infuriating was her helpless condition. It was difficult to appear righteously angry when her face barely cleared the surface. Exertion and excitement made her huff for every breath. "How can you be so mean? First you say I'm ugly, then you drop me in the water fully clothed, and then you pretend to drown? And I thought you were a nice person! You're horrible! Cruel!"

"Who said you're ugly?" He caught her by the waist and lifted until her head and shoulders rose out of the water. His hair lay slicked back from his high forehead. She could count the freckles on his peeling nose.

"Let go of me!" The grip of his hands sent her heart into spasms. Her corset's ribs bit into her flesh. She pulled at his fingers, kicking wildly.

He shook her. "If you don't hold still, I'll drop you back in the pool and you can find your own way out."

Her struggles ceased. She gripped his forearms, feeling iron beneath the flesh. *I can't cry! I must keep control.*

"Now who said you were ugly?"

"You did. That was unkind! I can't help having crooked teeth any more than you can help having red hair and freckles!"

He blinked. She saw his eyes focus upon her mouth. She clamped her lips together.

"I never noticed that your teeth are crooked."

"But you said . . ."

"I said I'd never seen a pout like yours. It's like a tornado brewing.

Wise people stay out of your way." He grinned. "I would never call you ugly. Your temper, however, deserves that designation, from all I hear."

Beulah gaped into his face.

"Go ahead and flay me alive. I can take it." He smiled.

Her mouth snapped shut. The backs of her eyes burned.

"I've got to put you down for a minute. My arms are giving out." He turned her to face away from him. She placed her hands on top of his at her waist, thankful for her trim figure and sturdy corset.

Hefting her back up, he slowly walked toward the far side of the little pool. As they passed the waterfall, Beulah looked up and felt spray on her face. "Wait!"

Myles stopped, lowering her slightly. Beulah reached out and touched the sheet of falling water, surprised by its power. "Ohhh, this is wonderful!" Rainbows glimmered in the misty water. She lifted her other hand, straining her upper body toward the falls.

"I can't hold you like this anymore," Myles protested, then let his arms drop.

Startled, Beulah caught hold of his wrists and began to protest; but Myles pulled her back, wrapped his arms around her, and supported her against his body so that her waist was at his chest level. "Go ahead and enjoy the waterfall," he ordered from between her shoulder blades.

Beulah's pounding heart warned her that she had exceeded the bounds of ladylike deportment. "Have you ever walked beneath it?"

"I have." She was sliding down within his grasp.

"Can you walk through it while holding me?" She looked over her shoulder at him and recognized the intimacy of the situation. His arms pressed around her waist and rib cage. He lifted his knee to boost her higher in his grasp.

"Are you—are you sure—are you sure you want me to?"

Seek ye the LORD while he may be found,
call ye upon him while he is near.
Isaiah 55:6

"P lease do!" she begged.

His arms shook both with strain and with excitement. Knowing he should flee temptation, Myles found himself unable to deny Beulah's request. Hopefully she would attribute his strangled voice to physical effort.

Again hefting her higher in his grasp, he walked toward the waterfall, feeling stones turn beneath his feet. Keeping one arm wrapped over his, Beulah lifted her other arm over her head to greet the cascade as it tumbled over their heads. Water filled their ears, noses, and eyes, dragged on their clothing, and toiled to pull them under. When they emerged on the far side, Beulah coughed. Water dribbled from her every feature. She had slipped down within his grasp, her bonnet was gone, and her arm now clung around his neck. Long eyelashes clumped together when she blinked those glorious brown eyes. Her smile lighted up the grotto. "I will never forget this, Myles."

She was a slender girl, yet she felt substantial in his arms, better than anything he had ever imagined. Oh, but she was lovely with her questioning eyes and her lips that seemed to invite his kisses! Her free hand crept up to rest upon his chest; she must feel the tumult within. His breath came in labored gusts.

Shaking, he gripped her forearms and shoved her away. He shook his head to clear it, reflecting that another dunk under the waterfall might benefit him.

"Myles—" she began, then fell silent. Although she was obliged to cling to his arms to keep from sinking, he felt her withdrawal. Her chin quivered with cold.

God, help me! I love her so, the wild little kitten.

Without another word Myles hoisted her into his arms, this time in the more conventional carrying position, and slogged across to the far shore. When Beulah turned to crawl up the bank, he caught a glimpse of her face. "Beulah?"

Her booted foot slipped and thumped him in the chest. With a soft grunt, he caught hold of her ankles and gave her an extra boost until she could sit on the mossy bank.

Water streamed from every fold of her clothing. Her hair dripped. Her face was crumpled and red. Her woeful eyes turned Myles to mush.

"Are . . . are you all right?" Assorted endearments struggled on his lips; he dared not speak them aloud. He touched her soggy boot, but she jerked it away, staggered to her feet, and rushed off along the bank of the creek.

❧

When Myles emerged from the forest near Fairfield's Folly, Watchful rose from her cool nest beneath the back porch and came to greet him, tail waving. Thankfully she was not a noisy dog. Myles left the jug on the porch and turned to leave, but the kitchen door opened.

"Hello, Myles."

Myles removed his hat as he turned. "Hello, Mrs. Watson."

Violet Watson cradled Daniel against one shoulder, jiggling him up and down. "My, but it's hot today! I happened to see you out the kitchen window." Her blue eyes scanned him. "I see you've been for a swim."

"Yes, Ma'am."

"I must admit, a dip does sound tempting. So Beulah reached you men with the water and cookies?"

"Yes, Ma'am. Please extend my thanks for all of her thoughtfulness."

Violet smiled. "I'll do that. She must still be reading at the pond. That girl does love to read, and she seldom finds time for it these days.

I'm afraid I depend greatly on her help around the house. Maybe I need to give her more afternoons off like this."

Myles nodded, feeling dishonest. He knew Beulah had returned home already, for he had followed her wet trail through the forest. She must have sneaked inside. "I enjoy reading, too."

"Really? Do you also enjoy music? Beulah and I are both fond of music, but we have so little opportunity to hear good music around here."

His ears grew warm. "I enjoy music." Realizing that he was rubbing his stomach, he whipped the offending hand behind his back. Violet didn't seem to notice.

She leaned against the doorframe. "I play the piano a little. Obie bought me a lovely instrument for Christmas, you know, but I do not do it justice. Beulah plays better than I do. Do you sing or play an instrument?"

"Yes, Ma'am."

"I'm thinking of planning a music party after harvest, just for our family and a few friends. Might you be willing to join us?"

"I'd be honored, Ma'am." Myles shifted his weight. "I must be going. Have an errand to run."

"Are you going to see Cyrus Thwaite? That poor man has been so lonely since his wife died. I'm certain he doesn't eat well. Let me pack you a sack of cookies for him."

Myles handed over the empty cookie sack. Little Daniel reached for it, trying to bring the strings to his open mouth.

When Violet returned the full sack, she gave Myles a sweet smile. "Good-bye, and thank you."

❧

Myles's mare whinnied as she trotted up the Thwaite drive. "Hello the house!" Myles called. Swinging down in one easy motion, he left his mare's reins hanging. A knock at the door brought no response. Myles entered, feeling mildly concerned. Cyrus seldom left his farm since his wife Hattie died last spring.

Myles scanned the kitchen, taking a quick peek into the pantry. The sacks of flour and sugar he had delivered the week before had not been touched. Only the coffee supply had been depleted. Dirty cups were stacked in the dry sink, but few plates had been used. He set Violet's sack of cookies on the table.

"Cyrus?" he called, quickly inspecting the rest of the untidy house. Stepping outside, Myles felt the relief of fresh air. A breeze had risen, swaying the birches beyond the drive. "Cyrus?" he bellowed, heading for the barn.

There—he heard a reply. From the barn? Myles broke into a jog. Chickens scattered as he approached the barn door. The cow lowed, turning her head to gaze at him. "Why aren't you out at pasture?" Myles left by the barn's back door. "Cyrus, where are you?"

"Here, Boy." Cyrus waved from across the pasture. He appeared to be leaning on the handle of a spade. At his feet lay a gray mound. Two vultures circled overhead, and crows lined the nearby pasture fence. The swaybacked old mule must have keeled over at last. But by the time Myles crossed the field, he realized that the animal had met a violent death. Its body was mauled.

"What happened?"

Cyrus lifted a long face. "You know how he could unlatch doors; he musta let hisself out last night, poor ol' cuss. Myles, I may be crazy, but this looks like a bear's work to me." He lifted a silencing hand. "I know there ain't been a bear in these parts since Hector here was a long-eared foal, but what else could break a full-growed mule's neck like this?"

Myles studied the claw marks on the animal's carcass. "Why would a bear want to kill an old mule? Surely it might have found better eating nearby." A suspicion popped into his mind.

"Mebbe it's sick or wounded or plain cussed mean. Would ya help me bury what's left Hector?" Cyrus looked halfway ashamed to ask. "Cain't jest see m'self leavin' him for the vultures and coyotes. Thought I'd bury him on this here knoll."

Myles nodded and returned to the barn for another spade.

To give Cyrus credit, he worked harder at eighty than many men worked at thirty; but his body lacked the strength to lift heavy loads of dirt. All too soon he was obliged to sit down. "Was a time I could work like you, Boy, but that time is long past." He wiped his forehead with a grimy handkerchief. "I been putting lots of thought into what's to become of this here farm. Hattie wanted to leave it to Obie, but I don't see much point in that. He's already got more land than he can work."

Myles paused for a breather, leaning on his spade. One callused hand absently rubbed his belly. "You might sell it and live in town. Bet you'd enjoy living at Miss Amelia's boardinghouse, eating her good cooking morning and night. Lots of company for you there."

Cyrus looked pensive. "You paint a tempting picture, Myles boy. I reckon I'd like that mighty well, but I can't see myself selling this farm. Hattie and me built it up when we was young, expecting we'd have a passel of younguns. Never did, though. I figure this land is worth more to me than it would be to a stranger. It's played out. We planted it so many years, took all the good right out'n it."

Myles began to dig again. "I hear there're ways a man can put soil right again by planting other things like beans and peas in it. Some scientists claim it'll work."

Cyrus shook his white head. "I'll never see the backside of a plow again. But if you had a mind to buy, I might reconsider selling. I'd rest easy knowing it was in your hands, Myles." His eyes drifted across the weedy pasture to stump-ridden fields beyond.

"If I—" Myles stopped working to stare at his spade. "You'd sell to me?"

"That sounds about like what I said, don't it? This place needs someone who'll put work and love into it. You've done a sight of work hereabouts already, but I know you've been itching to do more, to make the place what it oughta be. You're a good man, Myles Trent, and I think you're a man God will use—no matter if folks claim you don't believe in Him. I know better."

Myles met the old man's gaze. "How do you know?"

"You're plumb full of questions that demand answers, and you ain't the kind who'll quit before he finds them answers. God promises that a man who seeks Him will find Him, if he searches with all his heart."

Myles shifted his grip on the handle. "I can't buy your place, Cyrus. No money. I've laid a little by each year, but not enough."

Cyrus pondered, deepening the lines on his brow. "Don't know why, but I got this feeling about you and my farm, Myles. I think God has something in mind, though I cain't begin to tell you what it is."

A deep sigh expanded Myles's chest. When he exhaled, his shoulders drooped. "Unless He plans to drop a fortune into my lap, I'll be a hired hand till the day I die."

"You might could marry rich," Cyrus suggested with a wicked grin. "Naw, I don't mean it. You find yourself a good wife and make this place into a proper home again."

Myles quickly began to dig. Cyrus chuckled. "Why is finding a wife such a chore for you young fellers? I just up and asked Hattie to wed me and got us hitched. No fuss and feathers about it, yet we stayed happy together sixty years. Bet there's more'n one lady in town who'd be eager to accept a fine feller like you. Why not chance it? Might want to wash up first; try hair oil and scented soap. Females like such things."

"A man doesn't want to marry just any woman," Myles objected. His thoughts whirled.

Scented soap. Van Huysen's Soap.

Money. His money.

Farm. His farm?

"Why not? One woman is same as another." Cyrus's grin displayed almost toothless gums. "Comely or homely, fleshy or scrawny, they kin all keep a man warm on long winter nights. Hattie was never what you might call comely, but then I weren't no prize winner myself!" He cackled. "One woman—that's all you need."

When the hole was deep enough, Myles dragged the carcass over and shoved it in. "That should be deep enough to keep varmints from digging ol' Hector up," he said. Cyrus helped him fill in the hole and tamp it.

"Hope that bear took off for foreign parts," Cyrus remarked. "We don't need a killer loose in these woods."

"I'll warn our neighbors about the possibility of a renegade bear.

Want to come to supper at Miss Amelia's boardinghouse with me to-night?"

Cyrus's faded eyes brightened. "That'd be fine. You got a buggy?"

"We can hitch my mare to your buggy," Myles said. "I'll talk with Buck about getting you another mule or horse. You can't stay out here alone with no transportation."

∼❧

On the way to town, Myles's mare tossed her head and tucked her tail whenever he clucked to her. "Cholla takes being hitched to a buggy as an insult," Myles explained when Cyrus commented on the mare's bad mood.

"Is she yours or Obie's?"

"Mine. Caught and tamed her myself out in Wyoming. Not so pretty to look at, prickly like the cactus she's named for, but she's got legs like iron and a big heart." Myles fondly surveyed his mare's spotted gray hide, wispy tail, and unruly mane.

"And a kind eye. You can tell a lot about a horse by its eyes," Cyrus added.

Miss Amelia Sidwell greeted them at her boardinghouse's dining room door. "Pull out a chair and tuck in. Evenin', Myles. You been taking too much sun."

"You're looking pert today, Amelia," Cyrus commented. "Fine feathers make a fine bird."

Miss Amelia appeared to appreciate the compliment, favoring the old man with a smile. Her blue-checked apron did bring out the blue in her eyes. "What brings you to town, Cyrus? Ain't seen you in a spell." Her voice was as deep as a man's.

"Your cooking draws men like hummingbirds to honeysuckle," Myles assured her, straddling his chair. He returned greetings from other diners, most of whom he knew.

A stranger stared at him from across the table. Myles nodded, and the gentleman nodded back, then looked away.

Amelia scoffed. "Hummingbirds, indeed. More like flies to molasses, I'd say." She ladled soup into Cyrus's bowl. "Got more of you blowflies than I kin handle these days. I'm thinkin' of hiring help."

"You, Amelia?" Boswell Martin, the town sheriff, inquired in his wheezy voice. "I can't imagine you finding help that would suit. What female creature ever found favor in your eyes?"

Never pausing in her labors, Amelia snapped back, "Miss Sidwell to you, Boz Martin—and I'll thank you to keep your remarks to yourself. If that's a chaw in your cheek, you'd best get yourself outside and rid of it. I never heard tell of a man eating with tobacco tucked in his cheek, looking like a hulking chipmunk. If you don't beat all!"

The sheriff meekly shoved back his chair and stepped outside while the other diners struggled to hide their mirth. Myles again met the gaze of the dapper gentleman with bushy side-whiskers. The two men shared an amused smile.

"I ain't never seen you before, Mister." Cyrus directed his comment toward the stranger. "You new in town or jest travelin' through?"

"I arrived in town Tuesday," the gentleman replied. "I am George Poole, lately from New York. I have business in this area."

"Welcome to Longtree, Mr. Poole." Cyrus and Myles reached across the table to shake the newcomer's hand. Poole's handshake was firm, his gaze steady.

The sheriff returned to the table and began to shovel food into his mouth.

"Boz?" Cyrus said. "I lost my mule today—looked like a bear's work."

Sheriff Martin gave the old man a skeptical look, still chewing.

Cyrus forestalled the inevitable protest. "I know there ain't been a bear in these parts for twenty years, but I know what I seen. The varmint broke ol' Hector's neck and left huge claw marks. I'm thinking you ought to organize a hunt before the critter tears up more stock."

Martin nodded and spoke around a mouthful of stew. "I'll get right on it."

"Don't talk with your mouth full," Amelia ordered, reaching over the sheriff's shoulder to place a freshly sliced loaf of bread on the table. Within moments the platter was empty. "You lot behave like hogs at a trough," the gratified cook growled.

"Talk of bears puts me in mind . . . that circus left Bolger this morning," one diner said. "I heard rumors they lost an animal in this area. Did you hear anything about it, Sheriff? Last thing we need in these parts is a roaming lion."

This time Boz swallowed before he spoke. "Nope. Ain't heard a thing."

Again Myles recalled his circus friend Gina Spinelli's slip of the tongue about a rogue bear, but he said nothing. Surely a missing circus bear would have been reported to the authorities. Or would it?

Mr. Poole turned his steel blue eyes upon Miss Amelia. "That was a wonderful meal, Madam. The best meal I've eaten in many a year."

Amelia fluttered. "Why, thank you, Mr. Poole. I'm right glad you liked it. I've got apple dumplings and cream in the kitchen."

"May I take my dessert later this evening? I'm afraid I cannot swallow another bite at the moment." He laid his folded napkin beside his empty plate and pushed back his chair. When he stood, the top of his head was on a level with Amelia's eyes.

Work-worn hands smoothed her starched apron. Myles noticed that her gray hair looked softer than usual; she had styled it a new way instead of slicking it back into a knot. "Certainly, Mr. Poole. You let me know when you're ready for your dessert."

Poole excused himself from the table and left the room, apparently oblivious to the stunned silence that followed Amelia's reply. "But, Amelia—" the sheriff protested.

"Not another word from you." She withered him with a glance. "Not a one of you what cain't fit in your dessert when it's offered. A fine gentleman like Mr. Poole isn't used to stuffing his face, so's a body must make allowances." With a sweep of her skirts, Miss Amelia returned to her kitchen.

Sheriff Martin scowled. "That woman's gone plain loco. A few bows and compliments, and even the best of women plumb lose their heads."

"Jealous, Boz? Maybe you'll get further with the lady if you try bowing and complimenting." Old Cyrus chuckled. "Wouldn't hurt to bathe if you're right serious about courting."

Boz's already florid face turned scarlet. "Reckon she'd take notice?"

"A woman likes it when a man takes pains on her account. Amelia likes things clean and neat."

"Clean" and "neat" were two terms Myles would never have applied to the sheriff. He was startled by the concept that Sheriff Martin wished to court Miss Amelia. Not that the man was too old for marriage—Boz hadn't yet turned fifty. But hard-boiled Martin had never struck him as the marrying kind.

Then again, what made any person wish to marry? A craving for love and companionship, he supposed. The longing to be needed, admired, and desired. The urge to produce children to carry on one's name. Myles could appreciate the sheriff's inclination.

"I'm thinkin' on asking her to the church social Friday," Boz growled, shoving food around on his plate. "How you think I oughta go about it, Cy?"

Enjoying his new role, Cyrus sized Boz up, rubbing his grizzled chin. "You need to head for the barber for a shave and trim, then buy yourself new duds. And no tobaccy. Amelia hates the stuff. Might better drop it now than later."

Boz rubbed his plump jowls with one dirty hand, making a raspy noise. He nodded. "I'll do it." Amid raucous ribbing from the other men at the table, the sheriff rose, hitched up his sagging belt, and headed for the door.

"No dessert, Boz?" Amelia stood in the kitchen doorway, a loaded plate in each hand.

"Not tonight. Got business to attend. Thank you for a wondrous fine meal, *Miss Sidwell*." Boz bowed awkwardly and made his exit.

Shocked by his unaccustomed formality, Amelia stared after him, shrugged, and plopped dumplings in front of two diners. When she served Myles and Cyrus, she fixed Myles with a shrewd eye. "You takin' Marva Obermeier to the church social, Myles? She's counting on it."

The fork stopped halfway to his mouth, then slowly returned to the plate. "Miss Obermeier?" His stomach sank. "Why would she expect that?"

"You'd be knowing better than I," Amelia snapped and headed back to her kitchen.

Myles gave Cyrus a blank look. The old man lifted a brow. "It's all over town, Myles. Didn't you know?"

The dessert lost its appeal. "I think I've only talked to her twice."

"You mean to say you ain't sweet on her?"

"No. I mean—yes, that's what I mean to say; no, I'm not sweet on her. I hardly know the woman."

"I reckon you'll be getting to know her real soon." Cyrus chuckled.

5

Wrath is cruel, and anger is outrageous;
but who is able to stand before envy?
Proverbs 27:4

*C*yrus was no prophet, but he came uncomfortably close. And "uncomfortably close" was an apt description of Marva herself. The blond lady was not unattractive; in fact, in her rosy, plump, blond fashion, she was pretty.

"I'm so happy to see you here tonight, Myles. You've been neglecting church lately." She wagged a finger in his face and moved a step closer. "My papa says I should claim you for my partner at charades."

Myles took a step back. "Why is that?"

"He says you're a natural performer. Have you ever been on the stage?" Marva spoke above the noisy crowd, leaning closer.

"In a way," Myles hedged, shifting backward. "Have you?"

Marva chuckled in her throaty way. "I? Not unless you count school recitations. I play piano in church, but that's different. No one looks at me. Are you warm, Myles? Would you like to step outside for a while?" She stepped closer to make herself heard.

"No, no, I'm fine." Myles moved back and bumped into the wall. He cast a desperate glance around, only to spy Beulah across the room. She sipped lemonade from a cup, then laughed at a comment from her companion. Myles felt a pinch in his chest at the sight of Al's broad shoulders and smooth dark hair. So Beulah had come to the social with Al. The romance must have revived.

"Myles?" He heard someone repeating his name and struggled to focus on Marva's blue eyes.

"Myles, are you all right? You look pale all of a sudden."

"Maybe I do need fresh air." He walked to the door, wishing he could bolt. Across the porch and down the steps, between small clusters of talking, laughing people—fresh air at last. He drew a deep breath and lifted his gaze to the evening sky. A few pink stripes still outlined the horizon; stars multiplied above them.

"It's a lovely night, Myles. I'm glad you brought me to see the sunset." Marva spoke at his elbow, linking her arm through his. "Do you want to take a walk?"

Considering his options, he accepted. "Why not?" He started across the yard surrounding the building that served Longtree as both church and schoolhouse.

Marva trotted to keep up. "Slow down, Myles! We're not racing. Wouldn't you like to stroll away from other people where we can talk?"

"The games will start soon. Wouldn't want to miss them." Myles shortened his stride, but maintained a rapid gait.

Marva began to puff. "I had no idea you enjoyed games so much, Myles. Aren't we rather old for such things?"

"You never outgrow having fun. They're having a spelling competition tonight along with charades." Fun was the farthest thing from his mind at the moment. Surviving the evening without a broken heart would be challenge enough.

When they returned to the steps, Myles escorted Marva through the door. A large woman greeted her. "Marva, Darling, you look lovely tonight. I'm sure Myles thinks so!" Without waiting for a response, she rambled on. "I was just saying to Ruby that your recipe for corn fritters is the best I've ever tasted. You add bits of ham to the mix, right?"

While the women discussed cooking, Myles melted into the crowd. "Pardon me. Pardon," he repeated, trying not to be pushy. Arriving at the refreshment table, he reached for a glass of lemonade.

"Hello, Myles." His outstretched hand froze in place as he recognized the pink taffeta dress across the serving table. Slowly his gaze moved up a slender form to meet eyes like chips of black ice. Beulah held a ladle in one hand, a cup in the other. "Are you having a pleasant evening? Miss Obermeier looks particularly lovely tonight, flushed from the cool night air."

Myles wanted to return a snappy remark about Beulah's equally blooming complexion, but his mouth would not cooperate. Was it her beauty that immobilized him, or was it her chilly stare?

"Would you like two cups of lemonade?"

"One will do. Uh, do you need help? I mean, with serving?" He worked his way around the table until he stood at her side. Was this a good time to apologize for throwing her into the pond?

She studied his face with puzzled eyes. "No, but you could offer to fetch more lemonade. Mrs. Schoengard and my mother are mixing more at the parsonage. We spent half the day squeezing lemons. I never want to do that again. Caroline Schoengard, you know, the pastor's wife?" she added in answer to his blank look.

"Oh. Yes. Are you having a nice time?"

"It's all right. Far more people showed up than were expected. Poor Mrs. Schoengard was distraught until Mama offered to help. Will you get the lemonade for me? This bowl is nearly empty."

"Right away." He thought he heard Marva call his name as he stepped out the back door, but he pretended not to hear. What a joy this evening would be if he could spend it at Beulah's side! How he longed to partner her at games, to share casual conversation and develop a friendship, to have talk circulate town that Myles Trent was sparking Beulah Fairfield.

Violet met him at the parsonage door. "Why, Myles, how nice to see you!"

He doffed his hat. "Beulah sent me to help. Is the lemonade ready? Her bowl is empty."

"Wonderful! Caroline," Violet called back over her shoulder, "people are drinking the lemonade even without ice."

"I haven't heard any complaints," Myles said. "Lemonade is a treat. Just right to wash down the sandwiches and fried chicken."

"Hello, Myles." The pastor's wife appeared in the kitchen doorway, wiping her hands on a towel. "A Chicago friend of my husband shipped the lemons to us. Wasn't that kind? Far more than our family could use." A lock of blond hair clung to Caroline's forehead.

"You must get off your feet for awhile, Caroline," Violet fussed over her pregnant friend.

"I'm fine." Caroline ignored her and led Myles to the kitchen. "Thank you for the help, Myles. We were about to send for someone to carry this kettle."

Myles wrapped his arms beneath the kettle's handles and lifted. Lemonade sloshed against his chest. Violet gasped. "I knew we should have put it into smaller containers. I'm sorry, Myles. That thing is so heavy—"

"It's all right. If you'll open the door . . ." Myles walked through the house, across the dark churchyard, and up the church steps. Violet and Caroline called further thanks after him, but he was concentrating too hard to reply.

Beulah backed away from the serving table while Myles emptied his kettle into the cut glass punch bowl. Only a few drops trickled down the kettle's side to dampen the tablecloth. Several gray seeds swirled at the bottom of the bowl. "There." Myles set the kettle on the floor and brushed at his shirt. Already he felt sticky.

"You've spilled lemonade all down the front of you; but then, you've probably noticed," Beulah remarked.

"I couldn't help it. Did pretty well coming all that way with a full kettle."

Beulah picked up a napkin and rubbed at his spotted sleeve. "Yes, you did. Thank you, Myles." Her gaze moved past him. "Marva is looking for you."

He cast a hunted glance over one shoulder. "Guess I'd better run. If she asks, tell her I got covered in lemonade and decided to go home."

"You mean, for good?" Beulah's eyes were no longer icy. Her hand touched his forearm. What was it about her mouth that made him think of kissing every time she spoke to him? "Won't you come back?"

Myles placed his other hand over hers and squeezed. "By the time I came back, the party would be about over. It's all right. I'm no socialite anyway. Never have been."

Someone asked for a cup of lemonade. Beulah poured it with shaking hands while Myles admired the downy curve of her neck. The pastor stood up to announce the start of the spelling match, and the milling crowd began to shuffle.

"If you leave, how will Marva get home?" Beulah asked beneath the buzz of conversation. He bent to listen, and her breath tickled his ear. His hand cupped her elbow. Did he imagine it, or did she lean toward him?

"The same way she came, I guess. Why?"

Beulah bit her lip, studying his face. Myles swallowed hard. Suddenly she bent over the table to wipe up a spill. Her voice quivered. "People never will learn to clean up after themselves. Thank you for your help tonight."

"My pleasure. And Beulah . . ." His courage expired.

"Yes?" She looked up for an instant, then dropped her gaze and licked her lips.

"Miss Beulah, may I have some lemonade?" Across the table, a little girl smiled up at Beulah, revealing a wide gap between her teeth.

"Certainly! Looks like you've lost another tooth, Fern. Are you competing in the spelling bee tonight?"

"Of course, Miss Beulah. You sure do look pretty. Wish I could put my hair up."

"It won't be too many years until you can. And thank you."

Beulah filled another cup. "You were saying, Myles?" She took hold of his wrist and pulled his hand away from his stomach. He hadn't even realized he was rubbing it again.

Heat rushed into his face. "Nothing important. I'll see you around." He didn't want to sound like an echo of little Fern. Beulah wasn't just pretty, she was beautiful tonight with her gleaming knot of dark hair, satin skin, full red lips, and those eyes that took his breath away . . . but he had no idea how to tell her so without sounding foolish.

She faced him. "Oh. Well, good night." Her lips puckered, suspiciously resembling a pout. A fire kindled in Myles's belly, and his hands closed into fists. The intent to drag her outside and bare his soul, come what may, began to form in his mind.

"Ready for the spelling bee, Beulah?" Al asked, sliding behind the table to join them. "Hey, good to see you here, Myles! I saw Marva a minute ago. Better start making your move; you know, like we talked about." He gave Myles a wink and an elbow to the ribs.

"Oh. Yeah." Myles said.

"Myles is just leaving," Beulah said in a voice like ice cracking. She linked arms with Al. "I've been looking forward to this all day," she cooed, gazing up with limpid eyes.

Al blinked in surprise, then grinned. "Me, too!"

Myles stared, his fists tightening.

"Don't stand there like a stone statue, Myles; go find Marva," Al advised. "You and I have the prettiest gals in town."

Myles skulked out the back door, his heart dragging in the dust. He vaulted to his mare's back and wheeled her toward the street.

"Leaving already, Myles?"

"Sheriff Boz? What are you doing out here?" He reined Cholla to a halt. She champed her bit and pawed at the gravel road.

"Patrolling the town. It's my job."

"Miss Amelia turned you down," he guessed. "I saw her with that New York man tonight."

Boz hooked his thumbs in his sagging gun belt. "Marva turn you down?"

"I've never asked her anything," he grumbled. "Better luck next time, Boz."

"Nothing to do with luck. I been praying for a good wife, and Amelia's the one God showed me." He rubbed his chin. "It'll just take time to convince her."

∼❧

"But, Beulah, you promised to be my partner!"

"I told you, I've got a headache. Ask Eunice; she's good at charades." Beulah slumped into a chair behind the serving table and rubbed her temples. "You already won the spelling competition. Isn't that enough?"

Al propped big fists on his hips. "How can a headache come on that fast?"

She shot him a sour look. "You expect me to explain a headache? It's all this noise, and I can hardly breathe."

He folded his arms across his chest and stared down at her. "I'd be happy to take you outside. Beulah, the games won't be any fun if you don't play. I'll sit with you until you feel better."

"No! Please leave me alone. I think I'll go over to the parsonage and ask Mrs. Schoengard if I can lie down."

Al helped her to her feet. "I'll walk you there."

He was so considerate that Beulah could not be as uncivil as she felt. As they passed the line of tethered horses and buggies, she looked for Myles's spotted mare. Cholla was gone. "Does Myles really plan to court Marva?" The question could not be restrained.

"I guess so. I . . ." Al gave her a sideward glance. "Why?"

"I wondered why he left so abruptly right after you advised him to 'make his move.'"

One side of Al's mouth twitched. "No matter what the man says, I think he's afraid of women. He's all right with girls like you and Eunice, but a real woman scares him speechless. Maybe I'll give him more advice and see if I can help."

Beulah reared back. "Albert Moore, I'm eighteen now, and I'll have you know that I'm just as much a woman as Marva Obermeier is!"

"Don't you think I know you're a woman? Beulah, that's what I've been trying to talk with you about these past few weeks, but you'll never give me a chance." On the parsonage steps, Al pulled her to a halt and gripped her shoulders.

Beulah flung his hands off. "That was a cruel thing to say, Al," she raged. "Myles doesn't see me as a little girl, even if you do! Leave me alone. I don't want to talk to you tonight."

The door swung open. Violet appeared, pulling on her gloves. "Is the party over? I was just heading that way—Beulah?" She stepped back as Beulah rushed into the house, gripping her head between her hands.

6

Casting all your care upon him; for he careth for you.
1 Peter 5:7

eulah was in her kitchen garden picking yet another batch of green beans for supper when Al caught up with her late the following afternoon. "I did it." He slapped a pair of leather gloves against his thigh.

"Did what?" Beulah asked coldly, adding two more beans to her basket.

"I finally told Cousin Buck about my mother's letter and my plan to go to California. He's disappointed in me for 'running out on my responsibilities,' as he phrases it. But, Beulah, when *will* be a good time to go back? My parents will die of old age before it's ever a convenient time."

"It is a difficult situation for you," Beulah agreed, trying to forget her grudge and be courteous. "I imagine Papa will calm down and begin to see your side of the situation. Presently he is thinking only of the work involved for him in keeping two farms running. Do you think you might sell off stock?"

"Our Jerseys? Never! We've worked years to build up our herd. Now that we have a silo for storing feed, we can keep our cows producing milk over the winter. This is not the time to cut back."

"But if there is no one to milk the herd, I can't see—"

"Myles will be here to milk them. Now that the creamery has opened, our farms should start pulling a profit instead of barely keeping us out of debt."

"Then this is poor timing for you to leave your farm, Al. It sounds to me as if you need to make serious choices about which is more important to you, your farm or seeing your parents."

"Nonsense," Al said. "After we bring in the crops, one man can keep the farm going over the winter. There's no reason Myles can't keep things rolling until my return. He should be pleased to have a steady job. During the past few winters he's had to cut ice blocks on the lakes or work up north in the logging towns to support himself."

Beulah turned back to her beans. "Papa Obie says Myles has worked hard for three summers and has little to show for it. Papa thinks you and he ought to grant Myles some land to start up his own farm, or at least give him a partnership. I heard him talking about it with Mama." There was a buoyant feeling in her chest when she spoke Myles's name.

A line appeared between Al's thick brows. "I don't like that partnership idea. Myles is a good fellow, hardworking and honest, but the Bible says we should not be unequally yoked together with unbelievers."

"Myles is not a believer?" Her voice was dull, giving no evidence that an ice pick stabbed at her heart.

Al lifted a significant brow. "Buck hopes that in time God will reach Myles's heart, but I haven't seen any change." He reached over to pick himself a ripe tomato. "If Myles wants land of his own, he should homestead somewhere. There is plenty of land for the taking in this country if a man has the ambition to find it for himself. Why should I give him any of mine?"

"I thought you wanted him to stay here and milk your cows. He can hardly homestead for himself while he's doing your work." *Myles cannot leave, not ever!*

"True," Al admitted. "But he has plenty of time; he's not old." He tossed and caught the tomato with one hand.

"You're younger than Myles," Beulah observed.

"Why are you so interested in Myles Trent?" The tomato slipped from his hand and smashed into the dirt. "First last night, and now today."

"What are you talking about?" Her cheeks flamed, but perhaps Al would not see. "I simply think your attitude is selfish. Kindly stop destroying my produce."

For a moment she heard only puffing noises as Al struggled to restrain hasty words. When he spoke again, his voice was humble. "I'm sorry I said that about Myles; he's a good fellow. Beulah, please . . . I didn't come here to argue. I need to talk with you. It's important."

"Al, I've got to go make supper; I've taken far too long picking these beans. Mama must be wondering if I ever plan to come back inside." She moved along the row of vegetables toward the house.

His mouth dropped open. "But, Beulah—" He started trotting along the outside edge of the garden to intercept her. "Honey, I tried to talk with you last night and you put me off. We can't go on like this! I've got something important to ask. Don't you want to hear?"

"Some other time, Al. I'll see you later." With an insincere smile, she darted up the steps.

Staring after her openmouthed, Al suddenly flung his hat to the ground and let out a roar. "That cuts it! I'm not even sure I want to marry you anymore, you . . . you . . . *woman!*"

❧

"So when are you getting married?" Eunice asked, plopping down on Beulah's bed.

"What?" Beulah stopped brushing her hair and stared at her sister.

"Didn't Al ask you to marry him?"

"Whatever gave you that idea? Do you want me to marry Al?"

"If you marry him, he can't go away." Eunice wrapped her arms around her knees and flung her head forward. Her brown hair, several shades lighter than Beulah's, draped over her knees and arms, hiding her face.

Beulah began to braid her hair. "I don't want to marry Al, Eunice." Red-rimmed eyes gazed from the mirror. Lack of sleep was catching up with her.

The girl's head popped up. She stared at Beulah between wavy locks. "That's silly. Everyone knows you're in love with Al. He's been courting you almost since we arrived in Wisconsin."

"I'm not in love with Al, and I don't want him to court me."

Eunice tossed her hair back. Anger sparked in her ice-blue eyes. "You're afraid to go to California, aren't you? I wouldn't be afraid. I'd go anywhere with Al."

"Then you marry him." Beulah smacked her brush down on the dressing table and rose. Her nightdress fluttered around her legs as she paced across the room. "I don't want to marry Al whether he goes or stays, Eunice. He is not the man I love." She rubbed her hands up and down her bare arms. What had happened to her gentle little sister? What had happened to the entire world? Everything seemed strange and mixed-up.

"Then who is? I can't imagine anyone nicer or handsomer than Al. You haven't got a heart, Beulah. I don't think you'll ever get married."

Beulah swallowed the lump in her throat. "I would rather be an old maid than marry a man I don't love. What has gotten into you, Eunice? This isn't like you."

Biting her lips, Eunice sprang from the bed and rushed out of the room. Beulah heard the girl's feet thumping along the hallway.

❧

Beulah lay in bed, staring toward the ceiling. *It's not as if I've never bickered with Eunice before, but this fight was different. What is wrong with me? Why do I hurt so much inside?*

There was a quiet knock at the door. "Come in."

Light streamed from the candlestick in Violet's hand as she peeked into the room. "I've just come from Eunice's room, and she told me of your quarrel. Beulah, do you need to talk?"

Beulah nodded, and a shuddering sob escaped. Rolling over, she buried her face in her pillow and cried out her misery. Warm hands rubbed her shoulders and stroked her hair.

At last Beulah turned back, mopping her face with a handkerchief. "Oh, Mama, I'm so unhappy."

"I know. Papa and I have been concerned about you."

"I don't know what to do."

"Tell me."

Beulah blew her nose and propped up on one elbow. She thought for a moment. "I don't know where to begin."

"Why not begin with what hurts?"

Beulah bit her lip. "I'm in love, Mama . . . and oh, it hurts so much! He sees me as just a girl—at least, Al says he does. And I think he doesn't respect me anymore because I touched him too much. And Al says he isn't a believer—but I can't believe he could be so nice and good if he isn't."

Violet frowned. "That cannot be true. Al has always proclaimed his faith in Christ, and we have no reason to doubt him."

"Yes, but he says Myles isn't. Mama, do you think he really wants to marry Miss Obermeier?"

Her mother blinked. "Beulah, do you mean to say you're in love with . . . Myles Trent?"

Beulah nodded.

"Oh, my!" Violet's shoulders drooped. "I had no idea. Papa told me . . ."

"Told you what? Don't you like Myles, Mama?"

"Of course I like him. He's a good man. Obie thinks highly of him. It's just that . . ." She couldn't seem to put her thoughts into words.

"He's only about twenty-five, and I'm eighteen now. Oh, Mama, just looking at him sets my soul on fire! I know he isn't handsome like Al, but he's so . . . so . . ."

Violet sighed. "I understand. He has the same masculine appeal as your papa. It's something about these cowboys, I guess. What did you mean by 'touched him too much,' Beulah?" Her voice sharpened.

Beulah studied her wadded handkerchief and confessed the waterfall story. "He didn't kiss me or anything, Mama, but I wanted him to." Her eyes closed. "Mama, he's so strong and gentle! It was the most wondrous moment of my life . . . and the worst. I can't help thinking about him all the time and wishing he would hold me again."

Violet brushed a hand across her eyes. "Oh, dear. I had no idea . . . What kind of mother am I to let this go on under my nose?" Her hand dropped to her lap and her shoulders squared. "Darling, you know that Myles has told your papa little about his past. It's not that we don't like him, but I fear he may be hiding from the law—you know, under a false name."

Beulah bolted upright. "Mama, how can you say such a thing? Myles has always been honest. Papa and Al trust him. And he is so polite. I know he has an air about him—sort of mysterious and danger-ous, I guess—but that doesn't mean he is a criminal!"

The line between Violet's brows deepened. "I don't mean to ac-cuse him, Dearest, but we cannot be too careful with our daughters. You are a beautiful young woman, and it sounds to me as if you tempted Myles almost beyond his strength to resist. If he does intend to marry Marva—which would perhaps be best for all concerned—you need to leave him alone."

"Mama, how can you say it would be best for him to marry Marva? I told you that I love him!" Beulah caught her breath on a sob.

Violet stood up and began to pace across the room. "But Beulah, what about Al? Eunice tells me that you don't want to marry him, but, Darling, he is steady and dependable—he's your friend, and he loves you. I can't help thinking . . . Well, to be perfectly candid, my dear, you have a tendency to be contrary. Are you certain you're not decid-ing against Al simply because everyone expects you to marry him?"

Beulah wrapped her arms around her knees and glowered. "Mama, Al is my friend, but he is more like an irritating brother than a lover. When we first met he treated me like fine china; then he got used to me and started acting like himself, and, honestly, Mama, he is so immature and annoying! I can think of few prospects worse than facing Al across the breakfast table every morning for the rest of my life."

Violet stared, shaking her head. "Oh, dear," she repeated. "I must talk with Obie. We may have to let Myles go . . . and that would be difficult, what with Al leaving for California soon. How could we find a replacement?"

Beulah scrambled to her knees, clasped her hands, and begged. "Mama, please don't send him away! He has done nothing wrong—it was entirely my fault!" She thumped a fist into her quilt. "And why shouldn't I marry him if I love him? Even if he sinned in the past, he is an honest man now, and he would be a good husband to me."

Violet seemed to wilt. "Beulah, how can you even consider marry-ing a man who does not love and serve God? I knew you had strayed from the Lord these past few years, but I thought you understood how vital shared faith is to a marriage."

Beulah sat back on her heels and hung her head. "You won't even give Myles a chance, will you, Mama? How can you be so sure he isn't a believer? He doesn't drink or swear or gamble, and there is goodness in his eyes." Resting her head upon her knees, she began to cry again.

Violet sat down and stroked the girl's long braid. "Beulah, I do want to give Myles a chance—he is a fine young man, and I can see why you admire him. I will ask your papa to talk with him about his faith and about his intentions toward you. But in the meantime, I think it would be best if you spent more time with your girlfriends and stayed away from Myles Trent. Not that we will ban him from the house, but . . ."

"Do you mean I have to hide if I see him coming?"

"I simply don't want you to seek him out, Dearest. If he approaches you, be gracious, of course, as I have taught you. Darling, I will be praying for wisdom and guidance—for your papa and me as well as for you."

She bent to kiss Beulah's damp cheek.

7

Let nothing be done through strife or vainglory;
but in lowliness of mind let each esteem other
better than themselves.
Philippians 2:3

"Thank you for coming, Mrs. Watson. And thank you for bringing Beulah. Maybe soon we'll be working on her wedding quilt." Sybil Oakley waved good-bye from her front porch as Violet clucked her gray mare into a quick trot.

Beulah waved to her friend until trees hid the girl from sight. "It's hard to believe Sybil is getting married." Beulah sighed.

"She has grown up quickly this past year. You know, many women would have flown into a temper if you'd pointed out flaws in their quilts. Sybil accepted your criticism graciously."

Beulah fanned herself. "I wasn't trying to be unkind."

"Neither were you trying to be kind. Darling, you must learn to think before you speak, or you'll chase away all your friends. You're gifted in many ways: beauty, talent, and intelligence. You don't need to point out other people's faults to make yourself look better."

Beulah was silent. The mare's hoofs clopped along the road, sloshing in occasional puddles. Maple and birch trees were beginning to show patches of yellow and red.

"I'm sorry, Mama. I'll apologize to Sybil next time I see her." Her voice was quiet.

"I've noticed that Al doesn't talk to you when he comes over. Did you quarrel with him, too?"

Beulah braced herself for a pothole in the road. "Not exactly. I think he's mad because I won't let him talk mushy to me. He tries to get romantic, and it makes me uncomfortable. He is my friend, and that's it."

"Have you told him how you feel?"

She wrinkled her nose. "No, but if he doesn't catch on by now, he's dumber than I think."

"Don't be unkind," Violet said. "You haven't told him about your infatuation with Myles, have you?"

"Mama, of course not! It's none of his business—and besides, I don't want to make him mad at Myles. I haven't seen Myles since the church social." Beulah felt glum.

"I did hear that he had dinner with the Obermeiers the other night. I hope he settles down with Marva. She needs a good man to love and spoil."

Beulah closed her eyes against a stab of jealousy.

↬

Singing to herself, Beulah wiped off the table. There was a quiet knock at the open kitchen door behind her. "Samuel is outside. He can play until dark," she called.

"Beulah?"

She spun around, putting a sudsy hand to her heart. "Myles?" It came out in a squeak. "I—I thought you were one of Sam's friends come to play. Papa Obie and Mama are at Cyrus Thwaite's house this evening, and Eunice is at a friend's house. It's just the boys and me at home," she babbled. "And the baby is asleep. I haven't seen you in weeks! Did you need to see my papa?"

Behind him, the sky was pink and filmy gray. A bat darted above the fruit trees, and a fox yapped in the forest. "No. I came to see you. I brought this." He held out a book. "Found it in Mo's pasture this morning. You dropped it that day, didn't you?"

That day—only the most important day of Beulah's life. Feeling conscious of her bare feet and loose braid, Beulah wiped her hands on her apron and reached for the book. "Thank you." It smelled warm, like sunshine and wildflowers. The cover was warped and the pages looked wavy.

"It got wet."

"I can still read it." She looked up.

What would Mama do? Shoulders back. Head high. Cool, even tones. Gracious and hospitable. "Will you come in for coffee and cookies?"

His boots shifted on the floorboards. "First I need to . . . to apologize for throwing you in the creek. That's been weighing on my mind. You were right to be angry—my behavior was inexcusable."

Beulah watched his right hand rub circles on his flat stomach. Why did he always do that? It made her want to touch him. *I can't love a man who doesn't serve God. I can't! Gracious and hospitable, that's all.*

"I forgive you. It was my fault, too. I threw water at you first."

"No hard feelings?"

She glanced up. The entreating look in his eyes reminded her of Samuel. "Would I ask a man to carry lemonade for me if I held a grudge against him?"

Myles smiled. "Guess not. Or maybe you knew I'd spill it all over myself and wanted to get back some of your own."

Beulah opened her mouth to protest, but Myles laughed. "I'm teasing. You're easy to provoke."

Warmth filled Beulah's heart and her cheeks. "So they say. I'm trying to improve. I wish you would smile and laugh more often. Your laugh makes me want to laugh. Now will you come in for coffee and cookies?"

His eyes twinkled. "Thank you. I will."

She lowered her chin and one brow. "What's so funny?"

"You. I'm glad you're back to normal. Those elegant manners make me nervous."

Beulah laughed outright. Forgetting her resolve to be aloof, she grabbed him by a shirt button and dragged him into the kitchen. Planting a hand on his chest, she shoved him into a chair. "Sit. Stay."

He seized her wrist in a lightning motion. "Bossy woman. If you request, I am your humble servant. If you order . . ." He shook his head. "Another dunk in the creek might be imminent."

"You use awfully big words for a hired hand." Beulah tugged at her arm. "Is that a threat?"

"A warning."

"I guess your apology wasn't genuine." She pouted, thinking how nice it would be to slip into his lap. He smelled of soap and hair oil. "Don't you want to be friends?"

Pressure on her arm brought her closer. "Is that what you want from me?" The low question set her heart hammering. His face was mere inches from hers. Beulah licked her lips.

Scrabbling claws skidded across the floorboards; then Watchful shoved her face and upper body between Beulah and Myles. Panting and wagging, the dog pawed at Myles's chest.

He released Beulah to protect his skin from Watchful's claws. "Down, Girl. I'm glad to see you, too." He forced the dog to the floor, then thumped her sides affectionately. Glancing toward the door, he said, "Hello, Sam."

Samuel stamped his boots on the porch, tossed his hat on a hook, and flopped into a chair. "Howdy, Myles. You come for cookies?"

"Just trying to sweet-talk your sister into giving me some. See if you can influence her."

Beulah propped her fists on her hips. "Not necessary. Samuel, you wash your hands first and bring in the milk, please." She moved to the stove and poured two cups of coffee.

The boy made a face at her back but obeyed.

"Bossy, isn't she?" Myles observed.

"You said it!" Samuel pumped water over his soapy hands, then ran outside to the springhouse.

Beulah's spine stiffened. She set a steaming cup in front of Myles. "Sugar? Milk?"

"Black is fine."

She felt his gaze while she took cookies from the crock and arranged them on a plate. "I'm not bossy," she hissed.

"Do you prefer 'imperious'?" His eyes crinkled at the corners. "You're rewarding to tease, and you somehow manage to be pretty when you're cross. Unfair to the male of the species, since you seem to be cross much of the time. I have observed, however, that your smile is to your frown what a clear sunrise is to a misty morning. Each wields its charm, yet one is far more appealing than the other."

Confounded by this speech, Beulah settled across from him. She was pondering an answer when Samuel clattered up the steps, carrying the milk. "Save some for me," he protested, seeing Myles pop an entire cookie into his mouth.

Still chewing, Myles wrapped his forearms around the plate of cookies and gave Samuel a provoking smile. "Mine."

Samuel pitched into him. Myles caught the boy's arms and held him off easily, but Samuel was a determined opponent. Beulah watched helplessly as they wrestled at the table. She rescued Myles's coffee just in time. "Boys, behave yourselves!"

The chair tipped over, and Myles landed on the floor, laughing. "Truce," he gasped. "I'll share."

Samuel was equally breathless and merry. "I beat you," he claimed. He thumped Myles in the stomach, and the man's knees came up with a jerk.

"Samuel! Don't be mean!" Beulah jumped to her feet. "Are you all right, Myles?"

Samuel gave her a scornful glare. "Don't be silly. I couldn't hurt him."

Myles sat up, resting an arm on his upended chair. "Aw, let her protect me if she wants to. I like it." Rubbing his belly, he smiled up at Beulah, and she felt her face grow warm.

Myles and Samuel talked baseball and fishing while they finished off the cookies. Sipping her coffee, Beulah listened, watching their animated faces and smiling at their quips and gibes.

"So where's Al?" Samuel looked at Beulah, then at Myles.

Beulah collected the empty dishes and carried them to the sink. Leaning back in the chair with an ankle resting on his knee, Myles stroked his beard. "Reckon he's at home."

"Why didn't he come with you?"

"He didn't know I was coming."

"He was here last night," Samuel said. "Eunice and I played marbles with him. Do you want to come play catch with me tomorrow?"

"Just might do that. Better enjoy free time while we have it. Harvest starts in a few days, and from then on, we work like slaves." Myles rose and stretched his arms. "Guess I'd better get on back."

"Bye, Myles." Samuel left the room without ceremony.

Taking his hat from the table, Myles twisted it between his hands.

"Thank you for the cookies and the good company, Beulah. Can't remember when I've had a nicer evening."

"I can't either." Beulah clasped her hands behind her. "I'm glad you came over." She backed away, giving him room to pass.

His eyes searched her face. "So am I." He clapped on his hat and disappeared into the night.

8

He healeth the broken in heart,
and bindeth up their wounds.
Psalm 147:3

apid footfalls approached the main barn from outside. "Myles? Al? Is anyone here?" Beulah called.

"I'm here," Myles answered. He set aside the broken stall door and rose, brushing wood shavings from his hands. "Al is out. Do you need him?"

Beulah stopped in the barn doorway, eyes wide, chest heaving. "I . . . well . . ." She hopped from one foot to the other, her gaze shifting about the barn. "Oh, what can it hurt? I need your help! Please come quickly, Myles."

"Are you ill? Hurt? Come, sit down here." He indicated the bench.

"No, no, I need help," she panted. "I found a cat caught by a fish-hook down near the beaver dam. Do you have something I can use to cut it loose?"

A cat? Myles put his hammer into his neat toolbox and selected a pair of pliers. After plucking his hat from a hook on the barn wall, he pulled it low over his forehead. "Lead on."

"I hope I can find the cat again." Beulah was beginning to catch her breath. Her bound braid hung cockeyed on the side of her head; her sunbonnet lay upon her shoulders.

"We'll find it." He followed her outside into blinding sunlight.

She pulled her sunbonnet back into place and retied the strings. "Do you like cats? I've never been fond of them, but this one purred when I touched it. Even if it hissed at me, I still couldn't leave it to die. Could you?"

"Of course not." Myles frowned, seized by a premonition.

When they entered the forest Beulah took the lead. Myles followed her slim form through the trees, keeping close behind her. He heard the cat wailing before they crossed the dam.

"Lucky you heard her instead of some hungry animal." Myles pulled aside branches. Sure enough, there was a familiar round face with the white blotch on the nose. Sorrow and horror formed a lump in his throat. "Hello, Girl. How long have you been here?" He snipped away a tangle of line until only a short piece dangled from the cat's mouth. Slipping one hand beneath her, he lifted Pushy free of the brush and cradled her in his arms. That rumbling purr sounded again, and the cat closed her golden eyes. Myles rubbed behind her ear with one finger, and she pushed her head into his chest. Dried blood caked the white bib beneath the cat's swollen chin. She made a little chirruping noise, her usual greeting.

He felt movement within her body, and the lump in his throat grew, making it difficult to speak. "I think she's expecting kittens."

"Really?" Beulah breathed out the word. "Can you help her, Myles?" She stroked the cat's side, then let her hand rest on Myles's arm.

"I'll try. Let's take her home."

Back in the barn's tack room, he dug with one hand through a box of medical supplies until he found a bottle of ointment. "Please find a blanket to wrap her in."

Beulah returned empty-handed. "The only blankets I can find are stiff with horse sweat and covered in hair. Will my apron do?" she asked, untying it.

He wrapped the cat in Beulah's calico apron, securing its legs against its body so that it could neither scratch nor squirm. Pushy let out a protesting howl, but relaxed and began to purr when he rubbed her head.

Beulah looked amazed. "This is the friendliest cat I have ever seen!"

Myles gave her a quick smile. "She's a special one. She won't stay wrapped up long, so we've got to work quickly. You hold her head up and her body down while I cut off the end of the hook."

Beulah did as she was told and watched him work. The cat struggled when Myles had to dig for the hook's barb, which protruded beneath her chin. Then *snip* and the barb fell upon Beulah's apron.

"Now we must hold her mouth open so I can slip out the rest of the hook." Myles demonstrated how he wanted Beulah to hold the cat under her arm. Once she had the cat in the right position, he pried its mouth open and struggled to grip the hook with the pliers. Pushy squirmed, gagged, and growled. Myles heard claws shredding Beulah's apron. His hat landed upside down on the floor.

"Got it." Myles held aloft the bit of wire and string. "Better get cotton over that wound before . . ."

Too late. Blood and pus oozed from the wound and dripped upon Beulah's lap. Myles snatched a cotton pad from the worktable and pressed it against the cat's chin. "Sorry about that."

Beulah said nothing. Her eyes were closed.

"Beulah? You . . . uh, might want to clean your dress there." He dropped cotton wool on the spot.

"I—I'm not very good around blood," she whispered.

Myles snatched the cat from her lap and pushed Beulah's head down toward her knees. "Lower your head until the faintness passes."

The apron dropped to the floor. Pushy struggled, trying to right herself. Her claws raked across his chest. "Yeow!" Myles tucked her under his arm, and she relaxed. "Stupid cat."

"Do you think she will live?" Beulah's voice was muffled.

"I hope so. Although I'm sorry about your dress, it's a good thing all that mess came out of her jaw. I'll put ointment on her face and hope her body can heal what we can't help."

"I've been praying for her." Beulah lifted her head. Her face had regained color. She took the jar of ointment and removed the lid.

"Have you? Good."

"Do you believe in God, Myles?" Beulah held out the jar.

"I believe there is a God."

She smiled. "I thought you must. Al said you weren't a believer."

He found it hard to meet her gaze. "Al can't be blamed for that. I guess I've been fighting God. Painful things happened in my past, and I blamed Him." Myles dipped a finger into the ointment. "I've had a lot of talks with Buck—Obie—about God."

"I know who you mean. All of Papa's old friends call him Buck—it's his middle name. So you don't blame God now?"

Myles evaded the question. "It isn't logical to blame God for the evil in the world."

"Feelings are seldom logical," Beulah said.

His hands paused. "True. Which is why it's dangerous to live by one's feelings." Myles held Pushy's head still as he smoothed ointment over her chin. She resumed her cheery purr.

"Pushy here must wonder why I am hurting her, yet she trusts me. This simple cat has greater faith than I do." There was a catch in his voice.

"She is your cat, Myles?"

"She lives in our barn. I named her Pushy because she finds ways to get me to pet her and feed her. I realize now that I hadn't seen her around for days, yet I didn't think to search for her." He fixed his eyes upon Pushy, trying to hide his face from Beulah. She would think he was foolish to become emotional over a cat. Pushy closed her eyes and savored his gentle rubbing.

So lightly that he scarcely felt it, Beulah skimmed his hair with her fingers. "You can't be everywhere and think of everything the way God does, Myles. I'm sure Pushy forgives you. You didn't intend to let her down. It was a human mistake."

"We humans make a lot of mistakes." Bitterness laced his voice.

"My mother says that's why we need to be patient with each other." She sighed. "People can be so annoying, and my first reaction is to say something nasty. My mother says it's because I'm proud and think myself better than other people."

Myles lifted his head until he could feel Beulah's touch. "Do you?"

"Think myself better? Sometimes I do," she said so softly he could hardly hear. Her fingers threaded through his hair. "Deep inside I know I'm not better, though. I don't like being mean."

Her touch made it difficult to concentrate. Myles closed his eyes. "You're being nice to me right now. My grandmother used to rub my head like this."

"You look as if you might start purring." Beulah laughed.

Hearing laughter in her voice, he smiled. "P-d-d-r-r-r. I can't do it like Pushy does."

Pushy climbed from his arms into Beulah's lap, tucked in her paws, and settled down to purr. The two humans paid her no attention. Myles shifted his weight and sat close to Beulah's feet. She put both hands to work, rubbing his temples and the nape of his neck. "I've got chills down my spine, this feels so good," he said, letting his head loll against her hands.

"Your hair ranges in shade from auburn to sandy blond."

"Yeah, but it's still red hair."

"Did you used to get teased about it?"

"My nickname was 'Red.'"

"The clown called you that, I remember."

"Antonio and everyone else at the circus. Wish I had dark hair and skin that didn't freckle."

"Like mine?"

"Yours or Al's."

"I used to get teased about my big teeth and about being skinny." She spoke quietly. "I've never told that to anyone but my mother before."

"It hurts, being teased." He reached back and patted her hand.

After massaging his shoulders for a few minutes, she touched the left side of his chest. "Is this your blood or Pushy's?"

Myles looked down, surprised to see a spot of red on his tan shirt. "Mine, I think. She scratched me."

"You had better put ointment on it," Beulah advised. She held out the jar.

Myles unbuttoned three shirt buttons, then his undervest and glanced inside. "It's nothing." He covered it up.

"Let me see."

"Yes, Mother." Feeling sheepish, he exposed the triple scratch, which was reddened and puffy. "I thought you couldn't bear the sight of blood."

"Turn this way." Beulah leaned over the sleeping cat and wiped a fingerful of ointment into the wound until his chest hair lay smeared and flattened across the scratches. "I've never done this before." She pursed her lips in concentration. Myles tried to swallow, but his mouth was too dry.

She looked up and smiled. "There, that should feel better soon."

The smile faded. "Did I hurt you? I tried to be gentle. Those scratches are deep."

"Uh . . . Pushy needs a drink." His voice sounded like gravel in a bucket. "I'll fetch milk from the springhouse." Myles scrambled to his feet and rushed from the barn, shaking his head to clear it. The temptation to haul Beulah into his lap and kiss her had nearly overcome his self-control.

He lifted the bottle of milk from its cold storage in the little manmade pool. Conflicting thoughts raced through his mind.

She doesn't know. She thinks I'm a Christian man like Buck and Al. If she knew me, really knew me, would she trust me, touch me with her dear hands? Myles shook his head, teeth bared in a grimace. *Antonio said I'm poison—full of bitterness and hatred. I would destroy her, the one I love. God, help me! I don't know what to do!*

He rubbed his face with a trembling hand. *Yes, I do know what I should do. If I were an honorable man, I would tell her to leave me alone, tell her to marry Al and be happy.*

When he returned to the barn, Beulah still sat on the bench with Pushy in her lap. The girl's eyes were enormous in her dirty face, and she was chewing on her lower lip. She opened her mouth, but Myles spoke first. "Sorry I took so long. Let's see if Pushy can drink this."

"She's asleep."

"I imagine she'll wake when she smells the milk. Set her on the floor here." He filled the chipped saucer.

Myles was right. Pushy was desperate for the drink, yet she could not lap with her swollen tongue. She sucked up the milk, making pained little cries all the while.

"I thought you were angry with me when you rushed outside," Beulah said.

"Why would I be angry?" Myles kept his eyes upon the cat.

"I shouldn't have touched you like that; you won't respect me anymore."

He let out an incredulous little huff, smiling without real humor. "Won't respect you? That's unlikely." He stared at a pitchfork, unwilling to grant her access to his chaotic thoughts. *Do you know what your touch does to me? Do you dream about me the way I dream about you?*

Could you be content, married to a wretched, redheaded hired man? What would you think if you knew my past?

"Does your stomach hurt?"

Myles snatched his hand from his belly.

"Eunice says you must be hungry a lot because you rub your belly so much."

He felt warm. "Nervous habit."

After several saucers of milk, Pushy made an effort to groom. As soon as she lifted her paw to her mouth she remembered the impossibility of using her tongue, but she wiped the paw over her ear anyway.

"Do you think her kittens will live?"

"I felt one moving while I held her. Unless she eats, she will not have milk enough for them." Squatting, Myles rubbed the back of the cat's neck with one finger, and the purr began to rumble. "I'll chop some meat for her tonight. It will have to be soft and wet. I'll keep her in my room until she is well. Poor Pushy. I think she has wanted to be my pet all this time, but I was too busy to notice how special she is."

"You *are* too busy. I hardly ever see you. I wish you would come by for coffee again some evening. My parents wouldn't mind." Beulah rose and shook out her rumpled apron. "I think even I would enjoy having a cat like this one. She's special."

Rising, Myles watched her fold the stained garment. She looked smaller without that voluminous apron. Her simple calico gown complemented her pretty figure. The sunbonnet hung down her back.

The ache in his soul was more than he could endure. *I'm not an honorable man. Al can't have her! I want Beulah for my wife. Whatever it takes, God. Whatever it takes.*

"Would you like to own Pushy?"

"I'm sure she will be happiest here with you." Beulah smiled. "I don't think my mother would want a cat. We already have one animal in the house, and that is enough. I had better be going home now. No one knows where I am. Take care of Pushy, Myles . . . and thank you for coming to her rescue. You may think I'm bossy, but I think you're wonderful!" Rising on tiptoe, she kissed his face above his beard.

He slipped his arms around that slim waist and pulled her close.

Her face rested within the open vee of his shirt; her breath heated his skin.

"Why did you do that?" Myles asked gruffly, his cheek pressed against her head.

"I saw my mother kiss Papa Obie that way not long after we met him." She sounded defensive. "She told me she did it to demonstrate gratitude for his kindness."

"No wonder Buck is besotted with your mother." Eyes closed tight, he spoke into her hair.

"I was trying to show affection." Beulah's arms wriggled free and slid around his waist. "Now I understand why Mama likes it when Papa holds her. It's nice."

When her hands pressed against his back, he released her and stepped away. "Come. I will walk with you as far as the dam."

Beulah looked shaken. Myles could think of nothing to say, so they walked in silence.

"Did I shock you?" she asked meekly.

"No."

Beulah had been walking ahead of him on the narrow path, but now she stopped to face him. "I wish I knew what you were thinking. Sometimes I feel as if you are laughing at me on the inside. I must seem young and naive to you."

"Believe me, I'm not laughing," he said. "Do I seem old and dried up to you?"

"Of course not, but you never seem happy. Even when you smile and laugh, there is sadness in your eyes." She tipped her head to one side and searched his face. "Do you ever wish you could talk with someone about . . . about things? I don't think I really know you, Myles. You're like a carrot—most of you is underground."

His lips twitched at her choice of analogy. Fear of overwhelming her prevented him from revealing even a fraction of his desire to be known and loved. "I'll let you know when the carrot is ready for harvest."

"Now I know you're laughing at me!" Dark eyes accusing yet twinkling, she gave him a little shove and hurried away along the trail. "Good-bye, Myles."

"Beulah?"

She glanced back.

"You can demonstrate gratitude to me anytime you like."

Aghast, she turned and ran into the woods. He chuckled.

9

Thou openest thine hand,
and satisfiest the desire of every living thing.
Psalm 145:16

Myles found the Bible in the bottom of an old saddlebag, smelling of mildewed leather. A spider had nested on the binding—years ago from the looks of it. The title page bore his name in his brother's hieroglyphic script: "Myles Van Huysen, from his brother Monte, 1875."

His squared fingertip caressed the page. "Monte." Memories assailed him: A childhood filled with Monte's derogatory name-calling and cruel tricks whenever Gram's back was turned. Years of adolescent jealousy and competition. Then Monte showing up at the circus—mocking, yet for once honest about his feelings and plans.

Myles stared vacantly at the saddlebag. In Monte's final days something had happened to change him, to turn him from his reckless ways. Was it the shock of finding himself a hunted man? Was it the realization that someone wanted to kill him? Myles shook his head. Danger had never fazed Montague Van Huysen.

He recalled faces around the campfire, cowboys of assorted sizes and colors squatting to drink scalding coffee before heading out to keep watch over the herd. Monte had smiled, a genuine smile containing no scorn, when he handed over the brown paper parcel. "Happy Birthday. The boys gave you a lariat, so I got you something you didn't want. It took me years to stop running from God; hope you're quicker to find Him."

Now, clutching the Book to his bare chest, Myles closed his eyes. "You were right, Monte. I didn't want it. Nearly tossed it away when I saw what it was. Wish I had. Stupid to carry an old book around with me all these years."

He opened it at random. "Isaiah. Never could make heads or tails of those long-winded prophets." Frowning, he looked at the heavy log beams overhead. "All right, God," he growled, "*if* You exist, explain Yourself to me. Beulah says I'm unhappy. Antonio says I'm carrying a burden of unforgiveness. I don't see how I can be held responsible for the wickedness of other people!"

Rising, Myles began to pace back and forth across the small room, his Bible tucked under one arm, a finger holding his place. "I'm not the one who sinned. First my mother gave up on living and left me to Gram. Then Gram favored Monte and made me work like a slave. Monte never gave me a moment's peace; then he followed me around the country all those years as if he really cared what became of me. It's his fault he got killed—" A surge of emotion choked Myles's voice. Grimacing, he struggled to hold back tears. Vehemently he swore.

Sorrow and loss were incompatible with his anger at Monte. Myles clenched his fists and screwed up his face. "I hated him, God! Do You hear me? I hated him! I'm not sorry he died." A sob wrenched his body. "I hate him for being such a fool as to get himself killed. I hate him for being an outlaw. I hate him for being so kind to me right before he died, just so I would mourn him!" Tears streamed down his face and moistened his beard.

He climbed onto his bed, bringing the Bible with him. Flat on his back with the Book lying open on his chest, he continued, "You tell me to forgive people if I want to be forgiven. Ha! What they did was wrong, God! I can't pretend it wasn't and absolve them from guilt." Self-righteousness colored his voice, yet speaking the words gave him no relief. "They didn't ask to be forgiven. They weren't even sorry. I hope they all burn in hell. What do You think of that?"

He pressed upon his aching stomach and groaned aloud. Antonio's words rang in his head: *"You cannot offer Beulah an unforgiving heart."* Poison. Hatred. The bitterness was eating him alive from within.

"Can You offer me anything better?" he demanded.

If I want God to explain Himself, I'd better read what He has to say. He's not going to talk to me out loud. As if this Book could answer any real questions.

His finger was still holding a place in Isaiah. Myles opened the Book, rolled over, and focused on a page. "'Ho, every one that thirsteth, come ye to the waters, and he that hath no money; come ye, buy, and eat; yea, come, buy wine and milk without money and without price,'" he read aloud.

How can he that has no money buy something to eat? His soul was thirsty, but this couldn't be speaking about that kind of thirst. Myles read on: "'Wherefore do ye spend money for that which is not bread? and your labour for that which satisfieth not? hearken diligently unto me, and eat ye that which is good, and let your soul delight itself in fatness.'"

So maybe it really is talking about feeding the soul. I suppose spending "money for that which is not bread" means trying to fill the emptiness inside with meaningless things. Maybe only God can fill that aching void, the hunger and thirst in my soul.

His gaze drifted down the page. "'Seek ye the LORD while he may be found, call ye upon him while he is near: Let the wicked forsake his way, and the unrighteous man his thoughts: and let him return unto the LORD, and he will have mercy upon him; and to our God, for he will abundantly pardon.'"

Myles stared into space and brooded. Much though he hated to admit it, his hatred and anger were wicked. He was that unrighteous man who harbored evil thoughts. He was in need of pardon.

He read on: "'For my thoughts are not your thoughts, neither are your ways my ways, saith the LORD. For as the heavens are higher than the earth, so are My ways higher than your ways, and my thoughts than your thoughts.'"

Myles snapped the book shut, eyes wide. A chill ran down his spine. There was his answer: God does not need to explain Himself. Period.

Myles suddenly felt presumptuous. Insignificant. Like dust. He tucked the Book under his bed, blew out the lamp, and lay awake until the early hours of morning.

∼❧

If Buck Watson was surprised when Myles started asking him questions about Scripture, he didn't say so. The two men spoke at irregular intervals, sometimes drawing a simple conversation out over hours.

"There are parts of the Bible I can't understand," Myles said as he raked hay on a newly cut field. He felt small beneath the dome of cloudless blue sky. Trees surrounding the pastures flaunted fall colors, reminding him of the passage of time.

"Such as?" Buck prompted.

The two worked as a team, tossing hay into a wagon. The mule team placidly nibbled on hay stubble. Myles looked at other crews around them, their burned and tanned backs exposed to the autumn sun. "I was always told to obey God's commands and He would take care of me. But the Bible tells many stories about good people who were killed or tortured. I've had bad things happen in my life. Wicked people seem to reign supreme; tornadoes, floods, and droughts come; and God sits back and does nothing. The Bible says God is the Author of good, not of evil. I know He knows everything and doesn't have to explain Himself to us lowly people, but my head still wants to argue the point."

"Man has free will to choose good or evil, and those choices can affect the innocent. The whole earth suffers under the curse of sin, and we all feel its effects. Sometimes God intervenes; sometimes He doesn't."

"But why? If He's all powerful, loving, and holy, why doesn't He prevent evil or crush wicked people?" Myles stabbed too hard, driving his pitchfork into the earth.

Buck considered his answer, brows knitted. "There are things we won't know until we reach eternity. You see, Myles, our faith is based not upon what God does but upon Who He is. God tells us that He is just, loving, merciful. We must take Him at His word and know that He will do what is best. He doesn't explain Himself. He doesn't guarantee prosperity and good health. But He does promise to be with us always, guiding and directing our lives for His purpose. Once you place your faith in Him, you will discover, as I have, that He never fails, never disappoints. He will give you perfect peace if you will accept it." Buck forked hay atop the mound in the wagon bed.

"Peace." Myles studied Buck's face and beheld that perfect peace in action. God's reality in Buck Watson's life could not be denied. There was no other explanation for the man.

Myles lifted his shirttail to wipe his sweating face. Over the course of the day, he had peeled down to an unbuttoned shirt. Buck worked shirtless; his shoulders were tanned like leather beneath his suspender straps. "I do want the kind of peace you have," Myles admitted. "I know I'm a sinner, but I'm not as bad as some people."

"When you stand before God, do you think He will accept the excuse that you weren't as bad as some other guy? What is God's requirement for entrance into heaven?"

"I don't know," Myles grumbled.

"Then I'll tell you: Perfection. No sin. None."

Myles jerked around to face his boss. "But that's impossible. Everybody sins. If that is so, then nobody could go to heaven."

A slow smile curled Buck's mustache. "Exactly. The wages of sin is death, and we are all guilty. Doomed."

Myles shook his head in confusion. "How can you smile about this? You must be wrong."

"No, it's the truth. Look it up for yourself in Romans." Buck's gaze held compassion. "But here is the reason I can smile: God loves us, Myles. He is not willing that any should perish. You see the quandary: God is holy—man is sinful. Sin deserves death—we all deserve death. No one is righteous except God Himself. Do you know John 3:16?"

Myles thought for a moment. "Is that the one about 'God so loved the world'?"

Buck nodded. " 'For God so loved the world, that he gave his only begotten Son, that whosoever believeth in him should not perish, but have everlasting life. For God sent not his Son into the world to condemn the world; but that the world through him might be saved.' "

Myles stared into space. "I think I'm beginning to see . . ."

"I would suggest that you start reading the book of Matthew. Read about Jesus, His life and purpose. He is God in the flesh, come to save us. Ask God to make it clear to you."

Myles climbed atop the pile in the wagon, arranging and packing the hay. His brow wrinkled in thought.

"Jesus died in your place, Myles, so you could go to heaven," Buck shouted up to him. "He loves you."

To Myles's irritation, tears burned his eyes. He turned his back on Buck and worked in silence. His work complete, Myles jumped down and leaned against the wagon wheel. A muscle twitched in his cheek, and his body remained taut. "I still have questions."

Gray eyes regarded him with deep understanding. "Nothing wrong with that. God wants you to come to Him with your questions."

Myles glanced at his friend and drew a deep breath. "Buck, I haven't forgotten your past. I don't know how you continued to trust God all those years, especially while you were in prison through no fault of your own."

"I had my ups and downs," Buck said. "Times of despair, times of joy. But I clung to God's promise to bring good out of my life. Sometimes that promise was the only thing I had left."

"But didn't you hate the men who did it to you? I mean, they're all dead now. You've had your revenge. Although I never understood why you went and tried to lead that rat Houghton to God before he died. I should think you would *want* him to rot in hell!"

Buck stopped working and studied Myles. "Hmm. I see." He rested both hands atop the rake's handle. "I tried hating, Myles. For months, I hated and brooded in that prison, vowing revenge on the lying scum who put me there. Then a friend read me a parable Jesus told about forgiveness; you can find it in the book of Matthew, chapter eighteen. That story changed my life."

Myles grunted. Forgiveness again. He didn't want to hear it.

Buck took a deep breath. "Myles, it comes down to one question: Are you willing to make Jesus your Lord or not?"

Myles stared at a distant haystack and brushed away a persistent fly. There was one thing he could do to make his past right. "I must return to New York."

Buck lifted one brow. "Oh?"

"I'll never have peace until I let my grandmother know where I am and apologize for running away. I can't bring my brother back for her, but I can give her myself. This is something I know God wants me to do." Myles slipped a hand inside his open shirt and scratched his shoulder. "Maybe I should write a letter. If I go back, I might lose everything that's important to me here."

Buck looked into his soul. "Beulah?"

"You know?"

"I'm not blind. Her mother asked me to question your intentions." Myles swallowed hard. "What about Al?"

"Wrong question. What about Myles? Listen to me, my friend. You can't make your heart right with God. Only Jesus can do that for you."

Myles's head drooped. "I know I'm not good enough for Beulah. A friend told me once that I would poison her with the bitterness in my heart. I've got to work this thing out with God."

Buck crossed his arms, shaking his head sadly. "Until you do, better leave Beulah alone."

Myles lifted his hat and ran one hand back over his sweaty hair. Then he nodded. Climbing into the wagon seat, he loosed the brake, called to the team, and headed for the barn. Buck moved to a new spot and began to rake.

Al and his crew waited near the barn to unload hay into the loft. After turning his load over to them, Myles watered his team at the huge trough. One mule ducked half its face beneath the water; the other sucked daintily. Myles pushed a layer of surface scum away with one hand, then splashed his face and upper body with the cold water. Much better. He slicked water off his chest with both hands, then plastered back his unruly hair.

Just as he finished hitching the team to an empty wagon, Beulah's voice caught his attention. There she was at the barn, serving cold drinks to the hands. Slim and lovely, dipping water for each man and bestowing her precious smiles. Myles suddenly noticed his raging thirst. Eyes fixed upon Beulah's face, he started across the yard.

Better leave Beulah alone.

Myles halted. Shaking his head, he closed his eyes and rubbed them with his fingers. The woman was like a magnet to him. Buck was right to warn him away from her. *Guess I'll have to do without the drink.* He jogged back to the wagon, leaped to its seat, and slapped the reins on the mules' rumps. "Yah! Get on with you."

"Myles!"

Shading his eyes with one hand, he looked back. Beulah ran behind the jolting wagon, her bonnet upon her shoulders. Water sloshed from the bucket in her hands. "You didn't get your drink. You can't work in this heat without it."

Myles hauled in the mules and wrapped the reins around the brake handle. She hoisted the bucket up to him. Myles took it, holding her gaze. "Thank you." Lifting the dipper several times, he drank his fill.

"Why didn't you come talk to me?" she asked. "I've hardly seen you for days and days. How is Pushy? Any kittens yet?"

"Not yet. She's healing well. She . . . she sleeps between my feet." Myles lost himself in the beauty of Beulah's eyes.

"Myles, are you feeling all right? Maybe you've had too much sun." Accusation transformed into concern. "Why don't you come inside for awhile. Your face is all red."

Temptation swamped him. What would it hurt to relax for a short time? When Beulah's gaze lowered, he realized that he was rubbing his belly again. She smiled when he began to button his shirt. "Don't bother on my account. You must be roasting." She touched his arm. "Your skin is like fire. Maybe you need another dunk under the waterfall."

Startled, Myles met her teasing gaze. "I washed in the trough. I'll be all right. Buck is waiting for me." His skin did feel scorched where her hand rested on his arm, but it wasn't from sunburn.

The smile faded as her eyes searched his face. "If you're sure . . . Myles, what's wrong?"

"I can't talk with you, Beulah. Not until—You don't even know me, who I really am."

"I know all I need to know. Did my mother tell you not to talk to me?" She sounded angry.

He studied her delicate hand, wondering at its power to thrill or wound him. "No."

"You're still coming to our music party Friday, aren't you?"

"I'll be there." He handed her the bucket. "Better get back to work." Holding her gaze, he tried to smile. "You, too. Lots of thirsty men around here."

She nodded and watched him drive away.

❧

Streams of milk rang inside a metal pail. Al spoke from the next stall. "I've got to leave soon in case we get an early snow. Thanks for all your help preparing this place for winter."

Myles grunted.

"I've given up on marrying Beulah. I don't know why I ever thought she'd make me a good wife. She's pretty, but looks aren't everything. A man wants a woman to be his friend and companion. Beulah flirts one minute and treats me like anathema the next. She about snapped my head off this afternoon. Something was tweaking her tail, that's certain."

Myles chewed his lip. "She hasn't been herself lately. She's got lots of good qualities."

Al snorted. "At the moment I'd be hard-pressed to name one."

"She's your friend. Don't say anything you'll be sorry about later, Al. Just because she isn't meant to be your wife doesn't mean she's not a good woman."

Al grumbled. "I know you're right. But still, I'm thanking the Lord that He prevented me from proposing marriage. What a fix I would be in if she had accepted!"

Myles leaned his head against a tawny flank, fixed his gaze upon the foamy milk in his bucket, and drew a long breath. "I'm thanking Him for the same thing."

"What did you say?"

"I said I'm thanking God that you didn't propose to Beulah."

"Thanks. Say, when did this come about, you talking to God?" Al's grinning face appeared above the stall divider.

"Recently. Been talking to Buck a lot. I've got a past that isn't pretty, but I know I need to make things right. I wrote a letter to my grandmother. Plan to mail it tomorrow when I go to town."

"Will you be able to keep my farm going this winter?"

"Not sure I should make promises at this point, Al."

He sighed. "I guess I understand. Wish I had peace about going to California. I don't feel right about it, and God isn't answering my questions."

As soon as he was alone, Myles allowed a grin to spread across his face. He punched the air in delight, kicked his feet up and stood on his hands, then dropped to his knees. "Thanks, God! I can hardly believe it, but thanks! Soon as I gave in to You and wrote that letter—whizbang! Al is out of the running! Now if I can sell my part of the soap business and buy Cyrus's farm, then . . ."

❧

"Myles, good to see you."

Pausing on the boardwalk in front of the general store, Myles stared at the speaker. The voice was familiar, but the face? "Sheriff Boz?"

Gone was the tobacco-stained walrus mustache. Looking pounds thinner, Boz Martin sported a crisp white shirt and string tie. The star pinned to his vest sparkled. His gun belt no longer completely disappeared beneath an overhanging paunch. He grinned, showing yellow teeth. Myles had never before seen the man's mouth.

"Don't know me, eh?"

"I haven't seen you at Miss Amelia's in awhile."

"Been staying away. I'm hopin' she'll be surprised, too."

"I'm sure she will be. You look . . . fine."

Boz stood taller, puffing out his chest. "Town's jam-packed with drifters, harvest workers. Lot of riffraff, if you ask me. We had to break up a fight at the Shady Lady last night. You hear about it?"

Myles shook his head.

Boz deflated slightly. "I'll be just as glad when that lot moves on. That New York character, Mr. Poole, left town last week, so I've got hopes Amelia will notice me again. Poole was mighty interested in you, Myles. Can't know why."

"How do you mean, 'interested'?"

"Asked a lot of questions around town. You going to Buck and Violet's party tonight? I can't make it, and neither can Amelia."

"That's too bad. Seems like half the town was invited. The Watsons have a lot of friends."

Peering intently across the street, Boz rose on tiptoe, fingering his gun belt. "That Swedish family south of your place lost a pig a few nights back. Looks like Cyrus's bear ain't left the county after all."

Myles turned to see what was distracting Boz, but saw nothing unusual. "Be glad to help on a hunt. We've been keeping our stock close to the barns, just in case."

"Ain't Al headin' west soon? Hear he's taking Beulah with him."

Myles fingered the letter in his pocket. "Al's catching the train south tomorrow. He's traveling alone."

Boz shifted to one side, frowning past Myles. "That so? Those two make a purty pair."

Blinking in surprise, Myles studied his friend's vacant expression. Another curious glance over his shoulder cleared up the mystery. On the walkway near the livery stable stood Miss Amelia, conversing amiably with the town barber. Myles shook his head and grinned. "Actually, Boz, I'm planning to elope with Beulah tonight after the party. We're moving to Outer Mongolia to open a millinery shop for disgruntled Hottentots."

"Yup. I saw that match coming almost as soon as she stepped off the train."

Myles chuckled. "Never mind. I'll see you later."

Still distracted, Boz waved two fingers. "Later, Myles."

When Myles left the general store, Boz had joined the conversation across the street. Smiling, Myles shifted his bundle under one arm. *Good old Boz. Hope he gets his Amelia.*

The letter was in the mail. Soon Gram would know both where Myles was and what had happened to Monte. *Is that enough, God?*

Cholla dozed at the hitching rail with her eyes half shut. "Howdy, Girl. Bought myself new duds for tonight. Hope you'll recognize me all duded up." The horse rubbed her ears against his hand and lipped his suspender strap. Myles's voice trembled with anticipation. "Think I'll stop at the barber next and get me a shave. Don't know if Beulah likes my beard or not, but I'm through hiding my identity. Maybe tonight I'll tell her about my past. Maybe she'll like the sound of 'Beulah Van Huysen.' "

"Myles!"

He turned on his boot heels. A buxom figure in a calico dress hurried along the boardwalk. Myles stiffened. He wanted to run, but his boots had grown roots.

"Goodness, but it's warm today," Marva panted, waving a hand before her flushed face. Her eyes were vividly blue. "They say it's going to storm tomorrow, maybe even snow, but I can't believe it! The trees still have most of their leaves. Mr. Watson got his corn in, didn't he? I saw the reaping machine pass our farm yesterday on its way out of town. Papa got our crops in days ago, but then he doesn't farm that much acreage."

She pressed white finger marks into his forearm and shook her head. "You're so brown, Myles, like an Indian! It's not good for fair-skinned people like us to take so much sun. I hope you wear your hat and shirt all the time."

Behind Marva, the Watson buggy stopped at the railing. Samuel and Eunice remained in the buggy while their mother stepped down and tethered her horse.

"Hello, Marva, Dear. So good to see you. Hello, Myles," Violet said in her gracious way.

"I'm looking forward to the party tonight, Mrs. Watson," Marva said as Myles tipped his hat. He tried to smile, but his face felt like dried clay. Marva chattered on, "This will be the social event of the season, I'm certain. I'm inviting Myles to join our family for supper before the party."

Violet gave Myles a look. "How nice! I look forward to seeing your parents, Marva. Is your mother better?"

"Much better, thank you. She and I have practiced a duet, and my papa brought out his fiddle for the occasion. I also look forward to hearing Myles sing. He has a marvelous voice." Marva took Myles by the elbow and pressed close.

Myles attempted to disengage his arm, but she clung tenaciously. Heat rose in his face.

He saw one delicate eyebrow lift as Violet met his gaze. "I, too, anticipate hearing you sing, Myles. Good day to you both."

Without moving away, Marva rattled on as if she had never been interrupted. "I'm sure you must be longing for good home cooking. It's been weeks since you visited us, and my papa keeps asking where you've taken yourself. I told him you've been harvesting for nearly everyone in the county, but he won't be happy 'til you join us for a meal. We can have supper first, then drive to Fairfield's Folly together." The dimple in her right cheek deepened. "What's your favorite pie?"

"Blackbottom. My grandmother used to bake it." Pushing at her hands, he detached himself from her grip. "Miss Obermeier, I really don't—"

"I'll do my best to equal your grandmother's pie. Where are you from, Myles? You seldom speak about yourself." Her gloved hand rested on his chest.

"There's little to speak of." Myles tried to slide the conversation closer to his horse. "Miss Obermeier, I don't think you—"

Marva followed. "Good friends don't use titles, Myles. Please call me Marva. I like to hear you speak my name."

"I must go now. Work doesn't wait for a man." Perhaps it was rude to mount Cholla then and there, but Myles was desperate to escape. Tonight was the night to let Marva know that his heart had already been bestowed elsewhere. His problem was how to communicate any message at all to a woman who never stopped talking.

"Be there at five." Marva rested her hand on his knee in a proprietary way. "Don't forget."

"I'll come after the cows are milked." He spun Cholla around.

Eunice and Samuel waved as Myles passed their buggy. "When's the wedding, Myles?" Eunice teased, and Samuel clasped his hands beside his face and batted his eyes in a fair imitation of Miss Obermeier. Had Myles not been so irritated, he might have been amused.

Glancing over his shoulder, he saw Marva laughing and waving at him. What had gotten into the woman?

Cholla sensed his anger and wrung her tail in distress. As soon as she passed the outskirts of town, Myles let out a "Yah!" Cholla leaped into a full gallop.

Beloved, let us love one another: for love is of God;
and everyone that loveth is born of God, and knoweth God.
1 John 4:7

Miss Obermeier finished playing a hymn. A patter of applause trickled through the room as she returned to her seat between Myles and her mother. She leaned over to whisper to Myles. He inclined his head to listen. Marva's pale hair gleamed, and her fair skin contrasted with Myles's ruddy tan.

"Wonder why Myles didn't wear his new duds," Al muttered as Cyrus Thwaite began a mouth organ solo of "Camptown Races."

Beulah met Al's gaze. "He bought new clothes?"

He nodded. "Today. A fancy suit, like for a wedding. Told me he had an announcement to make. I'm guessing there will be a wedding soon."

Beulah jerked as if she had been slapped.

"Maybe it didn't fit," Al mused. "Too bad. Marva looks like a queen, and Myles looks like . . . like a farmhand. I've got to help the man loosen up."

Eunice leaned around Al, frowning and holding a warning finger to her lips. "Don't be rude!" she whispered.

Beulah took shallow breaths. *I won't look. I cannot bear to see Myles sitting with that woman.* Her heart had started aching the moment she saw Myles hand Miss Obermeier down from a buggy, and the pain grew steadily worse. Marva's parents already seemed to regard Myles as a son-in-law.

He never made me any promises, yet I thought there was something special between us. Maybe he does think of me as a child to be amused.

Biting her lower lip, Beulah smoothed the skirt of her sprigged dimity frock. She had been so proud of this dress with its opulent skirts and tiny waist. Violet had fashioned a ruffled neckline that framed the girl's face, revealing the delicate hollow at the base of her throat and a mere hint of collarbone. Now the white ruffles seemed childish.

Marva's royal blue satin gown showed off her white shoulders. Beulah wondered that Marva could keep her countenance in front of Reverend and Mrs. Schoengard. "I think her dress is improper for an unmarried lady."

Al gave her a wry look. "Trust you to say so."

"Shhhh!" Eunice leaned forward again.

Beulah flounced back in her seat. *I was excited to have Myles come tonight. Now I wish he had stayed home. I wish I had never met the horrible man.*

David and Caroline Schoengard rose to stand beside the piano. Violet settled on the stool and opened her music. "We will sing 'Abide with Me,'" Caroline announced in a trembling voice.

Beulah watched the pastor shape his mouth in funny ways as he sang the low notes. Mrs. Schoengard was now heavily pregnant. Their voices were pleasant, but once in awhile Caroline strained for a high note and fell short.

Al shifted in his seat and tugged at his stiff collar while the Schoengards returned to their seats. "Is it almost over?" he whispered.

The only people present who had not yet performed were Al, Myles, and Obie. Beulah knew her stepfather could not carry a tune. He attended Violet's party to be an appreciative audience, he said. And Al would "rather be dead than warble in front of folks."

"Myles, will you play for us?" Violet requested. "Don't be shy; none of us are music critics."

Myles rose, approached the piano, and turned to face his small audience. Candlelight flickered in his eyes and hair. "I'll play, but I have something to tell all of you afterward." His gaze came to rest upon Beulah. "Something important."

She sucked in a quick breath, lifting one hand to her throat.

Myles placed the piano stool and seated himself. He drew a deep breath and flexed his fingers, seeking Beulah's gaze. The message she read in his eyes at that moment banished her jealousy and insecurity.

He began to play a lively composition. His hands flew across the keyboard with complete mastery. Broad shoulders squared, heavy boot working the pedal, he looked incongruous, yet perfectly at home. His very posture denoted the virtuoso.

Myles completed the piece with a flourish. "Schubert," he said into the ensuing silence. A murmur stirred the room's stuffy air as people audibly exhaled.

"Wow," Al said.

"That was unbelievable, Myles," Violet said. "Never before in my life have I heard—"

"I had no idea you knew how to play piano," Marva protested. "You always let me play and never said a word!"

"You never asked me," Myles said. "This is what I planned to tell you all tonight. My true name is Myles Trent Van Huysen, and during my childhood I was a concert pianist and singer. At age sixteen I ran away, and many years I have wandered the country seeking purpose for my life. Thanks to Buck Watson, I found that purpose here in Longtree. I apologize for keeping my identity a secret all this time. I was wrong to deceive you. With God's help, I am doing my best to make reparation to those I have wronged."

Obie and Al approached Myles with outstretched hands. Beulah watched the men clap Myles on the shoulders and embrace him, expressing forgiveness and acceptance. Soon everyone had gathered around the piano, eager to greet this new Myles.

Beulah joined the crowd, trying to appear happy. What did this mean? Was Myles planning to leave town and return to his concert career? He suddenly seemed far away and beyond her.

"Sing for us, Myles," Violet pleaded.

"Yes, please do," other voices chimed in.

"A love song," Marva requested.

"A love song." Myles appeared at ease in his new role of entertainer . . . but then, the role was not new to him. Acrobat, pianist, singer—what other surprises did the man hold in store? Was there anything he could not do?

Beulah recognized the tune he began to play, but never before had she heard such elegance in the old, familiar words. Myles affected a Scot's accent that would fool any but a native. His voice was smooth, richer than butter.

"O, my love's like a red, red rose,
That's newly sprung in June."

Beulah felt herself blush rose red when Myles caught and held her gaze.

"As fair art thou, my bonnie lass,
So deep in love am I,
And I will love thee still, my dear,
Till a' the seas gang dry."

He was singing the love song to her! Beulah gripped the piano case with both hands, feeling the music reverberate in her soul.

"And fare thee weel, my only love,
And fare thee weel a while!
And I will come again, my love,
Tho' it were ten thousand mile!"

The song ended. Myles lowered his gaze to the keys, releasing Beulah from his spell. "Hope you like Robbie Burns," he spoke into a profound silence. "It was the only love song I could think of at the moment. I know some opera, but didn't think you'd care to hear me sing in Italian."

Beulah drew a deep breath; it caught in her throat.

"Never cared much for fancy singing, but that beats all," Al admitted. "I think I'd be pleased to listen for as long as you cared to sing— and in any language you choose."

"How long had it been since you played the piano?" Violet asked.

Myles figured for a moment. "More than nine years. It's a gift, I guess—being able to play any song I hear. I didn't play those pieces flawlessly, of course, but usually I can play and sing almost anything after hearing it once or twice."

"Amazing! I heard no mistakes. Myles, you have thrilled our souls. Thank you for sharing your gift," Violet said. "I hope you know that you are part of our family, whatever your name."

The entire group murmured agreement.

"If anyone is thirsty or hungry," Violet continued, "we have cider and cookies in the kitchen. You are all welcome to stay as long as you like."

Everyone seemed to relax, and conversations began to buzz. Cyrus and Pastor Schoengard asked Myles to play requests, which he obliged. Strains of "My Old Kentucky Home" and "It Is Well with My Soul" accompanied the chatter. Samuel chased another boy into the parlor, laughing and shouting. Their mothers shooed the boys outside.

Beulah drifted toward the kitchen and claimed a cup of homemade cider. The drink felt cold and unyielding in her stomach, so she left her cup on the counter. She wanted to wander outside amid the fruit trees, but the night was cool and her dress was thin. She could retire to her room for the night, but that would negate any chance of talking with Myles. Wrapping a shawl around her shoulders, she took refuge on the porch swing.

The front door opened and closed. "May I speak with you?"

Startled, Beulah looked up. Moonlight shimmered on a full skirt and fisted hands. Marva's face was hidden in shadow.

"Yes."

The other woman joined her on the swing, making it creak. A moonbeam touched Marva's beautiful hair and traced silver tear streaks on her face. Muscles tensed in her round forearms as she repeatedly clasped her hands.

"Myles loves you." Marva gulped.

Beulah had no idea what to say. *Dear God, please help me to be kind and good.* She pulled her shawl closer and saw Marva do the same. They would both freeze out here on the swing.

"Are you going to marry Al?" Marva asked.

"No."

"Why not?"

"I don't love him that way."

Marva sighed. "You're so young. Do you have any idea what you want in a husband?"

"I know that I don't want to marry a man who is like a brother to me."

"So you would steal a man from another woman?"

Beulah stiffened. "Of course not! What a—" She nearly choked on her own hasty words. Maybe Marva's insinuation was unkind, but it was the desperate charge of a broken heart. What might Beulah be tempted to say under similar circumstances? She felt sudden sympathy for Marva.

"You already had Al. Why did you try to steal Myles from me?" Tears roughened Marva's voice.

"I didn't know you loved him, Miss Obermeier. I wasn't trying to be cruel to you, honestly!"

Marva covered her face with her hands. "It's not fair! It's just not fair."

Beulah patted Marva's shoulder. "My mother tells me that God is always fair. If He doesn't allow you to many Myles, then He must have someone better in store. You've got to trust Him, Marva. He doesn't make mistakes."

Marva lowered her hands and sucked in a quivering breath. "You're nothing like I thought you were, Beulah Fairfield. Everyone talks about your sharp tongue and quick temper. They must be jealous. You're really a sweet girl." Her tone was doleful. "No wonder Myles loves you. You're both pretty and nice."

"So are you," Beulah said. "Just now I asked God to help me be kind; it doesn't come naturally to me."

Marva gave a moist chuckle. "Me, neither. I came out here wanting to scratch your eyes out! It's easy for you to talk about God bringing someone better along; but when you get to be twenty-six with not so much as a whisker of a husband in sight, you'll know how I feel. Of course, you're likely to be married and a mother several times over by the time you're my age."

She stood up, leaving Beulah in the swing. "When my parents come outside, will you tell them I'm in the buggy?"

"I'll tell them. Are you sure you're all right, Marva?" She followed the older girl down the steps.

Marva shivered. "I'll recover. Humiliation isn't fatal."

"I don't know. I've come close to dying of it more than once."

Marva reached out and hugged Beulah. "Maybe my heart isn't as broken as I thought it was. I feel better already. Myles is a wonderful man, but he never did seem to care for my cooking, and sometimes when I talked to him I saw his eyes kind of glaze over. Guess I'd better be patient and wait for God's choice instead of hunting down a man for myself."

Beulah found it hard to restrain a giggle, but Marva waved off her efforts. "Go ahead and laugh. I know I'm silly." She grinned. "You know, I once even considered Sheriff Martin as a marriage prospect. I didn't consider him long, but the thought crossed my mind."

"Marva, he's old enough to be your father!"

Marva chuckled. "I know. Oops, here come my parents. You'd better get inside before you freeze. I'll see you at church, Beulah."

❧

"I would take it as a favor if you would sing in church," Reverend David Schoengard said in a hushed voice. "God could mightily use a talent like yours."

"I hope He will," Myles replied. "When the time is right, I will let you know."

"Don't wait too long," David advised.

"I am still learning what it means to honor Jesus as Lord. You know that story about the lost sheep? That's me."

"The church door is open to lost sheep."

A small boy tugged at the pastor's leg. "Dad, Ernie hit me."

"Excuse me a moment, please." David squatted to listen to his son. Myles scanned the room.

"Looking for Beulah?" Al asked. Leaning one elbow on the piano, he sipped a cup of cider. "She's talking with Marva, I think. I spotted the two of them on the porch swing not long ago. If you need help splitting up a cat fight, call on me."

"How did you—"

"Please, don't ask! Anyone with half an eye could have read the look on your face while you sang to Beulah tonight, old friend. I'm thinking you'd better soon have a serious talk with Buck, or he'll be after you with the shotgun." Al's grin was pure mischief. "I'm also thinking I'll have to miss that train tomorrow. Don't you want me to stand up at your wedding?"

"You're not angry?"

"Naw. When two people are right for each other, it's obvious. And vice versa. Beulah and I blended like horseradish and ice cream. You'll be good for her; she needs someone to keep her in line. You should have seen her writhing in jealousy when you showed up with Marva tonight." Al chuckled. "She must have been dying when I talked about what a handsome couple you and Marva made."

Myles felt his face grow warm. "I intended to tell Marva tonight—"

"I don't think you need to say a word. She knows. Her parents just left. They looked pretty sad."

His shoulders slumped. "They're good people, Al. And Marva's a nice lady. I feel bad about hurting her."

Al shrugged. "Some of us are slow to catch on. I wasn't the quickest hog to the trough, myself. Don't know why I couldn't see the attraction between you and Beulah before now. It sticks out like quills on a porcupine. But there will be another girl for me—one who appreciates my humor and thinks I'm great." He grinned.

Myles had to smile. "You're chock-full of brilliant analogies tonight. Porcupine quills?"

"So are you going to talk with Beulah or not?"

☙

He found Beulah on the porch swing. Watchful lay at her feet. The dog flopped a fluffy tail. "Isn't it too cold for swinging?" Myles asked.

Huddled beneath her shawl, Beulah stared up at him. "I guess it is. I needed a place to think, but I've discovered that the front porch isn't private."

Myles leaned a hip against the railing, gazing out past the barn. His left leg jiggled up and down. "Al told me Marva talked to you."

"She was crying at first, but when she left she was laughing. I like her, Myles. She is funny and nice. I think she could be a friend."

He shifted against the rail. "I was planning to explain to her tonight. About you and me, I mean."

Her voice was too bright. "I enjoyed your singing. I don't understand why you hid your talents for so long."

The comment interrupted his train of thought. "It's a long story."

From somewhere beyond the barn came a commotion. Watchful lifted her head, ears pricked. Myles followed the dog's gaze, but saw nothing. Hackles raised, growling softly, the dog trotted down the steps and headed for the barn. The white tip on her tail was visible after the rest of her disappeared.

"Myles?" Beulah stopped swinging and leaned forward. "What is it?"

Watchful began to bark. Myles had never heard such a noise—the dog sounded frantic, terrified. His ears caught the bawling of cattle, trampling hooves.

"I don't know, but I'm gonna find out."

Running feet approached, and two small figures appeared in the moonlight. Myles heard the boys panting before he could identify Samuel and his buddy, Scott Schoengard. "Myles!" Samuel said, stumbling up the steps. "There is something big in the yearling pen—something that roars!"

We roar all like bears. . . .
Isaiah 59:11

$\mathcal{I}$ called Watchful, but she won't come. Go save her, Myles! That monster will kill her!" Samuel was sobbing.

Myles threw open the front door. "Buck! Al! Trouble at the barn."

Buck snatched up a lantern and a rifle, tossing another gun to Myles. Al caught up with them halfway across the yard. The yearling pen was ominously quiet except for Watchful's shrill yelps. Leaning against the split rail fence, Buck lifted the lantern. On the far side of the pen, many wide eyes reflected the lamplight. A young cow bawled.

"Watchful, come." The stern command brought the collie to heel, ears flattened, tail between her legs. Every hair on the dog's body stood on end. She still yammered at intervals. "Hush, Watchful." Instant silence. She pressed against Buck's leg and shivered.

Buck unlatched the gate, and the three men stepped into the pen. Myles felt the hair on his nape tingle. A cursory examination of the corral revealed that the invader was gone.

Buck studied the muddy ground with a practiced eye. He pointed out bunches of woolly hair on a fence post along with glutinous streaks of blood. "It was a bear."

Myles counted the cattle. "One yearling missing. The Hereford-cross with the white patch on his left hip."

Al measured a print in the mud with his hand. "That was one big bear. It lifted that steer over the fence."

"We'll track it come morning. I don't follow giant bears into dark forests," Buck said with grim humor.

239

Al crossed his arms. "That monster could have come after one of the children."

"Sam and Scott were playing near the barn," Myles said. He swallowed a wave of nausea at the sudden mental picture of what might have been. "God must have been protecting them. I'll be ready for the hunt first thing tomorrow, Buck."

"Me, too."

Buck lifted a brow at his cousin. "Don't you have to get ready for your trip, Al? Your train leaves at four o'clock tomorrow afternoon."

Al glowered at the ground. "Might know I'd have to miss the fun. All right. I'll feed and milk in the morning, one last time, so you two can hunt."

Something cracked in the darkness near the gate. Watchful's ears pricked. The men spun around, guns lifted. A ghostly figure drifted closer. "It's me—Beulah."

"What are you doing?" Al snapped. "Don't you know there's a bear out here somewhere?"

Beulah clutched her shawl. "I didn't know until now." Her voice sounded small.

"Back inside, Beulah," Buck ordered. "Your mother will worry."

"I'll escort her." Myles stepped out of the corral.

"No lingering."

"Yes, Sir." Myles had never before heard that protective note in Buck's voice. He followed Beulah toward the kitchen door. She drifted beneath the apple trees, crunching leaves beneath her feet.

"I love all our trees and the beautiful fall color, but now comes the hard part—raking," she said in a quivering falsetto. "Did you like the cider? My mother and I made it from our apples."

Myles touched her arm. "Beulah."

She turned. Her eyes were dark pools in her pale face. "Oh, Myles, you aren't really going to hunt that bear, are you? I'm frightened!"

She cared! "I've hunted bears before. Buck and I will hunt this one down in no time. A few shots and it'll be over."

Her hand fluttered up to rest upon his chest. Myles wrapped his fingers around her upper arm. "Buck told me not to linger, but I must tell you tonight. I love you, Beulah. I want to marry you. I want it more than anything." His voice cracked.

He heard her suck in a quick breath. "Do you know God yet, Myles? Mama and Papa both told me to wait until you gave your life to Him. You said something tonight about making your peace with God's help. Did you mean it?"

"I did. I do. I wrote to my grandmother and apologized for running away. I imagine she will contact me soon, and I expect to make a quick trip to New York to wrap up business affairs." His voice trembled with eagerness. "I'm planning to buy the Thwaite farm, Beulah. For us. You and me. How does that sound?"

He wanted to hold her in his arms, but the rifle in his right hand made that impractical.

Beulah touched his beard with two fingers. "It sounds wonderful . . . but are you sure you want to be a farmer? You can do so many things. I've never known anyone like you."

"I'm sure." He leaned the rifle against the back steps and took Beulah into his arms. "Are you sure you want to marry a farmer?"

She captured his face between her hands and gently kissed his lips. "Please don't go away, Myles. Not ever."

"What?" he mumbled, conscious only of his need for another kiss. Her lips warmed beneath his, and her hands gripped his shoulders. Myles kissed her again and again until the cold, dark world faded away. Nothing existed except Beulah, sweet and pliant in his arms.

The kitchen door opened, catching them in a beam of light. "Beulah, it's time for you to come inside," Violet said.

The couple sprang apart, wide-eyed and breathing hard. Beulah grabbed for her falling shawl and rushed past her mother into the house.

"Myles, I believe you need to talk with Obadiah before you meet with Beulah again."

Myles heard the iron behind Violet's mild tone. Gathering his scattered self-control, he nodded and picked up the rifle. "This is Buck's."

Violet took it from him. "Al is waiting for you out front." She started to close the door then paused. "I know you love my daughter,

Myles, and I'm not opposed to the match. But as her mother, I must be careful of her purity."

Guilt swamped him. "I understand. I am sorry, Ma'am. It won't happen again."

"See that it doesn't. Good night, Myles Van Huysen."

❧

Myles stepped into predawn darkness, feeling the chill through his wool coat and gloves. A recent dusting of snow on the ground might make tracking more difficult. Cholla was displeased to see him so early, but she accepted her bit after Myles warmed it in his palm. "We're on a hunt, Girl. Like old times."

Cats waited around Cholla's stall, making noisy petition for milk. "Sorry, friends. No milk this morning." Myles thought of Pushy, still sleeping on his bed, and grinned. These cats would rebel for certain if they knew she got her own saucer of cream each morning and evening.

He tied a scabbard to his saddle and shoved his loaded rifle into it, then packed extra cartridges into his saddlebags. "Hope we're back in time to escort Al to the station." He would miss his young boss and friend.

Cholla broke into a canter, tossing her head and blowing steam. Myles hauled her back to a jog. "Too dark for that pace, my lady. We'll get there soon enough."

Buck waited in the yearling paddock. By the first light of dawn, he studied the bear's spoor. Buck nodded greeting as Myles joined him. "Big bear, like Al said. Amazing claw definition for a blackie. I'd say it was a grizzly if I didn't know better."

"Powerful, whatever it is, to carry off a yearling steer. It obviously has little fear of man."

"Makes my heart sit in my throat to think how the children have walked and ridden about the property at all hours these past weeks. And all the while this monster was afoot."

Myles had been having similar thoughts. "Have you heard the rumors that a bear escaped from the circus? If this is the bear I think it might be, our lives have been in constant danger. That grizzly hated people."

Buck swung into his saddle. His jaw clenched in a grim line. "Whether it is or whether it isn't, our job is to end the creature's life."

The bear's trail was easy to follow; it had dragged the carcass through grass and brush. Less than a mile up the creek, they found the remains of the young Hereford crossbreed. "There lies our next year's winter beef supply," Buck grumbled, still on horseback. "This bear has an eye for a tender steak."

Jughead and Cholla snorted and shied at the strong scent of bear. "Steady, Boy. That bear should be miles from here by now." Buck patted his gelding's neck, but the horse would not be quieted. "I don't like this." Buck exchanged glances with Myles, then studied the surrounding brush and trees. Plenty of hiding places for a bear.

Cholla reared slightly, eyes rolling. "What if it stayed around to eat from the kill again?" Myles asked and hauled his gun from its sheath.

Buck swung his mount around, rifle at the ready. "It could happen. This bear doesn't seem to follow standard bruin behavior. Let's see if he's still around." He gave a whoop.

"That should frighten every critter in the county," Myles chuckled. The laughter froze in his throat. Not twenty yards away, a huge cinnamon-brown form rose out of a patch of mist. The bear's roar was more than Cholla could endure. With a rasping squeal, she reared high, pawing the air. Myles forced her back down, but it was impossible to fire while fighting his horse. The bear made a short charge, then paused to rise up and roar again. Foam dripped from its open jaws.

A rifle cracked, and the bear flinched. Infuriated, it charged at Jughead. The mustang bolted with Buck sawing at his reins and shouting.

Myles brought his rifle around, but Cholla chose that moment to shy sideways into the trees. The shot went wild, and Myles lost a stirrup. Furious and frustrated, he decided to let the screaming horse loose and try his chances on foot. He leaped to the ground, and while the bear made a short dash toward Cholla, Myles fired. In his haste, he hit the hump on its back.

Instantly the bear spun around, spotted Myles, and charged with incredible speed. Myles caught a glimpse of flaming eyes, yellow tusks, and a red tongue. Without a thought he cartwheeled to one side, made a front roll, and propelled himself upward to catch hold of a tree branch. He swung his legs up as the bear charged beneath him, still roaring.

All well and good, but now his rifle lay on the ground. "Buck, I'm up a tree!" Could he be heard above the animal's fury?

The bear quickly figured out where Myles was and returned to the tree. Its roars were deafening, and it pushed against the tall pine, making it wave wildly. Then, to Myles's horror, the bear began to shinny its great bulk up the trunk. Even as Myles scrambled to move higher, one great paw slapped into his leg and pulled. He let out a shout, clinging to the trunk with all his strength. "God, help me!"

Shots rang out in rapid succession. Buck stood ten feet away in plain view, pumping bullets into the beast's back. The bear gave another roar, then a grunt, and dropped to the ground in a heap.

Myles hugged the tree trunk, laughing in hysteria. Relief made his arms go limp. Had he eaten breakfast, he would surely have lost it. Pain knifed through his leg. "Thank You, God. I'm alive."

"Amen." Buck's voice sounded equally shaky. "You all right, Myles? I'm so sorry—I never dreamed my yell would bring the bear down on you like that. I thought he had you for a moment there."

"I think he got my leg. That beast went up a tree like a squirrel—I've never seen the like."

"It is a grizzly. I guessed it from the tracks, but I didn't believe my own eyes."

Myles tried to climb down the tree, feeling weaker than a kitten. His leg was wet. His head felt swimmy. "Check its neck, Buck. I have an idea he's wearing a collar, or used to be."

Buck bent over the carcass. "Biggest bear I've seen in years." He reached a hand into the coarse fur. "You guessed it, Myles. A leather collar with a short length of chain. Those rumors about the circus bear were true. I can't believe no one reported this!"

"No doubt the owner feared negative publicity. They probably expected to find the bear before they left, but he was too smart for them."

"Maybe he was smart, but a circus animal wouldn't know how to survive in the wild. Stealing stock was his only option. Look how skinny—no fat surplus for hibernation. He would never have lasted the winter. I can't help feeling a little sorry for the old bruin." Buck shoved the inert body with his boot.

"Not me. This isn't the first time that old buzzard came after me." Myles released his hold on a branch and dropped to the ground. His leg buckled. He fell to his knees and grabbed it. The hand came away red. "Buck, I need help."

Rushing to his side, Buck pulled out a knife and cut away the trousers. The smile lines around his eyes disappeared. "Looks nasty. Got to stop that bleeding."

Peace I leave with you, my peace I give unto you:
not as the world giveth, give I unto you.
Let not your heart be troubled, neither let it be afraid.
John 14:27

While Beulah mixed pancake batter, gazing dreamily through a frosty windowpane, she saw Jughead trot into the barnyard, riderless and wide-eyed. "Mama!" Dropping her work, she raced upstairs. "Mama, Jughead came home without Papa. Something bad has happened, I just know it!"

Violet nursed Daniel in the rocking chair. Her body became rigid; her blue eyes widened. "Let's not panic. Papa might have released Jughead for some reason." She bit her lip while Beulah wrung her hands. "Send Eunice over to tell Al. He'll know what to do."

Dead leaves whisked across the barnyard, dancing in a bitter wind. Frost lined the wilted flower border, and ice rimed the water troughs. His reins trailing, Jughead hunted for windfalls beneath the naked apple trees. Beulah's gentle greeting made the horse flinch and tremble. He allowed her to take his reins, however, and seemed grateful for her attentions. She patted his white shoulder, feeling cold sweat beneath his winter coat.

In the barn, Eunice was saddling Dolly. Excited and frightened, the younger girl chattered. "Can you believe how cold it is today? And yesterday I didn't even carry my coat to school. Good thing there's no school on Saturday or I wouldn't be home right now. Good thing Al hasn't left yet. Maybe he'll decide not to go to California after all. Maybe . . ."

Beulah tuned out her sister's prattle. If anything had happened to Papa or Myles . . . Beulah hauled Jughead's saddle from his back and hung it on the rack. Would Papa want her to blanket the horse now, or was Jughead warm enough with only his winter fur? Taking the gelding to his stall, she slipped off his bridle. The slimy snaffle bit rattled against his teeth, but Jughead was too good-natured to hold that against Beulah. He bumped her with his Roman nose and heaved a sigh, seeking reassurance.

Beulah patted his neck and rubbed his fuzzy brown ears, resting her cheek against his forelock. "Papa will be all right, Jughead. Don't worry."

"I'm leaving now, Beulah." Dolly's hooves clattered on the barn floor as Eunice mounted.

"Be careful. And hurry, Eunice."

After Dolly galloped up the driveway with Eunice clinging to her back, Beulah closed the barn door and returned to the house. Her face felt windburned when she removed her wraps.

Wandering from room to room, she looked for chores that needed doing. No one was hungry for pancakes, so she covered the batter. At last she decided to bake bread and cookies. The men might come home hungry. Her thoughts kept returning to Myles and Papa.

Dear God, please keep them safe! I love them both so much.

While the bread rose and the first batch of cookies baked, she sat at the table and tried to soak up the stove's radiated heat. Wind howled around the eaves and rattled the windows. Beulah shivered.

Violet entered the kitchen and sniffed. "It smells good in here, Beulah. You've been working hard." She spread a quilt on the floor and set Daniel on it, handing him a spoon and two bowls for playthings. Sitting at an awkward angle, he crowed and waved both hands in the air. He grinned at his mother, and Violet smiled back.

Beulah stared. "How can you be so calm, Mama? Papa could be in terrible danger out there, and it looks like snow again!" She waved a hand at the window.

"God is with him, Beulah. I've been praying since you told me about Jughead, and God assures me that He is in control. Remember Philippians 4:6–7: 'Be careful for nothing; but in every thing by prayer and supplication with thanksgiving let your requests be made known unto God. And the peace of God, which passeth all understanding, shall keep your hearts and minds through Christ Jesus.' If I chose to worry about Obie every time he went into a dangerous situation, I would be in a home for the insane by this time." Violet smiled.

Daniel leaned too far forward and fell on his face. Unfazed, he grabbed the spoon and batted it against a bowl.

Beulah studied her mother's expression. "But how, Mama? How can you trust God this way? You can't see Him, and you know that bad things happen sometimes."

Violet poured herself a cup of coffee. "When you truly know the Lord, you know that evil and pain are the farthest things from Him. He is all the joy and meaning in life, Dearest. Without Him, life is nothing. It's the Holy Spirit Who gives us peace, Beulah, along with love, kindness, and every other spiritual fruit. He doesn't force Himself into our lives—we have to allow Him to fill and use us for God's glory."

Beulah removed the cookies from the oven and put in another batch. "Last night I asked God to help me be kind to Marva, and He did. I have given my life to Jesus, and I know He is working in me, but I don't have the peace I see in your life and Papa's. Most of the time I don't even want to be kind and good. Hateful things come out of my mouth before I think them through!"

Violet rose and wrapped an arm around her daughter's drooping shoulders. "Darling, don't you understand that all people are that way? None of us in our own strength can be always kind or loving or unselfish. Those traits belong to God alone. And yet God can use anyone who is willing to be used by Him. You say He helped you last night? Then you know He can change your heart when you allow Him."

"I'm willing right now, but I might not be tomorrow," Beulah admitted. "You know how ornery I am."

Violet squeezed the girl's shoulders. "Yes, the tough part is surrendering your will to His will. I understand entirely. Where do you think you got your ornery nature? It wasn't from your father."

"Then how do you do it, Mama? How can you be so full of faith and patience and everything?"

"Remember when Jesus talked about taking up our cross daily? He meant that every day we must die to ourselves and let Him live through us. That is the only way to have lasting peace and joy in your life—and it's the only way to have faith through any crisis. When you know God well, you will understand how completely He can be trusted with your life."

Beulah nodded, thinking over her mother's words. She sampled a cookie, chewing slowly. "Mama, I need to talk with you about Myles. Last night, right before you told me to—"

Watchful began to bark from her post at the back window.

"Someone is coming," Violet said. Both women rushed to look outside. Behind them, Daniel began to cry. Violet hurried back to pick him up.

"They're back!" Beulah exclaimed. "Al and Eunice are with them."

"Thank the Lord!" Violet rejoined her at the window.

"I'm going out there to greet them," Beulah declared. She hurried to the entry hall for a coat and hat, then rushed down the steps and across the yard. "Papa! Myles, are you all right?" Both men looked pale and drawn.

Obie caught her before she could spook the horses. "We killed the bear, but not until after he took a swipe at Myles. Got to get the doctor out here right away. Help us take Myles into the house, and I'll ride to town."

"I'll go with you," Al offered. "I'm not leaving today. I'll catch a train next week. I can't run off to California when Myles is hurt."

Nobody argued. Beulah rushed back to the house to inform her mother, and together they decided Myles should have Samuel's bed. The men carried Myles up the stairs just as Beulah tucked in the top bed sheet. The sight of his bloody boot and trouser leg stopped her breath for a long moment. "Oh, Myles!" she exclaimed. Her head began to feel light and foggy.

"It's not so bad. You should see the other guy." He gave her a crooked smile. "I'm pretty thirsty."

"I'll get you a drink. Do you want water or coffee or milk?"

"Water."

As she left the room, she heard her mother order quietly, "Al, help me cut the boot from his foot. Beulah, we need a basin of hot water."

"Yes, Mama." All the way downstairs and while she worked, Beulah prayed: *Lord, please fill me with your Spirit today and help me to show love, peace, joy, and every other fruit. Please help my dear Myles! Help the doctor to heal his leg like new. And please keep me from fainting when I see all that blood.*

She held the basin with towels to prevent sloshing water from burning her hands while she mounted the stairs. A bucket of cold water for Myles weighted her right arm.

"Put it there on the bureau," Violet said. "Thank you, Beulah. Al and Papa have gone for the doctor."

Beulah offered a dipper of well water to Myles. He propped himself on one elbow and drank. "Much better." When he returned the dipper, their hands touched. Beulah felt her lips tremble. She could not meet his gaze.

Beulah dropped the dipper into the bucket. On the floor at her feet lay the shredded shirt Obie had used to stanch Myles's blood. It was leaving a stain on the floorboards. Beulah closed her eyes and breathed deeply. *Don't think about it,* she told herself. She gingerly picked up the shirt and wrapped a clean sheet around it. Blood soaked through.

"You may toss out that old shirt." Violet was tearing a sheet into strips. "Then again, I suppose we can boil it and use it for rags."

Beulah trotted downstairs and put the bloody cloth in a pot to boil, then ran outside and was sick behind the withered perennial bed. Her head still felt light afterward, but at least her stomach had settled. The cold, fresh air helped.

"The bleeding has slowed," Violet was saying when Beulah returned to the room, "but you'll have to be stitched."

"I thought as much." Myles looked pale.

"Beulah, will you please check on Daniel?" Violet asked. "I think I hear him stirring."

Beulah gave Myles a longing look, then hurried to obey her mother.

Daniel had pushed up with both hands to peer over the side of his cradle. His little face was crumpled into the pout that always appeared just before he started crying. He grinned when he saw Beulah and flopped back down on his face, crowing and kicking at his blankets.

Beulah melted. "Oh, Sweetie, I do love you! I wish you would sleep right now, though."

"I'll take him for you, Beulah." Eunice stood in the doorway. Curls had escaped her braid to frame her round face, and the hem of her dress was soaked. Her blue eyes looked lost and lonely. "Is Myles going to die? You should have seen that bear. It was huge. Papa says it charged at Myles and he swung into a tree like a monkey." She wiped a fist across her eyes and sniffed. "Please let me take Daniel. I don't know what else to do." Tears clogged her voice.

A wave of love for her sister warmed Beulah's heart. "Myles lost a lot of blood, but I don't think he'll die. Of course you may take Daniel. You'd better change into dry clothes first. If you don't, you'll be coming down sick next thing, and we don't need that." Her voice softened. "Thank you for riding for help this morning. You're pretty wonderful."

Eunice's dimples appeared before her smile. She nodded and hurried to her room. Beulah settled into the rocking chair and cuddled Daniel close. He was too busy and awake to snuggle, so she let him sit up and amuse himself by playing with her buttons while she sang "Auld Lang Syne."

Eunice spread Daniel's blanket on the floor and set up his blocks before she took the baby from Beulah. "We'll be fine. I think the doctor is here; someone arrived just now."

"Thank God! And Eunice, Al decided he's not leaving today." Beulah smiled at the overjoyed expression on her little sister's face. "He'll catch the train next week."

Eunice caught hold of Beulah's skirt as she whisked past. "Beulah, I'm sorry I said you were heartless. You love Myles, don't you?"

Biting her lip, Beulah nodded. "But don't you tell anyone!"

The dimples appeared again. "I won't. He's not Al, but I like him a lot."

Peace filled Beulah's heart as she returned to Samuel's bedroom. Next thing she knew, she was being shooed from the room. How she wished Myles would request her presence! Not that Mama would have allowed such a thing. Not that Beulah could have endured the sights or sounds of a sickroom without passing out on the floor.

Beulah hurried to the kitchen to prepare more coffee and cookies for everyone. Someone—Eunice?—had removed the batch of cookies from the oven and punched down the bread dough. It was ready to bake.

Dear God, it's hard to be helpful when all I want is to be with Myles. I guess this is the best way for me to serve today. Please help me to have a cheerful attitude and to give thanks.

Obie and Al were grateful for the hot food. Beulah joined their sober conversation midway through and gathered that someone besides Myles was hurt. "*Who* got shot last night, Papa? What happened?"

Obie wiped his nose with a handkerchief. "The sheriff. One of those drifters who's been causing trouble in town all month had a drop too much at the tavern last night and took offense when Boz offered him a night's rest in jail. Before anyone could react, the man pulled a gun and shot Boz from point-blank range."

Blood drained from Beulah's face . . . again. "Will he live, Papa?" she croaked.

Obie shook his head. "They carried him home, and Doc dug out the bullet, but he's afraid it nicked a lung. Boz has powder burns on his chest, and he has trouble breathing."

Beulah bit her lips and screwed up her face. The tears overflowed anyway.

Obie patted her hand. "Miss Amelia is taking care of him while Doc is here with Myles. Boz couldn't ask for better care. We just need to pray. He has peace about eternity, thank the Lord." Obie drew a shaky breath and blinked hard. "He's my oldest friend. The deputy is keeping order in town for the present. The man who shot Boz is behind bars. I'm hoping to visit him after church tomorrow."

"I'll go with you," Al offered.

"You could take him some of my cookies." Beulah wiped her face with her apron and tried to smile.

～❧

Light snow fell Sunday, but Monday dawned clear and warmer. Eunice and Samuel threw snowballs back and forth as they left for school, but the snow blanket had dwindled to a few patches by noon.

While Mama nursed Daniel, Beulah peeked in to check on Myles. His foot lay propped on pillows. In repose, his pale face had a boyish look. His eyes opened, but Beulah slipped away before he spotted her. Violet had made it clear that Beulah was never to be alone with Myles in his sickroom.

Outside, Watchful began to bark. Beulah went to her own room and peered down at the driveway. "Mama, someone is coming. I don't recognize the horses."

Violet sounded harassed. "Would you greet our guest and make excuses for me, Dear? I'll be down when Daniel is finished."

Beulah untied her apron and hung it on a hook, patted her hair, and opened the door. An elderly woman stood on the top step. Behind her, the buggy turned around and disappeared up the driveway. "Hello, Dear. Is this Obadiah Watson's home?"

"Yes, it is."

Watchful suddenly rushed past the woman into the house, whisked Beulah's skirts, and bounded up the stairs. "I'm so sorry," Beulah gasped. "That was my brother's dog."

The lady straightened her bonnet. "Does a man named Myles Trent work here?"

"Yes, but he does not live here."

The lady's face fell. "But they told me . . . Oh, dear, and I let that hired rig go . . . I was so sure Myles would be here."

Beulah hurried to explain, "No, don't worry—you see, he is here right now. Upstairs in bed. He was injured the other day. Are you— Could you be his grandmother?"

The woman lifted a trembling hand to her lips. "Yes, I am Virginia Van Huysen. Is my grandson expected to live?"

Her tragic eyes startled Beulah. "Oh, yes!" she quickly assured. "He is recovering nicely. It was a bear that attacked him."

"I see." The woman looked bewildered. "My Myles was attacked by a bear?"

Beulah recalled her manners. "Please come inside. My mother will be down in a few minutes; she is caring for my baby brother. I'm sure Myles will wish to see you."

Mrs. Van Huysen gave her a weak smile and stepped inside. "I

253

hope so. I'm sorry, Child—it has been a long and tedious journey. My train arrived in town only this morning. Mr. Poole was supposed to meet me in Chicago, but he did not appear."

"I see." Beulah said nothing. She could neither ask questions nor remain silent. The lady seated herself on the horsehair davenport at Beulah's invitation. They sat and stared at one another.

"Would you like me to tell Myles that you have arrived?"

"He did not know I was coming." There was sadness in the woman's reply. "How old are you, Child?"

"Eighteen. I am Beulah Fairfield. Obadiah Watson is my stepfather. Myles has worked for him these past three years, mostly during the summers."

"I am pleased to make your acquaintance, Miss Fairfield. You are a pretty child. Do you play the piano?" She indicated Violet's instrument.

"A little. Nothing to compare with Myles. He played for us the other night for the first time. It was amazing."

Mrs. Van Huysen lifted her brows. "So, he still can play. Hmm. Did he sing for you?"

Beulah could not help but smile. "Yes! It was wonderful. He told us that he was a concert pianist in New York, and he told us his real name for the first time. Did you receive his letter?"

"Letter? Myles has not written to me in years."

"But he did! Just last week. He wanted to apologize to you for running away to join the circus when he was a boy. Did Myles live with you always?"

"The boys lived with me after their parents died."

"I didn't know his parents were dead. My father died years ago, but my mother is happy with Mr. Watson. He is a good father to us." Beulah paused. "Did you say 'the boys'? Does Myles have a brother?"

Mrs. Van Huysen suddenly rose. "Please take me to Myles now. I can wait no longer."

Beulah led her to the staircase. "This way, please."

Mrs. Van Huysen worked her way up the stairs. Beulah wanted to offer her arm for support but feared rejection. "This way," she repeated, pushing open the door to Samuel's bedroom.

Myles appeared to be asleep. Blankets covered him to the chin, and his eyes were closed. "Myles?" Beulah whispered, moving to the far side of the bed. He did not stir. The room still smelled of blood, ether, and pain.

Mrs. Van Huysen stood at his other side. "Myles, my dear boy!" Her lips moved, but no other sound emerged. Tears trickled over her withered cheeks.

Beulah touched Myles's shoulder. "Myles, wake up. There is someone here to see you." Her own eyes burned. "Myles!" She gripped his shoulder and shook gently. Her fingers touched warm bare skin. Startled, she jerked her hand away.

His eyes popped open and focused on her face. "Beulah. I was dreaming about you." His hazy smile curled her toes. His hand lifted toward her face.

"Look who is here to see you, Myles," she whispered, unable to speak loudly. She glanced at his grandmother, and a tear slipped down her cheek.

Myles turned his head. Beulah saw his eyes go wide, and his mouth fell open. A moment later he was sitting up, clutching Mrs. Van Huysen and nearly pulling the lady from her feet. "Gram!" His voice was a ragged sob.

Beulah crept from the room.

*Y*ou're so tiny, Gram. Did you shrink, or have I grown?"
Myles asked.

Virginia patted his hand and smoothed his forehead, just as she had during his childhood illnesses. She smiled, but her expression was far away. "You must tell me about Monte sometime, Myles. Right now is convenient for me."

He pulled his hand out of her grasp and ran it over his rumpled hair. "I know. I've been hiding things too long, from myself . . . from everyone." He drew a deep breath and released it in a sigh, praying silently for strength. "This won't be easy."

Virginia watched him with sad yet peaceful eyes.

"Monte was wild, Gram. I know you thought he was a good boy, but it was all a sham. He loved to gamble, drink, and smoke . . . although I can say with confidence that he was never a womanizer. You raised us to respect women, and Monte kept that shred of decency as far as I know. With his charm, he might have been worse than he was."

Tears pooled in his grandmother's eyes, but she nodded. "I knew, Myles. It nearly broke my heart to see the way you two boys fought and despised each other. I prayed for wisdom and did everything I could to encourage love and respect between you. It never happened. For some reason, Monte considered you a rival from the day you were born."

Myles sat stunned. "You knew? I thought you doted on him."

"Certainly. I doted on the both of you. What grandmother doesn't dote on her grandsons, flawed though they may be?"

"Then why did you keep me isolated from everyone except private tutors and force me to practice for hours every day? It was a terrible life for a boy! I thought you hated me and loved Monte."

Virginia looked stunned. "I wanted the best for you, Myles. God gave you a wondrous gift, and I felt it my duty to give you every opportunity to develop and enjoy that gift of music. I thought your complaints stemmed from laziness, and I refused to listen. Oh, my dear, how wrong I was! My poor boys!" Wiping her eyes, she insisted, "Tell me about Monte. I must know."

"When you sent him after me, he took advantage of the opportunity to sample every pleasure the world had to offer. He was delighted to escape his responsibilities. He did plan to return someday, but then circumstances prevented it."

Virginia shook her head. "I knew I had lost him. Releasing him to find you was a last effort to show him that I trusted and respected him as a man. He proved himself unworthy, as I feared. He did write to me occasionally over the years, however, as you did. I never understood why that precious correspondence ended."

Myles absently unbuttoned his undervest. "The last place we were together was Texas; you knew that much. We had a steady job brush-popping longhorns for a big rancher. Monte started running with a group of gamblers. They were the ruin of him. It wasn't long before he started rustling a beef here and there to support his habit, and the boss became suspicious."

Tears trickled down Virginia's cheeks again, but she nodded for him to continue.

Myles twined a loose string around his finger and tugged. "Then all of a sudden Monte changed. I don't know exactly what happened— well, maybe I do—but anyway, one day he was wild, angry, and miserable; the next day he was peaceful, calm, and had this radiant joy about him. He told me that he had made his life right with God. I thought he had lost his mind. Both of us hated church and anything to do with religion, yet here was Monte saying he had found Jesus

Christ. He tried to talk with me about God—even gave me a Bible for my birthday."

"Thank You, Jesus!" Virginia moaned into her handkerchief.

"One day we were riding herd, almost ready to start a drive north. Monte was across from me, hunting strays in the arroyos. A group of riders approached him. I took my horse up on a small bluff and watched. I had a bad feeling—something about the situation made me nervous. The best I can figure, the riders were men to whom Monte owed money, probably demanding payment. I saw Monte's horse rear up; Monte fell off backward and vanished. The sound of a shot reached me an instant later. Panic spread through the herd. Within seconds I was riding for my life, hemmed in on every side by fear-crazed longhorns."

The string broke free and his button dropped beneath the blankets.

"And Monte?"

"I never found him, Gram. By the time we got that herd straightened out—a good bit smaller than it was when the stampede started—we were miles from the location of the fight, and it was pouring rain. I hunted for days, but found no trace of Monte or his mustang. The horse never returned to the remuda; it must have died in the stampede, too."

Virginia sobbed quietly.

"I don't know if the men who killed Monte were aware that I witnessed his murder, but I didn't take chances. I was nineteen, scared, stricken with regret and sorrow. I hightailed it out of Texas and never went back. Once or twice I thought about writing to you, but shame prevented it. Not until God straightened me out this summer did I have the courage to confess my role in Monte's death."

"You weren't to blame, Myles." The idea roused Virginia from her grief.

He sniffed ruefully. "Had I not run away from home, Monte would never have been in Texas."

"Then he most likely would have died in a back alley in Manhattan. It is not given us to know what might have been, my boy. We can only surrender what actually is to the Lord and trust Him to work His perfect will in our lives." Virginia's voice gained strength as she spoke. "Monte is safe with the Lord, for which fact I am eternally grateful. Myles, Dear, can you ever forgive me for my failings as a grand-mother?"

Myles nodded. A muscle in his cheek twitched. "I forgive you, Gram. You meant well." He blinked, feeling as if a small chunk had broken from the burden he carried. To his surprise, forgiving his grandmother was an agreeable experience. Love welled up in his heart, and he opened his arms to her.

Weeping and smiling, Virginia fell into his embrace without apparent regard for her dignity.

❧

Beulah carried a tray upstairs and knocked at the closed door. The voices inside stopped, and Mrs. Van Huysen opened the door. "That looks lovely, Dear. Thank you." She stepped aside, and Beulah carried the tray to the bureau.

"Are you two having a good visit? Were you comfortable last night, Mrs. Van Huysen?"

"Yes, Dear. Thank you for the use of your bedroom. I'm sorry to put everyone to such inconvenience."

"It is no trouble. We are all pleased to meet Myles's grandmother."

More than a day had passed since Virginia's arrival. Beulah's family had begun to wonder if the two Van Huysens would ever rejoin the world.

Myles eyed the steaming bowls and the stack of fresh bread slices. "What kind of stew?"

Beulah felt her face grow warm. She gave his grandmother an uncertain glance. "Bear."

Virginia's face showed mild alarm.

Myles laughed aloud. "Poetic justice. I hope he was a tender bear. Don't worry, Gram; Beulah is the best cook in the state, with the possible exception of her mother."

"I don't doubt it."

"I hope it's good stew," Beulah said weakly. "Papa says the bear was skinny and tough. He showed me how to prepare it so it would taste better, but I don't know if you'll like it."

Myles shoved himself upright. "Beulah, will you ask Al to feed Pushy? She must be wondering what happened to me."

Beulah avoided looking at him. "Al says Pushy is lonely but well. She reminded him to feed her. No kittens yet."

"You need to take a look at the stitches in my leg, Beulah. There are fifty-seven. Doc did a great job of patchwork. Maybe you could learn a few new designs for your next quilt. Beulah sews beautiful quilts, Gram. She can make almost anything."

"Indeed?"

"Did you see the bear when they brought it in, Beulah? Wasn't he immense? You should have seen that monster climb a tree. He would have had me for sure if Buck hadn't packed him with lead. Say, that water looks good. Would you pour me a drink?"

Beulah felt his gaze as she poured two glasses of water from the pitcher. She glanced at his grandmother and caught an amused smile on the lady's face.

Virginia suddenly rose from her chair and smacked Myles's hand. "Stop that belly rubbing. Never could break you of that." She addressed Beulah obliquely. "Myles suffered chronic stomachaches as a child. He used to wake me every night, crying for his mother. At least he no longer totes around a blanket."

Myles slumped back against the pillows. "No secret is sacred."

Beulah smiled. He would be embarrassed for certain if she gave her opinion of his habit—she found it endearing.

"Myles was a sickly, scrawny child—all eyes and nose. It's amazing what time can do for a man. I never would have known you in a crowd, Myles—although one look into your eyes would have told me. Doesn't he have beautiful eyes, Beulah? They are like his mother's eyes, changing hue to suit his emotions. I would call them hazel."

"Sometimes they look gold like a cat's," Beulah observed.

"Has he told you that he was being groomed for opera? His beautiful voice, his ability to play almost any piece the audience might request, and his subtle humor packed in the crowds. He was truly a marvel—so young, yet confident and composed. Even as a little child, he was mature beyond his years. I thought I was doing the best thing for him, helping him reach the peak of his ability. How wrong a grandmother can be!" She shook her head sadly.

"We've already discussed this, Gram. It's in the past and forgiven, remember?" Myles sounded embarrassed.

"Myles told me about the letter he wrote last week." Virginia shook her head. "I never received it. My private detective, Mr. Poole, recently discovered Myles's whereabouts after long years of searching. I find it odd that Myles wrote to me even as I was coming to see him. But the Lord does work in mysterious ways."

"God told me to write to you, Gram," Myles said gruffly, "even though He knew you were coming."

"At any rate, I plan to telegraph Myles's old agent tomorrow and set up a return performance. The musical world will be agog; his disappearance made the papers for months. His reappearance will take the world by storm, I am certain."

"Gram," Myles began, sounding somewhat irritated.

Beulah backed toward the door. "That's wonderful. You had better eat before the stew gets cold. I'll be back for the dishes."

She heard Myles call her name as she ran down the steps, but she could not return and let them see her distress. *Myles is leaving!*

❧

"Beulah is a pretty thing and well-spoken," Virginia commented. "Exquisite figure, although I'm sure you have noticed that fact."

"I have."

"Your fancy for the child is evident, and even I can see why she attracts you." Her gaze shifted to Myles, and she pursed her lips. "The bluest blood in New York runs in Van Huysen veins."

"Blended with the good red blood of soap merchants, sea captains, and a black sheep or two. From all I hear, some of Beulah's ancestors might have looked down their aristocratic noses at one or two of my wild and woolly ancestors." His mustache curled into a smirk.

Virginia merely poked at her stew.

"So you like Beulah, Gram?" Myles dipped a chunk of bread into his stew and took a large bite.

"I suspect there is more to that inquiry than idle curiosity. Do you intend to wed the child?"

"I do." One cheek bulged as he spoke.

His grandmother considered this information. "Would she blend into our society, Myles? Her manners are charming, but they are country manners, nonetheless."

"If she won't blend in, then I wouldn't either. It's been a long time since I lived in your world." Myles ate with relish.

Virginia frowned. "Yours is a veneer of wilderness, I'm certain. Cultured habits will return, given the proper surroundings. I do hope you plan to shave soon. Facial hair does not become you."

"It was a disguise. Not a good one, but it fooled me." Myles smiled wryly. "All of this is immaterial, since, as you know, I do not intend to remain in New York. One farewell concert, sell the business, and back here I come to purchase a farm." His voice quivered with excitement.

Virginia lifted a trembling hand to her lips. "Um, Myles . . ."

"Buck Watson told me again and again that God blesses when we surrender our lives, and I'm living proof of that fact. It struck me one day that my resistance to facing my past was preventing me from having the future I longed for. You can stay in Long Island if you like, Gram, or we could sell that old house and move you out here. There's room in the Thwaite farmhouse, and I plan to build on anyway. The farm needs money and work, that's certain, but neither should be a problem."

Virginia finally succeeded in breaking into his soliloquy. "About the business . . . there is something you need to know, Myles."

❧

Beulah scooped the mess of raw egg and shattered shells from the hardwood floor and dumped it into a pail. Goo had settled in the cracks between boards.

"I didn't mean to, Beulah. The floor was slippery, and I fell flat."

Samuel hovered around her, shaking his hands in distress. "Mama needed those eggs. I feel awful."

Beulah sat back on her heels and sighed. "The chickens will lay more eggs tomorrow, I'm sure. We still have two from yesterday. Don't worry about it. I'm thankful you're not hurt."

Samuel crouched beside her. "Are you feeling all right, Beulah? Is Myles dying? Is Sheriff Boz dying? Why are you being so nice?"

Beulah frowned, then chuckled. "As far as I know, no one is dying. Papa says the sheriff is holding his own. I simply don't see any point in being angry about smashed eggs. You didn't intend to break them, and someone has to clean it up. I'm not busy right now like Mama is, so I'm right for the job."

Her brother laid a hand on her shoulder. "Thanks, Beulah. You're a peach." With a fond pat, he hurried from the room.

When the floor was no longer sticky, Beulah sat back with a satisfied sigh. "That wasn't so bad."

"Beulah," Samuel called from another room. "Mama wants you to collect the dishes from Myles's room. And can you set beans to soak?"

"I will." When the beans were covered and soaking, Beulah washed her hands and checked her reflection in the blurry mirror. Her hair was reasonably neat, and the chapping around her mouth had cleared. She touched her lower lip, recalling Myles's ardent kisses. "Will he ever kiss me again?" she whispered.

Glancing at the ceiling, she sighed again. *Lord, please give me peace about the future. I know You are in control, but I always want to know about things right now! Please help me to control my emotions around Myles and to seek Your will.*

Minutes later, Beulah knocked at the bedroom door. "Myles?"

Silence.

She pushed open the door. He lay with arms folded across his chest, staring out the window. "Myles, do you mind if I collect your dishes?"

He did not so much as bat an eye. Biting her lower lip, Beulah began to load the dinner dishes onto her tray. Mrs. Van Huysen had picked at her food. Myles must have enjoyed his stew.

"Please stay," Myles begged as Beulah prepared to lift the tray. He reached out a hand. She was startled to see that his eyelids were red and swollen.

"Myles, what's wrong? Where is your grandmother?" She wrapped his cold hand within both of hers. "Are you hurting?"

His other hand fiddled with a buttonhole on his undervest; the corresponding button was missing. "Yes." He pressed her hand to his cheek and heaved a shaky sigh.

"I'm so sorry!" Beulah settled into the chair beside his bed. "Would you like me to read to you?"

"No. Don't go so far away."

Beulah blinked. "Far? I'm right next to you. Where is Mrs. Van Huysen?"

"Lying down, I think. I don't care. Nothing matters anymore."

She reached out to feel his forehead. "You're cool and damp. Would you like another blanket?"

When she would have returned to the chair, he grabbed her around the waist and pulled until her feet left the floor. Sprawled across him, Beulah felt his face press into her neck. "Myles, let me go! What if my mother walked in right now? She would murder me!"

"I need you, Beulah. Just hold me, please! I won't do anything indecent, I promise."

Hearing tears in his voice, she stilled. "Myles, what is wrong?" Her hand came to rest on his upper arm. It was hard as stone. His entire body was as tense as a bowstring.

"Do you love me, Beulah?"

Her teeth began to chatter from pure nerves. Something was not right. She felt a terrible heaviness in her spirit. "Yes, I love you. I do. Myles, whatever is wrong? I'm frightened." Pushing up with one arm, she regarded his face. "You were bright and cheerful when I brought lunch. Is the pain that bad? I'll get Mama."

"No!" He gripped her wrist. His eyes were glassy and intense. "Will you marry me right away? We can start over somewhere else, maybe homestead a place."

She shook her head in confusion. "I thought you planned to buy the Thwaite farm and settle here. Why should we marry right away? You're acting so strange, Myles."

He emitted a bark of laughter. "Plans? I have no more plans. Not ever. Plans involve depending on someone else. I will never again trust anyone but myself. And you, of course. You'll be my wife. We can live by ourselves out West."

The dread in Beulah's chest increased. "Please tell me what has happened." She twisted her arm, trying to escape his viselike grip.

He suddenly released her and flung both forearms over his face. "Same old story. I trust someone, they let me down. Everyone I have ever depended on has failed me. Everyone. Most of all God. As soon as I start trusting Him even the slightest bit, the world caves in. If you desert me, too, Beulah, I think I'll crawl away and die."

She reached a hand toward his arched chest, then drew it back. "But God will never fail you. Why do you think He let you down?"

Myles sat up in a rush of flying blankets. Eyes that reminded Beulah of a cornered cougar's blazed into her soul, and an oath blasted from Myles's lips. His white teeth were bared. "Enough of this insanity! The entire concept of a loving, all-powerful God is absurd. A fairy tale we've been force-feeding children for generations. A superstition from the Dark Ages. I don't ever want to hear you talk about God to me again, do you hear?"

Beulah's mouth dropped open.

His fury faded. "Don't look at me like I'm some kind of monster! I need you, Beulah!" Flinging the blankets aside, Myles swung his legs over the far side of the bed and tried to stand on his good leg.

Seeing him sway, she sprang around the foot of the bed. "What are you doing? Myles, get back in bed or I'll call Papa." She stopped cold, realizing that he wore nothing but winter underwear. Hot blood flooded her face, and she rushed back to stand by the door.

He whipped a blanket from the bed and wrapped it around his waist. Jaw set, he hopped to the window and looked down on bare trees and blowing snow. "That's how I feel inside: cold, gray, and lifeless."

"That's because you've turned your back on God." Beulah was

surprised to hear herself speak. "What happened to you, Myles? Why are you acting this way?"

He huffed. "I'll tell you what happened. For years Buck has been telling me about God, about salvation. Finally I decided to try this thing out, trusting God. I wrote to Gram. I started giving God credit for the good things happening in my life. I even started believing that He was with me. When I read the Bible it was as if He talked to me."

Beulah studied his broad shoulders and felt her dreams crumbling.

"I began to believe that He had wonderful plans for my life— marriage with you, the farm I've always wanted, and friends who like me for myself, not because I'm a Van Huysen. I've never wanted the money; I've been proud to support myself and lean on no one . . . except maybe Buck. But since God told me to reconcile with Gram, I figured He must intend me to make use of my inheritance. I didn't want much; just enough to buy a farm and set us up with a good living. Then I found out that you loved me—life was looking incredibly good. Gram came, asked me to forgive her, and I did. Great stuff. Everything coming together."

He fell silent.

Beulah settled into a chair, hands clenched in her lap.

"Then the cannonball drops: There is no money. The family friend who ran the Van Huysen Soap Company mismanaged it into bankruptcy, sold out to another manufacturer, and is now president of that company. He swindled it all away and left Gram holding massive debts. She sold off most of our stock and commercial properties to pay the debts, then mortgaged the family house to pay for the detectives who found me. There is no money. None."

Beulah tried to sound sympathetic. "Don't the police know how that man cheated your grandmother? Isn't there something you could do to help her?"

"There is no money to pay for lawyers, and apparently Mr. Roarke covered his legal tracks. It looks as shady as the bottom of a well, but no one can prove anything."

"Poor Mrs. Van Huysen. I can understand why you are upset. Had you been there to keep an eye on the business, this might not have happened to her."

Myles turned to fix her with a glare. "Don't you understand, Beulah? Gram is fine; she still has the old house and a small stipend to live on. The money lost was *my* money! This is the end of *my* dream. I have no money to buy a farm, and I can't support a family on my pay as a hired hand. We cannot stay here. Either I must return to New York and try to break back into the music world—which would not be an easy task no matter what Gram says—or I must head out West and find land to homestead."

Beulah's chest heaved, and her heart thudded against her ribs. That heavy, ugly feeling weighed on her spirit. "So when it looks like God is answering your prayers the way you want, you believe in Him. As soon as things don't go your way, you decide He doesn't exist? That isn't faith, Myles. That is opportunism. And I thought *I* was a selfish person! I don't care what you decide to do. Whatever it is, you'll do it without me."

Picking up the tray, she stalked from the room.

And Jesus answered and said unto him,
What wilt thou that I should do unto thee?
Mark 10:51a

Al entered the sickroom without knocking. "Myles, you won't believe what happened!" Spotting Mrs. Van Huysen, he pulled off his hat. "Hello, Ma'am."

"Good morning, Albert," Virginia responded cordially.

"I sure enjoyed visiting with you last night. Myles, do you know this grandmother of yours whupped me at checkers? It was an outright slaughter."

"Myles never cared for the game," Virginia said when Myles remained silent. "He is good at chess, however." A moment later, she rose and gathered her embroidery. "I'll let you boys chat awhile." The door clicked shut behind her.

Al settled into the empty chair, long legs splayed. "It stinks in here. Like medicine."

Myles tried to scratch his leg beneath the bandage. The skin showing around the white cloth was mottled green and purple. "What's the news from town? Doc tells me it looks like Boz will pull through."

"If good nursing has anything to do with it, Boz will be back on his feet within the week. From all I hear, Miss Amelia treats him like a king." Al's eyes twinkled. "She had him moved to her boardinghouse, and her front parlor is now a hospital room. Nothing more interesting to a woman than a wounded man, but I guess you know all about that."

Myles grunted. "So what's your big news?"

Al slipped a letter from his chest pocket. "Today I got this letter from my folks asking me not to come west until spring. Can you be-

268

lieve it? Today! Think about it: If you hadn't let that bear rip your leg off, I would have been on my way by now and missed their letter. No wonder I didn't have peace about leaving! They don't even want me yet. I have no idea what I'll do with my farm next year, but it doesn't matter—God will provide, and I've got all winter to think and prepare. So if you need to go to New York, don't hesitate on my account."

Myles tried to smile. "That's good news, Al. I felt guilty about delaying your trip."

"Now that you're rich and all, you won't be needing a farm job, I reckon," Al said, looking regretful. "I feel funny about things I must have said to you in the last year or two, me thinking you had less education and fewer advantages than I had!" His grin was crooked. "That will teach me to judge people by appearance."

"You always treated me well, Al. You have nothing for which to apologize."

"Why are you so gloomy? Is your leg hurting?"

The innocent question sparked Myles's wrath. He bit back a sharp reply and folded his arms on his chest, staring out the window.

"Hmm. Beulah is moody, too. My powers of deduction tell me that all is not well in paradise."

"Shove off, Al. I'm not in the mood for your jokes." Myles scowled.

Al pursed his lips in thought. "Want to talk with Buck?"

"I want to get out of this house, pack up, and head for Montana."

"What happened, Myles? I thought your life was going great. Beulah loves you, you've cleared things up with your grandmother, you've got a music career and money to burn."

"I'm not rich, Al. The money's gone."

"Oh. All the money?"

"Every cent."

Al looked confused. "But Beulah wouldn't care whether you're rich or not. She loved you as a hired hand."

"Whatever I do, wherever I go, she says she's not going with me. Guess she only loved me if I stayed here in town." Bitterness left a foul taste in his mouth.

"That doesn't sound like Beulah. She could make a home anywhere if she set her mind to it, and she's crazy about you, Myles."

Myles gave a mirthless sniff.

"Sure you don't want to talk to Buck?"

"I know what he'll say. He will tell me I need to forgive those who have wronged me and give control of my life over to God. I've heard it all before."

Al lifted a brow. "Sooo, tell me what's wrong with that answer? Sounds to me as if the truth pricks your pride, Pal."

Myles rolled his eyes.

"C'mon, Myles. Think this through. Are you content and filled with joy right now?"

Myles slashed a glare at Al, but his friend never blinked. "Fine. Don't answer that. Think about this: How could your life be worse if God were in control of it?"

Myles opened his mouth, then closed it. His head fell back against the headboard. "I've never had control anyway."

"Exactly. You're at the mercy of circumstances with no one to turn to. The only things you can truly control in your life are your behavior and your reactions."

"Sometimes I can't even control myself."

"Without God, we're all losers. Look at Buck. The stuff that happened to him was like your worst nightmare. He could be the most bitter, angry person you ever met, but he chose to trust God with his life, and look at him now!"

Myles nodded. "And you, too. You didn't get angry about Beulah."

Al shrugged. "It wouldn't have done any good to get mad. Anyone can see she isn't in love with me, and to be honest, my heart isn't broken. The point is, once you decide to trust God with things, He turns your messed-up life into something great. I'm not saying you'd have it easy from then on, or that all your dreams would come true; but no matter what happens, your life would be a success. The Bible says in First Peter, 'Humble yourselves therefore under the mighty hand of God, that he may exalt you in due time.' You can never lift yourself up no matter how hard you try."

After a moment's thought, Myles lowered his chin and shook his head. "I don't see it, Al. I understand that God is far above me, holy and just, almighty and righteous, but loving? I don't know God that way. Sure, He saved me from the bear, but look what has happened to me since."

"When was the last time you read about Jesus?"

"The last time I read the Bible? I was reading in Genesis the other night."

"I think you need to read the Gospels now. The Old Testament is important, too, but you need to understand about Jesus first. Where is your Bible?"

"At our house next to my bed. Don't bring it here, Al. I want to go home. Can you talk Buck into taking me home? It's driving me crazy, being here in the same house with Beulah. She hasn't spoken to me since we fought yesterday. Gram is good to me, but I'm getting cabin fever."

Al looked into his eyes and gave a short nod. "I'll talk to Buck."

❧

Beulah watched the wagon disappear up the drive. Her eyes were dry. Her heart felt as leaden as the sky. Returning to her seat, she picked up her piecework and took a disinterested stitch.

Violet observed her from across the parlor. "The house already seems quiet, doesn't it? I will miss having Virginia around to chat with. She is the most interesting lady. She refused my offer to stay here. I hope she will be comfortable at the men's house. They don't have an indoor pump, you know, and the furnishings are rather crude."

"Is Daniel sleeping?" Beulah asked in her most casual tone.

"Yes. Samuel is at Scott's house, and Eunice is reading. Did you hear Al's news?" Violet snipped a thread with her teeth.

"Several times over. I told Eunice first; then she told *me* about three times so far. I'm glad he's not leaving for awhile. We would all miss him. I think Eunice has romantic feelings for Al."

Violet chuckled. "I've noticed. She has good taste. Maybe I'll have Albert for a son-in-law someday after all. I hope so. He's a dear boy."

Beulah concentrated on tying a knot. "She's only thirteen, Mama. Maybe I should have married him."

Violet's hands dropped to her lap. "Pardon?"

Beulah winced, wishing she had kept the stray thought to herself. "Al wouldn't marry me now if I proposed to him myself, and I'm not in love with him anyway, but I can't help wondering if I couldn't have been happily married to him. After all, lots of people make marriages of convenience and end up happy together. Al is annoying, but he's steady and safe."

Violet lowered her chin and stared at her daughter. "What about Myles?"

Beulah pressed her lips together and jerked at a tangle in her thread. "Myles is not the man I thought he was. He is selfish and bitter." She swallowed hard.

Setting aside her mending, Violet joined her daughter on the couch. "Tell me."

Beulah leaned against Violet. Her shoulders began to shake. Wiping her eyes, she grumbled, "I hate crying, Mama, but it seems as if every time I try to talk about something important, I start bawling."

"It's a woman's lot in life, Darling." Violet pushed a lock of loose hair behind her daughter's ear and smiled. "I understand, believe me."

Between sobs and sniffles, Beulah poured out her heartache and disappointment. ". . . so I told him he could go without me. I thought he was kind and wise, Mama, but yesterday he acted like a brute. And all because of some money he doesn't have. I'm so thankful I found out what he is really like before I married him!"

Violet stared at the fireplace, pondering her reply. "So now Myles is a brute. All the good things you loved about him mean nothing."

Beulah wiped her eyes and nose with a handkerchief. "I could never be happily married to a man with such a terrible temper, Mama. He swore in my presence and never apologized!"

"If Myles has truly turned his back on the Lord, then I agree that you should not marry him. But if, as your papa believes, he is on the verge of surrender, it would be a shame for you to give up on him. He adores you, Beulah, and I think he would make you an excellent husband."

Beulah's head popped up. "Mama! How can you say that after

what I just told you? He told me never to mention God's name in his presence again!"

"He was distraught. I'm sure he didn't mean it. I understand he had a long talk with Al about God this afternoon, and he plans to start reading the New Testament when he gets home today. Darling, every man has faults. I hope you realize that. Even Al would lose his temper, given the right provocation."

"Papa never shouts at you."

A dimple appeared near Violet's mouth. "No, but that's because he talks softly when he gets angry. The angrier he is, the softer his voice."

"You don't mean it, Mama," Beulah said, eyes wide.

Violet rubbed a little circle on the girl's back. "I mean every word. Darling, you had better learn quickly that only God can offer you complete security and contentment. No man can fulfill your every need, and most of them wouldn't want to try. The average man enters marriage thinking that a wife's purpose is to fulfill *his* needs. Unless you recognize the fact that all people are basically selfish, you will be in for a rude awakening when you marry. Myles has plenty of faults, but so have you, my dear."

"If people are so terribly selfish, how can a marriage ever be happy?"

"That's where the Lord makes a difference. In His strength, you and I can learn to love our men with all their human flaws and failings. That is one of the greatest joys of marriage: to give and give of yourself to please your beloved. Usually a good man will respond in kind, but you must understand that there is never a guarantee of this. Your part is to love at all times, without reservation."

Beulah wilted. "How can I do that, Mama? You know how selfish I am!"

"In the Lord's strength, Dear. If you truly love Myles, you will accept him just as he is and be grateful for the opportunity to shower him with the love and attention he craves from you. There are few things in life more fulfilling than pleasing your husband, Beulah." Violet spoke with the authority of experience.

Beulah sat straighter. "I want to be exactly like you, Mama. You make Papa so happy that he glows when you're near. I want to make Myles that happy."

Violet squeezed her shoulders. "That's my girl! Now you keep on praying for Myles, and when he is ready to receive your love, I think you will know it."

Beulah hugged her mother. "You're wonderful. I feel so much better! Now, I have this idea for my wedding dress that I've been wanting to discuss with you. Do you have a moment?"

Eyes twinkling, Violet nodded.

❧

Pushy kneaded a dent for herself in the middle of Myles's back. He groaned when she settled down. "You must weigh a ton, Cat. When are you going to fire off those kittens?"

Pushy purred, vibrating against him. "You really missed me, didn't you?" Her affectionate greeting had warmed his heart.

He returned to his reading. The book was fascinating. For the first time in his life, Myles could visualize Jesus among the people, teaching, healing, loving.

The parable of the unforgiving servant in Matthew, chapter eighteen, struck a nerve. He recognized himself in the cruel, vindictive man who punished a debtor after he himself had been forgiven a much larger debt. The simple story was an eloquent reprimand and admonition.

"I understand, Jesus," Myles said, bowing his head. "This story is about me. Please forgive me for my anger at Monte. I want to forgive him as You forgave me. If he's there with You now, please tell him for me. Tell him I love him. I forgive Mama for dying and leaving me behind. She must have been terribly lonely after Father was killed in the war. And I forgive Mr. Roarke for swindling us, too. I don't imagine he's deriving much true pleasure from his ill-gotten gains. I feel almost sorry for him. You know that the real reason I refused to forgive people all those years was pride. I thought I was better than others. I was wrong."

Humility was an easy burden in comparison to the bitter load he had carried for so many years. Myles felt free and relaxed, yet still rather empty.

"Where is the joy, God? Are You really here with me? What's wrong with me? Maybe I'm spiritually blind."

Pushy purred on.

Sighing, Myles returned to the Book. The story enthralled him, and when he reached the end of Matthew, he continued on into Mark, absorbed in the story of Jesus from a slightly different perspective. His eyes were growing heavy when he reached chapter ten, the story of blind Bartimaeus begging at the roadside.

Then, for some reason, he was wide-awake. His mind pictured the pitiful man in rags who cried out, "Jesus, Son of David, have mercy on me!"

Jesus stopped and asked the fellow what he wanted. Jesus didn't overlook the poor and helpless among His people. He cared about the blind man.

Myles read the next part aloud. "'The blind man said unto him, Lord, that I might receive my sight.

"'And Jesus said unto him, Go thy way; thy faith hath made thee whole. And immediately he received his sight, and followed Jesus in the way.'"

Myles stopped and read it again. Slowly his eyes closed and his hands formed into fists. The cry echoed from his own heart. "Lord, I want to see! Please, help me to see You as You truly are."

He contemplated Jesus. "The kindest man who has ever lived. He came to reveal You to mankind. He was Emmanuel—'God with us.' God in the flesh. So You *are* a God of mercy, patience, and infinite understanding. Lord, I believe!"

Myles wept for joy.

For I determined not to know any thing among you,
save Jesus Christ, and him crucified.
1 Corinthians 2:2

*H*is bandaged foot wouldn't fit into a stirrup, so Myles decided to ride Cholla bareback. A wool blanket protected his clothes from her sweat and hair, and he laid his walking stick, a gift from Cyrus Thwaite, across her withers. "Take it easy, Girl," he warned, gripping a hank of her mane in one hand as he sprang to her back and swung his leg over. "I'm running on one foot, so to speak." The swelling had receded and the vivid bruising had faded to pale green and purple, but Myles could put little weight on the foot as yet.

"Myles, you be careful," Virginia called from the front porch as he passed. "Visit your friend and the barber and come straight home. Do you hear?"

"I hear." Reining in the fidgeting mare, Myles grinned at his grandmother. He could endure her motherly domination for the sake of her good cooking and excellent housekeeping skills—abilities he had never before known she possessed. "You're quite a woman, Gram."

"Away with your flattery," she retorted, not before he glimpsed her pleasure.

Cholla trotted almost sideways up the drive, head tucked and tail standing straight up. Its wispy hair streamed behind her like a shredded banner. "You're a loaded weapon today, aren't you?" Myles patted the mare's taut neck. "Sorry; no running. The roads are too icy."

A few miles of trotting took the edge off Cholla's energy. She still occasionally challenged her master's authority, but her heart was no longer in it. Myles felt her muscles unwind beneath him.

Although it was good to be out in the open again instead of cloistered in his stuffy room, fighting the horse drained much of Myles's strength. When he dismounted in front of Miss Amelia's boarding-house, he lost hold of his walking stick. It clattered to the frozen mud. Cholla shied to one side, and Myles landed hard. His bad foot hit the ground. Clutching Cholla by the chest and withers, he gritted his teeth and grimaced until the worst pain had passed.

"Steady, Girl," he gasped. Balancing on one foot, he scooped up his stick. It wasn't easy to tether Cholla with one hand, but he managed. Hopping on one foot, using the stick for balance, he made his way to Amelia's porch.

"What on earth are you doing, Myles?" Amelia said, flinging open her front door and ushering him inside.

"I came to see Boz," Myles gasped. "Isn't he here?"

"You come on into the parlor and sit yourself down." Amelia supported his arm with a steely grip. "That's where Boz keeps himself." She lifted her voice. "You got a visitor, Sheriff. Another ailing cowboy on my hands. Just what I needed. You two sit here and have a talk. I've got work to do." Leaving Myles in an armchair, she brushed her hands on her apron, gave each man an affectionate look, and departed.

Boz drew a playing card from his deck, laid it on a stack, and gave Myles a crooked smile. "How's the foot?" His right shoulder was heavily wrapped, binding that arm to his side.

"Mending. You don't sound so good." Myles shifted in his chair.

Boz did not immediately reply. "I ain't so good, Myles," he finally wheezed. "Bullet nicked a lung and severed a nerve in my shoulder. It kinda bounced around in there. Doc did his best, but he doesn't expect I'll regain the use of my arm."

Myles blinked and stared at the floor.

"I know what you're thinkin'," Boz said. "Not much good in a one-armed sheriff. I reckon God has other plans for my future."

Myles met the other man's steady gaze. Slowly he nodded, amazed by Boz's cheerful acceptance of his fate.

"Amelia says I can work for her. She's been needing to hire household help, and she cain't think of anyone she'd rather have about the place."

"You?" Myles stared blankly until he caught the twinkle in his friend's eyes. "Boz, are you joshing me?"

The former sheriff's face creased into a broad grin. "She reckons it wouldn't be proper for me to stay here permanent-like, so she proposed marriage."

Myles began to chuckle. Boz put a finger to his lips. "Hush! Let the woman think it was all her idea, at least until after we're hitched."

Myles sputtered with suppressed merriment, and Boz joined in. Soon the two men were wiping tears from their faces. Boz groaned, holding his shoulder and wheezing. "Stop before you do me in."

The door opened, and Amelia backed into the room carrying a tray. "I brung you coffee and cakes." Her sharp eyes inspected their faces. "Doc says the sheriff needs quiet. Hope I didn't make a mistake by letting you in, Myles."

"He's all right, Amelia. Laughter is good for what ails a man. What you got there? Raisin cookies?" Boz perked up.

"Yes, and snickerdoodles. Mind you don't eat more'n is good for ya, Boswell Martin."

Nearly an hour later, Myles grinned as he heaved himself up on Cholla's back. "Next stop, the store, then on to the barbershop." The horse flicked her ears to listen.

Thank You for leaving Boz with us here on earth, Lord, Myles prayed as he rode. *And thank You for giving him his heart's desire. He's waited a long time for love, but from the look in Amelia's eyes while she fussed over him today, he's found it.*

Myles picked up his mail at the general store. There was a letter addressed in strange handwriting. Curious, he paused just inside the doorway, balanced on his good foot, and ripped open the letter.

Dear Myles,
    Antonio tells me what to write, and I do my best.
    Antonio pray for you every day. He say have you dropped your burden yet? I hope you do, Myles. We want your best for you.
    You can write us here in Florida. We stay until summer season open. We want to visit you, but have not the money.
    Antonio want to know if the bear was found. He feel bad

*about keeping it secret. Our circus, it was bought by another man
when the owner was put in jail. He cheat one man too many,
Antonio say. Things better for us now, but we want a home that
does not move.*

*Antonio speak much of settling down to open a bakery. Is
there need for a bakery in your town?*

God bless you.

Antonio and Gina Spinelli

Myles determined to write back at his first opportunity. Antonio
would be pleased to hear news of his mended relationship with God,
and if any town ever needed a bakery, Myles was certain Longtree,
Wisconsin, did.

As Myles rode past the parsonage, someone hailed him. He reined
in Cholla and waited for the pastor to approach. "Hello, Reverend."

David Schoengard's ruddy face beamed as he stood at Cholla's
shoulder and reached up to shake Myles's hand. "Good to see you
about town. We've been praying for you. From all I hear, yours was a
serious injury."

"Thanks for the prayers. God has been healing me . . . inside and
out."

David's eyes gleamed. "Ah, so the lamb has found its way home?"

"More like the Shepherd roped and hog-tied an ornery ram, flung
it over His shoulder, and hauled it home. I'm afraid I was a tough case,
but He never stopped trying to show me the truth."

The pastor chuckled. "I understand. Are you ready to profess your
faith before the church?"

Myles tucked his chin. "Is that necessary?"

"Not for your salvation, of course, but it would be a wonderful
encouragement to other believers to hear how God worked in your
life. I'm also hoping you'll honor us with a song someday soon."

Staring between Cholla's ears, Myles pondered. "I do need to ask
forgiveness of people in this town. Guess this is my chance. I'll do it,
if you think I should, Reverend."

"I appreciate that—and please call me Dave, or at least Pastor Dave.
I'm no more 'reverend' than you are." He patted Cholla's furry neck.

Myles nodded. "All right, Pastor Dave. Do I need your approval on a song?"

"I'll trust you to choose an appropriate selection. And thank you. Caroline will be excited when I tell her you agreed to sing."

"How is she doing?"

"She has a tough time of it during the last weeks before a baby arrives, but she handles it well. My mother is at the house to help out. She and Caroline are great friends."

David cleared his throat. "If you don't mind me asking, how are things between you and Marva? Or is it you and Beulah? Caroline and I were never sure."

Myles scratched his beard and took a deep breath. "Marva and I are friends. There never was more between us. And Beulah isn't speaking to me at present. I . . . uh . . . let's just say she got a glimpse of Myles Van Huysen at his worst, and she didn't care much for what she saw."

"I see. Have you apologized?"

"Not yet. I haven't spoken with her since God . . . since He changed me. I don't know how to approach her. I mean, she pretty much told me to leave her out of my future plans."

"The change in you could make a difference, Myles. Faint heart never won fair maiden."

"Yes, I need to figure out a plan. Right now I'd better be on my way. I've got orders not to dawdle."

"Your grandmother?" David stepped away from the horse. "I enjoyed meeting her last Sunday. Quite a lady."

Myles nodded. "Beulah is a lot like her. Feisty." He smiled. "If you think of it, I could use a few prayers in that area, too. You know, for wisdom and tact when I talk to Beulah."

"Every man needs prayer in the area of communication with women," David said with a straight face. "See you Sunday." With a wink, he turned away.

❧

Myles squirmed in the front pew, elbows resting on his knees, and rubbed one finger across his mustache. His chin felt naked, bereft of its concealing beard. His heart pounded erratically. Lines of a prepared speech raced through his head.

Marva Obermeier played the piano while the congregation sang. She never once looked in his direction. Myles could not sing. He knew he would be ill if he tried. Why had he volunteered to sing so soon? He wasn't ready. It was one thing to entertain a crowd for profit and another thing altogether to sing in worship to God while other believers listened.

"Relax, Myles. The Lord will help you." Virginia leaned over to pat his arm.

He nodded without looking up.

Was Beulah here, somewhere in the room behind him? Would she change her mind when she saw how God was transforming his life, or had he forever frightened her away? With an effort, Myles turned his thoughts and heart back to God and prayed for courage and peace. *This is all new to me, Lord. I feel like a baby, helpless and dependent. Can You really use me?*

His foot throbbed. He needed to prop it up again. Pastor David was making an announcement. Myles tried to focus his mind.

"A new brother in Christ has something to share with us this morning. Please join me in welcoming Myles Trent Van Huysen into our fellowship of believers."

Myles rose and turned to face the crowd, leaning on his crutch. Expectant, friendly faces met his gaze. He swallowed hard. "Many of you know that I have been living a lie among you these past few years. Today I wish to apologize for my deceit and ask your forgiveness."

There was Beulah, seated between her mother and Eunice. Her dark eyes held encouragement and concern. She pressed three fingers against her trembling lips.

"My grandmother, Virginia Van Huysen, has prayed for me these many long years. She never gave up hope that God would chase me down. I stand before you to confess that I am now a child of God, saved by the shed blood of Jesus Christ. My life, such as it is, belongs to Him forevermore. I do not yet know how or where He will lead, but I know that I will humbly follow." His voice cracked.

Marva sat beside her father in the fourth row. Although her eyes glittered with unshed tears, she gave Myles an encouraging smile.

"I'm having difficulty even talking—don't know how I'll manage to sing. But I want to share my testimony with a song."

He limped to the piano. After leaning his crutch against the wall, he settled on the bench. This piano needed tuning, and several of its keys were missing their ivories. One key sagged below the rest, dead. Myles played a prolonged introduction while begging God to carry him through this ordeal.

Lifting his face, he closed his eyes and began to sing Elizabeth Clephane's beautiful hymn:

"Beneath the cross of Jesus I fain would take my stand . . ."

Myles knew that the Lord's hand was upon him. His voice rang true and clear. The third verse was his testimony:

"I take, O cross, thy shadow for my abiding place—
I ask no other sunshine than the sunshine of His face;
Content to let the world go by, to know no gain nor loss,
My sinful self my only shame, my glory all the cross."

The last notes faded away. Myles opened his eyes. His grandmother was beaming, wiping her face with a handkerchief. He collected his crutch and stood. Someone near the back of the room clapped, another person joined in, and soon applause filled the church. "Amen!" Myles recognized Al's voice.

Pastor Schoengard wrapped an arm around Myles's shoulder and asked, "Would anyone like to hear more from our brother?"

The clapping and shouts increased in volume. " 'Amazing Grace.' " It was Cyrus Thwaite's creaky voice.

" 'Holy, Holy, Holy,' " someone else requested.

Pastor David lifted his hand, chuckling. "This is still a worship service, friends. Please maintain order and do not overwhelm our new brother." He turned to Myles. "Will you sing again, or do you need rest?" he asked in an undertone. "Don't feel obliged, Myles. There will be other days."

Myles stared at the floor, dazed by this openhearted reception. He smiled at the pastor. "It is an honor." He returned to the bench and began to play, making the ancient spinet sound like a concert grand.

16

But as it is written, Eye hath not seen, nor ear heard,
neither have entered into the heart of man,
the things which God hath prepared for them that love him.
1 Corinthians 2:9

*W*hoa, Girl." Myles hauled the horse to a stop and set the buggy's brake. On the other side of a pasture fence, Al and Buck kept watch over a smoldering fire, feeding it with branches and dead leaves. Smoke shifted across the sodden field, hampered by drifting snowflakes.

Myles hoisted a large basket up to the seat beside him, unlatched the lid, and peeked inside. Indignant yellow eyes met his gaze. "Meow," Pushy complained.

"I'll be right back, I promise. I need to talk to Buck for a minute. You should be warm enough in there." Leaving the basket on the floor, he climbed down and vaulted the fence, hopping on his good foot before regaining his balance.

Cold seeped through his layers of clothing. "Not a great day to be outside," he commented to the other men as he approached. "That fire feels good." He held out gloved hands to the blaze.

"Need to get rid of this brush before winter sets in for good," Buck answered, forking another bundle of dead leaves into the fire. Flames crackled, and ashes drifted upward. "This is the best weather for it. Little danger of fire spreading."

"Um, I need to talk with you, Buck. Do you have a minute?"

Al looked from Myles to Buck and back. "Need privacy? I can head for the house and visit the family."

Myles shifted his weight, winced at the pain in his leg, and tried to smile. "Thanks. Would you take the buggy, Al? I've got Pushy and the kittens with me—planned to let Beulah see them. I'm afraid they'll get cold."

Al smirked and shook his head. "You and those cats! All right, I'll deliver the litter to Beulah, but that's all. Should I tell her you're coming?"

Myles nodded. "Soon."

He stood beside Buck and watched Al drive away. The rooftop of Fairfield's Folly was visible through the leafless trees surrounding it. Smoke drifted from its chimneys. Myles could easily imagine Beulah working at the stove or washing dishes.

"How's the leg?"

"Better every day."

"Good. Violet is in town visiting Caroline and the Schoengard baby," Buck said. "Had you heard? Little girl, arrived last night, big and healthy. They named her Jemima after Pastor David's mother."

"That's wonderful! A healthy girl, eh?" Myles fidgeted. "Great news."

"Beulah is watching Daniel. Samuel stayed home from school; said he was sick. I have my doubts." A smile curled Buck's thick mustache and crinkled the corners of his eyes.

"Beulah is home?"

"That's what I said. Washing laundry, last I saw."

"I, uh, need to talk with you. About the future. I mean, about Beulah and me. I need advice."

Buck threw a branch on the fire. "I'm listening."

Myles shifted his gaze from the fire to the house to the trees and back to Buck. He crossed and uncrossed his arms. "I'm not sure where to begin."

Buck smiled. Sparks flew when he tossed a large pine knot into the blaze.

"I want to ask your permission to marry Beulah, but I don't know how soon I'll be able to support a wife. I must return to New York and give a concert tour. Along with a few remaining stocks and bonds and whatever is left from the sale of the family house after I pay off debts, the money I earn should be enough to purchase the Thwaite farm.

Cyrus agreed to hold it for me . . . at least for a few months." Myles spoke rapidly. Realizing that he was rubbing the front of his coat, he stuffed the errant hand into his pocket.

"Do you plan to propose before you leave or after you return?"

"I don't know." Myles rubbed the back of his neck, pushing his hat over his forehead. "Do you think she will accept my proposal at all? I mean, I haven't spoken with her—not a real conversation—since the time she blew up at me. I can't leave without knowing, but at the same time it would be tough to leave her behind once we're engaged. What do you think I ought to do, Buck?"

"Have you prayed about this?"

"God must be sick of my voice by now. I've been begging for wisdom and guidance. I feel so puny and stupid. After years of regarding God with—I'm embarrassed to admit this, but it's the truth—with a superior attitude, I'm feeling like small potatoes these days."

"God likes small potatoes. They are useful to Him."

Myles shoved his hat back into place. His smile felt unsteady, as did his knees. "If Beulah won't have me, I'll set up housekeeping with my grandmother. Gram has decided she likes Longtree better than New York, believe it or not. Most of her old friends have died, and she prefers to live out her earthly days with me here. She's a great lady."

"That she is. And what are her plans if you marry?"

"She would be willing either to settle in town at Miss Amelia's boardinghouse or to stay with us at the farm, whichever Beulah would prefer. Gram has money of her own, enough to keep her in modest comfort for life." Myles tossed a handful of twigs into the fire, one at a time. "Do you . . . do you think Beulah will see me today? I mean, is she still angry? I was terrible to her that day—I swore at her, threatened her, and manhandled her."

Buck shook his head. A little chuckle escaped.

"What are you thinking?" Myles asked in frustration.

"Beulah and her mother have been sewing a wedding gown these past few weeks while you've been stewing in remorse and uncertainty. She forgave you even before you professed your faith at church. Beulah's temper is quick, but she seldom holds a grudge. I hope you know what a moody little firebrand you're getting. That girl will require plenty of loving attention."

Myles gaped as a glow spread throughout his soul. "She's been making a wedding dress? For me?"

"Actually, I believe she intends to wear it herself," Buck said dryly.

Myles was too intent to be amused. "And I have your permission to propose?"

"You do. Violet and I are well acquainted with your industry and fidelity, my friend. You will be an excellent husband to our girl."

Myles stared at the ground, blinking hard. "And I had the gall to believe God had deserted me," he mumbled. Biting his lip, he turned away. "I don't deserve this."

Buck wrapped a strong arm around the younger man's shoulders. "I felt the same way when Violet accepted me."

"You did?"

Buck laughed aloud. "Go talk to the girl and decide together on a wedding date. It might be wiser to wait until your return from New York to marry; but then again it might be pleasant for the two of you to make that concert tour together—a kind of paid honeymoon. Beulah could be your inspiration."

Myles stared into space until Buck gave him a shove. "Get on with you. She's waiting."

❧

Beulah jabbed a clothespin into place, securing Samuel's overalls on the cord Papa had suspended across the kitchen. The laundry nearest the stove steamed. Beulah tested one of Daniel's diapers. It was still damp.

"You could at least try to talk to me," she accused the absent Myles. "How am I supposed to demonstrate unselfish love to a man I never see?" Her lips trembled. Clenching her jaw, she stabbed another clothespin at an undervest but missed. "No one tells me anything. For all I know, he's going back to New York without me."

Recalling Myles's singing in church, she brushed a tear away with the back of one hand. "He was so handsome. I hardly knew him without his beard. He looked like a stranger. And oh, his song made my soul ache." Pressing a hand to her breast, she allowed a quiet sob. "You have changed his heart, haven't You, God? Mama was so right. After all my accusations that Mama wouldn't give Myles a chance, *I'm* the one who quit on him at the crucial moment. Please let me try again, Lord."

Samuel's wool sock joined its mate on the line.

A whimper of sound escaped as Beulah's lips moved. "If you have changed your mind about me, the least you could do is come and tell me so. Oh, Myles, I love you so much!"

A lid rattled. "Who are you talking to, Beulah?" Samuel slipped an oatmeal cookie from the crock and took an enormous bite. Watchful sat at his feet, tail waving, hopeful eyes fixed upon the cookie.

Startled to discover that she was not alone, Beulah glared. "Myself."

"Finally found someone who wants to listen, hmm?" Samuel ducked when she threw a wet towel at his head. Laughing, he left the kitchen with Watchful at his heels.

"I thought you were too sick to go to school," Beulah yelled after him. "You'd better get in bed before Mama comes home."

She retrieved the towel, brushing off dust. Sighing, she decided it needed washing again. "My penalty for a temper tantrum."

Scraping damp hair from her face with water-shriveled fingers, she drifted to the window and stared outside. Movement drew her attention to her garden. A doe and two large fawns, dressed in their gray winter coats, nibbled at bolted cabbages. Resting her arms on the windowsill, Beulah felt her heart lighten. "Better not let anyone else see you," she warned the deer. "One of your former companions is hanging on the meat hook by the barn. We have plenty of venison for the winter, but you never know."

The animals' ears twitched. All three stared toward Beulah's window. After a tense moment, the doe flicked her tail and returned to her browsing. Then the three deer lifted their heads to stare toward the barn before springing away into the forest.

Watchful barked from the entryway, and Beulah heard a man's deep voice. Her hands flew to her messy hair, and her eyes widened.

"Al is here!" Samuel shouted. "He brought something in a basket."

"I'll be right there," she said, relaxing. It was only Al. "Why aren't you in bed, Sam?"

Samuel pounded upstairs, skipping steps on the way.

⟋

Myles lifted his hand to knock just as the door opened. Al waved an arm to usher him inside. "Enter, please. I'm on my way out. I'll take my mare back and leave the buggy for you. Want me to stable Bess before I go?"

Myles nodded as he limped inside. "Thanks, Al." He swallowed hard. "Where is Beulah?"

Al's grin widened. "In the parlor. Sitting on your bear."

"My bear?" Myles stopped, puzzled.

"It makes a nice rug."

"Oh, the bear."

Shaking his head, Al laughed. "Go on. Talking to you is useless." He clapped his hat on his head and slammed the door as he left.

Myles licked his lips and took a fortifying breath. *Lord, please help me.*

He stepped into the parlor. A shaggy brown rug lay before the stone hearth. Beulah sat Indian style in the middle of the bear's back, and in the hammock of her skirt lay Pushy and four tiny kittens. Firelight glowed in Beulah's eyes and hair. The cat purred with her eyes closed while her babies nursed.

"Myles!" Beulah's voice held all the encouragement Myles required. "You came."

Daniel lay on his back near the rug, waving a wooden rattle with one hand. At the sight of Myles, the baby rolled to his stomach and called a cheerful greeting. Myles bent to pick up the baby, enjoying the feel of his solid little body. Daniel crowed again and whacked Myles in the face with a slimy hand. Bouncing for joy, he dropped his rattle.

"I came. You like my kittens?" Favoring his left leg, he settled near her on the rug. Daniel wriggled out of his grasp and scooted toward the fallen toy. "I wanted you to see them before their eyes opened."

"They are adorable." Beulah lifted a black and white kitten. Its pink feet splayed, and its mouth opened in a silent meow. Pushy opened her eyes partway until Beulah returned her baby. "I love them, Myles."

Hearing a catch in her voice, he inspected her face. "What's wrong?"

"Does this mean you're leaving? You brought the kittens to me for safekeeping."

Myles noted the dots of perspiration on her pert nose, the quivering of her full lips. Tenderness seemed to swell his heart until he could scarcely draw breath. "No, my dearest. I simply wanted you to see them. I have just spoken to your stepfather, as your mother wisely advised."

Beulah's dark eyes held puzzlement. "You spoke to Papa?"

"Have you changed your mind, Beulah? Do you still wish to marry me? Can you forgive me for swearing at you and threatening you?"

She clasped her hands at her breast. "Yes, Myles! More than anything I want to marry you!" She started to rise then remembered the burden in her lap.

Chuckling, Myles scrambled to his hands and knees, leaned over, and kissed her gently. Below his chest, Pushy's purring increased in volume.

When he pulled away, Beulah's eyelashes fluttered. Her lips were still parted. He returned to place a kiss on her nose. "We need to talk, Honey."

"Your mustache tickles."

Just then, Daniel let out a squawk. Startled, Myles and Beulah turned. Only the baby's feet projected from beneath the davenport.

"Oh, Daniel!" Beulah cried. "He rolled under there again. Would you get him, Myles?" She deposited kitten after kitten in the blanket-lined basket. Pushy hopped in and curled up with her brood.

After crawling across the room, Myles took hold of Daniel's feet and pulled him out from under the davenport. As soon as he saw Myles, Daniel grinned. "You're a pretty decent chaperone, Fella," Myles said. "Better than Pushy is, at any rate."

Beulah hurried to scoop up her dusty brother. "He moves so quickly. I got used to him staying in one place, but now he's into everything."

"Can I come in yet? Are you done kissing?" Poised in the parlor doorway, Samuel wore a pained expression.

"Don't count on it," Myles said.

Beulah shrugged. "You might as well join us. You're no more sick than I am, you scamp. But at least this way you get to be first to hear our news: Myles and I are getting married."

Samuel stretched out on the bearskin, combing its fur with his fingers. "I know. I heard you."

"You were listening? Samuel, how could you?"

"Easy enough. I was sitting on the stairs." He lifted a gray kitten from the basket and cradled it against his face.

While Beulah gasped with indignation, Myles began to chuckle. He sat on the davenport and patted the seat beside him. "Come on, Honey. It doesn't matter. We've got important things to discuss." After depositing Daniel on the rug for Samuel to entertain, Beulah snuggled beneath Myles's arm and soon regained her good humor.

While Samuel played with kittens and Daniel rolled about on the floor, the lovers planned their future.

ℰPILOGUE

January 1882, New York City

*C*urled into the depths of a well-cushioned sofa, Beulah shut her book, smiling. Snow drifted upon the balcony outside her window, mounding on the railings like fine white sugar. Closing her eyes, she sighed in contentment. *Thank You, Lord. Married life is better than I ever imagined.*

The Van Huysens had opted to stay in one of the older hotels in the city. Its old-fashioned splendor was sufficient to please Beulah without overwhelming her. At times, especially around the holidays, she had suffered pangs of homesickness. But Myles's adoration, combined with the knowledge that this tour was temporary, soothed her occasional feelings of inadequacy and loneliness.

She slipped a letter from inside the book cover. There on the envelope her new name, "Mrs. Myles Van Huysen," was written in Mama's neat script. Beulah ran her finger over the words. She was eager to share family news with Myles that night after the concert. He was currently at the theater, practicing.

"Beulah?" A familiar voice called from outside the hotel door. Virginia did not believe in knocking. Beulah hurried to let in her new grandmother.

Virginia bustled into the room, her arms filled with packages. "I've been shopping. Wish you had come with me, but I still managed to spend a good deal. I want you to try this on." After dropping several boxes upon a table, she shoved the largest in Beulah's direction.

"What have you done, Gram?" Beulah chuckled. "What will Myles say?"

"I don't care what that boy might say. It's my money, and I'll spend it as I like." Spying the letter in Beulah's hand, she said, "So you've heard from your mother again? How is everyone back home?"

The crisp inquiry warmed Beulah's heart. She kissed Virginia's cheek. "I love you, Gram. Mama says to tell you 'hello.' They are all well. Daniel is pulling up to stand beside furniture now. Sheriff Boz and Miss Amelia have set February fourteenth as their wedding day, so we should be home in time for the wedding. Um, let's see . . . Eunice found homes for all four of Pushy's kittens. Mama and Papa are letting her keep the black one, Miss Amelia chose the black and white girl, and Mr. Thwaite picked the gray boy. Believe it or not, Al decided to take the black one with white feet! After all his teasing Myles about liking cats, he now has a pet cat of his own."

"That's so nice, Dear." Virginia smiled fondly at the girl. "Only a few days now until we'll all be on the train headed for Wisconsin."

"Will you be sorry to leave New York? You must miss your old house. Didn't it hurt to see strangers take it over?"

Virginia pursed her lips and gazed through the window at blowing snow. "For many years now New York has not seemed like home. Ever since the boys left me, I've been a lonely soul. My friends are all gone, and sometimes when I walked around that old house, I missed my dear husband Edwin so much. . . . I could picture John and Gwendolyn chasing up and down the stairs—they were our only children, you know. John was killed in the war, and Gwen died of cholera at age fifteen."

Shaking her head, she said firmly, "Dwelling in the past is detrimental to one's mental and spiritual health. Now I have Myles, you, and many friends in Longtree." Her expression brightened. "My life is in the future now. First in Wisconsin, then in heaven!"

Seeing Beulah dab at a tear, she started back into action. "Now take these boxes and try on the gown. It's only a short time 'til we must leave for the theater. Don't want to be late! I had a note from Mr. Poole this morning—he will be at the concert tonight. The man seems to take personal pleasure in Myles's success, which is not too strange considering his role in the boy's return to the stage. I hear it's another sold-out house. Myles's agent has been begging him to reconsider and stay on permanently."

Arms loaded with boxes, Beulah turned back to grin. "Poor man! He hasn't a chance against Cyrus Thwaite's farm."

⤫

Beulah perched on the edge of her seat, absently fanning herself. Her emerald taffeta evening gown rustled with every movement, but it was impossible to keep entirely still.

"Hard to believe it's snowing outside, isn't it?" Virginia leaned over to ask. She smoothed a bit of lace on Beulah's shoulder and smiled approval.

Beulah nodded in reply. The old lady's whispers were sometimes louder than she intended. Myles was singing a heart-wrenching aria from *Aida*, and Beulah wanted to listen.

"Hard to believe this is the last week of Myles's tour," Virginia commented a few minutes later while Myles performed Schumann's A Minor Piano Concerto. Again, Beulah nodded briefly.

After weeks of attending her husband's concerts, she still had not tired of hearing him sing and play. Each night Myles varied his repertoire. Always he sang opera, usually Verdi or Mozart; often he performed a few ballads and popular songs; most nights he took requests from the audience. Beulah's favorite part of each performance was discovering which hymn he would choose for his finale.

Tonight he sang "Holy, Holy, Holy." Beulah closed her eyes to listen without distraction. No matter how cross, irritating, or obstinate Myles might have been during the day, each night she fell in love with him all over again. He was so handsome, charming, and irresistible up on that stage!

"I think I'll head home now, Dear," Virginia said while Myles took his bow.

Beulah stopped clapping long enough to return the old lady's kiss. "Thank you so much for this marvelous dress, and the gloves, and the reticule, and everything! Your taste is exquisite. You are too good to me." Beulah smoothed the ruffles on her bouffant skirt.

"Child, it was my pleasure. I trust Myles will approve. I hope you know how thankful I am to have you for a granddaughter. Myles has excellent taste, too. Good night." She patted Beulah's cheek and bustled away. Although Myles often requested her to let him escort her home, Virginia maintained independence, insisting that she was perfectly capable of hailing a cab and returning alone to the hotel.

As soon as the red velvet curtain fell, Beulah gathered her things and hurried backstage. Myles waited for her in his dressing room, smiling in welcome.

"Do you like it?" Beulah twirled in place. "Gram bought it for me. Isn't she wonderful? Not that I'll find much use for an evening gown back in Longtree. Gram fixed my hair, too."

Myles's eyes glowed. "You are beautiful, my Beulah. More than any man deserves." His voice was slightly hoarse.

When he closed the door behind her, Beulah wrapped her arms around her husband's neck and kissed him. "Thank you, thank you for bringing me with you to New York. I wouldn't have missed this experience for the world," she murmured against his lips.

"You say that every night," he chuckled, pressing her slender form close.

"And every night I mean it," she insisted. Framing his face with her hands, she studied each feature. "Sometimes I miss your beard, but I do love how your face feels right after you shave."

"You're standing on my feet." He rubbed his smooth cheek against hers.

"That way I'm taller." She stood on tiptoe to kiss him.

He took her by the waist and lifted her off his feet. "How about if I bend over instead? These shoes were expensive, and my toes are irreplaceable." Smiling, he kissed her pouting lips.

Consoled, Beulah snuggled against him. "Darling, sometimes I don't want this honeymoon to end; other times I want so much to be back in Longtree, setting up our new home. But it will be hard to return to ordinary life after all this glitter and glamour."

"This has been a marvelous honeymoon tour, but I think we would soon tire of such a hectic lifestyle. Think of snowball fights, ice-skating on the beaver pond, and toasting chestnuts. We need to hike up the stream and visit our waterfall while it's frozen."

"And I am looking forward to experiencing everyday things as your wife," Beulah added. "Cooking breakfast for you in our own kitchen, washing your laundry, collecting eggs from our own chickens."

Myles hugged her close and rocked her back and forth. Secure in his arms, Beulah felt entirely loved.

"Yes, each day offers its own pleasures," he mused aloud. "Be content with the joys of today, Darling. This tour has been successful beyond my wildest dreams. I know God paved the way, and I'm sure we can trust Him to plan the rest of our future as well. We're making memories right now that we'll treasure for the rest of our lives. God is very good."

Logan's Lady

by Tracie J. Peterson

Dedicated to: Rebecca Germany,
one of my favorite editors.
Your friendship means a great deal to me and I
thank God upon my every remembrance of you.

Colorado, 1875

*A*melia grimaced as she heard her father and Sir Jeffery Chamberlain break into yet another discussion on the implementation of fertilizer to boost agricultural yields. *It was this dreadful country that did it,* she thought. *America! A country filled with barbaric men, ill-mannered women and positively rotten children.*

Shifting uncomfortably in the seat of their stage, Amelia wished fervently that if there were a God, He would reach down and smite the lot of them in order that she might be allowed to return home to England. But of course that wasn't going to happen because Amelia had firmly decided for herself that there was no God.

"I say, Chamberlain," her father stated with a marginal note of enthusiasm. "I believe we're slowing down."

"Yes, quite right," the younger man responded and peered out the window. "We've made an excellent way thanks to our time spent on the railroad. American railroads are quite the thing. Good money here, what?"

"Indeed, the stage coaches are just as abominable as those back home, but I believe their railway system to be quite superior," came the reply and the conversation erupted into a spirited discussion of the American rail system. Amelia sighed, adjusted her lace collar and waited for the announcement that they had arrived in some small, forsaken Colorado town.

She hadn't wanted to come on this trip to America. America had been the furthest thing from her mind, in fact, but her father was insistent and clearly closed the matter to discussion. Amelia's sisters

Penelope and Margaret were just as loath to travel, but they were quite interested in Sir Jeffery Chamberlain.

Amelia held a small wish that she could share their enthusiasm. After all, he was to become her husband. At least that was the plan as her father saw it, but Amelia had no intention of marrying the pompous man. Jeffery Chamberlain was a long time crony of her father's. He wasted his days doing as little as possible, furthering his already sound reputation of being a spoiled dandy. He had been knighted, but only because his mother held a tender place in the queen's heart. And, he owned vast estates with wondrous woods that beckoned the visitor to take a turn about, but those were his only redeeming qualities as far as Amelia was concerned.

Her father viewed him in a different light, however. Sir Jeffery Chamberlain was rich and popular with Queen Victoria's court. He had a sound education and a quick wit which had managed to keep him out of trouble on more than one occasion, and he was worth an enormous sum of money which could keep not only his own lands well-kept, but would surely flow over to his future father-in-law, Lord Reginald Amhurst, the sixth earl of Donneswick—should that need arise.

Staring hard at the man, Amelia noted all of his flaws. His nose was too long, his forehead too shiny. He had perfect white teeth which seemed to be constantly bared for all the world behind unflattering smiles and his beady eyes were placed too close together. Added to this, the man was an unmitigated bore.

Amelia shook her head uncomfortably and tried against the rocking and bouncing of the stage to look at the magazine she'd bought in Cheyenne. Flipping through pages of ladies' fashions, Amelia tried to rationalize her thoughts. *I cannot blame Father for setting out to arrange a marriage. It is done all the time in my circle of friends. Why, I don't even remember the last time one of my companions managed to marry for love, and not because the union was of financial benefit to one family or the other.* Some of her friends had grown to genuinely love their intended mates. Others had not. Her dear friend and confidant, Sarah Greene, had managed to find herself engaged to a charming man of wit and gentlemanly breeding and had quickly lost her heart. But that was not to be the case for Amelia. She could not find it in her heart to love Sir Jeffery, as he insisted they call him, nor did she think love would grow there for this man.

Amidst a roar of "whoa's" and a cloud of dust, Amelia realized that they had come to a stop. Ignoring her father's window description of the town, Amelia tucked the magazine into her bag. Immediately Penelope and Margaret began fussing and going on about the wilds of America.

"I suppose we might very well be scalped by Indians," Penelope said with a fearful expression. She allowed Sir Jeffery to assist her from the stage before adding, "We're so very glad to have your company, Sir Jeffery." She oozed congeniality and interlaced her arm with his. At seventeen she was more than a little bit aware of the power a young women's simpering could have over the male gender.

"It is my pleasure, Miss Penelope," he assured her.

Margaret, a year Penelope's junior, secured her place on the opposite arm of Sir Jeffery as soon as her father had helped her from the stage. "Yes, it would be quite frightful to have come all this way into the heart of the American wilderness with only Father and Mattersley to offer protection. Why, whatever would three women and two old men do should the heathens truly choose to attack us?" Mattersley, the other *old man* she referred to was the earl's manservant and constant companion.

Amelia watched all this through the open door of the stage. She rolled her eyes and sighed. *Indeed, what would Sir Jeffery, pompous dandy that he was, do in such a situation? Bore the poor Indians to death with questions of what fertilizer they were using on the Colorado plains?* She couldn't abide the simpering of her sisters and chose instead to remain in her seat on the stage until her father beckoned her forward.

"Amelia, allow me to help you down. Why, you've scarcely said two words since we left Cheyenne. You aren't ill are you? Taken with vapors, what?"

Amelia's pale blue eyes met those of her father's. "No, Father, I'm not at all indisposed. I simply have had my mind consumed with a variety of subjects."

Sir Jeffery untangled himself from Amelia's sisters and came to offer his hand. "May I accompany you to the hotel, Lady Amhurst?" he questioned with a slight bow. Amelia noticed her father's frown as if he could read the curt reply she was thinking. Containing her thoughts with absolute ladylike control, she nodded. "Of course. Thank you," she murmured, putting her gloved fingers into Jeffery's palm.

"I have arranged for us to have rooms at a boarding house here in Greeley," the earl began. "It's a temperance colony so there will be no wine with dinner, nor any after-dinner brandy, I'm afraid." Amelia, knowing her father's distaste for alcohol, realized that he said the latter for Jeffery's sake.

"Ah, the barbarians," Jeffery sighed and Amelia knew he meant it. To Jeffery, any measure of discomfort represented a less than acceptable social standing. And for Jeffery to be without his brandy was definitely a discomfort.

For a reason beyond her understanding, Amelia was put out at Jeffery's attitude. Not because of the alcohol—although she herself couldn't abide the stuff—no, it was more than simple issues of food and drink. Jeffery's entire demeanor put her at odds. Maybe it was just that she wanted to conflict with his ideals. Maybe it was the fact that she was completely disgusted with his companionship and still hadn't been able to get it across to either her father or Jeffery that she had no desire to marry.

Glancing upward, Amelia instantly felt the noon sun bear down on her. Grimacing, she opened her white parasol and lifted it overhead to ward off the harsh rays.

"Oh, Father," Penelope began to whine, "it's ever so hot here. Must we stand about as though we were hired help?" She looked for all the world as though she might faint dead away at any moment.

They were all quite used to Penelope and Margaret's displays of weakness, and for several moments no one said anything. Finally the earl motioned for his loyal valet, Mattersley, and gave him several coins. "See if you can't arrange for our things to be brought up." The man, close in age to his employer, gave a regal bow and set out on his mission. "There," the earl said, turning to the party, "I'd say that settled itself rather nicely. Let's make our way up, what?"

"Indeed," Jeffery answered as though his was the only opinion to be had. "This harsh American sun is quite hard on fair English skin." He said the words looking at Amelia, but she had the distinct impression they were given more in consideration of his own situation than of hers.

The dry, dusty streets of Greeley did nothing to encourage the entourage. The boarding house was a far cry from the regal estate they'd left behind in England. It wasn't even as nice as the furnishings they'd acquired in New York City or Chicago. In fact, Amelia knew it was by far the worst accommodations they'd known yet, and her opinion of America slipped even lower. Why, even when they'd toured India, they'd resided on lovely estates.

From the moment they walked into the questionable place, arguments ensued and miseries were heightened. The owners of the atrocious little house actually expected Amelia and her sisters to share one bed. The very thought of it caused Penelope to cry and Margaret to fan herself feverishly as though she might actually faint from the very suggestion.

"I believe we'd arranged to have all five of your rooms," the earl protested, combating a roving horde of black flies.

"Kain't hep it a bit, mister," the slovenly dressed proprietor announced. "I hed a man come in last night what needed a place to stay."

"This is Reginald Amhurst, the sixth earl of Donneswick," Chamberlain interjected angrily. "Lord Amhurst, to you."

The proprietor looked over the rim of his dirty spectacles. "Ferenors, eh? We gets 'em all kinds here. You sound to be them thar British gents. I guess the missus said you was comin'."

Amelia grew tired with the exchange and glanced around the room to where a crude painting hung at the base of the stairs. She studied it intently, wishing she could forget the heat. The picture fascinated her from afar, as it seemed to almost move with life. Stepping closer, Amelia found it half covered with pesky black flies. It was only then that she really noticed most everything suffered from such a fate.

"Excuse me," a stranger's voice sounded over her head. "This isn't an art gallery. Besides, I don't think old Farley's painting is all that interesting."

Amelia was so lost in thought that she hadn't realized she was blocking the stairway. She looked up with a surprised expression and found herself noticing the broad, muscular frame that accompanied the voice. The mustached mouth seemed to twitch a bit as though it might break into a laugh.

Without so much as a smile, Amelia backed away. "My pardon, Sir." Her voice was haughty and her look froze the man in his place. She still found it disconcerting to be openly addressed by men without a proper introduction. Childhood teachings were hard to lay aside, even for a holiday to America.

With a grin, he gave a broad sweep. "You are quite pardoned, Ma'am."

Amelia raised her handkerchief and turned away to keep from muttering something most unladylike. *Rude. That's what all Americans are.*

"Hey thar, Logan," the boarding house proprietor called as the man passed to the front door.

"Afternoon, Ted."

Amelia tried to watch the scene without letting the man called Logan see she was at all interested in the conversation.

"Logan, didn't ya tell me you was gonna be leadin' a group of ferenors up the mountains?"

"I did."

"Well, I think this here party be yer folks."

Logan eyed the group suspiciously as though he'd just been told that they were responsible for having robbed the local bank.

"You're Earl Donneswick?" Logan questioned Amelia's father.

"I am, indeed." Lord Amhurst replied, before Jeffery could speak. Amelia turned to watch the introduction. "This is Sir Jeffery Chamberlain, my man Mattersley, and my daughters."

Logan let his gaze travel around the room to each of the women before settling on Amelia. He smiled slightly when his blatant stare caused her to blush, then turned his attention to the matter at hand.

"I'm Logan Reed, your guide to Estes Park."

"Mr. Reed, we are quite anxious to be started on our journey. Can you advise us as to when we might expect to begin? The heat is positively wilting our ladies." Jeffery commented before the earl could do the same.

Logan looked again at the women. "Are you proposing to take your womenfolk along?"

"Indeed we are," the earl replied.

Amelia watched as Logan cast a skeptical glance at her. "There are places where we'll scarcely have a trail to follow. Packing into the Rockies isn't a Sunday school picnic."

"My daughters have climbed in the Alps, my good man. I assure you they are quite up to the challenge."

Logan's smile broadened. "If you say so. I just wouldn't want the ladies to get hurt." His gaze returned to Amelia who stuck her chin in the air defiantly and turned toward the fly-covered window.

"Lady Amhurst and her sisters are quite capable," Jeffery interjected irritably.

"Lady Amhurst? I thought you said your name was Donneswick."

The earl smiled tolerantly. "I am Reginald Amhurst, the sixth earl of Donneswick. I am called Lord Amhurst, but it is common when I travel abroad to have my title mistaken for my name. My daughters, of course, are called by the family name of Amhurst. A bit confusing for you Yanks, but nevertheless, easy enough to remember."

"With that matter resolved," Chamberlain stated in a cool, even voice, "when can we expect to begin? You surely can't expect us to remain in this poor excuse for a town for much longer."

"Whoa, now. Just hold on for a minute," Logan said raising his hand. Amelia glanced back over her shoulder, fascinated in spite of herself at the way Logan Reed seemed to naturally take charge. "We've got some ground rules to cover first and I don't think standing around the front door of Ted's is the place for it. Ted, can we use the dining room?"

"Sure enuf, Logan. Ya go right ahead." Ted seemed to be happy to rid himself of the commotion. "Ya want I should have the missus bring somethin' to drink?"

He addressed Logan, but it was Lord Amhurst who answered. "Yes, please have tea and cakes sent 'round."

Ted stared at the man for a moment, then turned to Logan. "It's okay, Ted. Why don't you just bring whatever's at hand." This the man understood and nodded agreement before taking himself off to the kitchen.

The party stared collectively at Logan, barely tolerating his breach of etiquette, but Amelia was certain that for Mr. Logan Reed, breaching etiquette was probably a daily routine.

"Come on this way," Logan ordered and led the way without even waiting to hear an approval from the earl or Jeffery. The entourage followed, murmuring among themselves as to the character and manners of the tall man.

"Everybody might as well sit down," Logan said, giving his well-worn hat a toss to the sideboard.

Amelia watched in complete amazement. At home, in England, her father would never have been addressed in such a manner. At home he commanded respect and held a position of complete authority. Here in America, however, he was just a man and it didn't matter in the least that he was titled.

While Amelia stood in motionless study, Logan pulled out a chair and offered it to her. Her blue eyes met the rich warmth of his green ones. She studied his face for a moment longer, noting the trimmed mustache and square, but newly shaven jaw.

"Thank you," she murmured and slipped into her chair without taking her gaze from his face.

"Now, we need to discuss this matter in some detail," Logan announced. He stood at the head of the table looking as though he were some famed orator about to impart great knowledge upon the masses.

"Mr. Reed," Amelia's father interrupted. "I have an understanding with the owner of several cabins in the Estes Park valley. He assured me that he would send a guide to bring our party to Estes. Furthermore, there is to be another family accompanying us; Lord and Lady Gambett and their two daughters."

Logan nodded. "I know about the Gambetts and was headed up to speak to them when you arrived. According to Ted, they're staying on the other end of town at Widow Compton's place. I suppose they're planning to bring their womenfolk along as well?"

"Indeed, they are. What, may I ask, is the difficulty here?"

Logan ran a hand through his brown hair and sighed. "The problem is this: I wasn't expecting to have to pack women into the mountains. No one mentioned women at all, in fact. I was told I'd be taking a hunting party to Estes. A hunting party seemed to lend itself to the idea of men."

Amelia suppressed a laugh and received the stunned glances of her traveling companions.

"You have something to say here, Miss . . ." Logan paused as if trying to remember which name she was to be addressed by.

"I am Lady Amhurst. Lady Amelia Amhurst. And while we're to discuss this trip, then yes, I suppose I do have a few things to say." She ignored the frown on her father's face and the "darling, please be silent" glare of Jeffery. "In England, women quite often ride to the hunt. We enjoy sporting as much as our menfolk. Furthermore, I assure you, we are quite capable of handling a gun, a mount, and any other hardship that might present itself on the trip."

"I'm glad to hear that you are so capable, Lady Amhurst. You won't be offended then when I state my rules. We will begin at sunrise. That doesn't mean we'll get up at sunrise, have a leisurely tea, and be on the road by nine. It means things packed, on your horse, ready to ride at sunrise. We'll head into Longmont first, which will give you a last chance at a night's rest in bed before a week of sleeping on the ground. If you're short on supplies you can pick them up there."

No one said a word and even Amelia decided against protesting, at least until she'd heard the full speech.

Logan continued. "It gets cold at night. We'll eventually be 7,000 feet up and the air will be thinner. Every morning you'll find hoarfrost on the ground so staying dry and warm will be your biggest priority. Each of you will pack at least three blankets and a canteen. Again, if you don't have them, pick them up here in Greeley or get them in Longmont. If you don't have them, you don't go. Also, there will be no sidesaddles available. You women will be required to ride astride, so dress accordingly. Oh, and everyone wears a good, sturdy pair of boots. This is important both for riding and for walking if your horse should go lame."

"Mr. Reed!" Lord Amhurst began to protest. "You cannot expect my daughters to ride astride these American horses. First of all it is most unacceptable and second, it—"

"If they don't ride astride, they don't go," Logan replied flatly. "Having them riding sidesaddle is more danger than I'm willing to take on. If you want them to come out of this alive, they need to have every possible chance at staying that way."

"Perhaps, Amhurst," Jeffery addressed him less formally, "we could arrange to employ another guide."

Logan laughed and crossed his arms against his chest. "I challenge you to find one. I'm one of only two in the area who will even bother with you people."

"And what, pray tell, is that supposed to mean?" Amelia interjected.

Logan met her eyes. "It means, I resent European tourists and rich socialites who come to take the air in my mountains. They don't care for the real beauty at hand and they never stay longer than it takes to abuse what they will before going off to boast of their conquests. I made a promise, however, to pack you folks into Estes, but you," he pointed a finger at each of the women, "are completely unsuited for the challenge. There are far too many things to consider when it comes to women. Your physical constitution is weaker, not to mention that by nature being a woman lends itself to certain other types of physical complications and private needs."

"See here! You have no right to talk that way in front of these ladies," Chamberlain protested.

"That is exactly the kind of coddling I'm talking about. It has no place on a mountain ridge. I am not trying to make this unpleasant, but we must establish some rules here in order to keep you folks from dying on the way." Logan's voice lowered to a near whisper. "I won't have their blood on my hands, just because they are too proud and arrogant to take direction from someone who's had more experience." He said "they", but his steely gaze was firmly fixed on Amelia.

"What other rules would you have us abide by, Mr. Reed?" the earl finally asked.

"No alcohol of any kind. No shooting animals on the way to Estes.

No stopping for tea four times a day and no special treatment of anyone in the party. If you can't cut it, you go back." Logan took a deep breath. "Finally, my word is law. I know this land and what it's capable of. When I tell you that something needs to be done a certain way, I expect it to be done without question. Even if it pertains to something that shocks your genteel constitutions. I'm not a hard man to get along with," he said pausing again, "but I find the institutions of nobility a bit trying. If I should call you by something other than by your privileged titles, I'll expect you to overlook it. During a rock slide it could be difficult to remember if I'm to address you by earl, lady, or your majesty. My main objective is to get your party to Estes in as close to one piece as possible. That's all."

"I suppose we can live with these rules of yours," Lord Amhurst replied. "Ladies, can you manage?" Penelope and Margaret looked to Amelia and back to their father before nodding their heads.

"Well, Amelia?" her father questioned and all eyes turned to her.

Facing Logan with a confident glare, she replied, "I can certainly meet any challenge that Mr. Reed is capable of delivering."

Logan laughed. "Well, I'm capable of delivering quite a bit, believe me."

2

melia spent the remainder of the afternoon listening to her sisters alternate between their praises of Sir Jeffery and their concerns about the trip.

"You are such a bore, Amelia," Penelope said with little concern for the harshness of her tone. "Why, Jeffery has simply devoted himself to you on this trip and you've done nothing but act as though you could not care less."

"I *couldn't* care less," Amelia assured her sister.

"But the man is to be your husband. Father arranged this entire trip just to bring you two closer. I think it was rather sporting of Jeffery to endure the open way you stared at that Reed fellow."

Amelia gasped. "I did not stare at Mr. Reed!"

"You did," Margaret confirmed. "I saw you."

Amelia shook her head. "I can't be bothered with you two twittering ninnies. Besides, I never said I approved of Father's arrangement for Sir Jeffery to become my husband. I have no intentions of getting closer to the man and certainly none of marrying him."

"I think Sir Jeffery is wonderful. You're just being mean and spiteful," Penelope stated with a stamp of her foot. A little cloud of dust rose from the floor along with several flies.

"If you think he's so wonderful Penelope, why don't you marry him?" Amelia snapped. The heat was making her grumpy and her sister's interrogation was making her angry.

"I'd love to marry him," Margaret said in a daft and dreamy way that Amelia thought epitomized the typical addle-brained girl.

"I shall speak to Father about it immediately," Amelia said sarcastically. "Perhaps he will see the sense in it." *If only he would.*

Margaret stared after her with open mouth, while Penelope took the whole thing with an air of indifference. "You know it doesn't matter what you want, Amelia. Father must marry you off before you turn twenty-one this autumn, or lose mother's money. Her fortune means a great deal to him. Surely you wouldn't begrudge your own father his mainstay."

Amelia looked at her younger sisters for a moment. As fair-haired as she, yet more finely featured and petite, Amelia had no doubt that they saw her as some sort of ogre who thought only of herself. Their mother's fortune, a trust set in place by their grandmother, was specifically held for the purpose that none of her daughters need feel pressured to marry for money. The money would, in fact, pass to each daughter on her twenty-first birthday, if she were still unmarried. If the girls married before that time, the money reverted to the family coffers and could be used by their father, for the benefit of all as he saw fit. Amelia knew it was this which drove her father forward to see her married to Sir Jeffery.

"I have no desire for Father to concern himself with his financial well-being. However, there are things that matter deeply to me, and Jeffery Chamberlain is not one of them." With that Amelia left the room, taking up her parasol. By the time she'd reached the bottom step she'd decided that a walk to consider the rest of Greeley was in order.

Parasol high, Amelia passed from the house in a soft, almost silent swishing of her pale pink afternoon dress. She was nearly to the corner of the boarding house when she caught the sound of voices and immediately recognized one of them to be Logan Reed's.

"You sure asked for it this time, Logan. Hauling those prissy misses all the way over the mountain to Estes ain't gonna be an easy ride," an unidentified man was stating.

"No, it won't," Logan said, sounding very disturbed. "Women are always trouble. I guess next time Evans sends me over, I'll be sure and ask who all is supposed to come back with me."

"It might save you some grief at that. Still," the man said with a pause, "they sure are purty girls. They look as fine as old Bart's spittoon after a Sunday shining."

Amelia paled at the comparison, while Logan laughed. How she wished she could face him and tell him just what she thought of Americans and their spittoons. It seemed every man in this wretched country had taken up that particularly nasty habit of chewing and spitting. *No doubt Mr. Reed will be no exception.*

"I don't think I'd compliment any of them in exactly those words, Ross. These are refined British women." Amelia straightened her shoulders a bit and thought perhaps she'd misjudged Logan Reed. Logan's next few words, however, completely destroyed any further doubt. "They are the most uppity creatures God ever put on the face of the earth. They have a queen for a monarch and it makes them feel mighty important."

Amelia seethed. *How dare he even mention the queen. He isn't fit to . . .* The thought faded as Logan continued.

"The Brits are the hardest of all to work with. The Swedes come and they're just a big bunch of land-loving, life-loving primitives. The Germans are much the same and always bring a lot of life to a party. But the Brits think everything goes from their mouth to God's ear. They are rude and insensitive to other people and expect to stop on a ledge two feet wide, or any other dangerous or unseemly place, if it dares to be time for tea. In fact, I'd wager good money that before I even get this party packed halfway through the foothills, one of those 'purty' women, as you call them, will expect to have tea and biscuits on a silver tray."

At this, Amelia could take no more. She whipped around the corner in a fury. Angered beyond reason and filled with rage, she took her stand. "How dare you insult my family and friends in such a manner. I have never been so enraged in all of my twenty years!" She barely paused to take a breath. "I have traveled all across Europe and India and never in my life have I met more rude and insensitive people than here in America. If you want to see difficulty and stubbornness, Mr. Reed, I'm certain you have no further to go than the mirror in your room." At this she stormed off, feeling quite vindicated.

Logan stared after her with a mocking grin on his lips. He'd known full-well she was eavesdropping and intended to take her to task for it quite solidly. The man beside him, uncomfortable with the display of temper, quickly excused himself and ran with long strides toward the busier part of town. When Logan began to chuckle out loud, Amelia turned back indignantly.

"Whatever are you snickering about?" Amelia questioned, her cheeks flushed from the sun and the encounter. Apparently remembering her parasol, she raised it to shield her skin.

"I'm amused," Logan said in a snooty tone, mocking her.

"I see nothing at all funny here. You have insulted good people, Mr. Reed. Gentlefolk, from the lineage of nobility, with more grace and manners than you could ever hope to attain. People, I might add, who are paying you a handsome wage to do a job."

She was breathing heavily. Beads of perspiration were forming on her brow. Her blue eyes were framed by long blond lashes that curled away from her eyes like rays of sunshine through a storm cloud. She reminded Logan of a china doll with her bulk of blond hair piled high on her head, complete with fashionable hat. Logan thought he'd never seen a more beautiful woman, but he still desired to put her into her place once and for all.

"And does your family consider eavesdropping to be one of those gracious manners of which you speak so highly?" he questioned, taking long easy strides to where she stood. Amelia recoiled as though she had been slapped.

"I see you find my words disconcerting," Logan said, his face now serious. Amelia, speechless, only returned his blatant stare. "People with manners, Miss," he paused, then shook his head. "No, make that Lady Amhurst. Anyway, people of true refinement have no need to advertise it or crow it from the rooftops. They show it in action. And they need not make others feel less important by using flashy titles and snobbery. I don't believe eavesdropping would be considered a substantial way to prove one's merit in any society."

Amelia found her tongue at last. "I never intended to eavesdrop, Mr. Reed," she said emphasizing the title. "I was simply taking in a bit of air, a very little bit I might add. Is it my fault that your voice carries above the sounds of normal activity?"

Logan laughed. "I could excuse a simple wandering-in, but you stood there a full five minutes before making your presence known. I said what I said, knowing full well you were there. I wanted to see just how much you would take before jumping me."

Amelia's expression tightened. "You couldn't possibly have known I was there. I had just come from the front of the house and I was making no noise."

Logan's amusement was obviously stated in his eyes. He stepped back to the house, pulling Amelia with him. Leaving Amelia to stand in stunned silence at his bold touch, he went around the corner. "What do you see, Lady Amhurst?"

Amelia looked to the corner of the house. "I see nothing. Whatever are you talking about?"

"Look again. You're going to have to have a sharper sense of the obvious if you're to survive in the wilds of Colorado."

From around the corner Logan waited a long moment before deciding he wasn't being quite fair. He reached up and adjusted his hat hoping his shadow's movement on the ground would catch her eye.

"Very well, Mr. Reed," Amelia sounded humbled. "I see your point, but it could have just as easily been one of my sisters. You couldn't possibly have known it was me and not one of them."

Logan looked around the corner with a self-satisfied expression on his face. "You're a little more robust, shall we say, than your sisters." His gaze trailed the length of her body before coming again to rest on her face.

Amelia turned scarlet and for a moment Logan wondered if she might give him a good whack with the parasol she was twisting in her hands. She did nothing, said nothing, but returned his stare with such umbrage that Logan was very nearly taken aback.

"Good day, Mr. Reed. I no longer wish to listen to anything you have to say," Amelia said and turned to leave, but Logan reached out to halt her.

She fixed him with a stony stare that would have crumbled a less stalwart foe.

"Unhand me, sir!"

"You sure run hot and cold, lady." Logan's voice was husky and his eyes were narrowed ever so slightly. "But either way, one thing you'd better learn quickly—and I'm not saying this to put you off again," he said pausing to tighten his grip in open defiance of her demand, "listening to me may very well save your life."

"When you say something that seems life-saving," she murmured, "I will listen with the utmost regard." She pulled her arm away and gathered her skirts in hand. "Good day, Mr. Reed."

Logan watched her walk away in her facade of fire and ice. She was unlike any woman he'd ever met in his life—and he'd certainly met many a fine lady in his day. She was strong and self-assured and Logan knew that if the entire party perished in the face of their mountain challenge, Amelia would survive and probably thrive.

He liked her, he decided. He liked her a great deal. For all her snooty ways and uppity suggestions, she was growing more interesting by the minute and Logan intended to take advantage of the long summer months to come in which he'd be a part of her Estes Park stay.

Logan stood in a kind of stupor for a few more minutes, until the voice of Lord Amhurst sounded from behind him.

"Mr. Reed," he began, "I should like to inquire as to our accommodations. The proprietor here tells me that you have taken one of the rooms intended for our use. I would like to have it back."

"Sorry," Logan said without feeling the least bit apologetic. "I'm gonna need a good night's rest if I'm to lead you all to Longmont. It isn't anything personal and I'm sorry Ted parceled out your evening comforts, but I need the room."

The earl looked taken back for a moment, apparently unaccustomed to his requests being refused, but nodded as he acquiesced to the circumstances.

Logan took off before the man could say another word. He could have given up the room easily, but his pride made him rigid. "Oh Lord," he whispered, "I should have been kinder. When I settle down a bit, I'll go back to the earl of Donneswick and give him the room." Logan rounded the corner of the house and found Penelope, Margaret, and Chamberlain sitting beneath the community shade tree. It was the only shade tree on this side of town. He couldn't help but wonder where Amelia had gone, then chided himself for even thinking of her. There'd be time enough on the trip, not to mention when they reached Estes, to learn more about her. He could take his time, he reasoned, remembering that Evans had told him the party would stay until first snow.

Whistling a tune, Logan made his way past Amelia's simpering sisters, tipped his hat ever so slightly, and headed for the livery. Lady Amelia Amhurst, he thought with a sudden revelation. "There's no reason she can't be my lady," Logan stated aloud to no one in particular. "No reason at all."

$$3$$

he following day brought the hunting party together. Lord and Lady Gambett arrived with their whiny daughters Henrietta and Josephine. Both of the girls were long-time companions of Penelope and Margaret, and their reunion was one of excited giggles and squeals of delight. Amelia stood beneath the shade of the community tree and waited for the party to move out to Longmont. She studied the landscape around her and decided she was very glad not to live in this dusty community of flies and harsh prairie winds. To the west she noted the Rocky Mountains and though they were beautiful, she would have happily passed up the chance to further explore them—if her father would have given her the option to return home.

Lady Gambett fussed over her daughters like a mother hen, voicing her concern quite loudly that they should have to wear such a monstrous apparatus as what the store clerk had called a "lady's mountain dress." The outfit appeared for all intents and purposes to be no different from any other riding habit. A long serviceable skirt of blue serge fell to the boot tops of each young lady, while underneath, a fuller, billowing version of a petticoat allowed the freedom to ride astride.

Amelia knew her own attire to be quite comfortable and didn't really mind the idea of trading in her dainty sidesaddle for the fuller and more masculine McClellan cavalry saddle. She'd heard Lady Bird speak of these at one of her lectures on the Rockies and just remembering the older woman made Amelia smile. Lady Isabella Bird was a remarkable woman. Traveling all over the world to the wildest reaches was nothing to this adventuresome lady. She had come to the Rockies only two years earlier on her way back from the Sandwich Islands. By sheer grit and force of will, Lady Bird had placed herself in the hands of strangers and eventually into the hands of no one at all when she took a rugged Indian pony and traveled throughout the Rocky Mountains all alone. Amelia admired that kind of gumption. She'd never dreamed of doing something so incredible herself, but she thought Lady Bird's accounts of the solitude sounded refreshing. Watching the stars fade into the dawn Amelia wondered to herself what it might be like to lay out on a mountain top, under the stars and trees, with no other human being around for miles and miles.

"You look pretty tolerable when you smile like that," Logan's voice sounded in her ear.

Startled, Amelia instantly drew back and lost the joy of her self-reflection. "Haven't you better things to do, Mr. Reed? As I recall, we were to be on our way by now. What seems to be keeping us?"

Logan smiled. "Loose shoe on one of the horses. Should have it fixed in a quick minute."

Amelia hoped this would end their conversation, but it didn't.

"You gonna be able to ride in that?" Logan asked seriously, pointing to the wind-blown navy blue skirt which blew just high enough to reveal matching bloomers beneath.

Amelia felt her face grow hot. "I assure you I will be quite able to ride. This outfit is especially designed to allow a woman to ride astride. Just as you demanded."

"Good. I don't want any of you dainty ladies to be pitched over the side."

Amelia jutted her chin out defiantly and said nothing. Logan Reed was clearly the most incorrigible man she'd ever met in her life and she wasn't about to let him get the best of her.

"Logan!" A man hollered and waved from where the others were gathered. "Horse is ready."

"Well, Lady Amhurst, I believe we are about to get underway," Logan said with a low sweeping bow.

❧

Amelia was hot and dirty and very unhappy when the party at last rode into Longmont, Colorado. The day had not been a pleasant one for Amelia. Her sisters had squabbled almost half the way about who was going to wear the blue-veiled straw riding bonnet. Penelope had latched on to it in Greeley, but Margaret had soon learned the benefits of her sister's veil and insisted she trade her. Margaret had protested that as the youngest, at sixteen, she was also the more delicate of the trio. Josephine, Margaret's bosom companion, heartily agreed. Pushing up tiny round spectacles, Josephine was only coming to realize the protection her glasses offered from the dust. While the others were delicately blotting their eyes with lace handkerchiefs, Josephine's eyes had remained a little more sheltered.

This argument over the bonnet, along with Logan's sneering grins and her father's constant manipulation to see her and Jeffery riding together, made Amelia want to run screaming in the direction of the nearest railroad station. But of course, convention denied her the possibility of such a display.

Glancing around at the small town of Longmont, Amelia was amused to see the townsfolk apparently could not even decide on the town's spelling. Some signs read *Longmount,* while others gave the title *Longmont.* The name St. Vrain seemed to be quite popular. There was the St. Vrain Cafe, the St. Vrain Saloon, and the St. Vrain Hotel which looked to her to be an oasis in the desert. Brilliantly white against the sun's light, the two story hotel beckoned the weary travelers forward and Amelia couldn't wait to sink into a hot bath.

Upon alighting from her horse, it was instantly apparent that Longmont suffered the same plague of black flies that had held Greeley under siege. The flies instantly clung to her riding habit and bonnet, leaving Amelia feeling as though her skin were crawling. The Gambett girls and her sisters were already whining about the intolerable conditions and although Amelia whole-heartedly agreed with their analysis that this town was completely forgotten by any kind of superior being, she refused to raise her voice in complaint.

"I assure you, ladies," Logan said with a hint of amusement in his tired voice, "this place is neither forsaken by God, nor condemned.

The people here are friendly and helpful, if you treat them with respect. There's a well-stocked hardware store down Main Street, and if you ladies wish to purchase another veiled bonnet, you can try the mercantile just over there."

The words were meant to embarrass her sisters, but as far as Amelia could tell, neither Penelope nor Margaret were aware of Logan's intent.

"Remember, this is one of those trips where you'll have to do for yourself," Logan said, motioning to the pack mules. "You might just as well get used to that fact here and now. No one is going to care for you, or handle your things, but you. You'll be responsible for your bags and any personal items you choose to bring on this trip. Although, for the sake of your horses, the mules, and even yourselves, I suggest you greatly limit what you bring along."

Jeffery immediately appeared at Amelia's side. "Never fear, Lady Amhurst, I am your faithful servant. You find a comfortable place to rest and I will retrieve your things."

Amelia watched Logan's lips curl into a self-satisfied smile. Obviously he had pegged her for one of those who would choose to be waited on hand and foot. What further irritated her was that if Logan had not been there, she would have taken Chamberlain up on his offer.

"Never mind that," she said firmly. "I can manage, just as Mr. Reed has made clear I must." She pulled down her bedroll and bags without another glance at Logan.

"Surely there is no reason you cannot accept my help," Jeffery spoke from her side. He reached out to take hold of her bedroll. "I mean to say, you are a gentlewoman—a lady. It is hardly something Mr. Reed would understand, but certainly it does not escape my breeding to intercede on your behalf."

Amelia wearied of his nonsensical speech. She glared up at Jeffery harshly and pulled her bags away from his hands. "I am of sturdy stock, I assure you. I have climbed in the Alps without assistance from you." She couldn't help remembering the bevy of servants who had assisted her. "I have also barged the Nile, lived through an Indian monsoon, and endured the tedium of life at court. I surely can carry baggage into a hotel for myself." The chin went a notch higher in the air and Amelia fixed her gaze on Logan's amused expression. "Perhaps Mr. Reed needs assistance with *his* things."

Jeffery looked from Amelia's stern expression to Logan's near laughing one. Appearing confused, he neither offered his assistance to Logan, nor did he protest when Amelia went off in the direction of the hotel, bags in hand.

The St. Vrain Hotel was no cooler inside than it had been outside. If anything it was even more stifling because there was no breeze and the flies were thicker here than in the streets. She turned at the front desk to await her father and struggled to contain a smile when he and Mattersley appeared, each with his own bags, and her sisters struggling dramatically behind them.

"Oh, Papa," Margaret moaned loudly, "you simply cannot expect me to carry all of this!" the earl rolled his eyes, bringing a broad smile from Amelia. The clerk at the desk also seemed amused, but said nothing. Amelia was thankful Logan Reed was still outside with the horses.

Jeffery strode in, trying hard to look completely at ease with his new task. He put his things down in one corner and announced he would go with Mr. Reed to stable the horses. Amelia was stunned by this. So far as she knew, Jeffery had done nothing more than hand his horse over for stabling since his privileged childhood. How she would love to watch him in the livery with Mr. Reed!

Amelia gave it no more thought, however, as the clerk led them upstairs to their rooms. She would share a room with her sisters again, but this time there were two beds. One was a rustic-looking, double-sized bed. It looked roughly hewn from pine, yet a colorful handmade quilt made it appear beautiful. The other, a single bed, looked to be even more crudely assembled. It, too, was covered with a multi-colored quilt, and to the exhausted Amelia, looked quite satisfactory. Other than the beds, the room was rather empty. There was a single night table with a bowl and pitcher of water and a tiny closet that was hardly big enough to hang a single dress within.

"Oh, such misery!" Penelope exclaimed and Margaret quickly agreed.

"How could Papa make us stay in a horrible place like this?" Margaret added.

"I think it will seem a great deal more appealing after you've spent two or three nights on the trail," Amelia said without asking her sisters' permission to take the single bed. She tossed her things to the floor and stretched out on top of the quilt, still dressed in her dusty clothes.

The bed isn't half bad, Amelia thought. *It beats being on the back of that temperamental mount Mr. Reed had insisted she ride.* Twice the beast had tried to take his own head and leave the processional, but Amelia, seasoned rider that she was, gave the gelding beneath her a firm understanding that she was to decide the way, not he. No doubt Mr. Reed had intentionally given her the spirited horse. *He probably hoped to find me sprawled out on the prairie ground,* she mused. *I guess I showed him that I can handle my own affairs.* It was the last conscious thought Amelia had for some time.

She had no idea how long she'd laid upon the bed. Her sisters had been arguing about who would sleep on the right side of the bed and who would go to search out another veiled bonnet. The noise was something she was used to—it was the silence which seemed to awaken her. Staring at the ceiling for a moment, Amelia tried to remember where she was and what she was to do next. She had no time for further contemplation, however, when a knock sounded at her door.

"Yes?" she questioned, barely cracking the door open.

A young woman wearing a starched white apron stood before her bearing a towel and bar of soap. "We've a bath ready for you, Lady Amhurst."

No announcement could have met with her approval more. Amelia opened the door wide and grimaced at the stiffness that was already setting into her bones. It had been a while since she'd been riding, what with the boat ride to America and the constant use of trains and stages thereafter.

"Thank you. Will you direct me?"

The woman, hardly old enough to be called that, motioned

Amelia to the room at the end of the hall. "I can get you settled in and take your clothes to have the dust beaten out. I'll bring you something else to wear if you tell me what you want."

Amelia stepped into the room and thought the steaming tub of water too good to be true. She immediately began unfastening the buttons of her half jacket. "You are very kind to arrange all of this for me. I must say the service here is quite good."

"Oh, it's my job," the girl replied. " 'Sides, Logan told me you'd probably want to clean up and he gave me an extra coin to make sure you were taken care of personally."

Amelia's fingers ceased at their task. "I beg your pardon? Mr. Reed paid for this bath?"

"Yes, ma'am."

Amelia hesitated, looked at the tub and considered her pride in the matter. The steaming water beckoned her and her tired limbs pleaded for the refreshment. She could always settle things with Logan Reed later.

"Very well." She slipped out of the jacket and unbuttoned her skirt. "If you'll bring me my black skirt and a clean shirtwaist, I'll wash out these other things." She would show Mr. Reed just how self-sufficient she could be.

"Oh no, ma'am. I can take care of everything for you. My mother does the laundry and she can have these things ready by morning. Pressed fresh and smelling sweet. You'll see."

Amelia reluctantly gave in. "Very well." She sent the girl off with her riding clothes, keeping only her camisole and bloomers. These she washed out by hand and hung to dry before stepping into the tub. With the window open to allow in the breeze, the items would dry by the time she finished with the bath. That was one of the nice things about the drier air of Colorado. Things took forever to dry back home in England. The dampness was nearly always with them and it was better to press clothes dry with an iron than wait for them to dry on their own. But here the air was crisp and dry and even in the heat of the day it was completely tolerable compared to what she'd endured when they visited a very humid New Orleans.

Sinking into the hot water, Amelia sighed aloud. How good it felt!

Her dry skin seemed to literally drink in the offered moisture. Lathering the soap down one arm and then the other, Amelia wanted to cry with relief. The bath was pure pleasure and she felt like the spoiled aristocrat Logan Reed thought her to be. After washing thoroughly, she eased back on the rim of the tub and let the water come up to her neck, soothing and easing all the pain in her shoulders. It mattered very little that Logan Reed had arranged this luxury. At that moment, the only thing that mattered was the comfort at hand.

When the knock on the door sounded, Amelia realized she'd dozed off again. The water was tepid now and her muscles were no longer sore and tense.

"It's me, Lady Amhurst," the voice of the young woman called. "I've brought your clothes."

"Come ahead," Amelia called, stepping from the tub to wrap the rough towel around her body.

The girl appeared bringing not only the requested skirt and shirtwaist, but Amelia's comb and brush. "I thought you might be needin' these too. I can help with your hair, if you like."

Amelia smiled. What a friendly little thing. She'd make a good chambermaid if she were a little less familiar. But that was the way of these Americans and Amelia found herself growing more accepting of it as the days wore on. To be friendly and openly honest was not a thing one could count on in the finer classes of people. Women of high society were taught to keep their opinions to themselves, and in fact, were encouraged to have no opinion at all. From the moment she was born, Amelia was strictly lectured that her father, and later her husband, would clearly do her thinking for her. Amelia had other ideas, however, and often she came off appearing smug and superior in her attitudes. People misjudged her confidence and believed her to think herself better than her peers. But it wasn't true.

Logan Reed came to mind. He, too, had misjudged her and her kind. Americans seemed more than happy to lend their opinion to a situation. Even this young woman gave her opinion at every turn. But, where Logan had made her feel quite the snob, this young woman made her feel like royalty. Then a thought crossed her mind and she frowned. "Did Mr. Reed pay for you to assist me with my hair as well?"

"Oh, no, ma'am. I was just thinking you might want some help what with it coming down in back and all. I can't do it up fancy like you had it, but I can help pin it up."

Amelia nodded. "Yes, I'd like that very much." The girl turned away while Amelia stepped into her underthings. They were a little damp and this seemed to make them cooler. Light was fading outside and Amelia knew it must nearly be dinner time. These Americans had the barbaric custom of eating a full meal not long after the time when she was more accustomed to tea and cakes. Supper at home was always an affair to dress for and always served late into the evening—sometimes even after nine. *Alas, yet another American custom to adapt to.*

The girl instructed Amelia to sit on a stool while she combed out the thick, waist-length tresses. Amelia prided herself on her hair. It was a light, golden blond which most all of her peers envied. To be both blond-headed and blue-eyed in her society, was to be the picture of perfection. Added to this was her, *how did Mr. Reed say it?* robust figure. Amelia smiled to herself. Many a glance had come to her by gentlemen too well-bred to say what Logan Reed had issued without the slightest embarrassment. She was robust, or voluptuous as her dear friend Sarah would say. When corseted tightly, she had a perfect hour-glass figure, well nearly perfect. Maybe time ran a little heavier on the top half than the bottom.

"There, how's that?"

Amelia took the offered mirror and smiled. The young woman had done a fine job of replicating her earlier coiffure. "It's exactly right, Miss . . ."

"Oh, just call me Emma."

"Well, thank you very much Emma." Amelia got to her feet and allowed Emma to help her dress. "Are the others going to bathe?"

"Oh, the menfolk went down to the steambath at the barbershop. The other womenfolk didn't seem to take kindly to my trying to offer up help, so I pretty much left them alone."

Amelia nodded and smiled. She could well imagine her sisters' snobbery keeping them from accepting the assistance of this young woman. And no doubt, Lady Gambett and her pouty brood had taken themselves off to a private wash basin. With a final pat to her hair, Amelia gathered up her things and followed Emma from the room. "You should see my father, Lord Amhurst, for the cost of this bath and my clothing being cleaned. Mr. Reed is no more than a hunting guide to our party and certainly has no call to be arranging my affairs."

Emma smiled. "Oh, that's just Logan's way. He's friendly like that."

"Well, I assure you I am not in the habit of allowing strangers, especially men, to be friendly like that with me. Please see my father with the bill."

Supper that evening was a surprisingly pleasant fare of roasted chicken, sage dressing, a veritable banquet of vegetables—mostly canned, but very tasty, and peach cobbler. Amelia had to admit it was more than she'd expected and only the thick swarm of hovering black flies kept her from completely enjoying her evening. That and Logan Reed's rude appraisal of her throughout the meal. He seemed to watch her as though she might steal the silver at any given moment. Amelia grew increasingly uncomfortable under his scrutiny until she actually found herself listening to Sir Jeffery's soliloquy on the founding of the London Medical School for Women and the absurdity of anyone believing women would make acceptable physicians.

"Why the very thought of exposing the gentler sex to such grotesqueries is quite abominable," Jeffery stated as though that would be the collective reasoning of the entire party.

Normally Amelia would have commented loud and clear on such outdated thoughts, but with Logan apparently anticipating such a scene, she chose instead to finish her meal and quietly excuse herself. This was accomplished without much ado, mainly because Lady Gambett opened the matter and excused herself first, pleading an intolerable headache.

Amelia soon followed suit and very nearly spilled over a water glass when she got to her feet. Her hands were shaking as she righted the glass. Looking up, she found Logan smiling. She had to get away from him quickly or make a complete fool of herself, of this she was certain.

Unfortunately, she was barely out the front door when Jeffery popped up at her side.

"Ah, Sir Jeffery," she said stiffly.

"Good evening, Lady Amhurst," he said, pausing with a smile, "Amelia."

She stiffened even more. Eyeing him with complete contempt she said nothing. There was no need. She'd often heard it said that with a single look she could freeze the heart right out of a man and Jeffery Chamberlain was certainly no match for her.

"Forgive me, Lady Amhurst," he said bowing low before her. "I sought only to escort you to wherever it is you might be going. The familiarity is born only out of my fondness for you and your good father's desire that we wed."

Amelia nodded. "You may be assured that those desires reside with my father alone. Good evening." She hurried away before Jeffery could respond. She hadn't the strength to discuss the matter further.

The evening had grown quite chilly and Amelia was instantly sorry she'd not stopped to retrieve a shawl. She was grateful for the short-waisted jacket she'd donned for dinner and quickly did up the remaining two buttons to insure as much warmth as possible. After two blocks, however, she was more than happy to head back to the hotel and remain within its thin walls until morning sent them ever upward.

Upward.

She glanced to the now blackened images of the mountain range before her. The shadows seemed foreboding, as if some great hulking monster waited to devour her. Shuddering from the thought, she walked back to the St. Vrain Hotel and considered it no more.

4

t was the wind that woke Amelia in the morning. The great wailing gusts bore down from the mountains causing the very timbers around her to shake and tremble. *Was it a storm?* She contemplated this for a moment, hoping that if it were, it would rain and drown out each and every pesky fly in Longmont. All through the night, her sleep had been disturbed by the constant assault of flies at her face, in her hair, and at her ears. It was enough to make her consider agreeing to marry Jeffery if her father would pledge to return immediately to England.

A light rapping sounded upon her door. Amelia pulled the blanket tight around her shoulders and went to answer it.

"Yes?" she called, stumbling in the dark.

"It's me, Emma."

Amelia opened the door with a sleepy nod. "Are we about to blow away?"

Emma laughed softly and pushed past Amelia to light the lamp on her night table. "Oh, no, ma'am. The wind blows like this from time to time. It'll probably be done by breakfast. Mr. Reed sent me to wake you and the other ladies. Said to tell you it was an hour before dawn and you'd know exactly what that meant."

Amelia frowned. "Yes, indeed. Thank you, Emma."

"Will you be needin' help with your hair and gettin' dressed?"

"No, thank you anyway. Mr. Reed made it quite clear that simplicity is the means for success on this excursion. I intend only to braid my hair and pin it tight. From the sound of the wind, I suppose I should pin it very tight." Emma giggled and Amelia smiled in spite of herself. *Perhaps some of these Americans aren't so bad.*

"Lady Gambett was near to tears last night because Logan told her that she and those youngun's of hers needed to get rid of their corsets before they rode another ten feet."

It was Amelia's turn to giggle. Something she'd not done in years. "Surely you jest."

"Jest?" Emma looked puzzled.

"Joke. I merely implied that you were surely joking."

"Oh, no! He said it. I heard him."

"Well, I've never been one to abide gossip," Amelia began rather soberly, "but I can well imagine the look on Lady Gambett's face when he mentioned the unmentionable item."

"She plumb turned red and called for her smelling salts."

"Yes, she would."

Glancing to where Penelope and Margaret continued to slumber soundly, Emma questioned, "Will you need me to wake your sisters?"

Amelia glanced at the bed. "No, it would take more than your light touch. I'll see to them." Emma smiled and took her leave.

"Wake up sleepyheads," Amelia said, pulling the quilts to the foot of the bed. Penelope shrieked a protest and pulled them back up, while Margaret stared up in disbelief.

"I believe you're becoming as ill-mannered as these Americans," she said to Amelia.

"It's still dark outside," Penelope added, snuggling down. "Mr. Reed said we start at dawn."

"Mr. Reed said we leave at dawn," she reminded them. "I for one intend to have enough time to dress properly and eat before climbing back on that ill-tempered horse."

Margaret whined. "We are too tired to bother with eating. Just go away, Amelia."

"Have it your way," Amelia said with a shrug. And with that she left her sisters to worry about themselves, and hurried to dress for the day. Pulling on black cotton stockings, pantaloons and camisole, Amelia smiled privately, knowing that she was quite glad for the excuse to be rid of her corset. She packed the corset away, all the while feeling quite smug. She wasn't about to give Logan Reed a chance to speak so forwardly to her about things which didn't concern him. Pulling on her riding outfit, now clean and pressed, she secured her toiletries in her saddlebags and hurried to meet the others at breakfast.

Much to her embarrassment she arrived to find herself alone with Logan. The rest of her party was slow to rise and even slower to ready themselves for the day ahead. Logan nodded approvingly at her and called for the meal to be served. He bowed ever so slightly and held out a chair for Amelia.

"We must wait for the others, Mr. Reed," she said, taking the offered seat.

"I'm afraid we can't," Logan announced. "You forget I'm experienced at this. Most folks refuse to take me seriously until they miss at least one breakfast. Ahhh, here's Emma." The young girl entered bringing a mound of biscuits—complete with hovering flies—and a platter of fried sausages swimming in grease and heavily peppered. It was only after taking one of the offered links that Amelia realized it wasn't pepper at all, but still more flies.

Frowning at the food on her plate, it was as if Logan read her mind when he said, "Just try to think of 'em as extra meat."

Amelia almost smiled, but refused to. "Maybe I'll just eat a biscuit."

"You'd best eat up and eat well. The mountain air will make you feel starved and after all the hard work you'll be doing, you'll wish you'd had more than biscuits."

"Hard work?"

Logan waited to speak until Emma brought two more platters, one with eggs, another with fried potatoes, and a bowl with thick white gravy. He thanked the girl and turned to Amelia. "Shall we say grace?"

"I hardly think so, Mr. Reed. To whom should we offer thanks, except to those whose hands have provided and prepared the food?"

For the first time since she'd met the smug, self-confident Logan Reed, he stared at her speechless and dumbstruck. *Good,* she thought. *Let him consider that matter for a time and leave me to eat in silence.* She put eggs on her plate and added a heavy amount of cream to the horrible black coffee Emma had poured into her cup. She longed to plead with the girl for tea, but wouldn't think of allowing Mr. Reed to see her in a weakened moment.

"Do you mean to tell me," Logan began, "that you don't believe in God?"

Amelia didn't even look up. "Indeed, that is precisely what I mean to say."

"How can a person who seems to be of at least average intelligence," at this Amelia's head snapped up and Logan chuckled and continued, "I thought that might get your attention. How can you look around you or wake up in the morning to breathe the air of a new day and believe there is no God?"

Amelia scowled at the black flies hovering around her fork. "Should there have been a God, surely He would not have allowed such imperfect creatures to mar His universe."

"You don't believe in God because flies are sharing your breakfast table?" Logan's expression was one of complete confusion. He hadn't even started to eat his own food.

"Mr. Reed, I believe this trip will go a great deal better for both of us if you will merely mind your own business and leave me to do the same. I fail to see where my disbelief in a supreme being is of any concern to you, and therefore, I see no reason to discuss the matter further."

Logan hesitated for a moment, bowed his head to what Amelia presumed were his prayers of grace, and ate in silence for several minutes. For some reason, even though it was exactly what Amelia had hoped for, she felt uncomfortable and found herself wishing he would say something even if it were to insult her.

When he continued in silence, she played at eating the breakfast. She'd hoped the wind would send the flies further down the prairie, but it only seemed to have driven them indoors for shelter. As the gales died down outside, she could only hope they'd seek new territory.

"I guess I see it as my business to concern myself with the eternal souls of mankind," Logan said without warning. "See the Bible, that's the Word of God . . ."

"I know what the Bible is perceived to be, Mr. Reed. I wasn't born without a brain, simply without the need for an all-interfering, all-powerful being."

Logan seemed to shake this off before continuing. His green eyes seemed to darken. "The Bible says we are to concern ourselves with our fellow man and spread the good news."

She put her fork down and matched his look of determination. "And pray tell, Mr. Reed, what would that good news be? Spread it quickly and leave me to my meal." Amelia knew she was being unreasonably harsh, but she tired of religious rhetoric and nonsensical sermons. She'd long given up the farce of accompanying her sisters and father to church, knowing that they no more held the idea of worshipping as a holy matter than did she.

"The good news is that folks like you and I don't have to burn in the pits of hell for all eternity, because Jesus Christ, God's only son, came to live and die for our sins. He rose again, to show that death cannot hold the Christian from eternal life."

Amelia picked up her thick white mug and sipped the steaming contents. The coffee scalded her all the way down, but she'd just as soon admit to the pain as to admit Logan's words were having any affect on her whatsoever. *The pits of hell, indeed,* she thought.

She tried to compose herself before picking the fork up again. "I believe religion to be man's way of comforting himself in the face of death. Mankind can simply not bear to imagine that there is only so much time allotted to each person so mankind has created religion to support the idea of there being something more. The Hindu believe we are reincarnated. Incarnate is from the Latin *incarnates,* meaning made flesh. So they believe much as you Christians do that they will rise up to live again."

"I know what reincarnation means, and I am even familiar with the Hindu religion. But you're completely wrong when you say they believe as Christians do. They don't hold faith in what Jesus did to save us. They don't believe in the need for salvation through Him in order to have that eternal life."

Amelia shrugged. "To each religion and culture comes a theory that will comfort them the most. In light of that, Mr. Reed, and considering the hundreds of different religions in the world, even the varied philosophies within your own Christian faith, how can you possibly ascertain that you and you alone, have the one true faith?"

"Are you saying that there is no need for faith *and* that there is no such thing as God?" Logan countered.

"I am a woman of intellect and reason, Mr. Reed. Intellectually and reasonably, I assure you that faith and religion have no physical basis for belief."

"Faith in God is just that, Lady Amhurst. Faith." Logan slammed down his coffee mug. "I am a man of intellect and reason, but it only makes it that much clearer to me that there is a need for God and something more than the contrivances of mankind."

Amelia looked at him for a moment. *Yes, I could believe this barbaric American might have some understanding of books and philosophies. But he is still of that mind set which uses religion as a crutch to ease his conscience and concerns.* Before Amelia could comment further, Logan got to his feet and stuffed two more biscuits into the pocket of his brown flannel shirt. Amelia appraised him silently as he thanked Emma for a great meal and pulled on his drifters coat.

"We leave in ten minutes. I'll bring the horses around to the front." He stalked out of the room like a man with a great deal on his mind, leaving Amelia feeling as though she'd had a bit of a comeuppance, but for the life of her she couldn't quite figure out just how he'd done it.

Emma cleared Logan's plate and mug from the table and returned to find Amelia staring silently at the void left by their guide.

"I hate to be a busybody, Lady Amhurst," Emma began, "but your family ain't a bit concerned about Mr. Reed's timetable and I can tell you from experience, Logan won't wait."

This brought Amelia's attention instantly. "I'll tend to them. Are there more of these biscuits?"

"Yes, ma'am."

"Good. Please pack whatever of this breakfast you can for us and we'll take it along. As I recall, Mr. Reed said there would be a good six miles of prairie to cross to the canyon."

"I can wrap the biscuits and sausage into a cloth, but the rest of this won't pack very good."

Amelia blotted her lips with a coarse napkin and got to her feet. "Do what you can, Emma, and I'll retrieve my wayward family."

❦

Ten minutes later, Amelia had managed to see her family to the front of the hotel. Penelope and Margaret were whining, still struggling to do something with their hair. Upon Amelia's threat to shear them both they grew instantly silent. Lady Gambett cried softly into a lace-edged handkerchief and bemoaned the fact that her nerves would never stand the jostling on horseback. Her daughters were awkward and consciously concerned about their lack of corseting, and Amelia had to laugh when she overheard Margaret tell Josephine that Mr. Reed was no doubt some kind of a devious man who would do them all in once they were far enough away from the protection of town. A part of Amelia was beginning to understand Logan Reed's misgivings about her people.

Logan repacked the mules with the baggage and items brought to him by the party, but Amelia noticed he was unusually tight-lipped. Light was just streaking the eastern skies when he hauled up onto the back of his horse and instructed them to do the same.

Amelia allowed Jeffery to help her onto her horse and winced noticeably when the softer parts of her body protested from the abuse she'd inflicted the day before. She said nothing, noting Logan's smirk of recognition, but her sisters and the Gambetts were well into moans and protests of discomfort. Logan ignored them all, however, and urged his horse and the mules forward.

❦

It wasn't yet ten o'clock when Logan first heard Amelia's sisters suggesting they stop. He couldn't help but cast a smug look of satisfaction toward Amelia when Penelope suggested they should imbibe in a time of tea and cakes.

He watched Amelia's face grow flush with embarrassment, but she said nothing, choosing instead to let her mount lag behind the others until she was nearly bringing up the rear of the party. Chuckling to himself, Logan led them on another two hours before finally drawing his horse to a stop.

Dismounting, he called over his shoulder, "We'll take lunch here."

It was as if the entire party sighed in unison.

Logan quickly set up everything they would need. He drew cold water from the mountain river which they'd followed through the canyon, then dug around in the saddle-bags to produce jerked beef and additional biscuits.

"You surely don't mean this to be our luncheon fare," Jeffery Chamberlain said in complete disgust.

The earl looked down his nose at the pitiful offering. "Yes, Mr. Reed, surely there is something better than this."

Logan pushed his hat back on his head. "We'll have a hot meal for dinner this evening. If we're to push ahead and reach our first camping point before dark, we'll only have time to rest here about ten, maybe fifteen minutes. It'll give the horses a well-deserved break and allow them to water up. The higher we go the more water you'll need to drink. Remember that and you won't find yourself succumbing to sorche."

"I beg your pardon?" Lord Amhurst questioned.

"Mountain sickness," Reed stated flatly. "The air is much thinner up here, but since you've traipsed all over the Alps, you should already know all about that. You need to take it slower and allow yourselves time to get used to the altitude. Otherwise, you'll be losing what little lunch you get and dealing with eye splitting headaches that won't let you go for weeks. It's one more reason I insisted the ladies dismiss the idea of corsets." Shudders and gasps of indignant shock echoed from the now gathered Gambett and Amhurst women. With exception of Amelia. She stood to one side admiring a collection of wildflowers, but Logan knew she was listening by the amused expression on her face.

Logan continued, trying hard to ignore the graceful blond as she moved about the river bank studying the ground. "As inappropriate as you might think my addressing the subject of women's undergarments might be, it is a matter of life and death. Up here beauty is counted in the scenery, not the flesh. The air is thinner and you need more of it to account for what you're used to breathing down below. Losing those corsets just might save your life. I wouldn't even suggest putting them back on after we arrive in Estes. The altitude there is even higher than it is here and I'd sure hate to have to run around all day picking up women in dead faints. Now I've wasted enough time. Eat or don't, the choice is yours. I'll water the horses and mules while you decide." He started to walk away then turned back. "I hate to approach another delicate subject, but should you take yourself off into the trees for privacy, keep your eyes open. I'd also hate to have to deal with an agitated mother bear just because you startled her while she was feeding her cubs."

With that said, he walked away grumbling to himself. These prim and proper Brits were more trouble to deal with than they were worth. This was the last time he'd ever act as a guide for anyone of English nobility.

He tethered his horse at the riverbank and pretended to adjust the saddle while he watched Amelia picking flowers and studying them with an almost scientific eye. From time to time, she drew out a small book and pressed one of these samples between the pages, before moving on to the next point of interest. He found himself admiring the way she lithely climbed over the rocks and couldn't help but notice her lack of fear as she neared the rushing river for a closer look.

As she held a leaf up to catch the sunlight, Logan was reminded of her atheistic views. *How could anyone behold the beauty of this canyon and question the existence of God?* It was one thing not to want to deal with God, or even to question whether He truly cared to deal with mankind, but to openly declare there to be no God—that was something he couldn't even fathom. Even the Indians he'd dealt with believed in God. Maybe they didn't believe the same way he did, but they didn't question that someone or something greater than man held the universe in order and sustained life.

Logan tried not to stare at Amelia, but he found himself rather helpless to ignore her. The other women were huddled together relaying their misfortunes, hoping for better times ahead and assuring each other that such torture could be endured for the sake of their menfolk. The men were gingerly sampling the lunch fare and after deciding it was better than nothing, they managed to eat a good portion before convincing the women to partake.

Logan wondered if Amelia would partake, but then he saw her draw a biscuit from the deep pocket of her skirt and nibble at it absentmindedly as she bent to pick up a piece of granite. *She is an industrious woman,* he thought, watching her turn the stone in her hand. *Who else could have gotten that sour-faced brood of travelers together in such a short time? Who else too, would have thought to get Emma to pack food for them to take, rather than whine and beg him to allow them a bit more time for breakfast?*

As if sensing his gaze upon her, Amelia looked up and met his stare. Neither one did anything for a moment and when Amelia returned her attention to the rock, Logan tried to focus on the mules. His stomach did a bit of a flip-flop and he smiled in spite of himself at the affect this woman was having on him. Stealing a sidelong glance he watched her cup water from the river's edge and drink. *Yes, Lady Amhurst is quite a woman.*

❦

"We'll be leaving in a few minutes," Logan announced to the weary band. "Take care of your needs before that." He walked to where Amelia sat quietly contemplating the scenery. "It's impressive, don't you think?" he asked, wondering if she'd take offense.

"Yes, it is," she admitted.

"Those are cottonwood trees," he said pointing out tall green-leaved trees. "Those with the lighter bark are aspen." He reached down and picked up a leaf. "This is an aspen leaf." Amelia seemed interested enough and so he continued. "I noticed you were saving flowers and if you need any help in identifying them later, I'd be happy to be of service. I'm pretty knowledgeable about the vegetation and wildlife in these parts." He tried to sound nonchalant for fear he'd frighten her away or anger her.

"I especially like those blue flowers," Amelia replied.

"Those are columbine. ''Tis said that absence conquers love! But,

O, believe it not; I've tried alas! its power to prove, But thou art not forgot.' A fellow named F. W. Thomas wrote that. It's from a poem called 'The columbine.' "

"How interesting." She said nothing more for a moment, then added, "What of those white ones with the short hairy stems?"

"Pasqueflowers. So named because they usually start flowering around Easter time. Comes from the Latin word *pascha* or the Hebrew *pesah* meaning 'a passing over', thus the Jewish feast of Passover and the Christian celebration of Easter, the death and resurrection of Christ." He really hadn't intended it as a mocking to Amelia's earlier lessons on *incarnate,* but even as the words left his mouth, he knew that was what they'd sound like.

Amelia stiffened, picked up her things and walked back to the horse without another word. Logan wanted to kick himself for breaking the brief civil respite from the tension between them. *Sometimes, Reed,* he thought, *you can sure put your foot in your mouth.*

5

melia tried not to remember the way Logan Reed had stared at her. Or how green his eyes were. Or how his mustache twitched whenever he was trying not to smile. She found herself unwillingly drawn to him and the very thought disturbed her to the bone. He was refreshingly different from English gentlemen and far better mannered than she'd given him credit for. His gruff exterior was mostly show, she'd decided while watching him help Lady Gambett onto her horse. He had tipped his hat and said something which had caused Lady Gambett to actually smile. Keeping these thoughts to herself, Amelia concentrated on the scenery around her.

"You are particularly quiet," Jeffery spoke, riding up alongside her. It was one of those rare places along the path that allowed for riders to go two abreast.

"I'm considering the countryside," she replied rather tightly.

"Ah, yes. America and her rough-hewn beauty."

Amelia frowned. "And what, pray tell, is that supposed to mean?"

Jeffery smiled tolerantly. "Simply that I'll be happy to return home to England. I'll be even happier when you reconcile yourself to our union and allow me to properly court you."

"I do not wish to discuss the matter."

"I know that very well, but I also know it is your father's intentions that we do so."

He lifted his face to catch a bit of the sun's warmth and Amelia was reminded of a turkey stretching his neck. *Perhaps he might let out a gobble at any moment.* She chuckled in spite of her resolve to be firm.

341

Jeffery lowered his head and stared at her soberly. "Have I somehow amused you?"

Amelia shook her head. "No, not really. I'm just a bit giddy from the thin air. I'm sure you will understand if I wish to save my breath and discontinue our conversation." She urged her horse ahead and was relieved when Jeffery chose to leave her alone

❧

Their stop for the evening came early. The sun was just disappearing behind the snow-capped peaks in front of them when Lord Amhurst's pocket watch read 3:35. Amelia slid down from the horse and stretched in a rather unladylike display. Margaret gasped and Penelope laughed, while the Gambett women were too intent on their own miseries to notice. Amelia shrugged off her sisters' questioning stares and began pulling her bedroll free from behind the saddle.

"Get your horses cared for first," Logan called out. "Take down your things and I'll come around and take care of the saddles and staking the animals out."

Moans arose from the crowd and Amelia wasn't sure but what even Mattersley was echoing the sentiment of the group. The older man looked quite worn and Amelia felt concern for him. He would die before leaving her father's side, and thus, he accompanied them whenever they traveled. But this time the trip was so much rougher. Amelia wondered if he would be able to meet the demands of the American wilderness.

"You did good today," Logan said, taking the reins of her mount. "If you think you're up to it, I could use some help putting up the tents and getting dinner started."

Amelia nodded and for some reason she felt honored that he'd asked for her assistance. While Logan removed saddles, Amelia went to Mattersley and helped him remove his bedroll. She didn't know why she acted in such a manner, but felt amply rewarded when Mattersley gave her a brief, rare smile. She took his mount and led it to where Logan was staking out Lady Gambett's mount.

"I see you're getting into the spirit of things," Logan said, quickly uncinching the horse.

"I'm worried about Mattersley. He doesn't seem to be adapting well to the altitude." Amelia looked beyond the horses to where Mattersley was trying to assist her father. "He won't be parted from my father," she added, as though Logan had asked her why the old man was along. "He is completely devoted to him."

"I can't imagine what it'd be like to have someone devoted to you like that," Logan replied softly.

Amelia looked into his eyes and found him completely serious. "Me either," she murmured. He made her feel suddenly very vulnerable, even lonely.

Logan's green eyes seemed to break through the thinly placed wall of English aristocracy, to gaze inside to where Amelia knew her empty heart beat a little faster. *Could he really see through her and find the void within that kept her so distant and uncomfortable?*

"My mother was devoted to my pa that way," he added in a barely audible voice.

Amelia nodded. "Mine too. When she died, I think of a part of him died as well. There is a great deal of pain in realizing that you've lost something forever."

"It doesn't have to be forever," Logan said, refusing to break his stare.

Amelia licked her dry lips nervously. "No?"

"No. That's one of the nice things about God and it isn't just a theory to give you comfort when somebody dies. If you and your loved ones belong to Him, then you will see them again."

Amelia swallowed hard. For the first time in many years, in fact since her mother's death, she felt an aching urge to cry for her loss. "My mother believed that way," she murmured.

Logan's face brightened. "Then half the problem is solved. She's in heaven just waiting for you to figure out that she knew what she was talking about. You can see her again."

Amelia's sorrow faded into prideful scorn. "My mother is entombed in the family mausoleum and I have no desire to see her again." She walked away quickly, feeling Logan's gaze on her. *How dare he intrude into my life like that? How dare he trespass in the privacy of my soul?*

~❧~

"Come on," Logan said several minutes later. He tossed a small mallet at Amelia's feet and motioned her to follow him.

Picking up the mallet, Amelia did as she was told. She wasn't surprised when she found Logan quite serious about her helping him assemble tents. He laid out the canvas structures and showed her where to drive the stakes into the ground. Pounding the wooden stakes caused her teeth to rattle, but Amelia found herself attacking the job with a fury.

Logan secured the tent poles and pulled the structure tight. To Amelia's surprise and pleasure, an instant shelter was born. Two more structures went up without a single mishap, or word spoken between them. Amelia was panting by the time they'd finished, but she didn't care.

Logan had sent the others to gather wood, but their production was minimal at best. When he and Amelia had finished with the tents, he then instructed the weary entourage to take their things into the tents.

"The ladies will have two tents and the men can use the other. It'll be a close fit, but by morning you'll be glad to rug up with the other occupants."

No one said a word.

Amelia took her things to the tent and started to unroll her bedding. "Leave it rolled," Logan instructed from behind her.

"I beg your pardon?" She pushed back an errant strand of hair and straightened up.

"Unrolled, it will draw moisture or critters. Wait until you're ready to sleep."

Amelia nodded. "Very well. What would you like me to do now?"

"We're going to get dinner going. Hungry?"

She smiled weakly. "Famished." In truth, she was not only hungry but light-headed.

"Come along then," he said in a rather fatherly tone. "I'll show you how to make camp stew."

"Camp stew?" she said, concentrating on his words against the pulsating beat of her heart in her ears.

He grinned. "Camp stew is going to be our primary feast while en route to your summer home. It's just a fancy way of saying beans and dried beef. Sometimes I throw in a few potatoes just to break the monotony."

Amelia allowed herself to smile. "At this point it sounds like a feast."

"You can take this to the river and get some water," he said, handing her a coffee pot. "I'll unpack the pot for the beans. You'll need to fill it with water first, then bring the coffee pot back full and we'll make some coffee."

She nodded wearily and made her way to the water's edge. Her head was beginning to ache and a voice from within reminded her of Mr. Reed's warning to drink plenty of water. Scooping a handful to her lips, Amelia thought she'd never tasted anything as good. The water was cold and clear and instantly refreshed her. With each return trip Amelia forced herself to drink a little water. On her last trip, she dipped her handkerchief in the icy river and wiped some of the grime away from her face. She drew in gasping breaths of chilled mountain air, trying hard to compensate for the lack of oxygen. For a moment the world seemed to spin.

Lowering her gaze, Amelia panicked at the sensation of dizziness. It seemed to come in waves, leaving her unable to focus. She took a step and stumbled. Took another and nearly fell over backward. *What's happening to me?* she worried.

"Amelia?" Logan was calling from somewhere. "You got that coffee water yet?"

The river was situated far enough away that the trees and rocks kept her from view of the camp. She opened her mouth to call out, then clamped it shut, determined not to ask Mr. Reed for help. Sliding down to sit on a small boulder, Amelia steadied the pot. *I'll feel better in a minute,* she thought. *If I just sit for a moment, everything will clear and I'll have my breath back.*

"Amelia?" Logan stood not three feet away. "Are you all right?"

Getting to her feet quickly, Amelia instantly realized her mistake. The coffee pot fell with a clatter against the rocks and Amelia felt her knees buckle.

"Whoa, there," Logan said, reaching out to catch her before she hit the ground. "I was afraid you were doing too much. You are the most prideful, stubborn woman I've ever met."

Amelia tried to push him away and stand on her own, but her head and legs refused to work together and her hands only seemed to flail at the air. "I just got up too fast," she protested.

"You just managed to get yourself overworked. You're going to lay down for the rest of the night. I'll bring you some chow when it's ready, but 'til then, you aren't to lift a finger." In one fluid motion he swung her up into his arms.

"I assure you, Mr. Reed—"

"Logan. My name is Logan. Just as you are Lady Amhurst, I am Logan. Understand?" he sounded gruff, but he was smiling and Amelia could only laugh. She'd brought this on herself by trying to outdo the others and keep up with any task he'd suggested.

"Well?" His eyes seemed to twinkle.

"I understand!" she declared and tried not to notice the feel of his muscular arms around her.

His expression sobered and Amelia couldn't help but notice that there was no twitching of that magnificent mustache. Sometimes, just sometimes, she wondered what it would be like to touch that mustache. *Is it coarse and prickly, or smooth and soft like the pet rabbit Margaret had played with as a child?*

He was looking at her as though trying to say something that couldn't be formed into words and for once, Amelia didn't think him so barbaric. These new considerations of a man she'd once thought hopelessly crude, were disturbing to her. Her mind began to race. *What should I say to him? What should I do? I could demand he release me, but I seriously doubt he would. And what if he did? Did she really want that?*

This is ridiculous, she chided herself. Forcing her gaze to the path, she nodded and said, "Shouldn't we get back? Maybe you could just put me down now. I'm feeling much better."

Logan gave her a little toss upward to get a better hold. She let out an audible gasp and tightly gripped her arms around Logan's neck.

"Don't!" she squealed with the abandonment of a child. Logan looked at her strangely and Amelia tried to calm her nerves. "I—I've always been afraid of falling," she offered lamely. "Please put me down."

"Nope," he said and started for camp. When he came to the edge of the clearing it was evident that everyone else was still collecting firewood. Logan stopped and asked, "Why are you afraid of falling?"

Amelia's mind went back in time. "When I was very young someone held me out over the edge of the balcony and threatened to spill me. I was absolutely terrified and engaged myself in quite a spell until Mother reprimanded me for being so loud."

"No reprimand for the one doing the teasing, eh?" Logan's voice was soft and sympathetic.

"No, she knew Jeffery didn't mean anything by it." Amelia could have laughed at the stunned expression on Logan's face.

"Not, Sir Jeffery?" he asked in mock horror.

"None other. I think it amused him to see me weak and helpless."

"Then he's a twit."

Amelia's grin broadened into a smile. "Yes, he is."

"Amelia! What's wrong!"

"Speaking of the twit," Logan growled low against her ear and Amelia giggled. His warm breath against her ear, not to mention the mustache, tickled. "Amelia's fine, she just overdid it a bit. I'm putting her down for a rest."

"I can take her," Jeffery said, dropping the wood he'd brought. He brushed at his coat and pulled off his gloves as he crossed the clearing.

"Well, Lady Amhurst, it's twits or barbarians. Which do you prefer?" he questioned low enough that only Amelia could hear.

Amelia felt her breath quicken at the look Logan gave her. *What is happening to me? I'm acting like a schoolgirl. This must stop,* she thought and determined to feel nothing but polite gratitude toward Mr. Logan Reed. When she looked at each man and said nothing, Logan deposited her in Jeffery's waiting arms.

"Guess your feelings are pretty clear," he said and turned to leave.

"But I didn't say a thing, Mr. Reed," Amelia said, unconcerned with Jeffery's questioning look.

Logan turned. "Oh, but you did." As he walked away he called back to Jeffery, "Put her in her tent and help her with her bedroll. I'll have some food brought to her when it's ready."

"He's an extremely rude man, what?"

Amelia watched Logan walk away. She felt in some way she had insulted him, but surely he hadn't really expected her to choose him over Jeffery. He was only a simple American guide and Jeffery, well, Jeffery was much more than that. If only he were much more of something Amelia could find appealing.

"Put me down, Jeffery. I am very capable of walking and this familiarity is making me most uncomfortable," she demanded and Jeffery quickly complied. She knew deep in her heart that Logan would never be bullied in such a way.

"Mr. Reed said to have you lie down."

"I heard him and I'm quite capable of taking care of myself. Now shouldn't you help get the firewood? Mr. Reed also said we were to expect a cold night." Jeffery nodded and Amelia took herself to the tent, stopping only long enough to give Logan a defiant look before throwing back the flaps and secluding herself within.

"Men, like religion, are a nuisance," she muttered as she untied the strings on her bedroll.

6

Morning came with bone-numbing cold and Amelia was instantly grateful for her sisters. Snuggling closer to Penelope, Amelia warmed and drifted back to sleep. It seemed only moments later when someone was shouting her into consciousness and a loud clanging refused to allow her to ease back into her dreams.

"Breakfast in ten minutes!" Logan was shouting. "Roll up your gear and have it ready to go before you eat. Chamberlain, you will assist in taking down the tents."

Amelia rolled over and moaned at the soreness in her legs and backside. *Surely we aren't going to ride as hard today as yesterday.* Pushing back her covers, Amelia began to shiver from the cold of the mountain morning. *Could it have only been yesterday that the heat seemed so unbearable?* Stretching, Amelia decided that nothing could be worse than the days she'd spent on the Colorado prairie. *At least here, the black flies seem to have thinned out. Maybe the higher altitude and cold keeps them at bay.* Amelia squared her shoulders. *Maybe things are getting better.*

But it proved to be much worse. A half-day into the ride, Amelia was fervently wishing she could be swallowed up in one of the craggy ravines that threatened to eat away the narrow path on which she rode. The horse was cantankerous, her sisters were impossible, and Mattersley looked as though he might succumb to exhaustion before they paused for the night.

When a rock slide prevented them from taking the route Logan had planned on, he reminded the party again of the altitude and the necessity of taking it easy. "We could spend the next day or two trying to clear that path or we can spend an extra day or two on an alternate road into Estes. Since none of you are used to the thinner air, I think taking the other road makes more sense."

Logan's announcement made Amelia instantly self-conscious. *Was he making fun of me because of the attack I suffered last night? Why else would he make such an exaggerated point of the altitude?*

"I do hope the other road is easier," Lady Gambett said with a questioning glance at her husband.

"I'm afraid not," Logan replied. "It climbs higher, in fact, than this one and isn't traveled nearly as often. For all I know that trail could be in just as bad of shape as this one."

"Oh dear," Lady Gambett moaned.

"But Mama," Josephine protested, pushing her small spectacles up on the bridge of her nose, "I cannot possibly breathe air any thinner than this. I will simply perish."

Logan suppressed a snort of laughter and Amelia caught his eye in the process. His expression seemed to say "See, I told you so" and Amelia couldn't bear it. She turned quickly to Lady Gambett.

"Perhaps Josephine would be better off back in Longmont," Amelia suggested.

"Oh, gracious, perhaps we all would be," Lady Gambett replied.

"But I want to go on, Mama," the plumper Henrietta whined. "I'm having a capital time of it."

"We're all going ahead." Lord Gambett spoke firmly with a tone that told his women that he would brook no more nonsense.

"Are we settled and agreed then?" Logan asked from atop his horse.

"We are, sir." Gambett replied with a harsh look of reprimand in Josephine's direction.

Amelia tried to fade into the scenery behind Margaret's robust, but lethargic, palomino. The last thing in the world she wanted to do was to have to face Logan. She was determined to avoid him at any cost. Something inside her seemed to come apart whenever he was near. It would never do to have him believing her incapable of handling her emotions and to respond with anything but cool reservation would surely give him the wrong idea.

Logan was pushing them forward again. He was a harsh taskmaster and no one dared to question his choices—except for the times when Jeffery would occasionally put in a doubtful appraisal. Logan usually quieted him with a scowl or a raised eyebrow and always it caught Amelia's attention.

But she didn't want Logan Reed to capture her attention. She tried to focus on the beauty around her. Ragged rock walls surrounded them on one side, while what seemed to be the entire world, spread out in glorious splendor on the other side. The sheer drop made Amelia a bit light-headed, but the richness of the countryside was well worth the risk of traveling the narrow granite ledge. Tall pines were still in abundance, as were the quaint mountain flowers and vegetation Amelia had come to appreciate. Whenever they stopped to rest the horses she would gather a sample of each new flower and press it into her book, remembering in the back of her mind that Logan Reed would probably be the one to identify it later.

Soon enough the path widened a bit and Amelia kept close to Lady Gambett, hoping that both Jeffery and Logan would keep their distance. Her father was drawn into conversation with Lord Gambett, and Lady Gambett seemed more than happy for Amelia's company.

"The roses shouldn't be planted too deep, however," Lady Gambett was saying, and Amelia suddenly realized she hadn't a clue what the woman was talking about. "Now the roses at Havershire are some of the most beautiful in the world, but of course there are fourteen gardeners who devote themselves only to the roses."

Amelia nodded sedately and Lady Gambett continued rambling on about the possibility of creating a blue rose. Amelia's mind wandered to the rugged Logan Reed and when he allowed his horse to fall back a bit, she feared he might try to start up a conversation. Feeling her stomach do a flip and her breathing quicken. Amelia gripped the reins tighter and refused to look up.

"Are you ill, my dear?" Lady Gambett asked suddenly.

Amelia was startled by the question, but even more startled by the fact that Logan was looking right at her as if awaiting her answer. "I . . . uh . . . I'm just a bit tired." *It wasn't a lie,* she reasoned.

"Oh, I quite agree. Mr. Reed, shouldn't we have a bit of respite?"

Lady Gambett inquired. "Poor Mattersley looks to be about to fall off his mount all together."

Logan nodded and held up his hand. "We'll stop here for a spell. See to your horses first."

Amelia tried not to smile at the thought of dismounting and stretching her weary limbs. She didn't want to give Logan a false impression and have him believe her pleasure was in him rather than his actions. Without regard to the rest of the party, Amelia urged her horse to a scraggly patch of grass and slid down without assistance. Her feet nearly buckled beneath her when her boots hit the ground. Her legs were so sore and stiff and her backside sorely abused. Rubbing the small of her back, she jumped in fear when Logan whispered her name.

"I didn't mean to scare you," he apologized. "I hope you're feeling better."

Amelia's mind raced with thoughts. She wanted desperately to keep the conversation light-hearted. "I'm quite well, thank you. Although I might say I've found a new way to extract a pound of flesh."

Logan laughed. "Ah, the dilemma of exacting a pound of flesh without spilling a drop of blood. The Merchant of Venice, right? I've read it several times and very much enjoyed it."

Amelia tried not to sound surprised. "You are familiar with Shakespeare?"

He put one hand to his chest and the other into the air.

" 'My only love sprung from my only hate! Too early seen unknown, and known too late!' " He grinned. " 'Romeo and Juliet.' "

"Yes, I know," she replied, still amazed at this new revelation.

" 'Hatred stirreth up strifes: but love covereth all sins.' "

Amelia tried to remember what play these words were from, but nothing came to mind. "I suppose I don't know Shakespeare quite as well as you do, Mr. Reed."

"Logan," he said softly and smiled. "And it isn't Shakespeare's works, it's the Bible. Proverbs ten, twelve to be exact."

"Oh," she said and turned to give the horse her full attention.

"I thought we'd worked out a bit of a truce between us," Logan said, refusing to leave her to herself.

"There is no need for anything to be between us," Amelia said, trying hard to keep her voice steady. *How could this one man affect my entire being? She couldn't understand the surge of emotions, nor was she sure she wanted to.*

"It's a little late to take that stand, isn't it?" Logan asked in a whisper.

Amelia reeled on her heel as though the words had been hot coals placed upon her head. "I'm sure I don't understand your meaning, Mr. Reed," she said emphasizing his name. "Now if you'll excuse me, I have other matters to consider."

"Like planting English roses?" he teased.

Her mouth dropped open only slightly before she composed her expression. "Have we lent ourselves to that most repulsive habit of eavesdropping, Mr. Reed?"

Logan laughed. "Who could help but overhear Lady Gambett and her suggestions? It hardly seemed possible to not hear the woman."

Amelia tried to suppress her smile, but couldn't. *Oh, but this man made her blood run hot and cold. Hot and cold.* She remembered Logan stating just that analysis of her back in Greeley. Just when she was determined to be unaffected by him, he would say or do something that made the goal impossible. She started to reply when Lady Gambett began to raise her voice in whining reprimand to Henrietta.

"It would seem," Amelia said, slowly allowing her gaze to meet his, "the woman speaks for herself."

Logan chuckled. "At every possible opportunity."

Lady Gambett was soon joined by Josephine, as well as Margaret and Penelope, and Amelia could only shake her head. "I'm glad they have each other."

"But who do you have?" Logan asked Amelia quite unexpectedly.

"I beg your pardon?"

"You heard me. You don't seem to have a great deal of affection for your sisters or your father. Sir Jeffery hardly seems your kind, although I have noticed he gives you a great deal of attention. You seem the odd man out, so to speak."

Amelia brushed bits of dirt from her riding jacket and fortified her reserve. "I need no one, Mr. Reed."

"No one?"

His question caused a ripple to quake through her resolve. She glanced to where the other members of the party were engaged in various degrees of conversation as they saw to their tasks. How ill-fitted they seemed in her life. She was tired of pretense and noble games, and yet it was the very life she had secured herself within. Didn't she long to return to England and the quiet of her father's estate? Didn't she yearn for a cup of tea in fine English china? Somehow the Donneswick estates seemed a foggy memory.

"Why are you here, Amelia?"

She looked up, thought to reprimand him for using her name, then decided it wasn't so bad after all. She rather liked the way it sounded on his lips. "Why?" she finally questioned, not truly expecting and answer.

"I just wondered why you and your family decided to come to America."

"Oh," she said, frowning at the thought of her father and Sir Jeffery's plans. There was no way she wanted to explain this to Logan Reed. He had already perceived her life to be one of frivolity and ornamentation. She'd nearly killed herself trying to work at his side in order to prove otherwise, but if she told him the truth it would defeat everything she'd done thus far. "We'd not yet toured the country and Lady Bird, an acquaintance of the family who compiled a book about her travels here, suggested we come immediately to Estes."

"I remember Lady Bird," Logan said softly. "She was a most unpretentious woman. A lady in true regard."

Amelia felt the challenge in Logan's words, but let it go unanswered. Instead, she turned the conversation to his personal life. "You are different from most Americans, Mr. Reed. You appear to have some of the benefits of a proper upbringing. You appear educated and well-read and you have better manners than most. You can speak quite eloquently when you desire to do so, or just as easily slip into that lazy American style that one finds so evident here in the West."

Logan grinned and gave his horse a nudge. "And I thought she didn't notice me."

Amelia frowned. "How is it that you are this way?"

Logan shrugged. "I had folks who saw the importance of an education, but held absolutely no regard for snobbery and uppity society ways. I went to college back east and learned a great deal, but not just in books. I learned about people."

"Is that where you also took up religion?" she questioned.

"No, not at all. I learned about God and the Bible from my mother and father first, and then from our local preacher. The things they taught me made a great deal of sense. Certainly more sense than anything the world was offering. It kept me going in the right direction."

Amelia nodded politely, but in the back of her mind she couldn't help but wonder about his statement. Most of her life she had felt herself running towards something, but it was impossible to know what that something was. Her mother had tried to encourage her to believe in God, but Amelia thought it a mindless game. Religion required you to believe in things you couldn't see or prove. Her very logical mind found it difficult to see reason in this. *If God existed, couldn't He make Himself known without requiring people to give in to superstitious nonsense and outrageous stories of miraculous wonders? And if God existed, why did tragedy and injustice abound? Why did He not, instead, create a perfect world without pain or sorrow?*

"I've answered your questions, now how about answering some of mine?" Logan's voice broke through her thoughts.

"Such as?" Amelia dared to ask.

"Such as, why are you really here? I have a good idea that Lady Bird has very little to do with your traveling to America."

Amelia saw her sisters move to where Jeffery stood and smiled. "My father wanted me to come, so I did. It pleased him and little else seemed to offer the same appeal."

"Is he still mourning your mother's passing?"

"I suppose in a sense, although it's been six years. They were very much a love match, which was quite rare among their friends."

"Rare? Why is that?"

Amelia smiled tolerantly. "Marriages are most generally arranged to be advantageous to the families involved. My father married beneath his social standing." She said the words without really meaning to.

"If he married for love it shouldn't have mattered. Seems like he did well enough for himself anyway," Logan replied. He nodded in the direction of her father in conversation with Mattersley. "He is an earl, after all, and surely that holds esteem in your social circles."

"Yes, but the title dies with him. He has no sons and his estates, well—" she found herself unwilling to answer Logan's soft spoken questions. "His estates aren't very productive. My mother had a low social standing, but she brought a small fortune and land into the family which bolstered my father's position."

"So it *was* advantageous to both families, despite her lack of standing?"

"Yes, but you don't understand. It made my father somewhat of an outcast. He's quite determined that his daughters do not make the same mistake. It's taken him years to rebuild friendships and such. People still speak badly of him if the moment presents itself in an advantageous way. Were we to marry poorly it would reflect directly on him and no doubt add to his sufferings."

"But what if you fall in love with someone your father deems beneath you?" Logan asked moving in a step. "Say you fall in love with a barbarian instead of a twit?" His raised brow implied what his words failed to say.

Amelia felt her face grow hot. *He is really asking what would happen if I fell in love with him.* His face was close enough to reach out and touch and as always that pesky mustache drew her attention. *What if?* She had to distance herself. She had to get away from his piercing green eyes and probing questions. "It could never happen, Mr. Reed," she finally said, then added with a hard stare of her own, "Never."

$$\binom{7}{}$$

*E*stes Park was like nothing Amelia had ever seen. Completely surrounded by mountains, the valley looked as though someone had placed it there to hide it away from the world. Ponderosa pine, spruce, and aspen dotted the area and Lord Amhurst was delighted to find the shrub-styled junipers whose berries were especially popular with the grouse and pheasants. She knew her father was becoming eager for the hunt. She had seen him eyeing the fowl while Jeffery had been watching the larger game.

They made their way slowly through the crisp morning air, horses panting lightly and blowing puffs of warm air out to meet the cold. To Amelia it seemed that the valley wrapped itself around them as they descended. Birds of varying kind began their songs, and from time to time a deer or elk would cross their path, pausing to stare for a moment at the intruders before darting off into the thicket.

Gone was the oppressive prairie with its blasting winds, insufferable heat, and swarming insects. Gone were the dusty streets and spittoons. This place was a complete contrast to the prairie towns she'd seen. Even the air was different. The air here, though thinner, was also so very dry and Amelia marveled at the difference between it and that of her native land. Already her skin felt tough and coarse and she vowed to rub scented oils and lotions on herself every night until they departed. But departing was the furthest thing from her mind. What had started out as an unpleasant obligation to her, was now becoming rather appealing. She found herself increasingly drawn to this strange land, and to the man who had brought them here.

She silently studied Logan's back as he rode. He was telling them bits and pieces of information about the area, but her mind wouldn't focus on the words.

What if she did fall in love with a barbarian? What if she already had?

❦

The lodge where they'd made arrangements to stay was a two story log building surrounded by smaller log cabins. Lord Amhurst had arranged to take three cabins for his party, while Lord and Lady Gambett had decided to stay in the lodge itself. Lady Gambett had declared it necessary to see properly to the delicate constitutions of her daughters. This thought made Amelia want to laugh, but she remained stoically silent. Delicate constitutions had no place here and it would provide only one more weapon for Logan Reed to use against them. She was bound and determined to show Logan that English women could be strong and capable without need of anyone's assistance. Amelia chose to forget that Lady Bird had already proven her case to Logan Reed two years ago.

"This place looks awful," Margaret was whining as Mattersley helped to bring in their bags.

Amelia looked around the crude cabin and for once she didn't feel at all repulsed by the simplicity. It was one room with two beds, a small table with a single oil lamp, and a washstand with a pitcher and bowl of chipped blue porcelain that at one time might have been considered pretty. A stone fireplace dominated one wall. Red gingham curtains hung in the single window and several rag rugs had been strategically placed in stepping stone fashion upon the thin plank floor.

"It's quite serviceable, Margaret," Amelia stated firmly, "so stop being such a ninny. Perhaps you'd like to sleep in a tent again."

"I think this place is hideous," Penelope chimed in before Margaret could reply. "Papa was cruel to bring us here, and all because of you."

This statement came just as Logan appeared with one of several trunks containing the girls' clothes. He eyed Amelia suspiciously and placed the trunk on the floor. "I think you'll find this cabin a sight warmer than the tent and the bed more comfortable than the ground," he said before walking back out the door.

Amelia turned on her sisters with a fury. "Keep our private affairs to yourselves. I won't have the entire countryside knowing our business. Mother raised you to be ladies of quality and refinement. Ladies of that nature do not spout off about the family's personal concerns."

Margaret and Penelope were taken aback for only a moment. It mattered little to them that Logan Reed had overheard their conversation. Amelia knew that to them he was hired help, no different than Mattersley. They were quite used to a house filled with servants who overheard their conversations on a daily basis and knew better than to speak of the matters, even amongst themselves. Logan Reed was quite a different sort, however, and Amelia knew he'd feel completely within his rights to inquire about their statement at the first possible moment.

"I suggest we unpack our things and see if we can get the wrinkles out of our gowns. I'm sure you will want a bath and the chance to be rid of these riding costumes," Amelia said, taking a sure route she knew her sisters would follow.

"Oh, I do so hope to sink into a tub of hot water," Penelope moaned. At seventeen she was used to spending her days changing from one gown to another, sometimes wearing as many as six in the same day. "I'm positively sick of this mountain skirt or whatever they call it."

"I rather enjoy the freedom they afford," Amelia said. Satisfied with having distracted her sisters, she unfastened the latches on the trunk. "But I would find a bath quite favorable."

They spent the rest of the day securing their belongings and laying out their claims on the various parts of the room. By standing their trunks on end they managed to create a separate table for each of them and it was here they placed their brushes, combs and perfumes. Helping Penelope to string a rope on which they could hang their dresses, Amelia realized they'd brought entirely too many formal gowns and not nearly enough simple outfits. *Where had they thought they were traveling? It wasn't as if they'd have anyone to dress up for.*

Logan came to mind and Amelia immediately vanquished his image from her thoughts. She would not concern herself with looking nice for him. Her father expected her to look the lovely English rose for Sir Jeffery. That was why the clothes were packed as they were. Her desires were immaterial compared to her father's.

"Amelia has twice as many gowns as we have," Penelope complained at dinner that evening.

Lord Amhurst gave her a look of reprimand, but it was Lady Gambett who spoke. "Your sister is the eldest, and by being the eldest, she is to have certain privileges afforded her. You mustn't complain about it for once she's married and keeping house for herself, you shall be the eldest."

This placated the petite blond, but Amelia felt her face grow hot. She was grateful that Logan was nowhere to be seen.

"I suggest we make an early evening of it," the earl said with an eye to his daughters. "There is to be an early morning hunt and I'm certain you won't want to lag behind."

Margaret and Penelope began conversing immediately with Henrietta and Josephine about what they would wear and how they would arrange their hair. Amelia could only think on the fact that she would be forced to spend still another day in Logan Reed's company.

"Papa," she said without giving the matter another thought, "I'd like to rest and walk about the grounds. Please forgive me if I decline the hunt."

The earl nodded, appraising her for a moment then dismissing the matter when Lady Gambett spoke up. "I will stay behind as well. I can't possibly bear the idea of another ride."

With the matter settled, the party dispersed and went to their various beds. Amelia faded to sleep quickly, relishing the comfort of a bed and the warmth of their fire. In her dreams she kept company with a green-eyed Logan, and because it was only a dream, Amelia found herself enjoying every single moment.

Logan was glad to be home. The valley offered him familiar comfort that he had never been able to replicate elsewhere. His cabin, located just up the mountain, wasn't all that far from the lodge where he'd deposited the earl and his traveling companions. But, it was far enough. It afforded him some much needed privacy and the peace of mind to consider the matters at hand.

Kicking off his boots, Logan built a hearty fire and glanced around at his home. Three rooms comprised the first floor. The bedroom at the back of the cabin was small but served its purpose. A kitchen with a cookstove and several crude cupboards extended into the dining area where a table and chairs stood beneath one window. This area, in turn, blended into the main room where the fireplace mantel was lined with small tin-type photos and books. A comfortable sofa, which Logan had made himself, invited company which seldom came, and two idle chairs stood as sentinels beside a crude book shelf. The tall shelf of books seemed out of place for the rustic cabin, but it was Logan's private library and he cherished it more than any of his other possessions. Whenever he went out from the valley to the towns nearby, he always brought back new books to add to his collection. This time he'd picked up an order in Greeley and had five new books with which to pass the time. Two were works by Jules Verne that promised to be quite entertaining. Of the remaining three, one was a study of science, one a collection of poetry, and the final book promised an exploration of Italy.

With a sigh, Logan dropped down onto the sofa and glanced upward. Shadows from the dancing fire made images against the darkened loft. The house was silent except for the occasional popping of the fire, and Logan found his mind wandering to the fair-haired Lady Amelia. He knew he'd lost his heart to her, and furthermore he was certain that she felt something for him. He wanted to chide himself for his love at first sight reaction to the delicate beauty, but there was no need. His heart wouldn't have heeded the warning or reprimand. Lost in his daydreams, Logan fell asleep on the sofa. He'd see her tomorrow before the party went out on the hunt, but how would he manage the rest of the day without her at his side?

❧

Amelia hung back in her cabin until well after her family had left for the hunting expedition. She was determined to keep from facing Logan Reed and having to deal with his comments or suggestions. She couldn't understand why he bothered her so much. *It wasn't as if he has any say in my life. It wasn't as if he could change my life, so why give him the slightest consideration?*

Making her way to the lodge, Amelia guessed it to be nearly eight o'clock. She could smell the lingering scents of breakfast on the air and knew that Logan had been right about one thing. Mountain air gave you a decidedly larger appetite.

"Morning," a heavy set woman Amelia knew to be the owner's wife called out. "You must be Lady Amhurst. Jonas told me you were staying behind this morning." Amelia nodded and the woman continued. "I'm just making bread, but you're welcome to keep me company."

Amelia smiled. "I thought to tour around the woods nearby, but I'd be happy to sit with you for a time, Mrs. Lewis." She barely remembered her father saying the place was owned by a family named Lewis.

The woman wiped her floury hands on her apron and reached for a bowl. "Just call me Mary. Mrs. Lewis is far too formal for the likes of me and this place."

Amelia sensed a genuine openness to the woman. "You must call me Amelia," she said, surprising herself by the declaration. The mountain air and simplicity of the setting made her forget old formalities. "What is it that you are doing just now?" she asked, feeling suddenly very interested.

Mary looked at her in disbelief. "Don't tell me you've never seen bread made before?"

"Never," Amelia said with a laugh. "I'm afraid I've never ventured much into the kitchen at all."

"But who does the cooking for your family?"

"Oh, we've a bevy of servants who see to our needs. Father believes that young women of noble upbringing have no place in a kitchen."

Mary laughed. "I guess I'm far from noble in upbringing. I was practically birthed in the kitchen." She kneaded the dough and sprinkled in a handful of flour. "Would you like to learn how to make bread?"

Surprised by an unfamiliar desire to do just that, Amelia responded. "I'd love to."

Mary wiped her hands again and went to a drawer where she pulled out another apron. "Put this on over your pretty dress so that it doesn't get all messy. And take off those gloves. It doesn't pay to wear Sunday best when you're working in the kitchen."

She turned back to the dough, while Amelia secured the apron over what she had considered one of her dowdier gowns. The peach and green print was far from being her Sunday best. Amelia tucked her white kid gloves into the pocket of the apron and rolled up her sleeves like Mary's.

"I'm ready," she said confidently, anxious to embark on this new project. Lady Bird had told her that only in experiencing things first hand could a person truly have a working knowledge of them. One might read books about crossing the ocean or riding an elephant, but until you actually participated in those activities, you were only touching the memories of another.

"Here you go," Mary said, putting a large hunk of dough in front of her. "Work it just like this." She pushed the palms of her hands deep into the mass. "Then pull it back like this." Amelia watched, catching the rhythm as Mary's massive hands worked the dough. "Now you do it." Mary tossed a bit of flour atop the bread dough and smiled.

Amelia grinned. "You make it look simple enough." But it was harder than it looked. Amelia felt the sticky dough ooze through her fingers and laughed out loud at the sensation. *Father would positively expire if he saw me like this.*

"That's it," Mary said from beside her own pile. "You can work out a great many problems while kneading bread."

"I can imagine why," Amelia replied. Already her thoughts of Logan were fading.

She worked through two more piles of dough with Mary's lively chatter keeping her company. When all of the dough had been prepared Mary showed her how to divide the mass into loaves. Placing the last of her dough into one of the pans, Amelia wiped a stray strand of hair from her face and smiled. It was satisfying work. Twenty-two loaves lay rising before her and some of them had been formed by her own hands.

"There are so many," she commented, noting some of the dough had been placed in pans before her arrival. Already they were rising high, while still others filled the lodge with a delicious scent as they baked.

"I've been collecting bread pans for most of my life. Working this lodge takes a heap of bread for the folks who stay, as well as those who help out. I alternate the loaves so that some are always baking or rising or getting kneaded down. Bread is pretty much alike the country over, so travelers take right to it when they won't eat another thing on the table. And, I sell a few loaves on the side. Menfolk around here don't always want to bake their own bread, so they come here to buy it from me." As if on cue the door opened and Logan Reed strode in.

Amelia stared at him in stunned silence, while Logan did much the same. A lazy smile spread itself under the bushy mustache, making Amelia instantly uncomfortable. "You don't mean to tell me that Lady Amhurst is taking lessons in bread baking?"

"She sure is," Mary said, before Amelia could protest the conversation. "Amelia here is a right quick learner."

"Amelia, eh?" Logan raised a questioning brow to keep company with his lopsided smile.

"Sure," Mary said, betraying a bit of German heritage in her voice. "She's a charming young woman, this one."

"That she is," he replied then turned his question on Amelia, "Why aren't you on the hunt?"

Amelia couldn't tell him that she'd purposefully avoided the hunt because of him. She tossed around several ideas and finally decided on the closest thing to the truth. "I wanted to tour about the grounds. I've had enough horsebacking for a while."

"I see."

For a moment Amelia was certain he really did see. His expression told her that he knew very well she'd made her decision based on something entirely apart from the discomfort of the old cavalry saddle.

"Why are you here? I thought you'd be off with the others." Amelia knew that if he had doubted the reason for her decision, she had just confirmed those doubts.

Mary looked rather puzzled. "He comes for bread. One of those menfolk I told you about." She nudged Amelia playfully. "He's needs a good wife to keep him company and make his bread for him."

"Mary's right. That's probably just what I need," Logan said with a knowing look at Amelia.

"If you'll excuse me Mary, I'm going to go clean up and take my walk. I appreciate your lessons this morning." Amelia untied the apron and put it across the back of a nearby chair, her kid gloves forgotten in the pocket.

"Come back tomorrow morning and we'll make cinnamon rolls," the heavyset woman said with a smile.

"Now there's something every good wife should know," Logan piped up. "Mary's cinnamon rolls are the best in the country. Why, I'd walk from Denver to Estes to get a pan of those."

"If time permits, I'd be happy to work with you," Amelia said and then hurried from the room.

Images of Logan Reed followed her back to the cabin where Amelia hurriedly grabbed her journal and pencil, as well as a straw walking-out hat. Balancing the journal while tying on the bonnet, Amelia quickened her pace and determined to put as much distance as possible between her and the smug-faced Mr. Reed. *Why couldn't he have just taken her party on the hunt and left her to herself? Why did he have to show up and see her wearing an apron and acting like hired help?* But she'd enjoyed her time with Mary, and she never once felt like hired help. Instead she felt . . . well, she felt useful, as though she'd actually accomplished something very important.

Making her way along a tiny path behind the cluster of cabins, Amelia tried to grasp those feelings of accomplishment and consider what they meant. Her life in England seemed trite when she thought of Mary's long hours of work. She was idle in comparison, but then again, she had been schooled in the graceful arts of being idle. She could, of course, stitch lovely tea towels and dresser scarves. She could paint fairly well and intended to sketch out some pastoral scenes from her hike and later redo them in watercolors. But none of these things were all that useful. Mary's work was relied upon by those around her. She baked their bread and kept them fed. She braided rugs and sewed clothes to ward off the mountain chill. She worked with the hides her husband brought back from the hunts. She knew all of this because Mary had told her so in their chatty conversation. *Mary's is not an idle life of appearances. Mary's life has purpose and meaning.*

Before she realized it, Amelia was halfway up the incline which butted against the Lewis property. She turned to look back down and drew her breath in at the view. The sun gave everything the appearance of having been freshly washed. The brilliance of the colors stood out boldly against the dark green background of the snow-capped, tree-covered mountains. The rushing river on the opposite side of the property shimmered and gurgled in glorious shades of violet and blue. But it was always the lighting which appealed her painter's eyes. The light here was unlike any she'd ever seen before. It was impossible to explain, but for a moment she felt compelled to try. She sat down abruptly and took up her journal.

"There is a quality to the light which cannot be explained. It is, I suppose, due to the high mountain altitude and the thinner quality of oxygen," she spoke aloud while writing. "The colors are more vivid, yet, if possible, they are also more subtle. The lighting highlights every detail, while creating the illusion of something draped in a translucent veil. I know this doesn't make sense, yet it is most certainly so." She paused and looked down upon the tiny village. She would very much like to paint this scene, but how in the world could she ever capture the light?

Beside her were several tiny white flowers bobbing up and down in the gentle breeze. She leaned over on her elbow, mindless of her gown and watched them for a moment. She considered the contrast of their whiteness against the green of their leaves and wondered at their name. Plucking one stem, she pressed it between the pages of her book, jotted a note of its location and got to her feet.

The higher she climbed, the rougher the path. Finally it became quite steep and altogether impassable. It was here she decided to turn away from the path and make her own way. The little incline to her left seemed most appealing even though it was strewn with rocks. The way to her right was much too threatening with its jagged boulders and sheer drops. Hiking up her skirt, with her journal tucked under her arm, Amelia faced the challenging mountainside with a determined spirit. She was feeling quite bold and was nearly to the top when the loose gravel gave way beneath her feet and sent her tumbling backward. Sliding on her backside and rolling the rest of the way, Amelia finally landed in a heap at the foot of the incline. Six feet away stood Logan Reed with an expression on his face that seemed to contort from amusement to concern and back to amusement.

Amelia's pride and backside were sorely bruised, but she'd not admit defeat to Logan. She straightened her hat and frowned. "Are you spying on me, Mr. Reed?" she asked indignantly from where she sat.

Logan laughed. "I'd say you could use some looking after given the scene I just witnessed. But, no, I didn't mean to spy. I live just over the ridge so when I saw you walking up this way, I thought I'd come and offer my services."

Amelia quickly got to her feet and brushed the gravel from her gown. Seeing her book on the ground she retrieved it and winced at the way it hurt her to bend down. "Your services for what?" she asked, hoping Logan hadn't seen her misery as well.

"To be your hiking guide," he replied coming forward. "It would sure save you on your wardrobe." He pointed to a long tear in the skirt of her gown. "Why in the world did you hike out here dressed like that?"

"I beg your pardon?"

"At least that riding skirt would have been a little more serviceable. You need to have sturdy clothes to hike these hills," he chided.

"I will hike in whatever is most comfortable to me, Mr. Reed."

"And you think corsets and muslin prints are most comfortable?"

Amelia huffed. "I don't think it is any of your concern. I'm quite capable of taking care of myself."

Logan rolled his eyes and laughed all the harder. "Yes, I can see that." He shook his head and turned to walk back to the lodge, leaving Amelia to nurse her wounded pride.

8

melia spent the rest of the morning making notes in her journal and contemplating Logan Reed. As much as she tried to forget him, she couldn't help thinking of his offer to be her hiking guide. *Logan knows every flower and tree in the area. He would certainly be the most knowledgeable man around when it came to identifying the vegetation and landmarks. If I am going to put together a book on the area it seems sensible to utilize the knowledge of the most intelligent man.*

The book idea wasn't really new to her. She'd been considering it since speaking with Lady Bird long before departing for America. Lady Bird told Amelia she should do something memorable with her time abroad. *Writing a book and painting dainty watercolor flowers seems very reasonable. Falling in love with a barbaric, American guide does not.*

Closing her book with loud snap, Amelia got to her feet. "I'm not in love," she murmured to the empty room. "I will not fall in love with Logan Reed." But even as she said the words, a part of Amelia knew that it was too late for such a declaration.

❧

At noon, she made her way to the lodge house where the hunting party had returned to gather for a large midday meal. Amelia saw that the hunt was successful, but for the first time she wondered about the business of cleaning the kill and how the skins of the animals were to be used afterward. She'd never given such matters much thought in the past. There was always someone else to do the dirty work.

"I say, Amelia, you missed quite a hunt. Sir Jeffery bagged a buck first thing out."

Amelia glanced at Jeffery and then back to her father. "How nice." She pulled out a chair and found Jeffery quickly at her side to seat her.

"It was a clean and easy shot, nothing so very spectacular," he said in false humility. "I could name a dozen animals that present a greater challenge to hunt."

"Perhaps the greatest challenge comes in bagging a wife, what?" Lord Amhurst heartily laughed much to Amelia's embarrassment and the stunned expressions of the others.

"Indeed true love is the hardest thing on earth to secure," Lady Gambett said in a tone that suggested a long story was forthcoming. She was fresh from a day of napping and eager to be companionable.

"Papa had a good morning as well," Penelope declared quickly and Margaret joined in so fast that both girls were talking at once. This seemed to be a cue to Josephine and Henrietta who began a garbled rendition of the hunt for their mother's benefit.

Jeffery took a chair at Amelia's right and engaged her immediately in conversation. "I missed your company on the hunt. Do say you'll be present tomorrow."

"I'm afraid I didn't come to America to hunt. Not for animals of any kind," she stated, clearly hoping the implied meaning would not be lost on Jeffery. The sooner he understood her distaste for their proposed matrimony, the better.

"What will you do with your time?"

Amelia folded her hands in her lap. "I plan to write a book on the flowers and vegetation of Estes Park." The words came out at just the exact moment that her sisters and the Gambetts had chosen to take a collective breath. Her words seemed to echo in the silence for several moments. Stunned faces from all around the table looked up to make certain they had heard correctly.

"You plan to do what?" Margaret asked before anyone else could give voice to their thoughts.

"You heard me correctly," Amelia said, taking up a thick slice of the bread she'd helped to make that morning. "The flowers here are beautiful and quite extraordinary. Nothing like what we have at home.

Lady Bird told me I should use my time abroad to do something meaningful and memorable. I believe a book of this nature would certainly fit that suggestion."

The earl nodded. "If Lady Bird believes it to be of value, then I heartily agree." With Mattersley nowhere in sight, he filled his plate with potatoes and laughed when they dribbled over the rim. "Waiting on yourself takes some practice." The dinner party chuckled politely and the mood seemed to lighten considerably.

As everyone seemed intent on eating, Amelia's declaration passed from importance and escaped further discussion. With a sigh of relief, Amelia helped herself to a thick slice of ham and a hearty portion of potatoes. Jeffery would think her a glutton, but let him. She was tired of worrying about what other people thought. She found it suddenly quite enjoyable to be a bit more barbaric herself. Almost guilty for her thoughts, Amelia's head snapped up and she searched the room for Logan. She knew he wouldn't be there, but for some reason her conscience forced her to prove it.

"So how will you get about the place?" the earl was suddenly asking and all eyes turned to Amelia.

"I beg your pardon, Papa?"

"How will you travel about to gather your flowers and such? Will you have a guide?"

Amelia felt the ham stick in her throat as she tried to swallow. She took a long drink of her tea before replying. "Mr. Reed has offered to act as guide, but I told him it wasn't necessary."

"Nonsense," her father answered. "If you are to undertake this project, do it in a correct manner. There is a great deal to know about this area and you should have a guide, what?"

"I suppose you are fair in assuming that," Amelia replied. "But I hardly think Mr. Reed would be an appropriate teacher on flowers."

Mary Lewis had entered the room to deposit two large pies on the table. "Logan's an excellent teacher," she said, unmindful of her eavesdropping. "Logan led an expedition of government people out here just last summer. He's got a good education—a sight more than most of the folks around these parts, anyway."

Everyone stared at Mary for a moment as though stunned by her boldness. "It seems reasonable," the earl said, nodding to Mary as if to dismiss her, "that Mr. Reed should direct you in your studies. I'll speak to him this afternoon and make certain he is reasonably recompensed for his efforts. Perhaps this evening at dinner we can finalize the arrangements."

Amelia said nothing. In truth, she had already decided to speak to Logan about helping her. She knew herself to be a prideful woman and what had once seemed like an admirable quality, now made her feel even more of a snob. Lady Bird had lowered herself to even help harvest the crops of local residents. How could she resist the help of Logan Reed, and possibly hope to justify herself. But just as her feelings were starting to mellow towards the man, he ruined it by joining them.

"Looks like you did pretty good for yourself, Amhurst," Logan said, taking a seat at the table.

Mary Lewis entered bringing him a huge platter of food. "I saved this for you, Logan."

"Much thanks, Mary." He bowed his head for a moment, before digging into the steaming food.

Everyone at the table looked on in silent accusation at Logan Reed. Even Mattersley would not presume to take his meals at the same table with the more noble classes. Logan Reed seemed to have no inclination that he was doing anything out of line, but when he glanced up he immediately caught the meaning of their silence. Rather than give in to their misplaced sense of propriety, however, Logan just smiled and complimented Mary on the food as she poured him a hot cup of coffee.

"Will Jonas be taking you out again tomorrow?" Logan asked as if nothing was amiss.

Amelia saw her father exchange a glance with Lord Gambett before answering. "Yes, I suppose he will. I understand you have offered to assist my daughter in gathering information for her book. I would like to discuss the terms of your employment after we finish with the meal."

Logan shook his head. "I didn't offer to be employed. I suggested to Lady Amhurst that I act as hiking guide and she refused." He looked hard at Amelia, but there was a hint of amusement in his eyes and his mustache twitched in its usual betraying fashion.

"It seemed improper to accept your suggestion," Amelia said rather stiffly.

"Nonsense, child. The man is fully qualified to assist you," Lord Amhurst stated. "I'll make all the arrangements after dinner."

Amelia felt Logan's eyes on her and blushed from head to toe. The discomfort she felt was nothing compared to what she knew would come if she didn't leave immediately. Surprising her family, she got up rather quickly.

"I beg your forgiveness, but I must be excused." Without waiting for her father's approval, Amelia left the room.

Much to her frustration, Jeffery Chamberlain was upon her heels in a matter of seconds. "Are you ill, Amelia?" His voice oozed concern.

"I am quite well," she replied, keeping a steady pace to her walk. "I simply needed to take the air."

"I understand perfectly," he replied and took hold of her elbow as if to assist her.

Amelia jerked away and once they had rounded the front of the lodge, she turned to speak her mind. "Sir Jeffery, there are some issues we must have settled between us."

"I quite agree, but surely you wouldn't seek to speak of them here. Perhaps we can steal away to a quiet corner of the lodge," he suggested.

Amelia shook her head. "I am sure what I desire to speak of will not be in keeping with what you desire to speak of."

"But Amelia—"

"Please give me a moment," she interrupted. Amelia saw his expression of concern change to one of puzzlement. She almost felt sorry for him. Almost, but not quite.

"You must come to understand," she began, "that I have no desire to follow my father's wishes and marry you." She raised a hand to silence his protests. "Please hear me out. My father might find you a wonderful candidate for a son-in-law, but I will not marry a man I do not love. And, Sir Chamberlain, I do not now, nor will I ever, love you."

The man's expression suggested anger and hurt, and for a moment Amelia thought to soften the blow. "However, my sisters find you quite acceptable as a prospective husband, so I would encourage you to court one of them."

At this Jeffery seemed insulted and puffed out his chest with a jerk of his chin. "I have no intentions of marrying your sisters," he said firmly. "I have an agreement with your father to acquire your hand in matrimony."

"But you have no such agreement with me, Sir Jeffery."

"It matters little. The men in our country arrange such affairs, not addle-brained women."

"Addle-brained?" Amelia was barely holding her anger in check. "You think me addle-brained?"

"When you act irresponsibly such as you are now, then yes, I do," he replied.

"I see. And what part of my actions implies being addle-brained?" she questioned. "Is it that I see no sense in joining in a marriage of convenience to a man I cannot possibly hope to love?"

"It is addle-brained and whimsical to imagine that such things as love are of weighted importance in this arrangement. Your father is seeing to this arrangement as he would any other business proposition. He is benefiting the family name, the family holdings, and the family coffers. Only a selfish and greedy young woman would see it as otherwise."

"So now I am addle-brained, whimsical, selfish, and greedy," Amelia said with haughty air. "Why in the world would you seek such a wife, Sir Chamberlain?"

Jeffery seemed to wilt a bit under her scrutiny. "I didn't mean to imply you were truly those things. But the air that you take in regards to our union would suggest you have given little consideration to the needs of others."

"So now I am inconsiderate as well!" Amelia turned on her heel and headed in the direction of the cabin.

Jeffery hurried after her. "You must understand, Amelia, these things are done for the betterment of all concerned."

She turned at this, completely unable to control her anger. "Jeffery, these things are done in order to keep my father in control of my mother's fortune. There hasn't been any consideration given to my desires or needs, and therefore I find it impossible to believe it has anything to do with my welfare or betterment."

"I can give you a good life," Jeffery replied barely keeping his temper in check. "I have several estates to where we might spend out our days and you will bring your own estate into the arrangement as well. You've a fine piece of Scottish land, or so your father tells me."

"But I have no desire to spend out my days with you. Not on the properties you already own, nor the properties which I might bring into a marriage. Please understand, so that we might spend our days here in America as amicably as possible," she said with determined conviction, "I will not agree to marry you."

Jeffery's face contorted and to Amelia's surprise he spoke out in a manner close to rage. "You will do what you are told and it matters little what you agree to. Your father and I have important matters riding on this circumstance and that alone is what will gain consideration. You will marry me, Amelia, and furthermore," he paused with a suggestive leer on his face, "you will find it surprisingly enjoyable."

"I would sooner marry Logan Reed as to join myself in union to a boorish snob such as yourself." Silently she wished for something to throw at the smug-faced Jeffery, but instead she calmed herself and fixed him with a harsh glare. "I pray you understand, and understand well. I will never marry you and I will take whatever measures are necessary to ensure that I win out in this unpleasant situation."

She stormed off to her cabin, seething from the confrontation, but also a bit frightened by Jeffery's strange nature. She'd never seen him more out of character and it gave her cause to wonder. She knew there had always been a mischievous, almost devious side to his personality. The memory of hanging over the banister in fear of plunging to her death on the floor below affirmed Amelia's consideration. Jeffery had always leaned a bit on the cruel side of practical jokes and teasing play. Still, she couldn't imagine that he was all that dangerous. He wanted something very badly from her father and no doubt he could just as easily obtain it by marrying one of her sisters. After all, they adored him.

Reaching her cabin, Amelia reasoned away her fears. Her father's insistence that she marry Jeffery was in order to preserve the inheritance. Perhaps there was some other legal means by which Amelia could waive rights to her portion of the estate. It was worth questioning her father. If he saw the sincerity of her desire to remain single, even to the point of giving up what her mother had planned to be rightfully hers, Amelia knew she'd have no qualms about doing exactly that.

"I would sooner marry Logan Reed." The words suddenly came back to haunt her. At first she laughed at this prospect while unfastening the back buttons of her gown. *What would married life be like with the likes of Logan Reed?* She could see herself in a cold cabin, kneading bread and scrubbing clothes on a washboard. She didn't even know how to cook and the thought of Logan laboring to choke down a meal prepared with her own two hands, made Amelia laugh all the harder.

The gown slid down from her shoulders and fell in a heap on the floor. Absentmindedly Amelia ran her hands down her slender white arms. Laughter died in her throat as an image of Logan doing the same thing came to mind. She imagined staring deep into his green eyes and finding everything she'd ever searched for. Answers to all her questions would be revealed in his soul-searching gaze, including the truths of life which seemed to elude her. Shuddering in a sudden wake of emotion, Amelia quickly pulled on the mountain skirt.

"He means nothing to me," she murmured defensively. "Logan Reed means nothing to me."

∼❧

Having dismissed himself from the dinner table on the excuse of bringing in wood for Mary, Logan had overheard most of the exchange between Jeffery and Amelia. At first he thought he might need to intercede on Amelia's behalf when Jeffery seemed to get his nose a bit out of joint, but the declaration of Amelia preferring to marry Logan over Jeffery had stopped him in his tracks.

At first he was mildly amused. He admired the young woman's

spirit of defense and her ability to put the uppity Englishman in his place. He imagined with great pleasure the shock to Sir Chamberlain's noble esteem when Amelia declared her thoughts on the matter of marriage. At least it gave him a better understanding of what was going on between the members of the party. He'd felt an underlying current of tension from the first time he'd met them, especially between the trio of Lord Amhurst, Jeffery, and Amelia. Now, it was clearly understood that the earl planned to see his daughter married to Jeffery, and it was even clearer that Amelia had no desire to comply with her father's wishes. *But why?* Logan wondered. *Why would it be so important for the earl to pass his daughter off to Chamberlain?*

"I would sooner marry Logan Reed." He remembered the words and felt a bit smug. He knew she'd intended it as an insult to Jeffery, but it didn't matter. For reasons beyond his understanding, Logan felt as though he'd come one step closer to making Amelia his lady.

9

In spite of her father's desire to have Amelia seek out Logan's assistance as her hiking guide, Amelia chose instead to hike alone. She was often up before any of the others and usually found herself in the kitchen of the lodge, learning the various culinary skills that Mary performed.

"You're doing a fine job, Amelia," Mary told her.

Amelia stared down at the dough rings as they floated and sizzled in a pool of lard. "And you call these doughnuts?" she questioned, careful to turn them before they burned on one side.

"Sure. Sure. Some folks call them oly koeks. The menfolk love 'em though. I could fix six dozen of these a day and have them gone by noon. Once the men learn doughnuts are on the table, I can't get rid of them 'til they get rid of the doughnuts."

Amelia laughed. They didn't seem all that hard to make and she rather enjoyed the way they bobbed up and down in the fat. It reminded her of the life preservers on board the ship they'd used to cross the Atlantic. "I'll remember that."

"Sure, you'll make a lot of friends if you fix these for your folks back in England," Mary replied.

Amelia couldn't begin to imagine the reaction of her "folks back in England" should they see her bent over a stove, laboring to bring doughnuts to the table. "I'm afraid," she began, "that it would never be considered appropriate for me to do such a thing at home."

"No?" Mary seem surprised. "I betcha they'd get eaten."

"Yes, I'd imagine after everyone recovered from the fits of apoplexy, they just might eat the doughnuts." She pulled the rings from the grease and sprinkled them with sugar just as Mary had shown her to do. It was while she was engrossed in this task that Logan popped his head through the open doorway.

"Ummm, I don't have to ask what you're doing today, Mary."

"Ain't me, Logan. It's Amelia. She's turning into right handy kitchen help."

Logan raised a brow of question in Amelia's direction. "I don't believe it. Let me taste one of those doughnuts." He reached out before Amelia could stop him and popped half of the ring into his mouth. His expression changed as though he were considering a very weighty question. Without breaking his stoic expression he finished the doughnut and reached for another. "I'd better try again." He ate this one in three bites instead of two and again the expression on his face remained rigidly set. "Mary, better pour me a cup of coffee. I'm going to have to try another one in order to figure out if they're as good as yours or maybe, just maybe, a tiny sight better."

Amelia flushed crimson and turned quickly to put more rings into the grease before Logan spoke again. "Now I know we'll have to keep this one around."

Mary laughed and brought him the coffee. "That's what I keep tellin' her. I don't know when I've enjoyed a summer visitor more. Most young ladies of her upbringin' are a bit more uppity. They never want to learn kitchen work, that's for sure."

Amelia tried not to feel pride in the statement. She knew full well that Logan had once considered her one of those more uppity types and rightly so. For the past few weeks even Amelia couldn't explain the change in her attitude and spirit. She found the countryside inspiring and provoking, and with each passing day she felt more and more a part of this land.

Not realizing it she shook her head. *I'm English,* she thought and turned the doughnuts. *I cannot possibly belong to this place.* She looked up feeling a sense of guilt and found Logan's gaze fixed on her. A surge of emotion raced through her. *I cannot possibly belong to this man.*

Swallowing hard, she took a nervous glance at her pocket watch. "Oh, my," she declared, brushing off imaginary bits of flour and crumbs, "I must go. I promised I'd wake Margaret by seven."

Mary nodded. "You go on now. I've had a good long rest."

"Hardly that," Amelia said and took off her apron. "I have been here three weeks and I have yet to see you rest at any time."

"I saw it once," Logan said conspiratorially, "but it was six years ago and Mary was down sick with a fever. She sat down for about ten minutes that day, but that was it."

Amelia smiled in spite of herself. "I thought so. Thanks for the lesson, Mary. I'll see you later." She hurried from the room with a smile still brightening her face.

"Don't forget," Mary reminded, "you wanted to start quilting and this afternoon will be just fine for me."

"All right. I should be free," she replied over her shoulder.

"Hey, wait up a minute," Logan called and joined her as she crossed from the lodge to the grassy cabin area.

Looking up, Amelia felt her pulse quicken. "What is it?"

"I was hoping you'd be interested in a hike with me. I thought you'd like to go on a real adventure."

Amelia's curiosity was piqued. "What did you have in mind?"

"Long's Peak."

"The mountain?"

Logan grinned. "The same. There's quite a challenging climb up to the top. If you think you're up to it, I could approach your father on the matter."

"He'd never agree to such a thing."

Logan's smile faded. "He wouldn't agree, or you don't agree?"

Amelia felt a twinge of defensiveness but ignored it. She found herself honestly wishing she could hike up Long's Peak with Logan Reed and to argue now wouldn't help her case one bit. "Without an appropriate chaperon, Logan," she said his name hoping to prove her willingness, "it would never be allowed."

Logan cheered at this. "So what does it take to have an appropriate chaperon?"

"Someone like Mary or Lady Gambett."

Logan nodded. "I guess I can understand that. I'll work on it and let you know."

Amelia saw him turn to go and found a feeling of deep dissatisfaction engulfing her. "Logan, wait."

He turned back and eyed her questioningly. "Yes?"

"I've collected quite a variety of vegetation and flower samples and I thought, well actually I hoped—" she paused seeing that she held his interest. "I was too hasty in rejecting your offer of help. My father wanted me to accept and so now I'm asking if you would assist me in identifying my samples."

"What made you change your mind?" he asked softly coming to stand only inches away. His eyes were dark and imploring and Amelia felt totally swallowed up in their depths.

"I'm not sure," Amelia said, feeling very small and very vulnerable.

Logan's lopsided grin made his entire face light up. "It doesn't matter. I'd be happy to help you. When do you want to start?"

"How would this morning work out for you? Say, after the others have gone about their business?"

"That sounds good to me. I'll meet you at the lodge."

Amelia smiled and gave a little nod. It had been a very agreeable conclusion to their conversation. She watched Logan go off in the direction of the lodge and thought her heart would burst from the happiness she felt. *What was it? Why did she suddenly feel so light?* For weeks she had fought against her nature and her better judgment regarding Logan Reed. Now, giving in and accepting Logan's help seemed to free rather than burden her.

She approached the cabin she'd been sharing with her sisters and grew wary at the sound of voices inside.

"Amelia is simply *awful*. She gives no consideration to family, or to poor Papa's social standing." It was Penelope, and Margaret quickly picked up the challenge.

"Amelia has never cared for anyone but Amelia. I think she's hateful and selfish. Just look at the gowns she has to choose from and you and I must suffer through with only five apiece. I'm quite beside myself."

"And all because Papa is trying to see her married to poor Jeffery. Why he doesn't even love Amelia, and she certainly doesn't love him. I overheard Papa tell him that he would give him not only a substantial dowry, but one of the Scottish estates, if only Jeffery could convince Amelia to marry him before we returned to England."

"She'll never agree to it," Margaret replied haughtily. "She doesn't care one whit what happens to the rest of us. She never bothers to consider what might make others happy. If she hurts Papa this way and ruins my season in London, I'll simply die."

Amelia listened to the bitter words of her sisters and felt more alone than she'd ever felt before. Her entire family saw her only as an obligation and a threat to their happiness. *Surely there is some way to convince them that I don't care about the money. All I really want is a chance to fall in love and settle down with the right man.* Instantly Logan Reed's image filled her mind and Amelia had to smile. She would truly scandalize her family if she suggested marriage to Mr. Reed.

The conversation inside the cabin once again drew her attention when Penelope's whining voice seemed to raise an octave in despair. "I hate her! I truly do. She's forced us to live as barbarians and traipse about this horrid country, and for what? So that she can scorn Sir Jeffery, a man in good standing with the queen herself?"

Amelia felt the bite of her sister's words. She'd never considered her siblings to be close and dear friends, but now it was apparent that even a pretense of affection was out of the question. Hot tears came unbidden to her eyes and suddenly years of pent up emotion would no longer be denied.

"Oh, Mama," she whispered, wiping desperately at her cheeks, "why did you leave me without love?" Gathering up her skirt, Amelia waited to hear no more. She ran for the coverage of the pines and aspens. She ran for the solitude of the mountainous haven which she'd grown to love.

Blinded by her own tears, Amelia fought her way through the underbrush of the landscape. She felt the biting sting of the branches as they slapped at her arms and face, but the pain they delivered was mild compared to the emptiness within her heart. Panting for air, Amelia collapsed beside a fallen spruce. Surrendering to her pain, she buried her face in her hands and sobbed long and hard.

It isn't fair. It wasn't right that she should have to bear such a thing alone. Her mother had been the only person to truly care about her and now she was forever beyond her reach. A thought came to Amelia. *Perhaps a spiritualist could put her in touch with her mother's spirit.* Then just as quickly as the thought came, Amelia banished it. In spite of the fact that spiritualists were all the rage in Europe and America, she didn't believe in such things. *Life ended at the grave— didn't it?*

"I don't know what to believe in anymore," she muttered.

She was suddenly ashamed of herself and her life. She wasn't really a snob, as Logan had presumed her to be. Her upbringing had demanded certain things of her, however. She didn't have the same freedoms as women of lower classes. She wasn't allowed to frolic about and laugh in public. She wasn't allowed to speak her mind in mixed company, or to have her opinion considered with any real concern once it was spoken. Amelia found herself envying Mary and her simple, but hard life here in the Rocky Mountains. The men around Mary genuinely revered and cared for her. Her husband had no reason to fear when he took a party out hunting, because everyone looked out for Mary.

I wish I could be more like her, Amelia thought, tears pouring anew from her eyes. She'd not cried this much since her mother's passing. Mother was like Mary. Amelia could still see her mother working with her flowers in the garden wearing a large straw bonnet cocked to one side to shield her from the sun, and snug, mud-stained gloves kept her hands in ladylike fashion. Amelia traced the fingers of her own hands, realizing that she'd forgotten her gloves. *Oh, Mama, what am I to do?*

Looking up, Amelia was startled to find Logan sitting on a log not ten feet away. "What are you doing here?" she asked, dabbing at her eyes with the edge of her skirt.

"I saw you run up here and got worried that something was wrong. Generally, folks around here don't run like their house is on fire—unless it is." He gave her only a hint of a smile.

Amelia offered him no explanation. It was too humiliating even to remember her sister's words, much less bring them into being again by relating them to Logan.

Seeming to sense her distress, Logan leaned back and put his hands behind his head. He looked for all the world as though he'd simply come out for a quiet moment in the woods. "There's an old Ute

Indian saying that starts out, 'I go to the mountain where I take myself to heal, the earthly wounds that people give to me.' I guess you aren't the first person to come seeking solace, eh?"

"I'm not seeking anything," Amelia replied, feeling very vulnerable knowing that Logan had easily pegged her emotions.

"We're all seeking something, Amelia," Logan said without a hint of reprimand. "We're all looking to find things to put inside to fill up the empty places. Some people look for it in a place, others in things, some in people." His eyes pierced her soul and Amelia looked away as he continued. "Funny thing is, there's only so much you can fill up with earthly things. There's an empty place and a void inside that only God can fill and some folks never figure that out."

"You forget, Mr. Reed," she said in protected haughtiness, "I don't believe in the existence of God." The words sounded hollow even to Amelia.

Logan shrugged. "You're sitting in the middle of all this beauty and you still question the existence of God?"

"I've been among many wonders of the world, Mr. Reed. I've traveled the Alps, as well as your Rockies, and found them to be extraordinarily beautiful as well. What I did not find, was God. I find no proof of an almighty being in the wonders of the earth. They are simple, scientifically explained circumstances. They are nothing more than the visual representation of the geological forces at work in this universe. It certainly doesn't prove the existence of God." She paused to look at him quite seriously. "If it did, then I would have to counter with a question of my own."

"Such as?"

"Such as, if the beauty of the earth proclaims the existence of God, then why doesn't the savagery and horrors of the world do as much to denounce His existence? This God you are so fond of quoting and believing in must not amount to much if He stands idly by to watch the suffering of His supposed creation. I've seen the beauty of the world, Mr. Reed, but so too, have I seen many of its tragedies and injustices. I've been in places where mothers murder their children rather than watch them starve to death slowly. I've seen old people put to death because they are no longer useful to their culture. I've beheld squalor and waste just as surely as I've seen tranquility and loveliness, and none of it rises up to assure me of God's existence."

"Granted, there's a lot wrong in this world, but what about the forces of evil? Don't you think evil can work against good and interfere with God's perfect plan? When people stray from the truth, the devil has the perfect opportunity to step in and stir up all kinds of chaos."

"Then your God isn't very strong, is He?" She lifted her chin a little higher. "As I recall, the devil you believe exists is a fallen angel named Lucifer. Is not your God more powerful than a fallen angel? Don't you see, Mr. Reed, these are nothing more than stories designed to make mankind feel better about itself and the world. The poor man trudges through life believing that even though he has nothing on earth, he will have a celestial mansion when he dies. A rather convenient way of bolstering spirits and keeping one's nose to the grindstone, don't you think?"

Logan shook his head. "You're talking about something you obviously know very little about. An eternal home in heaven isn't all that the repentant sinner has to look forward to."

"No?" She looked away as though studying the trees around them. "I suppose you will tell me that he can pray and have his desires magically met by a benevolent God who wants His children to live in abundance and earthly wealth."

"Not at all. God isn't in charge of some heavenly mercantile where you step in and order up whatever your little heart wants. No, Amelia, I'm talking about living in truth. Knowing that you are following the path God would have you travel, and in knowing that, you will find the satisfaction of truth, faithfulness, peace, and love."

"Oh, please," Amelia said meeting his eyes. "This is all religious rhetoric and you know it. The fact of the matter is that truth is completely in the heart and mind of the person or persons involved. I see the truth as one thing and you obviously see it as another. Do not believe I'm any less satisfied for the things I believe in, because I assure you I am not." She bit her lip and looked away. She could hardly bear to meet his expression, knowing that deep inside, the things she believed in were not the least bit satisfying.

As if reading her mind, Logan sat up and said, "I feel sorry for you Amelia. You are afraid to consider the possibility that there is a God, because considering it might force you to reckon with yourself."

"I don't know what you mean." She got to her feet and brushed off the dirt and leaves that clung to her skirt.

Logan jumped to his feet. "That's it. It's really a matter of you being afraid."

Amelia bit at her lower lip again and looked at the ground. "I need to get back. They'll have missed me at breakfast."

Logan crossed the distance to stop her. Putting his hand out, he took hold of her arm and gently turned her back to face him. "God can fill that void inside, Amelia. He can wrap you in comfort and ease your burden. He can be all that human folks fail to be."

Amelia pushed him away. She was, for the first time in a long, long time, frightened. Not of Logan Reed, but of what he represented. "I have to go."

"In a minute," Logan said softly. "First tell me why you were crying."

Amelia shook her head. "It was nothing. Nothing of importance."

Logan reached out and before Amelia could move, he smoothed back a bit of hair from her face and stroked her cheek with his fingers. "It's important to me." His voice was barely a whisper.

Amelia stared up at him and found herself washed in the flood of compassion that seemed to emanate from his eyes. Her mouth went dry and her heart pounded so hard that she was sure Logan could hear it. She struggled with her emotions for a full minute before steadying her nerves to reply. "I don't want to be important to you."

Logan laughed. "Too late. You already are."

Amelia balled her hands into fists and struck them against her side. "Just leave me alone, Logan. I can't do this."

Logan looked at her in surprise. "Do what?"

Amelia opened her mouth as if to speak, then quickly shut it again. She had nearly said, "Love you." Now, standing here in the crisp freshness of morning, Amelia knew beyond doubt, that Logan understood exactly what she'd nearly said. "I can't do this," was all she could say.

Logan backed away. "I have an idea. Why don't you come on a hike with me tomorrow? Your family and friends will be on an overnight hunt, I heard Jonas telling Mary all about it after you left the kitchen. We could spend the whole day gathering your samples and I could spend all evening telling you what they are."

"I don't think—"

"Don't think," Logan said with such longing in his voice that Amelia couldn't ignore his plea.

"All right," she said quickly, hoping that if she agreed to his suggestion he'd leave her alone. There'd be plenty of time to back out of the invitation later. Later, when she was calmer and could think more clearly. Later when the warmth of Logan's green eyes didn't melt the icy wall she'd built between them.

Logan's mustache twitched as it always did before his lips broke into a full smile. "I'm holding you to it."

Amelia nodded and started back down the mountain. Two things deeply troubled her. One was Logan's words about God. The other was Logan, himself.

10

ogan had spent a restless day and night thinking of what his hike with Amelia might accomplish. He saw the desperation in her eyes. He knew she longed to understand what was missing in her life. But how could he lead her to the truth about God, when she didn't believe in the validity of God? Usually, whenever he witnessed to someone, Logan knew he could rely on the Scriptures to give them something solid that they could put their hands on—the written word of God. That seemed to be important to folks. With Amelia's disbelief in God and her position that the Bible was nothing more than the collective works of men from the past, Logan felt at a loss as to how he could proceed without it. His mother and other Christians he'd known had assured him that all he needed was a faith in God and in His word. And even now, Logan believed that was still true. But what he couldn't figure out was how to apply it all and show Amelia the way to God. Somehow, he felt, he must be failing as a Christian if this simple mission eluded him. *How can I defend my faith in God and show Amelia the truth, when it is that very truth that makes her run in the opposite direction?*

Logan took up his Bible and sat down to a self-prepared breakfast of smoked ham and scrambled eggs. He opened the book and bowed his head in prayer. "Father, there's a great deal of hurt inside Amelia Amhurst. I know You already see her and love her. I know You understand how to reach her. But I don't know how to help and I seek Your guidance and direction. I want to help her find her way home to You. Give me the right words and open her heart to Your Spirit's calling. In Jesus' name I pray, Amen."

Logan opened his eyes and found comfort in the Scripture before him. "The Spirit itself beareth witness with our spirit, that we are the children of God," he read aloud from the eighth chapter of Romans. A peace came over him and he smiled. God's Spirit would speak for him. It wasn't Logan Reed's inspirational words or evidence that would save Amelia, it was God's Holy Spirit. The Holy Spirit would also show her the validity of the Bible. He needn't compromise his beliefs and put the Bible aside. Neither did he need to go out of his way to defend God. God could fully take care of all the details.

He almost laughed out loud at the way he'd taken it all on his own shoulders. It was typical of him to rush in and try to arrange things on his own. But now, he didn't have to and God had made that quite clear. Amelia Amhurst was here for a reason. Not for her father's matrimonial desires or Chamberlain's financial benefits in joining with her. Amelia was here because God knew it was time for her to come to the truth. The Holy Spirit would bear witness to Amelia that not only was God real, but that she had a way to reconcile herself with Him. With a lighter heart, Logan dug into his breakfast and prepared for the day.

❧

Logan whistled a tune as he came into the lodge through the kitchen. He found Amelia bent over a sink-full of dishes and paused to consider her there. Her blond hair was braided in a simple fashion to hang down her back and the clothes she wore were more austere than usual. She no longer appeared the refined English rose, but rather looked to be the descendant of hearty pioneer stock.

"I see you dressed appropriately," he said from behind her.

Amelia whirled around with soapy hands raised as though Logan had threatened a robbery. In a rather breathless voice she addressed him. "I borrowed some clothes from Mary." Gone was any trace of her agitation with him the day before.

"Good thinking." Logan felt unable to tear his gaze away from her wide blue eyes.

"She gave me some sturdy boots, as well." Amelia's voice was a nervous whisper as soap suds dripped down her arms and puddled onto the wood floor.

"You gonna be much longer with those?" Logan asked, nodding toward the sink, but still refusing to release her gaze.

"No. I'm nearly finished."

"I can help," he offered.

"No. Why don't you have a cup of coffee instead? I can see to this."

Amelia was the one who finally turned away. Logan thought her cheeks looked particularly flushed, but he gave the cookstove and fireplace credit for this and took a cup. Pouring rich, black coffee, Logan nearly burned himself as his glances traveled back and forth between Amelia and the coffee.

"How'd the quilting lesson go yesterday?" he asked.

"My stitches were as big as horses," Amelia admitted, "but Mary told me not to worry about it. She said it was better to work at consistency and spacing."

"Mary should know. She does beautiful work."

"Yes, she does." Amelia finished with her task and dried her hands on her apron. "I don't suppose I'll ever do such nice work."

"You don't give yourself enough credit. Look how quick you took to making doughnuts. When you reach Mary's age you'll be every bit as good at making quilts as she is."

"I seriously doubt that," she replied and Logan thought she sounded rather sad. "You see, once we return to England, I know it will hardly be acceptable for me to sit about making quilts and frying doughnuts."

"Maybe you shouldn't go back."

The words fell between them as if a boulder had dropped into the room. Sensing Amelia's inability to speak on the matter, Logan changed the subject. "Well, I have a knapsack full of food, so if you're ready—"

Amelia nodded and untied her apron. "Let me get my coat." She hurried over to a nearby chair and pulled on a serviceable broadcloth coat. The jacket was several sizes too big, obviously another loan from Mary, but Logan thought she looked just right.

Smiling he nodded. "You look perfect."

"Hardly that, Mr. Reed, but I am . . . well—" she glanced down at her mismatched attire and raised her face with a grin, "I am prepared."

He laughed. "Well, out here that suggests perfection. A person ought to always be prepared. You never know when a storm will blow up or an early snow will keep you held up in your house. Preparation is everything."

❧

The sun was high overhead before Logan suggested they break for lunch. Amelia was secretly relieved and plopped down on the ground in a most unladylike manner. The scenery around her was hard to ignore. The rocky granite walls were imposing and gave her a powerful reminder of how little she knew of taking care of herself. *What if something happened to Logan? How would I ever return to Estes without his assistance?*

"You up to one more thing before I break out the chow?"

Amelia looked up and hoped that the weariness she felt was hidden from her expression. "I suppose so." She made a motion to get up, but before she could move Logan reached down and lifted her easily.

"You look pretty robust," he said, dropping his hold, "but you weigh next to nothing. I've had dogs that weighed more than you."

Amelia thought it was a strange sort of observation, but then remembered back in Greeley when her beauty had been compared to a polished spittoon. "And I've had horses more mannerly than you," she finally replied, "but I don't hold that against you and I pray you won't hold my weight against me."

"You pray?" he said, acting surprised.

"It's a mere expression, I assure you. Now please show me what you had in mind and then feed me before I perish."

Logan took hold of her hand and pulled her along as though they traveled in this manner all of the time. He walked only a matter of ten or twelve steps, however, before drawing Amelia up to a frightening precipice.

"Oh, my!" she gasped gazing over the edge of the sheer drop. She clung to Logan's hand without giving thought to what he might think. "How beautiful," she finally added, gazing out beyond the chasm. A tiny ledge of rock stuck out some six or seven feet below them, but after that there was nothing but the seemingly endless open spaces below. Beyond them, the Rocky Mountain panorama stretched out and Amelia actually felt a lump form in her throat. There were no words for what she was feeling. Such a rush of emotions simply had no words. It was almost as if this country beckoned to her inner soul. She felt something here that she'd never known anywhere else. Not in the Alps with all of their grandeur. Not amongst the spicy, exotic streets of Egypt. Not even on her father's estate in England.

Her eyes scanned the scene and her mind raced with one pounding sensation. When her eyes settled on Logan's face, that sensation was realized in a single word. *Home. I feel,* she thought, *as though I've come home.*

For a moment she thought Logan might kiss her, and for as long a moment, she wished he would. She longed for his embrace. The warmth of his hand on hers drew her further away from thoughts of her family and England. *Is this true love? Are this man and this place to forever be a part of my destiny? Yet how could it be? How could I even imagine it possible?* She was a refined English lady—the daughter of an earl. She had been presented to Queen Victoria and had even made the acquaintances of the princesses.

Logan's voice interrupted the awe-inspired moment. "Come on, let's eat."

He pulled her back to the place where she'd rested earlier, and without ceremony, plopped himself down on the ground and began wrestling with the knapsack. Amelia was very nearly devastated. *Didn't he feel it too? Didn't he feel the compelling, overwhelming attraction to her that she felt to him?*

Chiding herself for such unthinkable emotions, Amelia sat down and took the canteen Logan offered her. She drank slowly, the icy liquid quenching her thirst, but not her desire to know more. *But what is it that I want to know?* She refused to be absorbed with questions of immortality and religious nonsense, and yet there were so many questions already coming to mind.

Logan slapped a piece of ham between two thick slices of Mary's bread and handed the sandwich over to Amelia. "It's not fancy, but I promise you it will taste like the finest banquet food you've ever had."

Amelia nodded and nibbled on the edge of the crust. She was famished and yet, when Logan bowed his head in prayer, she paused in respectful silence, not really knowing why. When he finished, he pulled out a napkin and revealed two pieces of applesauce cake.

"Mary had these left over from last night and I thought they'd make a great dessert."

"Indeed they would," Amelia agreed and continued eating the sandwich.

In between bites of his own food, Logan began sharing a story about the area. "This is called Crying Rock," he explained.

"Why Crying Rock?" Amelia asked, looking around her to see if some rock formation looked like eyes with water flowing from it.

"Legend holds that an Indian warrior fell to his death from that very spot where we stood just minutes ago. He had come to settle a dispute with another warrior and in the course of the fight, he lost his life."

"How tragic. What were they fighting about?" Amelia asked, genuinely interested.

"A young woman," he said with a grin. "What else?"

Amelia jutted out her chin feeling rather defensive. "How foolish of them both."

"Not at all. You see the warrior was in love with a woman who was already pledged to marry the other man. It was arranged by her father, but her heart wasn't in it. She was in love with the other warrior."

Amelia felt the intensity of his stare and knew that he understood her plight in full. She felt more vulnerable in that moment than she'd ever felt in her life. It was almost as if her entire heart was laid bare before Logan Reed. She wished she could rise up with dignity and walk back to the lodge, but she hadn't the remotest idea how she could accomplish such a feat. Instead, she finished her sandwich and drank from the canteen before saying, "Obviously, she lost out in this situation and had to marry the man she didn't love."

Logan shook his head. "Not exactly. After the death of her true love, she was to marry the victor in five days and so she brought herself up here and sat down to a period of mourning. As legend tells it, she cried for four straight days. The people could hear her, clear down in the village below and folks around here say at night when the wind blows it can still sound just like a woman crying."

"What happened after that?" Amelia asked, almost against her will.

"On the fifth day she stopped crying. She washed, dressed in her wedding clothes and offered up a final prayer in honor of her lost warrior," Logan paused and it seemed to Amelia that he'd just as soon not continue with the story.

"And?" she pressed.

"And, she threw herself off the rock and took her own life."

"Oh." It was all Amelia could say. She let her gaze go to the edge of the rock and thought of the devastated young woman who died. She could understand the woman's misery. Facing a life with Jeffery Chamberlain was akin to a type of death in and of itself. And then, for the first time, the realization that she would most likely be forced to marry Jeffery, truly sunk in. The tightness in her chest made her feel suddenly hemmed in. Her father would never allow her to walk out of this arrangement. There was no way he would care for her concerns or her desires to marry for love. The matter was already settled and it would hardly be affected by Amelia's stubborn refusal.

"You okay?" Logan asked softly.

She looked back to him and realized that he'd been watching her the whole time. "I'm, well—" she fell silent and tried to reorganize her thoughts. "The story was fascinating and I was just thinking that perhaps a book on Indian lore would be more beneficial than one on wild flowers."

Logan seemed to consider this a moment. "Why not combine them. You could have your flowers and identification information and weave in stories of the area. After all, the summer is coming quickly to an end and you've already done a great deal of work on the area vegetation."

"Would you teach me more about the lore from this area?" she asked, swallowing down the depression that threatened to engulf her.

"Sure," he said, so nonchalant that Amelia knew he didn't understand her dilemma.

No one understands, she thought as a heavy sigh escaped her lips. *No one would ever understand.*

11

week and a half later, Amelia watched as Mary finished packing a saddlebag with food. "Mary, are you sure that you and Jonas want to do this?" she questioned quite seriously. "I mean, Long's Peak looks to be a very serious climb."

"Oh, it's serious enough," she said with a smile. "I've made it four times before, I figure number five ain't gonna kill me."

"You've climbed up Long's Peak four times?" Amelia questioned in disbelief.

Logan laughed at her doubtful expression. "Mary's a great old gal and she can outdo the lot of us, I'm telling you."

Mary beamed him a smile. "He only says that 'cause he knows I'll cook for him on the trail."

Amelia was amazed. Long's Peak stood some 14,700 feet high and butted itself in grand majesty against one end of Estes Park. It was once heralded as one of the noblest of the Rocky Mountains and Lady Bird had highly recommended taking the opportunity to ascend it, if time and health permitted one to do so. Amelia was still amazed that her father had taken to the idea without so much as a single objection. He and Sir Jeffery had found a guide to take them hunting outside the village area. They would be gone for over a week and during that time he was quite unconcerned with how his daughters and manservant entertained themselves. After all, he mused, they were quite well-chaperoned, everyone in the village clearly knowing what everyone else was about, and the isolation did not afford for undue notice of their activities by the outside world. Logan had immediately approached him on the subject of Amelia ascending Long's Peak, with a formal invitation to include her sisters and the Gambett family. Lady

Gambett looked as though just thinking of such a thing made her faint and the girls were clearly uninterested in anything so barbaric. After a brief series of questions, in which Mary assured the earl that she would look after Amelia as if she were her own, Lord Amhurst gave his consent and went off to clean his rifle. And that was that. The matter was settled almost before Amelia had known the question had been posed.

"You've got enough grub here to last three weeks," Jonas chided his wife.

"Sure, sure," his Mary answered with a knowing nod, "and you and Logan can eat three weeks worth of food in a matter of days. I intend that Amelia not starve." They all laughed at this and within the hour they were mounting their horses and heading out.

"Some folks call it 'the American Matterhorn'," Logan told Amelia.

"I've seen the Matterhorn and this is more magnificent," she replied, rather lost in thought.

The valley was a riot of colors and sights. The rich green of the grass contrasted with wildflowers too numerous to count. But thanks to Logan, Amelia could identify almost every one of them and smiled proudly at this inner knowledge. She would have quite a collection to show off when she returned to England. For reasons beyond her understanding, the thought of leaving for England didn't seem quite as appealing as it always had before. She pushed aside this thought and concentrated instead on the grandeur of a blue mountain lake that seemed to be nestled in a bed of green pine.

The Lewises' dogs, a collie mix and a mutt of unknown parentage, ran circles around the party, barking at everything that crossed their path, often giving chase when the subject in question looked too small to retaliate. Amelia laughed at the way they seemed to never tire of chasing the mountain ground squirrels or nipping after the heels of the mule-eared deer.

As the sun seemed to fall from the sky in an afterglow of evening colors, Amelia felt a sadness that she couldn't explain. The emptiness within her was almost more than she could bear. She thought of her mother and wondered if she were watching from some celestial home somewhere, then shook off the thought and chided herself for such imaginings. No doubt they'd been placed there by the irritating con-versations of one Logan Reed. His beliefs seemed to saturate every-thing he said and did, and Amelia was quite disturbed by the way he lived this faith of his.

"We'd best make camp for the night," Logan called and pointed. "Over there looks to be our best choice."

Later, Amelia could see why he was so highly regarded as a com-petent guide. The area he'd chosen was well-sheltered from the canyon winds and had an ample supply of water. Added to this were feathery pine boughs, so surprisingly soft that when Amelia lay down atop her blanketed pine mattress, she sighed in unexpected delight. Staring up at the starry sky, Amelia uncomfortably remembered Bible verses from the thirty-eighth chapter of Job. Her mother had been particularly fond of these and had often quoted them when Amelia had questioned the 'how's' and 'why's' of God's workings.

"Where wast thou when I laid the foundations of the earth? declare, if thou hast understanding. Who hath laid the measures thereof, if thou knowest? or who hath stretched the line upon it? Whereupon are the foun-dations thereof fastened? or who laid the corner stone thereof; When the morning stars sang together, and all the sons of God shouted for joy?"

Her mother's explanation had always been that Amelia had no right to question God, and Amelia remembered countering that if God's position wasn't secure enough to be put to the test, then He wasn't as omnipotent and omniscient as people said. Suddenly, she felt very sorry for those words. Not because she believed in God's ex-istence, but for the sorrow she remembered seeing in her mother's eyes. Sitting up, she hugged her knees to her chest and watched the flames of their campfire for awhile.

You wouldn't be very pleased with me now, Mother, she thought. The flames danced and licked at the cold night air and when a log popped and shifted, Amelia jumped from the suddenness of it.

"I'm surprised you're still awake," Logan said, from where he lay watching her.

Amelia felt suddenly very self-conscious and shrugged her shoul-ders. "Just thinking."

Logan leaned up on his elbow. "Care to share it?"

Amelia smiled and the reassuring sounds of Mary and Jonas' snoring made her relax a bit. "I was thinking about my mother."

"I bet you miss her a lot," Logan offered.

"Yes, I do. It seems like she's been gone forever and it's only been six years. She was sick quite awhile before she died." Then as if Logan had vocalized the question, Amelia added, "Consumption."

"And she was a Christian?"

Amelia rocked back and forth a bit and looked up to the heavens. "Yes."

"So how is it that you came to believe there was no God?"

"He never listened when I prayed," she replied flatly.

"How do you know?"

"Because my mother died."

Logan said nothing for several moments, then sat up and added a few more pieces of wood to the fire. "Did your mother ever deny you something that you wanted?"

"Of course," Amelia said, not understanding his meaning.

"So why wouldn't God be inclined to do the same?"

Logan's eyes were intense and his expression so captivating that for a moment Amelia forgot to be offended. Instead she simply asked, "To what purpose? I was fourteen years old, my youngest sister was barely ten. To what purpose does a merciful God remove mothers from children?"

"Good question. Wish I had the answer."

Amelia felt instant disappointment. She'd fully expected one of those quaint Christian answers like, "God needed another angel for heaven." Or, "God had need of your mother elsewhere." Amelia knew better. Especially since she left three grieving children and a devastated husband.

"You seem taken aback," Logan said softly. "Did you expect me to tell you the mind of God?"

Amelia couldn't help but nod. "Most other Christians would have. They have their wonderful little answers and reasons for everything, and none of it ever makes sense. To me, if there were a God, He would be more logical than that. There would be a definite order and reason to things and of course, a purpose."

"And you think that's missing in our world?" Logan questioned seeming genuinely intrigued by the turn the conversation had taken.

But Amelia felt weary of it all. She was tired of seeking answers when she wasn't even sure what the questions were. She couldn't make sense of her life or of her mother's death, therefore, to cast her frustration aside seemed the only way to keep from going insane.

"I think," she said very softly, "that the world has exactly the order we give it. No more. No less. If people are out of control, then so too, the world."

"I agree."

"You do?"

Logan smiled. "Surprised?" Amelia nodded and he continued. "God gave mankind free will to choose Him or reject Him. A great many folks refuse Him and chaos and misery ensue. They seek their own way and call it wisdom when they settle in their minds how the universe has come together."

"But is your Christianity any different? Didn't you decide in your own way how the universe has come together?"

"No," Logan replied. "I decided to accept that God's way was the only way and that put the rest of my questions at rest."

"But don't you ever worry that you might be wrong?" Amelia asked, knowing that she was very concerned with her own version of the truth. Perhaps that was why she felt herself in a constant state of longing. There was an emptiness inside her that refused to be filled up by the reasonings and logic of her own mind, yet she didn't know what to put in its place.

Logan stretched back on his pallet. "I guess if I'd come to God as an adult, I might have wondered if the Bible was true and if God was really God. But I became a Christian when I was still very young and it was easy to believe what my parents told me about the Bible and faith. I can see where it would be a whole heap harder for you. You have a lifetime of pride and obstacles to overcome. Accepting that the Bible is true would mean that your life would change, and some folks aren't willing to risk what that change might entail."

He fell silent and before long, Amelia noticed that his breathing had grown deep and even. Lying back down on her own pine bed,

Amelia felt more lonely and isolated than she'd ever been in her life. *What if Logan was right?* her mind questioned. She quickly pushed the thought away. But as she drifted to sleep it came back in a haunting reminder that followed her even into her dreams.

~&

The next day, Amelia awoke before it was fully light. The night had turned cold and Amelia's teeth chattered as she dragged her blankets around her shoulders and went to throw more wood on the fire like she'd seen Logan do. The dying coals quickly ignited the dry wood and soon a cheery blaze was crackling once again. It was this and not any sound made by Amelia which caused the rest of the camp to stir.

Logan was first to sit up, rubbing his eyes and yawning. Mary and Jonas murmured good mornings to each other before Mary took herself off for a bit of privacy. Jonas didn't seem inclined to talk and Logan was already pulling out things for breakfast.

While they were all occupied, Amelia took herself off a ways in order to study the sunrise in private. At first the blackness gave way to midnight blue and then as the slightest hint of lemon coloring suggested light, it gave way to a turquoise and brightened as the sun stretched over the snowcapped peaks. *How beautiful!* She marveled at the glory of it all.

They quickly breakfasted and were on their way by seven, the sunrise permanently fixed in Amelia's mind. They made good time, passing an area Logan called "The Lava Beds." It was here that huge boulders mingled with small ones to create a strangely desolate stage. They were nearing the place where Logan had said they would have to picket the horses and climb, when dark clouds moved in and rain appeared imminent.

Logan immediately went to work to find them even the smallest shelter to wait out the storm. He finally found a suitable place where they would be snug under the protective ledge of a particularly wide rock shelf. Jonas and Logan picketed the horses, while Amelia and Mary carried their things to the rock. The heavens opened up, as if cued by their having found shelter, and poured down a rain of tremendous proportion. Lightning flashed around them just as Jonas and Logan came to join the women.

C-R-A-C-K! Thunder roared, causing Amelia to nearly jump out of her skin. It seemed as if they sat atop the world and the fullest impact of the storm was to be spent on them alone.

Logan grinned, and eased a little closer to Amelia. Another flash of lightning caused Amelia to put her hands to her ears and press herself tighter to the wall. She felt terribly embarrassed by her childish display, noting that Mary and Jonas had their heads together talking as though nothing at all was amiss. She rallied herself in spirit and was determined to display more courage when a blinding strike of lightning hit directly in front of them with its deafening boom of thunder.

Amelia shrieked and threw herself at Logan in such a way that she feared she'd knocked the wind from him. Hearing him groan, she pulled back quickly, but found his arm around her.

"Stay, if it makes you feel better. I promise, Mary and Jonas aren't going to care."

Amelia smiled weakly at Mary. "I've never been in a storm like this," she said, barely able to form audible words.

"Logan knows how they go," Mary replied, which seemed to offer Amelia approval for her actions.

Turning to Logan, Amelia temporarily forgot the storm around her and concentrated instead on the one in his eyes. Her heart pounded harder, while her breath felt as though it were caught around the lump in her throat. Licking her dry lips, she eased away and hugged her arms around her. *Better to find strength and comfort from within than to lose another portion of myself to this rugged mountain man.*

After a time the storm passed, but Logan judged by the skies that another would soon follow and the climb to the top of Long's Peak was postponed. As they descended back down the mountain, hoping to reach the heavy cover of pines before the next storm was upon them, Logan tried to treat the matter light-heartedly.

"We'll just try again later on," he said confidently. "Sooner or later, we're bound to get you to the top."

Amelia tried not to be disappointed. In truth, by this time her emotions were so topsy-turvy that she wasn't at all certain whether she cared if the trip were canceled or not. She rode sedately, saying very little except when addressed with a direct question. There was a great deal this trip had brought to mind and there was still the rest of the summer to think it through.

12

From that day, the summer passed much more quickly than Amelia had expected. Not a moment went by when she wasn't painfully aware that soon the snows would threaten to close off access to the plains. Soon she would be headed back to England and her marriage to Sir Jeffery. She tried to push down her fear, but it rose up like a phoenix from the ashes of her heart, threatening to slay her in mind and soul.

Her joy came in spending her days with Logan. With her father and Jeffery absorbed in their hunting and her sisters busy with the Gambett girls, Amelia found herself free to work with Mary each morning and then with Logan. She had copied down nearly every specimen of vegetation in the area, and Logan had taught her how to identify animal tracks and to mark her position from the village using the elements around her. She thought it almost her imagination, but swore her hearing had become better as she could make out sounds in the forested mountains that she'd never heard before. One day, when their water ran out, Logan had taught her how to listen for the sounds of water. Once she learned what it was that she was trying to hear, Amelia was amazed. The sounds had always been there, but she was just unaware of them. Before, the sounds in the air had come to her as a collective noise, but now she could separate the trickling of a mountain stream from the rustling of aspen leaves.

She had learned to depend more upon her other senses as well. Her sight and sense of smell were two things Logan said were absolutely necessary for staying alive. As they traipsed through the woods together he would often stop her and ask what certain smells were, and Amelia was quite proud to find that she was rapidly learning to identify each of these as well. Without realizing it, Amelia had spent the summer learning how to survive in the Rockies.

The bittersweetness of her circumstance, however, caught up with her one afternoon when her father sought her out.

"Amelia, we need to talk."

She looked up from where she was jotting down notes on a strange little bird which she had mistaken for a woodpecker.

"Just a moment Father," she said, finishing her notes. "I've identified that pesky noise we've lived with these months. You know that pecking sound that comes at all hours of the day and night?" She didn't wait for him to reply. "It seems that this bird is a chipping sparrow and it chips away all the time. It actually feeds its young even into adulthood when they are fully capable of feeding themselves. Isn't that fascinating?" This time she put the pen down and looked up to find her father's serious expression.

"Quite," was all he would reply on the matter before taking a seat across from her. "Amelia, you have sorely neglected the one duty I gave you—which was to allow Sir Jeffery to pay you court. I say, I've never seen a more stubborn woman in all my life, unless of course it was your mother."

Amelia smiled. "A high compliment if ever there was one."

The earl shook his head. "I'm afraid it wasn't intended as one. See here, I know how you feel about being forced to marry, but the truth is I can't have the family coffers being depleted because of your foolishness. Why any reasonable solicitor would allow your grandmother to set out a trust to unmarried daughters is beyond me. Why it positively reeks of inappropriateness."

"It was Grandmama's money, after all, and she was only worried that her family might find themselves in situations of desperation and heartache. Grandmama had found it necessary to marry a man she didn't love, and all for financial reasons. She didn't want the same fate to befall her daughter or her granddaughters, yet now you propose to do just such a thing in order to keep the money for yourself." Amelia knew the anger in her heart was rapidly flooding over into her tone of voice.

"You have no right to speak to me thusly," the earl said rather stiffly. "I have to do what I feel is right for the benefit of the entire family, not just one member."

Amelia shook her head. "No, Father, I believe you are considering only one member—yourself." She slammed her book shut, mindless of smearing the still damp ink. "I've tried to be orderly about this and I've tried not to bring you undue pain, but I must speak honestly here." She swallowed hard and thought of the conversation she'd overheard her father having with Jeffery the night before. Logan would chide her for eavesdropping, but this time it served to clarify the mystery behind her father's desperation to marry her to Jeffery.

"I know about your gambling debts," she began, "and the fact that you owe Sir Jeffery a great deal of money." The earl's eyes widened in surprise. "I'm not the simpleton you would give me credit for being. It wasn't hard to learn about this, nor was it difficult to learn that you had promised Jeffery land in Scotland, land I might add which has been in our family for generations and which must pass through the succession of marriage or death, rather than be sold.

"Furthermore, I know that Jeffery covets the land for his own purposes, some known to me and others I'm sure are unknown, but nevertheless he wants that land. So now we come to the inheritance my grandmother set in place, Pan inheritance which passed to my mother and made the prospects of marrying beneath our status not quite so distasteful."

The earl pounded his fists on the table. "Enough! You know very well that I loved your mother and she loved me. Ours was not a marriage for fortune and status and you know well how the name of Amhurst suffered for just such impropriety."

Amelia took a deep breath and sighed. "Yes, but I must ask if it wasn't worth it?"

Lord Amhurst said nothing for a moment. His expression fell and he too sighed. "I could lie and say that if given the choice to do it all over again, I would marry another woman. But the truth is, I loved your mother very much and I would not trade our time together."

"So why are you trying to force such a thing upon me? If I were to inherit my share of the trust, do you believe I would leave you to suffer? How heartless you must think me."

"Nay, I never thought you heartless, but your share of the trust would never pay back what I owe Chamberlain. I'm sorry, Amelia." His resolve seemed to return. "You will have to marry Sir Jeffery."

Amelia felt as though a noose were being slipped around her neck. She rose with as much dignity as she could muster. "Your foolishness, not mine, has caused this situation. I find it completely unreasonable that I should be the one to pay for your mistakes. Let Jeffery marry one of my sisters. They both seem quite head-over-heels in love with the man."

Her father shook his head. "He wants the land which is to pass to you, Amelia. It is the Scottish estate which passes to the eldest that appeals to him."

"So I am to be sold off for the price of land and the sum of gambling debts?"

"Call it what you will," her father replied in a voice that suggested deep regret, "but avail yourself to Sir Jeffery in a proper courting manner and settle your mind on the fact that this marriage will take place."

~&~

Later that week while dressing quietly for dinner, Amelia felt a desperation building inside that couldn't be cast away with the assurance that she'd somehow work things around to her way. Jeffery had lost little time in picking up his pursuit of Amelia and as his attentions became bolder, Amelia was forced to sequester herself in her cabin for fear of what he might do next.

Penelope and Margaret were already talking of returning home and of all the things they would do. Amelia tried to remember her own earlier desires to return to England, but they'd passed from existence and now she wanted instead to remain in Estes. It was almost humorous to her that in the three months they'd spent in America, and Estes in particular, her views about the barbaric ways of the Americans had changed. She had come to look at Mary as a mother image and she cherished the time spent under her tutelage. She'd learned to cook and bake, as well as sew practical garments and quilt. Mary had also shown her how to properly clean house and wash clothes. And when time permitted, Amelia had even taken lessons in tending the vegetable garden and livestock.

As she pulled on her gloves for dinner she looked at her hands and realized how worn and rough they'd become. Back in England her friend Sarah would be appalled at the sight of calluses upon a lady's fingers, but Amelia wore them as badges of honor. She'd earned those calluses by working at Mary's side and she was proud of what she'd accomplished.

"Oh do hurry, Amelia," Penelope whined. "We'll never be able to sit down to dinner if you don't finish getting ready."

"I for one, refuse to wait," Margaret said, grabbing her shawl. "Come along, sister. Amelia will bring herself when she's ready. Maybe we can corner Sir Jeffery and he'll tell us more tales of his adventures in China."

"Oh yes," Penelope said, nodding her head. "That would be grand."

They left Amelia in a rush of chatter and anticipation of the night to come. She stared after them through the open door and shook her head. If only she could feel such enthusiasm for Sir Jeffery, none of this might have ever happened. The afterglow of sunset left a haunting amber color to the sky over the mountains. The chill of autumn was approaching and with it came a longing that Amelia could not explain. If only they had never come to America she would never have laid eyes on the Rocky Mountains and never have met Logan Reed.

Logan.

Her heart ached from the very thought of his name. She was hopelessly in love with him, and yet, there was nothing to be done about it. Logan was as poor as a church mouse and he could never offer to pay off her father's debts the way Jeffery could. Her father owed Jeffery over seventy-thousand pounds and even with her trust, the debt would barely be half paid. It was rapidly becoming a hopeless state of circumstances.

"Well, well," Jeffery announced from the door. "I looked about for you and found you missing."

"With good reason," Amelia said rather angrily. "I wasn't yet ready to present myself at dinner."

Jeffery leered. "I could help you . . . dress."

"As you can see, I'm quite dressed and I suggest you keep your disgusting thoughts to yourself."

She moved across the room to retrieve her shawl and heard Jeffery close the cabin door. Turning around, she found that he'd already crossed the room. He took hold of her roughly and crushed her against him in a fierce embrace.

"Stop it, Jeffery!" she declared and pushed at his chest.

Jeffery only laughed and held her fast. "You mustn't put me off. We're to be man and wife after all. A kiss of passion shared between two lovers is quite acceptable."

"But you forget. I do not love you," Amelia answered, kicking Jeffery's shin as hard as she could.

He immediately released her and Amelia scurried from the room, panting for breath and close to tears. Jeffery had so frightened her with his actions that she was quite uncertain as to what she should do next. Fleeing into the darkness behind the lodge, Amelia waited until her breathing had calmed and her heart stopped racing. *What should I do? What can I do?* Her father had made it quite clear and there was no other answer. She waited several more minutes, knowing that she was keeping everyone from their meal, then with a sigh she went to face them all. Walking slowly, as if to her own execution, Amelia entered the lodge and the dining hall without the slightest desire to be among people.

"Ah, there she is now," Lord Amhurst announced. "Amelia, dear, come and join us in a toast."

Amelia looked up and found the entire party staring at her. Everyone seemed quite joyous and Jeffery stood with an expression of sheer pride on his face. They weren't apparently unhappy with her for the delay of their dinner and instead seemed extremely animated.

"What, might I ask, are we drinking a toast to?" she asked, hesitantly.

The earl beamed a smile upon her. "Sir Jeffery has told us that this night you have accepted his hand in marriage." Her father raised his drink. "We are drinking to you and Sir Jeffery and a long, happy marriage."

Amelia felt the wind nearly knocked from her. She looked from her father to Jeffery and found a sneering grin on his face. His expression seemed to say, "I told you I would have my way."

"Well, do come join us," her father said, rather anxiously. "We've waited all summer for this."

Amelia found it impossible to speak. A lump formed in her throat and tears were threatening to spill from her eyes. Without concern for appearances, she turned and ran from the lodge.

Fleeing down the stairs and into the night, Amelia barely stifled a scream as she ran full-speed into Logan Reed's arms. She couldn't see his face, but heard his chuckle and felt a sense of comfort in just knowing he was near.

"I'm so sorry," she said, trying to disentangle her arms from his.

"I'm not. Want to tell me what you were running from?" Amelia felt the tears trickle down her cheeks and a sob escaped her throat. Logan's voice grew more concerned. "What is it Amelia? What has happened?"

"Nothing," she said, unable to keep from crying.

He took hold of her upper arms. "You're crying, so something must be wrong."

"Just leave me alone."

His voice was low and husky. "Amelia, I care about your pain and so does God. He can help you through this, even if I can't."

She jerked away, angry at the suggestion. "If God cares so much about pain, then why does He let His children suffer? I'm going to my cabin," she declared and walked away.

Logan was quickly at her side and it wasn't until she'd opened the door to her still lighted cabin that she could see that he was smiling.

"What? Are you going to laugh at me now?"

"Not at all. It's just that I thought you didn't believe in God."

"I don't."

"Then why did you say what you did about God letting His children suffer."

"Because you are always throwing your religion and God in my face!" she declared. "You always fall back on that and always use that to settle every issue that has ever arisen between us."

"Because He is my foundation and my mainstay. God cares about your pain, but haven't you brought it on yourself? Don't you hold any responsibility for your own actions?"

"Oh, go away, Logan," she moaned in sheer misery. *Why did he have to say those things?*

With a shrug of his shoulders, Logan surprised her by turning to leave. "I'm gonna pray for you Amelia. I know you're having a rough time of coming to terms with God, but just remember, He already knows what's in your heart and He knows the future He holds for you."

With that, he was gone and Amelia closed the door to cry in earnest. *Why is this happening to me and what in the world am I to do about any of it?* Giving up on the world and conscious thought, Amelia stripped off her dinner clothes and pulled on a nightgown. Then, mindless of her sisters, she blew out the lamp and threw herself into bed to have a good long cry.

13

$\mathcal{W}$ell, if you ask me," Penelope began, "I think it positively scandalous the way you put Sir Jeffery off."

"No one asked you," Amelia said flatly. She busied herself with quilting and tried to ignore her sisters and the Gambett girls.

"Mother says it is outrageous for you to suppose you will get a better match than Sir Jeffery," Josephine Gambett said, pushing up her glasses. They immediately slid back down her nose.

"Yes, Mother believes you are seriously jeopardizing your family's position with the Queen. After all, Sir Chamberlain's mother is a dear friend of Her Majesty," Henrietta added, not to be outdone by her sister.

Amelia felt her cheeks burn from the comeuppance of these younger girls. She thought of a hundred retorts, but bit her tongue and continued stitching.

"I think it's pure selfishness on your part," Margaret said with a little stomp of her foot. "There are other people to consider in this situation."

Amelia finally set aside her quilting and looked hard at each of the girls. "If you'll excuse me, I believe I would prefer the company of adults." With that she got up and without any conscious plan to do so, made her way to the cabin her father shared with Mattersley. She knew he would be there cleaning his guns and in her mind she formed one last plan to plead her case.

"Father?" she said, knocking lightly upon the open door.

Mattersley shuffled across the room. His face looked pinched and his eyes were sunken. "Come in, Lady Amhurst. The earl is just now occupied with the weapons."

Amelia smiled at him. Even here in the wilds of America, Mattersley held to the strict code of English propriety. "Thank you, Mattersley." She started to walk past him then stopped and asked, "How are you feeling? You look a bit tired."

Mattersley seemed stunned by her concern. "I am well, Miss."

"You should have some time off to yourself," she said, glancing to where her father sat. "Father, don't you agree?"

"Say what?" the earl questioned, looking up.

"I believe Mattersley is working too hard and some time off would serve him well."

"Oh, well yes," her father said, genuinely seeming to consider this. "A capital idea! Mattersley, you go right ahead and take the rest of the day—"

"No," Amelia interrupted, "a day will certainly not afford him much of a rest. I suggest the rest of the week. He can stay up in the lodge. I know Mary has extra room."

"Oh." Her father seemed quite taken aback.

"There is no need for that, Sir," Mattersley said in a voice that betrayed his weariness.

"My daughter is quite right," Lord Amhurst answered, seeming to see the old man for the first time. "You've been out on nearly every hunt with us and working to keep my things in order. I can surely dress myself properly enough for the rest of the week, what?"

"Very good, Sir," Mattersley replied and Amelia thought it almost sounded like a sigh of relief.

"Well, now that this matter has been resolved," she began and took the chair beside her father, "I thought we might address another."

"Do tell?" the earl replied and continued with cleaning his shotgun.

"Father, I have come to plead with you one final time to release me from this preposterous suggestion that I marry Sir Jeffery." The earl said nothing and so Amelia continued. "I cannot marry a man I do not respect, and I hold not the slightest respect for Sir Jeffery. I also cannot bring myself to consider marrying a man I do not love."

"Such modern notions do you a grave injustice, my dear," her father replied. "My mind is set and this is my final word. You will marry Chamberlain. In fact, I've arranged for us to depart Estes in three weeks. We will travel by stage from Greeley to Denver and there you will be married."

"What! How can you suggest such a thing? Why that won't even allow for a proper wedding, much less a proper English wedding," Amelia protested.

"It is of little concern. Sir Jeffery and I discussed the matter and we both believe it to be to the benefit of both parties."

"What parties? You and Jeffery? Because, I assure you it will never be to my benefit." She got to her feet, trembling from her father's declaration. "I cannot understand how my own father would sell me into such an abominable circumstance."

"And I cannot imagine that I raised a daughter to be so defiant and disobedient," the earl replied, looking at her with a stern expression of dismay. "Your mother would not be pleased in the way you've turned out. Even she would find your temperament to be unwarranted."

"Mother would understand," Amelia said softly, the anger being quickly replaced by the realization that her father could care less about her feelings. "And once, when you and she were still together, you would have understood too."

She left the cabin and felt as though a damp, cold blanket had been thrust upon her shoulders. The weight of her father's sudden declaration was more than she'd even imagined him capable of turning out. Immediately her mind sought for some manner of refuge. *There has to be something I can do.*

She walked a ways up the mountain side and paused beside a formation of boulders and rock. Hiking up her skirt, she climbed to the top by inching her way along the crevices and hand-holds. Once she'd managed to achieve her goal, she sat down in complete dejection and surveyed the village below.

Three weeks was a very short time.

She sighed and thought of leaving Estes and knew that it was tearing at her in a way that she'd never prepared herself for. She would have to leave the clean, crisp mountain air and the beauty that she'd never grow tired of looking upon. *And for what? To return to the cold, damp English winters? To be the wife of that unbearably cruel bore?*

She felt a tear trickle down her cheek and rubbed it away with the back of her sleeve. She almost laughed at herself for the crude gesture. *In so many ways I've become one of them. How can I go back to England now?*

"I can't do it," she whispered. "I can't go back."

That left her with very few alternatives. She couldn't very well talk her father into letting her remain in America. Soon enough she would be twenty-one and her father would never allow that day to come without her being properly married to Sir Jeffery.

"I could run away," she murmured and the thought suddenly seemed very possible. *Logan has taught me how to find my way around,* she reasoned. *I could hide out in the mountains until after my birthday and then Father would have no choice.* But her birthday was the twenty-third of November and by that time this entire area would be snow-packed and frightfully cold. There was no way she would survive.

"But I don't want to survive if I have to marry Jeffery."

With that declaration an entirely different thought came to mind. Taking her own life could not be ruled out as a possible alternative. She thought of Crying Rock and the Indian maid who'd bravely gone to her death rather than face the unbearable ordeal of marrying a man she abhorred. *I'm no different than that woman. My sorrow is certainly well-founded. To leave this place, this lovely, wonderful place would be sheer misery.* And yet, even as she thought it, Amelia knew it wasn't just the place—it was Logan. Marriage to any man other than Logan was simply unthinkable.

"But he doesn't feel the same way I do," she chided. "He has his God and his religion and he doesn't need a woman who would fight him with intellectual words and philosophies." *No, Logan needs a wife who would work at his side, worship at his side, raise a family at his side. Logan would expect her to believe as he did, that God not only existed, but that He played an intricate role in the lives of His children. And that in doing so, He gave them a Savior in Jesus Christ.*

Something her mother had once said came back to haunt her. "Only the foolish man believes there is no God, Amelia. For the Bible says, 'even the demons believe in God, and they tremble'."

Amelia gazed out over the valley and sighed. Logan said she had but to open her eyes to the handiwork of God to realize His existence.

But how could she believe in God, much less in the need to worship Him and follow all manner of rule and regulation laid out in the Bible? To what purpose was there such a belief as the need for eternal life? Wasn't it just that mortal man could not stand to believe that his important life ended in the grave? Wasn't the idea of immortality something mankind comforted itself with in lieu of facing the truth that once you died, that was all there was? After all, most religions she'd studied had some form of immortality for their believers. It was rather like a parting gift from a high-society soiree. Something to cherish for those who had the courage to play the party games.

"I do not need such comfort," she whispered and hugged her arms close. "When my life is done, it is done and there will be no marriage to Sir Jeffery and no longing for what I can never have."

Suddenly it seemed quite reasonable to put an end to her life. In fact, it was almost calming. If there was nothing else to concern herself with, why not stop now? She'd seen more of the world than most people. She'd enjoyed the pleasures of the privileged life and she'd once known the love of good parents and siblings. *So what if I never know the love of a man—never know the joys of motherhood?* She wiped the tears which were now pouring freely from her eyes.

"I will go to Jeffery and plead my case before him. I will tell him honestly that I have no desire to marry him and suggest to him a different course," she told the valley before her. She climbed down from the rock and smoothed her skirt. "If he refuses to give consideration to my desires, then the matter will be resolved for me."

She thought that there should be some kind of feeling of accomplishment in making such a decision, but there wasn't. She felt empty and void of life. "I am resigned to do this thing," she said as an encouragement to her broken spirit. "There is no other way."

*S*ir Jeffery, I wonder if I might have a moment of your time," Amelia began one evening after dinner.

He seemed to sneer down his nose at her as though her request had somehow reduced her to a beggar. "I would be honored," he said and extended his arm for her.

Amelia, seeing all faces turned to behold her action, placed her hand upon his sleeve. "I suggest a short walk, if that would meet with your approval," she said cautiously.

"But of course, Lady Amhurst. I am your servant."

Amelia said nothing more, but allowed Jeffery to lead her amicably from the lodge.

"I must say this is a pleasant surprise. Dare I hope you're coming around to my way of thinking?"

Amelia let go of him and shook her head. "No, rather I was hoping to persuade you to my way of thinking."

"How so?"

"Sir Jeffery, I have no desire to marry you. I do not love you and I never will. I cannot make it any clearer on this point." She turned to him in the dim lamp light of the porch and hoped he would understand. "I know about your hold on Father and I know about your desire for the Scottish property." She held up her hand to wave off his question. "I overheard you two discussing the matter one evening. Therefore, I know, too, that you are not marrying me because of any great love, but rather because you want a good turn of business."

"Fair enough," Jeffery replied and leaned back against the porch railing. "But your knowing the circumstance does nothing to change my decision."

"But why not? Why not be an honorable man about this and allow Father some other means by which to settle his debt?"

"I'm open to other means. If you can put the seventy-thousand pounds in my hand, I'll call the entire wedding off."

"Truly?" she asked, feeling at once hopeful.

Jeffery sneered and laughed. "But of course, you can't put that kind of money in my hands, even if you inherit, can you?"

"Perhaps not right away, but I could put over half of it in your hands."

"What? And leave yourself with no income. If you do not marry, your father is sure to exile you to that pitifully cold Scottish estate you seem so inclined to hang on to. Without funds, how do you propose to live?"

"I hope to sell my book when we return to England. Lady Bird suggested—"

"No, Amelia. I will not call off this wedding on your hopes and the suggestions of Lady Bird."

"And there is no other way to convince you?"

"None. Now stop being such a foolish child about it all. You'll have the very best of everything, I assure you. And, if you're concerned about your freedom to find true love, I will even go so far as to say that as long as you are discrete about your affairs, I will be most tolerant of them."

Amelia was totally aghast. "I would never consider such a thing!"

Jeffery sighed and spoke tolerantly as though dealing with a simpleton. "It is done all the time, Amelia dear. Most of nobility take lovers because they've been forced into loveless marriages. I'm simply trying to offer you what would be an acceptable arrangement in lieu of your sacrificing to a marriage of arrangement."

Noises from the front of the lodge porch told Amelia that her sisters and their friends were making their way over to the Amhurst cabin. They were giggling and talking in rapid fire succession about some point or another. It probably amounted to nothing more than their ritual game of after-dinner whist. Amelia lowered her voice to avoid drawing attention to herself.

"I am appalled that you would suggest such a thing. Marriage is a sacred institution, not something to be flaunted about and infringed upon by numerous affairs."

"My dear, you are quite naive to believe such a thing. I had thought you to be more mature about these matters, especially in light of your disbelief in holy affairs. I thought you above all other women to be removed from such nonsense."

"Faithfulness has never been nonsense to my way of thinking."

"Ah, but it is your way of thinking that is keeping this matter unresolved. Your father has made up his mind to accept my generous offer. It will benefit all people in one way or another. Yes, even you will benefit, Amelia, and if you would but stop to think about it, you would see that I speak the truth. You might even come to enjoy my company after a time, and furthermore, to find pleasure in my bed."

Amelia dismissed such notions with her coldest stare. She hoped Jeffery felt frozen to the bone from her look. "I believe we've said all there is to say," she stated and turned to leave. Jeffery did nothing to stop her.

"You'll soon see for yourself, Amelia," he called after her, then laughed in a way that suggested he was very much enjoying the entire matter.

Amelia hurried to her cabin, fighting back tears and angry retorts. She knew that there was little to be done but accept her fate. Suicide seemed her only answer and her heart grew even heavier as she considered how she might accomplish such a fate.

"I want to wear the green one," Penelope argued and pulled the gown from Margaret's hold. Both sisters looked up guiltily as Amelia entered the room to find them fighting over her gowns.

When Amelia remained fixed in her place, saying nothing of reprimand, Penelope took the opportunity to explain. "There is to be a dance tonight. They're clearing the lodge's main room and Mary is fixing refreshments. It won't be as nice as a fancy ball, but I'm positively dying to dance. And Mr. Reed said the local men will come and serve as partners."

Margaret lifted her nose in the air and said, "I do hope they bathe. Some of these Americans seem not to know what a benefit water and soap can be." Her attitude suggested she might be reconsidering her appearance at the dance, but just when Amelia figured her to be absent, Margaret's expression changed to one of pleading desperation. "You simply must let us borrow your dresses. You have so many pretty gowns that you've not even worn and we've only those old things." She waved to a small stack of discarded gowns.

"Do whatever you like," Amelia finally said in a voice of pure resignation. "You may have all of my dresses for all I care. I won't be needing them anymore."

"You're only saying that to make me feel bad," Penelope said, puffing out her chest indignantly. "Just because you are marrying Sir Jeffery in Denver and will receive a new trousseau, you think you can be cruel."

"Yes, you are very mean-spirited, Amelia," Margaret agreed. "I think I've never met a more hateful person. You'll have Sir Jeffery and his money and go to court and spend your days in all the finery and luxury money can buy. We'll still be trying to make a proper match."

"Yes," Penelope added with a sigh, "and hoping that our husbands will be as handsome and rich as Sir Jeffery." Both of them broke into tittering giggles before Penelope sobered and tightened her hold on the gown as though Amelia might change her mind. "So you needn't be so smug Amelia. You may walk around with your nose in the air for all we care."

Amelia looked at them both. She was stunned by their harshness and hurt by their comments. These were her sisters and there had been a time when they were all close and happy. She remembered joyous times when they were little and she'd played happily with them in the nursery. She loved them, even if they couldn't see that. Even if time and sorrow had made them harsh, and strained their ability to be kind. She saw hints of their mother woven in their expressions. Margaret looked like their mother more than any of them, but even Penelope shared a similar mouth and nose. Amelia sighed. They should be close, as close as any three people could ever be. But they thought her a snob and a spiteful, prideful person, and perhaps they were right. It seemed only to fuel the idea that the world would be a better place without her in it.

Not wishing to leave them with a bitter memory of her, she offered softly, "I do apologize. I fear you have misjudged me, however. It was never my intentions to make you feel bad."

Margaret and Penelope looked at her in complete surprise. Amelia wondered if they had any idea of what she was about to do. They were so young and childish and probably concerned themselves only with what color would best highlight their eyes or hair. No doubt they prayed fervently that Amelia would allow Jeffery the freedom to dance with them and pay them the attention they so craved. *Will they mourn me when I am gone? Will anyone?*

"You don't care at all how we feel. All summer you've pranced around here like some sort of queen. Always you've had the best of everything and Father even allowed you to remain behind from the hunt when we had to drudge about this horrid country looking for sport!" Penelope declared.

"Yes, it's true!" Margaret exclaimed in agreement. "You had Jeffery's undivided attention and positively misused him. You have no heart, Amelia."

Amelia could no longer stand up under their criticism. She felt herself close to tears again and rather than allow them to see her cry, turned at the door to walk away. "You needn't worry about the matter any more," she called over her shoulder. "I'll take myself to the Crying Rock and relieve you of your miseries."

Crossing the yard, Amelia looked heavenward. A huge milky moon shone down to light her way and a million stars sparkled against the blackness. Mother had told her that stars were the candlelights of angels.

"But I can't see the angels, Mother," Amelia had said in her doubt and disbelief.

"We can't always see the good things at hand, but we can trust them to be there."

Amelia sighed and rubbed her arms against the chill. "You were wrong, Mother. There is no good thing at hand for me."

She made her way up the mountain through the heavy undergrowth of the forest floor. She only vaguely knew the path to the Crying Rock and hoped she'd find the right way. Tears blinded her from seeing what little moonlight had managed to filter down through the trees. She'd never been one given to tears, but during these few months in America she'd cried enough for a lifetime. Now, it seemed that her lifetime should appropriately come to an end.

Her sisters' harsh comments were still ringing in her ears and her chest felt tight and constricted with guilt and anguish. *Perhaps they're right. Perhaps I am heartless and cruel. The world would be a much better place without me.*

God cares about your pain. Logan's words come back to mind so clearly that Amelia stopped in her place and listened for him to speak. The wind moaned through the trees and Amelia realized that it was nothing but her mind playing tricks on her. *There is no God,* she reminded herself, chiding herself for being foolish.

"Even if there were," she muttered, "He wouldn't care about me."

~&

Logan leaned against the stone wall of the fireplace and wondered if Amelia would join in the evening fun. He'd watched her from afar and saw that her mind was overly burdened with matters that she refused to share. He'd prayed for her to find the answers she longed for.

Over in one corner, Lord Amhurst and Sir Jeffery were steeped in conversation and Logan couldn't help but watch them with a feeling of contempt. *What kind of man forces his child to marry against her will? Especially a man who represents nothing but fearful teasing from childhood and snobbish formality in adulthood.* He longed to understand better and not to feel so judgmental about Amelia's father and his insistence that she wed Jeffery Chamberlain. He knew very little except for what he'd overheard and none of that gave him the full picture. He'd tried to get Amelia to talk about it, but even when he'd caught her in moments where she was less guarded about her speech, she refused to share her concerns with him.

His mind went back to the conversation he'd overheard earlier that evening between Amelia and Jeffery. He'd been coming to the lodge and rounded the back corner just in time to hear Amelia tell Chamberlain that she believed in faithfulness in marriage. Chamberlain certainly hadn't, but it didn't surprise Logan.

"Well, well, and here come some of our lovely ladies now," the earl stated loudly.

Logan looked up to find Amelia's sisters flouncing about the room in their finery. Lady Gambett and her daughters were quick to follow them into the room, but Amelia was nowhere to be found.

"I say, Penelope," Lord Amhurst began, "isn't that one of Amelia's gowns?"

Penelope whirled in the pale green silk. "Yes, Father, it is."

"You know how particular your sister is about her gowns. It will certainly miff her to find you in it."

"She knows all about it," Penelope replied.

"Yes, Father, she does. In fact, this is her gown also and she told me I could wear it," Margaret chattered. "Although it is a bit large."

Logan smiled, seeing for himself that Margaret's girlish figure couldn't quite fill out the bodice. He could imagine Amelia growing impatient with them both and throwing the gowns in their faces. Sipping a cup of coffee, Logan tried to hide his smile and keep his thoughts to himself.

In one corner, several of the boys were tuning up their fiddles and guitars to provide the evening's music, while the earl exchanged formalities with the newly arrived Lord Gambett. They talked for several minutes while the ladies gathered around Jeffery, each vying for his compliments. Some of the local men straggled in and Logan nearly laughed aloud at the way they each paused at the door to shine their boots on the backside of the opposite leg. Never mind their jeans might show a smudge of dirt, so long as their boots looked good. Logan almost felt sorry for them, knowing that these prim and proper English roses would hardly appreciate the effort.

"We're certain to beat the snow if we leave at the end of next week instead of waiting," Logan heard Lord Gambett say.

"What do say you, Mr. Reed? Is the snow upon us?" Lord Amhurst suddenly questioned.

"It's due, that's for sure," Logan replied. "But I think you're safe from any real accumulation. We might see a dusting here and there, but it doesn't look bad just yet. Of course, with mountain weather that could all change by morning."

The musicians were ready and awaited some kind of cue that they should begin playing. The fiddle player was already drawing his bow across the strings in what Logan knew to be an American-styled call to order. He looked around the room and still seeing no sign of Amelia, questioned the earl about beginning the music.

"I see Lady Amhurst is still absent, but if you would like, the boys are ready to begin playing."

The earl glanced around as though Amelia's absence was news. "I say, Penelope, where is that sister of yours? She doesn't seem to be here."

Penelope shrugged. "She left the cabin after telling us to wear whatever we wanted. She was mean-tempered and said she wouldn't be needing these gowns anymore. We presumed she said that because of her marriage to Sir Jeffery. Don't you think it mean of her to boast that way?"

Lord Amhurst laughed. "At least she's finally coming around to our way of thinking, what?" He elbowed Jeffery and laughed.

"Indeed it would appear that way," the sneering man replied.

Logan hated his smugness and thought of his lurid suggestion that Amelia would come to enjoy his bed. Logan seethed at the thought of Amelia joining this man in marriage. He had worked all week long to figure out what he could do to resolve Amelia's situation. He couldn't understand her loyalty to a father who would be so unconcerned with her feelings, and yet he respected her honoring him with obedience. *Somehow there has to be a way to make things right for Amelia.* He thought of approaching the earl and asking for Amelia's hand, but he was already certain that the man would never consider him a proper suitor, much less a proper husband.

"I congratulate you, Chamberlain, on your powers of persuasion. You must have given her a good talking to in order to convince her to marry."

"Maybe it was more than a talking to," Lady Gambett said in uncharacteristic fashion.

The girls all giggled and blushed at this. They whispered among themselves at just what such possibilities might entail, while Jeffery smiled smugly and accepted their suppositions. Logan barely held his temper and would have gladly belted the grin off Chamberlain's face had his attention not been taken in yet another startling direction.

"But did Amelia say when she might join us?" the earl asked, suddenly seeming to want to push the party forward.

"No," Penelope replied, "she said she was going off to cry on some rock. I suppose she'll be at it all night and come back with puffy red eyes."

"Then she'll be too embarrassed to come to the party," Margaret replied.

Logan felt his breath quicken and his mind repeated the words Penelope had just uttered. *She said she was going off to cry on some rock.* *Did she mean Crying Rock?* He put his cup down and signaled the band to begin. He wanted no interference on exiting quickly and figured with the music as a diversion he could make his way out the back kitchen door.

He was right. Logan slipped from the room without anyone voicing so much as a "Good evening." His thoughts haunted him as he made his way to the end of the porch. He grabbed a lighted lantern as he jumped down from the steps. *She doesn't want this marriage and she knows about Crying Rock.* He mentally kicked himself for ever taking her there.

"Lord, if I've caused her to seek a way out that costs Amelia her life, I'll never forgive myself," he muttered.

15

s if drawn there by sheer will, Amelia finally made her way to Crying Rock. She stood for a moment under the full moon and looked down on the valley below. Across the mountains the moon's reflection made it appear as though it were day. The dark, shadowy covering of pine and aspen looked like an ink smudge against the valley. The mournful sound of the wind playing in the canyons seemed to join Amelia's sobs in sympathetic chorus.

Her gown of lavender crepe de Chine did little to ward off the bite of the mountain breeze. The polonaise styling with its full skirt and looped-up draping in back gave a bit of protection, but the wind seemed to pass right through the low cut bodice and was hardly deterred by the chiffon modesty scarf that she'd tucked into it. The finery of a Paris gown meant little to her now. *What good were such baubles when no one cared if you lived or died?*

She stepped closer to the edge and wiped her tear-stained face. *Father will be very unhappy when he learns what I've done. All of his plans will be for naught, and yet he'll still have his money and the land will pass to Penelope.* Perhaps her sister would go willingly into marriage with Sir Jeffery. Thinking of Jeffery made her stomach hurt. He was mean and crude and just standing over the dizzying drop made her remember his cruelty to her as a child.

"This thing must be done," she said to the sky and then sank to her knees in misery. *If only there were some reason to go on with life.* She simply couldn't see herself at Jeffery's side playing the innocent wife while keeping her lovers waiting in hidden rooms. Furthermore, to imagine, that Jeffery would entertain himself in such a manner bothered her pride more than she could admit. If Jeffery had at least loved her, it might have been possible to go into the marriage. But he wanted nothing more than her father's money and the manipulative power to control all that she would inherit. Amelia felt sick just imagining the arrangement.

"If God did exist—" she said softly and lifted her gaze again to the panoramic view of the mountains. She thought of Logan and all that he'd shared with her about God and the Bible. She thought of his faith to believe in such matters. He was totally unwavering, even when she made what she knew was a strong argument against his beliefs. Logan wouldn't argue with her about God. And it wasn't because Amelia hadn't sought to stir up a conflict now and then. Logan would merely state what he believed to be the facts and leave Amelia to sort through it herself. She remembered one conversation which had taken place several days earlier in which she had asked Logan how he could be so certain that he was right in his beliefs.

"How can you be so certain that I'm not?" he had questioned. "I'm willing to bet my life on my beliefs. Are you?"

Amelia felt a chill run through her at the memory. Was she willing to bet her life on her beliefs? Her mother's faith had been the foundation for their household. Her father had even admitted that it was one of the things which had attracted him to her in the first place.

"Mother, why did you have to leave us?" Amelia whispered. "Why did you have to leave me with so many questions? If God loves us as you always said He did, then why did He cruelly take you from the children who needed you? Where is God's mercy in that? Where is the love?"

The rustlings of the wind in the trees below were all that came back in reply.

"All right," she said giving in to the tremendous longing in her soul. "If You exist God, then why do you allow such tragedy and injustice? Why, if You are such a loving Father, do You allow Your children to experience such pain?" she paused in questioning and rubbed her arms against the mountain chill. "Why do You allow *me* to hurt so much?"

"I want to believe," she said and this time the tears came. "I want to believe." She sobbed and buried her face in her hands. "But it hurts so much and I'm so afraid that You won't be any more constant than Mother was. If I believed, would You merely go away when I needed You most, just as she did?"

A verse of Scripture from childhood from the last chapter of Matthew, came to memory. "And, lo, I am with you always, *even* unto the end of the world."

"But the world is filled with a variety of beliefs and religious nonsense," Amelia protested against the pulling of her spirit. "How can I know that this is real? How can I know that I am choosing the right path?"

Logan had said it was a matter of faith and in believing that the Bible was truly the word of God. Logan had also said that God proved Himself over and over, even in the little day to day points of life.

"God, if You are real," Amelia said, lifting her face to the starry, moonlit sky overhead, "then You must show me in such a way that I cannot miss it in my blind foolishness."

But even if God was real He wouldn't change my plight. What tiny thread of hope had begun to weave itself through her broken heart, snapped with this sudden realization. She was still facing her father's edict that she marry a man she didn't care about. She would still find herself headed back to England within the month. And, she would still lose the man she loved.

Logan came to mind with such a powerful urgency that Amelia no longer fought against it. She loved him as truly as she had ever loved anyone, and in many ways, intimate and frightening ways, she loved him more than she had ever loved anyone else. Logan was like no one else in the world. He cared to share his faith with her in such a way that it wasn't merely preaching for the sake of fulfilling his obligation to God—rather it was that his heart was so full to overflowing with love for his God and Savior that he couldn't help but share it.

Then too, Logan was perhaps the only man who had ever treated her with respect that didn't come from a sense of noble obligation. Logan spoke his mind and refused to play into her role of "Ladyship", but he also afforded her a kindness and gentleness, of spirit that only her mother had ever given her. But of course, that didn't mean he loved her and love was truly all that Amelia longed for in life.

"There is no reason to live without it," she whispered. "Oh, God, if You are real then give me a reason to live. Send me love. Real and true love. Please, let someone love me," she sobbed.

"I love you," Logan said from somewhere behind her. "Even more, God loves you, Amelia."

The sound of his voice startled her so badly that Amelia hurried to her feet, tangling her skirt around her legs as she tried to straighten up. Caught off guard by Logan and by the gown's hold on her, Amelia lost her balance and fell to the ground. The impact caused a piece of the rocky ledge to give way and Amelia felt herself slipping from the safety of Crying Rock.

Digging her hands into the rock and dirt, she thought, *Not now. I can't die now!* But even as the thought crossed her mind, she was more than aware of her dangerous situation. With what she thought would surely be her last breath, she screamed Logan's name.

"Amelia!" he cried out from overhead. "I thought I'd lost you!"

She pressed her body against the cold, hard granite and for the first time in her life began to pray earnestly. She barely heard Logan calling her name and refused to even lift her face to search for him overhead.

"Amelia, you have to listen to me," Logan said again. "Can you hear me?"

"Yes." She barely breathed the word.

As he moved overhead, bits of rock and dirt pelted down on her head causing Amelia to shriek in fear. "Don't be scared, Amelia, I'll soon have you right as rain."

She would have laughed had the predicament not been so grave. *Don't be scared?* She was long past scared. She was terrified to the point that she thought she might pass out cold and end any hope of her rescue.

"Listen to me Amelia. I can reach your hand if you lift your arm up."

"No, I'm not moving," Amelia replied, hardly daring to breath.

"You have to do as I say or you may well be on that ledge for whatever time you have left on earth."

She said nothing for several heartbeats and then spoke in a barely audible voice. "I can't do it, Logan."

Logan seemed not to hear her. "Look up and to your right. I'm reaching down as far as I can and I can almost touch your head. All you have to do is give me your hand. I promise I won't let you go."

"I can't do it," she repeated sternly.

"Yes, you can," he told her sounding so confident that she felt a surge of hope. "Trust me, Amelia. Have faith in me and what God can do."

Amelia felt the pounding of her heart and the fierce chill of the wind as it whipped up under her skirt from the canyon below. She wanted to believe that Logan could do what he claimed. She wanted to trust that God would honor her prayer of desperation.

Slowly, methodically, she released her grip on the rock. Her hands ached from their hold, but slowly she stretched her fingers until they were straight. She lifted her arm ever so slowly. She refused to look up, terrified that she would find the distance too far to make contact with Logan's hand. But then his hand clamped down on her wrist jarring her rigid body to her toes. Amelia had to force herself not to cry out.

"I've got you. Now just don't fight me and we'll be okay," Logan called down to her. "I'm going to pull you back up on the count of three. One. Two—"

Amelia's heart was in her throat. *If I die now there will never be any hope of reconciling myself to God.*

"Three!" Logan exclaimed and Amelia found herself being hoisted back up the rock wall. She heard her crepe de Chine skirt tear against the jagged edge and the loose dirt rolling off the ledge as Logan dragged her across it. In the time that it took to realize what had happened, Amelia lay atop the ground with Logan panting heavily at her side.

He jumped up quickly and pulled her away from the edge to more stable ground. Wrapping his arms around her, he held her in a trembling embrace that told her how afraid he'd been. He sighed against her ear and Amelia thought it all more wondrous than she could take in. She relished the warmth of his body against hers and the powerful hold of his arms. *He loves me,* she thought. If only she could stay in his arms forever.

Then, without warning, she started to giggle and then to laugh and Logan pulled away to look at her quite seriously. The thoughts flooding through her mind, however, would not let her even speak a word of explanation. It was almost as though the missing joy in her life had suddenly bubbled over inside.

"Amelia, are you all right?"

She nodded and continued to laugh so hard that tears came to her eyes.

"It's shock," he said authoritatively. "Come sit down."

Shaking, Amelia allowed him to lead her to a small boulder and sat willingly when he pushed her to do so. She was still laughing, however, at the very idea that she had asked God to give her a sign so clear that she could not miss the truth! What remained comical in her mind was that God could hardly have made it any clearer, and even Amelia, in her childish refusal to believe in His presence, was ready to admit her folly.

Logan sat down beside her and pulled her gently into his arms. She looked over and found his expression so fearful that it sent her into new peals of laughter.

"I'm sorry," she alternated between gasps and giggles. "It's just so, so—" her voice fell away in uncontrollable mirth.

"Amelia, honey, you've got to calm down," Logan said softly. Her hair had managed to come loose during her escapade up the mountain, and Logan methodically stroked it as if to calm her.

"It's just," she said, finally gaining control of her voice, "that I asked God to prove Himself to me. I asked Him for a sign that even I couldn't ignore and then He does just that, getting my full attention by dangling me over the ledge! Oh, Logan, don't you see how funny it is?"

Logan nodded and smiled. "I remember you asking Him for love, too."

This did the trick in sobering her completely. "Yes, I did." She looked deep into his eyes, unable to make out their brilliant green shading in the moonlight. "I'm glad you came."

"Me, too."

With their faces only inches apart, the kiss that followed seemed more than natural. Amelia felt Logan bury his warm fingers in her hair in order to slant her head just enough to give him free access to her mouth. She was stunned by the kiss at first, then a flaming warmth seemed to radiate out from where their lips touched. It flowed down through her body until Amelia wanted to shout aloud with joy.

"Amelia," Logan sighed her name as he pulled away from the kiss. "I love you, Amelia. Please tell me that you could love a barbarian."

She smiled. "I *do* love you, Logan Reed."

With this, he kissed her again, only this time less urgently and when he pulled away, Amelia could see that his eyes glistened. "I thought I'd lost you," he whispered.

"I couldn't see a reason to go on, but neither did I have the courage to put an end to my life," Amelia admitted.

"It doesn't take courage to kill yourself," Logan interjected. "That's the coward's way out."

"I was in such turmoil. I kept remembering the things my mother had taught me about God and the things you kept pushing in my face." At that she smiled and took hold of his hand. "Logan, you were right to keep after me. I've always known God existed, but I didn't want to admit it because if He existed in the power and glory people told me about, it also meant that He had the power to keep the bad things in my life from happening. But He didn't. He let Jeffery torture me as a child. He let my Mother die before I was ready to say good-bye to her and He left me to be forced into a marriage with a man I can't abide." She paused and searched Logan's face for condemnation. When she found only love reflected in his gaze, she continued.

"To believe in His existence meant I had to accept that He knew what was happening and that He stood by and let it happen. That seemed cruel and heartless to me. The God my mother had always told me of was merciful and loving. I couldn't accept that He would do such a thing or even allow someone else to do those things. Does that make any sense?"

"I think so," Logan replied. "But how about now? Those things haven't changed. And, there are still horrible tragedies in life. Tragedies that won't just go away overnight."

"That's true," Amelia said thoughtfully, "but I suppose I must simply accept that fact. I don't imagine life will always make sense, but what does make sense to me is that if there is a way to deal with the bad times in peace and confidence, then that's what I want. I've watched you all summer and your peace and assurance has driven me nearly insane."

He laughed at this and hugged her close. "Your uppity, stubborn 'I'll-do-it-myself' attitude has nearly driven me to drink, so I guess we're even." He ran his hand through the blond silk and smiled. "Oh, and I always wondered what you'd look like with your hair down and now I know."

"And what exactly do you know?" she asked impishly.

"That you are the most beautiful woman in the world," Logan replied. "What little of it, I've seen."

"There's no place else in the world as pretty as Estes, Logan, and no place I'd rather be."

"So what are we going to do, now?" he asked softly.

Amelia smiled and pulled back far enough to look into his face. "I'm ready to lay it all out before God, Logan. I'm ready to face life and march back down the mountain and do what I'm told to do." She bit at her lower lip and looked away before adding, "At least I think I am. It won't be easy to leave you."

"Leave me? Who said anything about you leaving me. I want you to marry me, Amelia."

She shook her head. "That, Logan, is impossible. There are things you don't know about which prevent my giving in to such a dream. And believe me, that is my dream. I would love to marry you and stay here in the mountains for the rest of my life. I know it deep down inside me, just as I know that I'm ready to accept Christ as my Savior." She paused feeling suddenly shy about her declarations. "But it is not possible for us to marry."

"With God," Logan said, reaching out to lift her face, "all things are possible. The Bible says so and I believe it with all of my heart, just as I believe you will one day be Mrs. Logan Reed."

Amelia felt tears come anew. She looked at him there in the moonlight and tried to commit to memory, every line and angle. She reached out and touched the mustache that she'd so often longed to touch and found it soft, yet coarse, against her fingers. Funny, but she'd not even noticed it when he'd kissed her.

She gazed into his eyes, seeing the longing and love reflected there for her—longing and love she held in her own heart for him. *How can I explain that I could never be his wife? How can I walk away from the only man I will ever love and marry another?*

As if sensing her thoughts, Logan took hold of her hand and kissed her fingers gently. "All things are possible with God," he repeated. "Not just some things, but all things."

"You don't understand, Logan. My father needs me to marry Jeffery. He owes him a great debt and Sir Chamberlain will brook no nonsense in collecting on the matter."

"Does he love you?" Logan asked quite seriously.

"No. I think that man incapable of love. But he does desire my land," she said smiling at the irony of it all. One man wanted her heart, another her land and she was stuck in the middle with her own longing and need and no one but God knew what that might mean to her.

"Do you love him?"

"Certainly not!" she declared with a look of horror.

"I love you, Amelia," He said simply. "I love you and I want to marry you, not for land or money or noble title, but because life without you would be unbearable. I think I fell in love with you the morning after our first all day ride. You tried so hard to keep from grimacing in pain as you got on that horse the next morning and I thought to myself, 'Here's a woman with real spirit.' Then I think I loved you even more when you went bustling around camp trying so hard to work at every job I gave you. I pushed you a bit too hard, but I got my reward. It put you in my arms."

"You asked me to choose between barbarians or twits," she murmured. "And you thought I chose Jeffery."

"No, I didn't."

"But you said—" she paused, cocking her head to one side as if to better understand him.

"I said that I could see you'd made your choice. I never said you chose Sir Twit. But I could see the argument you were having with yourself over feelings that you couldn't yet come to terms with. So I gave you over to him, hoping that the misery would drive you right back to me."

"I couldn't sleep that night for the things you made me feel," she admitted.

"Me either. So you see, I'm not ready to give up and say this can't be done. I'm quite willing to fight for you and pay off your father's debt if necessary."

"You can't. It's a great deal more money than either of us could hope to raise."

"How much?" he asked flatly, with a look of disbelief on his face.

"Seventy-thousand pounds."

"Done."

"Done?" she questioned. "Where in the world are you going to come up with seventy-thousand pounds?"

"Well, it probably won't be pounds, but American dollars will spend just the same."

She shook her head. "Don't joke about this."

"I'm not joking."

She could see by the serious expression on his face that indeed, he wasn't joking. "How are you going to come by seventy-thousand dollars or pounds?"

"I'll take it out of the bank."

"You mean rob it?" she asked in alarm.

Logan laughed until Amelia thought he would fall off the rock on which they were sitting. "No, silly. I'll withdraw that much from my account."

"You have that much money?"

"And a good deal more," he said soberly.

"But I thought—"

"You thought because I live here in Estes and lead guided tours into the park that I was too dirt poor to go anywhere else. Isn't that right?" She nodded, feeling quite guilty for her assessment. "Well, it isn't true. I've got more money than I'll ever need thanks to a little gold mine my father and I own. The truth is, I live this way because I love it. Estes is the only place in the world I ever came to that when I first laid eyes on it, I felt like I'd come home."

"Me, too," she whispered, barely able to speak. *Did God bring me here to bring me home to Him? To Logan?* It was more than she could take in all at once. *Is this how God is making Himself real in my life? To suddenly answer all my needs in one powerful stroke?*

Logan got to his knees and pulled her down with him. "First things first," he said, pulling her closer. "You said you were ready to accept Christ as your Savior, right?" Amelia nodded, forgetting everything else for a moment. "Then that is where we start our new life together," he replied and led her in a prayer of repentance.

16

*S*now blanketed the mountain tops while a light powdery dusting covered the valley below. They had left Estes days ago and Amelia felt an apprehension that grew into genuine fear. What if Logan couldn't convince her father to release her from the engagement to Sir Jeffery? What if Jeffery, himself, refused? With each step the horses took, with every descending clip of their hooves against the dirt and rocks, Amelia felt something inside her die.

She watched both men with anxious eyes, all the while praying fervently. Her father seemed mindless of her dilemma and Jeffery only appeared smug and self-satisfied with the circumstance. Logan promised that God would provide an answer and a way to see them through, but Amelia wasn't as steady in her faith as Logan and the possibility seemed completely out of reach.

Shortly before noon, Logan stopped the party to rest the horses and to Amelia's surprise he beckoned Sir Jeffery to follow him into the forest. Appearing quite annoyed with their barbaric guide, Jeffery did as he was bid, but not without a scowl of displeasure plastered across his aristocratic face. In a short while they returned to join the party and Jeffery seemed all smiles and satisfaction. Amelia was puzzled by this turn of events, but no more so than when Jeffery heralded her father and the two men began to have a feverish discussion. From time to time her father nodded and glanced in her direction, but no one summoned her or indicated a need for her presence and so Amelia remained with her horse, seeing to it that he was properly watered.

They remounted and made their way another hour or so, weaving back and forth across the St. Vrain River before emerging from the canyon to face some six miles of flat prairie land. Longmont would be at the end of that prairie ground and Amelia felt her hope giving way. Longmont represented the place where they were to take the stage to Denver and forever leave Estes, and Logan, behind them. She shuddered, fought back tears and prayed for strength to endure whatever God decided. And all the while she felt her heart nearly breaking with desire to turn around and run back to the safety of Estes.

How could she leave?

She glanced over her shoulder to the mountains. They seemed gray in the harsher light, and the chill in the air left little doubt that winter would soon be a serious business in the area. She gripped the reins tighter and ignored the single tear which slid down her cheek.

How could she leave Logan?

She watched him lead the way across the dried-out prairie and tried to imagine sitting in her damp, drafty English manor house without him. Months ago, she wouldn't have given a single shilling to extend her trip to America by even a day, and now she knew she'd gladly trade the rest of her life to be able to marry Logan and share even a few days as his wife.

"I say," the earl called out to his companions, "this place seems worse for the passing of time."

"Indeed," Lord Gambett replied, gazing about. "Not at all pleasant. It was hot and unbearable when we departed and now we find it dusty and devoid of life."

Amelia smiled at this. Months ago, she would have agreed with Lord Gambett, but now, with the training Logan had given her. Amelia observed life everywhere. Insects, animals, autumn vegetation. It was all there, it was just a matter of where you looked.

"Whoa," she heard Logan call to the party. She glanced forward to find that everyone had halted their horses on the edge of town. "I believe you all know your way from here," Logan said sternly. "Tie up your mounts in front of the hotel and take your personal belongings with you. I'll see to the horses and gear and meet you to settle up in about half an hour. I'll also bring your trunks at that time."

Everyone nodded and urged their horses forward to the hotel. Amelia saw her father and Mattersley press forward with Penelope and Margaret in tow, but she couldn't bring herself to join them. She stared, instead, at Logan astride his horse. Logan, whose face was tanned and sported a new two-day growth of beard. Logan, whose jeans accented his well-muscled legs and whose indigo-dyed, cambric shirt hugged him in way Amelia longed to imitate. He pulled off his hat, wiped his brow and finally noticed that she was watching him. With a grin, he replaced the hat and nudged his horse in her direction.

"You having trouble following directions again, Lady Amhurst?"

She felt a lump in her throat that threatened to strangle her. "No," she barely croaked out.

His mustache twitched as he broke into a broad smile. "Faith, Amelia. Have faith."

"It's stronger when I'm with you," she replied.

"Don't put your faith in me. Remember, your strength comes from God and He will help you."

She nodded. "Okay, Logan. My faith is in God." She spoke the words aloud hoping it would help her to feel more confident. "But how are we going to—"

"Don't worry about anything. Now join up with your family and I'll see you in half an hour." He winked at her before leading his horse off in the direction of the livery.

"Don't worry—have faith," she murmured and urged her mount forward. "Easier said than done."

❧

Half an hour later, Amelia was just as nervous as when she'd left Logan. Her father seemed preoccupied with some matter, while Sir Jeffery was suddenly paying far more attention to Penelope and Margaret than he'd done throughout the entire trip. When she could stand it no longer, Amelia went to the earl and demanded to know what was going on.

"Amelia, Sir Jeffery has agreed to release you from your engagement."

Her mouth dropped. Recovering her composure she asked, "He did? But what of the money?" At this Mattersley took several steps away from the earl and pretended to be preoccupied by studying the ceiling.

Her father shrugged. "He dismissed the debt as well. I have no idea what you said to him, Amelia, but there it is."

"But I don't understand."

"It would seem that you have won this round. I . . . well . . . perhaps I was overly influenced to marry you off because of the debt." He looked at her intently. "I never meant any harm by it, Amelia. I thought you could be happy in time. I suppose now you are free to remain unmarried."

"But what of the inheritance and your concerns for the family coffers?" she asked warily.

Weariness seemed to mar his brow. "You gave your word that you'd not see us suffer and I've always known you to be a woman of truth. Having you stay on with me as your sisters marry and leave, will no doubt be a comfort in my old age."

How strange, Amelia thought wondering how she might broach the subject of Logan's proposal and her own desire to remain in America. How could she explain the change in her heart when she'd been the one to protest leaving England in the first place?

"Ah, good, you're all here," Logan said, striding into the room as though he were about to lead them all in a lecture symposium.

Lord Amhurst looked up with Mattersley doing likewise, but Penelope and Margaret remained in animated conversation with Sir Jeffery. Lord and Lady Gambett stared up wearily from their chairs, while Henrietta and Josephine looked as though they might start whining at any given moment. Amelia dared to catch Logan's gaze and when he smiled warmly at her it melted away some of the fear she felt.

"Your trunks are outside," he announced, "and the stage is due in two hours. I'd suggest you take one of your breaks for tea and cakes before heading to Denver. There isn't much in between here and there, and you'll be mighty sorry if you don't."

"I believe this will square our account," Lord Gambett said, extending an envelope.

Logan looked the contents over and nodded. "This is mighty generous of you, Gambett." The man seemed notably embarrassed and merely nodded before muttering something about seeing to the trunks.

"And this should account for us," Lord Amhurst announced, providing a similar envelope.

Logan tucked the envelope into his pocket without even looking. "If you have a moment, I'd like to speak with you privately, Lord Amhurst."

"I dare say, time is short, speak your mind Reed. We haven't even secured our tickets for the stage."

"They're reserved in your name, I assure you. Five tickets for Denver."

"Five? You mean six, don't you? Or did you reserve Sir Jeffery's separately?"

"No, I meant five." Logan looked at Amelia and held out his hand to her.

Amelia hesitated only a second before joining Logan. Even Penelope and Margaret gasped at the sight of their sister holding hands with their American guide. Mattersley was the only one to offer even the slightest look of approval and that came in the form of a tight-lipped smile.

"I've asked Amelia to marry me, and she said yes. Now, I'm asking for your blessing, Lord Amhurst."

"Why I've never heard of such rubbish!" the earl exclaimed. "Amelia, what nonsense is this man speaking?"

"It isn't nonsense, Father." Amelia noted that her sisters had gathered closer, while Lady Gambett, seeing a major confrontation in the making, ushered her girls into the dining room. Jeffery stood by looking rather bored and indifferent. She smiled up at Logan and tried to calm her nerves. "It's all true. I would very much like to marry Logan Reed and since Sir Jeffery has kindly released me from our betrothal, I am hoping to have your blessing."

"Never! You are the daughter of an earl. You've been presented at court and have the potential to marry . . . well . . . to certainly marry better than an American!"

"But I love an American," Amelia protested. "I can do no better than to marry for love."

"I forbid it!"

"Father, I'm nearly twenty-one," Amelia reminded him. "I can marry without your consent, but I'd much rather have it."

"You marry this man and I'll cut off all inheritance and funding from you. You'll never be welcomed to set foot on my property again."

"Isn't that what Grandfather Amhurst told you when you decided to marry Mother?" Penelope and Margaret both gasped in unison and fanned themselves furiously as though they might faint.

The earl reddened at the collar and looked quite uncomfortable. "That was a different circumstance."

"Not so very different to my way of thinking." Amelia dropped her hold on Logan and gently touched her father's arm. "Father, don't you want me to know true love as you and Mother did?"

"And you love this man enough to lose your fortune?"

"She doesn't need a fortune," Logan interjected. "I have enough for the both of us." This drew everyone's attention. "Look, there doesn't need to be any pretense between any of us." Logan drew out two envelopes and handed them to the earl. "I won't take your money for the trip and you can give this back to Lord Gambett, as well. Also," he said, reaching in for yet another envelope, "this is yours Chamberlain. You will find one hundred-thousand dollars awaiting you at the bank in Denver."

"One-hundred thousand?" Amelia questioned.

Logan smiled. "I had to make it worth his trouble." Jeffery said nothing, but tucked the envelope into his pocket. Lord Amhurst stood staring at his own envelopes while Logan continued. "As I said, Amelia doesn't need the Donneswick fortune. She'll be well-cared for by me and she won't want for anything, unless of course, it's your blessing."

The earl looked positively torn and Amelia instantly felt sorry for her father. "I love him, Father," she said, tears glistening in her eyes. "You wanted me to marry before my twenty-first birthday and I'm finally agreeing to that."

"Yes, but—" he looked at her and suddenly all the harshness of the last year seemed to fade from his expression. He looked from Amelia to Logan, and seemed to consider the idea as if for the first time. "I say, you truly wish to be married to him and live here, in America?"

"I truly do." She leaned over and kissed her father on the cheek, whispering in his ear, "Logan makes me happy, Papa. Please say yes."

He smiled and touched Amelia's cheek. "You will come for visits, won't you?"

"Of course we will," she replied. "So long as we're both welcomed."

He sighed. "Then you have my blessing, although I offer it up with some misgivings."

"Oh, thank you, Father. Thank you!" Amelia gave him an uncharacteristic public embrace before throwing herself into Logan's arms.

Logan hugged her tightly and happily obliged her when Amelia lifted her lips to his for a kiss.

"Ah, I say," the earl interrupted the passionate display, "but I don't suppose we could find a man of the cloth in this town, what?"

Logan broke the kiss and nodded. "Parson's waiting for us as we speak. I didn't figure you'd much want to leave her here without seeing her properly wed."

The earl very ceremoniously took out a pocket watch and popped open the cover. "Then I say we'd best be going about it. I have a stage to catch shortly, as you know."

*E*PILOGUE

*T*thought you said May around here would signal spring," Amelia said, rising slowly with a hand on her slightly swollen abdomen. She looked out the cabin window for the tenth time that morning and for the tenth time found nothing but snow to stare back at her.

"Hey," Logan said, coming up from behind her, "we didn't make such bad use of the winter." He wrapped his arms around her and felt the baby's hefty kick. "See, our son agrees."

"What he agrees with," Amelia said in her very formal English accent, "is that if his mother doesn't get out of this cabin soon, she's going to be stark raving mad."

"We could read together," Logan suggested. "We could get all cozied up under the covers for warmth, maybe throw in some heated rocks from the fireplace to keep our feet all toasty—" His words trailed off as he nuzzled her neck.

"I believe we've read every book in the cabin, at least twice," she said, enjoying his closeness.

"We could play a game of cards. We could get all cozied up—"

"I know. I know," she interrupted. "Under the covers for warmth and throw in some heated rocks, but honestly Logan I'm going to throw one of those rocks through the window if we can't do something other than sit here and count snowflakes."

"Maybe, just maybe, if you can bear to be parted from me for a spell, I'll ride down to Mary's and see if she can come up here for a bit. Maybe you ladies could share quilting secrets."

"But I want to get out! I want to walk around and see something other than four walls and frosted windows. I may be with child, but

444

that certainly doesn't mean I'm without feet on which to walk. Please, Logan."

Logan sighed and laid his chin atop her head. "If you promise to dress very warmly and to wear your highest boots, and do everything I say, then I suppose I could be persuaded to—"

"Oh, Logan, truly?" Amelia whirled around causing Logan's head to snap back from the absence of support. "When can we go? Can we go now?"

Logan laughed, rubbed his chin and gave Amelia a look that said it all. She liked the way he was looking at her. It was a look that suggested that she alone was responsible for his happiness and if they remained snowed in the cabin for another six months, he'd still smile in just exactly the same way. He touched her cheek with his calloused fingers and smiled. "Good things take time, Lady Amhurst."

"Mrs. Reed," she corrected. "I'm happily no longer a lady of noble standing."

He grinned roguishly. "Oh, you're a lady, all right. But you're my lady now."

She smiled and felt a surge of joy bubble up inside her. "God sure had a way of getting my attention," she said, putting her hand over his.

"The stubborn, impatient ones are always the hardest," he whispered before lowering his mouth to hers.

Amelia wrapped her arms around Logan's neck and returned his kiss with great enthusiasm. She'd found the happiness that she'd never thought possible, and come September, she was going to have a baby. Logan's baby—and she was Logan's lady, and somehow that made the long winter seem not quite so unbearable.

An Unmasked Heart

by Andrea Boeshaar

To my faithful readers. Where would this writer be without you? Thank you for your cards and letters of encouragement. They are precious to me.

This story, *An Unmasked Heart,* is the last in my historical *McCabe Legacy* series. I hope you will enjoy reading it as much as I enjoyed writing it. I pray this, and all the others, *An Unwilling Warrior, An Uncertain Heart, An Unexpected Love,* and *An Undaunted Faith,* will be a blessing to you for years to come. I look forward to writing a new historical series some time in the future.

1

California, 1873

*T*he scene unfolding before her eyes was one Angelique Huntington had always tried to avoid when coming down to San Francisco's roughest district. Cigar smoke, like fog rolling in from the bay, swirled around the ceiling as the two gamblers faced each other. Their anxious hands twitched above their holsters, and Angie tried to sink deeper into the shadows of the Mad Dog Saloon. She'd been on her way out when she happened upon this most unfortunate encounter.

"Don't do it, you fool," a third man warned an angry-looking card player. "You draw on this fellow, and he'll kill you. Don't you know who this is?"

"Sure, I know," the first man slurred. "You just tol' me."

"Then use your head, Boy! You're in no shape for dueling tonight."

In reply, he swayed slightly and finger-combed his dirty blond hair off his forehead. He seemed to be rethinking his intentions.

Staring on, Angie pulled her dark, woolen cape more tightly around herself as the negotiator turned to address the second gunfighter. From her vantage point all she could see was the challenged man's back, his short, ebony hair, black shirt and trousers, and the bullet-laden gun belt strapped around his narrow hips.

"Please accept my apologies on behalf of my friend here, Mr. Montano," the peacemaker stated, perspiration dotting his balding head. "My friend has had too much to drink tonight, and he's always been a sore loser."

Montano? Angie perked up. She knew that name. How could she ever forget it?

"*Sí*, all is forgiven," Montano said in a deep, velvety-steel voice that held a hint of a Mexican accent. "But I suggest you take your friend home before he gets himself killed."

It's him, Angie thought. *It's got to be him.*

Slapping on his wide-brimmed hat, the intercessor grabbed hold of his blond crony and pushed him out the swinging saloon doors. Angie backed up into the corner by the staircase, praying she wouldn't be noticed. Then she regarded the man called Montano as he donned his hat and turned his back on the winnings. The raucous piano music resumed and the other patrons, some with painted-faced harlots in their laps, continued with their profane diversions.

At last Angie watched the dark-haired man leave the establishment. She quickly followed behind him. A cold drizzle had begun to fall. "Montano," she called. "Paden Montano."

He paused on the boardwalk and slowly turned around. A wary curiosity lighted his dark eyes.

Angie smiled. It was him all right. Slipping in between buildings and under an awning, she beckoned him into the darkness. When he stepped forward, she threw off the gray hood that had covered her blond hair.

"Sheriff? It's me. Angie Brown . . . except my last name is Huntington now."

"Angie?" His voice was but a whisper, and his face seemed a mask of incredulity.

"Remember me? You and Pastor Luke saved my life by staging my escape from Silverstone, Arizona, about six years ago."

"I remember you." He glanced at the saloon building, then back at her.

Angie smiled, but in the next moment her eyes grew wide as Montano seized her upper arms and shook her until she thought her brain would rattle loose.

"And after all that trouble," he said with an obviously clenched jaw, "you return to the lifestyle we sought to deliver you from?"

"No, no . . . you . . . have it . . . all wrong," she said. "Please stop. Let me explain."

He released her none too gently, and Angie swallowed hard.

"Sheriff," she said, feeling irritated, "I don't recall you ever being so quick-tempered."

"Then maybe it's a good thing I am no longer a sheriff. Now you have one minute to explain before I throttle you."

Angie gulped, knowing Paden Montano didn't make idle threats.

"Remember Bethany?" she began. "The young woman who was engaged to Pastor Luke back in Silverstone? Well, she reached out to me and shared her faith while I was a . . . a working girl, so periodically I do the same here in San Francisco. I come down here to tell these women that there is a better life awaiting them if they'll only trust Christ with their souls as well as their vocations. I'm a proprietress of a dress shop along with my stepsister, Veronica." Having stated the latter, Angie couldn't help raising her chin proudly. "The Lord has been good to me."

A small chuckle emanated from the darkly clad man before her. "My apologies . . ." He gave her a polite bow. "What did you say your last name is now? Huntington? I assume that's *Mrs.* Huntington?"

"Once more, you assume incorrectly, *Mr.* Montano," Angie quipped, feeling more at ease. "After Veronica took me in, I wanted a new last name to go with my new life so no one from my past would ever find me—accidentally or otherwise. Veronica decided that I should be introduced to San Francisco society as a distant relative on her deceased husband's side, and she very graciously shared her last name with me. Together, we operate the Huntington House Dress Shop."

"I stand corrected. Forgive me."

"Of course." Angie tipped her head and grinned. From the dimly lit street behind them, she could just barely make out Montano's swarthy features. "I can tell you haven't changed a whit. Same black mustache, same penchant for saloons, card games, gunfights . . . and black clothing." She paused, lifting a brow. "Except you're wearing your hair much shorter these days."

"*Sí*, you are right on that account, but you are wrong on all others." There was a grin in his voice. "I have changed. How could I not, living in the same town as Pastor Luke McCabe? He is a most convincing preacher. I became a Christian a few years back."

"Oh, that's wonderful." Angie's heart soared at the news. "I've prayed for you . . . for everyone in Silverstone."

"We have prayed for you, too." Montano glanced over his shoulder. "May I escort you home, Miz Huntington?"

"Yes, I'd like that, but . . ." She paused, nibbling her lower lip in consternation. "But if you're a born again believer, why were you gambling in a saloon—one that exploits women in such a wicked manner?"

"Because it is, unfortunately, a part of my job, Angie," he said in hushed seriousness, but reverting, nonetheless, to the familiarity they'd shared in years past. Taking her elbow, he guided her toward a nearby hackney. She told him her address and Paden called instructions to the hired driver.

Settling into the black leather seat, Angie watched as he sat down across from her. "What sort of business are you in?" she couldn't help asking.

"I don't recall you ever being so inquisitive."

She smiled her embarrassment, but felt oddly hurt at his mocking reply. She had shared her occupation with him. In fact, he'd demanded it! Silence filled the carriage as they rode the distance to Angie's home in the South Park district. After they'd jerked to a halt, she invited Paden in to meet her stepsister. "I've told Veronica all about you over the years."

"Perhaps another time," he said. His voice sounded almost tender.

"Will there ever be another time?" she asked boldly. "There are so many questions I want to ask you."

"Such as?" She saw his mustache twitch amusedly.

"Well, I'd like to know how Bethany is faring for one thing. How are the girls at Chicago Joe's? I find myself thinking of some of them . . . praying for them."

"Many of Chicago Joe's working girls accepted the Lord and found honorable employment in other cities. Chicago Joe went out of business in Silverstone, thanks to Pastor Luke." Paden grinned. "As for Bethany, she and the pastor married and the last I saw them, some two years ago, they had quite a collection of children."

"I'm very happy for them," Angie replied, unable to suppress the note of wistfulness as Paden helped her alight from the coach. "Thank you for passing all the good news on to me."

"My pleasure. *Buenos noches, señorita.*"

His tone now held a distinct note of finality, which, Angie told herself, was of no consequence to her, so she gave Paden a parting smile and climbed the steps to the front porch. Behind her, she heard the rhythmical clip-clop of horse hooves, echoing on the brick-lined street as the carriage drove away.

❧

Lord, I need a new profession, Paden silently prayed as the carriage rocked back and forth on its way to the Oriental Hotel. When Angie had questioned his faith earlier because of where she'd seen him— and with whom she had seen him—it fueled that nagging spark of shame Paden continually carried deep within his soul. His work often took him into dens of iniquity, and he knew it wasn't right to frequent them for the sake of gleaning information; but if he quit his job with Allan Pinkerton, what else could he do? He was, after all, one of the detective agency's most capable manhunters.

A vision of the lush, wide-open spaces he'd seen in northern Texas drifted across his mind. A ranch to call his own . . . yes, that would be nice. So why didn't he just quit this business and stake his claim?

Paden ruefully shook his head. He knew the reason. As always, another Pinkerton assignment would come his way and keep him busy. Too busy to dream. But it was time to settle down. Paden sensed it now as never before. He had to quit this line of work before he caught a bullet in his back. Tonight one of the gamblers recognized him as the former sheriff of Silverstone. Word would soon spread that he was in town, and if anyone besides San Francisco's chief of police knew he worked for Pinkerton, he'd be a walking target.

Lord, not only do I need a new job, Paden added to his prayer, *I need Your protection.*

❧

"How did your, um, meeting go tonight?"

Angie stepped into the foyer and smiled at her stepsister, knowing Veronica didn't approve of her ministry at the brothels, but she could hardly expect a more positive response since Veronica wasn't a Christian. Very simply, she didn't understand Angie's occasional visits to the worst part of town for the purpose of sharing God's Word.

"My meeting went very well," Angie replied, her smile broadening. "One of the working girls accepted Christ." She hung up her wrap, wrinkling her nose at the pungent smell of cigar smoke. She'd have to be sure to air her clothing.

"Who was the gentleman who saw you home tonight?"

"That was Paden Montano," Angie said, walking into the parlor. "Do you recall me speaking about him and Pastor Luke in Silverstone? They were the two men who helped me escape."

Veronica gasped and touched the cameo brooch pinned at the high neckline of her coral silk gown. "You don't say? He wasn't at one of those houses of ill-fame, now was he?"

"No, he . . . well, I'm not really sure what he was doing in that part of town tonight. In any event, Paden is no longer a sheriff and he's in San Francisco on business."

"Paden? Hm . . . I see." Wearing a troubled expression, Veronica smoothed back a lock of her honey-brown hair. "Do you think he'll keep quiet about your . . . your identity? I mean, he knows your past, Angelique," she stammered. "Do you think he'll spread it around the city and start a scandal?"

At the mere idea, a stream of terror coursed through Angie's veins. The one thing she feared above all else was that her past would somehow become public knowledge. "Paden won't say a word," Angie finally answered, praying it was so. "He's on my side. He helped me leave the sordid life I led. Besides, he's a Christian now."

"Yes, well, many a Christian has fallen from grace, if you know what I mean. Take my late husband, for example, the scoundrel." She blew out a derisive breath, then lifted a questioning brow. "Are you certain Mr. Montano can be trusted?"

"I'm as certain as I can be."

Veronica looked none too convinced; however, she didn't press the issue. "Would you care for some tea, Darling? And . . . oh! you simply must see the new pattern book I bought."

Angie nodded. "But first I'd like to change into something more comfortable. It's raining. . . ."

"Of course."

After a parting smile, Angie took the steps to her second-floor bedroom. The anxious knot in her chest began to loosen. She had nothing to fear from Paden Montano.

Or did she?

2

*A*ngie reverently slid her fingertips across the raspberry-colored silk lying on the long working table. "Beautiful," she whispered.

"Isn't that the most incredible fabric you've ever seen?" Veronica asked from across the shop.

"Most certainly." Angie unrolled several lengths from the bolt and held it under her chin. "I believe I'd like a dress of this color. Can't you just see a polonaise trimmed with a cream eyelet?"

"Oh, splendid, Angelique. Simply splendid."

Angie smiled, mentally creating the fitted bodice and cutaway skirt that would be worn over a matching underskirt. The polonaise would indeed be, as her stepsister said, "splendid."

Glancing around the shop, Angie's heart swelled with gratitude. God had been especially good in blessing her with this partnership. Veronica was the businesswoman and Angie the dressmaker. Together they were a successful team, serving only San Francisco's elite.

Against the far wall hung gowns in different sizes and a rainbow of colors—all Angie's handiwork. Women's "delicates" were kept in the back room and out of the sight of any gentleman who might step into the boutique, looking for a gift, like a lace handkerchief, an exquisite shawl, or a silk scarf for the woman in his life. Of course, Angie kept busy with special orders, too, such as trousseaus.

She refolded the pinkish-red cloth and pivoted. At the other end of the store, near the front door, stood a round, polished oak table bearing several pattern books. Two comfortable armchairs were positioned beside it. Presently, Veronica busied herself with straightening the ivory lace curtains that framed the plate window. She glanced out-side before looking over her shoulder at Angie. "Here he comes."

"Who?" Angie frowned. "You don't mean Captain Witherspoon."

"The very one. He's heading straight for our shop."

"Oh, my. . . ."

Angie's heart began to flutter in anxious excitement. Captain Gar-rett Witherspoon could turn any woman's head. He turned Angie's. Tall, broad-shouldered, with thick brown hair and serious hazel eyes, he made a handsome sight. Coupled with the fact that he was a capa-ble sailor who traveled the world over, he proved an interesting conversationalist—one whom Angie could listen to for hours. Best of all, Garrett professed Christ and said he came from a long line of En-glish believers who had immigrated to Maine after the Revolutionary War. Someday, he had told Angie, he meant to settle down on his fam-ily's land near the Atlantic. After he'd spoken those words, a certain light had entered his greenish-brown gaze, one that let Angie know the good captain had intentions of settling down with *her!*

But therein lay the problem, not that Angie wouldn't mind be-coming Mrs. Garrett Witherspoon one day; however, she feared his family would somehow discover her less than pristine background. Most of all, what would Garrett say when he found out he'd married his own Mary Magdalene? Would he understand? Would he love her all the more for it? Or would he eye her with contempt for the rest of their wedded days?

Angie knew she should tell him about her past herself, but a knot seemed to lodge in her heart each time she considered it. What would she ever do if Garrett ended his pursuit of her and sullied her reputa-tion around San Francisco—or around the world? She'd be ruined a second time in her twenty-five years. Once had been enough. It would be far better to forestall their budding romance now.

"Shall I make your excuses?" Veronica asked as if divining Angie's tumultuous thoughts.

"Yes, perhaps you should."

With that, Angie made her way into the back room where she touched her finger to her lips, motioning Mr. Lee, their hired Chinese security aid, to silence. He nodded agreeably and, once she felt satisfied that he wouldn't give away her whereabouts, Angie poured a cup of tea. When the tiny bell on the front door jangled, she strained to listen to the conversation between Garrett and her stepsister.

"Why, Captain, how nice to see you again."

"Thank you, Mrs. Huntington," came the resonant reply. "I wondered if Angelique is here."

"I'm sorry, but you just missed her."

"What a shame."

There was no mistaking the disappointment in Garrett's voice, and remorse filled Angie's being. She hated having any part of deceit. Moreover, she longed to have a husband and children someday, but it seemed her dream would never come true—not with her kind of history.

"I purchased four tickets to the theater tonight. There's a reception afterward, and I had hoped Angelique would accompany me. You, too, Mrs. Huntington . . . along with a cousin of mine. He just arrived in town."

"He?" Angie heard Veronica's chuckle of discomfiture. "Well, I . . . I don't know. That is, I don't care to be socially thrust into the company of a man whom I've never met."

"Pardon me, Madam, but I meant no such thing. I simply thought it would make for a pleasant evening."

"Hm . . . and what performance is it?"

"Shakespeare's *Twelfth Night*."

"Really? I adore Shakespearean comedies."

Angie nearly dropped her porcelain teacup. Was Veronica actually considering Garrett's offer?

Peeking out the curtained doorway, she saw the back of Garrett's wide shoulders beneath his navy blue wool coat as well as Veronica's contemplative expression. In truth, Angie had always thought her stepsister would make a perfect match for the dashing sea captain. Veronica's delicate, creamy features seemed to compliment Garrett's masculine ones; she was every bit as comely as he was handsome.

"I suppose we could accompany you and your cousin to the theater after all," Veronica stated at last, much to Angie's chagrin. She didn't want to go. The more time she spent around the captain, the more she fostered a hope in her heart that would likely end in tragedy. *Romeo and Juliet might be a more fitting production for this evening,* she thought wryly.

Veronica cleared her throat. "I'll inform Angelique. I'm sure she'll be thrilled."

"I'm hoping so," Garrett replied, and Angie noted the optimism in his tone. "We'll be by to collect you ladies around six o'clock this evening."

"Angelique and I shall be waiting."

When the bell on the door signaled Garrett's departure, Angie reentered the shop. "Sister dear, what have you done?" she asked Veronica, feeling miffed. "Seems it didn't do me a lick of good to conceal my presence."

"Oh, now, don't be cross. It's just one night, and we'll get to see *Twelfth Night* free of charge. Surely you can abide the captain's company one last time." She sighed, sounding weary. "And I will have to tolerate his cousin . . . whomever that may be. I sincerely hope he's not some blackguard."

Quietly, Angie resumed her work, knowing her stepsister could spot a blackguard a mile away. Veronica's late husband had fit the bill. Angie was just too glad that Sergeant William Huntington—Billy, to most—had passed by the time she arrived in San Francisco. Not that she wished death on anyone—especially if he wasn't a believer. Simply, she'd known too many blackguards in her life to ever want to meet another.

❧

Paden couldn't help the sardonic smile that curved his lips when his cousin began describing the woman in whom he was romantically interested. She was none other than Angie Brown, also known as Angelique Huntington. Smoothing down the corners of his mustache, Paden decided this could prove to be a most uncomfortable evening since it seemed Garrett knew nothing of Angie's past.

"If she agrees to marry me," he continued, "I hope to set sail at the end of the month—with Angelique on board. I hope to beat the bad weather and make it home by Thanksgiving."

"*Sí*, I hope all turns out well for you."

"I believe Mother will take to her immediately," Garrett stated confidently before grinning at Paden from across the carriage. "You'll see. Angelique is a sweet, Christian woman. She needs a man like me to protect her."

Paden inclined his head politely, wondering if his cousin knew anything about Angie's ministry at the brothels. It seemed she could hold her own if circumstances ever warranted it. However, Paden meant to speak with Angie about her venturing into that iniquitous part of town alone. She had to stop it before she got herself killed . . . or worse.

The carriage pulled to a halt in front of the Huntington ladies' narrow clapboard house with its ornamental gingerbread trim. Paden recognized the place from when he had seen Angie home safely several nights ago. Since it seemed important to Angie, he'd meant to pay her a call and meet her sister; but in his pursuit of Harry Munson, a gunman who'd been riding with the James Gang back in Missouri, Paden had been too preoccupied for socializing.

And then he'd met up with his cousin on his mother's side: Garrett Witherspoon.

Paden's mother had been reared in an aristocratic home. Her father, Paden's grandfather, was an eccentric with interests in Mexico and on one of his many journeys there, he'd taken along his lovely daughter, who wound up falling hopelessly in love with a vaquero named Alonso Montano. Despite her father's protests, Kathleen married the charming vaquero. Paden and his four sisters were the result of their union. While the Witherspoon family conceded the marriage, it never fully accepted Paden and his father into the fold. Nonetheless, Paden and Garrett became boyhood pals during the summers when Kathleen made the long trek from Mexico to Maine to see her relatives. The last time Paden had seen Garry was at the end of this country's Civil War. They'd both enlisted with the Union.

Walking up to the porch, Garrett knocked soundly at the front door. A pretty lady with honey-brown hair and who wore a stunning lavender gown answered. She then beckoned them inside.

"Goodness, but it's cool tonight," she said, making light conversation as the men entered.

"Yes, Ma'am," Garrett replied. Then he began making the introductions. "Mrs. Veronica Huntington, allow me to introduce my cousin, Paden Montano."

"A pleasure to meet you," he said, bowing courteously. He noticed the woman's slight frown of confusion.

"Paden Montano?"

"*Sí, señora.*"

Before another word could be uttered, Angie entered the parlor, looking more beautiful than any woman had a right to. Her golden-blond hair was swept up and pinned in back with tiny ringlets hanging behind one ear. She wore a deep blue dress, which accentuated her indigo eyes, and Paden felt momentarily awestruck—until he watched Garrett stroll to her side and usher her forward. Then reality set in. Angie would soon be betrothed to a member of the Witherspoon family.

"Angelique, I should like you to meet my cousin," he said, making the introduction.

Surprise entered Angie's gaze, then she paled visibly. "Your cousin?"

Paden stifled a laugh at her horrified expression. "Miz Huntington," he said with another mannerly bow, "I'm pleased to meet you." The latter he stated emphatically so she'd understand that he had not betrayed her confidence.

She relaxed somewhat, glancing from Paden to Garrett and back to Paden again. "You're . . . related? Cousins?"

"We sure are," Garrett said, with a friendly clap on Paden's shoulder. "But our family's genealogy will have to wait. If we don't hurry, we'll miss the curtain call."

Paden gave Angie an assured wink before offering his arm to a mystified Veronica. This evening would prove to be very interesting, he decided. Very interesting, indeed.

3

*P*aden was aware of Angie's troubled expression throughout the play and even afterward as the four of them sat around a small table in the opulent lobby of the theater, sipping punch and enjoying some cake. He noticed Angie didn't touch her dessert.

"Now, tell me again," Veronica said, "how are you two related?"

"We're cousins," Garrett explained. "My father and Paden's mother are siblings."

"You don't look alike." Veronica studied each man's facial features.

"Very true," Garrett answered once more. "I suppose that's because Paden resembles his father, and I resemble my mother."

"Reason enough," she said lightly, giving Angie a quick glance. Then she turned to Paden. "I understand you're in San Francisco on business."

"*Sí,* that is correct."

"What sort of business are you in?"

"That's the million-dollar question," Garrett said laughingly. "No one really knows what Paden does for a living." His hazel eyes were bright with curiosity. "Some say he works for the Mexican government. Some say he works for the United States federal government. Others believe he's a bounty hunter."

"Goodness! You're quite the mystery man, aren't you, Mr. Montano?" Wearing an amused grin, Veronica looked at Garrett. "Which do you think it is, Captain?"

"Knowing my cousin, I'd say he works for whoever is paying him the largest salary. But given that Paden is a Christian now, I'm less likely to believe the bounty hunter theory."

"And you are correct. I am not a bounty hunter," Paden replied, chuckling over all the conjecture. However, he didn't offer up further explanations. Gazing across the table, he noted that Angie hadn't even cracked a smile, but peered forlornly into her glass of fruit punch.

Garrett was obviously aware of his lovely escort's dampened spirits also, and a frown of concern furrowed his brows. He shifted in his chair, appearing uncomfortable. "Perhaps it's time to call it a night. I think these dear ladies are tired."

"I believe you're right," Paden said.

The men stood. Angie and Veronica rose as well. Then Garrett offered to fetch their wraps.

Once he was out of earshot, Paden gave Angie his full attention. "Why the long face tonight? Did you not enjoy the comedy?"

She met his gaze, her eyes searching his. "How can you ask me such a question?"

"I beg your pardon?"

Veronica cleared her throat. "You have to admit, Mr. Montano, your arrival in San Francisco is quite uncanny. I'm sure if I were Angelique, I would be wondering if you came to town to warn your cousin of her past."

"Warn my cousin?" As soon as Paden grasped her meaning, he shook his head. "No, no, no. You are mistaken. Both of you." Looking at Angie once more, he added, "My cousin and I met each other by chance, I assure you. Furthermore, Garrett has no idea you and I ever met before."

Angie merely shrugged. "Well, it doesn't matter anyway."

Paden narrowed his gaze, wondering over her reply.

"Come along, Dear," Veronica said, slipping a protective arm around Angie's shoulder. She led her through the waning crowd and toward the coat check where Garrett still stood in line.

Paden marveled in their wake. Suddenly, trailing an unscrupulous outlaw from state to state seemed an easier task than figuring out a woman's mind.

Angie couldn't sleep, so she felt grateful for Veronica's company as well as the chamomile tea steeping in the floral-patterned, porcelain teapot.

"Do you think Mr. Montano was lying when he said he didn't mention your past to the captain?" Veronica queried as she poured the fragrant brew.

Angie took the proffered teacup and saucer. "I've never known Paden to lie."

"Well, then, what's to fret about?"

"Nothing . . . everything!" Frustrated, Angie stood and began pacing the rose-papered room. "Oh, Veronica, I wish I didn't have to wear a mask and hope and pray that no one will find out about the woman beneath it—the woman with the despicable past."

Her stepsister gave her a sympathetic grin. "Worrying can't change a thing, so sit back down and drink some tea. After a good night's sleep, you'll feel better."

"But don't you see? Garrett is sure to propose marriage any day now. I'd love to accept, have children, live happily ever after."

"That could never happen," Veronica stated with an emphatic shake of her head. "The happily ever after part, I mean. You don't love Garrett Witherspoon."

"I love him as much as I could love any man."

"Nonsense. You're better off without him."

"But—"

"Angelique, I know what I'm saying. Marriage is . . . constraining."

"Not for Christians. You should hear how my pastor preaches on wedded bliss."

"If his wife preached on the subject, I might listen."

Veronica sipped her tea while Angie took her place in the parlor chair once more and then lifted her porcelain cup to her lips.

"You know, he is quite handsome, not to mention very charming."

"Who?" Angie asked. "Garrett?"

"No, no . . . Montano."

"Paden?"

"*Sí, senorita,*" Veronica quipped.

Angie swept her gaze upward.

"He's got a very straight, aristocratic nose, and his dark eyes don't seem to miss a thing." A faraway expression crossed her face. "When he looked at me, Angelique, it was as if he could see right into my soul."

"Don't be silly."

Veronica snapped from her musing. "Silly? Is that what you called me?" She shook her honey-brown head. "I'm extremely serious. Come now, admit he's attractive."

Angie couldn't lie. "All right. I admit it. He's a nice-looking man. But he's also very rugged, accustomed to wild places. He's had to be, living in the Arizona Territory all those years. Moreover, Paden Montano is a famed gunman."

Veronica leaned forward. "How many people do you think he's killed?"

"I'm sure I wouldn't know!" Angie frowned at her stepsister's curiosity. "You're not . . . interested romantically in Paden . . . are you?"

"Of course not." Veronica moved to pour herself another cup of tea. "I lived with one cruel man already, and I'm certainly not going to get myself involved with another."

Angie mulled over the reply. "Just for the record, I don't believe Paden is cruel," she stated at last. "He might not be the marrying kind, but he's not anything like your late husband. From what you've described, that man was downright mean."

"That's putting it mildly." Veronica paused, looking pensive. "May I ask you something extremely personal?"

Angie thought it over, deciding there wasn't much about her life, past or present, that her stepsister didn't already know. "Of course," she replied at last.

"Was Mr. Montano ever one of your, um, customers back in Silverstone?"

"No, never." Unbidden memories surfaced and Angie recalled the handsome, much sought after sheriff. Chicago Joe's girls had literally fought over him whenever he entered the brothel, although Paden often had a strong drink and a good card game on his mind, much to the prostitutes' disappointment.

Veronica replied with a dignified, "Hmph. I'm glad to hear it. I'd hate to think he was *that* kind of man."

"Even if he was, that part of his life is over now," Angie said. "Just as God delivered me from that horrible pit and miry clay, he saved Silverstone's former lawman. Paden said he's a Christian and, although I haven't had a chance to talk to him about it, I don't doubt his word."

"A Christian?" Veronica lifted her shoulders noncommittally. "Well, I suppose religion helps some people along." She sipped her tea, looking pensive. "You know, I'll never forget my first sight of you, standing on my doorstep, looking like a half-drowned kitten."

"I am forever indebted to you for taking me in," Angie stated sincerely.

"Indebted? Hardly. You proved yourself worthy of my attention and my home, and now we operate a thriving business together. We're friends. More than friends, we're sisters. And we're happy."

"Yes, we are . . . happy." Forging a smile, Angie brought the teacup to her lips. She felt like a hypocrite, for the hollowness in her heart didn't mirror the placid words she'd just spoken.

She wasn't truly happy. She wanted more. She yearned for a husband to cherish and protect her. She longed for a baby to cradle in her arms, a child to nurture and love.

And the only way she'd ever attain her desires was if she married Captain Garrett Witherspoon!

4

"   ngie!"

Hearing her name, she stopped on the boardwalk in front of an apothecary. She knew who had called her even before she turned around since no one in San Francisco called her "Angie."

"Good afternoon, Mr. Montano," she said in feigned formality. She still couldn't get over how different he looked without his long hair tied back at his nape with a leather band. In Silverstone, folks often remarked that Paden Montano could double as an Apache. But today, dressed in dark trousers, vest, white shirt, and black jacket, he appeared quite the refined gentleman—just as he had last night.

Holding his wide-brimmed hat in one hand, Paden grinned and gave her a courteous bow. All the while he eyed her closely, and Angie suddenly recalled what Veronica had said: *When he looked at me, Angelique, it was as if he could see right into my soul.* Yes, Paden definitely had that effect on a person.

"I wondered if I might have a few words with you," he told her now.

"Well, I am on my way to the bank—"

"May I accompany you?"

Angie shrugged. "If you'd like."

She began walking and Paden easily fell into step beside her. "You did not enjoy yourself last night," he began. "I have been wondering why."

"It's a long story, one I'm sure you don't have time for."

"On the contrary, I would like to hear it."

Angie paused in front of the bank. "Why?"

A softness entered Paden's dark eyes. "I care about you. I have

469

what you might call a vested interest in your life, both because I helped you escape from Silverstone and because my cousin plans to make you his wife." When she inhaled sharply, Paden added, "That should not come as any surprise to you."

"I'm not surprised . . . exactly. I simply didn't expect you to be so frank."

Angie glanced around nervously, hoping passersby couldn't overhear their conversation. Just across the street, she spied one of the "mud hens," a name given to women who gambled in mining stocks and who had lost all their money. Destitute, they begged coins off the more affluent who did their business in the city's financial district, but then they gambled away their handouts. A pathetic station in life, yet Angie knew the Lord could deliver any of those poor souls. Just as He had delivered her.

Angie swung her gaze back to Paden. "You don't think I'm good enough to marry Garrett, is that it?"

"I never said that." He shook his head in obvious disappointment. "Do your banking, *mi amada,* and when you are finished, we will sit down and discuss this matter over refreshments."

"I need to get back to the dress shop."

"I think we will talk first."

Angie opened her mouth to argue, but the severe expression on Paden's face made for a change of heart. "I'll be back shortly," she said.

"*Sí,* I will be waiting."

Inside the stately, red brick building with its ceramic-tiled floors and mahogany-paneled walls, Angie headed for the teller window. She'd nearly reached it when Mr. Rosewahl, the bank's president, caught her by the elbow.

"Did that man accost you, Miss Huntington?" he asked indignantly. Although he dressed impeccably, the man always reminded Angie of a large, balding bird. "I can summon the authorities if you wish."

"Excuse me?" she asked, frowning her confusion.

"That Mexican. Outside. Did he harass you in any way?"

Giving him a reassuring smile, Angie shook her head. "That's

Paden Montano. He's an acquaintance of mine, and he happens to be Captain Garrett Witherspoon's cousin."

"You don't say. . . ." Mr. Rosewahl's hawklike gaze darted to the shuttered window, opened just enough to reveal Paden's shadowy silhouette. "Montano, eh?"

"Yes, that's correct."

Mr. Rosewahl looked back at Angie. "Well, then, I guess there aren't any problems to report."

"No, Sir."

With a polite, parting smile, Angie walked the rest of the way to the window, where she made her deposit. Once the task was completed, she rejoined Paden on the boardwalk. "There's a small café up the street," she suggested. "We could talk there. I know Mrs. Tibbles serves up a fine cup of tea."

"Tea?" Paden arched dubious brows.

"Or a good, strong cup of coffee."

"*Sí,* that is more like it."

As they strolled amicably, side-by-side, Angie judged Paden's height to be no more than a few inches taller than her own five feet three inches. Garrett stood at least six feet. Regardless, Paden Montano seemed to exude the more commanding presence, even though his cousin governed numerous bawdy crewmen during his voyages. Mentally shaking herself, Angie wondered why she was even comparing the two men.

After they'd entered the café, Paden chose a quiet corner table in the far end of the sparsely occupied establishment. Preparing to seat himself, he unbuttoned his jacket, and Angie glimpsed the wide gunbelt strapped around his waist. Once more she questioned his occupation, mulling over the choices Garrett had listed last night. Employed with either the Mexican or American government? A bounty hunter?

"So what exactly is your business, Paden?" Angie couldn't help asking.

He grinned wryly. "What do you think?"

Mrs. Tibbles's youngest daughter, Susan, a brunette with unmanageable curls tucked beneath a white scarf, came over and took their orders. Then she strolled off in the direction of the kitchen.

"I think maybe you work for the army."

"I used to."

Angie felt herself grow frustrated. "Well, unless you tell me," she challenged, "I refuse to speak to you, and we can just sit here and drink our beverages in silence."

He sniffed loudly and appeared as though he were trying not to chuckle, which made Angie all the more irritated.

Susan reappeared, set down Paden's coffee and Angie's tea, then departed.

"I can't say I mind my *silent* view," Paden said emphatically, stirring sugar into his brew. "I think I could gaze at you for hours, Angie. You've become a very beautiful woman. My cousin is a lucky man."

Angie's face warmed with embarrassment.

"Which brings me to the reason I wanted to speak with you today."

Chagrin gave way to acquiescence. "Oh, fine. What is it you'd like to know?"

"It is more like what I want you to know. I have no intentions of betraying your confidence." He lowered his voice until it was but a whisper. "I will take the secret of your past to my grave."

"How comforting," she quipped.

Looking amused, he took a long drink of his coffee.

"But the fact of the matter is, Garrett is entitled to know before he . . . he marries me."

"True. But you must be the one to tell him."

"You make it sound so simple," Angie said, tasting the bitterness of her words. She gazed into her teacup for several long moments before looking back at Paden. "How do you think Garrett will react when he discovers the news?"

"That I cannot say."

"He's your cousin. Can't you give me some idea?" She closed her eyes as several anguished heartbeats elapsed. "Paden," she began again, "what is the Witherspoon family like? Will they accept me, knowing who I am? What I was?"

"They do not have to know. This matter is between you and Garrett. Although," he added, wearing a pensive frown, "my aunt Mary will probably want you investigated."

Angie groaned.

"But take heart," Paden stated lightly, "perhaps she will hire me to do the detective work."

Angie narrowed her gaze. "You're a . . . a detective?"

"*Sí,* I am a Pinkerton agent. But I trust you will keep my secret just as I have promised to keep yours."

She nodded, oddly impressed by the admission.

"I'm here in San Francisco searching for a renegade, but I do not want the fact uncovered just yet—for obvious reasons."

"I understand. I won't say a word. Not even to Veronica."

"*Gracias.*"

"Now, back to my question about the Witherspoon family . . ."

Angie took a deep stifling breath. "Do you think I'll fit in?"

"Surely my cousin has told you about his family."

"Yes. . . ."

"So the question is, do *you* think you'll fit in?"

"I . . . I don't know." She expelled a deep sigh. "I seem to vacillate on the subject. Perhaps I should abandon the idea of marrying Garrett altogether."

"You give up so easily. Isn't your love for my cousin worth braving a few patricians?"

"My love for him?"

"*Sí.*" Paden eyed her quizzically, causing Angie to look away and concentrate on her tea. "You don't love him?"

"Well, I . . . I like him very much," she said. Then suddenly she wanted to share her innermost thoughts with Paden. She had to unburden herself to someone and Veronica certainly wasn't any help. Besides, Angie felt certain she could safely confide in the ruggedly handsome man sitting across from her. After all, they were already keeping each other's secrets. What was one more? "I'm sure after we're married I'll love him. He's a Christian. He'll provide a comfortable lifestyle for me. He's everything a woman could want in a man. Surely, love will come."

"That is a big gamble."

"Yes, but how can I possibly lose?"

~&

As Paden drank his coffee and listened to Angie's faulty reasoning for marrying Garrett, he couldn't help feeling oddly hopeful. Last night he'd lain awake in bed, staring at the darkened hotel room's ceiling. All he could think about was Miss Angie Brown—that is, Miss Angelique Huntington.

Back in Silverstone, he'd sensed something special about the disheveled girl with haunted, blue eyes. She had stood apart from the other hardened females at Chicago Joe's—which was one of the reasons he willingly risked his life to help Angie escape from that profane lifestyle. Seeing her transformation, he knew the venture had been worth it. Except, he'd seen traces of that same futility in her gaze last night, and it disturbed him enough to lose precious hours of sleep. This morning, he felt strongly that he had to speak with her. Perhaps it had been spawned from sheer male pride, but Paden had wanted to be the one to rescue her once more.

This time, from a loveless marriage.

He listened as Angie admitted to wanting a husband, a family. She told him how in the past few years, God had healed her heart, her soul, and her mind. She now knew that not all men were lascivious creatures, and through several Bible studies, she'd learned the difference between fornication and the act of intimacy after marriage. However, Angie did not come out and directly state the latter. Rather, her face turned a pretty shade of crimson as she stammered out her meaning. Even so, Paden got the gist of it.

"I'm so embarrassed," she murmured. "I mean . . . bringing up that subject."

He gave her a patient smile. "If you were not blushing, I would not believe that the Lord restored your spirit. But I can see He has."

Angie looked relieved. "Nevertheless, Garrett deserves to hear the truth."

"I agree. So what's stopping you from telling him?"

"Fear, even though I know God doesn't give us the spirit of fear. Still, I can't seem to help it." Angie finished her tea. "What if Garrett spurns me and divulges my past to others, leaving me scandalized?"

"And you believe he might do that?"

"I don't know. I guess it all boils down to trust, doesn't it?" she said at last.

Paden nodded.

"I never realized it before, but I guess I'm afraid to trust Garrett."

"And trust is the cornerstone of a happy marriage, is it not?"

Angie arched a golden brow. "How'd you ever become so wise on the subject?"

Chuckling, Paden fingered his mustache. "I watched my parents. Never have two people loved each other more than my mother and father."

"That's really nice," she said, looking so misty, it caused Paden to wish he could pull her into his arms, soothe her fears and worries, and replace them with—

He shook himself mentally. What in the world was he thinking? It was one thing to save a woman from marrying the wrong man, and quite the other to step in as the groom.

He considered her, watching her strawberry pink lips as she spoke. Marry Angie. The idea was tremendously appealing. His past wouldn't frighten her, just as hers didn't shock him. Together they could make a life for themselves in Texas. Build a ranch. Settle down.

"Paden, did you hear me?"

He shook himself from his reverie. "I'm sorry. What did you say?"

"I said, I have to get back to the dress shop. Veronica will be wondering why I've been gone so long."

"Of course. Allow me to escort you."

"Thank you." She smiled, and Paden's insides warmed.

Dear God, what is wrong with me? he prayed as he paid for their beverages. He wasn't a man given to whimsical thinking. He was one who knew the cold, hard, even cruel realities of life. But, perhaps, it was time to do a little dreaming. And a little courting. True, he had courted a number of ladies in the past six years. Good, decent, pretty women, but none had the certain spunk he desired. He wanted a woman who would keep his life interesting, not bore him or nag him to an early grave. That woman was Angie. He could sense it. However, difficult as it may be, he had to stay out of the way until she made up her mind about Garrett—one way or the other.

"Paden?"

He started when Angie touched his arm. Then he noticed they stood in front of the Huntington House Dress Shop.

"You seem a million miles away," she said. "Is everything all right? Did I say something to offend you?"

"No," he assured her. He wanted to reach out and caress her cheek, feel its softness beneath his palm. Instead, he jammed his hands into his jacket pockets and resisted the urge. "I'm fine. Just thinking."

Angie's indigo eyes brightened. "If everything is all right, I guess I should get back to work. Thank you for listening to me babble on about my problems."

"It was my pleasure."

She smiled briefly before her expression changed to one of earnestness. "Garrett is coming to dinner tonight. Would you . . . would you come, too? I have a feeling he's going to propose, but with you there . . . well, it might buy me some time to pray about the situation further."

Paden thought it over and couldn't see any harm in it. "Thank you for the invitation. I would be happy to accept. What time, and where?"

"Our house and . . . about seven o'clock."

"I will be there."

5

$\mathcal{T}$he dinner table was lavishly outfitted with Veronica's best English dishes. White plates, bowls, platters, cups and saucers, having a rose motif and gold trim, added bits of color atop the pearly tablecloth. Beyond the dining room, in the kitchen, Tu Hing, the Chinese cook, busily prepared a scrumptious-smelling fare that caused Angie's stomach to rumble in anticipation.

"It's been quite awhile since we've entertained anyone other than the Ladies' Literary Society," Veronica stated, as she primped in front of the gilt-framed hall mirror. Dressed in a stylish, burgundy Gabrielle dress with white flounces, she ironically matched the rose-patterned wallpaper in the parlor and her exquisite dinnerware.

Angie grinned. "I hope you don't mind that I invited Paden."

"Not at all. In fact, it'll give me someone to talk to while you and Captain Witherspoon ogle each other."

"We do not 'ogle.' At least, I don't."

Veronica swung away from the mirror. "No, I don't suppose you do." She sighed. "Why haven't you severed this relationship, Angelique? Nothing will come of it. You said, yourself, the captain isn't likely to sympathize with your past. Why are you wasting your time . . . and his? There's no use in leading the poor man on."

Disappointment flooded Angie's being. Her stepsister's words rang true; unfortunately, Angie didn't feel quite ready to give up her dream of having a family of her own. "I . . . I'm still praying about . . . things," she stammered.

Veronica gave her a quelling look. "Angelique, I have protected you all these years. Remember the young banker who began calling on you? I put an end to that, now didn't I?"

"Yes, but that was different. Archie wasn't the man for me."

"And what about Mr. Morgan, the tailor?"

Angie wrinkled her nose in distaste. He hadn't attracted her in the least bit.

"And Mr. Parsons, Mr. Jensen, Mr. Smith . . ." Veronica counted the names on her long, tapered fingers. "Mr. Santiago, and that poor widower with all those smudge-faced brats . . ."

"I thought he rather preferred you, sister dear," Angie teased.

Veronica rolled her eyes, seemingly appalled. "My point is this—I have spared you numerous times from making a terrible mistake."

"Perhaps, but I wasn't interested in any of those other men."

"But you're interested in the captain? Still?"

Angie felt herself blush as she shrugged out a reply.

"Aren't you the least bit concerned that you'll return to your wanton ways if you're ever intimate with another man?" Veronica asked pointedly. "It's a sickness, you know."

Angie gulped down the sudden lump of revulsion rising in her throat. "No, Veronica, it's not a sickness. Not for me, anyway. What began as a state of hopelessness became a lifestyle of sin. I thought I was nothing. Nobody. I thought it was my fault your father, my stepfather, abused me after my mother died. But then a sweet little Christian schoolteacher by the name of Bethany Stafford showed me differently." Angie's voice softened, and she had to smile as she recalled her conversion experience. "Bethany said God loved me, that He created me before the beginning of time, and that He wanted me to be His child. All I had to do was—"

"Yes, yes, I've heard the rest before. You found religion." Strolling into the parlor, Veronica tossed an impatient glance over her shoulder. "For the record, my father was almost as despicable as my late husband."

Angie closed her eyes in a moment's anguish, wondering how that could be possible.

"So you see, we've both been brutalized by men. We're better off committing our lives to each other and our dress shop rather than husbands. Although, I must admit," Veronica added, peeking around the gauzy sheers and out the front window, "it is rather pleasant to be in the company of a handsome face now and then." Straightening, she looked across the room at Angie. "But the secret to happiness is remaining unmarried."

Angie nibbled her lower lip in consternation. Could her stepsister really be correct?

❧

"What are you doing here?"

Stepping up beside him on the Huntington ladies' front porch, Paden gave his cousin a sardonic grin. "I was invited."

"Oh? And might I presume Mrs. Huntington did the inviting?" Garrett asked with a conspiratorial nudge of his elbow. "She's a lovely widow, in spite of her audacious streak. Unfortunately, she's not a Christian."

"God saw fit to save me," Paden replied, "He can save anyone."

Garrett rapped on the heavy, oak door and grinned. "I can't argue with you there."

Moments later, Angie appeared in the entryway, bidding them welcome. One look at her, dressed in a lilac-colored gown, her blond hair tied back with violet ribbons, and Paden felt his mouth go dry. Next he watched in a mixture of awe and envy as his cousin took Angie's proffered hand and placed a light kiss on her fingertips.

"You're as enchanting as always, Angelique."

"You're too kind."

A blush crept up her cheeks before she glanced at Paden. He inclined his head politely.

Angie smiled. "Well, come in. Both of you. Come in."

Paden followed his cousin through the doorway and then, after Angie took their overcoats, he trailed Garrett into the parlor. There they found Veronica perched comfortably on the settee.

She smiled a greeting. "Would either of you care for a small glass of wine before dinner?"

Both men politely refused the offer. Making his way to an upholstered armchair, Paden took a seat, leaving the matching armchair for Garrett and the other half of the settee for Angie; but as it happened,

Angie strolled into the room and claimed the armchair. Still standing, Garrett rubbed his jaw in uncertainty.

"Lovely weather we're having," Angie began, smoothing her satiny skirts.

"Quite." Veronica appeared amused as she obviously noted Garrett's predicament.

Paden wanted to chuckle and he almost felt sorry for his cousin. Next, he decided that in spite of her impure past, there was still an element of naiveté about Angie. Obviously the Lord had restored that quality along with her soul.

Veronica cleared her throat. "Angelique, Dear . . ." She patted the place beside her.

After a frown of confusion and a glance at Garrett, Angie's cheeks turned a lovely shade of scarlet. This time Paden couldn't contain his amusement.

"I'm so sorry, Garrett," Angie gushed as she stood. "I don't know what I was thinking. I guess I wasn't thinking at all."

"It's been a long day," Veronica said. "We were very busy at the shop this afternoon."

"Well, then, this invitation to dine with the two of you is doubly appreciated," Garrett remarked, sitting in the armchair now.

"We love to entertain, don't we, Angelique? Why, we were discussing the very subject just moments before your arrival. Isn't that right?"

Paden watched Angie nod beneath Veronica's pointed stare. Then a few moments of weighted silence passed, marked by the slow ticking of the grandfather clock, poised in the corner of the parlor.

"Captain, when do you next set sail?" Veronica asked, breaking the uncomfortable lull.

"I hope to leave by the end of the month." He gazed at Angie with a longing in his eyes that Paden didn't miss.

She quickly looked away.

"I do hope you remember your promise to bring me some of that Oriental silk I've been hearing so much about," Veronica said.

"Oh, yes, Ma'am. That is, I'll bring you the fabric if I ever make the voyage to the Orient again. You see, I plan to sail back to Maine and spend some time with my family." Once more, Garrett's eyes lingered on Angie, although she kept her gaze riveted on her hands, folded neatly in her lap. She had undoubtedly grown uncomfortable with his unspoken solicitations.

Paden fingered his mustache and continued to gauge the situation. He found it curious that his cousin behaved like an infatuated schoolboy in Angie's presence when, in fact, he was known to make seasoned crewmen cower over their disobedience.

A Chinese man, wearing a starched, white apron over black apparel, suddenly appeared in the doorway. "Dinner is served," he announced with a polite bow.

"Thank you, Mr. Hing." Veronica stood and eyed her guests. "Shall we eat?"

❦

Picking at her fish, Angie inwardly cringed at the turn in the conversation. Veronica, in her usual probing manner, had begun to question Paden about his experiences in the Arizona Territory.

"I heard those Indians are savages!" Veronica declared, forking some fried rice into her mouth.

"Many are, but many are not," Paden answered.

"Personally, I would rather confront a hurricane than one of those murdering Indians," Garrett said. "I have heard horror stories from settlers and soldiers, alike. Some of the gruesome deaths they described are—"

"Are not for ladies' ears," Paden interjected.

Garrett had the good grace to look abashed. "My apologies, Angelique. Mrs. Huntington."

"Oh, don't worry. Angelique and I are made of sturdier stuff than that. Aren't we, Dear?"

She replied with a feeble nod.

"We read the *Chronicle* every day, you know," Veronica said from her place at one end of the table. "Besides, with all the riffraff in this city it's a wonder there are any decent citizens left at all. There are gambling dens by the dozens on the waterfront, and saloons, and bordellos. . . ."

Angie felt as though she might be sick.

"Of course, I've never been near any of those horrid establishments. I'll bet you didn't have to worry about such corruption in the Territory, did you, Mr. Montano?"

"On the contrary. We had our share of problems."

"Now, in what little town did you say you were sheriff?"

"Silverstone. Silverstone, Arizona."

"Yes, that's right," Veronica said, taking a sip of her tea. "It sounds like a mining town. What do you think, Angelique?"

She slid her gaze to Veronica's, wondering if her stepsister had gone mad. What could she possibly be thinking, bringing up Silverstone?

Tu Hing entered the dining room, carrying a carafe of coffee. Angie gave him a polite smile. She and Veronica never could get used to calling him by his first name, so they simply referred to him as Mr. Hing. She watched now as he dutifully filled the men's cups before retreating to the kitchen.

"Tell me, Mr. Montano, did you ever have any . . . adventures while you were sheriff?"

Paden grinned wryly. "*Sí,* I had a few." His eyes met Angie's from across the table and she saw pools of sympathy in their dark depths. Then he looked back at Veronica. "The territories are becoming famous for their *bandidos,* and several had the misfortune of straggling into my jurisdiction."

"Oooh, be still my heart," Veronica crooned, her hand fluttering to her chest. "If this were a novel, Mr. Montano, I'd just have to turn the page and read what comes next."

"Good thing it's real life," Angie muttered.

Sitting to Veronica's right, Garrett chuckled softly.

"Did you do anything heroic, Mr. Montano? Did you ever rescue anyone from danger?" Veronica asked emphatically.

Angie gasped, inhaling a sip of tea. Next, she proceeded to cough uncontrollably. Garrett was swift to come to her aid. When at last her choking subsided, she apologized to their guests before sending Veronica a warning glare. Her stepsister was treading on dangerous ground.

Veronica smiled back in feigned innocence. "Better now, Angelique?"

"Much," she stated, clearing her throat one last time. "Thank you."

Garrett reclaimed his chair. "Mrs. Huntington, I have a hunch Paden's life as Silverstone's sheriff was quite different than anything you might read in a dime novel."

"You think so?" Veronica turned her inquisitive, hazel eyes to Paden. "So no saving damsels in distress, hm?"

A slow smile spread across his face. "As a matter of fact, I can recall the rescue of one woman in particular."

Angie felt the blood draining from her face.

"Oh, do tell, Mr. Montano."

"She'd been captured by a band of Yuma," Angie heard Paden say over the anxiety roaring in her ears. "I had gotten to be on friendly terms with the Indians, and after three days, I managed to convince one of the braves to release the woman. She was then reunited with her husband and small children."

"How absolutely thrilling!" Veronica exclaimed. "Angelique, did you ever hear such a tale?"

"I'd rather not discuss it." Truth to tell, she'd heard sagas that would curl Veronica's honey-brown hair. But Angie would never subject her stepsister to such shocking accounts. She vehemently wished Veronica would cease her interrogation of Paden.

Lifting her linen napkin, Angie unwittingly dabbed her temples. They'd begun to throb.

"You're not coming down with one of your sick headaches, are you, Darling?" Veronica asked, her face a mask of concern.

"I'm all right."

"You do look a bit peaked," Garrett said with a troubled frown.

"Shall I get the laudanum?" Veronica asked sweetly.

Angie took several deep breaths. "I'm really fine," she assured everyone, but inside, she felt like sobbing. She hadn't escaped Silverstone; it still held her in bondage. What good was cultivating a new life if just below its surface lurked the demons from her past, ready to spring at any moment? Hadn't Veronica proved that much tonight?

"Miss Huntington?"

Paden's deep voice, spiked with its subtle Mexican accent, penetrated her tumultuous thoughts. She glanced at him expectantly.

"Perhaps a bit of air will do you some good."

"My cousin is right," Garrett said. He quickly rose from the table and helped Angie to her feet. "Some cool sea breezes will perk you right up, and I'm more than happy to accompany you. We'll stroll in the moonlight together."

Angie glimpsed the ardor shining in his brownish-green eyes and shuddered inwardly. If Garrett proposed, she knew she'd have to be completely honest with him. However, she didn't feel up to it. Not now. Not tonight. . . .

"A walk sounds pleasant enough to me," Paden said. "How about you, *Señora* Huntington?"

"Oh, well, I—"

"Good. Then it's settled." Paden pushed back his chair and stood. He grinned at Garrett's glowering countenance. "The four of us shall take a little moonlit stroll, *sí?*"

"*Sí,*" Angie replied quickly, a wave of relief pouring over her.

Making their way through the parlor, Angie paused near the front door to hand each gentleman his overcoat. As she gave Paden his, she managed to whisper, "You've been a veritable hero tonight. How will I ever thank you?"

Paden leaned forward and playfully chucked her under the chin. "Do not worry, my little *mariposa,*" he whispered back, "I will think of something."

6

The sun had long set when the group of four headed out on their stroll. Cool Pacific breezes blew wisps of Angie's hair onto her cheek and she brushed them backward. As they proceeded down one of San Francisco's many hilly, unpaved avenues, Angie gazed heavenward and found herself momentarily awestruck. The expanse of the dark sky was dotted with stars, reminding her of ivory sequins sewn onto endless yards of black velvet. *Lord,* she thought, *Your handiwork is perfect.*

Just then a passage in Psalm 8 came to mind. *"When I consider thy heavens, the work of thy fingers, the moon and the stars, which thou hast ordained; What is man, that thou art mindful of him?"*

And who am I, Angie wondered, *that the Creator of the universe would love me enough to die for my sins?*

"Fear not," came God's words from the first verse in Isaiah 43, *"for I have redeemed thee, I have called thee by thy name; thou art mine."*

I am God's, she marveled. *He called me by my name. He wanted me for His own. Me!*

It suddenly occurred to Angie that if she were good enough for God, she certainly ought to be good enough for the likes of Garrett Witherspoon. She looked at him askance, realizing he was explaining in great deal how sailors gauge the wind's velocity and how they rig up their sails accordingly.

Angie stifled a yawn.

"I have never been on a ship," Veronica said as they came up to a sandy knoll near the Golden Gate Park, which was still in the process of being developed. From their vantage point, they could see the crowded San Francisco Harbor. Beyond it was the strait called the

Golden Gate. Angie could vividly recall the trepidation and excitement she felt some six years ago as the ship bringing her to San Francisco cruised into the bay.

"I prefer to sail rather than travel by stage or even the railroad," Garrett declared.

"Really? I have only traveled on a miserable wagon train," Veronica said.

Lowering herself onto a large boulder, Angie listened as her stepsister and the captain discussed the advantages of journeying by boat.

Paden pointed to the place beside her on the rock. "May I?"

Angie nodded and scooted over to make more room for him.

The conversation between Garrett and Veronica continued.

"Would you like to know another secret?" Angie whispered to Paden. He turned his head and faced her. Beneath the moonlight, she saw him grin. "I get terribly seasick."

Paden's smile broadened. "Does my cousin know that?"

Angie shook her head.

"It's a long way from San Francisco to Maine."

"So I hear."

Paden chuckled.

"Do you get seasick?"

"No, but I get very bored. Nothing but sky and water to look at for days on end. The last time I sailed on a clipper, I was seventeen. I sailed to Maine with my mother to see her family."

"Did you and Garrett get along back then?"

"Oh, *sí,* we were *amigos* from the beginning. Garry and I spent many happy summers together, causing all sorts of mischief." Paden laughed softly. "But my grandfather, aunts and uncles, and several cousins did not like me because my father is Mexican. However, over the years, their hatred waned. Or I got used to it."

"Why did you keep going back if you knew your relatives didn't like you?"

"My father made me. You see, he didn't want my mother traveling all that distance alone."

"Oh, yes, of course. I can see the wisdom in his decision."

Angie looked over at Veronica and Garrett. They were still talking ships, masts, and now Veronica was asking about pirates. Angie sighed, wondering if it was such a good idea to share her novels with her stepsister. It seemed she took them far too seriously. Looking back at Paden, Angie asked, "You didn't have to go on a ship during your army days?"

"No. I was in the cavalry."

"Union?"

"*Sí.* I was twenty-three when I enlisted," he said wistfully. "I was naive and ready to take on the world."

"Twenty-three? I was only twelve." She tipped her head, considering him. "That would make you . . . thirty-six now?"

"Your arithmetic is very good, Miz Huntington," he quipped.

She smirked. "Paden Montano, how did you ever live to be thirty-six years old without getting married?"

He shifted his position on the rock and his shoulder brushed up against hers. "Like my cousin, I never found the right woman," he answered plainly. He paused before adding, "And don't think I haven't looked. Over the past several years, I've courted a number of proper, Christian women. But none sparked my interest . . . until recently."

Even in the darkness, Angie picked up something meaningful in his tone, his gaze. In a flash, she knew what it was. "Are you interested in Veronica?" she whispered.

Paden leaned forward so their noses touched. "No."

"Oh." Chagrined, Angie brought her head back.

He chuckled.

"But there is someone in whom you are interested, is that correct?"

"*Sí,* I think there is."

"Here in San Francisco?" Angie watched Paden's head nod. "Do I know her?"

"You are too inquisitive for your own good." Paden crossed one booted foot over his knee and leaned back farther, his hand on the rock, just behind Angie.

"I'm only asking because if I know her, I could tell you if she's worth pursuing."

"Oh, I know she is worth pursuing. She is a very special young lady." He leaned against her, playfully bumping her shoulder with his. "And I do not need a matchmaker, so don't even consider it."

Angie inhaled sharply. "I would never do such a thing!"

"Yes, you would. You're a woman. I have four sisters, so I know how you females think."

Angie folded her arms, lifting a defiant chin. Beside her, she heard another of Paden's chuckles. She bristled. "All right, Mr. Know-it-all, if I guess this woman's name, will you tell me if I'm right?"

Paden took several seconds to mull over the question. Finally, he agreed.

Angie searched her mind for the name of every unattached female she knew. There weren't many in San Francisco—decent women, anyway. Many bachelors in need of wives took to ordering them through the mail.

"Thelma Bobkins," Angie said.

"Never heard of her."

"Hmm . . . you can't possibly be interested in Mrs. Carlisle. Her husband passed last year, but she has to be at least fifty."

"No, not Mrs. Carlisle—whoever she is."

Angie was about to make another calculated assumption when Garrett interrupted their little game. "I think we should start heading back," he said. "The wind is picking up. Angelique, you should have told me you were freezing, sitting there on that cold, hard boulder."

"On the contrary, I'm quite comfortable, thank you."

Upon hearing Paden's discreet, little snort of amusement, she realized the folly of her remark. Since they'd been sitting so close together, Garrett obviously presumed she was huddling beside his cousin for warmth.

Angie quickly stood. "But, you're right, I do think it's time to get back."

"Yes." Garrett looked between the two of them before offering Angie his arm.

Slipping her hand around his elbow, she glanced at Veronica, whose expression said nothing as to how she might view the situation.

Angie decided to make it a point to ask later tonight, once their company departed.

The walk back seemed laden with tension. No one spoke, and Garrett kept up a lively pace, causing Angie to feel winded by the time they reached the house. On the front porch, he pulled her aside while Veronica and Paden went inside ahead of them.

"I must speak with you, Angelique."

"Tonight?"

"Yes. Right this minute."

Angie nibbled her lower lip indecisively. "Here? I'm freezing, remember?"

"Well, then, where? I have to talk to you . . . privately."

"How about tomorrow? No, it's Saturday and that will never do. Veronica and I have some orders to finish. How about Sunday after church?"

Garrett paused for a long moment, thinking it over.

"Surely whatever you have to discuss with me can wait until then," Angie added sweetly. "Can't it?"

His insistence dissolved before her very eyes. "Yes, I suppose you're right."

Angie smiled.

"We will both be in better frames of mind on Sunday, as you're shivering out here in the night air and I'm . . . well, I'm rather perturbed."

"Why is that?" She suspected the answer, but had to ask anyway.

To her dismay, he shrugged off her question. Then he surprised her further by whisking her into his muscled arms and kissing her soundly. Hard and possessively. When he released her, Angie stumbled backward. She touched her bruised mouth as tears gathered in her eyes. "How dare you treat me like that," she choked.

Garrett's reason quickly returned. "Angelique, I'm so sorry. . . ."

She barely heard the apology as she made for the door. She fumbled with the latch, but it soon opened and she ran into the house.

"Angelique, please—"

She ignored Garrett's calling her to come back and pushed past

Veronica and Paden. Lifting her skirts, Angie took to the steps, two-by-two, and headed for her room. There she flounced onto her bed, sobbing. Why did men have to be so boorish? Why couldn't they be kind and tender . . . gentle?

Then suddenly one thing became very clear in Angie's mind. Captain Garrett Witherspoon was certainly not the man for her!

7

*T*here, there, now," Veronica cooed, "don't cry."

Sitting on the edge of her bed, Angie dabbed her eyes with her hanky.

"You must admit, you and Mr. Montano did look quite cozy, sitting there on that rock. I can't really blame the captain for his jealous behavior."

"Veronica!" Angie gaped at her stepsister.

"Oh, now, I didn't say I condone it. I just . . . well, I understand, that's all."

"You're taking his side over mine."

"I'm doing no such thing," Veronica said. "It's just that after speaking with Captain Witherspoon tonight, I feel I know him better and he seems like an upstanding fellow; but then, of course, they all seem that way at first. Marriage must bring out the beast in men."

Angie ignored the remark. "What was the meaning of bringing up Silverstone tonight? You practically betrayed me in front of our guests. You, my most trusted friend. How could you do that to me?"

"Relax, my dear, I didn't set out to expose your past. I was merely testing Mr. Montano's integrity, that's all."

"And? Did he pass?" Angie couldn't keep the cynicism out of her voice.

"Yes, I suppose he did."

She cast Veronica a dubious look, and then several moments of silence passed between the two women. Angie played over in her mind the churlish way Garrett had kissed her good night.

Then suddenly beside her, Veronica started. Angie snapped out of her reverie. "Did you hear that?" Veronica asked in hushed tones.

"Hear what?"

"Upstairs. In the attic. It's him. I know it."

Angie inhaled deeply before letting out a slow breath. "Oh, not this again."

"Didn't you hear that thud?"

"No. And I've told you a million times, sister dear, that there aren't any ghosts up there. I haven't run into one yet."

Another bump, and this time Angie heard it, too. Veronica, however, nearly jumped out of her skin.

"It's the window," Angie said, recognizing the sound. "The breeze is out of the west tonight and likely blew it open. I'll run up and secure it."

"You are so brave."

Shaking her head at the foolishness, Angie grabbed the lighted lamp from the bedside table and headed for the stairs. A couple of years ago, she'd created her own sewing room up there, despite Veronica's superstitions and warnings. While Angie didn't believe in ghosts, per se, she believed Satan and his host were on their job twenty-four hours a day. Still, whenever Veronica's apprehensions began to affect her, Angie recalled the passage of Scripture that promised, "Greater is He that is in you than he that is in the world." No, Angie wasn't brave, but with the Holy Spirit's power, she had nothing to fear.

Reaching the dark attic now, she strode past a settee and several armchairs, each covered for protection with old linens. Beneath her, the floorboards creaked ominously, and she had to admit that by night this unfinished third story was, indeed, spooky. But, by day, Angie felt inspired by the breathtaking view of the ocean from her little sewing room at the front of the house. Entering her fabric-littered workplace, complete with dress forms, she saw that, as she'd suspected, the window had blown open. She shut and latched it tightly.

"Angelique?" Veronica's worry-riddled voice wafted up the stairway. "Are you all right, Dear?"

"I'm fine. It was the window we heard banging."

Lamp in hand, she made her way back downstairs. Veronica stood at the foot of the steps, waiting anxiously. For all her mettle, when it came to testing a man's integrity, Angie decided her stepsister was quite a goose concerning adventure novels and nighttime noises. There, Veronica's imagination excelled.

"Well, I think I'll turn in," Angie said. After a hug, she headed for her bedroom.

"Angelique?"

She paused, turning. "Yes?"

"I believe this is another of those times when having a man around might come in handy."

Angie had to grin. "Are you thinking of giving marriage another chance?"

"I . . . I don't know about that," Veronica stammered. "But I suppose we could board out the guestroom. Why most of the bachelors in San Francisco stay in boardinghouses. Perhaps Captain Witherspoon would—"

"Perish the thought! We're not set up for such an endeavor, and it wouldn't be proper to have him or any other gentleman living in this house in such close proximity to us—two unattached females."

"You're right, of course. I can't fathom why that notion went through my head."

I can, Angie mused as she padded the rest of the way to her room. Whenever she felt especially lonely, she meditated on the story of Adam and Eve in Genesis. God instituted marriage from the beginning. The Lord, Himself, performed the first wedding ceremony. It was right. It was good. God said so. And it was only natural for a woman to want to marry and raise children. Likewise, Angie deduced, a woman instinctively desired to be protected and cherished by the man she loved. Veronica was not immune to that innate yearning. Neither was Angie, and in her mind's eye she suddenly saw Garrett's serious eyes, strong chin, broad shoulders, and capable disposition. But as tempting as marriage to the captain seemed at this moment, Angie knew it wasn't God's will for her life. She sensed it now. Clearly.

But someday, she thought, crawling beneath the thick, down-filled comforter, someday the man of her dreams would walk into her life. He'd have a gentle hand, mild manner, a quiet voice, but unequivocal valor. He would accept her for who she'd been and who she'd become by God's grace. He'd love the Lord with all his heart, soul, and mind, and he'd love her so much, he'd die for her if he had to.

"Oh, for pity's sake," Angie murmured, rolling onto her side. "Now who's got the wild imagination?"

∾

The next day, Garrett stopped by the dress shop and asked to talk with Angie, but she had customers waiting to be fitted and couldn't get away. Veronica played mediator and the two of them seemed to have a beneficial conversation.

"He's ever so sorry," Veronica relayed at supper that evening.

"I believe he is, and all is forgiven." Angie paused to consider her stepsister for several long moments, before returning her attention to the seafood souffle that Tu Hing had prepared. "Your tone has changed. You no longer seem so opposed to Garrett. In fact, you seem rather for him . . . us."

"Well," she began, pressing back a stray lock of her honey-brown hair, "he strikes me as most sincere. One can't help feeling a bit sorry for the man. He is trying awfully hard to win your heart, you know."

"Yes," Angie agreed, "but unfortunately as time goes by, I feel less peace about marrying Garrett. And last night—" She sighed. "Last night I realized he's not the man for me."

"Surely a single kiss couldn't have frightened you that badly."

"No, not frightened exactly," she admitted, "but he manhandled me, don't you see? I promised myself when I left Silverstone that I would never again allow a man to take me or my affections by force, whether physically or emotionally."

"My dear, marriage cannot protect you from ever being in that situation again."

"Perhaps not," Angie said, thinking Veronica sounded more like her old self, "but God can. He'll protect me . . . and if it's His will that

I should marry, He'll lead me to the right man someday." She grinned. "But for now I have my work—and after today, I have a lot of work!"

"And you have me," Veronica added. "Don't forget me."

~❧

Sunday morning arrived and brought with it sunshine and a mild breeze. To Angie, it seemed a perfect day. She strolled to church with the Johnson family, who lived a few doors away. When they reached the small, brick house of worship near the Nob Hill area, Angie immediately saw Garrett's large frame folded into a pew about midway to the front. Beside him sat Paden. They seemed to chat amicably while Mrs. Matthison's fifteen-year-old daughter, Glenda, played the upright piano in the far left-hand corner of the sunlit sanctuary. Presently, she was plunking out "A Mighty Fortress Is Our God."

Angie slipped undetected into a pew across the aisle and two rows behind Garrett and Paden. Carla Chamberlain, a lovely new mother, was situated next to her and struck up a brief conversation about the weather and the diminishing Comstock Lode, but then Pastor Richards strode to the large, wooden pulpit. Smiling a greeting, the brown-eyed, copper-haired minister led them first in a few hymns before launching into his message.

"My dear friends," he began, "with the threat of economic depression looming over our city, we must remember what's really important in this life. . . ."

Angie listened intently, wondering what the monetary decline would mean for the Huntington House. She and Veronica had been hearing for some time that the decreased production of ore from the Comstock mine had significantly affected a number of San Francisco residents, but that wasn't anything new. With the rampant speculating of mining shares, many found themselves millionaires one day and paupers the next. Furthermore, the banks had seen their portion of fiscal peaks and valleys, too—so much so that Veronica felt leery of the financial institutions, but, at the same time, she acknowledged their importance in the community. Nevertheless, she insisted upon depositing only a fourth of their income from the dress shop, and the rest Veronica kept locked up tightly in a hidden safe at home.

Angie pushed aside her thoughts and forced herself to pay attention to the message.

"The Bible says one cannot serve God and money. You'll love the one and hate the other. Therefore we must lay up our treasures in Heaven." The reverend paused. "If Christ is our Joy, our Master, we can lose fortunes and still be happy."

Numerous voices in the sanctuary exclaimed, "Amen!" Angie inadvertently glanced across the aisle, only to find Garrett staring back at her. His hazel eyes seemed to beseech her. Obviously he felt badly about Friday night's miserable encounter. Angie returned an assuring smile, but then refocused on Pastor Richards, knowing the outcome of her meeting with Garrett later. If he proposed marriage, she'd have to decline. She didn't love him. She never would. *Lord,* she prayed, *I've trusted You with my soul. I trust You with my finances . . . certainly, I can trust You to bring me the right husband in Your perfect time.*

Pastor concluded his sermon and the congregation joined him in a hymn during the altar call. Several members went forward, and some even publicly announced that, regrettably, money had taken the Savior's place in their lives. The tearful smiles on their faces shone with divine forgiveness.

Once they were dismissed, Angie filed out of the pew. In the aisle, she met Garrett.

"I hope you still have time to speak with me, Angelique," he said in a formal, sophisticated tone, but his eyes were filled with anticipation.

"Why, yes, of course, Captain." Angie turned, and her gaze met Paden's. He nodded politely. She smiled a greeting. Looking back at Garrett, she said, "There's a small chamber in the rear of the church. Pastor Richards won't mind if we use it."

"Very good. Lead on."

She did, making her way through the throng of church-goers who were headed in the opposite direction.

"A bit like rowing against the tide," Garrett muttered near her ear as they inched forward. Finally, they reached the little room. The walls were unfinished and the air smelled musty. Angie took a seat on one of the long, wooden benches.

"I'll keep the door open for propriety's sake," Garrett said as he sat on the adjacent bench.

"Yes, please do."

A few moments of taut silence passed between them.

"I would like to start by begging your forgiveness, Angelique. I acted like a complete cad, taking such liberties with you Friday night."

"I have already forgiven you, Garrett," she said sincerely.

He smiled. "Thank you." He cleared his throat. "Now, as for the topic I wish to discuss with you. . . ."

Angie held her breath and sent up a quick prayer for wisdom.

"By now, you must know how I feel about you."

"Um, well, yes, I've gathered that you're quite fond of me."

Garrett grinned. "Fond, Angelique, cannot begin to describe my affections for you."

"I'm very flattered," she replied, looking down at her full skirt and picking at a piece of invisible lint.

He captured her hand in both of his, then sank to one knee. "Angelique, my sweet, I am in love with you. Say you'll marry me." He searched her face. "We'll sail off together, and once we're settled in Maine, I'll build you a home. Angelique," he whispered, "I will give up my career as a sea captain for you."

His words touched her heart in spite of her stiff resolve to turn him down. "Oh, Garrett, I—"

"Say yes."

Angie moistened her suddenly parched lips. "Garrett, I—"

"You're obviously speechless, my dear. A simple 'yes' will do."

"But—"

"Captain Witherspoon, sir?"

At the sound of the masculine voice coming from the doorway, Garrett swung his gaze around, and Angie looked up to find a young man standing there, his hat in hand. "Sir, I hate to disturb you. . . ."

Looking vexed, Garrett stood and brushed the dirt from his trousers. "What is it, Hopkins?"

"It's the *Jubilee,* Sir."

"What about her?"

"She's on fire."

"What? My ship's on fire?"

"Yes, Sir."

He turned to Angie with wide eyes. "Please excuse me."

"Of course."

Without another word, Garrett took off with the younger man running after him.

Angie sat back down, praying the fire would be extinguished soon and that Garrett's ship wouldn't suffer too much damage. Then she decided that refusing the dashing captain's marriage proposal wasn't going to be as easy as she imagined. He said he loved her. He'd give up his life on the sea for her. He'd make her a home. It was all she'd ever wanted to hear in a marriage proposal.

Couldn't I learn to love him, Lord? she asked her Heavenly Father. But the beat of her heart pounded out the answer: No, no, no, no, no, no, no.

Then suddenly a long shadow appeared on the dusty, plank floor in front of her. Glancing at the doorway, she saw Paden leisurely reclining against the wooden frame. He held his wide-brimmed hat in his hands and he wore a dark gray shirt, ebony vest, and jacket. His charcoal-colored trousers were neatly stuffed into shiny, black boots.

"Well?"

"Well, what?" Angie rose from the bench.

"Did my cousin propose as we suspected?"

"Yes. Unfortunately, his ship caught fire before I could give him my answer."

Paden shook his dark head. "Such a pity about his ship. I was the one who told Garry's first mate, Luther Hopkins, where to find him. I hope the vessel is not completely destroyed."

"Yes, I hope not."

Paden pushed himself off the doorjamb and stepped forward. "You look . . . worried, *mi amada.* What's wrong?" He stopped just inches away and stroked Angie's cheek with the knuckle of his forefinger.

"I'm just . . . thinking," she replied softly, unnerved by his touch and wondering why.

"Thinking of marrying my cousin after all?"

"Yes. I mean, no." She shook her head, feeling oddly flustered. Sidestepping Paden, she paused by the doorway. "What I meant is, I reconsidered briefly, but I really cannot accept. That's my final answer."

When no reply was forthcoming, Angie peeked over her shoulder at Paden. He grinned back at her. "Miz Huntington," he began on a formal note, "may I escort you home?"

Angie turned the rest of the way around, her skirts swirling at her ankles. She thought over his offer, his touch, his romantic Spanish endearments and narrowed her gaze suspiciously. "Paden Montano, are you flirting with me?"

"*Sí, señorita*. How could you tell?"

"Lucky guess," she quipped.

Smiling, Paden offered his arm. Angie threaded her hand around his elbow. They made their way back through the sanctuary and, walking up the aisle beside him, Angie experienced a strange stirring in her heart. Would she ever be a bride, stepping elegantly down the aisle, heading for the altar and not the front doors?

Lord, she prayed for the second time that morning, *I've trusted You with my soul. I trust You with my finances . . . certainly, I can trust You to bring me the right husband in Your perfect time.*

8

*O*utside, the sun shone brightly from its noonday perch in a blue, cloudless sky. Angie inhaled the fresh, sea air, but then noticed Paden's troubled expression. Following his gaze, she saw thick, black smoke towering into the air.

"I think the fire at the harbor is worse than we first suspected," he murmured. "And from the looks of it, I'd wager that Garrett's ship is not the only one involved."

Angie inhaled sharply, praying this fire wouldn't consume the city like the one back in '51. She'd heard horror stories about that day.

Paden turned to face her. "I'm sorry, but I need to go and see if I can help."

"I'm coming with you."

He looked as though he might argue the point, but then a hint of a grin caused his sleek, black mustache to twitch. "As you wish."

Taking her hand, he hurried to the corner, where he summoned a hackney. After they climbed in, Angie had several minutes to catch her breath before they reached the harbor. When the carriage pulled to a halt, Paden helped her down before giving the Chinese driver his fare. Next, he took hold of Angie's elbow and propelled her toward the chaotic scene.

Firemen shouted orders to each other while they manned the steam engines and hoses, aiming for the three smoldering vessels. The police kept spectators at a safe distance. Sailors ran up and down gangplanks, unloading precious commodities before the flames consumed them.

"There's Garry," Paden said, pointing off to the left. Then, with his hand beneath her elbow, he guided her forward, through the busy throng.

Garrett frowned, watching their approach. "What possessed you to bring Angelique down here? This is no place for a lady."

Angie glanced at Paden. "She insisted," he stated simply.

"Well, you could have refused to bring her," Garrett muttered before turning to Angie. "My dear, the docks are no place for a woman."

"But I wanted to help. Paden said he was coming, so I . . . I *forced* him to bring me along."

"You forced him, eh?" Lifting a brow, Garrett gave his cousin a doubtful look before bringing his gaze back to Angie. "That's kind of you, my sweet, but now the fire is out on the *Jubilee.* There's nothing more any of us can do at the moment. As you can see, there's extensive damage, but she's still afloat. I guess that's something to be thankful for."

Angie had never seen Garrett's ship before, and she guessed it had once been a fine-looking vessel. Now her masts were blackened and burned, although the bow seemed to have suffered the most damage.

"Doesn't look like we'll make it to Maine before Thanksgiving, Angelique," Garrett said, gazing at his clipper. "Not on the *Jubilee,* anyway."

She frowned at him, then looked at Paden, who gave her a curious glance.

"And she might not be worth rebuilding at this point," Garrett continued somewhat pensively before returning his attention to Angie. "But at least I have you. This loss is much easier to accept, knowing our future together awaits. And what's stopping us from seeking passage on another ship?"

Before Angie could reply, Paden cleared his throat loudly. "Is there something you haven't told me, Garry?"

"Why, yes, I guess there is." Lifting her hand and gazing into her eyes, he said, "I asked Angelique to marry me after church today, and she accepted."

"She did? Why, Miz Huntington," Paden drawled, "I'm surprised that you didn't tell me the good news, yourself. Congratulations."

"But I—"

"I think she's a bit overwhelmed," Garrett cut in, slipping his arm around Angie's waist. "In fact, I really ought to take her home. I'm sure this fire has upset her greatly."

"By all means," Paden replied.

"I am perfectly fine," Angie protested. She gave Paden a pointed stare, hoping he'd help her out of this most awkward position, but he merely glared at her, his expression unreadable.

Then before another word could be uttered, Garrett escorted her down the dock and away from the waterfront. He managed to hire a coach and assisted Angie inside. "I'm afraid I smell like a chimney," he said apologetically after he'd seated himself beside her.

"Garrett, there's been a terrible misunderstanding."

"With regard to my cousin? Oh, don't worry about him. I suspect he's been trifling with you, but that will change now that we're betrothed."

"But that's where the misunderstanding lies, Garrett. We're not betrothed. I never accepted your marriage proposal. I never had a chance."

"You didn't? I'm sure I heard you agree to become my wife."

"No," Angie replied, shaking her head, "you didn't hear that because I never said it."

"Well, say it now, my sweet."

"I can't," she said softly, ruefully. Her past flashed across her memory like a searing reminder not to even be tempted by this matrimonial offer. "Garrett, I can't marry you. I'm sorry."

His expression fell, and Angie felt terrible for hurting him. "I'm sorry," she stated again. "But I know it's not right. It's not God's will. I've prayed about it."

"And so have I!"

"Yes, but were you listening for an answer or were you telling the Lord your intentions?"

Garrett brought his chin back indignantly.

"I do that sometimes," Angie confessed. "I tell the Lord those things I wish to accomplish and ask Him to bless them, never thinking to ask if my plans are in accordance with His will for my life."

"I am sure I have not misunderstood my God," Garrett replied tersely.

Angie didn't reply. It seemed senseless to argue the point. A few moments of taut silence passed and then the carriage came to a stop. "Thank you for seeing me home."

Garrett took her hand. "Angelique, please—"

She pulled out of his grasp. "I'm so sorry. The last thing on earth I want to do is hurt you, but I can't marry you."

His features hardened. "Very well, Miss Huntington," he said in stiff formality. Then he climbed out of the hack and helped her down.

As soon as her feet touched the ground, Angie fled to the front door with tears of remorse stinging her eyes.

༺

Paden lurked in the darkness outside an impressive gentlemen's club. Hours ago, he'd seen Harry Munson enter with William Rosewahl, a bank president, and Hiram Littleton, a medical doctor. Both men were in the upper echelon of San Francisco's society. Andy's theory had been correct.

Paden recalled his first day in this city. He had walked into the police station and announced himself as an old friend of the police chief. That hadn't been a lie, either. He and Andy Stephenson had fought in the cavalry together, so when Paden informed him that he was employed as a Pinkerton agent and stated his business, Andy told him about the corruption going on among many of the city's affluent citizens.

So that explains why I couldn't find Munson among the gambling dens and saloons, Paden mused. The money Munson stole during the train robbery in Missouri had earned him a place with some of San Francisco's elite. Unfortunately, Paden couldn't get into the club to apprehend the renegade since it was a "members only" establishment. Obviously, Rosewahl and Littleton had sponsored Munson as their guest.

He waited, poised and ready, praying for protection. Paden knew he had to nab Munson soon. The longer the man went unchecked, the easier it would become for him to discover Paden's identity as a Pinkerton agent.

Just then, the doors to the gentlemen's club opened and out stepped two obviously intoxicated males, singing off-key at the top of their lungs. "Way down upon the Swanee River, far, far away, there's where my heart is turnin' ever, there's where the old folks stay. . . ."

Paden rolled his eyes and shook his head. The door to the club opened once more, and another man exited. It was Harry Munson.

Drawing his gun, Paden watched from the shadows as Munson headed in his direction, right behind the two drunks who continued to sing, "All the world is sad and dreary, everywhere I roam; Oh, brother, how my heart grows weary, far from the old folks at home."

As the group of three men neared, Paden suddenly recognized Garrett as one of the off-key vocalists.

Paden stood there, stunned. Garry? Drunk? How was that possible? However, in that moment of distraction, Munson turned the corner. Stepping out from the darkened alley, Paden followed him . . . until his cousin's voice halted him in his tracks.

"Well, if it isn't my favorite relative," he slurred.

Paden stopped and pivoted. The other drunken man had climbed into a carriage that swiftly went on its way down the street.

"You are a disgrace, Garry. Look at you," Paden said, disgusted. "You are a Christian man. You have no business getting drunk."

"I couldn't help it," he replied, slurring his words. "First the *Jubilee* and then Angelique. A man can only take so much. . . ."

"Come on. I will take you back to the boardinghouse."

"No, no, I can't go there. Mrs. Crabtree doesn't like to rent to men who indulge in spirited beverages, and I promised her I was not of that inclination. I wasn't, either . . . until tonight." Garrett grinned and swayed slightly.

"Then you will have to come to the hotel with me."

"I am forever indebted to your kindness," Garrett mumbled, tripping over every syllable.

Paden sighed and led him down the street to a waiting hack. "Take us to the Oriental Hotel."

The driver nodded.

Paden helped his brawny cousin into the coach and then sat opposite from him. "What happened with Angelique?"

"She turned me down," Garrett lamented. "She said she can't marry me."

The words echoed in Paden's mind. *She turned him down.* He couldn't help but feel elated at the news. Except, he shouldn't; his cousin was hurting badly. Then he realized that if he won Angie's heart, it would be a bittersweet victory.

Garrett narrowed his gaze. "It's your fault she turned me down."

"Mine?"

"Yes, yours. You . . . you charmed her, knowing she was the love of my life. You . . . you're nothin' but a philanderer."

Paden grinned. He'd been called worse. "And you, *Primo,* are very drunk. But you'll think clearer in the morning—after your headache subsides."

~❧~

Sunshine streamed through the open draperies of the hotel room, shining in Garrett's eyes. He moaned and Paden chuckled before swallowing the last of his coffee. He'd purchased a pot full of the steaming brew in the downstairs dining room and now poured himself a second cup.

"You had better wake up, or I'll drink all the coffee myself."

In reply, Garrett moaned again. "I'm sure thugs beat me to a pulp last night."

Paden chuckled again. "No, I'm afraid you were your own worst enemy."

"Apparently. I can't imagine what I was thinking. I have never been drunk in my life. I have never even touched liquor . . . before last night."

"I hope you will never touch it again."

Garrett squinted at him, looking as if it hurt to do so. "On my honor, I never will. The morning after is horrible!" He fell back on the pillows and groaned.

Smiling, Paden sipped his coffee. "Any news on what started the fire yesterday?"

"It was arson. Authorities have incarcerated the fellow—a disgruntled sailor who lost his job and decided to burn down the harbor."

"Hmm. . . ."

"I can't help but wonder why God allowed the *Jubilee* to be one of the vessels that burned. Why didn't the Lord protect it? He knows shipping is my occupation, my livelihood. Now that Angelique . . . well, it hardly serves my purposes to retire from my life on the sea."

Paden thought it over. "I'm afraid I don't have any answers for you."

"No, no one does. This is between my God and me."

"Perhaps so, but I do have a confession to make."

"Oh?"

"*Sí.*" Paden knew it had to be said. "I would like nothing better than to win Angie for myself."

"I figured." Garrett propped himself up on one elbow and strained to look at him through the bright sunshine. "Angie, is it?"

Paden shrugged.

"Well, I'll tell you one thing, she's a lady and she's not about to marry a gunfighter."

"True enough. That's why I have been thinking along the lines of buying land in Texas and settling down."

"You? Settle down?" Garrett laughed and collapsed against the pillows again. "Now that's funny."

"It is not half as amusing as you giving up your life on the sea," Paden returned.

"Touché," Garrett quipped. He was silent for several long moments. "I guess love has a way of warping a man's thinking."

"I guess it does."

"But you can't possibly be in love with Angelique. You hardly know her. You only recently met. You've seen her, what . . . twice?"

"And what do you know of her?"

"I know she's shy, sweet, in need of a man's protection."

Paden smirked, thinking about Angie down by the wharf, witnessing to the working girls.

"She's a Christian."

"Have you heard her salvation testimony?"

"Well, no . . . have you?"

"*Sí.*"

Garrett bolted upright, then winced. "You have?"

Paden nodded. "And what about her family background," he began carefully. "What do you know of it?"

"She's a Huntington, a distant relative of Mrs. Veronica Huntington, whose husband was killed at Vicksburg. He died a hero's death. The Huntington family is respected in San Francisco."

Paden pursed his lips thoughtfully. "Does Angie have sisters? Brothers?"

Garrett looked momentarily uncomfortable. "Not sure. Do you know?"

"If I recall, she only has one stepsister."

Garrett gave him an underhanded look.

"And you, of course, know the color of her eyes."

"Of course. They're . . . um, green, I think."

"They are dark blue, like the sky just as the stars begin to shine."

"You are so poetic," Garrett stated facetiously. "That's why the women adore you." He threw off the bedcovers and stood. "I knew Angelique's eyes were blue. I've seen 'em a hundred times. I just couldn't remember."

"Understandable."

"Tell you what, Paden. You go ahead and try to win Angelique's heart with your flowery words and Latin charm. She turned me down, so I guess that means she's fair game. But I'm not giving up that easily, and I will continue to pursue her . . . since it looks like I'm stuck in San Francisco for awhile anyway. Your job, whatever it is, will be taking you away soon, and then Angelique will forget all about the smooth-talking gunslinger who broke her heart. She'll realize that I'm the best man for her."

Paden thought it over, then shook his head. "No, I don't want a war over a woman to come between us, Garry. There has to be another way to settle this matter. We're family. We're blood."

He snorted derisively as he poured himself a cup of coffee. "Relatives or not, the war has begun."

9

og had rolled in off the Pacific as Angie made her way to the bank Monday afternoon. Because of the overcast sky, everything around her looked dismal. It matched her mood. She knew she'd done the right thing in turning down Garrett's proposal yesterday, yet she felt so disappointed. What if she never got another offer of marriage?

Veronica said she was better off "unattached." Perhaps she was right. A husband seemed like an awful lot of trouble.

Arriving at the bank, Angie pulled open the door and let herself inside. She walked to the window and made her transaction. When she turned to leave, Mr. Rosewahl stepped into her path. "Miss Huntington, how nice to see you today."

She smiled. "Why, thank you."

"The dress shop business is booming, I hope."

"We keep busy, yes." Angie was careful as to how she replied since Veronica refused to put all their income into the savings account. Mr. Rosewahl wouldn't be pleased to hear it, and he'd likely give the two of them a lengthy speech on the proper safekeeping of their funds.

"Glad to hear it," the man replied, staring down his beak-like nose at her. "And where is your Mexican friend today?"

"Excuse me?"

"That man you were with on Friday . . . what was his name? Montano?"

"Oh, yes."

"My wife thinks perhaps there are wedding bells in your future. She has this way of stargazing, you know."

Angie gave the man a polite smile. She'd told him before that she was a Christian and didn't believe in fortunetellers. Besides, Mrs. Rosewahl was forever saying that wedding bells were in her future.

"Mr. Montano might be the right one," the banker continued. "What does he do for a living?"

"Um . . ." While Angie had promised to keep Paden's secret, she knew she couldn't lie. "I believe he works closely with the United States government," she said diplomatically.

"Oh, really? How very interesting. Do you think he makes a good living?"

"I'm sure he does."

"Well, a woman has to be certain of these things before entering into marriage, Miss Huntington."

"Thank you for your concern, but I don't believe I'll be marrying Paden or anyone else very soon."

"But it's written in the stars, Miss Huntington. Now, about Mr. Montano . . . where is he from?"

"He was born in the United States and reared in Mexico."

"Ah, of course. Mexico."

Angie stepped toward the door. "Good day to you, Mr. Rosewahl."

"One more question, please. I hope you don't mind. I don't mean to be intrusive, I'm just . . . well, as you said, *concerned*."

She nodded, but suddenly something about this whole conversation made her very nervous.

"Is your Mr. Montano the same one who was a sheriff in the Arizona Territory? Silverstone, Arizona?"

Angie felt herself grow pale, sensing that Mr. Rosewahl had done some investigation work. She momentarily debated how to answer him. Then she decided honesty was the best recourse. "Yes, as a matter of fact, Paden was sheriff in Silverstone."

Rosewahl's eyes narrowed. "He's a renowned gunman, Miss Huntington. How could you possibly be acquainted with a gunman?"

She sighed, hoping she seemed nonchalant. "As I mentioned, he's Captain Garrett Witherspoon's cousin."

"Ah, yes, that's right. The captain. A pity about the fire at the docks yesterday. I hope his ship is unharmed. Any marital prospects there?"

"No, I'm afraid not. Now, I really must get back to the shop."

"Of course. Good day, Miss Huntington. I'm sorry to have detained you."

Angie left the bank, but as she strolled down the boardwalk, a dark foreboding crept up her spine. Of course, it wasn't a secret that Paden had been sheriff in Silverstone. That tidbit couldn't have been difficult to discover. Still, the fact that Mr. Rosewahl had found it out at all caused alarm bells to jangle in the depth of her being.

She increased her pace, then darted across the street and walked up the block to the Oriental Hotel. Reaching the four-story building, she entered the lobby and nearly collided with Garrett, who was on his way out.

"Angelique! I mean . . . Miss Huntington."

She inhaled sharply. "Good afternoon . . . Captain." She glanced over his attire and thought he looked a bit rumpled. Perhaps many of his belongings had been lost in the fire. Regardless, his thick, brown hair was neatly parted and combed. He looked clean-shaven and he smelled of masculine woodsy-spicy soap. Where had she smelled that fragrance before?

"The fog rolled in quickly, didn't it?" Garrett remarked, looking up at the sky.

"Yes, it did."

He nodded before glancing over his shoulder. "Do you have business here at the hotel?"

"Yes, I need to speak with Paden. Is he in?" Garrett's expression fell, and so as not to give him the wrong impression, Angie quickly added, "It's an official matter."

"I see. Well, I'm sorry to say that my cousin is not in his hotel room. I just came from there."

"Oh. You're looking for him, too?"

"Not really. It's a long story—one you would not be interested in hearing, I'm sure."

"I'll take your word for it." Angie gave him a little smile.

"You can leave a message for Paden at the desk if you wish."

She shook her head. "No need. It's not pressing. It can wait."

A soft light entered Garrett's hazel eyes and, once more, Angie noted how very handsome he was. Perhaps before rejecting his marriage proposal, she should have discussed the matter with Pastor Richards.

No, no . . . she'd made the right choice. Why was she second-guessing herself?

"May I escort you somewhere?"

"I suppose I'll just return to the shop."

"Well, how about that!" He grinned. "I'm heading in the same direction."

Angie smiled in skeptical acquiescence. Why was Garrett being so nice to her? She'd rejected him yesterday. She would have expected him to be cold and indifferent.

He offered his arm, and Angie looped her hand around his elbow. She sighed inwardly as they began to walk. She would just have to think of some other way to tell Paden about Mr. Rosewahl.

❧

As it happened, Veronica invited Garrett to dinner. He readily accepted and Angie was surprised that the evening passed as pleasantly as it did. Garrett refrained from giving her long, amorous looks which, in turn, made Angie feel more comfortable in his presence. They talked and laughed and enjoyed each other's company.

"He's really a very nice man," Veronica said once Garrett left.

Angie began climbing the stairs to her bedroom. "Does that surprise you, sister dear?"

Just behind her, Veronica produced a light, little flutter of a laugh. "As a matter of fact, it does."

Grinning, Angie gave her a quick, parting hug in the hallway. "Good night."

"Sweet dreams, Darling," she returned in a motherly tone.

In her room, Angie changed into her night clothes and brushed out her long hair. She felt bone tired from not having slept well the night before and yet she felt completely at peace, satisfied, and contented. In retrospect, Angie realized that she'd felt awful for hurting Garrett yesterday, but seeing as he'd taken the news so favorably, she was no longer riddled with guilt.

She crawled into bed and under the thick patchwork quilt that Veronica had painstakingly brought from back East. Closing her eyes, she said her prayers. *Thank You, Lord, for keeping me safe today. Thank You for blessing our business and putting food on our table, clothes on our backs. Thank You for Veronica and I pray for her soul, Lord. Please continue to work in her heart. Help me to be a good witness to her, a testimony of Your love. . . .*

On that thought, Angie drifted off to sleep. However, in no time, it seemed, she was awakened by an odd-sounding noise. She sat up in bed, straining to hear in the darkness, and the strangest sensation stole over her being. She sensed another's presence. Could there really be someone in her bedroom?

Fear paralyzed her for a long moment, but soon her wits returned. Then, just as she moved to get out of bed to investigate, a leather-encased hand clapped over her mouth. Angie's arms flailed as she fought her assailant, but he quickly over-powered her.

"Hush, *mi amada*," came the soft, familiar voice with its subtle accent. "It is I."

Angie relaxed slightly, her breath coming and going in quick spurts, while questions darted through her mind. Paden slowly lifted his gloved hand from her mouth and moved away. "What are you doing here?" she hissed at him. "You scared me half to death!"

A pause.

"Paden?" Angie's ire was rising quickly, but his next words cut to the quick.

"I've been shot. I am wounded. I need your help."

10

*Y*ou're hurt?"

"*Sí,*" Paden replied.

"Where? Is it bad? Why didn't you go to the hospital?"

"Shh, Angie, keep your voice down. No one must know that I am here. It's a long story, and I will explain, but first . . . please, if you could look at the gunshot wound. It's in my right arm . . . and my chest, I think."

Angie pulled on her robe, tying it at the waist. "You think? What do you mean, you 'think'?"

Paden just sighed, obviously in pain.

Assessing the situation, Angie decided the best place to tend to Paden was in her sewing room. Hurriedly, she ushered him up the stairs.

"How did you get into my bedroom?" she had to ask.

"I climbed onto the verandah, then in through the window."

Angie lit a lamp, feeling amazed. "You climbed to the second-story verandah with an injured arm?"

"It is incredible what a man can do when his blood is racing . . . and God's angels are guiding his every move."

"Yes, I suppose it is, although I don't approve of such behavior as climbing into a woman's bedroom in the middle of the night."

"*Sí,* I understand, and I would not have done it except for my desperate situation."

Somewhat appeased, Angie helped him take off his jacket, vest, and shirt, then evaluated his injuries.

"God was certainly protecting you," she said. "The bullet went clear through your arm, missing the bone. You were only grazed on

513

the right side of your chest—except you've got a good-sized gash there."

She led him across the room and helped him onto the fainting couch. He closed his eyes in obvious relief. However, Angie thought he'd lost a fair amount of blood, judging from his stained clothing and pallid complexion. She knelt beside him. "You need a doctor, Paden. Your wounds need to be properly cleaned, and the one in your arm needs stitching."

"You are a competent nurse, Angie," he replied without opening his eyes. "I know you have patched up gunshot wounds before."

"Sure," she remarked with a trace of cynicism, "except the last un-fortunate soul who I attended died on me."

"I promise I will not die."

After a dubious look, Angie took hold of some scrap material and bound the wound on his arm to stop the bleeding. "Why can't I fetch the doctor?"

"Because I cannot trust anyone right now. Harry Munson, the out-law I was hired to find, got away, and now he knows I'm after him. One of San Francisco's prominent doctors—a man named Littleton—was killed tonight, and a banker named Rosewahl was injured or may be dead."

Angie gasped. "Mr. Rosewahl?"

"*Sí*, I shot both men. I had no choice. It was an ambush, and I walked right into it. Munson drew on me first, but fortunately, his aim is not so good. Then Littleton and Rosewahl pulled out pistols, and . . . well, I had no other choice than to defend myself. I don't think there were witnesses, but I'm sure there are people in high places who would like nothing better than to slap me with a murder charge."

"Oh, Paden!" Angie felt afraid for him.

"Tomorrow, I will have to get a message to the chief of police. He is a friend of mine."

Angie nodded, realizing his dire predicament. "I'll help you."

"*Gracias.*"

"Oh, Paden, I hope I didn't aid the ambush."

"What do you mean?" he asked weakly.

"When I went to the bank this afternoon, Mr. Rosewahl asked me a host of questions about you. He knew you'd been the sheriff in Silverstone."

"What did you tell him?"

"Nothing he didn't already know. And I went to the Oriental Hotel looking for you, to inform you about the incident, but I ran into Garrett and he said you weren't there."

Paden let out a long, slow breath. "He lied to you. I was in my hotel room all afternoon."

"He lied?"

"*Sí*. He is determined to win your heart even though you turned him down once. He will not take no for an answer."

"Of all the despicable things!"

"Angie?" Paden's voice was but a whisper. "Could you sew me up before I bleed to death?"

"You're not going to bleed to death," she retorted. "No such luck."

His sleek, black mustache twitched as he grinned. Angie quickly made her way downstairs to fetch some supplies. When she arrived back at her sewing room, she coaxed Paden into taking a healthy dose of the laudanum she used to cure her sick headaches.

"You don't want to feel this, Paden. Trust me."

"*Sí*, I trust you."

His words had an odd effect on her heart. She felt flattered. Privileged. Paden Montano didn't trust just anyone.

Carefully, Angie began to clean his bloody wounds with hot, soapy water. By the time she'd finished, Paden was sound asleep, his chest rising and falling in deep, even rhythm. She prayed before she began to stitch the hole in his right arm. Piercing another human being with a needle made her queasy, but Paden was right: She'd done it before. Sometimes at gunpoint.

At Chicago Joe's house of ill-fame, Angie had been known for being handy with a needle, whether it came to sewing a hem or torn flesh. Gunfights were not uncommon among the desperados who frequented the establishment, and Paden, the town's only lawman, had his hands full. Most times, however, he let the riffraff shoot it out, figuring it saved him some work. Angie had always thought he was a fair man. Fair, but hardened. She supposed he had to be.

The night he and Pastor Luke came to rescue her had completely caught her unawares. She could still recall the way her heart had lurched at the sight of Paden stepping through the door of her dark, dingy room at the brothel. She'd respected him until that moment. However, he soon commanded her to pack her bags and informed her she was going out the window and into the waiting wagon in the alley below. Angie's head had spun with incredulity.

And now here he was, back in her life.

And now here she was, patching up another gunfighter.

Oh, Lord, when will it ever end?

Angie knotted off the end of the thread, deciding she'd done as good a job as any doctor. She wrapped a clean piece of material around Paden's upper arm. It would be a sufficient bandage. Rising, she stretched out the kink in her back and searched the attic for a blanket. She found one and covered Paden. Then, lamp in hand, she retired to her bedroom, making sure there were no telltale bloodstains on the floor for Veronica to find in the morning.

༺

When the first pinks of dawn lighted the eastern sky, Angie forced her weary body out of bed. Donning her robe, she hurried downstairs before Veronica awoke and before Tu Hing began his day by preparing breakfast. Finding the kitchen empty, Angie made a meal for Paden. Later, she would smuggle up some hot coffee. For now, this would have to do.

Reaching the attic, she set down the wooden tray she'd been carrying and examined her patient.

Paden cracked open one eye. "Have I died and gone to heaven? I see an angel."

Angie smirked. "Save your charm for some other poor, unsuspecting woman. It won't work on me."

"No? Such a pity."

"For whom?"

Fully awake now, Paden struggled to a sitting position. "Such sparring first thing in the morning is not healthy for a man."

"Neither are gunfights," Angie quipped. "Here, I brought you some breakfast."

Paden looked at the tray holding a plate of roasted chicken, rice, a chunk of bread, and half a jar of fresh milk. Then he inspected his arm and flexed his hand. Next, he tried to bend his arm at the elbow, but moaned in agony.

"I hope you didn't just burst all my stitches," Angie said, frowning at him. "That wound is going to take awhile to heal."

"*Sí,* I know. But I had to try it out."

Shaking her head at him, she pivoted. "I need to get dressed, but I'll try to bring you some coffee before I leave for the shop."

Paden caught her hand as she tried to leave. "Thank you, Angie," he whispered.

"You're welcome," she replied, feeling oddly unsettled.

He released her, and she continued on her way downstairs. Once inside her bedroom, she wondered why she had suddenly felt so flustered. Was Paden's gratitude so hard to accept? Or was it the way he'd looked right through her with those deep brown eyes of his?

Angie pushed her thoughts of Paden aside and pulled a dark gray skirt and white blouse from the polished oak wardrobe. After she'd dressed, she brushed back her hair, pinning it in a bun and adorning it with a silvery ribbon.

"Good morning, Angelique," Veronica said, meeting her in the hallway. "Did you sleep well?"

She stifled a yawn. "Actually, not. I hope you slept better than I did."

"I did, thank you." Veronica's greenish-brown eyes seemed to sparkle. "I had a lovely time last night. Would you like to know a secret?"

Angie smiled.

"I dreamt about Captain Witherspoon! I was Cinderella and he was Prince Charming. We were at a ball given by the Hathaways."

Angie couldn't help the little giggle that slipped through her lips.

"He asked me to dance, and I accepted. We waltzed all night long . . . and then I woke up."

"And you're not tired? After waltzing all night long?"

Veronica cast her glance from beneath lowered lashes. "It was a dream, Angelique. Nothing more than a silly old dream."

They sat down at their places in the dining room, and Tu Hing brought their tea. He greeted each lady with a polite smile before returning to the kitchen.

"You know, sister dear," Angie said, deciding to forget Garrett's lie from yesterday—at least for the time being, until she could confront him about it, "I always thought you and the good captain would make a handsome pair."

"Bite your tongue. It'll take a miracle for me to marry him or any other man."

Angie grinned and sipped her tea. Little did Veronica know that God was in the miracle business!

11

ngie managed to sneak some coffee up to the attic sewing room for Paden. Mr. Hing had seemed curious as to her request, since she wasn't a coffee drinker. Despite the questions so obviously swirling around in his head, he didn't speak his mind, for which Angie was grateful.

"*Gracias*, Angie."

"You're welcome," she replied, setting down the hot, steaming brew. "I also brought the newspaper and a Bible for you." She watched Paden flex his hand. "I hope you're planning to take it easy today."

"*Sí*, I don't have much choice." He met her gaze. "Therefore, I need another favor."

Angie folded her arms and lifted her chin, preparing herself. "Yes?"

"Could you take a message to the chief of police for me? His name is Andy Stephenson."

"I know what his name is. Doesn't everyone in San Francisco?"

Paden shrugged.

"What would you like me to tell him?"

He grinned. "Thank you, Angie. I am indebted to you."

She shook her head, unable to help the smile. "You saved my life, Paden. This is the least I can do for you. Now what's the message?"

"Tell Andy that I am alive, but wounded. Tell him I am the one who killed Littleton, and possibly Rosewahl. Please explain to him that it was self-defense. Then ask him to wire the Pinkerton office for me."

Angie nodded. "All right."

"Also let Andy know that I am willing to turn myself in if necessary. For now, it is best that I stay in hiding. I cannot defend myself, should I meet up with a desperado who wants to settle an old score."

Angie immediately felt concerned. "Is that likely?"

Paden shrugged. "It is always a possibility."

She frowned, thinking it must be an awful existence for Paden to have to constantly watch his back and be ready to draw. It was a lifestyle of which she wanted no part. Gunfighters and desperados . . . she'd had her fill of them.

"Well, I'd best get myself to the dress shop. Veronica is waiting for me."

"*Sí,* then you had better go. But one last question, *por favor.* Do I need to worry that your hired man or anyone else may come up here?"

"No. Veronica believes this attic is haunted by the ghost of her late husband and she's convinced poor Mr. Hing of it." Angie smiled. "No one will bother you up here."

"Except, perhaps, the ghost of Mr. Huntington."

"Why, Paden Montano, I would have never guessed you to be fooled by silly superstitions."

His wry grin told her that he was only teasing.

She smiled again and stepped toward the stairwell. "I usually have errands in the afternoon, so that's when I'll go to the police department. I'll try to get back here to sneak up some lunch for you."

"Don't worry about me, Angie. I will be fine."

"You'll rest?"

Paden grinned sheepishly. "I will rest."

Appeased, Angie made her way down two flights of stairs, grabbed her shawl by the front entrance, then left the house for the shop just a few blocks away.

It wasn't until midafternoon when Angie found time to leave the shop. At the bank, the clerk informed her that Mr. Rosewahl was at the hospital in grave condition. She lent a sympathetic ear, but said nothing about her knowledge of the incident. Then it was on to the police station. In discovering San Francisco's history, she'd learned that organized law enforcement had begun more than twenty years ago. Now however, there were rumors flitting about with regard to corruption among some of the officers. Veronica, especially, relished any gossip pertaining to innocent citizens who were incarcerated for crimes they never committed. Then, while they attempted to prove their guiltlessness, the renegade police raided the prisoners' homes, thieving and looting as they went. Angie was sure the stories were highly exaggerated because she'd never known anyone who had personally experienced such a thing. Nevertheless, she approached the uniformed gentleman at the front desk with caution.

"May I help you, Ma'am?"

"Yes. I'd like to speak with Chief Stephenson, please."

The young man shook his dark brown head. "Sorry, Ma'am. He's awfully busy today." He grinned charmingly. "Perhaps I can help."

"No, I'm afraid I need to speak with the chief."

"What about?"

"A personal matter."

"I see." The officer scratched his head and glanced over his shoulder and down a long hallway. "Well, like I said, he's awfully busy."

"I'm a friend."

The officer's brows shot up. "Oh?"

"Well, a friend of a friend, I guess you might say."

"A friend of a friend, eh? That sounds kind of suspicious to me."

Angie felt herself growing frustrated and nervous. She hadn't expected to be interrogated.

"What's your name, Ma'am?"

She nibbled her lower lip. Ought she give it to him? What if he were in on the corruption and made trouble for her and Veronica? Angie had the welfare of the dress shop to think about.

"All right, then, Ma'am. What's your friend's name?"

Once more, she hesitated. Would Paden mind if she gave his name or did he say he'd already given it. He'd seen his friend, the chief. Surely he'd been questioned, too.

"Now, look, Ma'am, I can't let just anyone see Mr. Stephenson. If you're *somebody*, perhaps—"

"Mrs. Paden Montano," Angie blurted without giving the matter a second thought. "Please tell the chief Mrs. Paden Montano is here to see him."

The officer gave her a once-over with a narrowed brown-eyed gaze, then looked increasingly suspicious.

"Just tell the chief I'm here to see him, all right?" Her patience was waning.

"Sure . . . Mrs. Montano."

Looking wary, the man left his perch and walked down the hallway, knocking on a door near the far end. Angie heard muffled voices and then another man joined the first officer and they both headed her way. Suddenly all the wild tales Veronica liked to tell swirled in her mind. Would they arrest her for trying to speak with the chief of police?

The second man approached. He was tall, distinguished-looking, and perhaps in his forties. His hair was russet with a mingling of gray. "Mrs . . . Montano?" He looked suddenly amused. "I understand you want a word with me."

"Are you Mr. Stephenson?"

"I am."

She glanced at the officer, situated behind his desk once more. "Could we speak privately?"

"Would you mind telling me what this is all about first?"

"It concerns my, um . . . husband."

"I see." A light of understanding flickered in his green eyes. "Follow me."

They walked through the corridor and Stephenson showed her into his office. Two black leather armchairs and a large desk piled with papers comprised most of the small room.

Stephenson closed the door.

"First, why don't you tell me who you really are. And I don't believe the Mrs. Montano bit . . . unless Paden got married in the last week."

"My name is Angelique Huntington. Veronica Huntington and I operate an elite dress shop on the edge of the financial district."

"Ah, I think I know the one. And how is it that you are acquainted with my friend, Paden?"

"Well," Angie began, taking a seat in the chair Stephenson offered,

"Paden is Captain Garrett Witherspoon's cousin, and the captain and I were . . . courting."

Nodding, the police chief sat down behind his desk.

"Paden came to me for help last night. He was wounded, you see. . . ." The entire story spilled from Angie's mouth. Several minutes later, she finished and glanced down at her gloved hands, praying she hadn't said too much. When she looked across the wide desk at Stephenson, he seemed deep in thought.

Finally he returned her gaze and sat forward. "I don't see how Paden is at fault if what you just told me is true. He obviously acted in self-defense. And I can vouch for him; he's not a cold-blooded killer. However, there are reasons that this situation must be handled with care and with the utmost discretion." Pursing his lips, he thought a moment longer. "Tell Paden that I'll wire Pinkerton and then, once we find out if Mr. Rosewahl is going to recover, I'll contact him."

"Until then?" Angie asked.

"Until then, he's to stay put."

"But he's in my attic, Sir."

"He'll have to stay there. I'll get his things out of the hotel and have them delivered to your dress shop under the guise of supplies or some such thing."

"I suppose that will be all right." Angie swallowed hard. She'd have to tell Veronica. And Garrett.

As if divining her thoughts, Stephenson added, "And no one else must know about his whereabouts. Is that clear?"

"But what about Paden's cousin? He'll wonder where he is. And what of Veronica, my relative and business partner?"

"You're a sharp lady," Stephenson said, rising to his feet. "Paden wouldn't trust you otherwise. You'll think of something." He chuckled. "*Mrs. Montano.*"

*A*ngie wasn't pleased with the situation. Not pleased at all. During her entire journey back to the dress shop, she wondered how she would keep Paden hidden from Veronica and Garrett. Then, once she arrived, Veronica informed her that "the good captain" was coming to dinner again tonight.

"You don't mind, do you, Darling?"

"No, no . . . of course not," Angie said reluctantly.

"He's quite amusing."

"Yes, I suppose he is."

"Do you think you'll change your mind about marrying him?"

Angie glanced across the shop at her stepsister. She was studying a swatch of lace at the front counter and appeared disinterested in her question's reply. However, Angie thought there had been a note of . . . something in her tone. Something that countered her impartial demeanor.

"No, I'll not change my mind, *Cinderella*. Prince Charming is all yours."

Veronica's honey-brown head snapped up. "Why, Angelique, you say the most outlandish things!"

She grinned. "You must be rubbing off on me, sister dear."

"I guess I must. But just remember, I'm a widow and widows get away with intrepid behavior."

"So do spinsters," Angie replied, lifting her chin.

Veronica looked aghast. "Spinster?"

"That's what I am, and that's what I'll always be."

"Hmph!" came Veronica's satisfied reply. "You're better off that way. You'll see."

Angie merely shrugged in silent disagreement before taking up the task of hemming Mrs. Garth's winter wrapper. It was a part of the woman's new wardrobe, purchased for her upcoming journey to London, England, with her husband.

Hours later, Angie and Veronica locked up the dress shop and ambled home, side by side. Upon their arrival, Tu Hing was given immediate orders for tonight's menu, and then Veronica dashed up the stairs to her room, insisting she must dress for dinner. Deciding to seize the opportunity, Angie followed the hired Chinese man into the kitchen.

"Mr. Hing, I'm famished. Could you prepare a plate of food for me?"

He bowed in acquiescence.

"But I'll eat tonight with Veronica and our guest as well."

He gave her a curious glance, but asked no questions. Within minutes, Angie was carrying a plate upstairs to the attic. "Paden," she whispered, announcing her presence, "it's me."

Entering her sewing room, Angie found him sleeping comfortably on the fainting couch. He'd managed to put on his shirt, though he'd torn away the right sleeve. She set down the plate and eyed the wound on his arm, realizing the makeshift bandage was bloodied. Kneeling beside the beige-upholstered lounge, she began carefully unwinding the material.

That's when Paden awoke and considered her through sleepy eyes.

"*Mi angel. . . .*"

Angie frowned at the reference, then touched her fingertips to his forehead. "Oh, no. I think you have a fever."

"I think it is just hot up here," he said with a sleepy grin. "And I am especially warm because I was exercising my arm."

"Yes, I can see that," she murmured, none too pleased, while inspecting his wound. To her relief, the stitches were still intact. "Paden, you've just got to take it easy."

"*Sí,* I found that out." A shadow of worry darkened his features. "My grip is very weak. I cannot even hold my gun for any length of time. I only pray the strength in this hand will return once my arm heals."

"You might help the Lord out and rest," Angie retorted.

Paden lifted a sardonic brow. "You are as cantankerous as any nurse I have ever known. Perhaps God is calling you to the medical profession."

"Not a chance. I'm happy in the dressmaking business." She stood and searched about for another piece of material to bind Paden's injured arm. When she found a long, cranberry-colored scrap, she knelt back down beside him. "I'm sorry to be so peevish."

"Apology accepted." He paused and Angie could feel the weight of his stare. "You look tired."

"I am, and Veronica invited Garrett to dinner again, so I won't be retiring for the evening any time soon."

"Let me get this straight. The reason for your discontent is because you're being forced to stay up late tonight . . . or is it that my cousin is coming for dinner?"

"Both."

"I see. Well, I'm glad to hear it. For a moment I thought, perhaps, you were angry with me."

Angie shook her head. "Not angry, but I've got bad news from your friend, Chief Stephenson. He says you've got to stay here indefinitely until Mr. Rosewahl's condition is known. Apparently, he is alive, but unconscious." She knotted off the material and sat back on her heels. "Mr. Stephenson said he'll gather your belongings at the hotel and have them sent to our shop. He knows where you are and promised he'd be in touch. Until then, no one else can know you're here."

Paden was momentarily silent as he considered the news. "I hadn't planned on staying here long. I never meant to be such a burden, Angie."

His rueful, dark eyes met hers, melting her heart. "You're not a burden," she said softly. "You're my friend." She smiled. "My *amigo*."

He stroked her cheek with the backs of his fingers. "What if I want to be more than just your friend?"

Angie's eyes widened. "But I thought you had a love interest here in San Francisco."

"I do, and I'm looking at her."

"Me?!" Angie cried, before quickly clapping her hand over her mouth, hoping Veronica hadn't heard the exclamation. After a moment's hesitation, she said, "Paden, you can't be serious."

"I am serious. But you look troubled."

Angie fretted her lower lip as she tried to select the right words. Finally, she decided to be brutally honest. "You're a gunfighter, Paden. I refuse to spend my life with a gunfighter."

"I am not a gunfighter—no more than any other man. I draw on no one, but I must defend myself."

"But your occupation—"

"It is temporary. I want to leave it behind and buy a ranch someplace where there is lush, green grass, cool streams, and tall evergreens. I am so tired of the brown desert."

As Angie listened, she thought it did sound rather inviting. San Francisco had scarcely any trees. Between the building going on within the city and the fire that ravished the land some twenty years ago, there was nary a tree to be found.

"You are thinking about it, *mi amada*."

"No, I'm not," she shot back. "And stop calling me that . . . *mi amada* . . . whatever it means." Angie didn't want to tell him it made her insides all quivery whenever those two words tumbled so eloquently from his lips.

"It is merely an expression of tenderness. Much like if your sister called you 'my dear.'"

"You're not my sister, Paden."

The corners of his mouth lifted, making him look amused. "*Sí*, that's true."

Angie rose from her place on the floor. "I need to dress for dinner," she said, changing the subject. "Garrett will be here soon."

"You are certain that you are not in love with him?"

"I'm certain. And I'm not in love with you, either." She hadn't meant to hurt him, but it was the truth and he needed to hear it.

To her surprise, Paden laughed.

"Shh, Veronica will hear."

"My apologies." He struggled to a sitting position, swung his legs off the fainting couch, and stood. Then he walked slowly toward her. "I know you are not in love with me . . . yet."

"Yet?" She arched her brows in question.

"*Sí*, I mean to charm you, Angie Brown, like you have never been charmed before."

She tried in vain to suppress a little smile. However, she soon realized this wasn't funny. "Paden, don't trifle with me."

"I am not trifling."

She tapered her gaze, gauging his expression. He seemed earnest enough. "Have you prayed about this?" she couldn't help asking.

"I have, and I will continue to pray."

Angie felt somewhat comforted by his reply. "And you really want to start a new life on a ranch?"

Paden nodded. "It is my dream."

She had to admit to being somewhat fascinated. "Will you tell me about it, about this dream of yours?"

"Of course."

"Angelique?" Veronica's voice wafted up the attic stairs. "Are you up there, Dear? It's after six and the captain will be here shortly."

"All right. I'll be down in a moment." She looked back at Paden. "I must go."

"I understand. We will talk later." Taking her hand, he brought her fingers to his lips. "*Hasta la vista.*"

Angie felt her knees begin to weaken. "I think you'll make quick work of this charm business," she said, withdrawing her hand.

"*Sí,* I hope so."

Shaking her head at her own gullibility, she strode to the stairwell as Paden's soft chuckle followed in her wake.

❧

Mr. Hing couldn't have prepared a more delectable meal. He had filleted and fried fresh fish and served it with a mound of rice mixed with onions, green peppers, and tomatoes. Garrett was a delightful guest, as usual, but Angie decided his charm couldn't hold a candle to his cousin's. While she ate, she couldn't help daydreaming, wondering what it would be like to marry Paden, leave the confines of the city behind, and live on a ranch. Have children. But could she fall in love with him?

Time would tell.

"Angelique, Dear?"

She snapped from her musings and looked at Veronica.

"The captain asked you a question."

Angie felt her face warm to a blush. "Forgive me. I guess my mind wandered."

"Quite all right." He smiled patiently. "I merely suggested a stroll after dinner."

"The three of us?"

"Ah . . . well . . ." Garrett shifted uncomfortably in his chair.

"You're very kind to offer," Angie went on, "but I'm not up to it. You two go ahead without me."

Two pairs of wide eyes stared at Angie. She blinked back, unsure of what she'd done. Then it struck her; Garrett wanted her company to himself. Angie dabbed at the corners of her mouth with her starched linen napkin and recalled Paden's statement about Garrett being determined to win her hand in marriage. Surreptitiously, she wondered if Garrett knew about his cousin's equivalent goal.

"It is a bit chilly tonight, Captain, don't you think?" Veronica stated politely. "Perhaps we could adjourn to the parlor and play checkers."

Angie had to smile at Garrett's obvious lack of enthusiasm. "Veronica is a marvelous musician," she said. "Maybe we can convince her to play the piano for us."

"I'd like that," he said, glancing Veronica's way.

The woman blushed to her honey-brown hairline. "Angelique, Darling, I don't play that well."

"Of course you do."

Veronica sent her a hooded glance.

Angie returned an innocent smile.

With the meal finished, the three ambled into the parlor, and

Veronica grudgingly took her place at the spinet in the far corner. After a few minutes of practice, she began to play a sweet melody that plucked at Angie's heartstrings. "What's the name of this piece?"

The question had been intended for Veronica, but Garrett replied. "It's called 'Lorena,' if I'm not mistaken. It was a song with a powerful punch to Rebel soldiers back in the war. Some became so lonesome when they heard it, they deserted their army."

"You're correct, Captain," Veronica stated with a quick glance over her shoulder. "It's one of my favorites."

"I've never heard you play it before," Angie remarked curiously.

"That's because it makes me sad. But tonight, for some reason, I felt like playing it." Then Veronica began to sing.

The years creep slowly by, Lorena,
    The snow is on the grass again;
The sun's low down the sky, Lorena,
    The frost gleans where the flow'rs have been.
But the heart throbs on as warmly now,
    As when the summer days were nigh;
Oh! the sun can never dip so low,
    A-down affection's cloudless sky.

"That is sad. I think I'm going to cry!" Angie declared, blinking back tears.

Garrett grinned sheepishly before he leaned back, crossed his booted foot to the opposite knee, and stretched his arm across the top of the settee. He appeared, in a word, comfortable. "How is it that a Rebel's song is your favorite, Mrs. Huntington?"

She stopped playing. "Angelique and I hail from Virginia, Captain."

Angie's melancholy vanished, and she laughed softly after glimpsing Garrett's surprised expression.

"Do you mean to tell me that I'm keeping company with Rebel women?" he teased. "I was a Union officer, you know."

"Take heart, Captain," Veronica crooned, "the piece was written by a Northerner and published first in the city of Chicago. Ironic that 'Lorena' was a favorite Confederate love song, don't you think?"

Garrett chuckled heartily. "Ironic, indeed." He glanced at Angie, who was seated across the room. "I'm glad the war is over and I hope never to see another one."

"Amen!" she exclaimed.

Veronica turned back to the piano and played the woeful love song once again, sending a wave of nostalgia crashing over Angie.

Her memories of the war included a sick mother and a ne'er-do-well stepfather. Just before the Civil War began, he got gold fever and moved his entire family to a boomtown in California. Veronica and her husband traveled across the country along with them, and both father and son-in-law panned for gold upon their arrival. Neither ever struck it rich as they'd planned, and both took up diabolical practices, such as drinking and gambling, as they traipsed from one mining town to the next, leaving their families to fend for themselves. Then, after Angie's mother died, her stepfather did the most despicable thing a man can possibly do: He violated his sixteen-year-old step-daughter. Grievously ashamed and believing that everything wrong in her step-father's life was her fault, Angie never told anyone about the abuse, and she continued to follow him from town to town, saloon to saloon. She was afraid to do otherwise. Finally, he ended up at Chicago Joe's and, in payment for a night of boozing and card playing, he virtually sold Angie into a life of prostitution.

"Veronica, stop playing that song, and don't play it ever again!"

Obviously startled, she paused in midchord, her fingers hovering above the ivory keys, and glanced over at Angie. "Whatever is the matter, Darling?"

"That song evokes horrible memories. Please, stop playing it this instant."

A light of comprehension entered her gaze. "Of course. Your request is my command. From this moment on, you'll never hear 'Lorena' in this house. How about a game of checkers?" She swivelled around on the piano stool. "Captain, you and I can begin, and the winner will play Angelique."

"All right."

Agreeable as he was, he looked a bit confused by Angie's outburst. She could hardly explain about her jaded past and how it still haunted her at the most inconvenient times. He'd never understand, and in that moment, Angie could only think of one man who would: Paden Montano.

*I*t's been an enjoyable evening, as usual," Garrett said as Veronica handed him his overcoat. "Thank you for inviting me."

"Our pleasure, Captain."

Angie hid a little smile, thinking her stepsister seemed on the verge of falling head over heels in love with the man. She'd caught Veronica gazing at Garrett tonight on several occasions, and there had been no mistaking the stars in her eyes.

"You'll have to come back and visit us soon," Veronica said invitingly.

"Yes, I'd like that." He turned and looked at Angie. "Good night, Angelique."

She effected a tight smile. "There is a matter I wish to discuss with you, Captain. It won't take long. Do you mind?"

"Not at all." In fact, he seemed rather encouraged, much to Angie's dismay.

She grabbed her shawl. "I won't stay out in the night air long," she said to Veronica, whose face fell with disappointment. "I won't be but a moment," she whispered in promise.

Her stepsister merely nodded.

Outside on the porch, Garrett smiled broadly as if he relished this moment alone with her. "What's on your mind? I hope it's the same thing that is on mine."

"I doubt it," Angie replied. She wetted her lips before continuing. "Garrett, why did you lie to me the other day, saying Paden wasn't in his hotel room when he was?"

Garrett looked taken aback by the question. "I . . . well, I . . ." He frowned. "How do you know I lied?"

"Paden told me."

"Perhaps he's the one who's lying."

"Is he?"

Garrett stared at her for several weighted moments, then shook his head. "All right, I'll confess it, for the sin has been pricking my conscience ever since. Yes, I lied. I couldn't seem to help it. The thought of you having anything to do with my cousin causes me to feel insanely jealous."

Angie nibbled her lower lip in consternation. "You need to ask God for strength to get over your jealousy. That's a sin unto itself."

"I know. I know." He glanced off in the distance, then swung his gaze back to her. "My cousin has designs on you, Angelique, in case you haven't noticed."

"Yes, I know," she answered candidly.

"You do?"

She nodded. "He told me."

"He did?" Once the reply registered, Garrett shook his head in irritation. "The knave. Well, I hope you won't be fooled by his philandering ways. He'll leave you brokenhearted, my dear. In fact, I suspect Paden has left town already. I stopped by the hotel late this afternoon and was told at the front desk that he had checked out."

"He'll be back," she stated simply, knowing she couldn't actually dispute the news without giving away important secrets.

"So, you've fallen for him already, eh?" Angie saw an angry muscle work in his jaw. Seconds later, his features relaxed and he stepped closer to her. "You're so young, Angelique," he said softly. "You're young and naive, and of course you'd succumb to Paden's practiced charm."

"You don't know me at all. I'm not as naive as you think. I haven't been a Christian for long and before my conversion I did some things . . . bad things."

"I could give a whit what's in your past. The Bible says old things pass away, behold all things become new after we accept Christ. I've

An Unmasked Heart

done some things in my life that I'm not proud of. I'm sure everyone has."

"No, you don't understand. I mean . . . what if you found out I did something horrible. Terrible."

A wry grin curved one side of his mouth. "Like what?"

Angie tried to conjure up something equally as appalling as her former lifestyle. "Well, what would you say if I told you I was once a female outlaw and ran with a murdering gang?"

Garrett dropped his head back and howled with amusement. "I'd say you and Veronica need to stop reading those silly novels." He chuckled again and sat down on the top stair.

Angie lowered herself down beside him, wondering what she could say, other than the truth, to dissuade him. "All right, I wasn't an outlaw," she said, her voice but a whisper, "but I'm not the woman you think I am. I have a . . . a past that I'm ashamed of."

"I told you, the past is the past," he replied in a steady tone, "and I could care less what's in yours. The woman you are today is the one I love."

Angie gulped. She couldn't believe what she was hearing. His words were like a sweet song to her ears. Still, she wasn't beyond the notion that if he really knew what she'd been, he wouldn't be saying he didn't care.

"Does Paden know about your past?"

"Yes. . . ."

Garrett turned to face her. "You told him the details?"

Angie shook her head. "I didn't have to. He knew me back then."

"Excuse me?" His eyes were wide with incredulity.

"I guess it's my turn to confess to some deceit. You see, my mother died, leaving me with a horrid stepfather who abandoned me in Silverstone. Paden was employed by the army and served as the town's sheriff at that time. He was the one who helped me leave and come here to San Francisco . . . and to Veronica." It wasn't the whole truth, but Angie congratulated herself on spilling that much to Garrett.

"Hm," he said, nodding, "this is beginning to make more sense. I

535

had wondered how my cousin could know so much about you in a matter of days."

"I begged him not to tell you anything. When I left Silverstone, I left nothing but wretchedness, and I've worked hard for six years to develop my relationship with the Lord and put my past behind me."

"From what I've heard of Silverstone, I can well imagine your desire to escape it. I'd rather battle the raging sea any day than be stranded in the sun-blanched, untamed territories." Garrett swivelled and took her hand in both of his. "Look, I don't care, Angelique. So you're not from high society. So you were forced to take up residence in a miserable place. All that doesn't matter now. You're born again."

"It shouldn't matter, you're right," Angie countered. "Unfortunately, my past will have lasting effects on me, I'm sure."

"You must put it all behind you, my dear."

Angie knew his suggestion was much easier said than done. "And what would your family say? Would they ever approve of someone like me—a woman with a tarnished history?"

"Is that what you're worried about?" Garrett chuckled. "Well, allow me to put your mind at ease. My family doesn't have to know all the whys and what-fors about your life. It'll stay between the two of us."

"And what if your mother investigates me to be sure I'm a suitable match for her son?"

Garrett shrugged. "We'll get married before we set sail to Maine."

With a long sigh, Angie realized Paden was right: Garrett wasn't about to take no for an answer. Even a partial truth hadn't deterred him.

"Promise me you'll reconsider, Angelique."

She pulled her hand from his grasp and an image of Veronica flashed across her mind. "I . . . I'm not the woman for you, Garrett."

"Yes, you are. You simply haven't realized it yet."

Angie stood. "All right. I'll reconsider," she said to forestall further debate. "But I can't guarantee I'll change my mind."

"It's enough for me to know you're at least rethinking my offer."

Angie nodded in agreement. "But you have to promise me something in return."

"Anything." His earnestness was endearing if nothing else.

She smiled. "Promise me you'll pray about this matter . . . with an open mind, asking the Lord to specifically show you if we're to marry."

"I promise to do exactly that."

Reaching for her hand, he brought it to his lips, placing a quick kiss on her fingers. Angie became immediately aware that the ardent gesture didn't hold the same effect as Paden's.

"Good night, Angelique."

"Good night," she replied, watching as he descended the rest of the stairs to the street. Turning on her heel, she reentered the house.

꿋

Sitting in front of the open attic window, Paden listened to the touching scene taking place two stories below. He knew he shouldn't eavesdrop, but he'd happened upon Angie and Garrett's conversation quite innocently, and now he couldn't seem to tear himself away.

Paden listened as she tried in vain to discourage his cousin, thinking that any man in his right mind would accept the rejection and let it go at that; but Garrett seemed dogged in his quest to win her hand in marriage, while Angie remained ever the diplomat. Another, weaker-willed woman, Paden decided, would most likely succumb to Garrett's impassioned pursuit. He grinned. But not Angie.

However, he heard her agree to reconsider. Was it a measure to put Garrett off, or did she mean it?

A cool ocean breeze sailed in through the window and Paden suddenly became aware of the throbbing in his arm. It tingled and ached right down to his fingertips, indicating obvious nerve damage. He only prayed it would heal. Lifting his arm by taking hold of his wrist, he tucked his hand through two buttons on his shirt, creating a makeshift sling. The pain eased somewhat. Then his side began to hurt where a bullet had grazed him, and he wondered if he'd cracked a rib in the process. His present discomfort combined with thoughts of Angie pushed him to the decision to call it quits with the Pinkerton Agency. He'd had enough gunfights to last a lifetime. It was time to settle down.

He heard footsteps and glanced toward the stairwell, where Angie soon appeared, balancing a large tray. In the other hand, she carried a lighted lamp. Paden smiled a greeting, then met her halfway, taking the lamp from her so as to ease her load. "What did you bring me?"

"Fish and rice," she replied, walking the rest of the way to the sewing room and setting down the tray. She turned and bestowed on him the loveliest of smiles. "Mr. Hing must think I've begun to eat like a moose since this is the second time this evening that I've asked him for a special meal, but I want you to regain your strength."

Paden grinned and placed the lamp on the table near Angie's sewing machine. "I appreciate your efforts."

Angie shrugged, looking a tad embarrassed, and it occurred to Paden that her cheeks suddenly matched the pink flounces and ribbons adorning her white dress. With her blond hair plaited and pinned on top of her head, she reminded Paden of a beautiful princess who'd just stepped from the illustrated pages of a fairy tale. Little wonder his cousin was so besotted with her.

"How's your arm?" she asked with a quizzical frown, seeing his hand inside his shirt.

"It hurts."

"Yes, I imagine. Would a sling help? I could make you one in a matter of minutes."

"*Sí*, Angie, that would help tremendously."

She gave him an accusatory glance. "You haven't been exercising again, have you?"

"No," he said with a grin. Then he raised his right hand. "On my honor I swear that I have been resting just as you instructed."

"Well, good."

Paden had to chuckle. "Does Garry know how bossy you are?"

Angie expelled an indignant huff, causing Paden to laugh all the more. "Shh, Veronica will hear."

"*Lo siento,*" he whispered. "I will try to be more quiet."

Sitting on the fainting couch, he watched as Angie unwound a yardage of material from a bolt, cut it, then began folding it. Next, she walked over to him and draped the fabric around his neck. After a few quick measurements, she took the cloth back to her sewing table and picked up a needle and thread.

"Paden, may I ask you a personal question?"

He debated the reply while watching her expertly weaving the needle in and out of what would soon be his new sling. "You may ask, but I may not be in a position to answer it."

She stopped her sewing and glanced across the room at him. "It's about love."

"What about it?"

"Well . . . how do you know if you're in love or not? I mean, you said you knew I wasn't in love with you . . . yet." She kind of smirked before taking up her needle again. "Are you in love with me, Paden? And if you are, how do you know you are?"

He grinned. "Nothing like a forthright woman to keep a man on his toes," he quipped. He rose and ambled to the window, staring out over the rooftops of San Francisco, trying to select the right words. "Let me see, how can I answer your question? Love, hm?" Turning, he faced her again. "I think love is a many-faceted emotion. Physical attraction, compatibility, and practicality are three of those facets. When I look at you, Angie, I like what I see. I would not mind waking up to find you lying beside me every morning."

"Paden!" She sounded properly chagrined.

"Well, you asked."

"Yes, I did, didn't I?" she muttered.

He chuckled softly, knowing that if she lifted her head from her sewing, he would see that her cheeks were as red as chili peppers. "Now, for compatibility," he continued, "you and I are very compatible. We seem to understand each other in a way that transcends mere interactions. For instance, in a glance I can tell what you feel in your heart . . . and, if I'm not mistaken, you can do the same with me."

She glanced at him, obviously calculating his words.

"As for practicality, you want to have a family, Angie, and I am more than ready to settle down. I am a man who adheres to his commitments and I am a Christian, so when I promise to be faithful, you can be assured I mean it. I'm also a capable man, and I'll earn a good living. I was reared on a ranch, so I know about horses, cattle, the annual drives, and the hard work." He paused before adding, "And if you don't know how to cook yet, you're smart enough to learn. I am not worried that I'll starve to death."

"Very funny," she shot at him. "For your information, I cook very well."

"See? There you have it. A future together is meant to be."

Angie tied off the thread, then lifted her scissors and cut it from the material. Rising from the wooden chair, she crossed the room and fitted him with his new sling. With his injured arm tightly secured now, he felt the pain slowly subside.

"Paden," Angie began, "your definition of love sounds too impersonal to me. You can't select a wife like you'd select a prized calf. There's got to be some feeling behind it—and more than mere physical attraction."

"True love takes time to cultivate, to grow and blossom."

She stared up at him, her blue eyes searching his face, searching for answers he didn't possess.

"Follow your heart, *querida*," he said, fingering several silky, gold strands near her temple which had come loose from their pinning. Then suddenly, he longed to kiss her, except he vividly recalled her adverse reaction to his cousin taking such liberties, and quickly squelched the desire. He was not, by nature, a patient man; however, he would bide his time for Angie's sake, so as not to scare her off.

"Have you ever been in love?" she asked, still gazing up at him sweetly.

He grinned. "I don't believe so . . . unless, of course, you want to count the time when I was seven and terribly infatuated with my schoolteacher, Margarita Benicia Carrillo. Alas, she broke my heart and ran off with one of the ranch hands."

Angie's eyes sparkled with amusement and when she smiled, it was as if the room filled with sunshine. Paden wondered if it would be so easy to bide his time after all.

As if divining his thoughts, she took a step backward. "I should go and leave you to eat your meal in peace."

Paden replied with a single nod.

"But, do you want to know a secret, first?"

"What's that?" he said, thoroughly enchanted by the young woman standing before him.

"I think Veronica has developed feelings for Garrett."

Paden raised curious brows. "Is that right?"

"Yes. I'd ask her about love, except I don't think she's inclined to discuss the subject. Not yet. But if I could get Garrett to—"

"Ah-ah-ah," he cut in on a warning note. "Do not play the matchmaker, or you will be sorry."

"I don't intend to play matchmaker," she replied indignantly. "I just want to help things along a bit."

"Stay out of the way, Angie. You will only hurt the ones you love by interfering. If God wants Garry and your stepsister together, He will work out the details. In fact, He has already."

She weighed his words, then nodded. "You're right. I guess I'm a romantic at heart."

Paden couldn't help teasing her. "Well, I am not a man opposed to romance. Save your antics for me."

She gave him a quelling look, and he laughed.

"Shh!"

"My apologies," he whispered.

"Angelique?"

Her eyes widened, and beneath the glow of lamplight, she resembled a little girl caught in the act of snitching a second cookie. "Coming, sister dear," she finally replied.

"I heard a man's voice up there."

Angie grimaced. "Um . . . it must have come from outside. Perhaps you heard Mr. Hing. In any case, I'll be right down." Whispering, she told Paden, "I'll have to take my lamp. It'll look suspicious if I show up without it."

"Do not worry. I have the one you brought up last night if I feel like reading. Otherwise, the moonlight coming through the window is bright enough by which to eat."

"All right, then." She gave him a parting smile. "Good night."

"Good night, Angie. Sleep well."

As he watched her departure, he felt oddly remorseful. He would miss her challenging inquisitions and delightful company. Her smile. Her twinkling, blue eyes. He hoped she would not stay away too long.

He moved toward the tray she'd left and had to grin at the sudden irony. He might have set out to charm Angie Brown, but it was she who had somehow taken hold of his heart.

And then he wondered if this is what it felt like to fall in love.

14

*V*eronica could not be placated; she insisted she had heard a man's voice in the attic. "It's him, Angelique. It's Billy!"

"No, it's not. I was just up there, and I promise I didn't see or hear that horrid man." Angie sighed. "He's dead, Veronica. He can't come back and haunt you. It's impossible."

"Then I'm going mad."

"No, no, there's a reasonable explanation for what you heard."

"What is it?"

Angie fretted over her lower lip, hovering between honesty and loyalty. "I can't tell you right now," she replied at last. "Please, don't ask me why. I promised I wouldn't say."

Veronica's features relaxed, and she suddenly appeared almost excited. "Is it a . . . a surprise?"

"Well, yes."

"Oh, I just love surprises! What are you up to, Angelique?"

"I told you, I can't say."

"Who are you hiding up in the attic? A carpenter? Is he restoring that old desk of my mother's—the one I'm so fond of? It's a sight for sore eyes, isn't it? It fell off the wagon twice on the journey across the country. Billy swore if it fell off a third time, he'd chop it to pieces and use it for kindling."

Angie inadvertently glanced at the ceiling, wondering if Paden could make himself useful and refinish wood, even though he could use only one arm.

"All right, Angelique. I'll let you have your fun. I won't snoop or question you further, but it is quite late for a man to be working in our house. I hope he doesn't plan to stay much longer." She chuckled.

"Oh, I can't fathom how you snuck a man in here, right under my nose. Mr. Hing must be in on your little secret." She laughed once more. "You're such a dear thing."

Angie produced a tiny smile and watched her stepsister retire to her room. She felt clammy from the stress of Veronica's interrogation. Short of lying, Angie didn't know how much longer she could hide Paden.

Entering her own room, she folded down the bedcovers, then began her nightly routine. Perhaps tomorrow, she thought, unpinning her hair, she would hear from Mr. Stephenson, and he'd tell her that Paden could safely be freed. As she picked up her silver-handled brush, she wondered why she felt a twinge of disappointment.

&

"Look what I brought for you ladies!" Garrett boomed as he entered the dress shop the next morning. "You're always feeding me, so I decided to return the favor."

Angie looked up from her hemming. "It smells delicious, whatever it is."

Veronica stood from the table at which she'd been sitting, scouring the latest Butterick pattern book, and met him at the door. "Cinnamon. I smell cinnamon."

"Indeed you do, Mrs. Huntington. And I've been told that these are the best frosted cinnamon rolls in the entire city."

"How thoughtful of you, Captain. Please come in." She turned. "Angelique, please set the tea kettle to boiling."

Angie lay aside the gown on which she'd been sewing and made her way to the back room. Just as she arrived, someone in the alley pounded on the back door. She turned to Mr. Lee, who dutifully answered it.

"I have a delivery for a Mrs . . . um . . ." The kind-faced, hired man, who appeared as though he might be someone's beloved grandfather, opened the order slip in his hand. "Mrs. Paden Montano."

"No one here by that name," the bulky security guard replied, closing the door.

"Wait!" Angie said. She gave Mr. Lee an embarrassed, little smile. "I know who that is. I'll accept the delivery."

He had the good grace not to ask, but assisted the older man with a valise. The contents, Angie suspected, were Paden's belongings from the hotel. Now how in the world was she supposed to get them from here to the house?

"Mr. Lee, would you mind terribly storing this large satchel in the far corner back there? I'll retrieve it later."

He silently nodded his acquiescence.

Angie peered out the curtained threshold to find Veronica and Garrett chatting amicably. She sighed with relief. At least they'd been preoccupied these past minutes, but how was it that Chief Stephenson sent something to *Mrs.* Paden Montano. That creature didn't exist. Although Angie had to admit, the name had a nice ring to it.

The water came to a boil and Angie finished preparing the tea before carrying it out on a large tray. Reaching the table, she set down her burden and placed cups and saucers in front of Veronica first, then Garrett. Next, she began to pour the tea, but when her gaze met the captain's angry stare, she gasped and missed his cup, spilling onto the table. Angie quickly soaked it up with one of the linen napkins on the tray.

"Mrs. Huntington just informed me of your little endeavor to surprise her. Is it true, Angelique, that you're harboring a man in your attic?"

She felt the blood drain from her face.

"He's working on Mother's desk. I'm sure of it," Veronica interjected. "I always guess secrets."

Angie laughed, but it sounded nervous to her own ears. "You shouldn't have told Garrett, you silly thing. Now he won't be surprised, either."

She chanced a look at him and he narrowed his gaze suspiciously. Suddenly Angie felt like her corset was much too tight.

"I, um, think I forgot something in the back room. Please excuse me."

She turned to go, but Garrett stood and quickly caught her elbow. "I think you need a bit of air, Angelique. You look rather . . . peaked." Before she could reply, he propelled her from the shop.

"Unhand me," she hissed.

He ignored her and led her down the boardwalk, past several curious pairs of eyes.

"You're hurting me, Garrett, and you're making a scene."

They rounded the corner and he stopped, placed his hands on her shoulders, and gave her a mild shake. "Where's Paden?"

"How should I know?"

"What are you up to?"

"Nothing."

"Who's in your attic?"

Angie swallowed the humiliation threatening to well in her eyes. "Veronica thinks the ghost of her late husband is up there. I've tried to tell her otherwise—"

"What do you take me for, a fool?"

At his harsh tone, Angie couldn't contain her tears any longer.

"Angelique, I want the truth."

"I . . . I can't tell you," she sniffled in reply.

Garrett straightened, and Angie realized she'd forgotten what an imposing figure he made. "If you won't tell me, I'll just have to find out for myself."

Pivoting, he took off walking in the direction of her home, and Angie debated whether he'd actually barge into their private residence and search the attic. But then, knowing his jealous temperament, she decided he would, and she made the choice to go after him.

"Garrett, wait. Please." He kept up his pace, and Angie had to trot to catch up. "I can explain everything."

Garrett refused to reply, although she saw an angry muscle work in his jaw. They neared her street, rounding another corner, and within minutes, Garrett was marching up to the front door with Angie, feeling winded, coming up behind him. He held out his hand. "I want your key."

"I don't have it," she replied honestly, breathlessly. "It's at the shop."

Garrett knocked loudly on the wooden door, while Angie prayed Mr. Hing was away at the market. Unfortunately, he answered, fulfilling his role as an occasional butler. To Angie's horror, Garrett pushed his way past the Chinese man, who began muttering in annoyance.

"It's all right, Mr. Hing," she tried to assure him, except she wasn't certain anything was "all right" at the present moment.

In reply, the dedicated employee shuffled angrily into the kitchen. Angie strode into the parlor and collapsed into an armchair. Moments later, she heard Garrett's thundering voice; he'd obviously found Paden. Then all was eerily quiet, and Angie hoped the two men hadn't killed each other.

Her temples began to throb. Leaning back in the chair, she rubbed them in a circular motion with her fingertips. Unfortunately, the throbbing soon became a pounding, and her laudanum was in the attic with Paden.

"Angelique?" Veronica's voice hailed her from the foyer. "Are you here, Angelique?"

"In the parlor."

Veronica sailed through the doorway. "I'm so glad I found you here. I was so worried, I closed the shop for the morning. Whatever is going on? Why was the captain acting so strangely?"

Angie stood, trying to ignore her brain-twisting headache. "Come along, I'll show you why."

Taking her stepsister's hand, she led her up one flight of stairs, but when they came to the steps to the next floor, Veronica balked.

"I am not going up there, Angelique."

"Yes, you are. There's nothing to be afraid of. I'll be right beside you, and Garrett is up there along with . . . well, you'll soon find out."

"But the ghost—"

"There is no such thing. Now it's time to face your fears, sister dear. Soon you'll see you've been afraid of nothing for years."

Grudgingly, Veronica ascended the steps. "At least I'm facing my fears in broad daylight," she muttered.

They reached the attic, and Angie felt her stepsister's grip tighten around her hand. "Don't be afraid."

Veronica gave her a skeptical glance, but Angie continued onward to the sewing room. They walked in, disturbing a discussion; however, Angie was pleased to see both men acting calm and civil, even though she hadn't forgiven Garrett for his gruff behavior.

Veronica gasped. "Why, Mr. Montano, what are you doing here? And your arm . . . whatever has happened?"

Angie sent Paden an apologetic look. "I couldn't keep your presence a secret any longer. I'm so sorry."

"Do not worry, *mi amada*. It could not be helped."

"What's going on?" Veronica asked once more.

"I'll let Paden explain," Angie said, spying the brown bottle of laudanum on the sewing table, adjacent to the fainting couch. She crossed the room and picked up her medicine. "By the way," she told Paden, "Chief Stephenson dropped your belongings off at the shop. They're in a valise in the back room." She glanced around the tiny group. "Now, if you'll excuse me, I must lie down. I've acquired one of my sick headaches."

"Of course, Darling," Veronica replied.

"Angelique, may I have a word with you before you leave?" Garrett asked.

"No, you may not," she snapped. "And I hope to never speak to you again!" With that, Angie spun on her heel and ran for the sanctuary of her bedroom.

15

aden relaxed on the settee in the parlor in the company of his cousin and Mrs. Huntington. It was nice to be out of seclusion, although he sorely missed Angie. She had remained in her room, nursing a headache, causing him some concern; but her stepsister insisted Angie's "sick headaches" were a fairly common occurrence and that she usually recovered within twenty-four hours.

"Would you like some coffee, Mr. Montano? Captain?" Paden politely declined, but Garrett accepted a cup. Veronica relayed the order to her Chinese employee.

"The meal was delicious," Garrett remarked.

"*Sí, gracias,*" Paden agreed. "Scrumptious fare, to be sure."

Veronica blushed prettily. "Oh, well, you're both quite welcome. But I enjoyed our dinner conversation the best." She turned to Garrett. "It seems I've developed a fascination for ships. Thank you for answering all my silly questions."

He smiled broadly. "Glad to oblige. Ships and the sea are two of my favorite topics."

Paden tried to conceal his mirth. It seemed Angie was right: Her sister did appear romantically interested in Garry.

He studied the two and thought they made a handsome couple. Both were kindhearted souls, although Veronica was still in need of salvation. Even so, had it not been for her compassion in seeing to it that Paden obtained his valise from the dress shop this afternoon, he would not be clothed in a fresh shirt and trousers tonight. And Garry . . . he had been extremely concerned about Paden's wounds.

So concerned, in fact, he forgot how angry he was that Paden had been hiding out in the Huntingtons' attic.

"It's such a shame Angelique didn't feel well enough to join us this evening," Garrett said. Sitting across the room from Paden, he shook his head. "I feel just awful. I acted like a veritable brute this morning."

Paden wasn't about to argue, having heard his cousin's side of the story. Little wonder Angie didn't want to speak to him.

"If she wasn't quite so spirited and independent, I wouldn't get so angry," Garrett mused aloud. "But I know she's young. . . ."

"Garry, your anger is your problem, not Angie's."

Garrett clenched his jaw in reply, although he appeared to be considering the remark.

"On the other hand, the captain is right. Angelique is somewhat vivacious and individualistic, but that's her creative nature," Veronica informed the men. "She has the most unique notions, and she's very talented with a needle and thread. Why, Huntington House Dress Shop was her brilliant idea. There I was, a widow with dwindling funds, unsure of what to do with the rest of my life. Then Angelique showed up at my door in need of a place to stay . . . why, she gave purpose to my life again."

Suddenly, a knock sounded at the front door. A look of surprise flashed across Veronica's face before she excused herself to answer it. When she left the room, Garrett shook his head, his expression one of disappointment. "Angelique needs a man with a firm hand to curb that independence of hers."

Paden chuckled. "I rather like an independent woman."

Garrett snorted. "Have you not read in the Scriptures that a wife is to submit to her husband?"

"Yes, but if I recall the passage correctly, the apostle Paul prefaces his instructions to wives by saying that both spouses must submit themselves to one another in the fear of God." Paden grinned. "Husbands have their own share of submitting to do—which was quite difficult for me to understand at first. You see, the home in which I grew up was quite patriarchal. My father was the ruler and my mother was to obey his every word. While he loved her deeply—still does—he could be a tyrant. Of course, he has tempered with age. But my mother was a bit like Angie, idealistic and independent, and I remember as a child—" He shook his head. "Ai-yai-yai! The sparks would fly between my parents."

"That's because she didn't submit to her husband."

"Partly true. But my father submitted to no one either . . . not even to the Lord."

Garrett sat back, looking agitated. He folded his muscular arms across his chest. "So what's your point, *Cousin?*"

"My point is that there must be a give and take in marriage. It cannot be so one-sided as one orders, the other obeys."

"Yeah? What makes you such an expert? You know no more about marriage than I do."

"True, but I know women. I lived with my mother and sisters, and I know a man has to approach females in a careful way if he hopes for a good response."

"All right, I agree with that much. But my 'approach,' as you call it, is much different than yours."

"*Sí,* it is—and look how Angie responds. If I may remind you, *Cousin,* she is currently not speaking to you."

Garrett opened his mouth in rebuttal, but Veronica suddenly appeared at the doorway. "Mr. Montano, the chief of police is here to see you." She looked a bit flustered. "He says he'd like to speak with you . . . in private."

Paden rose from his place on the settee. "Thank you, Mrs. Huntington," he said with a slight bow.

"I hope there's no trouble."

He gave her an assuring smile. "Do not fret. Andy Stephenson is a friend of mine."

"A friend?" She looked over her shoulder at her uniform-clad guest before turning back to him. "Oh. Well, then . . ." She smiled, looking both curious and concerned. "I'll leave you two to your conversation."

"*Gracias.*"

Stepping into the front hallway, Paden grinned at the sight of his longtime friend standing by the door.

"*Amigo,*" he greeted, "I would shake your hand, but as you can see, my right arm is in a sling and is temporarily out of commission."

Stephenson smirked. "Forget the handshake. I'm just happy to see you're alive."

"*Sí*, me, too."

The two men walked farther into the foyer so they wouldn't be overheard. "Listen, Pal," Andy began seriously, "I won't mince words; you need to get out of town. Fast. Rosewahl died this afternoon, and his son is distraught. He personally told me that he's looking to kill you and kill everything you love—just like you killed his father.

"Now, look, Paden, I've conducted an impromptu investigation, and I've found that Rosewahl and Littleton were involved in a mining speculation scheme. Rosewahl's bank was more or less the cover for the whole operation. Munson got involved when he came to town with his ill-gotten gains. Anyone with no conscience and a lot of money was welcome to join. When I told young Frank Rosewahl about the conspiracy, he refused to believe it and threatened to kill me, too, so I locked him up. But I don't know how long I can keep him behind bars. He's already hollering for his attorney, and our police force has many San Francisco residents suspicious because of lies and rumors that originated from men like Rosewahl and Littleton. They were in the upper echelon of society, well-respected in the business district by day and veritable thieves by night. Therefore, if I keep Frank in jail and his lawyer decides to smear our reputation further, we could end up with riots."

"I understand. Let him go," Paden replied, leaning against the balustrade at the foot of the staircase. "I have faced dangerous men who have wanted to kill me before. I'm not afraid. I will not run like a coward."

"But you can't defend yourself. You're injured."

Paden knew he had a point there.

"Look, my friend, take my advice. Get out of San Francisco, marry that little imp you sent into my station, and settle down somewhere."

"Little imp?" He grinned. "You mean Angie?"

Stephenson chuckled. "I do, indeed. She walked into the station and, in order to get around one of my officers, announced herself as Mrs. Paden Montano. When the news got out, it caused quite a few chuckles among my men who know you."

Paden grinned broadly, feeling oddly encouraged. "*Sí*, I'm sure it did. To tell you the truth, I have already proposed marriage to Angie and she is . . . considering my offer."

"So, you know this woman?"

He nodded.

Stephenson frowned. "How well do you know her?"

Paden lifted a brow. "I beg your pardon?"

"Well," he drawled, leaning against the wall and folding his arms across his chest, "after *Mrs. Montano* left the station, I did a little snooping and discovered she's got a couple of aliases. Her real name is Angela Sarah Brown, also known in San Francisco as Angelique Huntington."

"I know all about Angie's past."

"I figured maybe you did." Stephenson rubbed his jaw contemplatively. "But if you care a whit about this lady, you'll get her out of San Francisco before Frank Rosewahl's attorney digs up the same information and ruins her name and her reputable dressmaking business. The two of you have been linked together. You've been seen around town. Your first mistake was taking her into Tibbles' Café. That's the gossip capital of the Golden Gate. One of the serving girls reported seeing you and Miss Huntington engrossed in an intimate chat."

Paden sighed. He recalled the afternoon clearly. Angie had admitted that she didn't love Garrett, and it was then that Paden had begun to think along the lines of winning her heart for himself.

"What I'm trying to say is, if Rosewahl's attorney doesn't slander the Huntington name, Frank might harm her to get to you."

"Harm Angie?" He narrowed his gaze. "Young Rosewahl would be signing his own death warrant if he so much as touches a single hair on her head."

"You got it bad, don't you?" One corner of Stephenson's mouth went up slightly. "I can hardly believe my ears. I guess you're serious about this woman."

"I am serious. Very serious," Paden said with absolute certainty.

Stephenson leaned forward. "Then get out of town and take her with you."

He sighed. "I can't leave San Francisco. I haven't finished my job. I haven't let Allan Pinkerton down yet, and I don't plan to start now. I must apprehend Harry Munson."

"Munson?" Stephenson shook his head. "That man is probably long gone, and you can't ride off on a manhunt with a lady in tow. It's one or the other."

After inhaling deeply, Paden let out a long, slow breath.

"What's it gonna be?"

"All right, all right. I don't know how, but I promise that by this time tomorrow, Angie and I will have left San Francisco."

❧

"There's got to be another way!"

Paden sighed as he knelt before Angie, taking her hand in his. "Believe me, I thought of everything, including sending you to my family in Mexico. Unfortunately, that idea presents its own share of problems—the foremost being your travel from the coast to the ranch on which my father is foreman. It would not be safe. Finally, I shared the dilemma with Garry, and his suggestion makes the most sense."

"But I don't want to sail to Maine with him. Not only do I not love him, but I've decided that I don't even like him."

Paden smiled warmly, revealing white, even teeth, a contrast to his brown skin and swarthy features. "I am glad to hear that."

"This isn't funny, and it's not a game of win or lose."

He sobered. "You are right." He squeezed her hand gently, his forearm now resting on her knee. "Still, I think it's the only way. You will be safe and your reputation will be spared."

Tears filled Angie's eyes as everything inside her screamed against this plan. "Paden, I get awfully seasick."

"Garry says he knows of medicine you can take. He will purchase it for you at the apothecary before you set sail."

"But I don't want to go."

Paden sighed once more. "I'm afraid you have no choice."

"What about if I leave town by way of the stagecoach?"

"And where will you go?"

Angie's heart sank. She didn't have a reply. Beseeching him with her misty gaze, she said, "Can't I go with you . . . wherever you're going?" His moment's hesitation gave her reason enough to continue. "A ranch sounds very nice. I can cook, and I'm a hard worker. You said, yourself, that it's a practical solution. You want to settle down and I want a family."

"Unfortunately, I have a job to finish before I can make that dream become a reality."

Angie swallowed, feeling wounded by his words. "So what you're saying is, your job is more important to you than I am." She yanked her hand from his and stood, then strode to the parlor windows, her arms crossed in front of her.

"You are not making this easy."

"Easy?" She spun on her heel. "I am in peril because of you. This is your fault, and now, in spite of all your sweet-talk, you're deserting me. On second thought, it's worse than desertion. You're putting me on a horrible ship of all things! But that's just fine," she said, swatting at an errant tear, "because you will never be more than a gunfighter, Paden. You just proved it."

She marched out of the room and ran up the stairs, nearly colliding with Veronica in the hallway. Glimpsing her stepsister's troubled expression, Angie's tears burst forth unchecked. "I'm so sorry," she choked. "I never wanted to ruin the Huntington name."

"Don't be silly," Veronica replied with tears of her own. "You couldn't ruin it any more than my late husband. It's a respectable name because of you . . . us. Our shop."

Angie lowered her gaze, uncertain as to how to reply. On one hand, she appreciated Veronica's compliment, but on the other, she felt ashamed of her past.

"You know," Veronica said, using her lace hanky to dab her eyes, "you and I could set up shop somewhere else. I mean, there are other large cities and some with plenty more females than this one."

Angie blinked, feeling suddenly hopeful.

"And we're East Coast women, Angelique, born in Virginia."

"You want to go back to Virginia?"

Veronica shook her head. "There's nothing for us there anymore, but Maine . . . that is, we wouldn't have to go all the way to Maine, but if the ship is headed that way, perhaps we could get off in New York."

"New York . . ." Angie thought the plan had possibilities. New York was a fashion-conscious city if ever one existed.

"Should I find the captain and ask if he'll book passage for me, too?"

"Yes!" Angie exclaimed, hugging her stepsister around the shoulders. "Oh, but, on second thought . . . could we travel by stagecoach?"

"Darling, I would never survive the trip."

Angie wasn't convinced that she'd outlive the journey by sea; however, unlike Veronica, she had the Lord to rely on for grace and strength. Somehow she would manage.

"I can't believe that you're willing to leave your home for me."

"This place? With its haunted attic?" Veronica sniffed in mock indignation. "I will be glad to get rid of it." She became thoughtful for a moment, then looked as if she were making a mental list. "I'll have to hire an agent to sell the house and liquidate our shop."

"There are trunks upstairs."

"Gracious me! We've got a million things to do before we board this evening."

Angie grinned.

"First, I must find Captain Witherspoon." Veronica headed purposely for the stairwell.

"Tell him that I will not go without you."

She tossed a smile over her shoulder. "I'll be sure to relay the message."

$\mathcal{P}$ aden found Angie's aloofness quite disturbing, and it didn't help matters that his cousin gloated over the situation's outcome. "She's not talking to you either, Garry," Paden reminded him as they sat alone at the dinner table while the ladies packed their belongings upstairs.

"Ah, yes, but I have approximately two months to remedy that little matter."

His cousin's remark caused Paden to bristle. "Just remember, New York is now the Huntington women's final destination."

Garrett chuckled. "I have two months in which to correct that, too."

But could he? Paden had to wonder. Angie had seemed adamant about her feelings for Garry. Would she change her mind?

Just then something his mother liked to say flashed across his memory. *It's a woman's prerogative to change her mind.* The phrase used to infuriate Paden's father, largely because he knew with that kind of disclaimer, he'd never get the same answer one day to the next, and with five women in the house, that got to be quite disturbing.

Well, Paden wasn't going to take that chance with Angie. He needed some sort of pledge from her or he'd likely be *loco* for the next eight weeks.

"Excuse me," he said, wiping his mouth with his linen napkin before placing it on the table. He slid his chair back and stood. "I have some unfinished business to take care of."

Garrett shrugged. "Of course."

Walking away from the dining room, he thought he might like to physically wipe the satisfied sneer off his cousin's face. Pausing at the foot of the steps, he listened to the goings-on above him, noting the excitement in Veronica's voice and the dread in Angie's. She hated traveling by ship, but perhaps she'd fare better on this journey than the one she'd taken six years ago. Regardless, he couldn't let Angie board in a matter of hours, believing he cared about his job more than he cared about her. But how could he convince her otherwise? What could he possibly say? What could he give her? What promise could he make? And why did he feel so desperate to do . . . *something?*

Paden knew the answer to the latter; simply, it tore him up inside to imagine Angie married to his cousin or any other man. Taking the stairs two at a time, he reached the top landing and put his forefinger over his lips to silence Mrs. Huntington, who'd gasped in surprise at seeing him. "I need to have a few words with Angie," he whispered.

"Well, to be honest," she whispered back, "I don't know if she'll allow it."

"I have to try."

Hesitantly, Veronica nodded.

Walking the rest of the way to Angie's room, he strode in unannounced and closed the door behind him. He took in the sight of Angie, dressed in a fawn-colored traveling suit, her blond hair coiled at her nape, and he couldn't recall ever seeing a lovelier woman.

"Veronica, I—" Angie turned around, garments dangling over her arm, and inhaled sharply. "You! What are you doing here? Get out this instant!"

"I will leave as soon as I have my say."

After an indignant little huff, she gave him a look of acquiescence. "Very well, what is it?"

Paden stepped forward, feeling less surefooted than he had a moment ago. "Now that I have your attention, I am not sure how to begin."

She gave him a perturbed little frown.

"I don't think there were ever words created to express how I feel, what I must tell you."

Her expression turned from aggravated to curious.

"I loathe the idea of you sailing out of San Francisco because I know it will be months before I see you again. Yet, I cannot think of a better escape for you. I am comforted somewhat to know your stepsister will now join you, and my cousin will be a capable escort. But I will . . . miss you, Angie."

"You will?" she asked skeptically.

"*Sí*, I will. I only hope and pray that you will miss me half as much."

In reply, she glanced at the gowns draped over her forearm.

"And you are wrong about my job. It is not more important than you," Paden said, hoping to put all her doubts to rest. "But I have an obligation, and completing this assignment fulfills my obligation to Allan Pinkerton. Only then will I be free to begin a new life, a new career. Can you even try to understand why I cannot walk away, or in this case, sail away from my work? I must finish what I have begun."

She met his gaze, and Paden's insides twisted at the sight of the anguish in her blue eyes.

"Finishing this job means another gunfight," she said, "and next time you might not emerge the victor. Next time, you might be killed."

"It's always a possibility," Paden admitted. "But will you pray for me—pray for my protection?"

She weighed her reply. "Yes, I'll pray."

Encouraged, Paden took another step closer to her. "Will you wait for me, Angie? Will you promise not to marry someone else during the interim? As soon as I apprehend Munson and surrender him to the proper authorities, I will come to New York and find you. We will then resume our . . . um . . . courtship."

"Some courtship," she muttered.

"I will make it up to you."

She searched his face, gauging his words. "I have never known you to lie."

"I am not a liar, Angie. Besides, if I didn't love you, I would not feel so troubled about your departure, yet I know there is no other recourse."

She appeared momentarily stunned. "What did you say?"

"I said, I am not lying. . . ."

"No, no, after that. You said—" She blinked. "Did you say you loved me?"

Paden paused, realizing that's exactly what he'd said. Where had those words come from, except from his heart? "*Sí*, Angie, I love you," he said, knowing now he meant every word of it.

She tossed the dresses onto a nearby chair. "When? When did you know you loved me? How?"

Paden had to chuckle at her bewildered expression. "I don't know when or how, I just know that's the way I feel. And you? How do you feel about me?"

She thought a moment before narrowing her gaze. "I feel like I could shoot you myself for all the upheaval you've caused me."

With his right arm still in a sling, he managed to lift his hand to his heart. "Such words of ardor," he quipped.

She had the good grace to look chagrined. Then, on a more serious note, she said, "I honestly don't know how I feel. You will always be special to me because you helped me escape Silverstone, but I'm unsure if that constitutes love."

He nodded, disappointment swelling in his chest. But what had he expected? Closing the distance between them, he slipped his uninjured arm around her waist and pulled her close to him. To his relief, she didn't recoil. "How many men have told you they loved you, Angie, hm?" he fairly whispered against her velvety-soft cheek.

She half laughed, half grunted at the question. "Scores of men, most of them drunkards." The reply had a bitter sound.

Paden drew his head back slightly. "I think if I were in your position, I would not believe another man who touted those three little words, 'I love you.' How empty they must sound."

Tears sprang into her eyes, and Angie tried in vain to blink them away.

"And yet, you long to hear those words—no, you long to *believe* those words, believe the man who is saying them, don't you?"

Angie nodded, her gaze lowered, her fingers fidgeting with the fraying hem of his sling.

"So it is up to me to prove my love to you, and I gladly accept the challenge. All I ask is that you wait for me. Wait for a just a little while. Until Christmas. Can you promise me that?"

Still misty-eyed, she nibbled her lower lip in contemplation while Paden held an anxious breath. At last she nodded out a subtle, but affirmative, reply.

"So you give me your promise that you'll wait?"

"Yes," she said. "I give you my promise."

"And you will board the clipper with no complaints?"

"Yes, yes. . . ."

"Good. And I promise you, Angie, you will not be sorry."

She smiled, albeit weakly, and Paden longed to kiss her tremulous, strawberry pink lips and taste of their sweetness, but instead he stepped backward. Far be it for him to lose Angie's confidence now by succumbing to physical desire. No doubt, she'd been the recipient of such contrived devotion before. Even Garrett had taken something from her that she wasn't yet ready to give.

Backing up to the door, Paden bowed courteously. "We have an understanding then, *sí?*"

Angie suddenly appeared completely at ease. She smiled, and this time it heightened the hue of her eyes. "*Sí, señor.* We have an understanding."

~&

Angie couldn't believe how lighthearted she felt after Paden left the room. It was as if a huge weight had been lifted from her, setting her spirit free again. Perhaps her anger with Paden, her disappointment in him, had been the albatross around her neck. Regardless, she found herself greatly respecting the man now. He had somehow comprehended the deepest part of her, and metaphorically, he had touched upon a place where no man had ever dared. All that, and Paden hadn't even kissed her—even though she had found herself wanting to be kissed. Quite a surprise, since Angie never imagined herself longing for a man's lips to touch her own.

"Angelique?" Veronica stepped into the room, forcing Angie from her sweet reverie. "Is everything all right?"

"Oh, yes." Oddly, she felt herself begin to blush.

"Mr. Montano didn't upset you further, did he?" Veronica seated herself, smoothing out the skirt of her brown tweed, two-piece traveling dress.

"No." Angie stared at the mirror and hairbrush in her hand before setting them into the trunk. Peeking at her stepsister from beneath lowered lashes, she added, "Paden said he loves me."

Veronica lifted a pert brow. "Is that so? Well, add another man to the list. It gets longer every day."

Angie laughed softly at the retort.

"And if I recall, the captain's name is there among the others."

"Yes, but this is different, sister dear. Paden means it."

"The others don't? Surely Captain Witherspoon is as smitten as they come."

"But don't you see? He, like others, said he loves me solely because he wants to possess me and force me to be someone I'm not, nor ever will be. Paden, on the other hand, knows and accepts me for who I am—like you did when I showed up on your doorstep so many years ago."

"Hm, I've never heard you talk this way before."

"I've never felt this way before."

"This sounds serious and, goodness, I believe I see stars in your eyes!"

Angie laughed heartily at the remark, while Veronica chuckled along with her.

"Ladies?" Garrett's voice reverberated up the staircase. "We need to leave shortly."

All amusement vanished, and the frenzy of gathering belongings and packing trunks resumed.

At last, neither Angie nor Veronica could get another item into the three trunks they had between them. Paden and Garrett made three separate trips upstairs, each man taking an end of a large trunk, then another, and another, carrying them out to the awaiting carriage. In the parlor, Veronica gave Mr. Hing last minute instructions. He could remain on the premises until the agent sold the house, and he was to guard existing assets. Furthermore, Veronica urged him to get a message to Mr. Lee at the shop. The agent would take care of handling the merchandise, but Mr. Lee needed to be informed. With each command, the Chinese man bowed courteously, and Angie felt sad to leave him behind. If she wasn't mistaken, he looked a bit sorrowful, himself.

"Time to go," Garrett announced.

Stepping outside into the evening dusk, Angie glanced around for Paden. He couldn't have left already, not without saying good-bye. Or had they said their good-byes?

Suddenly she spied him on the far side of the carriage, astride his black stallion. He had taken his arm out of the sling and, clad in ebony trousers, vest, overcoat, and wide-brimmed hat, he looked very much like the handsome sheriff who had helped her escape Chicago Joe's house of ill-fame. How ironic that she was running away from her past for a second time. Well, she determined, there would not be a third.

"Angelique?"

Garrett held the door to the carriage open, waiting to help her inside. She accepted his hand and stepped up into the coach. Within moments, the hackney lurched forward, and they were on their way to the wharf. Positioned beside her stepsister, Angie could hear Paden's horse following them.

They arrived at the docks and, familiar with the procedures of loading and boarding, Garrett immediately located the ship on which he'd secured passage, commissioned uniformed stevedores to man the trunks. His own belongings, he informed them, had been stowed earlier.

"I guess we're ready to board."

"Will the ship leave tonight?" Angie asked.

"No, tomorrow morning, but Paden and I thought it was best if we settled into our cabins early. A mere safety precaution, considering the situation."

"This is terribly exciting," Veronica remarked.

"I'm glad you think so, Madame. Let's hope your enthusiasm rubs off on Angelique."

Glancing off in the distance, Angie viewed the gentle rise and fall of the tall-masted clipper and already she could feel her stomach begin to churn. She swallowed. "The Oriental Hotel would do nicely for tonight, I think." From behind her, Paden's soft chuckle wafted to her ears. She spun on her heel. "I've changed my mind. I'm not going."

"But our passages have been paid in full," Veronica said, while Angie stared up at Paden. "This is the only way to avoid possible danger."

Angie's pleading gaze remained locked with Paden's dark eyes. "You cannot change your mind, *mi amada*. We have an agreement, remember?"

"But—"

Paden shook his head, whispering, "You promised."

Garrett cleared his throat. "We're wasting time."

At that precise moment, a shot rang out, splintering the night air and sending a shiver of terror down Angie's spine. She heard Veronica gasp, heard a man's voice shout, "Get down!" Then one moment she was on her feet and the next she lay face down near a brick wall in front of which stood a row of barrels. She lifted her head and found Veronica in a similar position. Both Garrett and Paden were sprawled out beside them, guns drawn.

"You ladies all right?" Garrett asked.

Stunned, Angie nodded. Veronica did the same.

"See anything, Garry?"

"Nothing. But I think it came from behind that warehouse."

"I think so, too." Paden sighed wearily. "If the gunman is Rosewahl's son, I am the one he wants to kill, not the rest of you." He paused. "Garry, cover my back while I make my way to my horse. I'll ride off, and hopefully our assailant will follow. After I'm gone, you three make haste and get on board the ship."

"Sounds good," Garrett agreed.

"But your arm, Paden."

"It is all right." He turned slightly to face Angie and gave her such a long look that she wanted to cry. Glancing back at Garrett, he said, "Ready?"

"Ready."

"I can't watch," Angie murmured, pillowing her head on her arms. Next to her, she felt Paden rise and heard his boots as he ran along the dusty, brick-lined alleyway that paralleled the succession of warehouses on the wharf. Then gunshots. More gunshots. The sound was deafening, and Angie had to cover her ears.

"Dear Lord, please keep him safe," she prayed aloud. "Don't let him die, please don't let Paden die. I'll keep my promise. I don't care if I have to be seasick for six months straight. Just please let Paden live."

The acrid smell of gunpowder filled her nostrils, and then the shots faded into the distance.

"Whoever's out there is definitely after Paden," Garrett said. He stood and hoisted Angie and Veronica to their feet simultaneously. A smattering of spectators had begun to gather on the piers that jutted out to assorted vessels.

"Come on, ladies," Garrett said, brushing the dust from his trousers, "we need to board our ship."

17

hat about Paden?" Angie asked as Garrett ushered her and Veronica up the gangway and onto the clipper. The sun had set and now the stars twinkled overhead in the inky-black sky.

"Paden will be fine."

"But I'm worried."

Garrett paused on the deck. "This is typical for my cousin, Angelique. He's a gunfighter involved in some sort of risky business. He enjoys it. That's his vocation. That's his life. Now, mind you, I'm thankful he is a Christian," Garrett continued. "I no longer have to concern myself with the condition of his soul. But I'm sorry that my cousin has had time to work his wiles on you, my dear. Paden charms the ladies everywhere he goes."

"He did not work his wiles on me," Angie said, angrily pulling her elbow from Garrett's grip.

He gave her a sympathetic little smile before glancing at Veronica, who watched the exchange with an interested expression. "I think it would be best if we found our cabins," Garrett said at last.

"Good idea, Captain," Veronica replied.

He smiled kindly. "On this voyage, it would be best if you didn't call me 'Captain.' It may confuse other passengers. Besides, after this journey, my seafaring days are over. I sold the *Jubilee,* even in her sorry state, and I'm looking forward to a new life as a landlubber."

"Really? How very interesting. What will you do?" Veronica asked.

"I plan to stay in the shipping business, but I'll work in the offices with my father and grandfather instead of sailing around the world."

"Won't you miss all the excitement of the sea?" Veronica queried further.

Garrett chuckled. "I should say not. In many ways, my cousin and I are alike. We have remained unmarried so we could see what we wanted to see and do what we wanted to do. For myself, I have seen and done all I care to. It's high time for me to take a wife and settle down."

Angie purposely avoided his gaze as Garrett led them below deck and through an elegant central salon.

"My, but this is quite impressive," Veronica remarked, looking around the room with its mahogany woodwork, trimmed with polished brass.

Angie nodded, thinking this vessel seemed a far sight better than the schooner on which she'd sailed coming into San Francisco years ago.

"Just look at this long table," Veronica added. "And matching benches . . . is this where we will dine, Captain—I mean, *Mr.* Witherspoon?"

Again, he gave her a warm and patient smile. "Please call me Garrett. All three of us are practically old friends. But in answer to your question, yes, this is where we'll dine."

"And these doorways?"

"They lead to cabins, Mrs. Huntington," Garrett said, opening one of the doors. "Here's ours."

"Ours?" Angie asked, suddenly alarmed.

Garrett looked mildly chagrined. "It's the best I could do on such short notice. It's a cabin with a servant's quarters, but I think we'll be quite comfortable. Come, take a look."

Uncertain, she walked through the threshold behind Veronica and saw that the cabin was actually two rooms with a doorway dividing them. The first room, intended for a servant, was very small indeed, and had one berth. However, the second room was more spacious, having two berths against the porthole wall.

"This is fine, Capt—oh, I meant to say Mr . . . I mean, Garrett." Veronica blushed over her stammering. "And you must call me by my given name."

He chuckled. "Very well." He glanced at Angie. "Are the arrangements to your liking, my dear?"

"They're very appropriate, yes. Thank you." She noticed their trunks had already been delivered and, upon further inspection, decided this cabin would do nicely.

"There won't be a meal served tonight since no other passengers are expected to board, so I thought we could hire one of the crew to fetch us dinner from one of the restaurants in town."

"That sounds wonderful. I'm famished. How about you, Angelique?"

"Yes, I'm all for the idea. But I wonder," she said, turning to Garrett, "is it possible to find out if Paden is safe?"

He sighed, looking somewhat annoyed. "I think it's best if you forget about Paden."

Veronica stepped forward. "Cap—I mean, Garrett, I know Angelique will fret all night long unless we at least *try* to accommodate her." She smiled sweetly. "Please?"

He momentarily considered the request. "All right. I'll see what I can do. At the same time, I'll arrange for our food to be brought in."

"Thank you," Veronica replied. "You're very kind."

With a parting nod, he left their room. He traipsed through his own, entering the salon and closing the main door behind him.

"That man is incorrigible!"

"No, he's not, Angelique. He has been so helpful. What would we have done without him this afternoon?"

Angie didn't think she could rightly argue the point; Garrett had been extremely solicitous to both of them.

"And didn't he manage a gun well?" Veronica exclaimed, her hazel eyes brightening. "It must have been due to all his military experiences. Nevertheless, I felt ever so safe and protected. My, but we've had an awful amount of excitement these past two days, haven't we?"

Angie had to grin at her sister's rambling.

"Well, come and see what I bought for you this afternoon," Veronica said, unlatching the sturdy leather straps of one of the steamer trunks. "It's a gift."

"You shouldn't have, Veronica."

She shrugged. "I love presents, you know. So I bought us each a journal in which we can record our daily adventures—beginning with today's."

Angie took the proffered book. She liked to read, but didn't enjoy writing. Regardless, the gesture was considerate on her sister's part. "Thank you."

"You're very welcome. And look what else I purchased."

Angie glanced into the drawer of Veronica's steamer trunk. "Dime novels!"

"Yes. I bought penny dreadfuls by the dozen!" She laughed like a girl.

Angie shook her head. "Sister dear, these books are beneath us. We should be reading Charles Dickens or Nathaniel Hawthorne."

"Oh, what fun is that? I adore wild escapades. And just think, Angelique, we've lived through some of our own. We've traveled across the country by wagon train, and now we're sailing the ocean from coast to coast."

"Yes, I suppose we have seen our share of adventure." Angie couldn't stifle her smile.

"I should say so. Perhaps we should write our own dime novel." Veronica set her leather-bound journal on the lower of the two berths. "Since you're younger, you sleep on the top."

Still chuckling over the remark about writing a novel, Angie agreed.

"And you're not feeling the least bit seasick, are you?"

"Amazingly, no, but we're still docked. I only pray I feel good once we set sail."

"Pray . . ." Veronica paused. "You know, Angelique, it's been a long time since I prayed for anything."

Startled by the admission, Angie couldn't imagine her stepsister ever petitioning God for anything. "When was the last time you prayed?"

Veronica grinned. "Just this morning, actually. When Mr. Montano and the capt—I mean, Garrett—announced their plan to whisk you away from San Francisco, I begged God not to allow it. Then, after I realized there was no viable alternative, I prayed I could go along.

Before this morning, I hadn't prayed since the day I married Billy. I didn't want to marry him, you know. My father forced me into wedlock."

Angie grimaced.

"I asked God to somehow stop the ceremony, but He didn't. After that day, I gave up asking God for anything."

"Until this morning."

Veronica nodded. "Until this morning."

Angie stepped toward her. "Sister dear, I imagine God heard all your prayers, but I have learned that His ways are higher than our ways and that the Lord can use those unexpected, unexplained tribulations in our lives. Sometimes we don't know why He has allowed such trials for us to bear, and perhaps it's not for us to ever understand. We just need to trust Him."

"Coming from you, Angelique, I might believe it's true. You have suffered as much as I, if not more."

"But there was a reason for my suffering, one being that I became a Christian during those dreadful years in Silverstone. God knew I had to reach the depths of despair before I realized my need for His salvation." Angie paused, considering her stepsister for a long moment. "What about you, Veronica? Are you aware of your own need for salvation?"

She shrugged. "I'm not sure what I believe. Can there really be a heaven and a hell? Can hell be any worse than what I've lived through with my late husband, that scoundrel?"

"Of course it can. The Bible says it will be much worse."

Veronica waved a hand in the air. "Let's not talk of such things. This is an exciting, happy time for us, Angelique. We're about to embark on a new life in New York City, although, I must admit, our life in San Francisco these past years has been quite comfortable. Still, I never cared for California and all the boomtown trash who have taken up residence in the state because of the mining prospects."

Angie nodded, sensing the moment to witness for Christ had vanished. Walking to her own trunk, she opened it and began to unpack a few necessities. Veronica did the same. Shortly thereafter, Garrett returned and announced that their supper had arrived; they would eat in the salon.

Taking a place on the bench beside her stepsister, Angie helped herself to the flaky, white rice, boiled fish with lemon sauce, and buttered carrots. Garrett sat across from them and chatted amicably about how this vessel differed from his own *Jubilee*. He admitted he would miss her, saying his ship had been his prized possession for years, but now he looked forward to starting anew.

"How ironic, Angelique and I just discussed that very thing. While we are grateful for our years as successful shopkeepers, we're excited about what lays ahead of us."

Angie merely smiled at Veronica's comment, but inside, she struggled to trust the Lord with her future. Did it include Paden? Was he safe? Had he reinjured his arm? She hoped she'd see him again. Amazingly, it saddened her greatly to think she never would. Did that mean she loved him?

The answer, she knew, was in placing her entire being in God's faithful hands. He knew the plan for her life, and He would reveal it to her in His good timing.

~&

The next morning, the sun streamed through the porthole as Angie and Veronica dressed. Angie felt a touch woozy from the all night rocking of the ship, but managed to change from her white cotton nightgown into a two-piece, tan walking dress with flounces and buttons adorning the front. Veronica donned a beige and white plaid gown with yarn tassels. Comfortably attired, they knocked on the adjoining doorway. Hearing no reply, they stepped into the smaller cabin and found it empty. Entering the salon, they spied Garrett at the long, mahogany table, sipping coffee and reading the newspaper. Seeing their approach, he wiped his mouth with a napkin and stood.

"Well, good morning, ladies," he said exuberantly. "And a fine morning it is to set sail."

After politely greeting him, Angie and Veronica seated themselves on the benches across from him. Garrett offered them warm, frosted, raisin biscuits that he had procured from a nearby bakery.

"Why, thank you," Veronica said, helping herself to one of the doughy treats. "You are the most thoughtful man I have ever known."

Garrett seemed taken aback by the candid remark. "I was brought up to revere any woman under my care. My father and grandfather were good examples to me."

"Oh, I'm sure," Veronica replied. "I merely find it . . . refreshing, is all."

Garrett grinned slightly, then looked at Angie, who quickly lowered her gaze. *Lord,* she prayed, *please let him fall in love with Veronica and not me. Garrett doesn't "revere" me—he wants to mold and shape me into his own little puppet.*

Angie picked at her biscuit, thinking that Garrett was as handsome as a man could be, with his walnut-colored hair and hazel eyes, his broad shoulders and tall frame. His very presence seemed to fill the entire salon and, while Veronica seemed woman enough to go toe-to-toe with Garrett, Angie felt suffocated by his commanding aura.

Polite chitchat ensued, but Angie remained silent throughout the remainder of the meal. Once they had finished eating, Garrett escorted them up the companionway to the deck, where they happened upon nothing short of chaos. Busy stevedores carried trunks onto the ship and called to each other while passengers boarded. Several people stood against the polished rail, waving to loved ones.

Angie searched the shoreline for Paden, thinking perhaps he'd want to say one last farewell, but her heart sank when his face didn't appear in the crowd.

"Witherspoon!"

Hearing Garrett's name, Angie swung around to see a stocky man in a blue uniform approaching.

"Well, well, if it isn't Jake Lancaster."

The other man removed his cap, revealing a balding head, and shook hands with Garrett.

Grinning broadly, Garrett made the appropriate introductions. "Veronica and Angelique Huntington, may I present Captain Jake Lancaster. We're old friends."

The man bowed courteously. "I hope you'll find your voyage comfortable, ladies. If not, please let me know at once so I may remedy the problem."

"Thank you, Captain," Veronica replied.

Angie smiled.

"You know, Witherspoon, I think it's quite unfair of you to keep such beauties to yourself."

Garrett smiled amusedly. "I am the ladies' chaperone. I'm a lucky man."

"I should say you are!"

Angie saw Veronica blush at the same time she felt her own cheeks warming in embarrassment. She glanced away, just in time to see Andy Stephenson striding up the gangway. He caught sight of her and smiled, heading in her direction. "Good morning, Miss Huntington."

She nodded demurely, feeling slightly suspicious. What did the man want? Did it concern Paden?

"I'm glad I arrived before your ship set sail," Stephenson said. "I have an important letter for you."

"Oh?" Angie took the proffered envelope, noting its wax seal.

"Yes, Paden asked me to deliver it. He said to tell you he's alive and well. One of my officers arrested the snipers last night. They turned out to be none other than Frank Rosewahl's son and a few of his friends. They'll have their day in court. Meanwhile, Paden has left town on business. I gave him my word that I would personally deliver his letter to you."

"Thank you," Angie replied. She felt so relieved to hear Paden was all right that she held the letter to her heart. "Thank you very much."

The police chief grinned wryly. "My pleasure. I wish you an enjoyable voyage."

Angie smiled, then watched as Stephenson made his way off the ship. Only then did she become aware of the three pairs of eyes staring at her. Chagrined, she excused herself and headed for the cabin, where she could read Paden's letter in private.

18

ngie read and reread Paden's letter, thinking that if the ship hadn't already set sail, she might have changed her mind and gone ashore. Rising from where she'd been sitting on the berth, she walked to her trunk and placed the letter inside her Bible. Paden certainly had a way with words; his letter had warmed her heart and sent delicious tingles down her limbs. That man could charm the birds right out of the trees if he had a mind to. While Garrett continued to insinuate that Paden charmed all the ladies who crossed his path, Angie refused to believe it. It may have been so at one time, but Paden was a Christian now. Things had changed.

Remember your promise to me, Paden wrote. *I will not forget my promise to you. I could no more forget you, Angie, than I could forget the sun in the sky or my heart beating inside my chest. . . .*

Angie sighed dreamily. How utterly poetic. Placing her Bible on top of her trunk, she suddenly felt as though having Paden's promise in writing made it somehow official. Yes, she would wait for him, and the sooner she informed Garrett of her decision, the better. Perhaps he would finally give up his ideas of marrying her and set his cap for another woman—namely Veronica.

But she's not a believer, Angie reminded herself. Nibbling her lower lip contemplatively, she decided to take up the matter with the Lord. He was in the miracle business after all—and that's what this situation required: a veritable miracle.

Paden struck a match and lit a small fire, then put the skinned rabbit on a spit across the flames. Sitting down on the rocky terrain, he glanced at his horse, which grazed on sparse clumps of grass off in the distance. Darkness was rapidly descending on the California desert, and somewhere off in the lonesome vastness, a wolf howled. Paden's horse snorted nervously. "Do not worry, *Medianoche*," he told the animal, "I will not let any harm come to you."

Returning his gaze to the campfire, Paden thought over the events of the day. Once more, he had uncovered nothing. Weeks had passed and still no trace of Munson. Paden hated to admit it, but he'd lost the man. Had he even suspected this outcome, Paden would have gotten on that ship with Angie. By now, she was probably somewhere in the South Pacific, nearing Cape Horn, her journey half-completed. Paden prayed for her daily, hoping Angie wasn't too seasick. He also prayed Garrett hadn't convinced her to marry him.

Paden turned the spit, reminding himself that if their union was meant to be, God would see to it that Angie waited for him. She had promised, and Paden planned to hold her to it.

❧

"Well, good morning, Angelique. It's good to see you out and about. You must be feeling better."

Looking up from her Bible, she smiled weakly as Garrett approached. "I am a bit better, thank you."

He looked out over the deck. "Calm seas, blue skies—a beautiful day."

Angie sighed, thanking God that the ship wasn't rocking to and fro as it had for the past two or three weeks. She had been holed up in her cabin, retching from seasickness for the duration.

"It won't be long now," Garrett mused aloud, taking a seat beside her on the bench that was firmly bolted to the deck. "We have about three weeks left to go, assuming the strong winds hold and we don't run into any more choppy weather."

"Perish the thought!"

Garrett chuckled, and Angie moved over to accommodate his girth. Then she noticed how tan his hands and arms appeared against his white shirtsleeves, which he'd rolled to the elbow. She looked up past his broad shoulders and saw his thick neck and face were sun-bronzed, and his dark brown hair now had golden highlights. He was as healthy as she was ill.

He met her gaze, and Angie averted her eyes.

"I think it might be a good idea if we disembarked in Brazil and let you recuperate," he said, leaning forward, his forearms on his knees, hands folded.

"But that will prolong our journey and you said you wanted to be home by Thanksgiving."

"True, but you're looking terribly pale and I don't think we should take a chance on you losing more weight."

Angie wetted her dry lips, suddenly ashamed of how loosely her dress hung from her shoulders. She had tried in vain to conceal her thin form.

"There'll be nothing left of you by the time we reach Maine."

Angie's head snapped up. "Maine? But Veronica and I planned to go to New York."

"Well," Garrett said haltingly, "plans have changed."

"But—"

"Now, Angelique, don't argue with me. Veronica and I discussed this matter a week or so ago and decided it would be best for the two of you to spend the holidays with my family and me in Maine. It doesn't make sense for the two of you to arrive in New York City and have no place to go. You can't very well land in a foreign city and expect to open a dress shop without the proper contacts."

She swallowed a retort, sensing he was right. "But Paden said—"

"Angelique, my cousin can track an outlaw through the desert at night, don't you think he'll be able to figure out you're in Maine?"

She cringed at his brusque reply and looked down at her Bible in her lap.

"Oh, I'm sorry," Garrett said. "Call me a sore loser. Call me whatever you want, but it displeases me greatly that you have chosen him over me. He can't offer you what I can. A life of comfort, befitting of a refined lady such as yourself, as opposed to hard work in the grueling elements on the range with a gunfighter. What are you thinking, Woman?"

"I'm thinking I'm not as 'refined' as you've assumed."

"Oh, not that again." With a derisive grunt, Garrett stood and walked to the rail and looked out across the expansive blue-green sea. "I sincerely hope you've prayed about this," he called over his shoulder.

She nodded. All she had done was pray about her promise to Paden, and the one thing God continued to reveal to her was that she could not go on living a life of pretense the way she had in San Francisco. With Paden, she could behave like the woman God created her to be: Angela Sarah Brown. Paden knew her innermost, darkest secrets, and he said he loved her regardless. Conversely, if she explained the truth to Garrett, she truly believed he would never understand.

She watched as he turned from the rail. "And this is your final decision?"

Again, she nodded.

"Very well, Angelique."

She lowered her gaze, fingering the silver-edged pages of her Bible.

With a sigh, he strode to the bench and sat down again. "I still think we should get off when the ship docks in Rio de Janeiro so you can get some rest."

"No," Angie replied, "I don't want to be a bother."

"You're no bother." He paused, before muttering, "Besides, my cousin will skin me alive if I release you from my care looking like an emaciated waif."

At the facetious retort, a swell of laughter bubbled out of Angie. Then, glancing at him askance, she decided she liked Garrett a whole lot better when he wasn't in love with her.

❧

Paden sat in a comfortable chair in Allan Pinkerton's Chicago office. He supposed he hadn't exactly failed his last assignment, since Munson turned up dead in a mining camp in Arizona. The desperado had apparently gotten himself killed after a heated card game. However, the money he stole would never be recovered, and Paden felt like he'd botched the job for the first time ever.

"Never mind Munson, that two-bit criminal. I've got bigger plans for you," Allan Pinkerton said in his Scottish burr. A stocky man with balding head and bushy beard, he had emigrated to America nearly thirty years ago in order to escape arrest for his part in aiding revolutionists fighting for workingmen's reforms. During the Civil War, Pinkerton had set up a secret service for the Union Army before going into business for himself. "I would like you to open some remote offices in the West and train my agents assigned out that way. You're quick with a gun, you know the land, the people, and the Indians."

Paden mulled over the remark. True, his arm had healed, so he was still quick on the draw. Nevertheless, he felt he couldn't take the job. "That is a generous offer, *Señor* Pinkerton, but I am afraid I cannot accept."

"I pay my agents well, and you know it—but I will double your salary."

Paden sat forward and rubbed his neck in indecision. The position sounded like a good one, and it would remove him from the manhunts he had grown to despise. However, he'd promised Angie no more gunfights, and he didn't think she would view this opportunity as an adequate compromise, let alone a godsend.

"I'm sorry," Paden said at last, shaking his head, "the job is not for me."

"Think about it," Pinkerton replied. "I'll give you twenty-four hours."

He grinned, knowing "The Eye," a name by which Pinkerton was commonly referred to, did not like to hear no for an answer. Paden stood and shook his employer's hand.

"I'll look forward to hearing from you," the Scotsman said with a knowing grin.

Paden gave him a parting nod and left the office. Walking the short distance to his hotel, he stopped at the front desk to check for messages. Days ago he had wired a Pinkerton associate in New York, hoping for word on Angie's arrival and whereabouts. So far there had been no reply, and Paden had begun to feel impatient.

"Yes, Mr. Montano, this came for you a short time ago," the uniformed young man said.

Taking the proffered slip of paper, Paden politely tipped his hat to the clerk, then stepped away from the desk to read it. After scanning the note, he crumpled it and shoved it into his jacket pocket. The ship had come and gone, but Angie and Veronica Huntington were not among the passengers who disembarked. Paden knew what that meant. Garrett had obviously managed to persuade the ladies to change their minds and travel to Maine. Well, that wasn't so bad, he decided, leaving the hotel and heading for the telegraph office. Maine had been the original destination. He only hoped and prayed his cousin hadn't cajoled Angie into more than rearranging her itinerary.

❧

Looking out over the ocean in the chilly November breeze, Angie gripped the rail and watched as the clipper neared Maine's Casco Bay. It seemed so close, but the captain had said this morning it would be hours before they actually docked.

As she thought over her journey, Angie felt incredibly blessed to have fared so well on the last stretch up the Atlantic. Of course, two weeks in Rio de Janeiro had done wonders for her body and spirit. Since Garrett had been there several times, he had acquired just the right contacts to order the food they wanted to eat and arrange for travel to the sights they wanted to see—that is, the sights Veronica wanted to see. While Angie recuperated, Garrett had no choice but to escort and entertain Veronica on one adventure after the other. From the reports she'd heard from her stepsister, Angie could tell Garrett wasn't minding the company in the least bit. In fact, it seemed to Angie that Veronica and Garrett were falling in love.

Stifling a grin, Angie glanced to her distant right where even now the two stood engaged in some deep conversation. They made a handsome pair: Garrett in a crisp, white shirt, dove gray vest, black jacket, and matching pants turned into leather boots, and Veronica wearing her tartan plaid dress with its black velvet trim.

Just then the very object of her thoughts whirled around and, with tears in her hazel eyes, rushed past Angie. Garrett followed her, then stopped.

"What did you do?" Angie asked accusingly.

After a deliberate pause, he replied, "I merely stated the truth, Angelique." He turned to face her and his expression softened. "I suggest you go after Veronica and see if you can comfort her."

Angie nodded and strode quickly to their cabin. Inside, she found her stepsister standing with her head against the outer wall, weeping. "Oh, you poor thing, what's happened?"

"I feel like such a fool," Veronica said. Angie put her arms around her and Veronica cried on her shoulder. "I told Garrett I loved him. I couldn't help it. The words came out of my mouth as if by their own volition."

"I can hardly say I'm surprised by the admission."

"But, unfortunately, there is no happy ending to report. Garrett said a match between us isn't possible. I accused him of still being in love with you, but he said that wasn't the case." Veronica sniffed. "He—he led me to believe he had feelings for me," she stammered. "Oh, I knew all men were veritable beasts, yet I fooled myself into thinking perhaps Garrett was different."

Just as Angie felt her ire on the rise, she perceived the real dilemma. "He's telling the truth. I know what the trouble is. You see, there can't be a match between the two of you until you share Garrett's faith."

Veronica brought her head up, searching Angie's face. "Attending church is really that important?"

"It's more than just church attendance, sister dear. Salvation is all about seeing your need for the Savior, Jesus Christ, accepting Him and what He did on the cross, and having a personal relationship with Him."

With a sigh, Veronica stepped away and found her hanky. She dabbed the tears from her eyes. "Seeing my need for the Savior, hm?"

"That's right."

"And what, exactly, do I need Him for?"

"For eternal life in heaven. We're sinners and can't get there on our own." Angie wanted to be careful with what she said so that Veronica's decision to accept the Lord wouldn't be based on her love for Garrett, but on her love for God. "However, Jesus Christ died for you in the same manner He died for me . . . a sinner."

"Yes, yes, you've talked about sin before," Veronica stated impatiently, "and you said sinners can't go to heaven. But, Darling, I am not a sinner. I haven't done anything wrong. All the wrongs have been done to me. Why did God allow me to suffer?"

Angie shrugged. "I don't know for certain. Perhaps He wanted you to see your need for Him. I know for myself that when things are sailing along smoothly in my life, I tend to forget about the Lord and how much I need Him to guide and protect me; but when I'm in trouble, He is the first one I call upon."

"My father used to say that religion was for weak-minded people who turned into hypocrites every Sunday morning."

"Yes, well, your father was a—" Angie bit her lower lip to keep from spitting out hateful words. She had long ago forgiven the man for the diabolical deeds he'd inflicted upon her innocence, but there were occasions when anger, bitterness, and resentment arose along with the unwanted memories.

Please, Lord, she prayed, *take these unrighteous sentiments away from me. Heal my heart, my spirit, as you have done so many times in the past. . . .*

"Angelique?"

Opening her eyes from her momentary prayer, she looked at her stepsister.

"You have every right to loathe and despise my father."

"Not in God's eyes, I don't. Jesus said hatred is the same as murder."

"Surely not."

"And murder is punishable by death . . . eternal death."

Veronica opened her mouth to retort, then closed it again. Spinning on her heel, she paced the room before turning back to Angie. "I hated my late husband."

"Yes, I know. You've told me so."

"I still hate him."

Angie nodded. She could tell.

"But you see, I thought Garrett would change all that. I thought he would show me the love of a good man and dispel my unfavorable feelings for the male gender."

"Only Jesus can do that, sister dear. Not Garrett."

Veronica gave her a curious glance before Angie strode to her trunk and retrieved her Bible.

"Here, read the Gospel of St. John, chapter three. We can talk more afterwards."

Hesitantly, Veronica took the opened Bible and sat down on the lower berth. "I've never read the Bible before."

Angie gave her a patient smile. "I hadn't either, up until six years ago. My mother read it sometimes," she added wistfully. "Mostly just before she died. I had thought the Bible was for old and dying people, but I have since learned it's for all ages."

Veronica looked down at the Book in her lap.

"Will you read the chapter I've pointed out? I think it may answer some of your questions."

"Yes, I'll read it," Veronica promised. "I suppose it's time I find out what all this religion business is really about."

Angie smiled, then left the cabin, praying her stepsister would allow the Holy Spirit to show her the truth from God's Word.

$$\textcircled{19}$$

As it happened, there wasn't much opportunity to discuss spiritual matters with Veronica before having to prepare to disembark. However, Garrett seemed pleased with Angie's progress and promised to make time to address any further questions Veronica had once they were settled at his parents' home, located on the outskirts of Portland.

The ship docked and Angie, Veronica, and Garrett, along with all the other passengers, prepared to go ashore. Sunshine tried in vain to warm the crisp November day while the ship's canvas sails flapped noisily in the wind. The crew called to one another as the gangway was lowered, and soon people began to file off the deck.

Once on dry land, Angie's knees wobbled. If it hadn't been for Garrett's hold on her elbow, they surely would have buckled. A similar occurrence took place after they'd docked in Brazil. Angie realized Veronica was having the same problem. Garrett, on the other hand, being the seasoned sea captain that he was, found the matter amusing as he assisted both women into a hired carriage.

"You two rest," he said with a charming grin, "and I'll fetch our trunks."

Angie and Veronica replied with grateful nods. "I'm thankful the voyage has come to an end," Angie stated with a sigh, leaning her head back against the black leather upholstery.

"I'm rather disappointed," Veronica said. "I enjoyed every bit of our journey. However, I must say, I'm glad to be on the East Coast once again. I hadn't realized how much I truly abhorred San Francisco until I left the city behind me."

Angie smiled wanly, then closed her eyes.

"Will you miss it?"

Her eyes opening, she glanced at her stepsister. "Miss San Francisco?" Angie shivered and pulled her wool shawl more tightly around her shoulders. "I'll miss its warmer weather, that's for certain."

"It gets chilly in San Francisco, too."

"Yes, but not like this."

With her own shawl draped about her shoulders, Veronica shrugged. "Oh, what's a little cold weather that a cozy fire and cup of hot tea can't fix?"

"Wait until it snows," Angie muttered.

"Snow is lovely."

She shivered again.

Minutes later, Garrett appeared and the carriage rocked to and fro as the hired hands loaded the travelers' belongings on top of the vehicle. Then Garrett climbed in and they were on their way. As they bounced along the cobbled streets, he pointed out various sites of interest, such as Portland's college and a host of architecturally unique, red-bricked structures. He explained that a fire nearly twenty years ago had leveled much of the city.

Soon the buildings and houses grew farther apart as they left the bustling heart of town. Then Garrett pointed out his parents' home as the carriage made its approach. Peering out the window, Angie noted the house was square in shape and constructed with the region's ever-popular red brick. Nevertheless, it appeared to be a regal-looking estate, and Garrett boasted of the magnificent view of the Atlantic from its third floor observatory.

"I certainly hope we won't be an imposition," Veronica stated, wearing a worried little frown.

"Not at all. My family should be expecting us since I wired them when the ship last docked."

After the carriage halted in the circular drive, Garrett helped each woman alight. The front door swung open, and a stern-faced butler, primly attired in black and white, greeted them. "Master Garrett," he said, a slight grin curving his thin lips. "How good to have you home at last." He gave each lady a look of inspection before bowing courteously.

"Jarvis! My, but you're a sight for sore eyes." Garrett smiled broadly. "May I present the Huntingtons, Veronica and Angelique."

Again, the balding man bowed. "At your service."

"Please see to our things, Jarvis," Garrett instructed, "while I take the women inside before they freeze to death. They're accustomed to a warmer climate."

"Of course, Sir."

Garrett led Angie and Veronica into the large home, where a small reception awaited them in the foyer. After hugs and kisses from several ladies, Garrett received claps on the back from two males, one of whom resembled an aged version of Paden, and Angie stifled a little gasp upon seeing him. After introductions were made, she knew the reason for the resemblance; the man was none other than Alonso Montano, Paden's father.

"How wonderful to see you," Garrett told his uncle and aunt and two dark-eyed, female cousins, "but it's so late in the year for a trip from Mexico."

Glances were exchanged all around. "Garrett, Dear," his mother, Mary, began, "we've had a death in the family. Your grandfather. We tried to reach you after receiving your wire, but with no success."

"Grandfather is dead?" Garrett looked immediately stricken.

Angie's heart went out to him and the entire family.

"He died a couple of weeks ago, Son," John Witherspoon said. "I'm afraid you missed the funeral."

A shroud of sorrow descended on the little congregation.

"He died peacefully in his sleep," Paden's mother, Kathleen, said on a more positive note. "And he was eighty-nine, for pity's sake. No one lives forever."

"How true," John replied with a sad smile.

"We did reach Paden," Kathleen added. "He wired back to say he was on his way. We sent a return message telling him it wasn't necessary for him to make the journey. Unfortunately, we were told he had already left the hotel in Chicago."

"I suspect his arrival has to do with something more than just Grandfather's death." Garrett pulled Angie forward until she stood beneath Kathleen Montano's scrutiny. A lovely woman with dark brown hair, graying slightly at each temple, Paden's mother bore a striking likeness to her brother and Garrett. "Aunt Kathleen," he began again, "I think you and Uncle Alonso will want to get to know this lady."

"And why is that?" she asked curiously, her serious hazel eyes staring into Angie's.

"Because Paden has a mind to marry Angelique."

Gasps of surprise filled the elegant front hallway, and Angie felt her face flame with embarrassment.

"Well, Paden's wire suddenly makes more sense," John said with a huge grin. "He asked if someone named Angie had arrived, but we hadn't the foggiest idea to whom he referred. But now I understand— Miss Huntington, you are Paden's 'Angie.'"

"She is indeed," Garrett said, and Angie couldn't detect a single note of bitterness in his voice, for which she felt enormously grateful.

"I think my son has good taste in women," Alonso said with a thick Mexican accent. Smiling, he slipped his arm around his wife's trim waist. "His taste is almost as good as mine."

Angie felt her blush deepen.

Paden's sisters began speaking in such rapid Spanish, that Angie couldn't discern a single word. Their parents chuckled.

"My daughters both think it's about time Paden settles down," Kathleen translated with a hint of a smirk. "Two of his younger sisters are already married with children and Regina, here, is betrothed."

The ebony-haired beauty smiled shyly while her younger sister, Eva, gazed on with admiration shining from her dark gaze.

"This is quite the surprise," Mary said, her brown eyes searching her son's face. "And what about you? When are you going to get around to finding a wife?"

"I'm, um, working on it, Mother."

Angie glanced over just in time to see Garrett look at Veronica, whose cheeks now matched the crimson stripe in the foyer's multicolored wallpaper.

The butler came in from outside and offered to show Angie and Veronica to their room. "I hope you don't mind," Mary whispered as they started up the steps behind Jarvis, "but with all the Montanos here, you'll have to share a bedroom."

"We don't mind a bit," Veronica assured the older woman. "Angelique and I have been sharing a cramped cabin for months."

Mrs. Witherspoon looked relieved. "Thank you for your understanding."

"Thank you for your hospitality," Veronica returned, and Angie had the distinct feeling the two would get along very well.

∾

Paden watched from the train window as the picturesque landscape rolled by as if painted on a moving scroll. For all his musing, he barely saw it. Soon he'd arrive in New York, and if, after scouring the city, he didn't find Angie, he planned to wire his aunt and uncle once more. Why hadn't she been on that ship when it docked in New York, and why, if Angie hadn't disembarked there, wasn't she in Maine? Where else would Garrett take her? Yes, Garrett, his boyhood chum and favorite cousin—he was up to something. Paden sensed it.

He thought back to when they were boys, stirring up mischief in the streets of Portland. He recalled how their grandfather had showed obvious favoritism toward Garrett, acting as though he were almost ashamed of Paden. Always, Garry would share whatever trinket Grandfather had given him and, always, it was Garry who played the diplomat, saying things like, "Grandfather doesn't mean any harm, he's just old." When they got into trouble, Garry did the talking.

They grew and became young men and only saw each other every couple of years. Both Paden and Garrett had dreams of accomplishing more than the average man, but where Garry was a Christian and lived morally, thus dubbed "the good one," Paden experienced the darker side of life and, therefore, became looked upon by Grandfather Witherspoon as "bad blood." Even so, Garry continued to befriend Paden, risking Grandfather's wrath.

When the Civil War began, both Paden and Garrett enlisted. They kept tabs on each other and miraculously met up near the war's end. Garry persuaded Paden to take the train home to Maine with him, and Paden did. It was then that their grandfather's prejudice dissolved. At last, Paden felt accepted by his New England kin, although he knew he'd never fit into their family, their lifestyle.

Now Grandfather was dead. Paden felt a stab of remorse; he hadn't even told the old man about his conversion to Christ.

As he continued to reflect upon his life, thinking of his family, the Witherspoons, and specifically his cousin, Paden wondered if Angie wasn't better off marrying Garry. It was a heart-wrenching notion, yet it carried with it a ring of truth that Paden hated to realize. Once Angie glimpsed the Witherspoons' finery, an obscure, dusty ranch in Texas would no longer be appealing.

Even so, he had a promise to keep.

ngelique, I cannot believe I'm doing this."

She laughed. "I can't believe you are either. Now hold still."

Veronica complied, and Angie continued to pin together the white, satin fabric. "Life can change so fast."

"I'll say," Angie replied in spite of the straight pins between her lips.

"It seemed as though one moment I was in San Francisco, a lost widow, despising the idea of remarriage, and the next thing I know, I'm a Christian here in Portland, Maine, getting fitted for my wedding dress."

Angie grinned. She still couldn't get over her stepsister's conversion. She never thought she'd see the day, but one Sunday afternoon, nearly two weeks ago, Veronica asked Jesus to save her. As a result of the pastor's clear gospel message that morning, all the knowledge about God swirling around in Veronica's head found a home in her heart.

Garrett had been pursuing Veronica ever since.

"I've never experienced such peace," she stated, "as I've felt since trusting the Lord. Although I have shunned the idea of marriage, I have peace about taking my vows with Garrett. As you know, Angelique, it's one thing to love a man and quite another matter entirely to spend the rest of your life with him, but God showed me something remarkable from His Word."

Angie's smile broadened.

"It was in the Gospel of Matthew," Veronica went on, "I memorized the verse.

"'For this cause shall a man leave father and mother, and shall cleave to his wife: and they twain shall be one flesh? Wherefore they are no more twain, but one flesh.' Aren't those the most beautiful words you've ever heard? Two hearts joined as one, and God created it." Veronica sighed dreamily.

Angie nodded in agreement. "But I feel badly for you," Veronica stated with a frown.

Removing the pins from her mouth, Angie looked up from her kneeling position. "Why?"

"Well, all along I thought you would be the one to get married and leave me to plod through life on my own. Instead, it's me doing the very thing to you that I balked at and resented."

"Don't worry about me. Paden will come for me. He promised." When no response was forthcoming, Angie stood. "He promised, and I believe him."

"But, what if—"

"Don't say it. We could 'what if' all day and accomplish nothing."

"True, except circumstances might arise that are beyond your control. You heard Garrett last night. Paden is a gunfighter. Gunfighters can get hurt . . . killed."

"Veronica, why are you trying to discourage me? Paden's parents seem to like me. I get along with his two sisters. They all believe that if Paden said he'd come, he'll be here. In fact, they're so sure of it, they've postponed their return to Mexico. Besides, Paden asked me to wait until Christmas. I can at least do that, can't I? Tomorrow is Thanksgiving Day. That gives Paden more than a month."

Veronica shrugged slightly.

"And the Witherspoons have offered their hospitality to me for that length of time, so it's not as though I'll be destitute and on the street after you and Garrett marry." She resumed pinning the satiny material together. "If, after Christmas, Paden doesn't arrive, I'll put my name in at various dress shops here in Portland or even in New York. I'll find work." Angie wondered at the despair that filled her being after she'd spoken those words. Somehow, she couldn't bear to think of a future without Paden. Did that mean she loved him?

Again, Veronica didn't reply and Angie sensed there was something more troubling her stepsister. She ceased her pinning. "What is it, Veronica? Tell me."

"I feel awful," she said.

"Why? You're getting married to a handsome, wealthy man who adores you. Why should you feel awful?"

"It's twofold, really," Veronica confided. "First, I wish you were marrying a handsome, wealthy man who adores you, too, and secondly, I . . . I . . ." She swallowed hard. "I have a dreadful feeling Garrett still loves you."

"Hm . . ." Angie gave the notion a moment's thought. "Well, perhaps he does," she finally replied, grinning at the startled look on stepsister's face. "But it wouldn't be the same love he feels for you."

Veronica's expression relaxed a bit.

"If Garrett still loves me, it's a protective, older brother, perhaps even paternal love. That's not to say he wasn't infatuated with me at one time, but I believe those feelings have passed. He's realized that marrying me wasn't God's will and he's accepted it and moved on. I find that quite admirable, don't you?"

"If that's the truth, yes."

"Ask him," Angie said on a challenging note.

"I could never question Garrett about such a thing."

"I think you should. If you share your feelings with your fiancé, he'll share his heart with you, and your relationship will deepen."

Veronica grew momentarily pensive, then smiled. "How did you ever get to be so wise?"

Angie laughed. "I'm not, really. In fact, if I'm ever in your position and a bride-to-be, I'm sure I'll be running to you for advice."

"I hope you do, Darling."

"I will," Angie promised.

❧

Paden searched New York City and, as he suspected, Angie was nowhere to be found. According to plan, he wired his relatives in Maine. Their reply alleviated his worries about Angie, since it seemed she had arrived safely, but at the same time, the message caused his heart to plummet.

Angie here STOP *Garrett to marry soon* STOP *Please come* STOP

So, she decided to marry Garry after all, Paden mused, pacing his hotel room with angry strides. *She promised me she would wait, but she goes back on her word. If she is that kind of a woman, then I don't want her and Garrett is welcome to her!*

After a few more furious thoughts, he paused and realized he didn't mean a single word of any of them. Yet, this was exactly what he had figured would happen. Angie discovered Garrett could offer her more, and what woman wouldn't choose a life of comfort in a cultured city over a life of hard work in the untamed West? He couldn't blame her.

A wave of self-pity stole over him, and Paden considered contacting Allan Pinkerton and inquiring after that last job offer. He had turned it down, expecting to marry Angie and buy a ranch. But what good would owning land be without a wife . . . without Angie? These past months without her had amazingly caused him to love her more. But now . . .

He lowered himself onto the edge of the bed, feeling as discouraged as the prophet Elijah had been when he lay down under the juniper tree. *Take my life, Lord. What good am I, a no-account gunman?*

In the next moment, it was as though the Lord God spoke directly to Paden's heart. The words were not audible, but more like an impression stamped upon his spirit. *Stop feeling sorry for yourself and board the next train to Portland.*

"Was that a command, Lord?" Paden asked aloud. "And if so, what would You have me to do once I arrive?"

No answer followed, but Paden felt sure God was directing him to take those first few steps. With renewed determination, he shook off his despair, packed his belongings, and headed for the train depot.

~❧

The first days of December brought a snowfall, and the landscape looked as white and lovely as Veronica did in her wedding dress. It had been decided that Garrett's best friend and his wife would stand up as witnesses, and Veronica feared that Angie would feel hurt.

"You should be my bridesmaid," she had insisted, time after time. "I just wish I could make Garrett see my point of view."

"Not to fret," Angie replied. "Garrett explained his reasoning and I can accept it. He and this couple have been friends since elementary school, and over the years they prayed for Garrett's future spouse. They're delighted he has chosen you, sister dear. They should be in the wedding party, not me."

"Oh, Angelique . . ."

"Now, now," she warned, "a good wife must heed her husband's decisions without complaint."

Veronica grimaced, causing Angie to laugh, and once more she rejoiced in the fact that she wasn't the one marrying Garrett Witherspoon.

❧

The day of the wedding was frosty and cold. The sky looked gray and mean. However, an air of excitement crackled within the confines of the cathedral walls in which the Witherspoons worshiped.

Sitting beside Paden's family in the long, polished front pew reserved for Witherspoon relatives, Angie smoothed down the skirt of her blue taffeta gown with her white gloved hands. At that moment, the organ began to play. Paden's youngest sister, Eva, sitting to Angie's right, looked enamored by the procession until finally the bride and groom stood before the altar.

"*Bella*," Eva whispered. "She is so beautiful."

Angie nodded in agreement. She had never seen a lovelier bride than her stepsister. The lacy, white veil added a touch of mystery and romance. Angie felt glad she had convinced Veronica of that wonderful moment when Garrett would unveil the face of the woman beside him and kiss her, his wife.

The pastor began to speak, but suddenly a disturbance in the back of the sanctuary caused stirs and whispers to waft across the large congregation. "Stop the wedding!" came the sharp demand. "I am sorry, but I cannot let you do this."

Shocked, Angie felt her blood run cold upon hearing the man's familiar, strong, smooth voice with its subtle accent. Next she heard his booted footfalls echoing through the church as he strode up the aisle. She turned and saw Paden standing not ten feet away. He looked quite dapper in his formal, black garb, and Angie's heart melted at the sight of him.

To her left, Kathleen Montano gasped and tried in vain to get her son's attention. "What is he doing?"

"I . . . I don't know," Angie replied.

Sitting beside Kathleen, her husband began to whisper something in Spanish and Angie distinctly heard the word *"loco."*

"Ah, if it isn't my favorite cousin," Garrett drawled with a huge smile. "I had hoped you'd make it to town for my wedding."

"*Sí,* I made it. I always keep my . . . *promises.*"

Angie inhaled sharply and raised her gloved hand to her lips, suddenly realizing Paden thought she was Veronica. No wonder he looked so angry. "Oh, dear," she murmured softly.

Just then Veronica lifted her veil, uncovering a curious frown, and Angie thought the expression on Paden's face was priceless. It went from shock, to confusion, to utter chagrin.

Angie began to laugh softly.

"Why don't you have a seat," Garrett said, looking amused and pointing in the direction of the Montanos and Angie.

Paden wheeled to his left, and when his dark gaze met hers, Angie didn't know whether to continue laughing or weep for joy.

Bowing courteously to the bride and groom, Paden publicly apologized for interrupting the ceremony before making his way to the pew.

"Scoot over, *chica,*" he said softly to Eva, who did as he bid her, but not without tossing him an indignant glare. Obviously the young woman didn't appreciate being referred to as a "girl," even if it was by her older brother. He then placed a quick kiss on his mother's cheek before sitting down beside Angie.

Her heart pounded so hard, Angie was sure Paden would hear it. She threaded her hand around his arm and squeezed it, knowing the gesture would have to suffice for the embrace she longed to give him. With his right hand, Paden covered hers.

"For days I have been under the assumption you were marrying Garrett," he whispered so closely that she felt his warm breath on her cheek. "I was heartbroken, but then I decided I would make you look into my eyes and tell me you loved him more than me. Only then would I be satisfied. Only then would I step aside and allow you to marry him."

Angie shook her head. "I keep my promises, too, Paden."

He grinned and his dark eyes shone with affection. "So I see."

~❧

After the wedding ceremony, family members and guests were invited to a reception at the Witherspoons' stately home. It wasn't until much later in the evening that Paden and Angie found time to sneak away from the crowd. Taking her hand, Paden led her away from the congested front room.

"Where are we going?"

"You'll see," he replied.

Showing her through the kitchen, where the temperature soared from hot ovens and hired hands busily prepared one tray of delectable hors d'oeuvres after another, Paden escorted Angie into his aunt's private tea room in the back of the house. Then he shut the lead glass-paned doors. The tiny room had been enclosed with matching lead glass-paned windows and beyond them, outside, stood tall, snow-laden evergreens.

"I have you alone at last," Paden said with a grin, stepping toward her.

"Behave yourself, *Señor* Montano," Angie warned half-heartedly.

He feigned a look of indignation. "I always behave myself."

Closing the distance between them, he slipped his arms around Angie's waist. She allowed herself to enjoy the feeling of being held in his strong embrace. "I hope you missed me these past months."

Looking up into his shadowed features, she nodded. "I missed you very much." With her palms resting on his upper arms, Angie slid her hand over the spot where he had been shot. "Did your wound heal all right?"

Paden inclined his dark head affirmatively. "And you? Have you recovered from your voyage?"

"Barely."

He chuckled lightly. "I will never force you to sail again. From now on, we will travel by stage or the railroad."

"*Gracias.*"

Paden smiled, but soon grew serious once more. "There is a matter of importance I wish to discuss with you."

Angie lifted expectant brows.

"While I was in Chicago, Allan Pinkerton offered me an outstanding position. I would be training agents and opening offices throughout the West."

Angie felt her heart sink.

"He offered to double my salary."

She lowered her chin, hoping Paden wouldn't see her tears of disappointment. "I thought you wanted a ranch," she said in a strangled, little voice.

"What do you want, *querida?* Tell me. I want to hear it."

Angie swallowed her emotion. "I want a husband who loves me, children . . . I want . . ." She returned her misty eyes to his dark, probing gaze. "Oh, Paden, I want you. I love you. But I can't marry a gunfighter. I can't. I know my heart, and it would break each and every time you left me for one of your assignments."

"Then I suppose it is a good thing that I turned down the job."

Angie glared at him. "You're toying with me. How could you?" She pushed against him, but Paden refused to let her go.

"This is not a game, Angie, but I have longed to hear you speak words of love. Can you blame me?"

She ceased her struggles, considering him, and concluding that beneath the rugged, *vaquero*—like exterior, beat the heart of a sensitive, perhaps even vulnerable man.

"Tell me again," he urged. "Tell me you love me."

Angie's heart warmed to the request. *"Te amo,"* she murmured in his native tongue, knowing she meant each word. *"Te amo."*

"That is music to my ears," Paden replied as he gently touched his lips to hers.

"Excuse me. . . ."

Startled by the interruption, Angie stepped backward. Paden heaved a sigh of frustration before swinging around toward the doorway where Eva stood, grinning at the two of them. "What is it?" Paden asked.

"Madre says it's time to wish Garrett and Veronica farewell. They're leaving on their honeymoon."

"Yes, Paden," Angie concurred, touching his shoulder as he stood with his back to her. "We should see them off."

Paden nodded. "Very well. Tell Mother that Angie and I will be there shortly."

"Sí, I will do that," Eva said, closing the door once more.

Facing Angie again, Paden's features softened and he gave her a long look. "Will you marry me?" he asked. "Marry me, Angie, and I promise to love and cherish you for the rest of my life."

She smiled as happiness bubbled up inside her. "Yes, I'll marry you."

He pressed another kiss on her mouth, then on her cheek, her neck.

"Paden, you must stop," she admonished, although she wished otherwise.

He reluctantly complied. "When you are mine, Angie," he avowed, "I will have a lifetime to love you."

"And I, you."

Looking pleased, he looped her hand around his elbow and guided her to the foyer, where the newly married couple prepared to take their leave.

Stepping forward, Paden stuck out his right hand and Garrett clasped it. "After all that has happened between us, I hope we are still friends."

"Of course," Garrett replied, wearing an earnest expression. "You are more than my cousin. You are my brother—my brother in Christ."

Angie saw Paden smile broadly and then the men's formal hand-shake became something resembling an arm wrestling maneuver.

"Take care, and congratulations to you."

Garrett clapped Paden affectionately on the back with his free hand. "You, too, and, um, I imagine you'll be a married man by the time Veronica and I return from our trip to Europe."

"You had better believe it."

Veronica spun around and hugged Angie. "It's official? You're going to marry him?"

Angie nodded.

"I'm so glad." Veronica tightened her embrace. "I love you, Darling, and I promise to write."

Tears filled Angie's eyes. "I love you, too. Please say you'll visit me sometime . . . on our ranch."

"Mercy, no!" Veronica exclaimed, pulling back. "You must visit me here in Portland. I've had enough of the West to last me a lifetime."

"But, sister dear—"

"Perhaps we'll meet somewhere in between," Garrett suggested diplomatically, taking Veronica's elbow and drawing her right up beside him. "God willing, there will be ample time for us to discuss possible sites. But right now, my wife and I must be on our way." He gazed at Veronica. "My wife . . . those two words have an awfully nice sound to them."

Veronica smiled back adoringly.

Watching them, Angie sighed, feeling a swell of happiness mounting within her. She glanced at Paden, and reality struck: God had done exceeding abundantly above all she could ever ask or think. He had brought a man into her life who understood her, loved her, and one whom she could love in return. In the process, the Lord had made a way for her to escape her sorry past once and for all. With Paden at her side, Angie knew she could now brave the future with an unmasked heart.